The History of
Jemmy and Jenny Jessamy

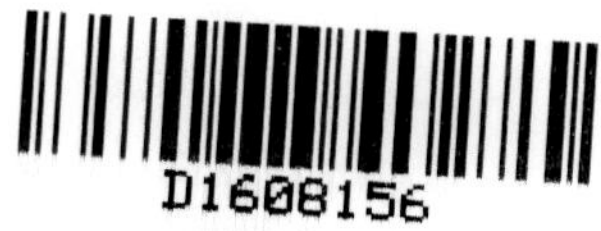

Eighteenth-Century Novels by Women

The History of Jemmy and Jenny Jessamy

By Eliza Haywood

Edited by John Richetti

THE UNIVERSITY PRESS OF KENTUCKY

Publication of this volume was made possible in part by a grant from the National Endowment for the Humanities.

Scholarly publisher for the Commonwealth,
serving Bellarmine University, Berea College, Centre College of Kentucky, Eastern Kentucky University, The Filson Historical Society, Georgetown College, Kentucky Historical Society, Kentucky State University, Morehead State University, Murray State University, Northern Kentucky University, Transylvania University, University of Kentucky, University of Louisville, and Western Kentucky University.

Editorial and Sales Offices: The University Press of Kentucky
663 South Limestone Street, Lexington, Kentucky 40508-4008
www.kentuckypress.com

09 08 07 06 05 5 4 3 2 1

Library of Congress Cataloging-in-Publication Data

Haywood, Eliza Fowler, 1693?-1756.
The history of Jemmy and Jenny Jessamy / by Eliza Haywood ; edited by John Richetti.
p. cm.
Includes bibliographical references (p.).
ISBN-13: 978-0-8131-2359-2 (acid-free paper)
ISBN-10: 0-8131-2359-3 (acid-free paper)
ISBN-13: 978-0-8131-9143-0 (pbk. : acid-free paper)
ISBN-10: 0-8131-9143-2 (pbk. : acid-free paper) 1. Courtship—Fiction. 2. Commitment (Psychology)—Fiction. I. Richetti, John J. II. Title.
PR3506.H94H48 2005
823'.5—dc22 2005022926

This book is printed on acid-free recycled paper meeting the requirements of the American National Standard for Permanence in Paper for Printed Library Materials.

Manufactured in the United States of America.

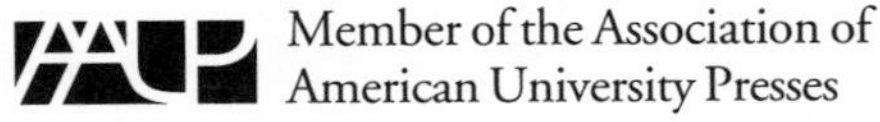

Contents

Introduction

I

In terms of sheer production of narrative prose fiction among eighteenth-century British writers, no one (not even Defoe) can rival Eliza Fowler Haywood (1693–1756). She burst onto the publishing scene as a novelist in her late twenties with the spectacular success of her three-part romance, *Love in Excess; or, The Fatal Inquiry* (1719–1720), which in the next few years was with Defoe's *Robinson Crusoe* and Swift's *Gulliver's Travels* one of the three most popular narratives of the first three decades of the eighteenth century. Very little, however, is known for certain about her birth and her early years before that entry into the world of romantic fiction. She may have been born in London, but it is more likely, says her most recent biographer, that she was born in the country, in Shropshire, and her family may have been fairly prominent or at least well connected there. Before her remarkable debut in the literary marketplace, Eliza Fowler seems to have been married to a Mr. Haywood and separated from him or left a widow.[1] In 1728, she wrote to a potential subscriber to her works that she had first become a writer after "an unfortunate marriage" that reduced her "to the melancholy necessity of depending on my Pen for the support of myself and two children, the eldest of whom is no more than 7 years of age." And in that same letter, she also explained that writing had been converted from an inclination to a necessity for her "by the Sudden Deaths of both a Father, and a Husband, at an age when I was little prepar'd to Stem the Tide of Ill Fortune."[2]

Nothing is known about her education, but we can be sure from reading her works that she was well versed in English poetry and drama and had a good knowledge of French and of French literature (she published some translations from that language), that she was, in short, intelligent and sophisticated. She may, it seems, have been more formally educated than most women, since in her periodical, *The Female Spectator,* she remarked of herself that she received an education "more liberal than is ordinarily allowed to Persons of my Sex."[3] What is certain about her early life is that as a young woman she became an actress and later a playwright as well, making her debut in Dublin in 1715 in Thomas Shadwell's adaptation of Shakespeare's *Timon of Athens.* According to Christine Blouch, she served a three-year apprenticeship in Dublin as an actress and when she returned to England in 1717 supported herself as an actress with provincial theater companies, but as she wrote in a letter in 1720, "The Stage not answering my Expectation, and the Averseness of my Relations to it, has made me turn my Genius another way."[4] Although she continued in the early 1730s to appear on the stage, sometimes in her own plays, from 1719 on she was known primarily as a writer. In her long career stretching over three decades as a professional author, she published more than thirty novels and novellas as well as translations of French fiction, four plays, some poems, six periodicals, and various political satires and miscellaneous journalism, including *The Female Spectator* (1744–1746), a monthly magazine written specifically for women.

During the 1720s, the high point of her popularity, she produced a steady stream of romance or amatory novels, most of them short enough to be more properly called novellas, and her work enjoyed considerable success as well as a measure of notoriety, especially if we judge by the publication in 1723–1724 of a sumptuous collection, *The Works of Mrs. Eliza Haywood, Consisting of Novels, Letters, Poems, and Plays* in four volumes (which went into a second edition in 1725), and then again in 1727 a two-volume collection of her *Secret Histories, Novels and Poems,* which by 1732 had reached a third edition. These are substantial collected volumes with elaborate prefatory material as well as a handsome engraved portrait of the author. Among the poems praising her in the preface to the four-volume collection is a tribute by the raffish poet Richard Savage (thought by some recent Haywood scholars to be her lover at the time), that speaks extravagantly of the special appeal of Haywood's amatory fiction for her many readers during those years:

As music fires, thy language lifts the mind.
Thy pow'r gives form, and touches into life
The passions imag'd in their bleeding strife:
Contrasted strokes, true art and fancy show,
And lights and shades in lively mixture flow
. . . .

Eliza, still impaint Love's pow'rful Queen!
Let Love, soft Love! exalt each swelling scene.
Arm'd with keen wit, in fame's wide lists advance!
Spain yields in fiction, in politeness, France.
Such orient light, as the first poets knew,
Flames from thy thought, and brightens ev'ry view!
A strong, a glorious, a luxuriant fire,
Which warms cold wisdom into wild desire!
Thy Fable glows so rich thro' ev'ry page,
What moral's force can the fierce heat assuage?[5]

In assessing this extravagant praise, one does well to remember the poet's intimate relationship with the novelist and the nature of such prefatory puffs. Nonetheless, Savage's evocation of Haywood's work is accurate enough, as it centers quite frankly on the erotic power of her imagination, her ability in her depictions of sexual passion to arouse and excite her readers, to warm "cold wisdom into wild desire," and his panegyric is full of images of a fire and heat in her "swelling" and "glowing" scenes that no moral reflection can extinguish or even temper. A slightly different description of her novels that describes them as less explicitly erotic and rather more sentimental and moral can be found in another prefatory poem prefixed to the four-volume collected works, "To Mrs. Eliza Haywood, on Her Writings," by one James Sterling:

Great Arbitress of Passion! (wond'rous Art!)
As the despotick Will the Limbs, thou mov'st the Heart;
Perswasion waits on all your bright Designs
And where you point the varying Soul inclines:
See! Love and Friendship, the fair Theme inspires
We glow with Zeal, we melt in soft Desires!
Thro' the dire Labyrinth of Ills we share
The kindred Sorrows of the gen'rous Pair;
'Till, pleas'd, rewarded Vertue we behold,
Shine from the Furnace pure as tortur'd Gold:
You sit like Heav'n's bright Minister on High,
Command the throbbing Breast, and watry Eye,
And, as our captive Spirits ebb and flow,
Smile at the Tempests you have rais'd below:
The Face of Guilt a Flush of Vertue wears,

And sudden burst th' involuntary Tears:
Honour's sworn Foe, the Libertine with Shame,
Descends to curse the sordid lawless Flame;
The tender Maid here learns Man's various Wiles,
Rash Youth, hence dread the Wanton's venal Smiles—[6]

Although many of Haywood's novels from the 1720s stick pretty closely to what was obviously an effective popular formula for amatory romance, Sterling's evocation of them makes it clear that her handling of that formula was complicated and often varied in significant ways. Basically, all of Haywood's novellas offer their readers the thrilling, sensational effects of sexual passion, which is evoked vividly as irresistible and turbulent, as a volcanic, all-consuming psychological event in a young woman's life. Steamy love affairs among members of an elegant and idle ruling class, often enough located in glamorously romantic French, Italian, or Spanish settings, are the defining subject matter of these stories. Aristocratic and libertine young men and inexperienced but susceptible young women of the same class are the prime actors in these dramas, with the men out to seduce and at times to abuse and abandon their eager and innocent victims. But many of these bodice rippers also feature a prominent sentimentality, as Haywood places extreme female suffering at their center, offering readers not just sexual excitement but affecting pathos or exquisite pity, tears as well as erotic thrills. And a good number of the novels also include variations on their central opposition of innocent female victim and worldly male seducer. Right from her debut novel, *Love in Excess,* which features Amena, an aggressively sexual woman, to the novella *Fantomina; or, Love in a Maze* (1724), whose remarkable heroine Fantomina assumes four disguises on four separate occasions to seduce a young man (Beauplaisir) with whom she is sexually obsessed, Haywood's novels regularly depict frank and openly aggressive female sexuality. A few of the other openly libidinous women in Haywood's novellas from this decade are what Jerry C. Beasley calls "monsters of aggression and ruthless exploiters of the power politics of sexuality," and as such he calls them "almost transvestites, duplicating in their behavior the vile excesses of the male libertines" who dominated the Haywoodian fantasy world.[7]

In another variation of the amatory formula, some of Haywood's stories strive for a measure of domestic realism, as she sets a few of them in a recognizable England (*The British Recluse; or, The Secret History of Cleomira, Suppos'd Dead* [1722]) or among the local urban middle or merchant class

(*The City Jilt; or, The Alderman Turn'd Beau* [1726], and *The Mercenary Lover; or, The Unfortunate Heiress* [1726]). And even the most melodramatic, lurid, and sensationalistic of them feature the usual cautionary label; they are, Haywood's narrator claims often enough, meant not to thrill or to arouse her readers but to warn the innocent and inexperienced among them of the perils of passion. It is hard to take such moralizing warning labels very seriously, although we can easily see how the eroticism of Haywood's fiction is intensified (as the Marquis de Sade's pornographic fiction such as *Justine, or The Misfortunes of Virtue* [1791] would show with shocking clarity later in the eighteenth century) by the spectacle of suffering virtue. At the least, we can say, pathos is as important as sex in her popular fictional formula and in its appeal, and in Sterling's words Haywood seeks to provoke in her readers "the throbbing Breast and watry Eye."[8]

Haywood herself in various prefaces to her novels as well as throughout many of the texts themselves defines her work as ultimately didactic, instructional in the mysterious ways of love, representations from the heart of how (primarily female) sexual passion works. Artless and spontaneous reporting or recording is Haywood's unconvincing characterization of her method as a writer, as she claims in effect to be no different from her various beleaguered young heroines. For example, in the preface to *The Fatal Secret* (1724), she dedicates the book to the Whig politician William Yonge (who was an enemy of Pope's political friends, Henry St. John, later Viscount Bolingbroke, and Bishop Atterbury), and in the process rather disingenuously or perhaps ironically describes herself as merely a woman writing about that which comes naturally to her. In what can only be taken as a bitter reflection on her exclusion from male privilege that would enable her to aspire to more exalted forms of writing, she comments on her special and humble situation as a female author, restricted to that topic, love, to which her sex gives her direct access:[9]

> Were there a Hope, tho' ne'er so distant a one, that I should ever be capable of any Performance worthy the Honour of your Patronage, it would not have been for a Trifle such as this I had entreated it: But as I am a Woman, and consequently depriv'd of those Advantages of Education which the other Sex enjoy, I cannot so far flatter my Desires, as to imagine it in my Power to soar to any Subject higher than that which Nature is not negligent to teach us.
>
> Love is a Topick which I believe few are ignorant of; there requires no Aids of Learning, no general Conversation, no Application; a shady Grove

> and purling Stream are all Things that's necessary to give us an Idea of the tender Passion. This is a Theme, therefore, which, while I make choice to write of, frees me from the Imputation of vain or self-sufficient:—None can tax me with having too great an Opinion of my own Genius, when I aim at nothing but what the meanest may perform.[10]

Haywood could not make claims like this for the novels she produced in the 1740s and after, when her subject matter widened and her style grew more varied and flexible. Looking back at the trajectory of Haywood's career, we can say that Sterling's emphasis in part of his verse tribute predicts Haywood's turn in the 1740s to moral-sentimental fiction when he speaks of her novels as filling "Honour's sworn Foe, the Libertine with Shame" and warning "the tender Maid" of "Man's various Wiles" and the "Rash Youth" of the "Wanton's venal Smiles." For this panegyrist, Haywood is the successor to Aphra Behn and Delariviere Manley, the two most prominent women writers from the recent past. Haywood clearly modeled some of her writing on Manley, for she wrote two "secret histories," *Memoirs of a Certain Island Adjacent to the Kingdom of Utopia* (1724) and *The Secret History of the Present Intrigues of the Court of Caramania* (1726), that were clearly meant by their mixture of sexual scandal and political gossip to remind readers of Manley's *New Atalantis* (1709–1710). Sterling's poem celebrates in the lines that follow a female literary tradition or succession, a proto-feminist scene in which Haywood rebels against the patriarchal exclusion of women from learning and by her genius makes herself worthy to receive the torch from her two predecessors as champions of women's writing:

> Sure 'twas by brutal Force of envious Man,
> First Learning's base Monopoly began;
> He knew your Genius, and refus'd his Books,
> Nor thought your Wit less fatal than your Looks.
> Read, proud Usurper, read with conscious Shame,
> Pathetick Behn, or Manley's greater Name;
> Forget their Sex, and own when Haywood writ,
> She clos'd the fair Triumvirate of Wit.[11]

To be sure, Sterling's feminized triumphal succession was not the standard narrative about Haywood and her two most prominent predecessors. By the third decade of the century and beyond, both Behn and Manley survived in literary memory for many as the disreputable and disgraceful female purveyors of scandalous and licentious writing. For example, in his Horatian imitation, "The First Epistle of the Second Book of Horace Imitated, To Augustus," Pope includes Aphra Behn ("Astrea") in a list of English dramatic failures, even among the best of them like Congreve, Farquhar, and Vanbrugh, but singles her out for the formulaic raciness of her plays: "The stage how loosely does Astrea tread, / Who fairly puts all characters to bed" (lines 290–91). Delariviere Manley, a writer for the Tories during the Queen Anne years, was in that capacity a friend and indeed a collaborator of Swift's, and he seems to have regarded her kindly. But early on in her career Haywood drew the special ire of Pope and Swift, partly because they thought that she had attacked the character of their friend Martha Blount in her secret history, *Memoirs of a Certain Island Adjacent to the Kingdom of Utopia* (1724), as well as Pope's neighbor and friend, Mrs. Henrietta Howard, in another scandal chronicle, *A Secret History of the Present Intrigues of the Court of Caramania* (1726), and partly owing to her friendship with their enemy, the dramatist and critic Lewis Theobald, Pope's censorious rival as an editor of Shakespeare's plays.[12] In a letter of October 26, 1731, Swift called her "a stupid, infamous, scribbling woman," although he claimed not to have read "any of her productions."[13] But Pope had already in Book II of *The Dunciad* (1728) ridiculed her mercilessly by depicting her as the prize for the winner in a urinating contest (part of the mock-epic Olympic games among the Grub Street Dunces):

> See in the circle next, Eliza plac'd,
> Two babes of love close clinging to her waste;
> Fair as before her works she stands confess'd,
> In flow'rs and pearls by bounteous Kirkall dress'd.
> The Goddess then: "Who best can send on high
> "The salient spout, far-streaming to the sky;
> His be yon Juno of majestic size,
> With cow-like udders and with ox-like eyes.[14]

As Pope has the commentator Martinus Scriblerus, his alter ego in *The Dunicad,* remark in a mock footnote to this passage, Haywood (and others like her) gave offense by writing "libellous Memoirs and Novels [that] reveal the faults and misfortunes of both sexes, to the ruin and disturbance, of publick fame or private happiness."[15]

As Pope's attack makes clear, in the mid-1720s Haywood was a busy, eminently successful writer, a highly visible professional, turning her hand to whatever the public seemed to want, and it is fair to say that as a popular author she had more readers than Pope. In its scabrous ferocity, his attack identifies Haywood as an important target for Pope's special satire of the popular literary marketplace of his day, a key symptom of what he and his fellow satirists thought was wrong with contemporary culture. Her prominent place in the poem (and in the frontispiece, depicting an ass loaded with various books by Pope's satiric targets, one of which is "Haywood's Novel" and another "Court of Caramania," one of Haywood's scandal chronicles) can be regarded as a tribute to her effectiveness and her popularity in the literary marketplace for which Pope and Swift had so much contempt. She moved in the literary demimonde of struggling and disreputable professional writers like Savage, that Grub Street that Pope ridiculed so memorably in *The Dunciad,* but she also counted among her friends quite respectable authors like Theobald and even more substantial literary figures clustered around the dramatist and poet Aaron Hill, whose circle included such figures as the poet John Dyer, the playwright and actress Susanna Centlivre, and the playwright David Mallet.[16]

Apparently undaunted by Pope's satire, Haywood continued to be an active professional in the literary marketplace, but as the 1720s came to an end her output declined somewhat from her earlier frantic pace. Perhaps the vogue for amatory fiction was subsiding, the market saturated one might guess, since she now began to turn to other formats and subjects of a more journalistic sort.[17] In 1732, for example, she wrote *Secret Memoirs of the late Mr. Duncan Campbell, the Famous Deaf and Dumb Man,* a Scotsman born deaf and dumb who claimed to have powers of second sight, and in 1735 a guide to the theater, *The Dramatic Historiographer; or, The British Theatre Delineated.* And in 1736 she wrote a vigorous and inventive political satire, *The Adventures of Eovaii, Princess of Ijaveo,* against Robert Walpole, head of the government and the most powerful politician in England. In the 1730s, she worked more in the theater, both as playwright and actress, as part of Henry Fielding's company of actors at the Little Haymarket Theater. Since 1724 or so she had lived in an intimate relationship with the playwright William Hatchett, and she appeared in several of his plays, such as *The Rival Father* (1730) and a musical version of Fielding's farce, *The Tragedy of Tragedies, The Opera of Operas* (1733), which she coauthored with him.

II

The decade of the 1740s marked a crucial shift in the narrative market, begun of course by the appearance in 1740 of Samuel Richardson's *Pamela,* which for many readers of the day inaugurated a startling, new domestic and psychological realism as well as a moral seriousness and decorum lacking in the amatory novella such as Haywood had produced. But for some rival writers, like Fielding and like Haywood herself, there was a morally disingenuous quality about Richardson's heroine that led them very quickly to produce parodies: in 1741, Fielding's *Shamela* and Haywood's *Anti-Pamela: or, Feigned Innocence Detected.* The subtitle promises what Haywood's romance novellas do not ever claim, veracity: "A Narrative which has really its Foundation in Truth and Nature; and at the same time that it entertains, by a vast variety of surprizing Incidents, arms against a partial Credulity, by shewing the Mischiefs that frequently arise from a too sudden admiration." Haywood's heroine, Syrena Tricksy, is a wickedly amoral and sexually scheming version of Richardson's innocent if resourceful and plucky heroine, and the readers likely to be warned against "a too sudden admiration" are men not women. Haywood turns the *Pamela* plot into a sexual picaresque or sex farce, with the young Syrena joining forces with her mother to swindle a succession of eager and gullible suitors. Unlike *Pamela,* the *Anti-Pamela* ends badly, with Syrena sent to prison as a prostitute and then exiled to Wales after she agrees never to return to London. A female picaresque narrative with a cunning prostitute for a main character, *Anti-Pamela* is a somewhat coarse and unappetizing book that quickly departs from the critique of Richardson's novel promised in the title to render a series of sexual escapades that are essentially swindles, as Syrena and her mother plot to squeeze all they can from her several suitors. Haywood, presumably, was gauging what her audience wanted, and perhaps she miscalculated since she never wrote again in this particular vein but turned to more sentimental and comically moral fiction.

Over the next ten years or so, in a sequence of four novels that ends in 1753 with *The History of Jenny and Jemmy Jessamy,* preceded by *The Fortunate Foundlings* (1744), *Life's Progress Through the Passions: Or, The Adventures of Natura* (1748), and *The History of Miss Betsy Thoughtless* (1751), Haywood can be said to have tried four fairly distinct narrative approaches, seeking in all of these to accommodate her work to the new kinds of novel writing that emerged in the 1740s in England as practiced by Fielding, Richardson, and Smollett.[18] In their alert diversity, these novels dramatize

Haywood's pragmatic professionalism, her adaptive skills to what the market place seemed to want. Each of these four represents a deliberate and inventive attempt to leave behind, in varying and increasing degrees, the febrile style and sensational subject matter of her works in the 1720s, to accommodate her narrative manner to the prevailing modes. As Mary Ann Schofield in her study of Haywood puts it: "sensational material has given way to moralistic reporting," and Haywood insists in these novels, says Schofield, that "she is dealing with real, not fictitious characters who can therefore be considered as good, moral, object lessons."[19] But she never attempted to imitate Richardson's grandly tragic epistolary manner as exemplified in his monumental *Clarissa* (1747–1748). Her model in terms of theme, narrative technique, and literary manner is clearly Fielding, of whose theater company at the New Theatre in the Haymarket during 1736–1737 Haywood was a member (even though he had earlier in 1730 satirized her in his play, *The Author's Farce* [1730], as "Mrs. Novel").[20] Like the author of *Joseph Andrews* (1742) and *Tom Jones* (1749), Haywood is in her later works, especially the last two, essentially a comic/sentimental novelist. This is not to say that she ever totally abandoned her melodramatic amatory subject matter, and *The Fortunate Foundlings* is the closest in spirit of her last works to her novellas of the 1720s. What it promises readers that is new on Haywood's menu is historical and social variety as the subtitle declares: "Containing Many wonderful ACCIDENTS that befell them in their TRAVELS and interspersed with the CHARACTERS and ADVENTURES of SEVERAL PERSONS of condition in the most polite Courts of Europe." And there is a good deal of historical variety of scene and situation in this novel, as Haywood's twin hero and heroine travel over most of Europe (separately), with Horatio serving in the Duke of Marlborough's army and enlisting in the army of the Swedish King Charles XII as his aide-de-camp. After fighting gallantly against the Russians, he winds up a gentleman-officer prisoner of war in St. Petersburg. Louisa, his sister, flees from the advances of the man who at the end of the book turns out to be their father and in the service of a rich widow falls in love with a French count in Vienna. As this compact summary of a book that has many more incidents may reveal, the book gives Haywood many opportunities to rehearse those emotional and amorous intensities she specialized in during the 1720s.

Haywood's next two novels, however, mark a decided shift away from that speciality, a real transformation in her fictional product. George Frisbie Whicher accurately called her next novel, the ambitious *Life's Progress Through the Passions: Or, The Adventures of Natura* (1748), "her emancipation from the traditions of romance."[21] Chiefly, such a characterization derives from the book's striking thoughtfulness, its intellectual ambitions in what amounts to a *roman à thèse,* as the author at the outset declares her purpose to explore through her hero nothing less than the "human mind," which in philosophic mood she says may be "compared to a chequer-work, where light and shade appear by turns; and in proportion as either of these is most conspicuous, the man is alone worthy of praise or censure; for none there are can boast of being wholly bright."[22] In his energy and variety of social and intellectual experiences and also in his insertion in contemporary upper-class English actuality of a sort (he goes to Eton, he takes the Grand Tour through Europe, he serves in Parliament), her hero anticipates some of Smollett's picaresque characters in *Peregrine Pickle* (1751) or *Roderick Random* (1748). On one level, Natura is also like some of the aristocratic libertines in Haywood's earlier novellas, and the novel recounts various sexual adventures, but the narrator also examines him as an instance of a complex and contradictory character, an opportunity for Haywood to ponder some of the mysteries and paradoxes of the human heart, the passions in this narrative including much more than sexual urges. As narrator, Haywood in *The Adventures of Natura* is intelligently thoughtful, her style and manner meditative and philosophical. Although the novel is packed with her characteristically fast-paced variety of scene and action and a good helping of her romantic and even erotic situations, the commentary on events is often elaborate, offering thoughtful generalizations about her character's behavior that go far beyond the psycho-sexual intensities of her earlier work. When she sends Natura on the Grand Tour of Europe, for example, his adventures are not purely amorous. When like many a good English traveler, he carefully examines Roman ruins in Lyon, the narrator generalizes and reflects on human curiosity and the thirst for new experiences:

> The drive of novelty is inherent to a human heart, and nothing so much gratifies that passion as travelling—variety succeeds variety:—whether you climb the craggy mountains, or traverse the flowery vale;—whether thick woods set limits to the sight, or the wide common yields unbounded prospect;—whether the ocean rolls in solemn state before you, or gentle streams run purling by your side, nature in all her different shapes delights; each progressive day brings with it fresh matter to admire, and every stage you come to presents at night customs and manners new and unknown before.[23]

To some extent, Haywood's next novel, *The History of Miss Betsy Thoughtless* (1751), is a retreat from the considerable originality (or downright strangeness) of *The Adventures of Natura.* But the critical consensus is that it is Haywood's best novel, and in terms of plausibility and moderate social and moral realism it is in fact the most accomplished and readable narrative she ever wrote. Betsy is a female version of Fielding's Tom Jones, a flirtatious coquette whose early life as an attractive young woman in the mid-eighteenth-century marriage market is a series of chaste love adventures (and even a near rape or two) with various men (including the love of her life, a Mr. Trueworth). This is capped by a disastrous marriage arranged for her by her brothers to the aptly named worldly Mr. Munden, who proves unfaithful and tyrannical (even at one point attempting to pimp her for his own advancement to a nobleman) but who, conveniently, dies at last of dissipation after the book's extended evocation of the woe that can be in marriage, allowing Betsy to marry in due course the newly widowed Trueworth. *Betsy Thoughtless* is both a comic and serious novel, combining the playfully ironic and almost parodic style and manner she may have absorbed from Fielding's novels with the female conduct book moral and social complexity that is a sign of Richardson's influence on mid-century domestic narrative.[24] As Haywood herself summarizes her heroine's character, it is volatile, mixed, and immature at first: she "was far from setting forth to any advantage the real good qualities she was possessed of: on the contrary the levity of her conduct rather disfigured the native innocence of her mind, and the purity of her intentions."[25] But Haywood is at pains to stress the native intelligence and good sense of her heroine, who "had a fine understanding and a very just notion of things," wanting only "to reflect on the many follies and deceits which some of those who call themselves the beau monde are guilty of, to be enabled to despise them."[26] *Betsy Thoughtless* is a genuinely insightful rendering of mid-eighteenth-century manners, sexual and marital, among the middle and upper classes. In the course of her flirtatious adventures that include a few real sexual threats, Betsy becomes with accumulated experiences more thoughtful or prudent, and for the most original part of the book, her disastrous marriage to Mr. Munden, her story provides a study of unhappy married life that is as good as any similar representation in mid-eighteenth-century fiction.

III

Of her last four novels, the most neglected during the revival in the last twenty years of scholarly and critical interest in Haywood (especially from feminist critics) has been *The History of Jemmy and Jenny Jessamy* (1753), perhaps because it has not been reprinted in a modern annotated edition such as this one. It seems, however, to have been read until the end of the eighteenth and into the early nineteenth century, with the last edition published in 1785. Indeed, Sir Walter Scott could count on his readers recognizing it when he referred with amused contempt to "the whole Jenny and Jessamy tribe" of authors of sentimental novels, although in some ways this novel is hard-edged and realistic rather than sentimental.[27] And in *The Newcomes* (1853–1855), Thackeray assumed that his readers would know what one of his characters is talking about when he fulminates against the fantasy of marriage for love, "this fine picture of Jenny and Jessamy [he gets the names wrong, of course, which may mean that Thackeray hadn't actually read the novel!] falling in love at first sight, billing and cooing in an arbour, and retiring to a cottage afterwards to go on cooing and billing."[28] Thackeray's Lord Kew not only has the names wrong. Jemmy and Jenny do not fall in love at first sight but rather grow up together, and they will, we can be sure, live after their marriage not in a cottage but in a substantial London town house and an elegant country estate. Haywood's novel by the mid-nineteenth century seems to have been remembered rather than read, and Thackeray's characterization of it shows that it was associated, loosely and vaguely, with sentimental romantic novels.

Neither purely sentimental nor romantic, Haywood's last novel is thus very much worth reading, since it represents a significant (and of course final) variation in her novelistic style. Like its immediate predecessor, it is most of the time couched in Fielding's bantering manner in an allusive, brightly sophisticated, and often chatty and familiar style (although there is a good deal of moralizing, sometimes fairly heavy and even ponderous). Featuring a large cast of characters in addition to the two titular ones, the narrative is leisurely, including many interpolated stories of female distress, some of them reminiscent of Haywood's early amatory novellas of seduction and betrayal and of unhappy married life or patriarchal tyranny that forces young women into marriage, and all of them to that extent related as negative or destructive opposites to the situation of the two main characters. And in the end several of these stories are directly related to the main plot, which includes a number of surprising coincidences that help to defeat those who would keep Jemmy and Jenny apart. The action moves around England, from London to Oxford to Bath and thence to Paris and back to London, where most of the novel takes place.

The main plot revolves around Jenny and Jemmy's long-delayed marriage, as they decide to wait to see if their affection for each other is genuine and as obstacles to it arise. There is at last a culminating duel with the main villain of the piece, the final complication for their long-postponed marriage, that puts Jemmy in great danger and forces him to flee to France.

Overall, the narrative is handled with a fairly light touch, as Haywood the narrator (in Fielding's manner) comments ironically and directly to her readers on characters and action, as well as occasionally on her own efforts as narrator. Yet Haywood is at times reluctant to concede Fielding's dominating influence or to place herself entirely in the camp of the comic novel. Here is the heading to chapter XVIII of volume III: "Contains none of those beautiful digressions, those remarks, or reflections which a certain would-be critic pretends are so much distinguish'd in the writings of his two favorite authors; yet, it is to be hoped, will afford sufficient to please all those who are willing to be pleased." In fact, the narrator of *Jemmy and Jenny Jessamy* gives a good deal of narrative space and expressive freedom over to the discourse of its characters, as the novel renders dialogue at some length and features much epistolary communication, the plot turning at several points on fabricated letters that nearly succeed in tearing the lovers apart. One might even say that Haywood allows her serious and exceedingly sober heroine to influence her own narrator's flippant discourse, and there are times when her own moralism turns somber, almost Johnsonian in its mature pessimism:

> According to all the observations which reason and a long experience has enabled me to make, happiness is a thing which ought to be totally erased out of the vocabulary of sublunary enjoyments;—the human heart is liable to so many passions, and the events of fortune so uncertain and precarious, that life is little more than a continued series of anxieties and suspence:—what we pursue as the ultimate of our desires, the summum bonum of all our wishes, fleets before us, dances in the wind, seems at sometimes ready to meet our grasp, at others soaring quite out of reach; or, when attain'd, deceives our expectations, baffles our high-raised hopes, and shews the fancy'd heaven a mere vapour. (II, v)

Haywood's narrator in *Jemmy and Jenny Jessamy* varies the tone and emphasis, from light social satire to psycho-sexual and moral ruminations such as this as she considers the twisted motives and secret desires of some of her characters. For example, at the beginning of volume II, she puts it this way as she examines the passions of the young widow, Lady Speck, resolved not to marry again and yet attracted to a young libertine, Celandine, and jealous of the innocent Jenny to whom this young man makes advances:

> There are so many secret windings, such obscure recesses in the human mind, that it is very difficult, if not wholly impossible, for speculation to arrive at the real spring or first mover of any action whatsoever.
>
> How indeed should it be otherwise, as the most virtuous and the most vicious propensities of nature are frequently in a more or less degree lodged and blended together in the same composition, and both equally under the influence of a thousand different passions, which disguise and vary the face of their operations, so as not to be distinguish'd even by the persons themselves. (II, I)

On the face of it, that is an odd comment, in a book where social comedy and satire dominate, in a story whose plot depends upon the predictable vices of libertines like Celandine and the equally standard and comically repetitive urges, weaknesses, and vanities of just about all of the other characters. The bright sophistication of Haywood's narrator is, in fact, balanced against those dark and threatening realities of lust and avarice that underlie such traditional comedy and social observation, that may be said always to constitute the underside of privileged upper-class life such as this novel and many other eighteenth-century novels of manners examine and critique.

It may be significant that *Jemmy and Jenny Jessamy* is the only one of Haywood's novels in which the main characters do not have quasi-allegorical names but real Christian names and an actual, if uncommon, surname. Both protagonists differ in their psychological plausibility, their mild thoughtfulness and self-control, from most of the other lesser or supporting characters, especially several libertine villains, such as Bellpine and Celandine, who act as nearly successful opponents of the two young lovers. Although he is no saint, Jemmy Jessamy is the most sympathetic and the most plausible male character Haywood ever imagined. Many readers will think of Fielding's Tom Jones as they observe Jemmy's easy and impulsive sexuality. He is described in the first volume as "a man of pleasure," who "did not live without many transient amours" (I, xiv). Near the end of the second volume, Haywood insists that Jemmy is drawn to the life: "let his actions speak for themselves; and if they cannot shew him so wholly blameless as could be wish'd, from the frailties of youth and nature, they will at least defend his character from the more gross imputations of perfidiousness, ingratitude, and deceit" (II, xix). The book's plot turns mostly on his gradual reformation from mildly rakish man about town into the ardent lover and contented bridegroom of his childhood friend. For her part, Jenny shares the stage just about equally with Jemmy. She is rendered as sweet but not naive or foolish like Betsy Thoughtless, moral and pure but pensive and observant of the trivial and sometimes vicious social scene around her. She is worldly enough to be wise to the sexual double standard that allows Jemmy to have affairs while she holds herself aloof from other suitors in anticipation of their marriage. As one of the female characters, Lady Speck, concludes to Jenny when it is discovered that Jemmy may be romantically involved with a singer in London: "In good truth we women have nothing to do with the men's affairs in this point before marriage;—and as I now begin to believe, in spite of all I have heard to the contrary, that he addresses no other woman than yourself upon honourable terms, these are but venial transgressions, which you ought to overlook till you have made him your own" (II, ix).

Early in volume I, Haywood almost seems to be repudiating her former approach to character as she introduces her two lovers, who have been brought up together by their families and through that long association "it became a kind of second nature in them to love each other, the affection they began in infancy, grew up with their years; and if what they felt as they approach'd nearer to maturity did not amount to a passion, it was at least somewhat more than is ordinarily found between a brother and a sister" (I, i). As we learn at the outset, they are affianced in childhood by their wealthy fathers, who hope that they will decide to marry when they come of age (when Jemmy is twenty-one and Jenny seventeen). Both fathers die before that date, but the two children are left very well off. The narrator describes the couple as compatible personalities, spirited and lively rather than priggish or solemn: "both of them were gay and volatile almost to an excess,—both lov'd the pleasures of the town, yet never pursued them so far as to transgress the bounds of strict virtue in the one, nor honour in the other" (I, iv). Their relationship serves as nothing less than a corrective to extravagant notions of what love should be:

> Neither of them were possess'd of any strong passions; and though the affection they had for each other was truly tender and sincere, yet neither of them felt those impatiencies,—those anxieties,—those transporting hopes,—those distracting fears,—those causeless jealousies, or any of those thousand restless sensations that usually perplex a mind devoted to an amorous flame;—he was not in the least alarm'd on finding she was frequently visited by some

> of the finest gentlemen in town; nor was she at all disconcerted when she was told he was well received by ladies of the most distinguish'd characters.
>
> I am well aware, that many of my readers will be apt to say,—people who could think and act in the manner I have describ'd, either had no charms for each other, or seem'd incapable of loving at all;—and I am ready to confess, that according to the receiv'd notions of love, there was a seeming inconsistency in this conduct, and had more the appearance of a cold indifference than the warm glow of mutual inclinations.
>
> Yet that they did love each other is most certain, as will hereafter be demonstrated by proofs much more unquestionable than all those extravagancies;—those raging flights commonly look'd upon as infallible tokens of the passion, but which, how fierce soever the fires they spring from may burn for a while, we see frequently extinguish of themselves, and leave nothing but the smoke behind. (I, iv)

This is quite a declaration or indeed something like a recantation of the former views of the "Great Arbitress of Passion" (as James Sterling had called Haywood in his poetic tribute), who might be said to have had a great deal to do in her earlier work precisely with perpetuating those "receiv'd notions of love" on which she pours scorn here, but in fact this analysis of her main characters as embodiments of love as it actually exists is the unifying thread of the novel. Near the end of many trials and troubles for the lovers, Haywood seems to be warning skeptical readers that the attraction between these two is indeed genuine and enduring. Her language here modifies the traditional amatory rhetoric of flaming passion. "And now let those readers, who in the beginning of this history were apt to look on Jemmy and Jenny as two insensibles, acknowledge their mistake, and be convinced that flames which burn with rapidity at first are soonest wasted, and that a gentle, and almost imperceptible glow of a pure affection, when once raised up by any extraordinary incident, sends forth a stronger and more lasting heat" (III, xi). *Jemmy and Jenny Jessamy* aspires, consistently, to a moderate social realism that is just a bit purer than that in *Betsy Thoughtless,* as Haywood purges her narrative (or at least the personalities of her main characters) of just about all of the old melodrama and extravagance of her earlier romance fiction. Such a revision is not surprising, since like all novelistic realism from Cervantes's *Don Quixote* on, Haywood's thrives on a refinement or indeed a rejection of romance. In this case, interestingly enough, it is her own version of romance and sexual sensationalism that is renounced.

Despite its title, *The History of Jemmy and Jenny Jessamy* is in fact a series of histories of a wide circle of privileged, leisure-class young people, friends and acquaintances of the two central characters. But the novel takes in as well the important interpolated stories of various interesting and distressed female strangers who turn up in the narrative. The whole is a collection of interlocked stories and related incidents, a rendering of a social world that is broader and more diverse than anything that Haywood had attempted before. It is also for Jemmy and Jenny primarily a series of lessons about the woe that is in contemporary upper-class marriage, as both of them from the very beginning of the novel have encounters and experiences with various kinds of marital dysfunction among their friends and acquaintances and in the tales told by strangers. Just at the beginning of the novel, several of Jenny's friends arrive as she and Jemmy are discussing their marriage plans, and they deliver themselves of some gossip about a tremendous three-day row between a well-known married couple, Lord and Lady Fisk. Jemmy and Jenny find this a sobering lesson about the dangers of hasty marriage and resolve to make themselves "well vers'd in all those things, whatever they are, which constitute the happiness" of marriage. And so Jenny proposes that since "this town is an ample school, and both of us have acquaintance enough in it to learn, from the mistakes of others, how to regulate our own conduct and passions, so as not to be laugh'd at ourselves for what we laugh at in them" (I, v). Haywood thus turns her novel into a deliberate survey on the part of her two main characters of the nature of marriage as it exists around them in London among their class and an exploration in that light of their own future compatibility for that state. For example, right after making this plan, Jenny visits the Marloves, a young married couple (Mrs. Marlove is all of sixteen) who are at each other's throats. And "the sagacious Jenny" (as the narrator, almost mockingly, calls her) is moved to moralize in what will be her characteristically sententious, not to say solemn, manner: "This naturally led her into reflections on the folly of two persons uniting themselves together by the solemn ties of marriage, without having well consider'd the duties of the state they were about to enter into, and confirm'd her in the resolution she before had taken of living single, till she was as well assured, as human reason could make her, that both herself and the man who was to be her husband, were equally qualified to render each other truly happy" (I, vii). And Jemmy attends a party for a couple who have been separated for fourteen years and now to the great satisfaction of all their friends have been reconciled. Jemmy looks around the room, watching for signs of marital discontent: "according to the agreement made between him and Jenny,

[he] kept an observant eye on all those whom he found were married, and easily perceived, by the looks which one of them in particular frequently gave his wife, that they were far from living together in a perfect harmony" (I, vii).

Not all of these observations of marital life are controlled, and some experiences lead to danger, dismay, and confusion. For Jenny, one of the most dangerous occurs near the end of volume I and is a curious mixture of marital negative exemplum and amatory melodrama. In its interruption of the graceful and glamorous hedonistic daily routine of the main characters with an inserted narrative of pain, suffering, and betrayal, this incident is also typical of the structure of the novel, which moves along placidly until unexpected treachery or violence intervenes. Jenny travels to Bath as part of a group led by the young widow, Lady Speck, and including her sister, Miss Wingman, and three male gallants, Lord Huntley (in love with Miss Wingman), Sir Robert Manley (who is in love with Jenny), and Mr. Lovegrove (in love with Lady Speck). The narrator describes their daily routine this way: "Since the adventure of Celandine the ladies had lived for some days in an uninterrupted scene of gaity;—every day,—almost every hour, brought with it some new pleasure or amusement" (II, v). The Celandine whom the narrator refers to is a handsome libertine who has attached himself to this party of pleasure, and he is clearly marked as trouble from his arrival: "it would have puzzled even his best friends and greatest admirers, if ask'd the question, to have found any one virtue in him to compensate for a thousand vices; he was vain to an excess, ungrateful, insincere, incapable either of love or friendship; a contemner both of morality and religion; in fine, he was a libertine profess'd" (I, xxiii). As Celandine strolls with Jenny in the gardens, his advances to her quickly grow more importunate and then rudely physical, but at that moment a woman jumps out of the bushes and rushes at Jenny with a knife. Disarmed by Celandine, "the furious stranger" soon thereafter offers her history to Jenny and her friends. This distraught young lady reveals herself to be Celandine's spurned mistress, one Mrs. M——, who had been seduced away from her husband and then abandoned. Her tale is, however, more complicated and circumstantial than the usual story of seduced female virtue. Left an orphan, she marries Mr. M——, who in the first days of their marriage is all ardor but whose passion cools with time. One of Mrs. M——'s friends suggests that she carry on a flirtation to make him jealous and restore his initial passion, and so Mrs. M—— involves herself with Celandine, her husband's protégé. But she is soon in love with the younger man, and in due course her husband catches them in flagrante and banishes her from bed and board. Predictably, Celandine tires of her quickly, but she follows him to Bath, determined to kill him and enraged to madness when she sees him with Jenny. In the aftermath of this incident, Jenny grows even more concerned about the state of the social world around her, recalling a disastrous marriage she had heard about when she was younger and reflecting at length on the delusive snares of sexual attraction: "it is the mind which ought to be the chief object of our attention; it is there alone we are either beautiful or deform'd; and the pains we take to ornament and embellish that nobler part of us will not be thrown away" (II, ii).

For his part, as he lives the life of a wealthy young man about town in London, Jemmy observes a number of unhappy marriages as well. One, especially, stands out and leads him to confirm in his own mind his plans to marry Jenny. In one of the many comic domestic scenes that the novel features, Jemmy's friend Mr. Kelsey is frustrated by his pious wife, who puts her devotions before her domestic duties. So when he brings Jemmy home to supper, the meal is ruined, overcooked, and ill attended to. Jemmy reflects at length on this incompatibility: "he concluded, that good nature and similitude of dispositions, tho' the last things consider'd, and seldom if ever enquired into by the persons about to be united, were indeed the chief ingredients to make their future happiness." And he reasons further that Jenny is perfect for him: "she had never betray'd a too strong attachment to any one thing; no caprice, no whimsical flights, no affectation, no pride of exciting the envy of her own sex, or of giving pain to those of the other; in all her words and actions she preserved the happy medium of neither being too gay and giddy, nor too sullen and reserv'd; nor was all this mere outward shew; he could not suspect her of disguise, as he had known her before she could arrive at the power, even if she had the will, of pretending to be other than she really was" (I, xvi).

From the beginning, Haywood's novel offers readers through the narrator's own reflections and then by means of her thoughtful hero and heroine an elegant moralism and slightly satirical rendition of leisure-class life such as Haywood had depicted in *Betsy Thoughtless.* This depiction of a social world is often a matter of using the various young people Jemmy and Jenny meet as satirical foils for their own attractive and sensible personalities. For example, early in volume I, with Jemmy at college in Oxford, Jenny decides to visit her school friend Sophia, who lives in the country, "some one or two and twenty miles distant from London, where she had received several pressing invitations to come, but had hitherto been prevented from complying by one accident or other" (I, ii). And while she is there, Sophia's brother, Rodophil, arrives with his fiancée, and their chit-chat evokes a trivial, empty world of irresponsible leisure-class youth. Rodophil's fiancée responds to Sophia's protest that they have arrived without notice:

> "Nay, as to that matter, child," cried the lady in a very familiar, and indeed, somewhat of a hoydenish tone, "you have nothing to accuse him of on this account, for I assure you neither of us thought of being here to-night, two hours before we set out from London; but I know not how it happen'd, but we were both in a frolicksome humour; he swore he would have me, and I swore if he had, he should run away with me;—the impudent thing took me at my word,—sent in a minute for a landau and six,—thrust me into it, and hurried me away without any farther preparation than just as you see." (I, ii)

This young lady, clearly, is socially gauche and as it turns out morally unsound. The narrator observes her behavior at dinner that night and comments from Jenny's perspective: "the insolence of flatter'd beauty, and the vanity of imagining, that she could do nothing unbecoming in her, made her act and talk in so affected, and so odd a fashion, as greatly defaced all the charms she had received from nature" (I, ii). Silly, voluble, and ill-mannered at table, she is greeted by Jenny's eloquent silence, but when she accuses our heroine of bashfulness, Jenny is roused to respond: "as her silence was occasioned only by the other's excess of volubility, the usual vivacity of her temper was rous'd by this reproach" (I, ii). Very shortly, it transpires that Rodophil's fiancée is already married to one La Val, but she declares that it was the result of a whim and since it was not consummated it can easily be dissolved. Rodophil, as Sophia tells Jenny, had only wanted to marry this young lady for her fortune, but he is now too disgusted with her to go through with it and leaves for a friend's house. This is the first of many scenes that Jenny will witness that will educate her in female folly, and thoughtfully serious as she already is, she draws the moral:

> "Who can be assur'd,"—said she within herself, "till experience convinces them, that they themselves may not be guilty of the same irregularity of humour, tho' their prudence, and the fears of censure may keep them from exposing the weakness of their resolution!—We all of us are liable to change in trifling matters, and frequently despise to-morrow what we lik'd to-day;—I see no reason, therefore, that we have to depend on our own hearts in things of the greatest importance."
>
> Jenny could not, in spite of the gaiety of her temper, forbear falling

> into little reveries of this nature, whenever she consider'd herself as entering into a state, from which there is no relief but the grave; or, what to a woman of any delicacy, is yet worse,—a divorcement. (I, iii)

A scene like this sets the pattern of the novel in Jenny's half of it: she observes romantic and marital life around her and draws sober lessons from it all, establishing herself as a font of good sense in a world where just about all the other young women she meets are foolishly thoughtless or feckless. Perhaps as a deliberate contrast with Betsy Thoughtless and other impressionable heroines, Jenny rejects conventional views of love: "she had heard and read much of the effects of love, and the fatal consequences which had sometimes attended a disappointed flame; and therefore had always consider'd that passion as a thing of too serious a nature to be sported with; and that it was an action highly ungenerous and cruel to encourage the growth of it in any heart, without having the power or inclination of making an adequate return" (I, xxii). In a comedy of contemporary upper-class manners, Jenny is (what Burney's Evelina will be more than twenty years later) somehow beyond or above those manners, a moralizing spectator and self-counselor rather than a full participant in the fairly decadent social life around her. For one early example, she recounts to Jemmy how at a gambling party she had lost some twenty pounds, all she had about her, when she was accosted by a nobleman, the Earl of ——, who proposed to give her more money to gamble with. Jenny tells Jemmy how shocked she is, not just at the impropriety of the offer but the Earl's amorous hyperbole as he makes the offer. Her response is indignant and independent: "Never was any poor creature so overwhelm'd with different passions as I then was; amazement, shame, disdain, and rage, at once rose in my bosom, and almost stopp'd the passage of my breath. I forgot all respect of his birth and place; and throwing the purse he had given me upon the floor,—'carry your offers,' said I, 'to those who want them, I despise both them and the hand from which they came'" (I, xi).

She tells this story to Jemmy, who has just recounted another tale of amorous intrigue about a lady given to gambling who repays her benefactors with sexual favors, although he neglects to tell her that he himself has enjoyed the lady's gratitude. The reader has already heard this story, of the beautiful Liberia, who is addicted to gambling and loses more in a year than her husband's rent rolls produce. After losing a considerable sum to Jemmy at a gambling house, she takes him home and beds him. But when Jemmy returns the next day, she greets him coldly and explains that their dalliance was purely a business matter, payment for the debt she owed him. Later that day, Jemmy discovers from an acquaintance that this sexual reckoning for her gambling losses is her common practice. Liberia's response to the amorous Jemmy is crisp and worldly, frank and matter-of-fact in the manner of a Restoration comedy, from a world that would shock Jenny if she were allowed to see it in all its confident and self-seeking amorality:

> But how unspeakable was his surprise, when, going to take her in his arms, she started back, and with a countenance all awful and austere, "Hold off, Sir," said she, "this is a familiarity neither becoming you to take, nor me to grant": the confusion he was in not permitting him to make any immediate reply; "I do not now," continued she, "owe fifty pieces to you."
>
> "No, Madam," reply'd he, a little recovering himself; "but you owe me a heart in return for that I have devoted to you."—"I have nothing to do with your heart, resum'd she; and as for mine it is my husband's due."—"If you really think so, Madam," cried he, "wherefore did you flatter me last night with having so large a part?"—"What happened last night," said she, "was merely accidental; I had lost all my money, and the debts we contract at play, you know are debts of honour; but where my own is not concerned, be assured I shall always have a just regard for that of my husband's." (I, x)

Jemmy seems to move confidently in this world of amoral pleasure-seeking and rough-edged dialogue, but Haywood wants us to know that he is not entirely defined by it, that he is in his fashion true to Jenny even as he is tempted by sexual opportunity. Jemmy's essential decency and openness are established by the contrast between him and characters like Liberia. He is relatively innocent and trusting in a world where such qualities are dramatized by the novel as dangerous, and for all his worldliness Jemmy's judgment as we are shown is faulty. Thus, his best friend is one Bellpine: "Jemmy had contracted a very numerous acquaintance since his father's death, many of whom had a large share of his esteem and friendship; but there was one above the rest whose humour and behaviour he was particularly taken with, and with whom he conversed with the most unreserved freedom" (I, xii). Bellpine is Jemmy's opposite number in some revealing ways. Like Fielding's Blifil, he is a hypocrite, a designing and calculating figure, deprived of his future substance by the marriage of his eighty-year-old uncle to a young woman of nineteen and now looking around for ways to improve his prospects. Bellpine possesses "many accomplishments both natural and acquired; but had no fund either of honour or generosity; he knew perfectly well how to insinuate himself into the good graces of those he convers'd with; but thought himself not bound to make an adequate return for any favours he received from them; all his wishes were center'd in self-gratification, and no consideration for others had ever any weight to make him desist that favourite pursuit" (I, xii). Introduced to Jenny by the trusting Jemmy, Bellpine sets out to sabotage Jemmy's engagement to his Jenny, with a view to marrying her himself. Counting on Jemmy's love of music, he contrives to introduce him to a well-known singer, Miss Chit, and when that plot fails he resorts to other stratagems such as a forged letter to Jenny. In the end, of course, his plot fails, and it will come as no surprise that all obstacles are overcome at last and the two titular lovers finally marry, along with their young friends, Lady Speck and Mr. Lovegrove, and Miss Wingman and Lord Huntley.

But before that happens, both Jenny and Jemmy grow wiser, learning deep and formative lessons not just about matrimony but also, crucially, about themselves. Jemmy, for example, is at last in the final volume of the novel redeemed from his impulsive, casual sexual affairs by experiencing a deep concern for Jenny's feelings when he learns of Bellpine's plot to slander him with Miss Chit:

> What was wanting in the violence of that passion he had for her was abundantly made up with tenderness;—he trembled not for himself but her;—conscious of his innocence, he had no cause to dread the reproaches she might meet him with; but was ready to sink under the apprehensions of what she endured, till he was fully clear'd of this unjust accusation.
>
> It was not that he first began to feel that burning impatience to be with her which all lovers pretend to have, though few perhaps, very few, in reality experience;—it was not that he so much languish'd to feast his eyes upon her beauties, or his ears with her wit and engaging conversation, tho' both had charms for him preferable to those of any other woman in the world; but it was to ease her of all suspence in regard to his integrity; and convince her, by the most unquestionable testimony, that he was incapable of love for any but herself. (III, v)

As one might expect, Jenny's thoughts are deeper, more reflective and objective, less selfish, more generalized and serious. In one of the most horrifying of the interpolated stories, Jenny's friend Sophia describes her swindle and seduction by a brutal army officer, Willmore, who after proposing marriage brings her to a brothel, borrowing from her a thousand pounds to purchase a commission. Sophia barely escapes and learns that her money, most of her small fortune, is irrecoverable. Near the end of the novel, she tells her story to Jenny and resolves to retire to a convent on the continent. Jenny's reflections after Sophia leaves include horror and pity, as well as puzzlement that her friend should trust someone she barely knew, but she also muses on the intertwinings of fate and circumstances in an individual's moral life:

> "How can I be certain," pursued she, "that in the same circumstances I should not have acted in the same manner that poor Sophia has done?—I have been defended from the misfortune that has befallen her;—first, by my father's care in training me up to love where interest and convenience would accompany my passion,—and afterwards by the well proved fidelity of the man ordain'd for me:—had I been left to my own choice, who knows what might have happen'd? (III, xvii)

In the self-consciousness of its main character, *The History of Jemmy and Jenny Jessamy* articulates the central concerns of the eighteenth-century novel about personal agency. A bit further on, Jenny returns to the topic and pities her friend once again but also shows an understanding of the particular circumstantiality that is crucial for understanding character and action:

> "Yet—why do I think this way," cried she again, "the circumstances of my fortune have render'd me no competent judge of the passion I pretend to condemn?—much certainly may be said in defence of poor Sophia,—her heart was tender, unprepossess'd, and ready to receive the first impression;—she had convers'd little with the world, was entirely ignorant of the artifices which the villainous part of mankind are capable of putting in practice to deceive our sex, and had no friend to advise or warn her against the danger;—I should therefore, perhaps, be no less inexcusable in censuring this unhappy creature, than she is in having yielded to that fatal impulse, by which so many, and some too of the best understanding, have been seduced." (III, xxi)

Jenny, in short, comes to understand the necessity of experience, of immersion and critical involvement in the world in order to evade its traps and temptations. One can say that she is the most sophisticated character in the novel, a real advance on Haywood's female characters from her early days as a producer of romance fiction. She embodies a sophistication that is far from cynical or merely worldly but is, rather, deeply moral and moderate. For a striking instance of this, consider the scene in volume II when she receives a letter (actually forged by the villainous Bellpine) from a woman who claims that Jemmy has made advances to her and is about to break off his relationship with Jenny. Her response to this letter is a matter, essentially, of stylistic sophistication that enables her to resist her initial, understandably alarmed, and even potentially hysterical response: "On the first reading this letter, new alarms, new doubts, new jealousies, instantly fill'd the head and heart of Jenny; but on a second perusal there seem'd to her something too romantic in the expression, as well as purport of it, for her to believe it founded upon real fact; and she began to fancy it was either intended by her enemies as an insult, or by her friends as a jest" (II, xvii).

The narrator herself, in contrast, tends to offer readers cool epigrams and moral-psychological maxims about timeless patterns in human beings, especially as she contemplates the behavior of the less savory characters. For example, when Bellpine learns that Jemmy is going to visit Jenny at Bath rather than continuing his affair with his old uncle's young wife, he is surprised that Jemmy has not lied to him, because "men who are themselves deceitful, are always slow in giving credit to the sincerity of others" (III, iii). This narrator is as worldly wise as the most jaded of her characters, and thus she remarks of Jemmy as he sets about arranging an amorous rendezvous: "With the pleasures of an amorous intrigue there will be always some mixture of fatigue"(II, xxvii). This generalizing habit is regular and confident for the narrator: "Every passion of the human mind," she remarks as Jemmy has to fly to France after wounding Bellpine in a duel, "gains double energy by our own endeavours to conceal it;—like fire, which being smother'd for a time bursts out at last with greater violence" (III, x). Or, earlier, she comments as Jemmy's affections for Jenny begin to waver when he meets an old flame, now married to an old nobleman, in London: "Yet see the swift vicissitude, and how suddenly the rolling tide of inclination is capable of overturning those designs which even we ourselves have believed were founded on the most solid basis, and impossible to be shaken" (II, xxviii). And, indeed, her habit of poetic and dramatic quotation (chiefly from Restoration dramatists and poets like Dryden) underlines her somewhat cynical and universalizing view of things as repetitive or recurrent. Although it is sentimental and melodramatic by turns, and although it is perhaps longer than it should be, *The History of Jemmy and Jenny Jessamy* is of great interest for students of the British eighteenth-century novel, especially in the context of Haywood's earlier work, in its balancing of this objective moralism of the narrator and the subjective growth in specifically novelistic terms of its heroine's response to her experiences in a particularized social world. Haywood's Jenny is in this way, paradoxically, far ahead of her creator in terms of moral and social sophistication.

Notes

1. George Frisbie Whicher's *The Life and Romances of Mrs. Eliza Haywood* (New York: Columbia University Press, 1915) was until recently the only biographical/critical study of Haywood's work, and it is a useful and thorough, if dated and deeply condescending, monograph. Our current revised and more careful understanding of Haywood's life is owed chiefly to the pioneering scholarship of Christine Blouch. See her essay, "Eliza Haywood and the Romance of Obscurity," *Studies in English Literature 1500–1900,* 31 (1991): 535–52. Blouch quotes a letter that Haywood wrote in 1728 to an unidentified potential subscriber to her works in which she states: "my maiden name is Fowler, and [I] am nearly related to Sir Richard of the Grange," whom Blouch identifies as Richard Fowler of Harnage Grange, Shropshire, who had a sister, Elizabeth, christened on January 12, 1692/3. Blouch, "Eliza Haywood," 537.

2. Quoted by Blouch, "Eliza Haywood," 537, 539.

3. Cited by Blouch, "Eliza Haywood," 537.

4. Christine Blouch, "Introduction," *The History of Miss Betsy Thoughtless* (Peterborough, Ontario: Broadview Press, 1998), 9.

5. "To Mrs. Eliza Haywood, on her Novel, Called, The Rash Resolve," from *The Works of Richard Savage, . . . With an Account of the Life and Writings of the Author, by Samuel Johnson.* A New Edition, 2 vols. London, 1777. This poem appeared first in the 1723 collected edition of Haywood's works. When he became a friend of Pope a few years later, Savage turned against Haywood, and in 1732 in a note in his poem, "An Author to be Lett" subjected her to a torrent of abuse: "When Mrs. Haywood ceas'd to be a Strolling Actress, why might not the Lady (tho' once a Theatrical Queen) have subsisted by turning Washer-woman? . . . But she rather chooses starving by writing Novels of Intrigue, to teach young Heiresses the Art of running away with Fortune-hunters, and scandalizing Persons of the highest Worth and Distinction." Cited in Whicher, *Life and Romances,* 125–26.

6. Quoted from the 1732 edition of *Secret Histories, Novels, and Poems,* in my *Popular Fiction Before Richardson: Narrative Patterns 1700–1739* (Oxford: Clarendon Press, 1969; rpt. 1992), 180–81.

7. *The Injur'd Husband; or, The Mistaken Resentment* and *Lasselia; or, The Self-Abandon'd,* edited by Jerry C. Beasley (Lexington: University Press of Kentucky, 1999), Introduction, xvi.

8. There is a valuable recent trend in feminist criticism and scholarship dealing with women's amatory fiction from the late seventeenth and early eighteenth century, like Haywood's, which finds in it subversion and resistance to masculinist and oppressively narrow constructions of the feminine. For example, according to Ros Ballaster, Haywood substitutes the patent fictionality of her novellas for the real world, thus reinscribing the truth of women's oppression at the hands of men and compensating them with the

pleasures of fiction. Such an approach finds an intellectual and especially a political complexity in works that are in other ways transparently simple, so that even formula fiction becomes a profound intellectual gesture full of meaning. See Ballaster, *Seductive Forms: Women's Amatory Fiction from 1684 to 1740* (Oxford: The Clarendon Press, 1992), 169. See also the fine essay by Toni O'Shaughnessy Bowers, "Sex, Lies, and Invisibility: Amatory Fiction from the Restoration to the Eighteenth Century," in *The Columbia History of the British Novel,* ed. John Richetti (New York: Columbia University Press, 1994), 50–72, which suggests that Haywood (and other women amatory novelists in the early eighteenth century) explore the complicated interplay of rape and seduction. And in her recent book, *Authorship, Commerce, and Gender in Early Eighteenth-Century England: A Culture of Paper Credit* (Cambridge: Cambridge University Press, 1998), Catherine Ingrassia finds that Haywood's narratives revise literary tradition by interrogating cultural norms and encouraging "alternative (and potentially empowering) models of behavior for women" as they "validate desire as a motivating force" (84). Ingrassia also links Haywood's fiction to what historians call the "financial revolution" that began in England in the early years of the eighteenth century, whereby a new credit-based economy emerged. In feeding the sexual fantasies of her readers, Haywood mimics the fanciful constructions of credit and speculation; the very limitations of her fictions, its extravagance and representational thinness, force her "readers to invest in the story and to expend emotional and imaginative currency" (88).

9. See my essay on Haywood's self-characterization in the context of women's writing in the early eighteenth century, "Voice and Gender in Eighteenth-Century Fiction," *Studies in the Novel* 19 (1987): 263–72.

10. Eliza Haywood, *The Fatal Secret* (London, 1724), n.p.

11. Quoted from the 1732 edition of Haywood's *Secret Histories, Novels, and Poems,* in my *Popular Fiction before Richardson,* 180–81.

12. For details on Haywood's scandal mongering, see Beasley, *Injur'd Husband,* xii.

13. Swift to Lady Howard, *The Correspondence of Jonathan Swift,* ed. Harold Williams (Oxford: Clarendon Press, 1963), 3:501.

14. *The Dunciad,* II, 149–56, edited by James Sutherland (London: Methuen, 1963), 119–20. Elisha Kirkall (1682–1742) had engraved Haywood's likeness for the four-volume collection of her works first published in 1723–1724. In his original version in three books, the passage was even coarser, including the following lines removed from the four-book *Dunciad* of 1742 that I have quoted: "Pearls on her neck, and roses in her hair, / And her fore-buttocks to the navel bare."

15. *The Dunciad,* ed. Sutherland, 119, note 149.

16. Haywood's reputation as an immoral and scandalous writer survived into the middle of the century. Jane Spencer quotes Samuel Richardson writing in 1750 to one of his female admirers, Sarah Chapone, about some scandalous women's memoirs by Laetitia Pilkington, Constantia Phillips, and Lady Vane, whose works are so immoral that he declares they make "the Behn's, the Manley's and the Heywood's, [*sic*] look white." See *Aphra Behn's Afterlife* (Oxford: Oxford Univ. Press, 2000), 62.

17. Pope's great enemy, the unscrupulous and inventive bookseller Edmund Curll, published a response to *The Dunciad,* entitled *The Female Dunciad,* which contained among other pieces a novella by Haywood, *Irish Artifice; or, The History of Clarina,* which

as George Frisbee Whicher explains had nothing to do with Pope or *The Dunciad*. See Whicher, *Life and Romances*, 123–24.

18. I have discussed this aspect of Haywood's career, as well as *The Fortunate Foundlings* and *The Adventures of Natura* in an essay, "Histories by Eliza Haywood and Henry Fielding," in *The Passionate Fictions of Eliza Haywood: Essays on Her Life and Work*, ed. Kirsten T. Saxton and Rebecca P. Bocchicchio (Lexington: University Press of Kentucky, 2000), 240–58.

19. Mary Ann Schofield, *Eliza Haywood* (Boston: Twayne Publishers, 1985), 87.

20. On Haywood's relationship with Fielding, see J.R. Elwood, "Henry Fielding and Eliza Haywood: A Twenty-Year War," *Albion* 5 (Fall 1973): 184–92.

21. Whicher, *Life and Romances*, 157. Whicher says that Haywood "here for the first time becomes a genuine novelist" as she strives not to idealize or glorify life but to "depict the actual conditions of life." But his praise is qualified, and he is careful to observe that the book is "artificial in design and stilted in execution" (157).

22. *Life's Progress Through the Passions: Or, The Adventures of Natura* (London, 1748), 2.

23. *Life's Progress Through the Passions: Or, The Adventures of Natura* (London, 1748), 101–2.

24. Elwood notes that the German edition of *Betsy Thoughtless* was presented as a work by Fielding. See, "Henry Fielding and Eliza Haywood," 191–92.

25. *The History of Miss Betsy Thoughtless*, ed. Christine Blouch (Peterborough, Ontario: Broadview Press, 1998), 223–24.

26. *The History of Miss Betsy Thoughtless*, 212.

27. Cited by Jerry C. Beasley, "Eliza Haywood," in *Dictionary of Literary Biography*, vol. 39, pts. 1 & 2, British Novelists 1660–1800, ed. Martin C. Battestin. (Detroit: Bruccoli Clark, 1985), 258.

28. William Makepeace Thackeray. *The Newcomes: Memoirs of a Most Respectable Family* (London: Smith, Elder, and Co., 1890), chap. xxx, 298. The novel was originally serialized from 1853–1855.

Chronology

ca. 1693	Born in London, Eliza Fowler, daughter of a shopkeeper or merchant, Robert Fowler. Or perhaps in Shropshire to the Fowlers of Harnage Grange. Her biographers are unable to say with certainty who her parents were.
1715	Acts in Thomas Shadwell's adaptation of Shakespeare's *Timon of Athens* in Dublin. She may have married while working in Dublin, but that is merely conjecture by her recent biographers.
1719–1720	*Love in Excess; or, The Fatal Inquiry*, three volumes *The Life of Duncan Campbell*, a pamphlet on a deaf-mute who claimed to have the gift of prophecy
1720	*Letters from a Lady of Quality to a Chevalier* (sold by subscription), Translated from French In 1719–1720, Haywood was associated with a number of London literary figures, including the dramatist and poet Aaron Hill, the poets Richard Savage (probably her lover at the time) and John Dyer, and the playwright David Mallet
1721	*The Fair Captive*, a play, produced at Lincoln's Inn Fields. Separated, it may be, from her husband, supporting herself and two children by her efforts as novelist and dramatist
1722	*The British Recluse; or, The Secret History of Cleomira, Suppos'd Dead* *The Injur'd Husband; or, The Mistaken Resentment*
1723	*Idalia; or, The Unfortunate Mistress* *Lasselia; or, The Self Abandon'd* *The Rash Resolve; or, The Untimely Discovery* *A Wife to be Lett* (a comedy that Haywood herself acted in at Drury Lane) *The Works of Mrs. Eliza Haywood, Consisting of Novels,*

Letters, Poems, and Plays (three volumes), including a prefatory poem by Richard Savage in praise of her work

1724 *Poems on Several Occasions*, Vol. IV of *The Works of Mrs. Eliza Haywood, Consisting of Novels, Letters, Poems, and Plays*

The Arragonian Queen: A Secret History

Bath Intrigues: in Four Letters to a Friend in London

La Belle Assemblée: or, the Adventures of Six Days (translation from French)

Fantomina; or, Love in a Maze

The Fatal Secret; or, Constancy in Distress

The Force of Nature; or, The Lucky Disappointment

The Masqueraders; or, Fatal Curiosity

Memoirs of the Baron de Brosse

Memoirs of a Certain Island Adjacent to the Kingdom of Utopia (scandal chronicle in the manner of Manley's *New Atalantis*)

A Spy Upon the Conjurer; or, a Collection of Surprising Stories . . . relating to Mr. Duncan Campbell

The Surprise; or, Constancy Rewarded

The Tea Table (periodical paper)

Broke off her relationship with Savage and began a twenty-year intimate relationship with the dramatist William Hatchett, who probably fathered one of her illegitimate children

1725 *The Dumb Projector; Being a Surprizing Account of a Trip . . . made by Duncan Campbell*

The Fatal Fondness; or, Love its Own Opposer

The Lady's Philosopher Stone; or the Caprices of Love and Destiny (translated from French)

Mary Stuart, Queen of Scots

The Tea-Table; or, A Conversation Between some Polite Persons of Both Sexes, at a Lady's Visiting Day

The Unequal Conflict; or, Nature Triumphant

1726 *The City Jilt; or, The Alderman Turn'd Beau*

Cleomelia; or, The Generous Mistress

The Distress'd Orphan; or, Love in a Mad-house

	The Double Marriage; or, The Fatal Release
	Letters from the Palace of Fame
	The Mercenary Lover; or, The Unfortunate Heiress
	Reflections on the Various Effects of Love
	The Secret History of the Present Intrigues of the Court of Caramania (another scandal chronicle)
1727	*The Fruitless Enquiry; Being a Collection of Several Entertaining Histories*
	The Life of Madam de Villesache
	Love in its Variety; Being a Collection of Select Novels (translated from Spanish)
	The Perplex'd Dutchess; or Treachery Rewarded
	Philidore and Placentia; or, L'Amour Trop Delicat
	Secret Histories, Novels, etc. (two volumes)
1728	*Irish Artifice; or The History of Clarina*, in *The Female Dunciad* (written in response to Alexander Pope's satiric representation of Haywood in *The Dunciad* (1728)
	The Disguis'd Prince; or, The Beautiful Parisian (translated from French)
	Persecuted Virtue; or, The Cruel Lover
	The Agreeable Caledonian (Part II, 1729)
	Some Memoirs of the Amours and Intrigues of a Certain Irish Dean
1729	*The City Widow; or, Love in a Butt*
	The Fair Hebrew; or, A True, but Secret History of Two Jewish Ladies
	Frederick, Duke of Brunswick-Lunenburgh (a tragedy, staged at Lincoln's Inn Fields for two performances)
1730	*Love Letters on all Occasions Lately Passed Between Persons of Distinction*
	Haywood satirized as "Mrs. Novel" in Henry Fielding's comedy *The Author's Farce*
	Performed the role of Briseis in William Hatchett's *The Rival Fathers*
1732	*Secret Memoirs of the late Mr. Duncan Campbell, the Famous Deaf and Dumb Man*
1733	*Opera of Operas*, with William Hatchett, musical

	adaptation of Henry Fielding's *Tragedy of Tragedies* (1731), with music by John Frederick Lampe
1734	*L'Entretien des Beaux Esprits, Being the Sequel to La Belle Assemblée* (translated from French)
1735	*The Dramatic Historiographer; or, The British Theatre Delineated*
1736	*The Adventures of Eovaii, Princess of Ijaveo* (an anti-Walpole satiric fantasy)
1737	Member of Henry Fielding's acting company at the Little Theatre Haymarket, appeared as Mrs. Screen in Fielding's *Historical Register for the Year 1736*, and as the Muse in his *Eurydice Hiss'd*
1741	In business as a publisher, until 1749 or longer, under the Sign of Fame in Covent Garden
	Anti-Pamela; or, Feigned Innocence Detected
	The Busy-Body; or, Successful Spy
1742	*The Virtuous Villager; or Virgin's Victory* (translated from French)
1743	*A Present for a Servant-Maid; or, the Sure Means of Gaining Love and Esteem*
1744	*The Fortunate Foundlings*
	The Female Spectator (periodical paper, published from 1744–1746)
1746	*The Parrot With a Compendium of the Times* (weekly periodical, August 2 to October 4)
1747	*Memoirs of a Man of Honour* (translated from French)
1748	*Epistles for the Ladies*
	Life's Progress Through the Passions; or, the Adventures of Natura
1749	*Dalinda; or, The Double Marriage*
	A Letter from H——G——, Esq.
1750	Arrested by the government and held in custody for several weeks for writing *A Letter from H——G——, Esq*, a political and Jacobite pamphlet
1751	*The History of Miss Betsy Thoughtless*
1752	*The History of Jemmy and Jenny Jessamy* (dated 1753)
1753	*Modern Characters; Illustrated by Histories in Real Life, and Address'd to the Polite World*

1754	*The Invisible Spy. By Explorabilis*
1755	*The Wife*
1756	*The Husband. In Answer to the Wife*
	The Young Lady

Haywood dies, London, February 25, 1756, and is buried in the churchyard of St. Margaret's, Westminster.

Note on the Text

I have transcribed this edition from a copy of the 1753 first edition of the novel in the University of Pennsylvania library: *The History of Jemmy and Jenny Jessamy. In Three Volumes. By the Author of The History of Betsy Thoughtless* [London: Printed for T. Gardner, at Cowley's Head, facing St. Clement's Church, in the Strand; and sold by all Booksellers in Town and Country, 1753]. There was a pirated Dublin edition in two volumes published that same year. Haywood's novel was reprinted by Gardner in 1769 in two volumes and again in 1785 by a publisher named Harrison, this time in three volumes. That same year it was also issued as part of the *Novelists Magazine*. The novel was also translated into German in 1777 and into French in 1779. It has been reprinted only once since then, in 1974, in a facsimile edition without any annotation, part of the Garland Press series, "Foundations of the Novel" (New York: Garland Press, 1974).

For clarity and ease of readability, I have changed the punctuation of quotations in accordance with modern usage, and I have capitalized titles such as "Mr.," "Sir," and "Lord." I have, however, retained all the rest of the original punctuation and spelling (although occasionally I have silently corrected what are clearly misprints), and I have also eliminated the long "s." I have also made some of the spellings of proper names consistent. For example, in this edition the first volume spells a character's name "Bellpine" but then in the second and third volumes changes it to "Belpine." I have made that "Bellpine" throughout.

The

HISTORY

of

Jemmy and Jenny Jessamy

IN THREE VOLUMES

By the AUTHOR of

The History of Betsy Thoughtless

The HISTORY of *Jemmy and Jenny Jessamy*

Volume I

Contents to the First Volume

Volume I / 7

CHAPTER XXVI

Will gratify the reader's impatience with the conclusion of Mrs. M——'s history; and also with what effects the recital of it produced in the minds of those who heard it.

The

HISTORY

of

Jemmy and Jenny Jessamy

Chapter I

May more properly be called an introduction to the ensuing history, than a part of it.

Jemmy and Jenny Jessamy, were originally descended from two male branches of the same family, as it may be reasonably supposed, they both being of the same name, and having the same escutchion;—but to trace how far the relationship between them was removed, would require much time and trouble in examining old records, memorandums, and church registers, and cost more than the acquisition would be worth, as it could not be found any way material to the history.

It shall therefore suffice to say, that Jemmy was the only son of a gentleman of a competent estate, and Jenny sole daughter and heiress of a wealthy merchant;—that their parents had always called cousins,—had lived with each other in the most perfect friendship, the tokens of which each seemed equally desirous should continue beyond the grave; and, to this end, resolved on a marriage between their children, provided that when they arrived at years of maturity, neither of them should have any objection to such an union.

As this agreement was very early made, and the accomplishment of it was seriously wished for by both parties, all imaginable care was taken to excite in the children a mutual affection for each other, and to make the name of love familiar to them long before they knew what was meant by the words, much less could have any notion of the passion,—depending on this maxim of the poet:

> Children, like tender oziers, take the bow,
> And as they first are fashon'd still will grow.[1]

Jemmy, who had four years the advantage of Jenny, was taught to call her his little wife, even while in her cradle, and Jenny no sooner began to speak than she was made to say she loved her husband Jemmy in her heart.

As their years increas'd, and they became capable of receiving the first rudiments of education befitting their different sexes, Jemmy was sent to Eton, and Jenny to a boarding-school at a small village not far from London; but to atone for this separation, they were instructed, by those who had the care of them, to write little epistles to each other, which they dictated in terms suitable to their age and innocence, and served to keep alive that spirit of affection, which had been inculcated in their more early infancy.—When the times of breaking up[2] allowed them to return to their friends, they were seldom asunder,—they partook together all those diversions prepared for them by their indulgent parents, and sometimes Jemmy, and sometimes Jenny, were at the head of the feast,—all others being but their invited guests.—Jemmy was continually presenting Jenny with some curious new invented toy, and the first fruits of Jenny's handy work, was a fine embroider'd waistcoat and cap for Jemmy.

By this means it became a kind of second nature in them to love each other, the affection they began in infancy, grew up with their years; and if what they felt as they approach'd nearer to maturity did not amount to a passion, it was at least somewhat more than is ordinarily found between a brother and a sister.

The two fathers, however, were highly contented with the effect their endeavours had produced in the hearts of their children, and doubted not but by the prudent measures [that] had been taken in the education of both, they should one day see them make very shining figures in the state of marriage, which they resolved should be delayed no longer than till Jemmy had arrived at the age of one and twenty, at which time Jenny would be some months past seventeen.

But how uncertain is life!—how fallible the prospects it presents!—it often happens that when they seem most near, they either vanish of themselves, or we are suddenly snatch'd from them:—the father of Jenny, though a man whose healthy constitution, according to all appearance, promised a much longer date, died in an apoplectic fit, and she became an orphan three years before the time prefix'd for the completion of her marriage.

This fatal accident must necessarily involve the tender and affectionate heart of this young girl in very great affliction; but it was less severely felt, as she had always been bred to look on the father of Jemmy as a second parent to herself;—she, therefore, hesitated not to commit the large fortune she was left mistress of entirely to his care, and chose him for her guardian, according to the forms of law.[3]

Soon after her father's death, finding she had attain'd all those accomplishments that could be taught her in a boarding-school, she removed from thence, and with the approbation of her guardian, went to live with a family where she had a much better opportunity of seeing the world, and knowing how to conform herself to the customs and manners of it, than ever she could have done by the precise rules observed in the place she came from.

Jemmy had some time before left Eton, and was gone to Oxford, in order to finish his studies; but he obtain'd leave from the head of the college to make frequent visits to London,—induced thereto, by the double obligation of testifying his duty to his father, and affection to his mistress;—to these two motives, a third, perhaps, might be added, equally prevalent with either of the former,—that of partaking the pleasures of the town, of which he was no less fond, than most others of his sex and age.

He was but just return'd to the university, from whence he had made a pretty long excursion, when he was suddenly recall'd to London:—The old gentleman was seiz'd with a pluretic fever,[4] which, notwithstanding all the remedies proper in such cases were apply'd, made so swift a progress towards his heart, as threaten'd an immediate dissolution;—it indeed proved so, for tho' Jemmy, on the melancholy news, took horse the same moment, and rode post to town, he arrived but just time enough to see this best of fathers breathe his last.

The pangs of death were on him, yet were his senses perfect;—on his son's approach, a gleam of satisfaction diffused itself through all his late disordered features;—he collected all the strength that was left in him to raise himself a little, and taking hold of Jemmy's hand, and joining it to that of Jenny's, who sat weeping by the bed side,—"My dear children," said he, "I regret the loss of life for nothing so much as because I shall be deprived of seeing that happiness, which I hope you will soon enjoy together";—he would have added something more, but his voice forsook him, and he expired that instant.

Few young heirs look upon any thing as a real matter of affliction, which makes them masters of themselves and fortunes; but Jemmy was of a different way of thinking, he had a great share both of good sense and good nature; and besides what filial duty demanded from him, love and gratitude for the indulgence with which he had always been treated by his father, made him lament his loss with the most unfeign'd and poignant sorrow.

Jenny was also very deeply affected at this event; she had been truly sensible of the value she ought to set upon so faithful a guardian, and so sincere a friend; and while she used her endeavours to give his son some consolation, stood in almost equal need of receiving it herself.

The prudent old gentleman, tho' perhaps without any apprehensions of being so near his end, had some months before made his will, by which it appeared, on examination, that he had appointed trustees to manage both for his son and intended daughter-in-law, in case he should die before they arrived at the age of acting for themselves, and also, that by his great economy, he had saved out of the receipts of his estates several considerable sums of money, which he had placed in the publick funds,—so that Jemmy found himself in possession of a much larger fortune than he had imagined, or had been made to hope for.

Soon after the melancholy solemnity of the funeral was over, he returned to Oxford; but stay'd no longer there than was necessary to take a decent leave of the gentlemen of the college, and other students with whom he had contracted the most intimacy.

But none of his friends or acquaintance, either wonder'd at, or condemned the haste he made to quit the university, not doubting but the sole motive of his doing so was the laudable affection for the lady intended to be his future bride.

Chapter II

Contains the narrative of a very odd adventure, but perfectly a'-pro-pos, tho' at present it may perhaps appear a little foreign to the business in hand.

During the short time that Jemmy stay'd at Oxford, his fair mistress took it into her head to make a visit to a friend in the country, about some one or two and twenty miles distant from London, where she had received several pressing invitations to come, but had hitherto been prevented from complying by one accident or other.

This was a young lady, for whom Jenny had as great a regard as for any one of her female acquaintance;—they had received part of their education together, and tho' Sophia, for so she was called, being somewhat older than Jenny, had much sooner left the school, yet their intimacy was not broke off by this separation, and they continued to see each other as often as opportunity permitted;—but the brother of Sophia, who was a batchelor, having prevail'd with his sister to come down, and take upon her the management of his house, had now occasioned between these ladies an absence for many months.

It is not, therefore, to be doubted, but that Jenny found herself very sincerely welcome.—Sophia omitted nothing that might convince her that she was so;—and as nothing more truly demonstrates the cordiality of the heart, than an open and undisguised behaviour, these ladies reciprocally related to each other all the little accidents that had befallen either of them since last they parted.

Among other things that Sophia communicated to her fair guest, she told her that her brother was about marrying, and at present was in London, prosecuting his addresses for that purpose, to a young lady of condition, "which," said she, "if he succeeds in, I shall not long be a resident in the country, as he then will have no farther occasion for my assistance, nor should I chuse to continue in the house with a sister-in-law."

"I sincerely wish him all the happiness he can hope for," replyed Jenny, "not only as he is your brother, but for his own sake also,—since I believe there are few men who deserve more":—"we are both extremely obliged to you my dear," returned the other, "but I fear——"

She was going on with something, which it is likely would have let Jenny into the quality and character of the intended bride, but was interrupted by a servant, who came hastily into the room, and told her that his master was just alighted at the gate, out of a landau and six,[5] and had brought a very fine lady home with him.

"Bless me," cried Sophia, in a great surprise, "the thing we were speaking of is certainly completed; but come," continued she, "let us go down to receive them, and be convinced."

In speaking these words she took Jenny by the hand, in order to do as she had said, but was prevented by the sight of her brother and the mistress of his affections, who had come laughing up, and were already on the top of the stair-case; on which she retired some paces back to give them room to enter.

This gentleman, whom I shall distinguish by the name of Rodophil, immediately presented Sophia to the lady, saying, "This, Madam, is the sister I have often mentioned to you": they then saluted each other with a great deal of politeness, while he paid his compliments to Jenny; but had no sooner done so, than turning to Sophia, "I am come a little unexpectedly upon you, sister," said he; " but, to make amends, have brought home a lady, who will be so good to take off your hands the trouble of managing my family."

"I am very ready to resign my place," reply'd she with a smile, "to one who, I doubt not, but will much better fit it; but Sir," pursued she in the same gay air, "I think you should have put it in my power to have given you the last cast[6] of my office, in a more elegant manner, than I am now capable of doing in this sudden surprise."

"Nay, as to that matter, child," cried the lady in a very familiar, and indeed, somewhat of a hoydenish[7] tone, "you have nothing to accuse him of on this account, for I assure you neither of us thought of being here to-night, two hours before we set out from London; but I know not how it happen'd, but we were both in a frolicksome humour; he swore he would have me, and I swore if he had, he should run away with me;—the impudent thing took me at my word,—sent in a minute for a landau and six,—thrust me into it, and hurried me away without any farther preparation than just as you see."

"Then the ceremony is not yet perform'd," said Sophia; "No," reply'd her brother, "but I hope to-morrow morning will put a final end to my suspence, and make me happy in my utmost wishes;—What say you, Madam," pursued he to the lady—"shall it not be so?"—"What occasion has the man to ask any questions!"—answered she, patting him on the cheek, "you have got me into your possession here, and must even do with me what you will."

Soon after this Sophia withdrew, to give the necessary orders for preparing supper, which, in spite of her being taken so unawares, was served up in a manner that shew'd there was little need of the apology had she made on the first entrance of her new guest.

Nothing was wanting to complete the elegance of the table, but a little more politeness of behaviour in the person, for whom chiefly such care had been taken in furnishing it;—but, tho' she was the daughter of a nobleman, and could not fail of having had an education suitable to her birth, yet the pride of blood,—the insolence of flatter'd beauty, and the vanity of imagining, that she could do nothing unbecoming in her, made her act and talk in so affected, and so odd a fashion, as greatly defaced all the charms she had received from nature.

"You are very ugly, Rodophil," would she cry; "I wonder what it is I like you for"; then rejoin'd with the same breath, "well, you are a dear bewitching toad, however"; one moment she would push him from her, swearing she hated him,—the next pull him towards her, protesting he could not be too near;—her discourse to the ladies was also of the same piece: she told Sophia, she had a pair of fine eyes, but did not look as if she knew she had any such things in her head; and laugh'd at Jenny, as having reason to accuse nature for not having endued[8] her with the talent of elocution.

Jenny, indeed, spoke but little the whole evening; but as her silence was occasioned only by the other's excess of volubility, the usual vivacity of her temper was rous'd by this reproach, and she reply'd, with some tartness, "Madam, if Sophia and myself were half so conscious as your ladyship seems to be, of having every thing we said approv'd of, we should certainly be all speakers and no hearers, and consequently this gentleman here be in danger of losing one of his senses, if a man in love can be supposed to have any."

The lady, in spite of all the assurance she was possess'd of, could not avoid appearing a little disconcerted at what Jenny had said;—Rodophil perceiving it, thought himself obliged, as a lover, to take up the word, and turning to Jenny; "Madam," said he to her, "the man who has the honour to be capable of distinguishing the perfections of that lady, must certainly be supposed to have no senses for any thing but her."

Jenny made no other reply to this, than that she doubted not but his passion was worthy of the object that inspired it; and, after a few hours past in a conversation not material enough to be repeated, Sophia conducted the mistress of her brother to an apartment she had caused to be got ready for her; and, through respect to him, waited in the room till she had seen her into bed.

Jenny having always been a sharer with Sophia in the same bed, when they were together at the boarding-school, would not hear of sleeping apart from her during the time she stay'd in the country, not only to avoid giving any unnecessary trouble to the family, but also because she was willing to lose as little of her company as possible.

Though the night was pretty far advanced when the ladies went into their chamber, neither of them had the power to close their eyes without discovering to the other some part of their sentiments in relation to the intended bride.

That a young maid of quality should suffer herself to be conducted in so odd a manner by a gentleman to his country seat, and that she should behave towards him in so affected, and indeed so confident a fashion, in the presence of two persons of her own sex, whom she had never seen before, had something in it so new, and so strange to them, that they could not well find words to express their astonishment.

"It must certainly be an excess of love," said Jenny, "that can oblige a man of Rodophil's good understanding to bear with such extravagancies in the woman he makes choice of for a wife."

"As for love," replied the other, "I believe that is quite out of the question; I think I may be pretty positive, from a thousand circumstances, that my brother is neither charmed with the beauties of her person, nor blind to the follies of her temper;—but he imagines,—how rightly I cannot as yet take upon me to determine, that her fortune, her birth, and the interest of her family will compensate for all other deficiencies."

Women, for the most part, are but too justly accused of being severe on the foibles of each other; and some will have it, that they even take a malicious pleasure in finding something to condemn; but it was not by this propensity that either of these ladies were instigated;—the one, who loved her brother extremely, was sorry and ashamed at having observ'd such errors in a woman who was to be his partner for life;—and the other, more through good-nature than the contrary, was vexed when any opportunity for censure presented itself.

Rodophil, however, full of the thoughts of being a bridegroom, quitted his bed much sooner than he was accustomed to do, and went to a neighbouring clergyman, who having licences[9] always ready by him, got one immediately fill'd up with the two parties names; and as the thing was to be private, promis'd to bring a friend with him, who should officiate in giving the lady's hand.

Sophia also rose very early that morning, being willing, in spite of her dislike to this match, to do it all the honour in her power, and that the shortness of the time would admit her.

None of the family were sluggards on this occasion,—all appeared in their several stations alert and chearful; sprightliness sat on every face, excepting that of the intended bride; but never was there so strange,—so sudden a transformation in any one person,—she that had the evening before been so wildly gay and volatile, even to a ridiculous excess, was now become quite moped and stupid;—twice had Sophia been in her chamber before she could prevail on her to leave it and come down stairs; and when Rodophil accosted her with the usual salutation of the morning, and told her it was the happiest he had ever seen, she made no answer, nor scarce vouchsafed to look upon him.

On the sight of the clergyman and his friend, who came exactly at the time they were expected by Rodophil;—"What is all this for?" said she sullenly;—"I won't be married":—"Not married, Madam,"—cried Rodophil, "you are not certainly in earnest":—"Indeed, but I am,—so pray let the parson go about his business; for he has none with me at this time."

"What is it you mean, Madam?"—demanded Rodophil, so much confounded that he could scarce utter these few words:—"I have told you," answered she, "that I won't be married,—at least at present;—therefore send away the man."

"I am sorry, Sir," said the reverend divine,—"that you did not take care to be better acquainted with the lady's mind before you gave us the trouble of waiting on you";—and, with these words, went hastily out of the room, followed by the gentleman he had brought with him, equally affronted as surpriz'd.

Rodophil went after them, to make the best apology he could for the caprice, as he then imagined it, of the lady's humour:—Sophia and Jenny were all this time in such a consternation, that they could only look sometimes on the person who had occasioned it, and sometimes on each other, without being able to speak a single syllable.

Rodophil return'd, and with a countenance which testify'd the resentment of his heart,—"Madam," said he to the lady,—"what have I done to deserve that you should treat me in this manner?—What motive could induce you to render me the jest of the whole country?"

"If you thought me unworthy of the honour I solicited,"—pursued he,—"wherefore did you encourage me to hope it?—assign at least some reason for so strange a reverse in your behaviour towards me."—These questions, and several others to the same purpose, being repeated over and over, she at last reply'd,—that she would satisfy him, but no body else.

Sophia, on hearing this, started immediately from her seat, crying:—"Oh, Madam, we will be no hindrance to the eclaircisement[10] my brother has so much right to expect";—in speaking this she left them together, taking Jenny with her.

Her curiosity was, however, raised to a pitch too high not to inspire her with an eagerness to be one of the first at the explanation of this mystery,—it presently came into her head, that there was a closet which opened from the passage, and was divided from the room where Rodophil and the lady were but by a thin partition, and guessing her friend's impatience by her own, they both went together, as softly as possible, into this little recess, where, putting their ears close to the pannel of the wainscot, they could easily distinguish what discourse passed on the other side.

As in reaching this place, they were obliged to take a circuit through a gallery of a pretty large extent, they lost some part of what had been said, but arrived timely enough to be witnesses of the main point, and to which all that had pass'd before could have been only the prelude.

"Married!"—they heard Rodophil cry, with a voice sonorous enough to have been audible at a much greater distance,—"death and furies,—when, where,—to whom!"—"You have no occasion,"—replied the lady, "to put yourself into this violent agitation,—I dare say I may be easily unmarried again."

"Confusion," rejoin'd Rodophil,—"what trifling is here! Married,—and may be easily unmarried again;—for heaven's sake, Madam, explain the meaning of all this, if there be really any meaning in what you say?"

"Have a little patience,"—replied she,—"I will tell you everything:—you must know, that Captain La Val, persuaded me one day to go with him to May-Fair Chapel,—where a man in a black coat read something over to us,—it was the marriage ceremony I think;—for my part, I did nothing but laugh all the time, yet the creature has ever since taken it into his head to imagine I am his wife."

"Very likely, indeed," said Rodophil scornfully,—"and what followed?"—"Nay, what signifies what followed," cried she, "the business is to get this foolish marriage dissolved; which I think may easily be done, especially as there were no witnesses, and we now heartily hate one another."—"Were these always your sentiments?"—demanded Rodophil;—"No," answer'd she,—"he pretended a furious passion for me, and I lik'd him well enough,—but he is now as indifferent as most other husbands, and I have never been able to endure him since I came acquainted with you;—therefore, my dear Rodophil, help me to get quite rid of him."

"As how pray?"—said he:—"Oh, I have contrived the means,"—answer'd she,—"you must send him a challenge, I know he does not love fighting, tho' he has made two campaigns, and I believe will be glad to relinquish me rather than come to tilt-work;[11]—but if he should venture, you will certainly have the better; for I am told he does not understand the sword."

"I am highly obliged to you, Madam," reply'd he, with the extremest disdain, "for the undertaking you would engage me in;—but really it is not my humour to risque my own throat, or attempt cutting that of another man's in the hope of becoming master of his property; and am so far from envying the good fortune of my rival, that I wish him all the happiness a man can enjoy with a lady of your consummate virtue and discretion."

"Ungrateful creature," cried she, bursting into tears, "is this the love you have profess'd for me, or a recompence for the proofs you have receiv'd of mine?"—"Oh, Madam,"—replied he, still more contemptuously, "you will find I know how to set a just value on such love as yours,—the landau that brought us is not yet return'd, and is at your service to conduct you to your husband's arms, or where-ever you think proper."

On this she call'd him monster,—villain, and all the names that rage and disappointment could suggest;—but he, little regarding what she said, rung the bell for a servant, and order'd the landau should be immediately brought.—Our fair eve-droppers thought this a proper cue for enterance, and came forth from their concealment:—"Sister," said Rodophil, "I leave you to take care of this lady, who seems a little disorder'd;—I am going out."

Sophia, after her brother had left the room, began to say some civil things, in order to moderate the distraction she appeared in; but she answer'd not a word; and, as soon as the landau was at the gate, flung herself into it without any farther ceremony:—but what effect her behaviour had on the minds of those she left behind, the reader will presently discover.

Chapter III

Is of still more importance than the former.

Though Rodophil, as Sophia had told Jenny, was not possess'd of any real passion for this capricious lady, and had been instigated merely by the prospect of advantage to make his addresses to her, yet was he so much chagrin'd at being exposed, by her folly, to the ridicule of the neighbourhood, from the thought it could not be kept a secret, that he went directly to the house of an intimate friend, and would not be prevailed upon to return to his own for a considerable time.

As for the two young ladies, the consternation they were in at what they had seen and heard, is not to be describ'd;—nothing but the conviction of their own senses, could have made either of them believe it possible, that a person, such as had just now left them, could have acted in the manner she had done.

The discourse they had together, after she was gone, was suitable to the occasion.—"I know,"—said Sophia,—"that there are some men who have so much vanity and assurance, that they will take no denial, nor quit their pretensions without some extraordinary method be taken to compel them to it; but I can assure you this was not the case with my brother;—I have very good reasons to believe she made him the first advances; and am certain, that if she did not, she at least highly encouraged his addresses."

"That you may not think,"—continued she,—"that I am excited to speak in this fashion through the natural affection to my brother, I will shew you a letter, which he happening to drop, I took up, and never return'd; because I was unwilling to let him know I had seen it."

In speaking these words she took a paper out of her pocket, and put [it] into Jenny's hands, which the young lady hastily opening found the contents as follow:

To * * * * * * * Esq;

I have had a thousand lovers, but never found one so easily repuls'd—if you had lov'd me with half that violent passion you pretended, you would have remember'd what the poet makes Jupiter say of our sex,

> I gave them but one tongue to form denials,
> And two fine eyes to yield a kind compliance.[12]

Mine must have been very unintelligible indeed, if they did not inform you that my heart was far from being displeased at the fine things you said to me;—Were you then to take it for granted, that I did not like you because I told you so, and gallop immediately out of town, as if absolutely despairing ever to obtain me?—Faint-hearted creature!—I pity your want of spirit;—a man of courage would have been more enflam'd by resistance, and never given over till he had gained his point.

I know this is going a great length, and may encourage you to boldnesses, which, perhaps, I should not be very ready to forgive; but I have said it, and do not think it worth while to spoil another piece of paper with writing to you in a different manner, so you must put what construction you please upon words: if you venture to town again upon the receipt of this, it is possible you will have no reason to repent your journey; but I promise nothing further, than that it depends entirely on yourself to continue in the good graces of

* * * *

P.S. I have made an appointment with some ladies to go to Vaux-Hall[13] the day after to-morrow;—they will have all their pretty fellows with them, and if you come time enough, I should chuse rather that you should squire me thither than any other man of my acquaintance.—Adieu.

"Upon this summons,"—said Sophia,—"my brother went directly to London, and you may suppose met with no unkind reception from the lady, by what you have been witness of."

"Yes, my dear,"—cried Jenny,—"I have, indeed, been witness of much more than I could ever have imagined in woman, much less in any one who pretends to the least share of honour or reputation."

This adventure, it is certain, had made a very extraordinary impression on the mind of that young beauty,—she had a strong discernment, and an uncommon quickness of apprehension,—she had easily discover'd, that the lady they were speaking of, tho' vain and affected to an excess, wanted not wit, but judgement, and that the errors of her conduct, in regard to La Val and Rodophil, were not owing so much to her folly, as to the inconstancy of her nature.

"Who can be assur'd,"—said she within herself, "till experience convinces them, that they themselves may not be guilty of the same irregularity of humour, tho' their prudence, and the fears of censure may keep them from exposing the weakness of their resolution!—We all of us are liable to change in trifling matters, and frequently despise to-morrow what we lik'd to-day;—I see no reason, therefore, that we have to depend on our own hearts in things of the greatest importance."

Jenny could not, in spite of the gaiety of her temper, forbear falling into little reveries of this nature, whenever she consider'd herself as entering into a state, from which there is no relief but the grave; or, what to a woman of any delicacy, is yet worse,—a divorcement.

She could not keep herself from uttering some part of her thoughts on this subject to Sophia; "Inconstancy," replied she, "is certainly a very great weakness; yet what security can be given by the wisest of us all, that we never shall be guilty of it?—it is an involuntary error; the effect of a sudden object, that when we least think of it, strikes upon the senses,—confounds the understanding, and leads the inclination astray, before people will know what they are doing."

"Since it is so,"—said Jenny,—"and may as well happen after marriage as before, I think it is best not to marry at all, as the consequences of such an accident would then be terrible indeed." "Then you would chuse to avoid a certain good,"—cried Sophia, laughing,—"rather than run the risque of falling into an uncertain evil?—but I do not regard what you say on this head,—we may talk as we will, but when it comes to the point, we shall do just as nature prompts."

Thus did the odd event of Rodophil's courtship furnish out both serious and pleasant matter of conversation for these two ladies while they continued together;—but Jenny, who had not intended her visit should be long, took her leave on the third day, and return'd to London,—where a second discovery fell in her way, which greatly corroborated those sentiments which the first had begun to inspire her with.

There are few milliners of more reputation in their way among the beau monde[14] than Mrs. Frill;—Jenny had been her customer ever since she had left her boarding-school, and happening now to go to her shop for some things she wanted, found her behind the counter very busy, and bustling among her shelves and band-boxes,—a thing very extraordinary with her, as she was pretty far advanced in years,—was infirm, and had always kept an extremely adroit shop-maid, who was used to take the trouble of the most part of the business off her hands.

"Bless me,"—cried Jenny,—"'tis a kind of prodigy to see you below stairs,—especially at this time in the morning;—pray where is Mrs. Becky, that you are obliged to fatigue yourself in this manner?"

"Ah, Miss Jessamy,"—reply'd she, puffing and blowing like a pair of bellows that has lost its wind,—"Becky has play'd the fool with herself,—she has left me, and is gone into keeping."[15] "Into keeping,"—cried Jenny!—"I should never have suspected it;—I thought Mrs. Becky[16] had been defended by the plainness of her person as well as by her virtue, from all attacks of that nature:—but pray who is the man?"—"I was of your opinion,"—said Mrs. Frill,—"but Sir J— * * * has found charms in her, and she in him;—he has taken fine lodgings for her, and they are almost always together."

She had no sooner mentioned the name of Sir J— * * *, than Jenny burst into exclamations;—she knew very well that he had loved, to the most romantic height the lady who was now his wife;—that he had not been marry'd to her more months than it had cost him years of courtship to obtain her;—that she was a person whose beauty,—accomplishments,—virtue and good nature rendered her every way deserving of all the affection he had profess'd for her;—and now to hear he had so early falsify'd his vows, seem'd a thing so strange,—so incredible, that she could scarce believe her ears, or that Mrs. Frill was not mistaken in what she said;—she asked over and over if she was sure the thing was true, and desir'd her to repeat all the particulars she knew concerning this surprising affair;—to which the other comply'd in these terms:

"You must know, Madam," said she, "that I had a very curious French capuchin,[17]—never was there a greater beauty of its kind,—it was wrought by a nun of quality to be disposed of for the benefit of the poor; scarce a flower that grows but was represented in their proper colours, intermix'd with gold and silver;—I shew'd it to such of my customers as I thought most likely to be the purchasers,—they all admired it, but did not care to give the price, tho' nothing ever was so cheap; for I asked no more than fifty guineas;[18]—but the truth is, most of them had lost a great deal of their money at play,[19] and you know, Madam, that makes ill for us trades-people.—I had kept it above a week, and fearing it would be blow'd upon,[20] proposed a raffle, and got ten ladies to subscribe five guineas a-piece; but when the day came appointed to decide to whose lot the prize should fall, one of them sent me word she had changed her mind, and could not come.

"This a little vex'd me,"—continued she;—"but rather than lose all, was determined to make up the deficiency myself, when luckily this very Sir J— * * * stept in;—as he was a married man, I ventured to ask him if he would not try his fortune for a present to his lady;—he readily agreed, and in fine[21] won it;—I offer'd to send it home, but he told me I need not give myself that trouble, for his man should call for it the next day, which Becky told me he did; but you will find by the sequel that he intended no such thing."

"About a week after, as near as I can remember," went she on,—"this audacious young hussy pretended to go on a visit to a relation, but came not home the whole night; which very much surprised me, and as she never had been guilty of the like before, made me fear some accident had befallen her; but the next morning I received a letter from her, which I will read to you."

In speaking these words, she took a paper out of her pocket, and read these lines:

TO MRS. FRILL.

MADAM,

I beg your pardon for quitting your service in so clandestine a manner; but I had an offer which I did not think proper to refuse;—I have a quarter's wages in your hands, and that, I hope, will make amends for my going without warning:—pray be so good to send my box by the bearer.—I am,

MADAM,
. your humble servant,
to command,
REBECCA TRIP

"I was very much amaz'd, as you may easily believe,"—resumed she,—"at the impertinence of the creature in writing to me in this manner; however, [I] had presence of mind enough to ask the porter from whence he brought the letter, and he readily told me from one Madam Trip, in South-Audley-Street;—on which I presently guess'd her situation, though not the person who had occasioned this change in it."

"But I continued not long in this suspence,"—pursued she,—"one of the ladies, who had been so unfortunate to lose her five pieces[22] at the raffle, told me she had met her in the mall, dress'd in a very rich brocade short sack[23] and petticoat, and that very capuchin Sir J— * * * had won; and I soon after heard, by one who is acquainted with the person at whose house she lodges, that she passes there for a relation of that gentleman's, and that he visits her every day."

Mrs. Frill had just finish'd this little narrative when a lady came into her shop,—after the usual compliment,—"I have been just giving,"—said Mrs. Frill to her,—"this young lady an account of the change of Becky's circumstances; and I assure your ladyship have had much ado to make her believe the veracity of it":—"I am sensible,"[24]—reply'd Jenny,—"that things of this nature too frequently happen;—but I confess, that to find a man who loved to that degree Sir J— * * * has done, should act in such a manner is very astonishing to me."

"For my part,"—said the lady,—"I see nothing astonishing in it, except his want of taste,—for as to his keeping a mistress, it could not be expected to be otherwise; that woman is a fool who thinks to keep a pretty fellow to herself in a town like this;—'tis true his wife is a very fine woman,—but he has had her, and variety has its charms for us all."

"In some things it may, Madam,"—answered Jenny,—"yet I cannot help thinking that inconstancy, either in man or woman, argues a very weak mind."—"Lord, miss, you talk like one that knows nothing of the world,"—cry'd the other,—"I have been married these three years, and am wise by experience;—it is not in nature for two persons always to be pleasing to each other;—but if you will not take my word for it, I hope you will believe Cowley, who was certainly as great a judge of love as even Ovid himself."

> The world's a scene of changes, and to be
> Constant in nature were inconstancy;
> For 'twere to break the laws herself has made;
> Our substances themselves do fleet and fade:
> The most fix'd being still does move and fly,
> Swift as the wings of time 'tis measur'd by:
> To imagine then that love should never cease,
> Love, which is but the ornament of these,
> Were quite as senseless as to wonder why
> Beauty and colour stay not when we die.[25]

Not this authority, nor all the arguments the lady could bring, who possibly was herself a proof of what she urg'd, could make Jenny recede from her opinion, or give up the point, the dispute between them continued till other company coming in put an end to it.

Though, by the whole deportment of Jenny, there seem'd to be but little share of earth in her composition, yet had she her serious moments;—what she had seen at the house of Rodophil, and been told of at Mrs. Frill's, came often into her mind; and she began to fear, from these two instances, that inconstancy was a frailty to which human nature was but too liable, and the reflections she made upon it had no small influence on her future conduct towards Jemmy, to whom it is now high time we should return.

Chapter IV

Will probably occasion various conjectures on what is to come.

A very small share of experience and observation may serve to inform us, that there is no passion of the soul which more easily wears off than that of grief for the death of friends; and indeed it is highly reasonable that is should be so,—religion obliges us to a perfect resignation to the decrees of providence;—philosophy teaches us that it is weak and unbecoming the dignity of our species to bewail woes, which in their very nature are irredeemable;—and the laws of society forbid us to indulge any emotions that might enervate our abilities, and render us less useful to the community.

Whether any arguments, drawn from the above considerations, could claim a part in enabling Jemmy to recover his former vivacity, I will not take upon me to determine; but, certain it is, that in a very short time nothing of the mourner, except the habit, was to be seen about him.

It would have been somewhat strange, indeed, if a gentleman, not yet quite one and twenty, possess'd of a very plentiful estate, and master of accomplishments to recommend him to the best company, should have had any leisure for melancholy reflections in a town like London, so abounding with every thing that can entertain and raise pleasing sensations in a youthful heart.

In the midst of all the various amusements he gave into, his dear Jenny, however, was not forgot,—scarce a day past over without his visiting her once, if not more, in some one part of it;—they behaved to each other in the same fashion they had always been accustom'd to do,—quite open and free, without the least breach of innocence or modesty;—kind without any mixture of dissimulation, and obliging without taking any pains to be so.

Scarce are there any where to be found two persons whose dispositions so exactly tally'd;—both of them were gay and volatile almost to an excess,—both lov'd the pleasures of the town, yet never pursued them so far as to transgress the bounds of strict virtue in the one, nor honour in the other;—both had an affluence of wit, and a great talent for ridicule; and both had too much good nature and generosity to extend that propensity to the prejudice of any one:—in fine, they were what the poet says,

In all so much alike, each heart
Seem'd but the others counter part.[26]

To the foregoing character of them might also have been added, that neither of them were possess'd of any strong passions; and though the affection they had for each other was truly tender and sincere, yet neither of them felt those impatiencies,—those anxieties,—those transporting hopes,—those distracting fears,—those causeless jealousies, or any of those thousand restless sensations that usually perplex a mind devoted to an amorous flame;—they were happy when they met, but not uneasy when they parted;—he was not in the least alarm'd on finding she was frequently visited by some of the finest gentlemen in town; nor was she at all disconcerted when she was told he was well received by ladies of the most distinguish'd characters.

I am well aware, that many of my readers will be apt to say,—people who could think and act in the manner I have describ'd, either had no charms for each other, or seem'd incapable of loving at all;—and I am ready to confess, that according to the receiv'd notions of love, there was a seeming inconsistency in this conduct, and had more the appearance of a cold indifference than the warm glow of mutual inclinations.

Yet that they did love each other is most certain, as will hereafter be demonstrated by proofs much more unquestionable than all those extravagancies;—those raging flights commonly; look'd upon as infallible tokens of the passion, but which, how fierce soever the fires they spring from may burn for a while, we see frequently extinguish of themselves, and leave nothing but the smoke behind.

All the formalities of a first and second mourning for the dead being over, every one now expected they should soon see the completion of a marriage they knew had been so long intended;—Jemmy also had some thoughts of it himself, and began to consider on such things as were proper to be done previous to the solemnity.

On looking over his father's papers he had found marriage articles between him and Jenny, with a deed of settlement on her by way of dower,[27] which the old gentleman had caused to be drawn up some time before his death;—these writings he now put into his pocket and carried them to her, in order for her approbation.

"What are these?" cry'd she, when he presented her with the packet:—"They are what concern you as nearly as myself,"—replied he,—"therefore, I would have you examine the contents at some leisure hour, and let me know if you think there is any thing in them that requires alteration or amendment."

"They ought to be things of great consequence, indeed, by their bulk,"—said she smiling, and beginning to unfold the parchment,—"you know,"—resumed he with the same gay air,—"for what we are design'd by both our fathers;—and I suppose mine, as being your guardian also, thought himself the most proper person to decide the terms on which we should come together."

"I have no reason,"—answered she,—"to suspect either his justice or good will towards me;—however, I will take the first opportunity of seeing what he has done for me on this score";—in speaking this she lock'd the writings he had brought in an escrutore[28] that was plac'd just behind her;—then turning hastily to him,—"but, my dear Jemmy,"—continued she,—"you must excuse me for this evening;—you must know I have promised some company to go to Ranelagh,[29] and I believe they are already beginning to expect me."—"It happens very luckily,"—said he,—"for there are three or four young fellows of us, who have promised to give some ladies the music on the river tonight,[30]—and I could not have stay'd above three minutes longer with you; for they depend upon me to see the hands all ready,—so, my dear Jenny, I will not detain you;—farewel."—"Farewel Jemmy," rejoined she,—and with these words both ran down stairs together;—he went into one chair[31] and she into another, to fulfil their several engagements.

The next day they saw each other again, as usual,—after some little chit chat on ordinary affairs, he asked her if she had found time to look over the writings he had brought the day before;—"Yes,"—answer'd she, "I breakfasted on them this morning";—"Well,"—cried he,—"what objections have you to make?"—"None at all,"—reply'd she,—"I rather think your father has made a better provision for me than my own would have desired or expected."

"Then I suppose there is nothing left for us to do,"—said he,—"but sign and seal, and go together before a parson."—"Some people may say so,"—reply'd she;—"but for my part I am of a quite different opinion, and think there is a great deal for us both to do before we come to the words,—to have and to hold."

"I easily comprehend what you would be at,"—resumed he laughing;—"new cloaths for ourselves and servants,—some addition to the equipage,[32]—a more fashionable chariot,—another pair of horses perhaps." "Hold,—hold,"—cried she interrupting him,—"I have no such stuff in my thoughts, I do assure you;—what I mean is infinitely more material than all you have mention'd;—and that is,—the being certain within ourselves of never repenting the engagements we are about to enter into."

"Repenting,"—said he,—"there is no danger of that I believe;—I will promise you to make as good a husband as I can,—and I am sure you will make a good wife."—"That is all as chance directs,"—answer'd she,—"we may think perfectly well at one time, and act very ill at another; in fine, my dear Jemmy,"—continued she,—"I think we ought to know a little more of the world and of ourselves before we enter into serious matrimony."

"Why faith, Jenny,"—answer'd he,—"I cannot help saying but that you are in the right;—I should not much like, methinks, to be quite so soon the father of a family."—"And I should hate to be called mamma,"—rejoin'd she,—"before I arrive at an age to write myself woman."

"I wonder,"—pursued she,—"how people can resolve to cut themselves off from all the pleasures of life, just as they are beginning to have a relish for them;—how should I regret being confin'd at home by my domestic affairs, while others of my sex and age were flaunting in the mall,[33] or making one at the rout[34] of a woman of quality?—and how would it mortify you to hear the ladies cry disdainfully, 'Jemmy Jessamy is a very pretty fellow;—but he is married,'—and then toss up their heads, and in contempt of you turn the doux yeux[35] on the next man in company, though perhaps he happens to be one of the most insignificant fops that the follies of the times ever fashioned, and without any one merit to recommend him but merely his having no wife?"

Jenny, who had always somewhat amiably striking in her eyes and tone of voice, appeared at this instant so particularly brilliant, that Jemmy could not forbear catching her in his arms with the utmost rapture,—crying at the same time,—"I shall little regard the contempt of all the women in the world, while blest with the kindness of my dear,—dear Jenny."

"And I think too,"—reply'd she, returning his embrace, and looking on him with a most enchanting softness,—"that I could forgo all other joys of life for those of my dear Jemmy's love; yet after all,"—continued she,—"we may both of us be deceived in our own hearts;—I have heard the wife say, that nothing is so difficult to acquire as the true knowledge of ourselves,—and who can tell what time and accidents may produce!"

Here Jemmy was beginning to make the most fervent protestations, that it was not in the power of fate itself to occasion the least alteration in his present sentiments on her account:—and Jenny was half persuaded, by what she felt in her own breast, that an affection, grounded and habitual as theirs had been, was incapable of varying on either side;—so that if this tender conversation had continued but a very little longer, it is highly probable they had agreed to put the finishing stroke to the work, their parents had labour'd for, by an immediate marriage.

Of this, however, there can be no positive assurance, as it was broke off by some company coming in;—but whether fortunately or unfortunately for the lovers, this interruption happen'd in so critical a moment, the reader, if he has patience to wait, will in the sequel of this history be inform'd.

Chapter V

Is somewhat more explicit than the former.

The persons who had surprised our lovers in the midst of the most interesting discourse they ever yet had entertain'd each other with, were two young ladies of Jenny's intimate acquaintance;—they had been driven out of the park by a shower of rain, and could not go home without calling on her, to communicate something which they thought would be equally diverting to her as it had been to themselves.

On seeing Jemmy with her,—"We have catch'd you alone together," said one of them, "and it is happy for you that you have been so, as nothing but the pleasure of each other's company, could have attoned for what you have lost by not being in the mall to-night."

"As how pray?"—demanded she,—"Lady Fisk,"—resumed the other,—"Oh, such fleering,[36]—such pointing,—such an universal titter as soon as ever she appear'd!"—"Lady Fisk,"—cried Jemmy, interrupting her,—"I am afraid, Madam, your intelligence is stale,—that lady has play'd over all her tricks long ago, and can do nothing new for us to laugh at."

"You are quite mistaken, I assure you," answer'd she;—"she has now, as Colly says, outdone all her usual outdoings, as you will be obliged to confess when you have heard the story."[37]

"What," cried he,—"can any thing go beyond her adventure in Covent-Garden,[38]—where she went in men's cloaths,—pick'd up a woman of the town, and was severely beaten by her on the discovery of her sex?"

"Or what happened to her at Bartholomew-Fair,"[39]—said Jenny,—"where being a little too pert with some young apprentices, who had attack'd her as a lady of pleasure, a riot ensued, and she was glad to produce her seal with the coat of arms upon it, and a letter she had received that day from her lord, to prevent being lodg'd that night in the watch-house,[40] and carried before the sitting alderman next morning."

"Neither of these exploits,"—reply'd the lady that had spoke first,—"comes up to what we have to tell you, or gave her half the mortification;—it would be the first story in the world if one could but find out the beginning;—but the misfortune is, that nothing but the catastrophe as yet is come to light."

"It is but half a story then, at best," said Jemmy laughing;—"but let us hear it however."—"I should not have kept you so long in suspence my dear, if this thing here,"—cried she, giving Jemmy a slap on the shoulder with her fan,—"had not interrupted me;—you must know, that some night last week Lord and Lady Fisk had a most terrible quarrel,—they were just going into bed,—she was undress'd all but her under petticoat;—what she said or did to provoke him to such wrath Heaven knows; but he push'd her out of the chamber,—drove her down stairs, and in that condition turn'd her into the street, charging the porter not to open the door on any account."

"Never was the pride and spirit of any lady so humbled as her's,"—continued this talkative lady;—"after finding that knocking and calling loud was to no effect, she condescended to put her mouth close to the key-hole of the door, and beseech the porter, in the most submissive terms, to let her in, though it were no farther than the hall; while her remorseless lord looked through the window, and insulting her distress, told her it was a fine night, and that it was good for her ladyship's health to be thus alfresco."[41]

"After having had his fill of laughter at the miserable plight to which she was reduced, he consented to her admittance;—she was no sooner within the doors than she flew up stairs;—the dispute between them was renewed with almost the same vehemence as before;—he loaded her with a thousand foul names;—she, in return, called him toad,—devil, and every thing her passion could suggest;—till having both rail'd themselves out of breath, they agreed to go into bed together, in order to finish the quarrel."

"But now comes the jest,"—went she on,—"How long a time do you think it took up to compose this difference? why no less than three whole days and nights successively; during all which space the chamber door was never opened, but to take in some refreshment, which was placed for them in the next room: this evening was the first of their appearance since their resurrection from the sepulchre of down; my lord received such congratulations upon it as made him glad to quit the park; but her ladyship, having somewhat more assurance, stay'd till the change of weather obliged her, as well as ourselves, to take shelter in our chairs."

"I cannot help confessing,"—said Jemmy, "but that there is somewhat pretty extraordinary in this affair, and also that one of them has a greater share of complaisance than I suspected; since it is plain that which ever of them was in fault the other did equal penance."

A good deal of pleasantry passed on this adventure, during the whole time the ladies stayed, which indeed was not very long;—they had here opened their pacquet,[42] and were upon the wing to carry it to those other of their acquaintance to whom they thought it might be equally new and agreeable.

The ladies had no sooner taken their leave, than Jenny began to animadvert, with more strength of reason than could have been expected from a person of her years, on the ridiculous fact they had been relating;—"You hear, Jemmy," said she, "what unaccountable things married people are sometimes guilty of;—instead of living together in a mutual harmony, it seems methinks as if they took a kind of pleasure in making each other wretched;—and sure they must do so, or they would not thus expose themselves to the contempt of the world, and become the jest even of their own servants, who must necessarily be the first witnesses of their folly."

"We ought not, however," replied he, "to lay on marriage the blame of all those preposterous things we see acted in that state, by persons we have been speaking of;—because long before their enterance into it, both of them behaved in such a manner as to shew they were wholly govern'd by caprice, and not by that farcical passion which many people are possessed of, in a more or less degree, for making a great noise, and being talked of in the world, tho' it is only for foibles, which one would think they should rather labour to conceal."

"But I must own," continued he, "that I have sometimes been very much surprised at the little concord I have observed between persons whose principles, humours, and behaviour, in the general, would make one imagine them equally qualified to give each other perfect happiness."

"What you say is extremely just," cried Jenny, "and I have often had occasion to make the same reflections;—it follows then, that every one before they engage in marriage should be well vers'd in all those things, whatever they are, which constitute the happiness of it;—this town is an ample school, and both of us have acquaintance enough in it to learn, from the mistakes of others, how to regulate our own conduct and passions, so as not to be laugh'd at ourselves for what we laugh at in them."

"Spoke like a philosophoress," rejoined Jemmy; "and upon second thoughts I agree with you, that as every thing is ready for us, and we can marry when we will, it will be best for us both to stay till we have got some farther lights into the mysterious duties of the conjugal union."

Jenny, who as yet had not the least inclination to enter into the serious road of matrimony, and would have been equally loath to have appear'd too refractory, if he had insisted on the performance of the covenant made between their fathers, was quite transported to find his sentiments so conformable to her own on this head; but forbore testifying all the satisfaction she felt, for fear of making him call in question the sincerity of her affection for him.

She only told him, that she was certain it would be for their mutual interest to do as he had mentioned;—on which he pursued his discourse in these terms:

"But, my dear Jenny," said he, "as learning will not come of itself, and we should be equally perfect in the different parts we are to act together hereafter; suppose we should resolve to communicate to each other all the discoveries we are able to make, among the several families that either of us converse with, and also all the confidences which are reposed in us;—by this means I shall be acquainted with all the humours of your sex, and you no stranger to those of mine; so that neither of us will be at a loss to bear with the foibles which nature or custom may have implanted in the other; besides," added he, "this is no more than practising before-hand one of those points, which, as I take it, is very essential to the happiness of both a husband and a wife,—which is the having no reserve."

"I am charm'd with your project," answer'd she; "but then each of us must be sure to preserve an inviolable secrecy in what has been imparted by the other, which is another main essential towards conjugal felicity."

Jemmy having assured her, that whatever she said to him on this account should be no more than talking to her own heart, they were beginning to divert themselves with the idea of the many whimsical passages they should have to recite to each other, when a footman brought a letter to Jenny,—the contents whereof were as follow:

To Miss Jessamy.

Dear creature,

If this finds you at home and disengaged, I flatter myself you will immediately comply with the request it contains;—I am now alone, and in a situation which requires both consolation and advice, neither of which I can hope for more effectually than from the friendship with which you favour me;—I would have waited on you, but am prevented by reasons which you will be no stranger to on seeing me. I am,

with the most perfect amity,
my dear Miss Jessamy,
yours, &c.
E. Marlove.

P.S. If I am unhappily deprived of your company to-night, I beg you will not fail coming as early as possible in the morning; for I am all impatience to let you into the history of my misfortunes.

"See here,"—said she, giving the letter to Jemmy,—"fortune already is likely to present me with something that may be worth your knowledge;—the lady who writes in this manner has honour and virtue;—she has been but four months married to a gentleman whom she preferred to a great number of other admirers, and who seems passionately fond of her;—you will not wonder that I am in as much haste to hear the occasion of her complaint, as she is to tell it me."

She then ordered a chair to the door, and calling for her gloves and capuchin, hurried them on while he was reading; the motive which carry'd her away was too agreeable for him to offer to detain her; and they parted without farther ceremony than a kiss, and good night.

Chapter VI

Contains some things well worthy of being seriously attended to, by those especially for whose service they are chiefly inserted.

Though Jenny had not doubted, by the lady's letter, but that something very extraordinary and perplexing had happen'd to her, yet she was far from expecting to find her in the condition she now did.

That half distracted fair one was lying extended on a couch,—her hair loose and hanging in wild disorder over her face,—her lovely eyes pouring forth tears,—all her features distorted with excess of passion, and every symptom of despair, grief, and rage about her.

Jenny was quite frighted; and indeed, who that had beheld her in this manner, but must have thought the most terrible accident imaginable had befallen her! "Ah, my dear Miss Jessamy," said she, as soon as she saw her enter, "how charitable is this visit to the most undone, forlorn, and miserable woman upon earth!"

"Bless me,"—cried Jenny, seating herself near her,—"what can have occasioned this sudden change in your late happy condition?"—"Oh, I will tell you all," replyed the other; "but when you shall hear how I have been treated by my ungrateful,—my perfidious husband, you will forswear marriage, and curse the whole race of false dissembling man."

"I sent for you,"—continued she,—"to make you the confidante of my resentment, as you have always been of my love; for this unworthy man, whom from my slave is now become my tyrant; and, instead of studying how to please me, has the insolence to attempt making me subservient to his will, and to contradict me even in things where every woman has a right to rule,—Could you ever have believed it, my dear Miss Jessamy,"—went she on,—"the vain creature imagines I have love enough for him to be satisfied with whatever he does?"

"I thought, indeed," said Jenny, "that both of you had love enough to be satisfied with what the other did;—But pray what may be the subject of the present dispute between you?"—"Oh such a gross affront upon my understanding, my humour,—my every thing that is dear to woman-kind," reply'd Mrs. Marlove,—"But of what nature?"—again demanded her impatient friend.

It was in vain she repeated the question over and over for several times successively, Mrs. Marlove was too much overcome by her passion to be able to give any direct account of the occasion, and all that could be gather'd from her incoherent exclamations was, that a favourite servant of Mr. Marlove's had quarrelled with her waiting-maid;—that she had insisted on the man's being turn'd away, and he as strenuously that she should part with her maid;—that very high words had rose on this occasion;—that he had endeavoured to exert the authority of a husband, and she to maintain the respect and complaisance due to a wife; and that after having absolutely refused to do as she desired, he had flung out of the house in very great discontent.

She was but just beginning to enter somewhat farther into the merits of the cause, when a servant put his head between the door, and told Mrs. Marlove, that the cloth was laid for supper,—and that his master was come home.—"Well, and what of that?" cried she hastily. "Nothing, Madam," said the man, "only my master desires that your ladyship and the young lady will be pleased to walk down."—"Tell him,"—reply'd she, with the utmost disdain in her voice and countenance,—"that I am not pleased to do any thing that he desires; and that I will neither eat nor sleep with him while he keeps that fellow Jonathan in the house."

On this, he said no more but withdrew, and Mr. Marlove came up in a moment after;—his looks express'd the utmost discontent;—he saluted Jenny, however, with respect, and then turning to his wife:—"I am surprised, my dear," cried he, "that you should expose yourself in this manner: family disputes ought to be discuss'd in private; it is impertinent to trouble our friends with them, and ridiculous to make our servants the witnesses of them;—for Heaven's sake, therefore, consider a little.—"

"I shall consider nothing," said she interrupting him, "but your unkindness and ingratitude;—What," pursued she with vehemence,—"to refuse me in so poor a trifle as the dismission of a servant?"

"Trifles, Madam," answer'd he very gravely, "when insisted on too peremptorily, become things of consequence; besides, you have often heard me say this man lived with my father;—that when I went abroad he gave him to me as the choicest present he could make; that he attended me in my travels through the greatest part of Europe; and that I have experienced his love and fidelity to me in a thousand instances:—it would therefore be highly unjust and ungenerous in me to turn him off; and I can look upon it as no less unreasonable in you to request it merely on the idle complaints and tittle-tattle of a chamber-maid."

"That chamber-maid,"—said she in the most haughty tone,—"while she belongs to me, is at least upon a level with your valet,—though in spite to me, I suppose, you have now raised him to your house-steward."

Mr. Marlove grew very red at these words, and was about to have made some reply, which perhaps might have heighten'd the quarrel, when the person who had been the occasion of it enter'd the room.

He was a grave, well look'd man, and had a certain open honesty in his countenance, which answer'd to the character given of him by his master.

"Sir," said he to Mr. Marlove, bowing in the most respectful manner,—"I have never known in my whole life so real a grief as I now feel, in finding myself the unhappy cause of any disagreement between your honour and my lady;—I therefore most humbly beseech you will be pleased to permit me to quit the house directly; for it is not fit your honour's peace of mind should suffer any disturbance, or my lady the least uneasiness, even for a moment, on so worthless a subject as myself."

"How, Jonathan," demanded Mr. Marlove, "are you in such haste to leave my service, that you would go before I am provided with a proper person to supply your place?"—"Oh, there is no reason for detaining him on that account," cried Mrs. Marlove, "my Abigail has a brother just now come out of place;—by the character I have heard of him he will be extremely fit for you, and we can have him at a minute's warning."

"'Tis very likely,"—reply'd he;—then having paused a little on what his wife had said;—"Well, Jonathan,"—pursued he, "we will talk farther on this matter to-morrow; but leave the room, and bid somebody send Abigail hither." Mrs. Marlove exulted within herself on hearing him speak in this manner, and pulling Jenny by the sleeve,—"My dear," cried she to her in a low voice, "I shall conquer this domineering husband at last."

Abigail immediately obeying the summons, that had been sent for her; "Well, Abigail," said Mr. Marlove, with half smile; which she then took for an indication of his being in great good humour with her; but, as it afterwards proved, was no more than a sarcastick sneer, "I am told you have a brother perfectly qualified for my service."

"Yes, please your honour," answer'd she simpering; "and, though I say it, as clever a fellow as ever stepp'd in shoe-leather; he can comb a wig to a charm, and buckle[43] too upon occasion; he does every thing in taste, I assure your honour;—besides, he is a spruce young man, and a thousand times fitter to attend your honour than the old formal creature you have now."

"It may be so," said Mr. Marlove; "but I have no business for him, nor have you any in my house longer than this night; therefore pack up your trumpery and be gone to-morrow morning": she was opening her mouth to speak, but he prevented her by saying, in a stern and resolute voice, "No raparties,[44] minx, I will have no incendiaries in my family;—out of my sight this moment and come into it no more."

Though scarce any creature was ever endow'd with a greater share of confidence than this wench, yet was she now so terrified at the looks of her master, that she durst not utter a single syllable while in his presence, and contented herself with muttering all the way she went down stairs, what she had not courage to say loud enough to be heard.

But it is altogether impossible to describe the rage Mrs. Marlove was in at this last proof of her husband's resolution; which was the more insupportable to her, as she had not above a moment or two before flattered herself with a belief that he was inclinable to conform to her desires.

She would have spoke, but excess of passion choak'd the passage of her words;—she flew into her chamber and threw herself upon the bed, where she certainly would have fallen into a fit, if Jenny, who had immediately follow'd her, had not cut the laceings of her stays,[45] in order to give her air.

On this she began to revive a little, and Abigail that instant coming up gave her a glass of cold water, which perfected the cure:—the first use she made of her received breath was to inveigh against the injustice, as she term'd it, of her husband:—Jenny was endeavouring to persuade her to more moderation, but was interrupted in the midst of what she was saying by Abigail.

"Nay, Madam," cried that malapert[46] huzzy, for that matter my lady has as much reason to be vex'd as I;—for my part, I do not know what my master means by using me as he has done;—he gives himself strange airs, methinks: I am sure it is not like a gentleman to shew so little respect for a servant."

These saucy reflections brought Mrs. Marlove more to herself than all the assistance that had been given her; angry as she was with her husband, she could not bear to hear him mentioned by such a creature in the manner she now did. "Airs," cried she,—"respect,—was ever any thing so ridiculously impudent! Sure, wench, thou hast forgot that the gentleman thou speakest so contemptuously of is my husband."

"No, Madam," answered she, bridling up her head, "I forget nothing that I ought to remember; and I must say again, that it does not become him to treat either you or me so unhandsomely as he has done."—"What, does the odious thing pretend to make comparisons?" cried Mrs. Marlove; and, provoked beyond all patience at the insolence of her deportment, snatch'd a powder-box from off the dressing-table and threw it at her head,—saying, at the same time, "Be gone this instant;—I shall keep no such bold-face about me."

"Bold-face, Madam," returned the audacious creature; "very pretty truly; but don't think I shall beg to stay; there are other places to be had, and I do not value."—She would have ran farther on in the same strain, if the sudden appearance of her master had not stopp'd her mouth, and made her think proper to go out of the room.

Mr. Marlove being heartily ashamed that Jenny had been witness of this foolish affair, resolved to salve it up, if possible, before she went away; and, to that end, came into his wife's chamber; chusing rather to recede a little from what he thought his just prerogative as a husband, than suffer her to depart with the notion of his having asserted it too far.

As he came into the room at one door Abigail was going out at the other;—he easily perceived, by her countenance, that some brulée[47] had happened between her and her lady, which taking for a good omen of succeeding in his design, he approach'd Mrs. Marlove; and, with an air perfectly degagée[48] and unembarras'd, "I hope, my dear," said he, "you are by this time convinced, that your maid had a farther view in quarreling with Jonathan than she pretended, and also how little she deserves you should espouse her cause."

"She has been impertinent, indeed," answer'd she; "but it is no wonder that she is so; when a woman is ill treated by her husband, she can expect no other than to be so by her servants also; and it is to you,—to you alone, that I either have, or shall hereafter be deprived of the respect due to me from our domestics."

"Accuse me not," said he, "of a thing so contrary to my nature;—your merits, and my just sense of them, will always engage me to behave towards you, both in public and in private, with all the complaisance and tenderness that man can pay or woman can expect."

"Then you would not contradict me in trifles," cried she, a little soften'd. "I will contradict you in nothing," said he, "that my reason will permit me to grant, or your own, on mature deliberation, induce you to desire.—As for the present dispute between us," continued he, "I only beg you will defer any farther speech of it till to-morrow; and if, in that time, you do not find cause to alter your opinion, I shall endeavour to accede to yours."

"A very fair proposal, indeed, Sir," said Jenny smiling; "and, my dear Mrs. Marlove, if you do not accept it I shall lay the whole blame of all the disagreements that may hereafter happen between you entirely on your ill-nature."

"That is a very severe inference," reply'd she; "however, to oblige you, I shall comply with Mr. Marlove's request."—"I am glad to obtain it at any rate," cried he;—"and I hope we may now go down to supper, which has waited for us this half hour."—Mrs. Marlove said she did not care for eating, and desir'd they would excuse her absence; but, by the intreaties of her husband, and some little pleasantries Jenny made use of on this occasion, she was at last prevailed upon, and they all went down together into the parlour.

Jenny kept an observant eye over both the husband and the wife all the time they were at table; and, as she was happy in a penetration, which few of her sex, especially at her years, can boast of, easily perceived that though he behaved with a politeness beyond what could have been expected after what had pass'd, and she seemed to have abated a great part of her late haughtiness and resentment, yet neither of them were sincerely inclined to submit to the will of the other, in any thing which was not entirely agreeable to their own.

The apologies they made to her, however, on the account of the unpleasing entertainment she had met with in this visit, with her obliging answers to them in return, and repeated good wishes for their future peace, engrossed a great part of their conversation during the whole time she stayed.

But the night being pretty far advanced, when supper was ended she took her leave of the half reconciled pair, and went home full of those reflections which, on the scene she had been witness of, must naturally have occurr'd even to a person of a much less considerative disposition.

Chapter VII

Affords fresh matter for edification to those who stand in need of it, as well as entertainment to such who do not.

Jenny had an infinity of good nature, and was extremely troubled at the disagreement she had seen between two persons whom she thought had been entirely happy in being united to each other:—the more she ruminated on the behaviour of Mrs. Marlove, the more she found in it to condemn; but then she was also equally surprised to find so great a change in that of her husband; she had frequently been in their company while in their days of courtship;—she had seen him humour all the little whims and caprices which the vanity of flatter'd beauty had made her guilty of;—she had heard him praise even her very foibles, and seem charmed with what the rest of the world most blamed her for.

"Good God," cried she to herself, "how strange a reverse does marriage bring! who that sees a man a husband would ever think he had been a lover?—till she was a wife, he would not have presumed to argue with her on any point she took upon her to assert;—he would not then have opposed his reason to any folly she committed; 'tis true she has insisted on a thing, which he must have been both ungenerous and weak to have comply'd with; yet would he once not have dared to have contradicted her in much greater matters:—if she is proud,—imperious and vain, it is on his own too obsequiousness [*sic*] he ought to lay the blame. Oh, why will men endeavour to persuade us we are goddesses, only to create themselves the pains of convincing us afterwards that we are but mortals!"

"Yet after all," said she again, "we know that the extravagant encomiums so lavishly bestowed upon us before marriage, are mere words of course; the homage,—the submissions paid us by the lover, all form and empty shew; and, as they are put in practice only to sooth our vanity, ought not to deceive our understandings so far as to make us imagine we either deserve, or have a right to expect the continuance of them, when the motive that induced them is no more.—Marriage, as it removes all coyness and reserve in the women, so it destroys all suspence in the men:—he is then in possession of his wishes, has done with hopes and fears; and sollicitations of course must also cease."

"Stripp'd, therefore, of that imaginary authority with which we once flatter'd ourselves, it is certainly the business of our sex to endeavour, by the most soft and obliging behaviour, to preserve and improve, if possible, the love of him, whom it is no longer in our power to awe by a contrary way of acting."

"A too great tenaciousness of our own merits," pursued she; "the pride of doing whatever we have a mind to, and of imposing the laws of our own will on that of the lover, may be submitted to while we are mistresses; but will never be borne with when we are wives:—the men, conscious of that superiority which custom and the matrimonial covenant has given them, never fail to exert it, and opposition on our side is struggling against the stream, and but serves to shew our weakness the more in the vain attempt."

"In my opinion," went she still on, "the way to accomplish what we aim at, is not to urge it with too much vehemence, even in the most reasonable things, much less can we expect success when we insist on such as are in themselves unjustifiable:—as in the case of Mrs. Marlove; and I much fear, that if many contests of this nature happen, they will by degrees weaken her husband's affection for her; perhaps, in time, utterly destroy it, and render her both unhappy and unpitied."

In this manner did the sagacious Jenny reason within herself upon the cause in question; and upon the whole, her judgement entirely acquitted Mr. Marlove of all blame, and gave the verdict against his too assuming wife, for whose late behaviour she could find no excuse, except her extreme youth, and inexperience of the temper of mankind, that lady being but sixteen, which was two years short of the age she had attain'd herself.

This naturally led her into reflections on the folly of two persons uniting themselves together by the solemn ties of marriage, without having well consider'd the duties of the state they were about to enter into, and confirm'd her in the resolution she before had taken of living single, till she was as well assured, as human reason could make her, that both herself and the man who was to be her husband, were equally qualified to render each other truly happy.

She longed, however, to see Jemmy, that she might relate this story to him, and hear his sentiments upon it; but she saw him not all the next day, which a little surprised her, as four and twenty hours seldom passed over without his making her one visit, if no more; the accident, which now occasioned his absence so much longer than usual, was, indeed, of a pretty particular nature;—it was this:

On his coming home the night before he found a letter that had been left for him, requesting his company at an entertainment to be given the next day on a very extraordinary occasion, by a gentleman who had been an intimate acquaintance of his father's;—the invitation was too pressing for him to refuse complying with it, which otherwise he would gladly have done, as he expected not to find any guests there suitable to his age or humour.

He found himself, however, agreeably deceived in this conjecture, and was surprised, on his entrance into a spacious room, to see it fill'd with a very brilliant company of both sexes, who being assembled in order to celebrate the most joyous circumstance that can happen in private life, came with a sincere resolution of contributing every thing in the power of each to do honour to the feast prepared for them.

But not to keep the reader in suspence, the person who made this invitation was a gentleman of birth and fortune;—he was married in his youth to a lady of celebrated beauty, and every way his equal; but, through a too great love of pleasure on his side, and some errors in conduct, though without any breach of virtue on her's, they had been separated for fourteen years, without the least probability of being reconciled, and even less of their ever living together again, as all the interposition of their friends for that purpose, during so long a space of time, had been in vain, and was, at last, entirely given over:—the unhoped for event, notwithstanding, came to pass;—both parties were alike touch'd with a just sensibility of their former mistakes, and return'd to the embraces of each other, with more ardency of affection than that with which they had first met in marriage.

There is certainly nothing which so much demonstrates the sincerity of our reformation, as a free confession that we have been in the wrong.—"I was," said the gentleman, "in possession of a treasure before I had attain'd to an age capable of knowing the true value of it; I wore it as an idiot does a diamond, careless on my arm, and liable to be snatch'd from me by the first person who admired its lustre;—but heaven has preserved it as a blessing for my riper judgement."

He concluded these words with kissing his lady's hand, and then went on, "I was," continued he, "one of those thoughtless wretches, which the poet, doubtless, had in his eye when he wrote these lines:"

Fictitious joys allur'd my dazzled senses,
And led them in the mistic maze a while;
Beguil'd with empty air, my restless heart
Still after some untasted pleasure roam'd;
But now the wanderer seeks his peaceful home,
And there finds all it vainly sought abroad.[49]

"I cannot suffer you, my dear," said the lady, with a most becoming smile, "to take upon yourself the whole blame of that unhappy disagreement, which has so long divided us;—I also have had my share of guilt, though in a different way from yours;—if you have been too gay, I have been too inconsiderate;—I have endeavoured not to make home delightful to you;—I rather, by a thousand impertinencies and follies, render'd my presence tiresome; I had no idea of the duties of my place, but behaved, when set at the head of a family, as I had done in the nursery, and expected to be humour'd in the same manner."

Thus did this lately re-united pair equally condemn themselves for the miscarriages of their past conduct; but, while they were speaking, there were not a few in company of both sexes, who hung down their heads, as conscious of not being wholly free from the errors they heard mentioned.

Jemmy, according to the agreement made between him and Jenny, kept an observant eye on all those whom he found were married, and easily perceived, by the looks which one of them in particular frequently gave his wife, that they were far from living together in a perfect harmony; tho', as he had never seen either of them before, and was wholly unacquainted with their circumstances, conditions, or humours, it was utterly impossible for him to guess from what latent cause the discord he discover'd proceeded;—but as it was the husband who seem'd most dissatisfied, he concluded, without knowing any thing of the matter, that it must be the wife who was to blame.

The men are apt to be too partial to one another on this score:—in the little time that Jemmy had at present for reflection, these lines of Mr. Dryden's came directly into his head:

Few know what cares a husband's peace destroys,
His real griefs and his dissembled joys.[50]

It is altogether impracticable for married people, when so unhappy as to have any real or imagined cause of complaint against each other, to keep the uneasiness they labour under from being visible to the world;—however perfect, as to other things they may be in the art of dissimulation, in this, spite of their utmost endeavours, the sentiments of their hearts will break out;—every look,—every gesture, betrays the inward pangs they feel;—which shews, that of all circumstances of discontent, those of marriage are with the most difficulty sustain'd.

Jemmy was afterwards informed, that the last mention'd gentleman was one of the many whom, it is not in the power of fortune to make happy;—that he took a kind of gloomy pleasure in creating to himself ideal ills, and then started at the apparition, which nothing but his own productive fancy had conjured up.

His wife was far from being a beauty; and as to her person, she had received no more from nature than would just serve to make her pass for not disagreeable; as to her behaviour, it was affable and chearful, but withal extremely modest; for as she never affected a too great reserve, so she was equally free from all that had the appearance of levity; but neither the little power her eyes had of captivating, nor the prudence of her carriage, could hinder him from imagining every man that looked upon her had a dishonourable design towards her, and also that she had no disinclination to encourage it.

The whole of the entertainment concluded with a kind of ball; and as there were more gentlemen than ladies present, the cloudy husband, with two others, retired to one corner of the room, and sat drinking to the healths of those that danced.

It was by mere accident, and without the least design on either side, that Jemmy had for his partner the wife of this suspicious gentleman;—but it was pleasant enough for those who sat near him to observe with what eagerness his eyes pursued each motion in them, which the regulation of the dance required,—how his colour changed,—how his lips trembled, whenever that couple set to each other, or turn'd hands; it was in vain they fill'd his glass and reminded him of the neglected toast, though it were even that of the royal family;—he thought of nothing but his wife, and seeing her, as he imagined, encouraging the dumb courtship of a person who would invade his rights, he had no longer patience, and the second dance was but just led up when he rose from his seat and said he must go home, for he had letters of importance to write, which till that moment he had forgot.

This put all into disorder;—the gentleman who had made the invitation would fain have persuaded him to stay, but was silenced by the other, urging the necessity of his departure:—the lady then told him, with a great deal of politeness, that if they must be so unhappy to be deprived of his company, she hoped they should not also lose Mrs.——, who she supposed had no letters to write.

"No,—no Madam," replied he, with very great emotion, "my wife may stay if she thinks proper; I do not want her, not I":—she was advancing to take her leave while he was speaking, nor would suffer herself to be prevailed upon, by all the lady could say, to stay behind her husband; but it was easy for any one to see her inclinations took the contrary part, and denied herself the satisfaction such good company afforded, merely through the apprehensions of paying too dearly for it when she came home.

Thus industriously do some people labour to bring on what most they would avoid;—if this lady had been possess'd of a little more beauty, or to speak more justly, had she been mistress of a less share of discretion, there were, doubtless, some in company who would have been excited, by the jealousy of her husband, to have attempted that chastity he took such ridiculous measures to preserve.

As it was, however, the behaviour of the husband served to render him contemptible in the eyes of every one, and that of the wife to give her charms, which otherwise could not have been remark'd in her.

The sarcasms pass'd on this unhappy self-tormented gentleman would be too tedious to repeat, yet were much shorter, than they otherwise would have been, if the music's sprightly sounds had not reminded the company, that their feet at that time demanded more employment than their tongues.

It is not to be doubted but that on going home every one made their several remarks on what they had seen, but the mind of Jemmy was affected by it in a particular manner, as he considered all that had presented itself to him that day concurred to make up one great instructive lesson for himself.

Chapter VIII

Will occasion various speculations in the inquisitive reader.

When our pair of lovers came to relate mutually to each other the foregoing narratives, they were both of opinion, that most of the disagreements that happened in marriage were occasion'd chiefly by the parties entering into that state too early, and too precipitately.

"If your friends, who now so much rejoice in being reunited," said Jenny, "had taken care before marriage to attain those qualifications necessary for the performance of the duties required from their respective stations, they would probably never have fallen into those errors which caused their separation.

"Nor would their guest," continued she, "be so unreasonably jealous of his wife's conduct, if, previously to his becoming a husband, he had made himself well acquainted with her principles and disposition, and also equally so with his own humour."

"Nor would Mrs. Marlove," replied Jemmy, "if she had at all studied the temper of mankind, have been so vain as to expect the same submission from her husband as she received from him while her lover;—much less have pretended to contradict him in things where it was not her province to interfere."

"Right," resumed she smiling, "and you may now easily perceive the advantage it is to us not to hurry ourselves into wedlock, as too many people do, without reflecting [on] what they are about, or being any way prepared to make the noose set easy."

"Then you persist in your resolution," rejoined Jemmy, "of not being married yet a while?" To which she answering in the affirmative, and repeating the arguments she had before made use of in her vindication, he readily enough yielded to the justice of her reasons; but that he did so was not so much owing to his discretion, as to another motive, which, though Jenny was ignorant of, it is not convenient that the reader should be so.

He had, in reality, met with some adventures of late which had given him too high a relish for the modish pleasures of the town for him to be able to quit them without reluctance, and which he had too much good sense not to know it would ill become him to indulge the pursuit of after he should be a married man.

Among the many places of diversion this great and luxurious town abounds with, Lady Racket's assembly has been always look'd upon as the most general rendezvous for all the young and gay of both sexes.

Jemmy went frequently thither, and it happening that one evening the company playing very high, he was stripp'd of all the money and bank notes he had about him, which amounted to a considerable sum.

A little vex'd at his ill fortune he was retiring to a window,[51] in order to compose himself, when the sound of a female voice very loud made him turn his head; he found it proceeded from Liberia,—the celebrated Liberia, who having been playing at another table, had lost all her money, and had not temper to bear it.

"Was ever such cursed luck!" cried she, starting up from her seat, "I have not a single stake left;—I have a good mind to make a solemn vow never to touch a card again." "Patience,—patience, Madam,"—said Jemmy, advancing towards her;—"behold in me your brother in affliction; these things will happen if we depend on the blind goddess."[52]—"Have you lost all your money too?" demanded she. "Every doit,[53] upon my soul," reply'd he; "so neither of us have any thing to do at present but to observe the fate of others."

"That would be an insipid way of killing time indeed," said she; "suppose you and I should set down to picquet,[54] as we both are in the same condition, and can play with nobody else."—"With all my heart," answered he, "and stake honour against honour."—"Perhaps that would be just nothing at all," cried she laughing.—"I dare trust yours," rejoined he, "if you will put the same confidence in mine."

"It would be ungenerous in me," reply'd she, "not to return good opinion with good opinion;—but I think it is against the rules of gaming to play merely upon credit;—I will set my solitaire[55] against that ring you have upon your finger."

Jemmy had a great regard for this ring, not so much for the intrinsic value of it, though it was a fine diamond, as because it had been his father's, who had given it to him some little time before he died: a moment's recollection, however, served to make him know what he should do on this occasion; and he reply'd with great alertness,—"Madam, I heartily agree to your proposal, with this proviso, that which ever of us is the winner, the stakes may be redeemable;—nor would it be fair in me to play with you on any other terms, as your solitaire is worth much more than my ring."

"Well, it shall be just as you would have it," reply'd she, "twenty guineas shall be the event";—to which Jemmy agreeing, they sat down to a table which some company had just quitted; she pluck'd off her solitaire and he his ring, both the pledges were laid under the candlestick, and to play they went;—fortune, for several deals, seem'd dubious in whose favour she should decide; but at length, after a hard fought battle, gave the victory to Jemmy.

"Was ever any thing so unluckly," said she, "but I won't give out, come, Sir," continued she, shuffling the cards, "twenty guineas more;—or, if you please, thirty; I shall then either be indebted fifty pieces to you, or have a claim on you for ten."

Jemmy would fain have persuaded her to give over, but she would hear nothing he said on that score; they cut the cards, poor Liberia, had the advantage of the deal, but was nothing a gainer by it, she had not even the satisfaction of a second struggle; he immediately produced point—queen—and quatorze,[56] without the trouble of playing a card.

"Confusion," cried she, bursting into tears, "sure all the stars in the firmament have conspired this night against me!" With these words she rose from table; "you have won, Sir," pursued she, "I know your directions, and will send the money in a day or two." She stayed not to hear what answer he would make, but flew out of the room with an air which denoted the utmost agitation of mind.

Liberia had a great share of beauty, and Jemmy of good nature; the distress she appeared in render'd her more lovely in his eyes than ever he had thought her; his heart was that instant fill'd with emotions she had never before inspired it with;—he followed, with the solitaire in his hand, and overtook her as she was passing through a room in order to reach the stair-case.

"Madam," said he to her, "I cannot suffer that beautiful neck should be without so becoming an ornament, even for the smallest space of time; I beseech you therefore, to resume this jewel, and also to assure yourself, that I dare take your word of honour as a sufficient security for a much greater sum than the trifle to which fortune has just now entitled me."

"No Mr. Jessamy," answer'd she, "that must not be, my lord is at present out of town, or if he were at home, I should not chuse to acquaint him with my losses at play;—it is also improper for me to let the steward know any thing of the matter;—it may be longer than I could wish, or you perhaps expect, before I can, with any convenience, discharge my obligation;—so desire you will say no more, but keep the pledge till in my power to redeem it."

All this was delivered in a voice so broken and hesitating, that Jemmy easily perceived by that, as well as by her looks, that it was with the utmost reluctance she refused the offer he had made, though her pride would not suffer her to accept it.

Something, which the reader will presently discover, coming that moment into his head, "Since you insist, Madam," said he, looking tenderly on her, "and will needs force me to retain something of yours in my hands, consent, at least, that I exchange this mortgage for some other, if you will permit me to wait on you home, and look over your trinkets, I shall certainly find somewhat that will please me as well, and you can much better spare."

"I must not reject every thing you propose," replied she with a half smile, and then received the solitaire from him, which he assisted her in replacing, and while he was doing so gave her neck a gentle pressure, which she was not so insensible as not to know the meaning of.

There needed no more,—she gave him her hand to lead her down stairs,—her own chair waiting in the hall she went into it, and he follow'd in a hackney.[57]

On coming to her house, she conducted him directly to her dressing room, where her woman being sitting at work, she bad[e] her set a bottle of wine on the table, and retire till call'd for,—saying she had some accounts to settle with that gentleman.

This attendant was no sooner withdrawn than the reduced Liberia opened a little cabinet, which contain'd her jewels.—"Here, Sir," cried she, "are all the toys of this nature I am mistress of."—Jemmy scarce vouchsafeing a glance towards them, reply'd,—"They must be fine, indeed, since owned by you, and must dazzle the sight of a man less knowing than I pretend to be in what is truly valuable;—but what is all the lustre they can boast while you are in presence?—How faint are the rays of the diamond to those your eyes send forth!—how insipid,—how weak is the glow of the ruby to these lips!"

He began this speech with looking intently on her face, and finding nothing there to discourage his attempt, concluded it with throwing his arms about her waist, and giving her more lively indications of his sense of the perfections he had praised, than all in the power of language could have done.

They were alone,—a couch was in the room, she resisted not his encroachments, and one moment gave him the full possession of a happiness, which not half an hour before he had not even the least thought of ever solliciting.

Scarce had he time to express the transports of his gratitude for the unhoped favours he had received, when Liberia, hearing the sound of voices on the stairs, rang her bell to know who was there; on which her woman immediately came in, and told her that two ladies, who had been at Lady Racket's assembly, and seeing her leave the company so abruptly, had call'd to know the occasion, fearing she might be indisposed.

"Lord, how impertinent is some people's friendship!" cried Liberia;—"Why did you not tell them I was well, but very busy?" "I did so, Madam," reply'd the other, "and that you was shut up in your closet, writing letters; but they insisted on seeing you,—ran up stairs in spite of me, and are now in the drawing room."

"Well,—there is no remedy for these things," said she, "I must go to them, or they will burst in upon me here; you'll excuse me, Mr. Jessamy,—it is highly improper you should be seen";—then turning to her woman; "shew him down the back stairs," added she, "with as little noise as you can."

She said no more, but went out of the room to receive her company, and Jemmy suffer'd himself to be conducted by her woman in the manner she had order'd.

Chapter IX

Has something in it of the marvellous.

Though Jemmy had as small a share of vanity in his composition as any man that ever lived, yet it would have been a thing almost supernatural in him, if an adventure, such as he had just now met with, had not elated a heart so unexperienced as was his;—Liberia was a woman of distinction, young, beautiful, and had every requisite to render her the delight and admiration of mankind; to what else then, but a peculiar liking of his person and behaviour, could it seem possible to him to impute the concessions she had made?

It is not to be understood, however, that the pleasing sensation he felt at this event proceeded from the gratification of any passion he had entertain'd for the lady, who so highly had obliged him;—no, on the contrary, his affection for Jenny was a sure defence from the attacks of any other charms; he had often seen Liberia, had thought her a fine woman, as every one did; but he had never been touched with the least spark of an amorous desire on her account; nor, on looking on her, had even consider'd the difference of sexes: but though what had happened between them was merely casual on his side; yet he could not help believing, that it was a previous inclination on her's which alone could have excited her to act in the manner she had done.

The hurry in which they were compell'd to part, took from him all opportunity to testifying that desire of continuing a correspondence with her, which otherwise, he thought, she would have had reason to expect; and which even gratitude, politeness, and even common good nature, would have exacted from him.

He therefore went the next morning to her house, certain in his mind of meeting with a reception suitable to the kindness she had given him such proofs of the night before;—she was just dress'd, and going to court; but, on his sending up his name, gave orders for his admittance; the servant who introduced him immediately withdrawing, he approach'd to salute her with the air and freedom of a favour'd lover.

But how unspeakable was his surprise, when, going to take her in his arms, she started back, and with a countenance all awful and austere, "Hold off, Sir," said she, "this is a familiarity neither becoming you to take, nor me to grant": the confusion he was in not permitting him to make any immediate reply; "I do not now," continued she, "owe fifty pieces to you."

"No, Madam," reply'd he, a little recovering himself; "but you owe me a heart in return for that I have devoted to you."—"I have nothing to do with your heart, resum'd she; and as for mine it is my husband's due."—"If you really think so, Madam," cried he, "wherefore did you flatter me last night with having so large a part?"—"What happened last night," said she, "was merely accidental; I had lost all my money, and the debts we contract at play, you know, are debts of honour; but where my own is not concern'd, be assured I shall always have a just regard for that of my husband's."

In spite of the consternation Jemmy was in, he could not refrain smiling at the distinction this lady made, and with an air, which had something of contemptuous in it, "I thought Madam," said he, "that the honour of the husband and the wife had always been inseparable."

"They are so, I allow," answer'd she; "but necessity sometimes compels a woman to do what otherwise she would not be guilty of; therefore I beg you will think no more of what has happened, it was a foolish affair indeed; but as it cannot be recall'd, should be forgotten."

He was about to make some reply, which it is likely would not have been very pleasing to her, but she went to the door and call'd to know if the chariot was ready, and being told it was, "Adieu, Mr. Jessamy," said she, "I am obliged to attend the princess; I hope whenever we meet, you will always treat me as the wife of Lord * * *."

She had no sooner spoke these words than she shot like lightning out of the room, leaving Jemmy in a situation of mind not easy to be described, or even conceived, by any one who has not been under the same circumstances.

It was not that his pride was so much mortifyed at this unexpected rebuff, as his comprehension was confounded at its being given; the more he endeavoured to fathom the mysterious meaning, the more he was absorb'd in wonder; in fine, he knew not what to think, nor by what motive to account for a proceeding so strange, so contradictory to the very nature of the sex.

The first shock of any thing is very difficult to be conceal'd;—the spirits, when suddenly alarm'd, are in a hurry for a while, then sink into as extreme a languor.—Jemmy dined that day at a tavern, by an appointment he had made with some gentlemen of his acquaintance; but neither their conversation, nor the glass which went briskly about, had the power of dissipating his chagrin, or driving Liberia entirely from his thoughts.

The least air of seriousness in persons of an extraordinary vivacity cannot fail of being taken notice of;—Jemmy was looked upon as the life and soul of all the company he went into; and now to find him, instead of inspiring others with good humour, stand in need of being inspired himself, made every one desirous of knowing what had occasioned this sudden transformation; but the affair was not a thing proper to be talked on, and he evaded giving any direct answer to the questions put to him on this head.

He did not long, however, preserve a taciturnity on this occasion, which was pretty painful to him;—the company being broke up, and only one gentleman, with whom he had a greater intimacy than with any of the others, staying behind, he could not forbear speaking of what so much engross'd his thoughts; in fine, he related to him the whole history of his late whimsical adventure, concealing only the name of the heroine concern'd in it.

But how strangely was he disappointed, when instead of hearing his friend express some astonishment, as he expected he would have done, at an event so new and uncommon, he only burst into such a violent fit of laughter as hindered him from speaking for some moments.

"What," cried Jemmy, "I suppose the story I have been telling you is too romantic to be believed, and you suspect I have been endeavouring all this while to impose upon your understanding an invention of my own, in the room of a real fact?"

"No, upon my word," reply'd the other, "I am so confident of the truth of all you have repeated, that upon occasion I would be your voucher for every particular of it;—but what made me so merry was, the great care you have taken in keeping the name of this fine lady a secret;—What will you say now," continued he, "if I tell you at once that I am very certain no woman but Liberia is capable of behaving in the manner you have describ'd?"

Liberia herself had scarce given Jemmy more surprise than his friend did in mentioning her as the person they were talking of. "Liberia," cried he, "What have I said to raise such a conjecture in you?"

"Nothing, upon my soul," answer'd the other; "you have nothing to accuse yourself of in this point, and might have told the story to five hundred people without any one of them being able to guess at the woman;—it is not my penetration but my experience, has let me into the secret of this matter;—and to make you master of an other, I must tell you that I have been beforehand with you."

Jemmy, not perfectly comprehending these words, asked what he meant? "It happen'd," said he, "the other day, that one evening I play'd at the same table with this extraordinary lady;—I swept the stakes, and she being out of cash, we went on upon credit;—fortune still was on my side;—she lost a considerable sum to me, which I had the same equivalent for that she bestow'd on you; and when I waited on her some days afterwards, in order to repeat my devoirs, received also just the same repulse you did, and found that it was her humour;—no play—no love."

"Then neither of us," cried Jemmy, "are oblig'd for the favours we have receiv'd to an amorous inclination on her part." "No, faith," reply'd his friend, "I rather take her to be one of the insensibles that way;—but her lust of gaming is insatiate;—she would be eternally at it,—there all the passions of her soul are center'd; and though at present a profest enemy to religion, would be the greatest devotee imaginable, were she once persuaded there were gaming-tables in heaven."

"In fine, my dear Jemmy," pursu'd he, "the case stands thus,—she loses more at play in one month, perhaps than the rent-roll of Lord * * *'s estate produces in a year; and being, either through fear or tenderness, unwilling to make him acquainted with her ill luck, prudently takes the method you and I have experienced, of satisfying the winners, and thinks herself no ill wife in so doing; since she forfeits her husband's honour only to preserve his peace, and never repeats her transgression with the same man, unless compell'd to it by a second necessity of the like nature."

Jemmy being now, by this detail, entirely freed from the perplexity of thought which the first surprize at the strangeness of Liberia's behaviour had involved him in, it is not to be doubted but that these two young gentlemen were pleasant enough on the affair in question, and mutually laugh'd at each other for the disappointment each of them had received, in imagining they had been favoured with a peculiar liking by that lady.

Neither of them having any engagements on their hands, they pass'd the whole evening together till the night was very far advanced, and called them to repose; during all which time little else but Liberia was talked on.

But as the repetition of a conversation, founded on such a topic, might not be very agreeable to such of our readers as we should be most studious to oblige; and besides, would be not at all material to the business of this history, we may reasonably hope being easily excused for passing it over in silence.

Chapter X

Affords but small matter of entertainment; yet, if well consider'd, may be of singular use to some readers.

There is a certain haughty surliness almost inherent to old age, which will not let people, when they come to be any thing advanced in years, allow the least share of understanding in those of a younger sort;—they treat them as mere idiots, incapable of comparing,—judging, or even of knowing right from wrong.

But this is a partiality which betrays that want of discernment in themselves which they accuse in others;—if youth, through too much fire, is adicted to vanity, rashness and impetuosity; age, through too much phlegm,[58] is no less liable to peevishness,—obstinacy, and pride;—in both, the faults of constitution have but too great an effect upon the will, and deprive reason of half its force.

The faculties of the mind certainly decay, and grow weaker in proportion as the vigour of the body is impair'd;—a keenness of conception,—a readiness of thought, and what is generally call'd wit, are the gifts of youth;—when the organs, through which the soul is said to operate, are in their full strength as nature made them, unobstructed by diseases, and unworn by time.—Age is chiefly wise by experience, and by improving those observations, which a long series of years had treasured up.

It must therefore be allow'd, that young people are far from being incapable of making the most just reflections; but the baits of sense;—the excitements of pleasure, and the whirl of a thousand different passions, which incessantly agitate the ideas, prevent those reflections from making any lasting impression, and consequently from being of any real use in regulating their actions;—so that they can be said to be discreet only by starts; and it is in this alone that all the boasted advantages of age consists.

Nothing was ever more strictly true than what that celebrated poet, Mr. Dryden, says, when speaking of the difference between youth and age, he expresses the whole sense of the argument in these two equally elegant and comprehensive lines:

Experience vainly in our youth is sought,
And, by age purchas'd, is too dearly bought.[59]

Our Jemmy was one of those who never did any thing which reason could condemn, without being immediately self-convicted and ashamed of his error, though, as I said before, through the fire of youth,—the enchantments of pleasure, and the prevalence of example, he could not sometimes avoid falling again into the same.

As to play in particular, without any extraordinary propensity of his own, he was frequently drawn in to make a party at several gaming-tables, both private and public, yet did he never reflect on what money he had lost without being convinced he could not have disposed of it a worse way;—nor did he ever win of any gentleman, whose circumstances he knew could not well bear a diminution, without being shock'd to the soul or having been one of those who had contributed to his misfortune.

He was perfectly sensible both of the vice and folly of gaming, as at present practiced among almost all degrees of people; and stood amaz'd whenever he recollected, that he had seen men of the first figure and fortune in the kingdom, not only condescend to mix in company with the common sharpers and gamblers of the town, but also to make use of the same low arts they did, in order to force chance as it were, to be their friend.

He could not think, without a mixture of pity and contempt on those, who neglecting the accounts of their estates, and trusting all to their stewards and bailiffs, boasted how well they were served in Mr. Hoyle's[60] calculation in the cutting of a pack of cards, and swear five pieces an hour was too small pay for the instructions of so learned a doctor in the great, mysterious, and most polite science of gaming.

He very often run over in his mind all the various amusements of the town; and on comparing them with this of gaming, none of them seem'd to him to have so small a plea for engrossing either the time or attention of a man of sense and honour.

"Every other pleasure or diversion," said he within himself, "have something in them deserving of that name; they either regale the senses, or exercise the body, or relieve the mind; but gaming is the contrary of all these; it impedes the gratification of our most natural appetites, it enervates the limbs with too long sitting, it racks the brain with cares, it fills the bosom with anxieties, and in fine, is a fatigue, which were it not the effect of our own free choice, would be intolerable."

"Nor is this all," would he sometimes add; "an inordinate love of gaming certainly proceeds from avarice, the most sordid passion of the heart, and consequently destroys all that is generous, noble, and sincere; deadens that social feel, that kindly warmth, which nature has implanted in us towards our fellow creatures; and renders the man devoted to this vice capable of no other wish than to enjoy the infamous triumph of bearing off the spoils of him he plays against, though it should even happen to be one he calls his friend, or one who must be entirely ruined by the loss of what he is now in possession of, through the favour of fortune, or a superior skill in the destructive art."

He concluded from all this, that to undo others, or be undone oneself, was the almost certain consequence of gaming high; for which reason he made many resolutions to avoid it as much as possible; and indeed persisted in them more than could be well expected from a man of his gay temper, and who, by the company he kept, was continually surrounded with temptations of that sort.

But if he thought the love of play so pernicious a thing in those of his own sex, in what light must he behold it in regard to those of the other?—He had read some old musty authors, who maintained that modesty was the peculiar characteristic of womanhood; that an innocence of deportment was the chief beauty of a virgin; and economy in private, and a decent reserve in public, that of a married woman; and he could not get it out of his head but that these maxims were just contrary, as they were to what he had seen practiced at play by some ladies, who pass for patterns of politeness and fashionable good breeding; and in comparing the difference, he could not forbear crying out,—"Sure, when these books were wrote, gaming was a thing never heard of among women!"

These having always been his notions, it could not be otherwise but that the example of Liberia must greatly contribute to fortify them in him, as he had now experienced what he had many times been told by those better acquainted with the ladies, that those debts, which are called debts of honour, are frequently discharged by loss of honour.

"What an amiable figure in life might this woman make," said he, speaking of Liberia, "if it were not for this mad attachment to gaming?—I dare believe she has no vicious inclinations of her own, and her quality and marriage with Lord * * * defends her from all impertinent addresses of our sex.—How strange then is the infatuation which compels her to run the fatal risque of being reduced to yield such condescentions, as otherwise her pride would scorn, and her virtue shudder at!"

He never ruminated in this manner without falling immediately after into a profound reverie, which whoever had seen him in would not have taken him for that gay, laughing, spirituous creature he appeared at other times; but it generally happens that persons of that humour, when they think at all, think more deeply than those of a heavy and phlegmatic disposition.

The many mischiefs which sometimes befall the fair sex, by indulging themselves in this dangerous amusement, made him tremble for Jenny; he knew she play'd occasionally, but though he had never heard her testify any extraordinary pleasure in it, yet he could not assure himself that she might not, by degrees, be drawn into a better liking of it, and consequently become liable to the same inconveniencies, to which so many others of her sex were every day subjected.

Love, friendship, and the consideration of his own interest and honour, as Jenny was one day to become his wife, obliged him therefore to do every thing in his power to prevent so great an evil; nor could he think of any method more effectual for that end, than by reminding her, in a delicate way, and without seeming to do it with design, of the dangers to which women who love play, could not fail of being exposed.

He had no sooner thought on this, than he resolved to put it into immediate execution; and to give the greater weight to what he intended to say, ransack'd his memory for all the alarming circumstances of a gaming-table, that he had ever either seen or heard of.

Chapter XI

A little more to the purpose.

Jemmy knew that his fair mistress kept a great deal of company, and that most of her afternoons were taken up with giving and receiving visits;—

whenever, therefore, he had any particular conversation to entertain her with, he always went to her in a morning; the business he had now to communicate seeming to him of too much importance to be delay'd, his impatience carried him thither more early than was his custom; yet had he not the satisfaction of finding her alone; the two lovely daughters of Mrs. G—— were just gone up stairs before him; but he was not much disconcerted at their presence, as he saw they were in their deshabillee,[61] and he could not doubt but that the hour of the day would soon call them home, in order to ornament those charms which were too much admired not to make them desirous of shewing them to the best advantage, whenever they appeared in public places, which they seldom or rather never fail'd to take all opportunities of doing.

These ladies, whose history it is probable will some time or other make a very interesting figure in the world, were distinguish'd more by the name of the two beautiful sisters, than by that of their family; they were, indeed, lovely beyond what language can describe, or fancy, without seeing them, delineate; both of them were tall, finely shaped, of a most graceful air, had the most regular features; eyes at once commanding and attracting love and admiration; and so equally had nature dealt her bounties to them, that hard it is to say which of them excell'd in any one of those perfections which each possess'd in so lavish an abundance.[62]

But being so alike beautiful was certainly a misfortune to them; for each seeming most lovely when the other was away, yet neither of them having the preference when together, the beholder's eye was kept in a continual motion, without knowing on which to fix; and this it was, which, join'd with some other considerations not my business to enquire into, that perhaps kept them much longer from being married, than many who have not the thousandth part of their power of charming.

This consideration, however, seem'd to have but little weight with them; they lived in the most perfect harmony, were rarely seen asunder,— whether at the play, the opera,—the court,—the Mall,—Vaux-Hall,— Ranelagh, in all places of resort they were inseparable as the twin stars that grace the zodiac.

In fine, so much the same in every respect was this pair of charmers, that if Mr. Waller had lived in their days, one would have imagined he could have no other in his eye when he wrote these lines:

Not the silver Doves that fly,
Yoak'd in Cytharea's car;

Not the wings which soar so high,
And convey her son so far,
Are so lovely, sweet and fair,
Or do more ennoble love,
Are so choicely match'd a pair,
Or with more consent to move.[63]

Fortunately for Jemmy's design, it so fell out that the conversation turn'd chiefly on the subject of gaming on account of a certain lady, who having no more than five and twenty hundred pounds per annum, had, according to her own confession, lost nine thousand in one season at play.

Jenny express'd, with so much warmth and spirit, the contempt she had of those who made a kind of business, or trade, as it were of this amusement, as sufficiently denoted the sincerity of her heart, while she was speaking, and gave Jemmy an infinite satisfaction in hearing her.

The two beautiful sisters made but a very short visit, as Jemmy had conjectured, and after they were gone, he resumed the topic they had all been talking on; "You women," said he smiling, "have much the advantage over us men; some of you, at least, have been ingenious enough to have found out a very easy method of discharging all the debts they contract at play: I could give you," continued he, "a thousand instances of what I say; but shall content myself with only one, in which a friend of mine made me the confidant, and on whose veracity I dare as much depend, as if I had been in his place, and one of the chief parties concern'd in it."

Finding Jenny look'd earnestly upon him all the time he had been speaking, and seem'd in a disposition to give attention to every thing he said upon that subject, he went on, and related to her, with as much brevity and modesty as such an affair would permit, all that had pass'd between himself, Liberia, and the other gentleman, who had been a sharer with him in the favour of that lady, hiding from her only the names and some few circumstances which might have given her room to guess more than he wish'd she should do.

Jenny was shock'd to the very soul at this recital; she had been witness of many extravagancies that women, who devote themselves to gaming, are often guilty of; she knew very well that they reduced themselves to great streights, sometimes even to the total ruin of their own and husbands fortune; but could never have imagined that any of them, merely for the sake of play, would have proceeded to those frightful lengths she now was told of.

After having expressed some part of her astonishment and indignation at such a depravity of nature, "How ought," cried she, "every one to guard against the first approaches of this dangerous propensity!" and then again, "bless me!" added she, "how can any one, who has a tongue to speak, and common sense to dictate what they say, lavish those hours in gaming, which might be pass'd in an agreeable and improving conversation! If no other ill consequences than barely loss of time attended it, methinks it were enough to hinder any one, not altogether void of reason, from pursuing, with the eagerness some do, an amusement at the best trifling and idle."

It is not to be doubted but that Jemmy was quite transported, at finding in his fair mistress sentiments so just and so exactly conformable to those he had, with the greatest ardency, wish'd she should be inspired with; he had no words which seem'd to him sufficient to praise, as they deserved, her prudence and penetration, yet said enough on that occasion to put her modesty to the blush.

"Do not fancy me to be possess'd of more merit than I have," answer'd she; "I believe that many of our sex, with as little inclination as myself to play, have been enticed to it by the examples of those whom we are so silly as to think it an honour to imitate, even in their vices; whatever we see practiced by those of the great world becomes a law to us of the inferior class; and I can tell you, that it is not to my own judgement, but to mere accident, that I am brought to a more reasonable way of thinking."

"You must know," continued she, "that a lady, who is a distant relation of mine, took me with her one evening to the route[64] of a person of condition; there was a prodigious deal of company, three large rooms made into one, and no less than fourteen tables set out for different sorts of gaming;—every body played, and though I never was fond of cards, yet was ashamed, in so public an assembly, not to do as others did, so engaged myself with a party who were sitting down to whist: either through want of skill, or attention, I soon lost twenty pieces, which was all I had about me at that time; but having no notion of giving over, as the others were for continuing, I went to my cousin, who was at quadrille[65] at another table, in order to get a fresh supply from her; but, to my great mortification, found she was entirely stript as well as myself; there was none of the company, with whom I was intimate enough to become a borrower."

"I must confess," pursued she, "that I then was silly enough to be heartily vex'd at this disappointment, and retired to the other end of the room, debating within myself whether I should go quite away, or stay to see how my cousin would behave, who I found was still at play with the same party she had been engaged in. As I was in this perplexity, the Earl of * * *, who had betted at our table, and been witness both of my ill luck and present confusion, came towards me, and putting a purse, that seem'd very weighty, into my hand, which he held fast grasp'd between both his,—'It is pity,' said he, 'that so fine a young lady should be deprived of her diversion on any account whatever, much less on that of a little paultry cash; accept these few pieces, they may be more lucky to you than your own; but if it prove otherwise, command as many from me as you shall stand in need of.'"

"I protest to you," went she still on, "that I was so confounded at finding my self accosted in this manner, that I had neither courage nor presence of mind enough to resent at first so impudent an overture, as I ought to have done; and it was the simplicity of my behaviour which, perhaps, encouraged him to proceed; for I only asking what his lordship meant, he reply'd with an air and voice sufficiently explanatory of the base thoughts he had of me. 'I mean to devote myself, and all I have, at the altar of your charms; happy if you smile upon the sacrifice.'

"Never was any poor creature so overwhelm'd with different passions as I then was; amazement, shame, disdain, and rage, at once rose in my bosom, and almost stopp'd the passage of my breath. I forgot all respect of his birth and place; and throwing the purse he had given me upon the floor,—'carry your offers,' said I, 'to those who want them, I despise both them and the hand from which they came.'

"With these words I burst from him and rejoin'd the company; my cousin was still playing, having borrow'd of some person she was acquainted with, and I kept leaning over the back of her chair all the time we stay'd; his lordship pass'd by me more than once, and discover'd by his looks that he was no less affronted at my behaviour than I had been at his, which, contrary to what it is likely his vanity might make him imagine, gave me more satisfaction than discontent.

"I was, however, very much agitated to think that any man, how great soever, had dared to treat me with the freedom he had done; on coming home I complained of it to my cousin, but she only ridiculed me for it; told me I was a novice in the ways of the town; that if she had been in my place, she would have taken his money and laugh'd at him afterwards for bestowing it; for which I liked her so ill, that I have ever since avoided her as much as possible."

"Thus you see, my dear Jemmy," added she, on concluding her little narrative, "that my dislike of gaming is not owing to my prudence in considering the folly of it, for I confess I never thought much about the matter, but merely to my Lord * * *'s behaviour; for certainly no young woman of common modesty, if treated as I was, will ever indulge herself in an amusement that renders her virtue liable to be exposed to such insolent attacks."

It was not in the power of all she could say, however, to make Jemmy desist from giving her the praises she deserved, nor from entertaining in his mind the most high idea of her understanding, as well as her virtue, insomuch, that could he have thought himself equally qualified in what might be expected from a husband, as she was in every thing that could be wish'd for in a wife, he would have seen no reason for delaying their mutual happiness one moment.

But a just consciousness of some little frailties, which afforded him too much pleasure to be able as yet to rectify, made him forbear to press her on the subject of their marriage for the present.

Chapter XII

Contains a very notable instance of friendship a-la-mode.

While our lovers were thus endeavouring to form their minds in such a manner as should enable them to render each other perfectly happy, when they should come to be united together, there were not wanting some who made it their chief study to contrive the means of separating them for ever.

Jemmy had contracted a very numerous acquaintance since his father's death, many of whom had a large share of his esteem and friendship; but there was one above the rest whose humour and behaviour he was particularly taken with, and with whom he conversed with the most unreserved freedom.

This gentleman, who was called Bellpine, was descended from a very ancient family, and had been, through the extravagance and ill management of his father, deprived of all that ought to have been his patrimony, except two hundred pounds a year, which had been settled upon his mother by way of jointure,[66] and could not be dissipated.

He had, notwithstanding, been flatter'd with the expectation of being one day in possession of an estate of near three thousand pounds per annum, being the undoubted heir of an uncle, who having lived a batchelor till a very advanced age, there was not the least probability of his ever changing his condition, and much less of his having any children, even in case such a thing should happen; and this dependance it was that hindred him from being bred up to any business or profession, and also gave him an air of self-sufficiency, in some measure conformable to the fortune he so reasonably hoped to become master of.

This uncle, however, to the extreme surprise of all that knew him, at the age of eighty-two, and equally laden with infirmities and years, took it into his head to marry a daughter of one of his tenants in the country,—a girl scarce nineteen.

An accident such as this, could not, when it happen'd, but give a very great shock to Bellpine, as he could not assure himself but that, in spite of his uncle's great age, a child, some way or other, might come, and cut him off at once from the inheritance he had been made to depend upon; yet did he not suffer his spirits to sink on this occasion, he rather exerted them all, in order to find some means to remedy, or, at least, to abate the asperity of this disappointment; the most feasible ones, he thought, would be to procure, if possible, some genteel employment about court, and, at the same time, make his addresses to some lady of an handsome fortune for a wife.

He was solliciting at the levees[67] of the great for the accomplishment of his first project; and casting about in his mind where he should direct his courtship with the most probability of succeeding in the other, when he commenced an acquaintance with Jemmy; chance brought them at first together, and a mutual liking of each other's conversation, by degrees, grew up to that intimacy between them already mention'd.

Jemmy was of the most open communicative disposition that man could possibly be; he had very few affairs in life which he made secrets of to any of those whom he call'd his friends; but with Bellpine he maintain'd no reserve; he made him the confidant of all his looser pleasures, his foibles, his very thoughts were not conceal'd from him; it therefore may be supposed that he disguis'd not the honourable affection he had for Jenny, the care that both their parents had taken to bring them up in notions of being united together when they arrived at years of maturity, and also the reasons urg'd on her side, and agreed to on his, for delaying, for some time, the celebration of their nuptials.

As his heart was warm with a passion, which duty and the custom of looking on her as the person ordain'd for his wife, had at first inspired him with, and a just sensibility of the many amiable qualities she was mistress of, had afterwards greatly heighten'd in him, he spoke of her in a manner sufficient to inflame the heart of the hearer with envy at his happiness; in this, indeed, it must be confess'd that he shew'd more sincerity than prudence; but as one of our poets observes,

> Those free from guile themselves, can scarce believe,
> That others will be false.[68]——

Nor was this all; he contented not himself with giving him a bare idea of what she was, he introduced him to her acquaintance, he frequently made him a partner in his visits to her, recommended him as a person highly worthy of her esteem and friendship; and, in fine, spoke of him in terms which obliged her to treat him as such; little, alas, suspecting that while doing this he was whetting the edge of a sword that might one day be pointed against his own bosom.

Bellpine was far from being the man the honest heart of Jemmy mistook him for; he was possess'd, it is true, of many accomplishments both natural and acquired; but had no fund either of honour or generosity; he knew perfectly well how to insinuate himself into the good graces of those he convers'd with; but thought himself not bound to make an adequate return for any favours he received from them; all his wishes were center'd in self-gratification, and no consideration for others had ever any weight to make him desist that favourite pursuit.

Being of a disposition such as I have described, it is not to be wonder'd at that the fine person and large fortune of Jenny should make him envy the happiness of him who was to be the possessor of that double treasure; he lov'd her on the score of her beauty, her wit, and the many amiable qualities he had observed in her; but adored her as being the mistress of what he so much wanted; and fill'd with the idea of those advantages he might reap in an alliance with her, made him resolve on the attempt, and to take all the methods his inventive fancy could inspire to alienate her affections from his friend.

He had often heard Jemmy say, that the agreement between them for protracting the celebration of their marriage had been first proposed by her; from whence he concluded, that the passion she had for him as not so violent but that it might be easily withdrawn, if she was once made to believe there was a decay in the love he profess'd for her.

He was sensible, notwithstanding, that there required a more than common share of caution and address in the management of this design; he saw very well, that Jenny had a great deal of sagacity, and penetration; it behoved him therefore, either to throw such a temptation in Jemmy's way as should render him in effect ungrateful and perfidious, or contrive such appearances of his being so as could not be discover'd from reality by any human wit.

With the first of these measures he commenc'd the prosecution of his design, though of the two the least feasible to be accomplish'd, as it was very difficult to find a woman who excell'd Jenny in any one perfection, that can attract the eye, or captivate the heart; "Love," said he within himself, "is seldom so much the effect of reason as of fancy, and if I can be so lucky as to present an object capable of firing the heart of this too happy rival with an amorous flame, and she has virtue or cunning enough to refuse the gratification on any other terms than those of marriage, it may so happen, that all the merits of Jenny, and his engagements with her, will be too light to over-balance inclination."

He knew that Jemmy was extremely fond of music; he had seen him in the utmost raptures on hearing a melodious voice, or an instrument finely play'd upon; and it was by this bait he hoped to allure Jemmy from his vows; or, at least, to draw him into such a manner of behaviour as should picque the pride of Jenny, and render her indifferent towards him.

To dissolve the cement of that tender affection, with which they now regarded each other, would go a great way towards gaining the point he aim'd at; he flatter'd himself, that if he could once set them at variance, he was at present enough in Jenny's favour to be able to obtain the first share of her tenderness, when taken off from the man who now engross'd it.

The person, whose charms he intended as the snare to entrap the constancy of Jemmy, was call'd Miss Chit; she pass'd in the opinion of most people, for the daughter of a gentleman distinguished in the world for nothing so much as for being her father; but it was whisper'd, by those who pretended to be conniossieurs in the secret intrigues of the great, that she really sprung from parents of a much more elevated station.

She was young, handsome, well shaped, and though of somewhat too diminutive a stature, had an air and mien extremely strieking; she wanted neither wit nor assurance to set off the talents she was mistress of to the best advantage; she was a great courtier, and perfectly skill'd in all the rudiments of modish good breding; but the chief inducement that Bellpine had to make choice of her as the instrument of his purpose was this; nature had given her a voice that seem'd the very soul of harmony, and when accompanied by her harpsichord, which she finely touch'd, the mellifluous sounds had power to calm the most raging passions of the mind, and convert all into love and soft desire; so that what the poet says of Mira might be justly enough ascrib'd to her,

> The wretch, who from her wit and beauty flies,
> If she but reach him with her voice, he dies.[69]

Bellpine frequently visited this lady, and was welcome to her on account of his facetious conversation, and the intelligence he pick'd up among his acquaintance, and was continually bringing her the intrigues of the town. As he was well received by her, he could not fail of being so by her father, who, it was easy to perceive, was but the second person in the family; standing as he did with both, it cannot be supposed he wanted interest to introduce any one he thought proper to her acquaintance.

He would not, however, proceed too abruptly in the affair, as it might have spoil'd all, if either party had suspected him of design; but watch'd an opportunity, when they were talking one day of music, to ask Jemmy, in a careless manner, as it were by chance, if he had ever heard Miss Chit sing and play?

"No," reply'd he, "but I have heard she does both to very great perfection." "I wonder," said the other, "that you should not have the curiosity to be judge of her skill that way yourself, as you are so great a lover of music!"

"I have not the honour to be at all known to her," return'd Jemmy, "nor have even ever seen her, any more than en passant, once or twice I think at court, and two or three times in the mall with Lady Fisk."

"I am pretty free there," cried Bellpine, "and if you have an inclination to hear this female Orpheus[70] of the town, will take you with me, and also engage she shall give you a touch of her harmony both vocal and instrumental; for, to do her justice, she has not the least reserve in this point; her harpsichord is never out of tune, nor her voice disconcerted with a cold."

Jemmy express'd a great deal of satisfaction at this offer, but gave much more than what he felt himself to his pretended friend, who look'd on the ready compliance he found in him as a happy beginning of the enterprize he had projected; so both being of the same mind, they agreed to meet at White's[71] the next day, and then proceed on their visit to the lady.

Chapter XIII

Is full of remarkable and interesting particulars.

Bellpine had no occasion to make any previous apology to Miss Chit for bringing a friend with him to visit her, having already taken that liberty, without her being displeased with it, in favour of several of his companions, who had testified to him a desire of becoming acquainted with her.

But it was not in this manner he chose to introduce Jemmy;—the plot he had laid required they should appear as agreeable as possible to each other;—it was therefore highly necessary to prepossess her with such an idea of the person she was to see, as should make her neglect nothing that might set off all the charms she was mistress of to the best advantage.

Having well considered within himself under what character a man was likely to appear in the eyes of a young,—gay,—vain woman, he went to her pretty early in the morning, and began with telling her he was come in behalf of a gentleman, who had entreated him to be his intercessor for permission to wait on her with him that afternoon.

This formal speech, from a man whose usual deportment might rather be accused of too little than too much ceremony, made her laugh very heartily:—"Bless me,"—said she,—"what romances have you been reading!—we are not sure running back to the days of Oroondates and Statyra;[72] if you have any friend to bring here, what need all this prelude? You know very well that every one you introduce is welcome."

Bellpine on this threw off the serious air he had affected, and resumed that free and undaunted one which was most natural to him, "Faith, Madam," answer'd he, "I can easily join with you in laughing at myself; I know I must make an odd figure in the grave strain, by the pains I took in putting it on; but I thought as I was one of Cupid's harbingers, my message ought to be deliver'd in somewhat above the common phrase."

"A harbinger from Cupid," cried she; "I find then you would persuade me you have this commission to me from a lover." "Most certainly," answer'd he, "from one who is three parts so at least; he is already charmed with your face, your air, your shape, and there is only wanting your fine voice to complete the conquest."

"Of whom?" demanded she; "'Tis fit I should know the name of this new vassal." "Have a little patience," said he, "and I will tell you every thing; in the first place he is a young heir, lately come to the possession of an estate sufficient to support a coach and six; in the next he is handsome, well made, has as genteel an address as any man about town; lastly, he is allow'd to have wit, honour, and good nature, and his name is Jessamy."

"I have seen that gentleman," return'd she, somewhat seriously; "and believe you have done him no more than justice in the representation you have made of him; but I have been told he is deeply engaged, and on the point of being married to a young lady of his own name; I think they call her Miss Jenny Jessamy."

"Nothing in it, upon my honour," cried Bellpine; "I can aver to you from my own knowledge, that there are no two people in the world of different sexes that have a more perfect indifference for each other; there was, indeed, such a thing intended for them by their fathers; but the old men are both dead, and you know, Madam, we young folks are apt to pay but little regard to the injunctions laid upon us by those who are no longer in a condition to resent our disobedience.

"It is true," continued this artful deceiver, "they see each other very frequently, hold a good correspondence, converse as friends; but without one grain of inclination on either side. I am very well assured, by what I have heard both of them declare, that should either of them insist on the performance of the covenant made between their parents, an eternal breach must infallibly ensue."

Jemmy and Jenny Jessamy kept too much company not to be well known in the polite world; their characters, their fortunes, and their mutual engagements, were no secret; they were the subjects of conversation among many who had not the least personal acquaintance with either of them; and it was a matter of surprise to every one that a marriage, which had so long ago been projected, was not as yet consummated.

As no body had pretended to discover any reason for this unaccountable delay, Miss Chit might easily give credit to that which Bellpine now assigned for it. Bellpine watch'd her every look, and perceiving that his insinuations had wrought thus far on her belief, proceeded to what now seem'd to him a task not difficult to be accomplish'd; that of persuading her Jemmy in reality felt some beginnings of a passion for her.

"You cannot imagine," said he, "with what raptures he expresses himself concerning you; the first time he saw you was at court; I was with him the same evening, and he could talk on nothing but you the whole time we were together.—'What eyes she has,—how bright, how sparkling,—what a mouth,—how finely turn'd,—how delicate is her shape,—how enchanting is her air!'"

"Hold, Mr. Bellpine," interrupted she, putting her hand before his mouth, "for the sake of curiosity no more; if you go on at this rate I shall know all before-hand, and he will have nothing new to say to me when he comes."

"Nay," rejoin'd Bellpine, "I do not suppose he will say much to you at this first visit, nor perhaps at the second, or even at the third. I have been told, by those who have experienced the passion, that a true lover never gets courage to declare what he feels to his mistress till half the town are appriz'd of it by his behaviour; but," pursued he, "you will have penetration enough to read in his looks what his lips wants boldness to reveal."

"Pish," said she, "do you think I shall give myself the trouble to examine his looks? It will be time enough for me to attend to them when his tongue shall have explain'd the dictates of his heart."

They had some farther discourse on this head, and in spite of the careless air Miss Chit affected to put on, the cunning Bellpine saw the impression his words had made upon her; and, after adding all that he thought necessary for strengthening it in her, took his leave, highly applauding himself in his mind for what he had done.

He met Jemmy at the appointed hour at the chocolate house,[73] and about tea time went with him on their purposed visit; on his sending up his name they were immediately shew'd to the room where Miss Chit was sitting; when he found, by the great care she had taken in her dress, and the exactness of every thing about her, that he had not flattered himself with a vain conjecture, but that she was indeed as desirous as he could wish of appearing lovely in the eyes of this new guest.

Jemmy, being presented her by Bellpine, saluted her with the utmost gallantry; she received him with a becoming modesty, which, notwithstanding, had something of inviting in it; the conversation at first turn'd only on general topics; but Bellpine would not suffer it to continue so, and told her, in his usual free manner, that he should not think himself forgiven for the liberty he had taken, till she had obliged both him and his friend with a song and a touch of her harpsichord.

To this she replied, with a sprightly tone of voice and gesture, that whatever he might think of her, she had too much complaisance for a stranger, who seem'd so well to deserve it, not to do every thing in her power to render the visit he had favour'd her with agreeable to him.

In speaking these words she sat down to her instrument, and, without waiting for any more intreaties, began to sing one of the most favourite airs in Mr. Handel's last oratorio.[74]

As she had in reality a very fine voice, great skill in music, and played admirably well, there was no occasion that Jemmy should stretch truth to a pitch too high in expressing the pleasure he took in hearing her.

But it was not in mere words alone he testified the mighty influence that the well concerted notes had over him;—he languished,—he died,—his soul seem'd all absorb'd,—dissolv'd in extacy;—and he not only spoke, but look'd in such a manner as without being prepossess'd, as she was, with an opinion of his having a passion for her, might well make her believe she had other charms for him besides those of her voice and skill in music.

As often as she gave over, Bellpine press'd her to renew the harmony; and sometimes Jemmy assumed the boldness to second a petition, which he was ever sensible was made entirely on his account. The lady was not refractory to their united intreaties, and continued playing till her father came into her room.

The usual compliments being past, they all sat down and enter'd into conversation; but whatever subject was started by the old gentleman, either the one or the other of Miss Chit's visitors had the address to turn it on the praise of music, and the perfection which she had attain'd to in that science.

Jemmy said many things which might seem extravagant on this occasion; but thinking he had stay'd long enough for a first visit, rose up and was preparing to take his leave, when Mr. Chit, who had been tutor'd before-hand by his daughter how he should behave, would not suffer him to speak of going, seiz'd upon his hat and gloves, and said that if his daughter had afforded them any entertainment, it was owing to him for having provided the best masters for her; and he therefore expected they would recompence him for it, by giving him their company the remainder of the evening; adding, that supper was just ready to be served up.

Jemmy would fain have excused himself, as he had an appointment which he was very unwilling to break; but there was no resisting the present kind compulsion, especially as Miss Chit condescended to join her intreaties with her father's; he therefore comply'd and contented himself with sending an apology to those who expected his coming.

The collation prepared for them was so elegant, the old gentleman's conversation so facetious, and his daughter's music so delightful, that the night was almost lost in morning-dawn when Jemmy and his false friend came away; but what use the latter made of this long visit the reader will very soon discover.

Chapter XIV

Seems big with the promise of some mighty matters hereafter to be brought to light.

It was so very late when the little company broke up, that Bellpine had no opportunity of putting any questions to Jemmy concerning his sentiments of the lady he had introduced him to; and as they lived different ways, took leave of each other at Mr. Chit's door, without any farther speech that night.

Full of impatience, however, for the success of his pernicious plot, he went pretty early the next morning to his house; and, according to his wish, found him quite alone, and not yet ready to go abroad.

He was scarce sat down, when he had the satisfaction of hearing Jemmy himself prepare the way for the conversation he intended to entertain him with, by thanking him for the pleasure he had enjoy'd the night before through his means.

"I wish from my soul," reply'd this wicked incendiary, "that it were in my power to procure you a much more ample and substantial one; music indulges no more than a single sense, Miss Chit has charms that might engross the whole five.—Ah, Jemmy,"—continued he, embracing him, "what a heaven it would be, after an hour or two of dalliance, to be lull'd to sleep by that angelic voice, pressing at the same time the ruby lips whence the transporting sounds proceeded! and then, ye gods, awake to a new raptures and repeated bliss."

Jemmy laugh'd heartily at the extasy which the other affected to feel through the force of imagination. "You wish me a happiness," cried he, "yet speak, methinks, as if you could not avoid being one of those who would envy me the possession of it; but my dear friend," added he, "you have no need to be under any apprehensions on the score; for to deal sincerely, I like Miss Chit as a musician, but shall never think of her as a woman."

These words gave a most terrible shock to the high-raised expectations of Bellpine; but, as he was master of an uncommon share of artifice, and an equal presence of mind, it was easy for him to conceal one emotion under the shew of another; and, starting back with a well counterfeited surprise, "Impossible," cried he, "you cannot sure be so insensible, so altogether untouch'd with charms that half the town are running mad after!"

"You know," answer'd Jemmy, with a very serious air, "I am under engagements elsewhere, which will not permit me to make my addresses to her or any other woman upon honourable terms; and I cannot suppose they would be accepted by Miss Chit if offer'd with a view of a different nature."

"I cannot flatter you so far as that, indeed," reply'd he, still disconcerted, and more so, when Jemmy hastily rejoin'd, "I wonder, Bellpine, that having so just a sense of the lady's merit, you never made your court to her yourself?"

On an interrogatory so unthought on, all his audacity forsook him; he was silent for some moments, but at length recovering himself, his ready wit furnish'd him with an excuse which seem'd plausible enough, and was certainly the only one that could have had the least appearance of sincerity.

"I shall disguise nothing of the truth from you," said he; "to be plain then, it is my vexatious circumstances which alone deter me; since my uncle has taken a step that may possibly deprive me of the inheritance I was born to expect, I have no dowry to offer with my services; a woman that has money demands a jointure adequate to the sum she brings; and for me to marry one whose only portion is her beauty and good qualities, would render both her and myself for ever miserable; so that whether Miss Chit is, or is not a fortune, she is quite out of the question with me as a wife."

He spoke all this with so much seeming candour and openness of heart, that Jemmy thought himself more than ever confirm'd in the opinion he had always entertain'd of the good sense and honour of his friend; and readily agreed with him, that where a marriage was consummated between two persons, neither of whom had a sufficient competency, it could not fail of making both parties equally unhappy, and also of entailing lasting wretchedness on their posterity.

Bellpine soon grew weary of this discourse, as it had no connexion with his present views; and therefore made his visit much shorter than he at first had intended it, and retir'd to a place where he might give a loose to his discontent, and contrive some other means of bringing his designs to perfection, since those he had already essay'd had proved so ineffectual.

As it was not in his power to make Jemmy become guilty in fact, his next resource was to make him appear so: to blacken him by any ill report directly to Jenny herself, he knew would be in vain, and treated with contempt by a woman of her penetration; he therefore took a more artful and more sure, tho' slow method of infusing the poison of jealousy and indignation into her soul; he gave it out in whispers, inuendoes, and dark hints, among those whom he found fond of scandal and of explaining mysteries of that kind, that Jemmy had an utter aversion to Jenny in his heart; that he was seeking some excuse to break entirely with her; and that it was Miss Chit who had caused this change in him; he had no great cause to doubt but that this rumour would spread from one to another through the town, and become so much the universal secret, that it could not fail of reaching Jenny's ears; and then he concluded that it would, by degrees, steal itself into her belief.

As Jemmy was a man of pleasure, and did not live without many transient amours, it may seem a little strange to some people that Bellpine, who by his intimacy with him, could not be a stranger to the errors of his conduct, did not chuse to get communicated to Jenny such things as a very small enquiry would convince her were true, rather than endeavour to alarm her with reports which had no foundation in fact.

But this was not Bellpine's way of reasoning; he rightly judged, that a woman of Jenny's understanding might easily be brought to forgive the frailties of youth and nature in a man of Jemmy's gay and volatile disposition; but would be irreconcileable, implacable, if once made to believe he address'd any other upon honourable terms.

It is easy for persons capable of inventing falshoods to propagate them in such a manner as to make them pass current for a time, and yet avoid any detection of their being the authors of it; it is not by saying directly a thing is so, that a story so much gains credit, as by half words,—winks,—nods, and other such like gestures;—these are the traps which catch the unwary, and give an air of reality to that which has no existence. Bellpine at least was well versed in this art, and practised it with such success as to the matter in question, and was so far from being suspected of having raised this report, that he has often been ask'd by those who heard from other hands what his opinion was concerning the truth of it.

Jenny, on account of her many accomplishments and good nature, was so generally beloved by those who knew her, and her character in such estimation with those who were not personally acquainted with her, that none could hear, without the most extreme surprise, that she was about to be forsaken by a man who from his very infancy had been taught to look upon her as his future wife, and for whom she made no secret of having the most tender affection.

But whenever this subject was mention'd to Bellpine, as it frequently so happen'd, he affected to hang down his head and be entirely silent; or, if desir'd by some one or other of the company to speak his thoughts, "I am no judge of the affair," would he say, "Mr. Jessamy is my friend, and I should be loth to think him capable of a bad action; Miss Jenny is certainly a fine girl, and so is Miss Chit; if he has changed his sentiments he doubtless has his reasons, but I know nothing of it."

His intimacy with Jemmy was so well known, that these undeterminate answers from him gave more credit to the story than the most positive assurances given by any other person could have done.

Nor was this all; to give the greater appearances of the truth of what he thought it was so much his interest to have believed, he contrived it so that Jemmy and Miss Chit should frequently be seen together in public places, though, for the most part, they met without the least design on the side of either of them.

Jemmy, indeed, could not avoid being somewhat accessary in corroborating the aspersion cast upon himself, as he had been introduced to that young lady, and received by her in the manner above-mentioned, the complaisance due to her sex and rank, join'd to the pleasure he took in hearing her sing and play, oblig'd him sometimes to visit her; Bellpine was generally with them; and when he was so, always found some pretext or other to draw them out where he knew there would be people who would not fail to take notice of their being together.

It requires more pains to be a villain than some people may imagine; besides imposing upon Jemmy, and making him act in a manner which shew'd his sentiments to the world far different from what they were in reality, Bellpine had also another card to play, which cost him little less contrivance.

As he had possess'd Miss Chit at first with a belief that Jemmy was seriously inspired with a passion for her, and knew very well that gentleman's behaviour had not at all been conformable to the assurances he had given her on his account, it behoved him to reconcile this contradiction so as not to leave her any room to suspect the deception he had put upon her.

He therefore continued, day after day, to carry her some fresh intelligence of the fine things Jemmy said of her; and insinuated that there was a design on foot, which, when once executed, would afford him a plausible pretence for breaking off entirely with Jenny; and that then he would avow his passion and declare himself devoted only to her.

Whether this young lady was absolutely convinced of the truth of what he said, I will not take upon me to determine; because, indeed, it is highly probable she never gave herself the trouble to examine the consistency of the story.

Dangerous, however, might such an imposition have been to some ladies, to have been flatter'd with the hopes of an alliance with a man such as Jemmy, perfectly agreeable in his person, accomplished in his manners, and opulent in his fortune; and then to find at once all those golden expectations vanish into air, might certainly have been fatal in its consequences, to a heart young, tender, and unexperienced in deceit.

Happy was it for Miss Chit, in this point at least, that the variety of company, the many fine things said to her by persons of condition, and particularly the devoirs,[75] whether feign'd or real, of a certain foreign minister, hinder'd her from being too attentive to the idea which the artifices of Bellpine might otherwise have engross'd her with.

Chapter XV

Contains an example that for a woman to be too good is not one of those things which are impossible to be found in human life.

Though the foregoing report, began and industriously propagated by Bellpine, had spread itself through all the acquaintance both of Jemmy and Jenny, yet did it not presently reach the ears of either of them; and they went on, as they had been accustom'd to do, communicating to each other every little adventure which fell into the way of each, provided they were such as might be, in any measure, conducive to the important end proposed, that of rectifying or improving their minds.

Among the many they recited to each other, some of which were too trifling to be inserted here; Jemmy happen'd upon one of a most extraordinary nature, and therefore must not be omitted; it was this:

He had been for some time pretty conversant with a gentleman named Kelsey; he was a man of family, fortune, good sense, and a very agreeable companion; but one thing was said of him, that, in the opinion of all the discreet part of his acquaintance, tarnish'd the lustre of all his other qualities,—that of his being a very bad husband to a most deserving wife.

This lady, to whom he had been married scarce a year, was very young, beautiful, and had every thing in her person requisite to make her beloved; and was in high estimation for the strictness of her virtue, her piety, and the affability of her behaviour; how could it then but seem strange to Jemmy, that two persons of the characters these bore in the world should not live happily together? He never heard any mention of the disagreement between them, without feeling a kind of painful curiosity for the cause, but he could find none who were able to give him any information in that point, tho' every one spoke loudly of the effects.

Chance at last presented him with the wish'd for discovery: a gentleman of distinction, a distant relation of Jemmy's was to have a private concert at his own house; Jemmy was one of the invited persons, with leave to bring any friend with him whom he should think proper; on which he made choice of Kelsey, and accordingly made him a visit on the morning of the day appointed, to desire he would accompany him to this entertainment, if not previously engaged to any other place.

Mr. Kelsey thank'd him for the obliging offer he had made him, reply'd, that he had no engagement at all upon his hands; "but if I had," said he, "I should be tempted to break through it, since I am certain none could afford me so much real pleasure as that of waiting on Mr. Jessamy any where; but more expecially," continued he, "on an occasion so perfectly agreeable to my taste."

Jemmy, after having made a suitable return to this compliment, was preparing to take leave, and desir'd that they might meet at White's chocolate-house about six; but the other would not suffer him to depart in this manner, he insisted on his staying to dine with him, and pass the time where he was till the hour arrived in which they should adjourn to a place more agreeable.

Jemmy would have excused himself from dining, as he had not the honour, he said, to be known to his lady:—to which Mr. Kelsey answer'd, that his wife was not ignorant of the respect due from her to any of her husband's friends.

The curiosity that Jemmy had for being an eye-witness of a lady's deportment whom he had heard so much of, and as yet had never seen, she seldom appearing in any public place, prevail'd with him at length to comply with her husband's request; they amused themselves with looking over some fine pieces of music, which Mr. Kelsey had that morning brought home in score, till three o'clock, at which hour he had order'd dinner to be ready.

The clock having struck, that gentleman conducted his guest into the next room, where they found the sideboard set out, the cloth laid, the corks of the bottles drawn, and every thing prepared for dinner being served up; but no servant was in waiting; all was hush'd and silent as tho' they had just rose from table, instead of not being as yet set down.

Mr. Kelsey waited some minutes, but at last rung the bell, on which the butler came up; on being ask'd if dinner was not ready, he reply'd with some hesitation, that he would enquire of the cook, and then went hastily away; soon after Mr. Kelsey rung again, and another servant appear'd, to whom his master making the same demand as to the former, answer'd bluntly, that his lady was not yet come out of her closet;[76] "Go then and call her," said Mr. Kelsey:—the fellow went, but returned immediately, and said the door was lock'd, and tho' he had both knock'd and call'd could get no answer; on which Mr. Kelsey grew extremely red, and begging pardon of Jemmy for leaving him alone a moment flew up stairs himself.

Jemmy was very much surpris'd at all this, but had not time to make any reflections on it; Mr. Kelsey came presently down follow'd by his lady, a very lovely woman, indeed; but seem'd greatly disconcerted: Jemmy advanced to pay her the civilities of a stranger, which, in spite of the confusion she was in, she receiv'd with the utmost sweetness and good breeding, and they all sat down to table.

The first course was served up in an instant; the garnishing of the dishes was elegant enough and inviting to the appetite, as doubtless what they contain'd would also have been, if not so much prolong'd beyond the necessary time: Mr. Kelsey stuck his fork first into one thing and then into another, then threw it down, bit his lips, and seem'd in very great emotions.

Jemmy could be at no loss to guess the occasion; and, to palliate the discontent he saw him in, help'd himself pretty plentifully out of that dish which was nearest to him; but never was any thing so spoil'd, the truffles, morelles,[77] artichokes, and other such things as should embellish the sauce were in a manner dissolv'd in it, and the meat itself wanted little of being so too, so that nothing but the bones discovered what it was.

Yet Jemmy fell to eating heartily, crying it was very fine, that it was dress'd exactly to his taste; but this politeness in him did not restore the good humour of his friend; the lady too was in some pain on seeing the ill effects which her staying too long in the closet had produced; and, addressing herself to Jemmy, "I am afraid, Sir," said she, "that your complaisance at this time gets the better of your sincerity; what is here is very much over done; but I hope we shall not find every thing so."

As she ended these words a servant set a fine hare upon the table, and Mr. Kelsey perhaps flattering himself that his wife might be a true prophetess on this occasion, took up his knife and fork once more, in order to carve; but the skin was so dried by being kept at a distance from the fire, that he found some difficulty to penetrate it, and when with much labour he had done so, the flesh beneath fell spontaneously from the bones, and indeed was almost fit for pulverizing.

Mr. Kelsey, who was naturally fiery, and apt to kindle on every little provocation, now lost all patience; he flung the dish from him with such a vehemence, that but for the footman's agility in catching it between his hands it must have fallen on the floor.

The lady, who was all confusion, said she was sorry and ashamed that it had happened so: "S'death,[78] Madam," cry'd he, starting from the table, "does it ever happen otherwise? If you had even common decency, you would not treat me in this manner: can you find no time to pray but just when dinner is coming upon table? Must my appetite continually be starved, my peace destroy'd, my reputation scandalized, my friends affronted, and all through your unseasonable devotion?"

"It is mighty well, my dear," reply'd she rising, "it is mighty well; but I shall say no more; it is from heaven alone that I must seek support, under the ill humour and intemperance of a husband": then turning to Jemmy, ask'd his pardon for what had past, and went hastily out of the room with eyes all bathed in tears.

"Would to heaven I had never seen your face," cry'd Mr. Kelsey furiously, and stamping with his foot as she was going out; but she took no notice either of his words or actions, and pass'd on as fast as she could: he continued walking about the room with gestures which evidently denoted the inward rage he was possess'd of, while Jemmy labour'd, tho' for some time in vain, to convince him that he was in the wrong to put himself into such agitations on account of an accident.

"Call it not accident, Mr. Jessamy," reply'd he, "what you have now been witness of has been almost every day repeated ever since our marriage. Oh," continued he, almost raving,—"how I could curse the hour,—the day,—the institution,—sacred as it is call'd, that join'd together two such opposites?"

At last, however, the consideration he had for his friend got the better of the resentment he had against his wife, and setting down again and making Jemmy do so also: "I know not," said he, "whether I shall ever be forgiven for the rudeness I have been guilty of; you have, indeed, suffer'd too much through the folly of my wife, and I ought not to have prolong'd your pennance by my ill humour, notwithstanding the justifiableness of it had, I been alone."

He then, without waiting for Jemmy's reply, call'd to the butler and ask'd him if there were any cold meats in the house that might supply the difficiency they had sustain'd: the man on this ran down stairs, and presently return'd follow'd by another servant with a large ham, of which a very little had been cut. "Come my dear friend," said Mr. Kelsey, "a cold repast is better than none at all; this we had yesterday and could not be spoil'd, tho' the chickens about it fell to pieces of themselves, like the hare you just now saw."

He said no more, but fell heartily on the ham before them; Jemmy, who for all his complaisance had made but a half dinner, follow'd his example; and a dessert, consisting of tarts, pitty-patties,[79] Jellies, fruits, and such like things, being afterwards placed upon the table, neither of these gentlemen had any reason to complain of their bad living that day.

When the cloth and servants were withdrawn, and the bottle and the glasses were the sole witnesses of their conversation, Jemmy finding the other was now in a disposition to bear it, began to rally him a little on the subject of his late disquiets: "Faith," reply'd Mr. Kelsey, "I have a true English stomach of my own, and cannot bear the least disappointment in victuals; and this fervour of devotion takes my wife at such odd periods, that whether I have company, or am oblig'd to go out on business at an appointed hour, never can be certain that dinner will be served according to the time.

"This unhappy humour in her," continued he, "it is that drives me so much abroad, I am compell'd by it to entertain my friends at a tavern, to transact all my affairs there; and sometimes indeed, to refresh my own senses with peace, and a bit of meat dress'd as it ought to be. How is it possible I should love home, when the very person in whose power it chiefly is to render it agreeable, exercises that power rather to create disgust than liking? I once loved her, and none but she herself could have wean'd my heart from the tender passion I had for her; but besides, whenever I complain of what you have seen, and some other irregularities in domestic life, she bursts into tears and reproaches; accuses me of unkindness, of intemperance, of prophaness to heaven, of regarding too much the things of this world, and such like stuff, which if I fly to avoid, I am at least justified in the poet's words."

> Clamours our privacies uneasy make,
> Birds leave their nests disturb'd, and beasts their haunts forsake.[80]

Jemmy, who could find little to say in the defence of Mrs. Kelsey, and had too much complaisance and good nature to say any thing against her, artfully waived the conversation and started more agreeable subjects, between which and the bottle they pass'd the time till the hour arrived which call'd them to the concert.

This being an entertainment adapted to the taste of both these gentlemen, 'tis not to be doubted but the pleasure they received in it attoned for all the mortifications of the preceding day; but, as it presented nothing material enough to acquaint the reader with, we shall make no further mention of it.

Chapter XVI

Treats only on such matters as it is highly probable some readers will be apt to say might have been recited in a more laconic manner, if not totally omitted; but as there are others, the author imagines much the greater number, who may be of a different opinion, it is judged proper that the majority should be obliged.

Jemmy, to whom the riddle of Mr. Kelsey's disagreement with his wife was now fully explain'd, no sooner found himself at home and alone, than he began to make the serious reflections both on the accident he had been witness of, and the real source from whence such unfortunate effects were originally derived.

"It is not," said he within himself, "it is not youth, beauty, wealth, nor even a mutual affection in the parties before marriage, that is sufficient to constitute their happiness, when once enter'd into that state; neither Mr. Kelsey nor his wife are wanting in any of those endowments or accomplishments which one should think necessary to endear them to each other; yet how miserable are they! It must therefore be, that a conformity of principles, a parity of sentiments and humours, and a certain sympathy of soul, ought to be the first links in the hymeneal chain; and without them, all the others fall to the ground and have no power to bind."

"I think," continued he, "that my friend has every requisite for making a good husband, were it his lot to have been united to a woman of his own gay temper; and the lady, who now creates such uneasiness both to herself and him, would certainly have made no less excellent a wife had she been married to an enthusiast."[81]

On reasoning farther, under various discontents that so frequently disturb'd the felicity of conjugal life, he concluded, that good nature and similitude of dispositions, tho' the last things consider'd, and seldom if ever enquired into by the persons about to be united, were indeed the chief ingredients to make their future happiness.

These considerations led him into an examination of Jenny's behaviour, even from her infancy, with much greater attention than ever he had done before; and the more he did so now, the less he could find to wish were chang'd; nothing had ever appear'd in her which seem'd to him to stand in need of the least rectification; she had never betray'd a too strong attachment to any one thing; no caprice, no whimsical fights, no affectation, no pride of exciting the envy of her own sex, or of giving pain to those of the other; in all her words and actions she preserved the happy medium of neither being too gay and giddy, nor too sullen and reserv'd; nor was all this mere outward shew; he could not suspect her of disguise, as he had known her before she could arrive at the power, even if she had the will, of pretending to be other than she really was.

Though he was in no haste to be married; yet, as he intended nothing more than being so, one time or other, great cause had he to thank heaven for being so peculiarly propitious in the lot ordain'd for him; nor was he insensible or ungrateful for the bounty, and had so true an esteem and affection for his dear Jenny, that we may almost give it to the reader for a certainty, that no temptation whatever could have made him entertain the least thought of any other woman for a wife.

He went pretty early the next morning to her apartment, which he seldom fail'd to do, when he had no farther business than to give her the bon jour;[82] but never when he had any thing to communicate in relation to the agreement made between them: he knew indeed, that she had very little occasion for any lessons of improvement from the faults of others; but he took an infinite pleasure in hearing the judicious observations she always made on every occurrence that presented itself to her.

He met her at the door, her chair waited, and she was just ready to step into it, "You are going out, I perceive," said he, "and I will not detain you": "Indeed but you shall," reply'd she; "I was only going to chapel, which I can do as well in the afternoon."

"But how," rejoin'd he, "shall I answer to myself for being an impediment to any act of religion?" "Religion," cried she, "does not enjoin us to be rude or unkind to our friends; and I know not if a just observance of the duties of social life be not a more acceptable sacrifice to the Deity than all the oraisons our lips can utter."

She said no more; but having dismiss'd the chairmen made Jemmy go up stairs, where she instantly follow'd him; as soon as they were sat down, "I dined yesterday," said he smiling, "with a lady who would have thought herself guilty of the extremest impiety and prophaness to have shewn half that complaisance to her husband, which I have just now received from you."

"She must then have very little affection for him indeed," replied Jenny; "and also be equally ignorant of the laws of the institution by which, as I take it, she is bound to oblige and to obey him in all reasonable things; but I see," continued she, "by your countenance that you are big with some new intelligence; so pray don't delay letting me have it."

Jemmy then made her an exact recital of the entertainment he had met with at Mr. Kelsey's; the brulee between the husband and the wife; the impatience of the one, and the provocation given for it by the other: Jenny laugh'd heartily at the beginning of this story, but grew more grave towards the latter end of it, and perceiving he had concluded, gave her sentiments on what he had been telling her in these terms:

"Can any one take this for piety?" said she; "I would not be so uncharitable as to think Mrs. Kelsey an hypocrite, but certainly such a behaviour has nothing in it of the air of true devotion." To which he reply'd, that he must do her the justice to believe, from what he could gather from the discourse he had afterwards with her husband, who was not in a disposition to be more favourable than the occasion requir'd, that all the mistakes she is guilty of proceed intirely from too warm a zeal in what she thinks the duties of religion.

"There are hours enough," said she, "to be spent in prayer, without breaking in upon those which the economy of the family requires; I am far from depreciating religious worship, but there are times for all things, and Mrs. Kelsey makes choice of such as are so utterly improper, as if it really arises from piety, renders it, in my opinion, such a kind of piety as has little merit in it."

"I am rather afraid," continued she after a pause, "that through sloth, and a certain indolence of nature, she neglects paying that tribute to heaven which is due from every reasonable creature at fit times; and at length, remembering her omission, runs to wipe off one fault by committing a still greater; for I would fain know, whether driving a husband to the extremes you say Mr. Kelsey is guilty of, be not a much worse error than even not praying at all?"

"For my part," added she with a more gay air, "I should have no notion of saving my own soul by doing what I saw would infallibly ruin another's; especially that of a person in whose happiness, both here and hereafter, I ought to take so great an interest."

Jemmy had a very high regard both for the mysteries and duties of reveal'd religion; though, like most other gay gentlemen of his age, he was little practis'd in the rules: but had he been a more strict observer of church discipline, he could not well have disapproved of the sentiments Jenny had declared; he told her she had argued like a casuist, and that he was sure there was never a clergyman in England but must agree with her on this point.

"I do not know that," answer'd she; "but I can tell you I durst not speak in the manner I have done, without thinking I had sufficient authority for it, from a little account given to my father, by a very learned and worthy divine, of one of his parishoners; I was very young when I heard it, but as it has made a lasting impression upon my mind, if you will afford me your attention I will repeat it."

Jemmy having assured her she would confer a very great obligation on him by so doing, she went on with her discourse in this manner:

"The reverend gentleman I have mention'd," said she, "was not only an excellent preacher but also an excellent man; all his actions were so many precepts, and his example a kind of living law; for there was no virtue which he laboured to inspire in others that he did not in the highest degree put in practice himself."

"He frequently favour'd my father with his company," continued she, "they were extremely intimate, and when the two good old gentlemen got together there never was any gap in conversation: one evening, in particular, he came to our house and my father, who was at church that day, and found a very thin congregation, was beginning to lament to him the decay of religion; to which the doctor reply'd in these terms; I think I remember his very words."

"'Aye, Mr. Jessamy,' said he, 'I am afraid indeed that religion is at a very low ebb at this time; but we must not always impute the want of it to those who we do not see constantly at public worship, even though we should know they were not detain'd from it by any infirmity either of mind or of body; there are a thousand accidents which may intervene, and withhold them from the discharge of this duty; nay, in some cases it may so happen that it is even laudable to be absent: you look surprised, Mr. Jessamy,' continued he, perceiving my father did so; 'but I can easily convince you of the truth of what I say: I came now from visiting a lady, who till within this month, or thereabouts, has not been at church for near seven years; though before that time no body more constantly attended; and yet I firmly believe that there is not a better or a more pious woman in the world.'

"These last words were far from lessening the astonishment my father had been in from the beginning of this discourse; but he would not interrupt the doctor, who went on thus:

"'To ease you of the suspence which I find I have raised in you,' said he, 'know, Mr. Jessamy, that this excellent lady flew not from divine service to pursue the pleasures of the town, nor to gratify any sensual inclination of her own, but to shut herself up in a close room with an aged parent, who, press'd beneath the weight of years and infirmities, unable to go out herself, and equally unwilling to receive any visits from those who knew her in a more sanguine state, had no consolation but in the dutiful cares of this beloved daughter, who was continually employ'd about her administering every thing in her power for her relief.'"

"It is impossible for me," said Jenny, pursuing the thread of her discourse, "to remember half the encomiums he made on this act of filial piety; but this I know, that I have ever since been fully convinced, that while we are here upon earth all the prayers we can make to heaven will be insufficient to attone for neglecting to discharge, as well as is in our power, the duties of our several stations."

Jemmy was now about to tell her how much his opinion, in this point, concided with what she had deliver'd; but she happen'd to be in a very talkative humour, and this being a subject which in her serious moments had frequently occurr'd to her, she would not quit it for the sake of hearing any praises given to herself.

"There are some people," resumed she, "who are hypocrites without knowing themselves that they are so; they fast, they pray incessantly, they are abundant in giving to charitable uses, and do many other great and laudable actions; but then they do them not so much for the sake of the religion that enjoins us to do all the good we can, as for the sake of gratifying their own vanity in being able to perform more than their neighbours."

"This is ostentation," cried Jemmy, interrupting her, "and I am afraid that too many of those great actions, so hyperbolically extoll'd in panegyrick, if search'd into the bottom, would be found to proceed from no other source."

"Ostentation," answer'd she, "is different from the propensity I mean; ostentation, as I take it, is rather an ambition of appearing better in the eyes of others than we either are or will take any pains to be in fact; but what I am speaking of is an innate triumph of the heart; a mental exultation within ourselves in the imagination that we in reality excel other people; and this I think may be call'd a spiritual pride."

"I have heard such strange stories," continued Jenny, "such unaccountable instances in relation to this same spiritual pride among the nuns abroad, as I should have look'd upon to have been mere inventions to depreciate and ridicule that way of worship, if they had not been solemnly averr'd to me by a lady who is herself a Roman Catholic, was two years a pensioner in a monastery at Paris, and an eye witness of the truth of what she said."

Here she was preparing to repeat some of those particulars which the lady had made her acquainted with; but was prevented by a servant who came into the room to call her down to dinner, on which Jemmy, as she was a boarder, took his leave probably with less reluctance if the subject they had been engaged in had happened to be one of a more entertaining nature.

Nor will the reader find any reason to be greatly dissatisfied at the breaking off a conversation which could be little improving, as an excess of devotion is not among the reigning errors of the present times.

Chapter XVII

Will in all likelihood appear, to the greatest part of our readers, a good deal more interesting than the former.

After that conversation which had engross'd the whole of the preceding chapter, a multiplicity of engagements, of one sort or other, so took up Jemmy's time, that he could not find one hour to visit his beloved and most deserving mistress for three days successively; but on the evening of the latter he found, on his coming home, a little billet from her which had been left for him in the afternoon, the contents whereof were as follows:

To James Jessamy, Esq;

Dear Jemmy,

A proposal has been made to me which before I accept of am desirous to acquaint you with; if this is so fortunate as to find you at home [I] shall be glad of seeing you this evening; if not, [I] expect you will not fail of calling on me in the morning as early as you can; because I have promised to give my final answer some time to-morrow. I am,

With all sincerity,
Dear Jemmy,
Yours, &c. &c.
J. Jessamy

On the first mention of this billet, after an absence of so unusual a length between these two lovers, when in the same town together, I dare believe that many of my female readers expected to find it fill'd either with reproaches or complaints; or, perhaps with a mixture of both; but Jenny was of a different complexion from the generality of her sex, she could love without anxiety, and glad as she was whenever she saw the object of her passion, was never angry or unhappy when she saw him not.

If all women could bring themselves to behave in the manner Jenny did, I cannot but think they would find their account in it, not only in the tranquility of their own minds, but also in rendering more permanent the affection of the man they loved; doubts, suspicions, and jealousies, though arising from a tender cause, frequently hurry the person possess'd of them into such furious marks of resentment, as, if the lover has the least inclination to break off, gives him a fair pretence of doing so.

The guilty heart, which perhaps might be in time reclaim'd by its own consciousness of being in the wrong, is often hardened by unbraidings; there is a certain pride and obstinacy in some natures which will not bear reproof, and makes them persist in the errors which themselves condemn, only because they are condemned by others.

But if the man, who knows he justly merits all the reproaches he can be loaded with, can so ill endure rebuke, how shall the innocent, the faithful lover support it; to be accused of a crime his very apprehension shudders at, to be treated by the woman he adores with sullen coldness, and with causeless testimonies of suspicion, must give him the most poignant inquietude; and though he may submit to it at first, and be even pleased, as imagining such a behaviour an indication of the most tender passion in his mistress; yet, when he finds all his endeavours to calm the tempest in her soul are fruitless, he will at last, especially if he is a man of sense and spirit, be wearied out, as the poet truly says,

> Small jealousies, indeed, inflame desire;
> Too great, not fan, but quite put out the fire.[83]

Or as another, in my opinion, more emphatically expresses his sense of the matter:

> 'Tis just, when doubts without foundation grow,
> Those who believe us false should find us so.[84]

But I have seen too much how far the power of jealousy, a passion truly call'd the poison of love, operates on a female mind, not to be sensible that all the advice I can give on this occasion will be entirely thrown away; and that I have more reason to ask pardon of my fair readers for this digression, than to flatter myself they will be any way profited by it.

To return therefore to the business of my history; it was too late when Jemmy received the abovemention'd summons from his mistress to attend her that night; but he comply'd with it very early the next morning, according to her request; and indeed much sooner than she could reasonably have expected he would be stirring.

He found her incompassed with trunks and ban-boxes,[85] and very busy in packing up her apparel: "You have found me preparing for a journey," cry'd she, "which notwithstanding I would neither resolve upon, nor promise to take without receiving your approbation of it."

"You surprise me," said he,—"a journey; and wait for my approbation of it."—"Yes,"—reply'd she, "it was to that end I sent for you in such a hurry; but sit down and I will tell you all."—Jemmy then took a chair, and she placing herself in another opposite to him, began as follows:

"You must know," said she, that I din'd yesterday, by invitation, at Lady Speck's;—her sister, Miss Wingman, was with her; they are both going to Bath to-morrow, and were very urgent with me to accompany them:—As I never saw that place, and have heard so much of it, I must confess I should be well enough pleased to go thither; especially when I have the opportunity of being escorted by three or four stout fellows with fire-arms, by way of defence from the gentlemen collectors of the road."[86]

"I know," replied Jemmy, "that Lady Speck will abate nothing that she thinks becoming her quality, and always travels in a genteel manner.—And so you set out to-morrow?"

"I do not tell you I shall set out at all," answer'd she, "for I am not yet determined."—Jemmy then ask'd her on what motive she hesitated.—"Can you not guess?"—cry'd she, looking kindly on him—"No upon my honour," said he,—"Then you are not so just to me as you ought to be,"—returned she gravely;—"you might have thought I would agree to nothing of this nature, without having first consulted you."

"Me," cry'd Jemmy, "did you not tell me you should like to go?"—"Yes," replied she, "but as I suppose, according to the footing on which we now stand, that it will be my duty hereafter to submit my inclinations to the regulation of your will, I thought it proper to give you a previous sample how easy it will be for me to do so. In fine, my dear Jemmy, I will not go without your consent; nor even without your approbation."

"This is indeed a proof of tenderness," cry'd he, "which I could not expect, nor can any way deserve, unless it be by joining my entreaties with the ladies, that you will not refuse their request." In speaking these words he rose from his seat and snatch'd her to his arm with an infinity of transport and affection.

"Then you are willing," said she, returning him his embrace, "to part with me for the long space of six or seven weeks at least? For they do not purpose to return sooner."

"I will not pretend to be so much the master of myself," said he, still holding her by the hand, "as to be perfectly content during such a separation as you have mention'd; but I can see no reason to put my patience to so severe a trial; I might follow you directly, but it happens unluckily that my steward whom I have sent for comes to town to-morrow, and the affairs I have to settle with him will detain me for some days; but I believe I may flatter myself with seeing my dear Jenny at Bath within a fortnight at the very farthest."

"May I then expect you?" cryed she, with a voice which express'd the utmost satisfaction. "You may not only expect but depend upon my coming," answered he; "you have the greatest security for it that is in nature, which is that of my own inclination."—"Believe me, my dear Jenny, that I never was easy when absent from you for any length of time;—the thoughts of you still mingled with all the little sports and recreations of my childhood; and now when riper years have made me more truly sensible, of the perfections you are mistress of, I feel it would be an utter impossibility to live without seeing you."

She answer'd these fond expressions with others no less endearing; after which, she told him, that since he agreed to her going, and had promised to follow, she would send immediately, and let Lady Speck know she should be ready to attend her ladyship next morning.

Jemmy then left her to do as she had said, and went home to dress; but return'd in the evening, and staid supper with her, when nothing passed of consequence enough to trouble the reader with, except his renewing the assurances he before had given her of seeing her at Bath as soon as his business was dispatch'd.

Chapter XVIII

Contains a brief account of Jenny's journey to Bath; and also some passages which happen'd on her arrival there.

Jenny, though she had all the reason imaginable to be pleased with this excursion, not only in the gratification of her curiosity in the sight of a place she had heard so much of, but also in the society of the company she went with; of whose characters it is highly proper to give the reader some account.

Lady Speck had been the wife of a person of great distinction, whom she lost in the first year of their marriage; but as love had not been in the least consulted by either party in the formation of that union, so grief had for his death little effect, either on the delicacy of her complexion, or the sprightliness of her humour; she had also some consolations which many widows want; for besides a very large jointure settled on her by her marriage articles, she was now in possession of an estate of near two thousand pounds a year, by the demise of an uncle.

The age of this lady did not exceed twenty-five; Miss Wingman, who was her sister by her mother's side, was six or seven years younger, and a great heiress; both of them had a great deal of wit and vivacity, but though they saw all the gay company in town, and convers'd freely, neither of them had been guilty of any thing that could call their conduct in question, or cast a blemish on their reputations.

These ladies, to whose characters I should also have added that of being very agreeable in their persons, could not fail of attracting a great number of admirers; and as their going to Bath was no secret, those who were most eager to prove the sincerity of their attachment, thought they could not do it a better way than by following them.

But there were two who distinguish'd themselves from all the rest of their competitors, by a particular act of knight errantry, these were Mr. Lovegrove and Lord Huntly; the one had for some time made his addresses to Lady Speck, and the other either was, or pretended to be passionately devoted to her sister.

These gentlemen, who were intimate friends, and the mutual confidants of each other's passion, contrived a little plot of love and gallantry between them, the idea of which gave them as much pleasure as they doubted not but their mistresses would receive in the execution of it.

Having taken care to inform themselves as exactly as possible of the time in which the ladies were to set out, they left London some hours sooner, and arrived at Maidenhead[87] early enough to accomplish what they had projected.

They put up at the first great inn in the town, and having given orders for a very elegant dinner to be prepared, posted themselves in a room that looked towards the road, that they might be ready to intercept the ladies, in case they should not intend to bait at this place.

This precaution was necessary, for Lady Speck's Jehu[88] was driving furiously on, as they generally do when passing through any town or village where they have not orders to stop.—The gentlemen saw them at a distance, and immediately sallied out. Lord Huntley's two servants laid hold of the bridles of the fore horses, and one of Mr. Lovegrove's, with an authoritative voice, call'd to the coachman to draw back the reins, their principals at the same time advanced at the coach door, and accosted those within it, in these terms:

"We arrest you, ladies, in the name of love," said Lord Huntley; "that God, so universally obeyed, has commission'd us, his faithful votaries, to stop your farther progress without his special leave";—"Ceres and Bacchus are too of the party," added Mr. Lovegrove, "and it would be in vain for you to think of resisting their united influence."

That momentary surprise which the ladies were in at the first stoppage of their coach vanish'd on the sight of the persons who had occasion'd it; and Lady Speck, who happen'd to sit on that side where they were, answer'd with a great deal of spirit, "We have nothing to do with the mischievous little deity;[89]—but as to Ceres and Bacchus, they are beneficent powers, and I think we ought to shew them some complaisance;—"What say you ladies?" continued she, turning to her sister and Miss Jessamy; the latter of whom, being wholly unaquainted with the gentlemen, made no reply, nor indeed had she time; for Miss Wingman presently took up the word, and said, "Nay sister, I think we have no choice to make; we are taken prisoners and must submit to the laws of the conquerors."

The coach door was then open'd, the ladies were handed out and conducted into a room, where they found the tablecloth laid, and sideboard set forth with as much elegance and propriety as if they had been in their own houses; but as they came somewhat sooner than the gentlemen expected, Mr. Lovegrove left Lord Huntly to entertain them for a moment, while he went down to give orders for hastening dinner.

As he was returning from this little expedition a post-chaise,[90] attended by one servant, came galloping into the yard of the inn; the person who alighted from it was Sir Robert Manley, a very great acquaintance of Mr. Lovegrove's; they immediately saw each other, and mutually advanced with open arms.

On putting the question to each other concerning the rout they were pursuing, Lovegrove related in a few words the method that Lord Huntly and himself had taken, to ingratiate themselves into the favour of their mistresses.

"You are happy fellows," said Sir Robert, smiling, "I am for Bath too; but you see how forlorn and solitary my journey will be in comparison of yours, who carry along with you those pleasures I am obliged to go in search of."

Mr. Lovegrove then told him, there was a third lady in company, "who young and handsome as she is," said he, "is like to have but a dull time of it, as my lord and I have our particular attachments; therefore, if I could prevail on you to join us, we should be all right, and more at liberty to indulge our several inclinations."

"I understand you," replied the baronet, "and was never backward in my life to come to the relief of a distressed fair one; I shall find something or other to say to her, while you are entertaining your mistresses."

On this the other purposed that he should prosecute his journey with them, in Lord Huntley's landau; to which he also agreeing, discharg'd in the same instant the post-chaise that had brought him thither, and they went up stairs together to join the company.

"I have staid a long time," said Mr. Lovegrove, presenting Sir Robert, "but have brought my excuse in my hand."—This gentleman was particularly known to Lord Huntley, and no stranger to Lady Speck and her sister, and was received by them with all imaginable demonstrations of satisfaction; but Jenny, not having the least personal acquaintance with him, said no more that what bare civility demanded from her to a man of his rank and character.

The conversation, during the time of dinner, becoming extremely gay and spirituous, our young heroine however bore a part in it, with so much wit and vivacity, which, added to her other charms, could not fail of captivating almost any heart, not already strongly prepossess'd in favour of another object;—his lordship and Mr. Lovegrove were defended, not only by the ideas, but also by the presence of their mistresses; but what the heart of Sir Robert Manley felt on the sudden rush of such united perfection, will very shortly be discover'd.

It would be quite needless to tell the reader that the table was elegantly serv'd for no one can suppose that gentlemen, who had taken so much pains to acquire an opportunity of entertaining their mistresses, would omit any thing for that purpose which the place they were in was capable of furnishing.

The same spirit of gallantry continued during the whole journey;—wherever they baited, which was as often as any agreeable prospect invited; the ladies had nothing to pay, either for themselves, their servants, or their horses;—as they travell'd very leisurely they found, on their arrival at Bath, their women attendants, who had come down with their luggage in the stage coach, had been there some hours before them, and prepar'd every thing necessary for their reception at the lodgings which Lady Speck had previously taken care to secure.

It being towards evening when they came into the town, the gentlemen, after seeing their fair companions safe into their apartments, withdrew, on pretence of leaving them to take that repose which the delicacy of their constitutions might require; but, in reality, to go about the execution of a project they had all three been concerting on the road, and which they imagined would give the ladies a second surprise, no less agreeable than the former.

They had been told there were a company of players, and a tolerable good band of musick, at that time in town; and as these people were to be employed for what they had design'd, they went directly to the theatre, and hired such of them as they found most fit for their purpose; which was no other than to compliment the ladies on their arrival, in a manner altogether new and unexpected.

Lord Huntley, who was a native of the kingdom of Ireland, had brought over with him a little musical interlude, which had been exhibited at a marriage feast where his lordship had been a guest.

As they were upon the subject of gallantry, he proposed to Mr. Lovegrove to entertain the ladies with this piece, by way of giving them their welcome to Bath, in case they should be able to procure people to perform the parts.

The personages which composed the drama, were Love, Honour and Pleasure.—Mr. Lovegrove was charm'd with the thought; and Sir Robert Manley said, that nothing could be more suitably adapted to the design they were at present upon.

The play-house, as I have already said, supply'd them with performers better than they could even have hoped for in that place;—a flaxen hair'd boy, with sparkling eyes,—cheeks which imitated the new blown rose, and an admirable voice, was chose to represent the God of soft desires.—A man of a most graceful aspect, and who had great skill in music, was to appear in the character of Honour.—A very beautiful young woman, and who also sung well, was to assume the name of Pleasure; and seemed, by her looks and manner, to be capable of giving a very just idea of the character she bore.

These people, properly habited and equipp'd for several parts they were to act, and attended by musicians with various kinds of instruments, were all placed in a close arbour, at the farther end of the garden belonging to the house where the ladies lodged; the mistress of which Lord Huntley had acquainted with the design of surprising the ladies with a morning's entertainment, and conducted them in through a back door with secrecy, according to the directions given her by his lordship.

Every thing being thus prepared, a servant was dispatch'd to the ladies, with the compliments of Lord Huntley, Mr. Lovegrove, and Sir Robert Manley; and entreating permission to wait on them, which being granted, they all immediately went;—the latter of these gentlemen having perhaps, as strong an attachment to be of the party as either of the former.

Scarce were the first salutations over, when the concert began, with an overture of wind and string instruments, accompanied with an harpsicord; —the ladies started;—"Bless me!" cry'd one;—"What's this?— Musick,"— cry'd another,—"and so near us,—where can it come from?"

"The sounds," said Mr. Lovegrove, "seem to me to proceed from behind the house."—"Certainly 'tis so," rejoin'd Lord Huntley,—"I fancy, ladies, you will hear it more distinctly in the next room." In speaking these words, without staying for permission to do so, he threw open the folding doors and they all ran in.

But how prodigiously were the fair audience surprised, when, on drawing up the windows, they saw the garden planted on each side with musicians, who all, at sight of them bow'd with the most profound reverence almost to the earth, in token that it was to them their present labours were devoted.

"What can this mean?" said Lady Speck.—"Here are those coming," reply'd Mr. Lovegrove, "who I believe will explain the mystery." There was time for no more on either side: Honour rush'd forth from his leafy covert, conducting little Cupid by the hand, and both advanced together to the middle of the alley; where, after making their obeisance to the windows, they began a duet, expressing the advantages each of them received by the fellowship of the other. Love confess'd that his darts carried gall instead of honey into the heart they reach'd, when not under the direction of Honour;—and Honour acknowledged, he never appear'd so truly amiable as when accompanied by Love.

They had no sooner ceased than Pleasure came tripping out, and told them, in a cantato, whenever they two were united, she must necessarily follow with all the sweets of nature.—They made her suitable answers in recitativo.[91]—After which the whole was concluded with a grand chorus.

This entertainment had all the effect that could be wish'd for by the contrivers of it;—Jenny was charmed with the elegance of the design,—Miss Wingman with the words, and Lady Speck with the musick.—In fine, they all seem'd to vye with each other in giving the greatest praises to it.

While they were thus expressing their satisfaction, the gentlemen put their heads out of the window, and Lord Huntley, in the name of the rest, said to the actors:—"We shall see you this evening at the theatre, and make our acknowledgements for the trouble we have given you; in the mean time you may carry with you the glory of knowing your performance has been approv'd of by the finest ladies in the world."

On this the players, after making a low bow to the company, retired, and were conducted out of the garden by the gentlewoman of the house, through the same gate by which they had enter'd.

A piece of gallantry, so flattering to the vanity of the young and gay, could not but receive from Lady Speck and her sister, all the retributions[92] it demanded from them;—and Jenny, though far from thinking herself a party interested in it, said a thousand fine things in its praise.

Charm'd as the lovers were with the gracious acceptance their mistresses vouchsafed to what they had done, their politeness reminded them, that they had already transgress'd the usual boundaries of a morning's visit; therefore they took leave till a more convenient hour of the day should permit them to return.

Chapter XIX

Treats of many things, which tho' they may seem at present less affecting than some others, yet are very necessary for the reader to be acquainted with, before we proceed farther into the history.

Youth, beauty, and wit, have deservingly a very powerful influence over the human heart; and every day, experience obliges us to own, that wealth, without the aid of any of these, is of itself sufficient to captivate;—it supplies all other defects;—it smooths the wrinkles of fourscore;—it shapes deformity into comeliness, and gives graces to idiotism itself; as it is said by the inimitable Shakespear:

> Gold! yellow, glittering, precious gold!
> Gold! that will make black, white; foul, fair; wrong, right;
> Base, noble; old, young; cowards, valiant![93]

But when the gifts of nature are join'd with those of fortune, how strong is the attraction!—How irresistible is the force of such united charms! According to the words of the humorous poet:

> Hence 'tis, no lover has the power
> T' enforce a desperate amour,
> As he that has two strings to's bow,
> And burns for love and money too.[94]

We ought not therefore, methinks, to judge with too much severity on the vanity of a fine lady; who seeing herself perpetually surrounded with a crowd of lovers, each endeavouring to excel all his rivals in the most extravagant demonstrations of affection, can hardly believe she deserves not some part, at least, of the admiration she receives.

But what pretence soever we may make to excuse the weakness of exulting in a multiplicity of lovers, it is still a weakness which all imaginable care ought to be taken to subdue; as it may draw on the most fatal consequences both on the admirers and admired:—What duels have been fought!—What torrents of blood have been shed in the mad-brain'd fury of jealous rivalship!—And how often have we seen the idol fair herself, who lately triumph'd in the pains she gave, neglected in her turn,—deserted and abandon'd to the last despair!

But this is only for such whom it may concern; the ladies I am at present speaking of were of a different stamp; Lady Speck had something of a pretty particular nature, both in her humour and character, as the reader will hereafter be informed; in the mean time [he] must content himself with a small sketch of both.

She liked a freedom of conversation with the men, but then she liked that conversation should be general; she took neither pride nor pleasure in the particular devoirs of those who profess'd themselves her lovers; and the encouragement she gave to the addresses of Mr. Lovegrove and others, was not the effect of any coquetry in her disposition, but was occasion'd merely by her policy, as she thought such a behaviour would be the best means to conceal a secret inclination she had entertain'd in favour of one; which inclination many reasons forbid her to make known, or even to be guess'd at.

Miss Wingman was of a humour so very volatile, that it was quite out of her power to think seriously for a minute together on any one thing whatever, and love the least of all took up her attention;—always pleased,—always happy, she neither plumed herself on the new conquests she acquired, nor regretted the loss of those slaves, who, weary of their bondage, shook off her chains.

As for the heroine of this history, her early engagement with Jemmy was so well known, that it had hitherto defended her from all attacks, either to put her constancy to the trial, or shew the world in what manner she would behave amidst a plurality of lovers.

But now the time was come in which this young lady was to give most substantial proofs, not only of her affection and fidelity to the man whom she looked upon ordained to be her future husband, but also of her generosity and gratitude to those to whose passion she had it not either in her power or inclination to make an adequate return.

As all the arts of love and wit were put in practice by Lord Huntley and Mr. Lovegrove, in the court they made to their respective mistresses, Sir Robert Manley thought it would ill become a man of his years and character to let a fine lady sit neglected by, especially one who appear'd so deserving as Jenny did, of all that could be said in her praise.

But though the compliments he entertain'd her with had at first no other foundation than mere gallantry, yet the manner in which she received them, and the answers she gave, were such as would have rendered it impossible for him to have withstood the charms of her tongue, even had he been unsusceptible to those of her eyes.

In fine, none of the perfections she was endowed with were lost upon him; he soon found the full effects of a passion he had been only sporting with, and might say with Cowley,

> Unhurt, untouch'd, did I complain,
> And terrify'd all others with my pain;
> But now I feel the mighty evil,
> Ah there's no fooling with the devil:
> In things where fancy much does reign
> 'Tis dangerous too cunningly to feign;
> The play at last a truth does grow,
> And custom into nature go.[95]

Love, tho' it may be counterfeited so as not to be, without great penetration, discover'd to be false, cannot, wherever it is sincere, be wholly conceal'd; Sir Robert's two friends perceived the change in him before he was quite assur'd of it in himself:—they were a little pleasant with him on the occasion; but at the same time acknowledged, that the beauty and merit of Miss Jenny Jessamy demanded all the respect that could be paid to her.

Sir Robert on this readily confess'd, that he had never seen a young lady whose person and accomplishments gave a more fair prospect of making compleatly happy the man who should possess her; "But," said he, "I have been told somewhat of an engagement she is under, and I should be sorry to appear either unjust in attempting to invade the property of another, or so weak as to give up my heart entirely without a possibility of having it well receiv'd."

Lord Huntley and Mr. Lovegrove were neither of them ignorant of what he meant; but the former having heard, in casual conversation, some of those whispers which the artifices of Bellpine had circulated through almost all companies, cried hastily out, "If a match between Miss Jenny and a young heir of her own name be the sole impediment to your making your addresses to her, I believe I may venture to assure you, from very good hands, that it is quite broke off; and that for some time they have neither regarded nor treated each other with any thing more than a bare civility."

"Your lordship's intelligence," said Mr. Lovegrove, "seems to me agreeable to reason on the nature of the thing; the marriage was agreed upon by their parents before the young people were capable of judging for themselves, as now they are arrived at years of maturity, I see no cause, except a disinclination on the one side or the other for delaying the consummation of what was so long ago projected."

People easily believe what they wish, and indeed there was so much appearance of reason in the inference Mr. Lovegrove had drawn, that it is not to be wonder'd at that the young baronet readily gave into it.

But he was still better satisfied, when, after having declared how happy he should think himself in an assurance of Jenny's heart being disengaged, Mr. Lovegrove told him, that since he found he was so serious in the affair, he would speak to Lady Speck, and endeavour to come at the certainty.

"And I," cried Lord Huntley, "will sound Miss Wingman on the occasion; I believe she will make no scruple to inform what she knows of it; and as she is nearer to her own years than her sister may be supposed to be, yet deeper in her secrets and confidants."

It would be superfluous to repeat the many retributions Sir Robert made to the gentlemen on the friendly part they took in his interest; so I shall only say, they were such as became the mouth of a man very much in love, and who scorn'd to make use of any dishonourable or ungenerous means for the attainment of his wishes.

Chapter XX

Is taken up with a conversation of very great importance.

Neither Lady Speck nor her sister were ignorant of those reports which had been so maliciously spread, concerning a change in the sentiments of Jemmy;—they had heard it averr'd by several of their acquaintances, as a thing past all dispute; but as their fair friend had never made them the confidants of her imaginary misfortune, they thought it too tender and delicate a point to be touch'd upon in her presence, and had always carefully avoided giving her the least hint that they had been told of such a thing.

It was owing however merely to the esteem and friendship they had towards her, that had induced them to persuade her to accompany them to Bath, believing that the pleasures of that place might keep her from resenting too deeply an indignity which few women are able to support with patience.

Regarding her in the affectionate manner they did, it could not but afford them a good deal of satisfaction to be inform'd by Lord Huntley and Mr. Lovegrove of the new conquest she had made; judging, as they reasonably might, that the offer of a heart, such as that of Sir Robert Manley, would fully compensate for the loss they supposed she had sustain'd by the infidelity of Jemmy.

Both these ladies assured not only their lovers, but Sir Robert himself, of the part they took in his interest, and that they would lay hold of the first opportunity to speak to Jenny on the affair, in such terms as should seem to them most effectual to convince her that she ought not to slight a proposal which could not but prove for her honour and advantage to accept.

They were punctual to their promise; the next morning, as they were sitting all together at breakfast, Lady Speck introduced what she intended to insinuate, by making some observations on the temper and behaviour of mankind in general; till by degrees she fell insensibly, as it were, and without seeming to have any design, into very great commendations of Sir Robert Manley; saying, that she thought that he had more virtue and fewer faults, than most men of her acquaintance; and then ask'd Jenny what was her opinion of him.

"Really, Madam," reply'd she, "I pretend to very little judgment of mankind, especially in those I have known so short a time; but by what I have seen of Sir Robert, he appears to me to have honour and good sense, and also to be well natur'd."

"You have named," said Lady Speck, "the three grand requisities for making a good husband; and I hope that the object of his affections will soon be convinced that he is possess'd of them, as well as with an infinity of love."

"Is Sir Robert then about marrying?" demanded Jenny.—"I cannot say absolutely about it," return'd Lady Speck; "for I am pretty certain he has not yet assumed courage enough to make any declaration of his passion; all I know is, that he is most violently in love."

"He is undoubtedly a very fine gentleman," said Jenny, "and if his passion be sincere and honourable he shall have my good wishes for his success." "As to his success," resum'd her ladyship, "it depends entirely on yourself;—for I assure you, it is with you he is in love."

"With me! Madam," cry'd Jenny, very much astonish'd, and setting down her dish of tea;—"What does your ladyship mean?"—"I mean as I have said," replied the other;—"but if you have a mind the intelligence should be repeated, I will oblige you so far as to assure you, that it is with your individual self Sir Robert Manley is in love."

"I perceive," said Jenny, "your ladyship is pleased to divert yourself this morning at my expence."—"No, I protest," return'd Lady Speck, "I was never more in earnest in my whole life."—"Indeed," rejoin'd Miss Wingman, "I can vouch for my sister's sincerity in this point;—Sir Robert has made Mr. Lovegrove and Lord Huntley the confidants of his passion; and I believe you will very soon hear it from his own mouth."

"I hope not," answer'd Jenny, in a very reserved tone;—"for if Sir Robert has in reality any such inclinations towards me as you mention, he should at least, methinks, have the prudence to keep them to himself, as he cannot but know my hand has long since been destined to another."

"Say rather," cry'd Lady Speck, "intended to be given; for it is not in the power of parents to make their children's fate;—they often decree for us what we do not think fit to comply with even while they live, to awe us into obedience by their frowns; but when they are dead, and we are left to the management of ourselves, we children pay not much regard to the injunctions of those who are no longer in a condition to thwart our inclinations."

"That may be the case sometimes Madam," said Jenny; "but I should be sorry to be among the number of those who verify it; our parents have not only an undoubted right to dispose of us, but also are much better judges of what will make our happiness than ourselves can pretend to be."

"All this is very true," cry'd Miss Wingman very briskly, "but how much soever those who would pass for the discreet part of our sex may picque themselves upon their implicit obedience in this point, I believe the men will not be found altogether so sanguine in the performance of their duty."

"No, no," reply'd Lady Speck, "inclination does all on their part;—it is not virtue,—it is not wit,—it is not beauty,—it is not all the perfections that Heaven and nature can bestow,—but fancy,—partial fancy, by which the heart of man is influenced; and that woman who perseveres in her affection for a lover, who either never did, or having once done so, ceases to regard her as he ought, discovers a meanness of spirit which must render her contemptible, both in his eyes and those of all her acquaintance."

Jenny, whose penetration few things escaped, presently comprehended that this discourse was aim'd to raise some suspicions in her mind concerning the constancy of Jemmy; and looking on such an attempt as highly injurious both to herself and him, answer'd with somewhat of what the French call a fierty[96] in her voice and countenance, in these terms:

"The more ridiculous it appears," said she, "the more reason has Mr. Jessamy and myself to thank Heaven for directing the care of our indulging fathers to cast our lot where there is no danger of such a misfortune happening to neither of us."

Lady Speck and Miss Wingman looked on each other with some amazement while Jenny was speaking, as not well knowing what to think; but after a pause of some minutes, "Some people," said Lady Speck, a little scornfully, "take a pride in being blind to what half the town has long since seen and laugh'd at." Here she stoped, and Miss Wingman, who was the more spiritous of the two, and a good deal nettled at the tart manner in which Jenny had spoke, cry'd out, "Dear sister, I beg you will shew Miss Jessamy the letter your ladyship received since our coming down to Bath; it is the duty of her friends to force open her eyes, as she seems obstinate to shut daylight out."

"It is a thing I have been very loth to mention," resum'd Lady Speck, "and now do it with an extreme reluctance; but since there is no other way to convince you that the world is not so ignorant as you imagine, of the inconstancy and perfidiousness of Mr. Jessamy, read that,—and cease for the future to offer any thing in the vindication of so unworthy a man."

In speaking these words she took a letter out of her pocket and put it into Jenny's hand, which that young lady opening, with an agitation of spirits very unusual with her, found it contain'd as follows:

To the Honourable Lady Speck, at Bath.

Madam,

As I know very well that minds truly benignant and humane, like your ladyship's, take a pleasure in every opportunity of doing good, I shall make no apology for the trouble of this anonymous epistle; especially as it is wrote with a view of serving a young lady, who so well deserves and possesses so much of your ladyship's kind wishes as Miss Jessamy.

But not to keep your ladyship in suspence, permit me to acquaint you that Mr. Jessamy, who for sometime has made his private addresses to Miss Chit, has now taken the opportunity of your fair friend's absence to avow publickly his passion for that young person. Some people will have it, that every thing is already so far concluded upon between them that a marriage will very shortly be consummated; but this I will not pretend to affirm: it is certain, however, that he loves her; and that a little skill in music, out-ballances, in his giddy fancy, all the real merits of the beautiful and accomplished Miss Jessamy.

I know not whether she is as yet appriz'd of his infidelity, or has even any suspicions of it; but the less she is so the more will it shock her tender nature to find, at her return, that he is married, or about being married to another.—How could her gentle heart support the sudden disappointment?—How bear the double pangs of the indignity offer'd to her love and beauty?—Fatal, alas, might be the consequences of such a stroke, if not previously prepar'd and arm'd against it!

It depends greatly on your ladyship to shield that injured innocence from being too deeply affected with her misfortune; and as her case must touch every one who has a soul capable of social commiseration, I take the liberty, with all submission, to entreat you, Madam, to give her such warnings of her fate as may render the certainty, whenever it shall arrive, less heavy to be borne;—if once thoroughly persuaded there is a probability of his being false, it will at least take off the alarming surprise of finding he is so; and the more early she is brought to suspect his baseness, the more opportunity she will have to exert the good sense she is mistress of, in despising instead of lamenting it.

The manner in which this is most proper to be done will best be determined by your ladyship's superior judgement: I only beg that the above hints may be received, in an assurance that they proceed from a heart truly devoted to honour and virtue, and entirely free from all views but such as may be conducive to promote the cause of those noble principles.

I am,
With a profound respect,
Madam,
Your ladyship's
Most humble,
Most faithful
And obedient servant.

P.S. Your ladyship will pardon the concealment of my name for the present, as an advice of this nature might probably subject the person who gives it to many great inconveniencies, if known before the affair to which it relates is absolutely concluded and past beyond all possibility of denial.

Scarce had Jenny patience to go through with this invidious scroll;—"Good God," cry'd she, to Lady Speck;—"who is it can have the baseness to assert such monstrous untruths, or the presumption to attempt making your ladyship's good nature the dupe of a design so villainous, and withal so mean?"

Then immediately recollecting what had just now been told her concerning the passion Sir Robert Manley had entertain'd for her, she hesitated not a moment to accuse him of having taken this method to alienate her affections from Jemmy; and looking on the contrivance with that contempt and indignation it really deserved, began to reproach in terms the most bitter that could issue from a mouth so little accustom'd to invectives.

The two ladies seem'd quite astonish'd at her behaviour, and both join'd to endeavour to convince her of the injustice to Sir Robert, who they believed had too much honour to attempt the gaining of his point by a way so abject and so unworthy of his character; and to clear his innocence, assured her that they had heard an account of Jemmy's infidelity from many hands before they had left London; or that Sir Robert had ever seen her face.

All they could say, however, was insufficient to make Jenny recede from her opinion; the dispute grew pretty warm, and would probably have run to greater lengths, if it had not been seasonably interrupted by some company coming to visit them.

Chapter XXI

Gives an account of some passages, which, added to the former, affords our heroine much matter of discontent.

Jenny had been so much discomposed and ruffled at the discourse of the ladies, and the letter shewn to her by them, that neither her natural sprightliness and gayety, nor all the efforts her reason made, were sufficient to re-settle in her mind that happy serenity she enjoy'd before.

She had not the least tincture of jealousy in her composition; she had always depended on the sincerity of Jemmy, and as yet was far from believing that he could be false; but it vexed her to be told that others thought him so; that he pass'd in the eyes of the world for an inconstant and ungrateful man; and what was still more insupportable, that herself was look'd upon as a slighted and forsaken mistress.

Pity is so near a-kin to contempt, that few women of spirit can bear it; even those who have the least share of vanity, I believe, would rather chuse to be envy'd and hated for having too much the power of pleasing, than commiserated for their want of it.

The affection she had for Jemmy was not of the fond and foolish nature as to make her wish to be for ever in his sight; she had been absent from him more weeks than she had now been days, without the least repining or inquietude; but on the hearing of this story she could not keep herself from being excessively impatient for his coming down to Bath;—not that she desir'd his presence to clear any doubts of her own, but that his behaviour might convince the company she was with of their mistake as to his fidelity.

The promise he had made of following her when she left London, and which had since been confirmed by two several letters she had received from him, made her expect his arrival would be very soon, and she was pleasing herself with the thoughts how that event would make Lady Speck and Miss Wingman ashamed of having too rashly given credit to a calumny, which she doubted not but they would then see had not the least foundation.

But this was a satisfaction which vanish'd in a very short space of time; a few hours made her know that she must wait much longer than she had imagined for the completion of what at present her pride made her so ardently desire.

The evening of that very same day, whose morning had occasion'd in her breast these various perturbations, presented her with something which was far from lulling them to rest.—Just as she was going to the assembly-room with the ladies and some other company, the post brought her a letter, the contents whereof were these:

To Miss Jessamy, at Bath.

Dear Jenny,

I am in so ill a humour, that I believe it would be utterly out of my power to write to any one person in the world except yourself; and yet it is almost entirely on your account that I am thus disconcerted. This you may think a paradox, but I shall soon explain the riddle.

For three whole days successively I have been every hour expecting the arrival of my steward; but last night, instead of himself I received a letter from him, acquainting me that having been obliged to make a seisure on one of my tenant's effects, that affair would of necessity detain him at least seven or eight days longer.

Judge how severely this accident has mortify'd me, as it deprives me so much longer than I hop'd of the pleasures of the Bath, and what is infinitely more valuable to me, the sight of my dear Jenny;—console me as often you can with your letters;—it is in them alone I can take any true satisfaction during this enforced absence.—Farewel;—I flatter myself there is no need of fresh assurances to convince you that I am,

With the warmest affection,
My dear Jenny's
Most devoted and
Obedient servant,
J. Jessamy.

P.S. My friend Bellpine, who is now with me, desires you will accept his compliments and best wishes;—we are just going together to hear a fine piece of music, if my chagrin does not turn the notes into discord.—Once more for this time,—my dear Jenny,—adieu.

Jenny withdrew to a window to take just a cursory view of this epistle; for being waited for by the company she could not, without a breach of civility, give herself time to examine it with that strictness the present situation of her mind inclined her to do. She was, however, sufficiently mistress of the sense of it to perceive she must not expect to see him at Bath so soon as she wish'd; and this delay, as my fair readers will easily believe, gave no small mortification both to her pride and love.

The assembly was more than ordinarily brilliant that night; but not all the diversions and gallantries of the place could dissipate the gloom that hung heavy on her spirits, and as she was an ill dissembler, was but too visible in her countenance.

It was not that in the slight perusal she had been able to give Jemmy's letter she had found any thing to confirm the informations of Lady Speck and Miss Wingman, but the delay of his coming, at a time when she thought his presence so necessary to clear both his own and her reputation, that alone gave her these inquietudes; and the disappointment was more grievous, as it was the first she as yet had ever met with.

Not all her efforts could enable her to behave with her accustomed vivacity that night;—she bore very little part in the conversation;—was wholly unattentive to the music, as well as the fine things said to her; and whenever she spoke, it was in such a manner as made it easy to perceive she would rather have chose to have remain'd silent.

Conscious of this defect, and finding herself altogether unfit for company, she pretended a violent head-ach, and retir'd some hours before the usual time.

On her coming home she shut herself up in her own apartment, and gave strict orders to her maid that no one should disturb her; then fell to examining, with the utmost exactness, every sentence of the letter which had created in her so much uneasiness;—she compared it with the others she had received from him since her arrival at Bath, and found it nothing different either in the stile or manner;—till coming to the postscript, the mention he made of going to hear a fine piece of music, she suddenly cry'd out,—"That music perhaps may be perform'd by Miss Chit; a story, such as I have been told, could not certainly be raised without some little truth for its foundation."

But this fit of jealousy lasted scarce a moment, "How unjust and foolish am I!" said she: "I know he loves music, but what then? If being mistress of that accomplishment had given Miss Chit, or any other woman, the preference to me in his esteem, he would have been entirely silent on the pleasure he was going to take; the guilty always carefully avoid speaking on the theme which calls their crime in question."

In this favourable disposition she might perhaps have continued, if a thousand instances of the deceit and perfidy of men in the affairs of love, which she had either heard or read of, had not immediately presented themselves to her remembrance, and reminded her that she ought not to be too secure; that the passion of love, like the wind, blew where it listed, and that, as the poet says:

Man is but man, inconstant still and various,
There's no to-morrow in him like today;
Perhaps the atoms rolling in his brain
Make him think honestly this present hour:
The next a swarm of base ungrateful thoughts

May mount aloft,
Who would trust chance, since all men have the seeds
Of good or ill, which would work upwards first.[97]

Yet for all this could she not bring herself to believe him absolutely false; if one moment accused him in her thoughts, the next acquitted him; but what gave her the greatest perplexity of all was, the difficulty she found in guessing by whom or to what end this aspersion had first been raised, and how it came to be so spread.

She thought that neither Jemmy nor herself had done any thing to incur the malice of the world, so far as that even any one person should be desirous of rendering them unhappy; "It cannot therefore be," cried she, "but that some vile self-interested view must be the source of all this; no body sure would be at the wicked pains to separate two persons whose hearts from their infancy have been united by the strictest bonds of love and friendship, merely for the sake of mischief; no, it is utterly impossible that human nature can be so depraved."

This reflection leading her still farther on, she began to argue within her mind for what end a contrivance to part her and Jemmy could be form'd, and found none so conformable to probability, as that the author of it aimed to be in the place either of the one or the other.

As for her own part, the engagements between her and Jemmy were so well known that no man had ever made his serious addresses to her, and if Sir Robert Manley had now any such intentions, the character of that gentleman would not permit her to believe he could be capable of making use of base means for the forwarding his wishes; besides, Lady Speck and Miss Wingman had assured her, in the most solemn manner, that they had heard the report before their coming down to Bath, or that he had ever seen her.

It rested therefore, that it must be on the account of Jemmy that all this had happen'd; she knew very well that he convers'd freely with the ladies, he had never made a secret to her of his doing so, and it seem'd not in the least improbable, that some one among them might like him but too well, "Perhaps," said she, "Miss Chit herself mistaking for love what he means only as gallantry, might have the vanity to boast of having inspired him with a real passion."

"The smallest hint," continued she, "that such a thing is,—or possibly may be, passes with many people for an undoubted fact.—And who knows but the whisper of Jemmy's imaginary infidelity may have been carried from one to another till it reach'd the ears of some person, who more compassionate than wise, wrote to Lady Speck in the manner I have seen."

Thus did she endeavour to dive into the bottom of this mysterious affair, assigning for it every cause that reason or her fertile imagination could suggest;—yet wavering still, and uncertain on which of them she should fix, her mind at length grew quite fatigued with the unavailing search; and she resolved to wait till time should bring to light what all her penetration could not at present enable her to discover.

In this manner was the sweetest and most serene temper in the world disconcerted and thrown off its byass, by the dark villainy of a man whom she had not the least suspicion of.—She went to bed however, and for ought I ever heard to the contrary, slept as well as if nothing had happen'd to perplex her waking thoughts.

Chapter XXII

Affords some very useful and exemplary hints to young persons of both sexes; which if they are not the better and wiser for, it is wholly owing to themselves, and not the fault of the author.

That only true composing draught, an unforced natural slumber, so effectually lull'd the mind of Jenny that when she arose the next morning the anxieties of the preceding day were scarce remember'd by her; or if they were, it was but to wonder at herself for having yielded to their force.

"As I think," said she, "that I may be pretty confident the story I was told yesterday has nothing of reality in it, but is a most vile and notorious falshood; how silly was I to give myself any pain concerning either, by whom or on what motive it was invented?"

"There are some people," said she, "who seem to be born with a propensity to mischief. I remember that when I was at the boarding-school a thousand little quarrels happen'd between the girls, which were occasion'd merely by the lying insinuations of some among us, who took a wicked pleasure in giving pain to others."

"Too many in the world," continued she, "when arrived at years of maturity, instead of endeavouring to correct, take pains to improve and cultivate this cruel disposition in themselves, till even it becomes a science; and the more vexation they create to those who are so unhappy to be of their acquaintance, the more proofs they imagine they give of their own ingenuity and fertility of invention."

"How stupid then is it," went she still on, "to give ear to every idle tale? It is joining with the adversaries of our peace;—aiding those malicious efforts, and giving them a triumph over us, which otherwise all they could do would never be able to obtain: we certainly ought not to believe ill of any one without the testimony of our own senses to confirm the truth of that report; but more especially it behoves us to reject with the utmost contempt whatever has a tendency to create a disagreement between us and those we love."

Thus did her good understanding and strength of reason enable her to get the better of all these doubts and jealous apprehensions, into which young persons of her sex are for the most part too liable to fall. She past a good deal of time in this sort of conversation with herself; and would not, perhaps, have broke it off so soon, if she had not been interrupted by Lady Speck's woman, who came into the chamber to enquire after her health, and to let her know that the ladies waited breakfast for her.

She obey'd the summons immediately, and appear'd so very sprightly, that Lady Speck and her sister had not the least room to imagine that the disorder she had complain'd of the night before had been occasion'd by any thing they had said to her in relation to Jemmy.

A succession of visitants, one after another, came in all that whole day, some of whom stay'd to accompany them to the long room;[98] but Jenny, who had never fail'd to answer every letter she had received from Jemmy by the very first post, would not now be more remiss; and excusing herself for a few minutes retired to her chamber and wrote to him in the following manner:

To James Jessamy, Esq;

My dear Jemmy,

I am very sensible that I am quite wrong to add to the vexation you express, by giving you any knowledge of mine;—yet it is not in my power to forbear telling you, that this delay of your journey hither has involved me in disquiets altogether new to me;—I know not how it is, that I never so much wish'd to see you as I now do.

I should be sorry if you neglected any affairs of consequence on my account; but be assured however, till you come, all the amusements, all the pleasures with which this place abounds, and I am continually surrounded with, will lose their relish and be insipid to me.

Such a confession would seem extremely aukward from the pen of a woman, were we not upon the terms we are, or had we been brought up in a different manner; but from my infancy I have been made to think it was my duty to conceal from you no part of my sentiments; and you have often told me, that the same principles were instilled in you:—As I have the most perfect confidence that you are no less punctual in your obedience to this injunction than myself, I am not afraid or ashamed of giving you all the testimonies of my affection that honour and virtue will permit; and more, I am certain, you will never desire.

I shall say nothing to urge you to as speedy a dispatch as possible of the business that detains you from me; I am too well acquainted with your sincerity to doubt if your heart is not already here, and shall therefore endeavour to console myself till your arrival with your letters, as you tell me you shall do with those you receive from me. I am,

With an attachment
Which only yourself can break,
My dear Jemmy,
Your most affectionate
And ever faithful
J. JESSAMY.

P.S. If I have express'd too much impatience in the above, excuse it on the account that hitherto, unaccustom'd to disappointments, I am the less able to sustain them with that fortitude and resignation I ought to do.

Having finish'd this little epistle, and given orders that it should be carried to the post-office, she return'd to the company, who by this time were ready to adjourn to the assembly;—she went with them, and few women there appear'd to more advantage than herself.

Sir Robert Manley, to whom neither Lady Speck nor Miss Wingman had related any part of the rebuff they had received from Jenny on his score, was very impatient to make a declaration of his passion to her; but though he had seen her three times that day at home,—in the walks,—and at the assembly, yet no opportunity proper for his purpose had presented itself.

He complain'd of his ill luck to Lord Huntley and Mr. Lovegrove, who, after consulting with the ladies what could be done for the advancement of the interest of their friend in this point, it was so contrived amongst them, that she should be left alone with him as if by accident.

But this could not be done with so much art as to elude the discernment of Jenny; she easily perceived with what intent first one and then another slipt out of the room, till none but herself and Sir Robert were left in it. She could not help smiling within herself to think that all this mighty pains was taken only to shew Sir Robert that he had nothing to hope for from her; and was not at all displeased with having it in her power to convince that gentleman, that the affection between herself and Jemmy was too strongly cemented to be shaken by the amorous attacks of any pretender whatsoever.

I am afraid that, on computation, the number of those ladies would be found but small, who, in this giddy and unthinking age, are not fond of making new conquests; though render'd, by even the most solemn engagements, utterly incapable of accepting the trophies presented them:—Jenny, however, had nothing of this vanity in her composition,—she had heard and read much of the effects of love, and the fatal consequences which had sometimes attended a disappointed flame; and therefore had always consider'd that passion as a thing of too serious a nature to be sported with; and that it was an action highly ungenerous and cruel to encourage the growth of it in any heart, without having the power or inclination of making an adequate return.

Sir Robert Manley was a person whose addresses might have gratify'd the pride of any woman, who placed her glory in seeing herself admired: Jenny was sensible of his merit, but the more she was so, the more she thought herself obliged to prevent him at once from indulging any fruitless expectations.

He had no sooner made her an offer of his heart, and was just beginning to assure her how much, and how eternally he was devoted to her, than she stopp'd the progress of his declaration, by asking him, with a very reserved air,—If he were really in earnest?—To which he answering in the affirmative, and annexing the most solemn protestation of the truth,—"Then Sir," said she, "I am equally sorry and astonish'd, that a gentleman of so much good sense and honour in other things, should forget himself so far as to entertain any thoughts of this kind for a woman, who, he cannot but have heard, has from her very birth been allotted for another."

The manner in which these words were deliver'd giving a double energy to the meaning of them, had a prodigious effect on the person to whom they were directed;—though a man of great presence of mind,—bred in high life, and perfectly acquainted with the world, he could not keep himself from being a little abash'd at receiving so grave and so severe a reprimand from a lady of Jenny's years and inexperience.

But soon recovering himself,—"Madam," said he,—"I beg you will do me the justice to believe, that however ardent my passion is, I would scorn to attempt the gratification of it by any ways which my honour or my reason should condemn:—that I love you, is most true; yet would I chuse rather to consume through the force of an inextinguishable flame, than to make the least encroachment either on your virtue or your peace."

"I do not indeed deny," continued he, "but that I have been told somewhat concerning an agreement made for you in your extreme youth; but as no consequence has since happen'd of that agreement, I flatter'd myself that your heart approv'd not of the choice made for you,—was at full liberty to elect for itself, and that no impediment lay in the way of my ambition, but my own unworthiness of obtaining so inestimable a jewel."

He concluded these words with a deep sigh, and a bow full of the greatest tenderness and respect; the grateful soul of Jenny was a little touch'd at his behaviour, and she immediately replied with an extreme sweetness;—"Were there no other bar than what you last mention'd, Sir," said she, "I believe there are few women, of any penetration at least, to whom your heart would be an unacceptable present; and I shall rejoice to see it bestow'd where equal worth and unpre-engaged affections may crown the utmost of its wishes."

"Ah, Madam!" cry'd Sir Robert, "Why is this enchanting goodness lavish'd on a man who cannot thank the bounty? All my desires, alas! are center'd in yourself; and to wish me happy with any other object, is but to wish me wretched.—But tell me,—tell me," pursued he,—"Are you in earnest, absolutely determined to give your hand to this too fortunate rival? Is it a thing mutually resolved between you?"

Jenny, knowing very well what he had been inform'd of concerning the supposed infidelity of Jemmy, was charm'd with his politeness in imputing the delay of their nuptials rather to an indifference on her side than a dislike on his; and now more desirous than ever of entirely stifling all fallacious hopes, which in the end might prove destructive to his peace, compell'd her modesty to confess to him, that she really loved Jemmy, and that her inclinations would have prefer'd him to all the men in the world, even though they had not been destined for each other by their parents.

Sir Robert could not hear this declaration without pain; but being fully persuaded in his mind, by what Lord Huntley, Mr. Lovegrove and others had assured him, that Jemmy but ill repaid the tenderness of his fair mistress, he assumed courage enough to offer a second petition to her consideration.

"Well Madam," said he, after a little pause, "I will not presume to call in question the merits of the man whom you are pleased to favour, I will believe him as deserving as I am sure he is happy; yet if any accident, yet unforseen, should happen to disunite you, if any thing, impossible as it may seem, should render him ungrateful for the blessing he enjoys, might I not hope my love, my truth, my perseverance, would in time find some room in a corner of that heart which doubtless then would have exterminated its first ideas."

This insinuation was far from working the effect it was intended for; Jenny was highly offended at it, and turning from him with somewhat of a disdainful air; "To demand a promise," said she, "on suppositions without foundation, is so chymerical as scarce deserves an answer; but Sir Robert, on this you may depend, that whenever Mr. Jessamy shall prove unworthy of my love, I shall, instead of giving him a successor in my heart, detest and avoid all mankind for ever."

Sir Robert was now conscious he had gone too far, and desirous of perserving her esteem, if he could not gain her affection, endeavoured all he could to excuse the rashness of his late suggestion, which possibly he succeeded in better than he imagined, as Jenny was sensible it was wholly owing to the base reports that had been raised; she would not however, seem to forgive too easily any reflection cast upon her dear Jemmy, but continued in the same serious deportment till the return of the company put an end to all discourse between them on this score.

Chapter XXIII

Relates how, in the compass of an hour, Jenny met with two surprising adventures of very different kinds; and the manner in which she behaved in them, with some other no less extraordinary particulars, which the reader will doubtless be puzzled to know the meaning of.

After what had pass'd between Jenny and Sir Robert, that gentleman thought it would be in vain to prosecute his suit; his friends also, to whom he imparted the conversation he had with her, were of the same opinion; and the report of Jemmy's inconstancy began now to lose much of the credit it had obtain'd among them.

Sir Robert, whose esteem for Jenny was not at all diminish'd by her late behaviour towards him, tho' it had made him endeavour to overcome his passion for her, omitted nothing in his power to reconcile himself to her good graces; which he at length effectually did, by giving her the strongest and reiterated assurances that he would never more attempt to interrupt that affection, which he now seem'd to believe mutually existing between her and Mr. Jessamy.

The same easy freedom of conversation, which had reign'd among this amiable company since their first coming down to Bath, was now again restored; but it lasted not long, accidents on accidents, in which every one had a share, immediately fell out, and turn'd all into discord and confusion.

Among the croud of guests who were every day at the tea-table of Lady Speck, there was a gentleman named Celandine; he had but lately return'd from making the tour of Europe, and like Clodio in the play,[99] pretended to be acquainted with all the intrigues of the several courts he had been in; he was gay, spiritous, had some wit, and abundance of assurance; which, with the affectation of great good humour, made him pass for a very agreeable companion, and particularly entitled him to the favour of the ladies; many of whom thought the loss of reputation no disgrace when forfeited on his account.

He was certainly very much indebted to nature for a handsome person, and to education for all those modish accomplishments which with unthinking people are apt to cast a lustre even to the worst qualities of the mind; his example was at least a proof of this melancholy truth; for it would have puzled even his best friends and greatest admirers, if ask'd the question, to have found any one virtue in him to compensate for a thousand vices; he was vain to an excess, ungrateful, insincere, incapable either of love or friendship; a contemner both of morality and religion; in fine, he was a libertine profess'd.

His family was ancient and honourable, and from thence descended to him a very large estate, which, without doing one generous or benevolent action, he seem'd to take abundance of pains to get rid of by the most unheard of, and ridiculous extravagancies and vagaries.

The reader will perhaps imagine, that a character such as this, deserved not so particular a description; nor should I have troubled him with it had there not been an absolute necessity of my doing so, for reasons which will presently appear.

Jenny was at home alone one day; Lady Speck and Miss Wingman were gone into the walks, but some letters she had received from London, which required immediate answers, had hinder'd her from accompanying them; having finish'd what she had to do before they return'd, she went down into the garden, in order to refresh her spirits after the fatigue they had undergone, by her writing so much longer than she was accustom'd at one time.

She took a short promenade in the great alley; but being in a contemplative mood, retired into the arbour at the farther end of it; where, as the reader may remember, the performers in Lord Huntley's interlude had been conceal'd; there could not, indeed, be a more proper scene for indulging meditation, and she was just beginning to fall into a very agreeable resvery, when on a sudden Celandine appear'd at the entrance of the leafy bower, and accosted her with these lines, translated by himself, from a French poet:

So look'd Pomona when Vertumnus came,
And with immortal raptures clasp'd the dame.[100]

As great a favourite as this young gallant was with most of the women of his acquaintance, Jenny had never been able to endure the sight of him, on account of his pert confident behaviour; but his presence was now doubly unwelcome to her, as there was nobody but herself to entertain him, or to bear a part in the impertinent freedoms of his conversation, and she could not forbear giving him a look which might have dash'd the boldness of any other man, and made him quit the place.

But Celandine, as has been before observ'd, and Jenny in this visit experienced to her cost, was none of those who were capable of being aw'd either by looks or words; full of his own merit, and puff'd up with frequent successes among the fair, he thought the whole sex at his devotion; that no woman could withstand his charms, and that the coldness Jenny had always treated him with was no more than an affectation of modesty in public, which on his making the first overtures of a passion for her would vanish in an instant, and she would drop into his arms as rain does from the firmament.

"How kind is fortune to me," said he, approaching her, "in giving me this opportunity of speaking in private to my angel." "If you are indebted to fortune for no greater favours," replied Jenny, "you have but small cause to thank her bounty: But pray," continued she, "how came you to be out of the walks this fine day, when all the world are there?"

"I might ask you the same question," answered he, "and equally wonder why I find the enchanting Miss Jessamy here, mopeing in a solitary shade, and neglecting to increase the number of her conquests, and add new triumphs to her eyes;—but I'll tell you," pursued he, catching hold of her hand,—"it was fate,—propitious fate, ordain'd it so for both our happiness;—some kind good natured demon put it into your head to stay at home, and in mine to seek you here."

He concluded these words with throwing one of his arms about her neck, and began to kiss her with vehemence: hard is it to say, whether surprise or rage, at being treated in this manner, was most predominant in her soul;—she broke from him, and starting some paces back, "What means this rudeness?" cried she,—"Give not so harsh a name," rejoin'd he, "to the emotions of the most tender passion that ever was."—"A passion for me," said she, in a voice full of disdain. "Yes,—for you," reply'd he, staring her in the face,—"Did my eyes never tell you the secret of my heart?" "No, really," said she,—"I never examine into the mysterious dialect, nor desire to have it explain'd."

With these words she was going hastily out of the arbour, but the nimble Celandine at one jump got between her and the entrance, and in spite of all the resistance she could make, forced her back to the bench where he had found her sitting.

"No more prudery," cry'd he,—"this pretended coyness,—we are now alone, and the means of being so are not easy to be found in such a place as Bath;—do not then, by this unseasonable reserve, make me lose the golden glorious opportunity that Heaven has sent, of giving you the most substantial proofs how much my soul adores you,—how much I prize you above that Heaven itself."

It is impossible to paint the distraction Jenny was in, as it was for her to express it, or relieve herself from the impending danger to which she was reduced. They were at too great a distance from the house for her cries to alarm the family;—he held her fast down on the seat, with his hands on both her shoulders, she could only call him monster, villain;—while he, regardless of her reproaches, utter'd things which made her modest heart shudder at the sound of.

To what horrid freedoms he might have proceeded is uncertain; a sudden rustling among the branches, which twined about the latticed arbour, made him relax the hold he had taken of his fair captive, and turn to see what had occasion'd this interruption. Jenny lost not the instant of her release, but rather flew than ran out of that detested place, when, just at the entrance, she was met by a woman, or to speak more properly, a fury, arm'd with a penknife, which she had doubtless plunged into the bosom of the defenceless fair, if Celandine, who was close behind, had not been very quick in wresting it from her hand.

"What fiend, thou cursed creature," cry'd Celandine, "has prompted thy malice to attempt this execrable deed?" "What fiend but thyself,—thou worse than devil," answer'd she, almost foaming at the mouth with passion. Jenny stay'd not to hear what further pass'd between them, but ran screaming down the alley; Lady Speck and Miss Wingman, accompany'd by Mr. Lovegrove, enter'd the house at that very moment, and were the first who came to her assistance.

Never were three people in greater consternation than they; Jenny, with arms extended and garments all disorder'd, crying out for help;—Celandine at some distance, with the utmost confusion in his looks and at his feet a woman, who seem'd either dead or in a swoon;—in vain they inquired the occasion of all this;—Jenny was incapable of speaking, by the fright which yet hung upon her spirits;—the intended murderess by the condition she was in, and Celandine by his guilt.

Mr. Lovegrove, who had more presence of mind that any of the rest on this occasion, finding no answers were given to their interrogatories, stept forward to convince himself if the person who lay upon the earth were alive or dead; and this action of his 'twas that probably recover'd Celandine the use of his tongue; but the first and only token he gave of it, was to say, it was a mad woman, who had some how or other gained admittance; and to desire the servants might be order'd to carry her out of the house.

Mr. Lovegrove having found the person he spoke of in this manner was only in a fainting fit, cry'd out, "Whatever she is, her figure, as well as the present condition she is in, seems to demand rather compassion than contempt."—On this Lady Speck and her sister ran to assist the charitable endeavour he was making for her recovery: but Jenny still kept at a good distance; and Celandine, who, for all his impudence, was not provided with fit answers to the questions which were like to be put to him, took the opportunity of their being thus engaged to sneak off, without giving any notice of his going.

By this time the woman of the house, with all the servants, were got into the garden, and among them the unhappy stranger was carried into a parlour and laid upon a couch, where proper remedies being apply'd, she came a little to herself.

Chapter XXIV

Contains some part of the history of the furious stranger, as told by herself.

The company, to whom Jenny had now related the dangers she had escaped, were very impatient to know the whole of this adventure; and perceiving the person chiefly concerned in it was recover'd enough to be able to satisfy their curiosity, began almost all at once to ask what had induced her to attempt such an act of barbarity; but the unfortunate creature had not the power, for a considerable time, of making any other answer than a torrent of tears, which gush'd from her eyes with such rapidity as drew compassion even from Jenny herself.

The violence of that passion however, which so long had stopp'd the passage of her words, having found this vent, she entreated their pardon for the disturbance she had caused, and thanked the charitable relief that had been offer'd her, in terms so polite as made every one see she was not of the lowest rank in life.

Then turning to Jenny,—"But it is you, Madam, I have most offended," said she; "Oh! had I perpetrated the horrid deed, Heaven sure must have decreed some new and yet unpractised torture for a crime like mine":—Here she ceased to give way to some sighs, which were just then forcing themselves from her afflicted bosom,—after which,—"Yet, that Heaven to whom I now appeal," cry'd she, "is witness for me, as well as my own conscious soul, that I was clear of all malice, all premeditated design against you:—When I drew that cursed knife, I meant not to hurt your innocence, but to do justice to myself on the villain that was with you:—Some demon in that instant sure, turn'd my erring arm from its intended mark to save his brother fiend."

"Who is this fiend,—this villain you are speaking of?" cry'd Lady Speck with some emotion.—"Oh! there is no name so foul,—so black as he deserves," reply'd the other;—but if you would paint a wretch, in whom all vices, all corruptions meet as in their center,—then call him Celandine."

"Oh! ladies," continued she, in the extremest agonies, "Why will you suffer such a serpent near you?—Wherever he comes he brings destruction with him, and bitterness of heart with everlasting infamy, are the legacies he leaves behind!"

It is probable she would have run on with these exclamations much longer, if Mr. Lovegrove had not reminded her, that as the person was not there, she would do better to inform the company of the cause of her complaint against him; "For," said he, "you neither can be justified nor he condemn'd in our opinion, without your letting us into the secret of his crime."

"Alas!" answer'd she, bursting again into tears, "neither his crime nor my shame are secrets to the world; and as I am before persons of so much honour and goodness, I have reason to hope that a perfect knowledge of those unfortunate circumstances which brought on my undoing, will entitle me rather to compassion than at all add to the contempt the late behaviour I have been guilty of must have excited."

The ladies then, as well as Mr. Lovegrove, assured her, that she could no way so well atone for the confusion she had given them, as by making them a faithful narrative of the motives which had induced her to it.

On this she endeavour'd to compose herself as much as possible, and after a pause of a few minutes, in order to recollect the passages she was about to relate, began to do as she was desired, in these or the like terms:

The History of Mrs. M——

"I will not detain your attention," said this afflicted woman, "with any impertinent particulars concerning a wretch so unworthy as myself; but beg you will afford a patient hearing of such as are absolutely necessary for the better understanding my unhappy story.

"I was the only daughter of a gentleman, who, being a younger son, had no other dependance than a post in one of the public offices; as he lived up to the height of his income, I was left at his decease, which happen'd when I was about seventeen years of age, with no other portion than a genteel education, some houshold furniture, and a few jewels. I had lost my mother in my infancy, so that I was altogether an orphan;—my father's brother, though possess'd of a large estate, declin'd taking any care of me; and I know not what would have become of me, if an aunt, by my mother's side, had not been so good to admit me into her family to preserve me, as she said, from falling into those temptations to which a maid of my years, and accounted not ugly, was liable to be exposed.

"I had not lived quite two years with this kind relation, before some business brought frequently to her house a gentleman call'd Mr. M——, who you must doubtless have heard of, as he makes a pretty considerable figure in the law;—he took a great fancy to me at first sight, which afterwards grew up into a passion;—in fine, he loved me upon the most honourable terms; ask'd leave of my aunt to make his addresses to me; the match was too advantageous for a girl in my circumstances to be refus'd; she press'd me to it, and as neither his person nor conversation were disagreeable to me, I consented, and in a short time became his wife.

"Few women, I believe, can boast of more happiness than I enjoy'd during the first seven or eight months of our marriage; my husband seem'd to have no other study than that of obliging me; he was continually forming some new schemes of delight and entertainment for me; he never heard of any ornament of dress or furniture, in use with the beau monde,[101] but he bought and brought it home to me; he could scarce bear losing the sight of me a moment; and indeed, gave me more of his company than could well be spared from his avocation.

"But the extremes of any thing are seldom lasting; this exuberance of transported love, this frenzy of passion, if I may call it so, vanish'd by very swift degrees; as sudden coldness almost at once succeeded, he treated me civily, 'tis true, retrench'd no part of my expences, denied me nothing that I ask'd; but yet I found a mighty difference between this and his former behaviour. Ah, how dangerous it is for men to begin with demonstrations of a fondness which they cannot persevere in; I was young, vain, inconsiderate; I expected the same assiduity to please, the same raptures as at first, and could not brook the disappointment.

"I complain'd of this change of my condition to a female friend of more years and experience than myself; at first she laugh'd at me, and told me that nothing was more common, and that she had often wonder'd Mr. M—— held out the honey-moon so long.

"This putting me beyond all patience, 'Do not be so much out of humour,' said she; 'your cause is but the same with other women, and I believe I can direct you to a course that will infallibly retrieve all; it is the nature of mankind,' continued she, 'to be rampant in the pursuit of their wishes, but languid in the full possession of them; you must give your husband room to apprehend he is not so secure of your heart as he has imagined; toy with some pretty fellow before his face, send often for him, and affect to be uneasy till you see him; this will rouse your husband if any thing will do it; jealousy new points the darts of love, and whets the edge of satiated desire, according to the poet:

They dearly prize, what they once fear to lose.'[102]

"I greedily swallow'd this false doctrine," continued Mrs. M—— with a deep sigh, "and immediately resolv'd on making the experiment: Celandine, whose person I have no occasion to give a particular description of, as you all know him, seemed form'd by nature for the purpose I intended.

"He came frequently to our house, my husband always treated him with the extremest respect, as indeed he had good reason to do, being indebted for his first setting out in the world, in the handsome manner he did, to the father of Celandine, whom both his parents had served, the one in quality of a steward, the other of house-keeper; the favours conferr'd on Mr. M——, even from his infancy by that old gentleman, were such as made many people suspect there was a nearer affinity between them than was for my mother-in-law's honour to acknowledge; be that, however, as it may, it is not my business to inspect into the faults of others, but bewail my own.

"I had hitherto behaved towards my husband's young patron, for so he always call'd him, with the reserve becoming the married woman; but now, according to the pernicious advice I had received, I put on the most light airs before him; and look'd and talk'd in such a manner as might have made a man, of much less vanity than he is endued[103] with, imagine me to be most passionately in love with him.

"Whether my husband had really too much indifference for me to regard any thing I did, or whether he thought the extraordinary civilities I shew'd to his friend were merely to oblige him, I cannot be certain; all I can say is, that he took not the least notice of this change in my conduct, nor could I perceive any alteration in his carriage to me upon it.

"But Celandine, who thought me all devoted to him, was not of a humour to lose any part of the triumph of his new conquest; he assiduously watch'd every opportunity of being alone with me, return'd the pretended advances I had made him with all the ardour of a man transported with them; till at last my heart became susceptible of the guilty flame, and what I had so fatally affected grew into reality; in fine, I loved him, was too weak to resist the dictates of my passion, and became a prey to the worst monster that ever wore the shape of man."

Here Mrs. M—— became unable to proceed, she was not so entirely lost to all sense of honour and virtue as not to feel an extreme shock at the remembrance of what she was about to repeat; shame and confusion overwhelm'd her heart, and threw her into a second fainting, from which she was not without some difficulty recover'd.

Chapter XXV

Contains a continuation of Mrs. M——'s adventures.

The unfortunate Mrs. M——, having once more regain'd the power and utterance, made a handsome apology for that interruption which grief and shame had occasion'd in her recital, and then prosecuted it in the following manner:

"It may seem strange, perhaps," said she, "that with my innocence I should lose all discretion too; yet so it was, fond even to madness of my undoer, and self satisfied with my crime, I thought of nothing, regarded nothing, studied nothing, but how to gain fresh opportunities of repeating it: whenever my husband was abroad, as of late he had but too often been so, I sent over half the town in search of Celandine; if he was not found, the ill humour I was in sufficiently testified to all about me my impatience for the disappointment; and whenever he was with me, we were constantly lock'd up together, and all who came to visit were deny'd access."

"All this, as may easily be supposed, could be no secret; some of my acquaintance contented themselves with shunning my conversation; others still kept me company, but it was only to have the more opportunity of seeing and exposing my folly: I became the derision even of my own servants, as I easily have perceived by the little obedience they paid to my commands and the pert answers they gave, which were also accompanied with fleering countenances and malicious grins, whenever I went about to exert my authority over them as a mistress. Oh, how great was my infatuation! I can now, with astonish'd eyes, behold all these things distinctly; but at that time was blind to all that conduced not to the gratification of my love; or, as I then flatter'd myself, rewarding that of the man whom I consider'd as the most faithful, as well as the most charming of his sex."

Here the tears began again to flow, but she soon dry'd them up, and pursued the thread of her discourse.

"My husband, I believe," continued she, "was the last person sensible of the dishonour I had brought upon him; but he could not long escape the hearing of what, had he not been blinded by his too good opinion either of myself or Celandine, he needed not to have been told. I am apt to think however, that he gave not an entire credit to the story, for if he had he would not have taken the pains he did to be convinced.

"He left Celandine with me one day, pretending that some very extraordinary business call'd him abroad; but, instead of going out, went and conceal'd himself in a closet within our bed-chamber, into which, thinking ourselves perfectly secure, we retir'd soon after his supposed departure: we had not been there many minutes before he rush'd out, and surprised us in a manner as could admit no doubt of the crime we were guilty of; Celandine snatch'd up his sword which lay in the window, and immediately drew it, expecting he should have occasion to use it; but my husband in the same moment eased his apprehensions on that score, by saying, with a voice which had more of grief than anger in it,—'Put up, Sir, I have not forgot the obligations I have to your family, and am only sorry to find you have taken this method to acquit me of them; all I desire is, that you will leave my house directly, and that from henceforward we may be utter strangers.'—Celandine was in too much confusion to make any answer, and went away with all the speed he could.

"As for my wretched self,—fear, which one would think should rather have given wings to my feet, and made me fly the presence of an injured husband, riveted me to the bedside on which I was sitting; my blood was all congeal'd, my spirits ceas'd to operate; he upbraided my ingratitude and perfidiousness in terms which I must confess they merited; I heard all he said, but had it not in my power to make the least reply, or to excuse, or defend my crime, had it been in words to do either; but at that time I was indeed bereft of speech as well as motion. Having vented some part of his indignation in revilings, he flung out of the room, and left me in the condition I have described.

"No stupidity sure ever equalled mine; a death like numbness had seiz'd all my faculties; what little sense I had was bewildered and confused; I could not even reflect on the misfortune to which my folly had reduced me, much less contrive any means to render them more supportable.

"How long I remain'd, or how much longer I should have remain'd in this lethargy of mind I know not; but it was almost dark when I was rous'd out of it by the sudden appearance of an elderly woman, a relation of my husband's, who with a stern voice and countenance told me, that she was sent by him to take care of his family; and that I must immediately go out of the house.

"This message, and the manner in which it was deliver'd, stung me to the very soul; rage and disdain now quickened every nerve, I was all on fire, and raved against Mr. M—— in terms which would have made any one who heard me think that it was myself, not he, who was the injured person.

"To this she cooly answer'd, that it was not her business to argue with me on these points; that she had discharged her commission in signifying my husband's pleasure to me; which, since I did not think fit to comply with, he must come himself and put an end to the dispute; adding, that he was not far off, and she would send directly for him.

"All my courage again forsook me, the sight of my husband at this time was more dreadful to me than any thing I could suffer in being banish'd from him; besides, my reason now convinced me, that after so full a detection of my crime, I could not hope to live under the same roof with him; at least not till a long series of penitence and submissions should give me a title to his forgiveness; I therefore called the woman back, perceiving she was going to do as she had said, and told her, that since it was my husband's will I should depart, I would not provoke him by my disobedience.

"In speaking these words I started up, went to the drawers, put a night-mob[104] in my pocket, hurried on my capuchin, order'd a coach to be call'd, and seem'd in as much haste to be gone as my husband was to get rid of me; while I was doing this his kinswoman desired I would take the keys with me, saying, that if I sent them in the morning, she had orders to let me have everything belonging to me.

"'Very well,' reply'd I carelessly, 'I shall know in the morning what I have to do.' The coach being at the door I stept hastily into it, and made the fellow drive me to a milliner's in Covent-Garden, whose customer I had been for a considerable time.

"I chose this woman's house for an asylum in my present distress, not daring to apply to any one of my relations; nor did I think it proper as yet to trust her with the whole secret of my guilt and my misfortunes; I only told her, that I had a quarrel with my husband and had swore not to sleep with him that night; so desired she would be hospitable enough to afford me a bed, as I knew she had one to spare.

"The former part of that night I past in the most cruel agitations, but towards the latter grew somewhat more composed; the vivacity of my temper represented to me, that I was not the first woman who had liv'd in a state of separation from her husband; that the discourse of these things was soon over; that I had a lover who would always supply me with the necessaries of life; and that the loss of reputation would be attoned for by the endearments of so worthy a man: thus, alas! was my judgement misguided by my fond passion for that ungrateful wretch.

"I dispatch'd a messenger to him next morning, he came immediately, desired I would provide a handsome lodging for myself; and assured me, with a thousand protestations, that his purse and his person should always be at my devotion: notwithstanding this I wrote to my husband, excusing my transgression as well as I was able; he sent me all the things I had left behind; but return'd for answer to my letter, that he was determined never to see my face again; and that all he would do for me was to pay for my board, on condition I would retire to a farm-house an hundred and fifty miles from London, and never more come back.

"Gladly therefore I accepted of Celandine's offer,—hired an apartment, and thought myself as happy as a woman in my circumstances could be.—I was, indeed, but too well satisfied with my condition;—I wanted for nothing that I desired, and had more than I could have expected of the company of the man I priz'd above the world:—but alas! these golden days were of a short continuance,—too soon I found, by sad experience, that a lover, as well as a husband, could grow cool on a sure possession.

"I cannot, however, accuse him of being a niggard to me in his allowance for my support; but loving him to that excess I did, it was an adequate return of love which alone could make me truly blest.

"At last he talk'd of going to Bath; I testify'd an extreme desire of accompanying him; but he endeavour'd to put me off, by pretences which seem'd to me very trifling, till I insisting upon his taking me with him, he plainly told me that I must not think of it, for he was to go with persons by whom it was wholly improper I should be seen. I wept, but he was not softened by my tears, only laying ten guineas on the table bid me console myself with that till his return, and then took his leave with the same careless air as he could have done of the most slight acquaintance.

"Judge how severe a stab this must give both to my love and pride;—I saw, by the manner of his refusing, that there was something more at the bottom than he made shew of, and resolved to fathom it whatever should be the event;—accordingly, as he left London one day in a post-chaise I follow'd the next in the stage-coach."

Here the reflection on those wild lengths, to which the folly of her passion had transported her, made her again unable to proceed, and the company were obliged to give a truce to their curiosity till she recover'd herself enough to go on with her narrative, in the manner which will be seen in the succeeding chapter.

Chapter XXVI

Will gratify the readers impatience with the conclusion of Mrs. M——'s history; and also with what effects the recital of it produced in the minds of those who heard it.

The unfortunate Mrs. M—— having dried up her tears, and made the best apology she could to the ladies for this interruption, resumed her discourse in these words:

"I took up my lodgings on my arrival here," said she, "at the inn where I alighted, and sent immediately in search of Celandine;—he came the next day, but his looks, before he spoke, made me know how little he was pleased with seeing me, 'I thought Madam,' said he, 'I said enough to prevent you from coming hither; and am surprized you should act in a manner so contrary to my inclination.'

"I told him, that I found it impossible to live so long a time without him; and a great deal of such fond idle stuff, which he as little regarded as indeed it deserved;—he insisted on my return to London the next morning; which after some tears, I at last promised to do, on condition that he would dine with me that day. It was with some difficulty I prevail'd upon him to give me his company, even for the few hours I requested it;—nor would I have taken so much pains to obtain so small a favour, if I had not flatter'd myself with being able to win him yet further to my purpose.

"But my hopes deceived me,—in vain I try'd all the arts that love inspir'd me with,—he was inflexible to all my intreaties,—unmoved by my indearments, and treated all I said to him on the score of my staying here with so much contempt, that the pride and spirit which my passion for him had but too much quell'd, began to rouse themselves in me;—I told him that he had no right to prescribe the place of my residence; that Bath was equally as free for me as for himself; and that I would not leave it. On this he started up, and with a countenance full of spite—''tis very well,' said he, 'you then may stay, but I fancy you will find it extremely difficult to support yourself either here or any where else without my assistance, which you may be assured I shall never afford to one who acts in opposition to my will.'

"The consideration of my wretched circumstances made me tremble at this menace, and again reduced me to submission; I implored his pardon for the rashness of my passion, and promised I would hereafter do in every thing as he would have me; this pacified him; and sitting down again, 'I would have you,' said he, 'behave like a reasonable woman, and one who knows the world; our amour has been of a long continuance, and you cannot expect a man like me should always confine himself to one object; to deal sincerely with you, I am here on the invitation of a woman of condition, whom I have the good fortune to be well with; if you offer to interfere with my pleasures I have done with you for ever; therefore, it depends entirely on yourself to keep me your friend or not.'

"It is amazing, even to myself to think how I had the power to conceal the agonies which rent my heart at this impudent declaration; yet it is certain that I did so: I avow'd to do every thing he required of me, and to regulate my conduct henceforward so as never to offend him; he seem'd pleas'd with my assurance, put five guineas into my hand to defray the unnecessary expence, as he called it, of my coming hither, gave me a kiss, wish'd me a good journey to London, and then left me to indulge the transports of a rage the more violent for having been suppress'd.

"I did not, however, waste much time in giving way to emotions which would neither avail my love or my revenge; to think of doing what I had promised to him was far from me; I resolved to see the face that had supplanted me in his affections; how afterwards I would behave I did not then consider: this was the first great point on which my soul was fix'd; and to accomplish it went that evening and hired a lodging in the most private part of the town: the people of the house, on my signifying to them that I wanted an adroit boy, or young fellow, to run on errands and wait on me while I stay'd at Bath, were so kind to help me to one exactly fit for my purpose; he had been a waiter in a coffee-house last season when Celandine was here, and knew him perfectly well.

"The chief business I employed him in was to stand centry near the house where Celandine lodg'd, to watch him wherever he went, to find out the names and characters of the persons he visited, and to bring me an exact account.

"By the diligence of this emissary I discover'd that he visited here every day; that he constantly attended three ladies from hence to the walks—the long room—the play, and all public places; that one of these ladies he seem'd most particularly attached to; and that she was call'd Lady Speck."

Mr. Lovegrove turn'd his eyes on Lady Speck, at these words, with some surprise; she was in a good deal of confusion and cried out, "Your spy was mistaken in his intelligence in this point, his attachment was equal to us all, and I dare say was equally regarded."

"Pardon me, Madam," resumed the unfortunate historian; "I knew not then, nor am yet certain to which of you the name of Lady Speck belongs; you will not wonder, that in those moments of my jealous rage, I wish'd destruction on the charms that had undone me; but this unlucky day above all I was least able to command my passion; the boy brought me word that he had seen Celandine in the walks with two of you, whom presently he quitted and hurried to this house; on which I concluded the third lady who stay'd at home, and to whom he was in so much haste to retire, was the person who I should henceforth look on as my rival; and at that instant fired with emotions, to which reason can set no bounds, I muffled myself up as you see, ran through the streets like one broke loose from Bedlam;[105] on my coming here I found the door open, a servant-maid was doing something in the hall, and on my enquiring for Celandine she told me he had come a little before, and she believed was then in the arbour at the lower end of the garden, for she had seen him pass that way; I flew directly to the place she mention'd; but the fury I was in had so blinded me that I did not readily perceive the entrance; I heard the voice of my perfidious lover, and thrust my head through the lattice and my whole body had certainly broke through that slender partition, if those who occasion'd my despair had not that moment rush'd out of the place: at this sight distraction took possession of my brain; all hell and its worst furies were in my heart; I drew my penknife, resolved to sheath it in the villain's breast; but I know not how it was," continued she, addressing herself to Jenny, "you, Madam, were nearest to me, and the blow I meant for him, in my mistaken rage was aim'd at you: what follow'd I am wholly ignorant of; for my disappointed rage recoiling upon myself, together with the rude blow the villain gave me in wresting the penknife from my hand, stopp'd all the springs of life, till your charitable endeavours put them again in motion, and called me back to sense, to shame, to misery, and the racks[106] of thought."

Thus did Mrs. M—— conclude her tedious narrative; but did not give over speaking till she afresh intreated pardon of the company for the disturbance she had occasion'd in the family, and of Jenny in particular, who had suffer'd most through the extravagance she had been guilty of; to which that young lady, with a great deal of sweetness, tho' not without some blushes at the remembrance of Celandine's behaviour, reply'd in these terms: "I can easily forgive the fright you put me into," said she, "as I know not but it was your seasonable interruption which chiefly preserved me from a worse mischief than that which I was threaten'd with by your mistaken jealousy."

"I did not know, my dear," said Miss Wingman with a gay air, "that the inclinations of Celandine were devoted to you; or that he left us so abruptly in the walks on purpose to have the pleasure of entertaining you alone." Jenny was about to make some answer, but was prevented by Mr. Lovegrove, who hastily taking up the word, cried out, "'Tis difficult, Madam, to know the real inclinations of a man such as Celandine; for I take him to be one of those so elegantly described by Mr. Rowe in his play call'd the *Fair Penitent*:"

> A singing, dancing, worthless tribe they are,
> Who talk of beauties that they never saw,
> And boast of favours that they ne'er enjoy'd.[107]

In repeating these lines he fix'd his eyes on Lady Speck, who seeming more than ordinarily pensive, and making no answer, he went on; "The poet," resum'd he, "throughout that whole performance, shews himself very much a friend to the ladies, especially when [he] gives them this advice:"

> Were you, ye fair, but cautious whom you trust,
> Would you but think how seldom fools are just,
> So many of your sex would not in vain,
> Of faithless men and broken vows complain.
> Of all the various wretches love has made,
> How few have been by men of sense betray'd;
> Convinc'd by reason, they your power confess,
> Pleas'd to be happy as you're pleas'd to bless,
> And conscious of your worth can never love you less.[108]

Here ensued a silence, which perhaps had continued yet longer if it had not been broke by Miss Wingman, that young lady having her thoughts more at liberty than any of the rest of the company, and who indeed loved talking so well, that it was a pain to her to forbear it for any considerable time. Turning towards Mrs. M——, "I am surprised, Madam," said she, "that your unfaithful lover having the confidence to avow his guilt, by telling you that he came down to Bath on the invitation of a woman of fashion, that you had not the curiosity to ask him the name and quality of the person for whose sake you were undone; since he had so little discretion as to let you into one part of the secret, he would certainly have made you acquainted with the whole, if you had desired it."

"It must be confess'd," rejoined Jenny, "that such an enquiry would have been highly natural in Mrs. M——; and, if answer'd to her satisfaction, might have saved her the trouble of employing an emissary to watch the motions of Celandine; but for my part, I have little cause to wish it had been so; since it was to her mistaken jealousy I was indebted for the seasonable relief I received from the insolent impertinencies of that vain and unworthy coxcomb."

"It is also possible, Madam," cried Mr. Lovegrove, in an extraordinary emotion; "such an eclaircisement might have been attended with worse consequences than you think on. Who can tell," added he with still more vehemence, "but that he might have mention'd the name of some lady who wants not an admirer zealous enough to have vindicated her reputation at the expence of his own life or that of the traducer?"

"I know not," replied Mrs. M—— sighing, "what consequences may have been prevented, or what might have ensued by the discovery of my rival; but this I am certain of, that I was so shock'd at his ingratitude, so astonish'd at his assurance, and so terrified with his menaces, that I had then neither presence of mind nor courage to put the question to him."

Lady Speck, who had not spoke one syllable for a considerable time, now affected a prodigious gaity du coeur,[109] "The demand you mean," said she, "I believe would have been to very little purpose; I dare answer Celandine would have been strangely puzzled to have informed you in any particulars of the fond lady for whose sake he came to Bath; men of his romantic disposition worship images of their own formation; boast of visionary favours, and take as much pleasure in the shadow as others do in the substance."

"True, Madam," cried Mr. Lovegrove gravely; "but if they should happen to assign real names to their ideal mistresses, what but the blood of such a villain could attone for his presumption?"

No reply was made to this; and Mrs. M—— thinking it would best become her to take leave of the company, which she did in the most respectful manner, every body assured her they pity'd her misfortunes, and that they sincerely wish'd something might happen to extricate her from the labyrinth in which she was at present involv'd.

After she was gone, there soon remain'd none but Miss Wingman and Jenny to maintain a conversation; Mr. Lovegrove, a good deal disconcerted at some passages he had heard related by Mrs. M——, pretending business call'd him, went away; and Lady Speck, who was extremely out of humour, and had been at some pain to conceal it, took this opportunity of retiring to her closet, in order to compose the troubles of her mind.

End of the First Volume

The HISTORY of *Jemmy and Jenny Jessamy*

Volume II

Contents to the Second Volume

The

HISTORY

of

Jemmy and Jenny Jessamy

Chapter I

Discovers something which may serve to prove, that though love is the original source from which jealousy is derived, yet the latter of these passions is the most difficult of the two to be conceal'd, and also less under the government of reason.

There are so many secret windings, such obscure recesses in the human mind, that it is very difficult, if not wholly impossible, for speculation to arrive at the real spring or first mover of any action whatsoever.

How indeed should it be otherwise, as the most virtuous and the most vicious propensities of nature are frequently in a more or less degree lodged and blended together in the same composition, and both equally under the influence of a thousand different passions, which disguise and vary the face of their operations, so as not to be distinguish'd even by the persons themselves.

It has already been observ'd, that there were some peculiarities in the humour and conduct of Lady Speck, which she had policy and prudence enough to conceal entirely from the world; and though not the most intimate of her acquaintance, nor even her sister, could ever penetrate into the secret motives of a behaviour, which to them seem'd frequently pretty strange, it is fit the reader should not be deny'd that satisfaction, at least as far as the above-mentioned premises will admit.

As her ladyship had found very little happiness in marriage, she had been too much rejoiced at being released from that bondage by the death of her husband, ever to think of entering into the same state a second time; but having observ'd that this was commonly the profession of all widows, and as commonly ridiculed by those who heard it, she forbore making any mention of her resolution in this point.

She had very little vanity in her composition, but loved a variety of company;—she was pleas'd to find herself continually surrounded by a crowd of gentlemen; but had been equally, if not more so, if they had visited her on any other score than that of courtship: she behaved to each of them so much alike, that jealousy was a thing unknown among these rivals; and as none of them had any great cause to hope, so likewise none of them thought he had cause to despair of being one day the happy man; and her youth,—her beauty,—her wit,—her fortune, made her appear too valuable a prize not to persevere in the pursuit of.

Thus easy, thus happy in herself, and delightful to all that saw her, did she live and reign the general toast and admiration of the town; when Celandine arriv'd from his travels, full fraught with all those superficial accomplishments so enchanting to the unthinking part of the fair sex.

What attracts the eye is too apt to have an influence over the heart;—his agreeable person,—his gaudy equipage, and the shew he made, dazzled the senses of even those who most affected to be thought wits;—he was the theme of every tea-table, and the chief object for whom the arts of the toylet[2] were employ'd.

Lady Speck had heard much of him before she saw him, but he was soon introduced to her acquaintance by a lady who frequently visited her, and had always spoke wonders in his praise; whether it were that she was prepossess'd by the good opinion she found others had of him, or whether it was to himself alone he was indebted for the impression he made on her is uncertain; but nothing can be more true, than that at first sight she felt for him what she had never done for any man after whole years of assiduity.

It is also altogether as impossible to determine if it was by any kind looks he perceived in her towards him, or by the great confidence he had in his own merits, that he was emboldened to declare himself her lover; it was, however, either to the one or the other that she owed the triumph of this new conquest, and he had not made her many visits before she was confirm'd of it by the most violent protestations that tongue could utter.

It seem'd, notwithstanding, extremely strange to her, that amidst all the testimonies he endeavour'd to give her of his love, he never once mention'd marriage; but, on the contrary, would frequently in her presence ridicule the institution,—say it was a clog upon inclinations, and only fit to link two people together who had no notion of the true joys of love, or of living politely in the world.

He often had the impudence even to repeat to her, in justification of his prophane position, all the lines he could remember from any of the poets who had exercised their talents in satirising that sacred ceremony; particularly these of Mr. Dryden:

Marriage, thou curse of love, and snare of life!
That first debas'd a mistress to a wife!
Love, like a scene, at distance should appear,
But marriage views the gross-daub'd landscape near.
Love's nauseous cure! thou cloy'st whom thou should'st please,
And when that's cur'd, then thou art the disease;
When hearts are loose, thy chain our bodies ties;
Love couples friends, but marriage enemies.[3]

But his behaviour on this score gave her not the least disgust towards him;—she was herself an enemy to marriage;—and besides his estate, though large, was not an equivalent for that she was in possession of; nor was any part of his character such as she thought becoming a man whom she would make a husband of;—she nevertheless loved him, nor took any pains to repel the kindness which every day grew stronger for him in her heart;—she was amused with his conversation, delighted with his addresses, look'd on him as a pretty plaything,—a charming toy which it would be doing too great a violence to her humour to throw away.

All this will doubtless give the reader no very favourable idea of her virtue; but we will suppose it was only a platonic liking she had for him:—how far indeed, the dangerous liberties she allow'd herself to take with him might have carried her, if they had been continued much longer, no one can pretend to say.

She was not, however, so much lost in the tender folly she indulg'd, as not to be perfectly sensible that the manner in which she conversed with Celandine could not, if known to the world, but occasion a great deal of discourse, little to the advantage of her reputation; and that it behoved her, above all things, to keep this secret of her soul from taking air:—to do this, she put in practice all the arts that a just fear of censure could inspire her with.—When Celandine was present with other company she affected to rally, and turn into bagatelle[4] every thing he said or did; and when he was absent, to ridicule those vanities and fopperies which she had understanding enough to see in him, though not in reality to condemn him for.—She not only treated those gentlemen, who before made their addresses to her, with a greater shew of favour than she had been accustomed to do; but also encouraged every new offer of that kind that was presented to her; and this conduct proved effectual for the purpose she intended it, that no one person suspected Celandine was among the number of her lovers, much less that he was the darling favourite of her bosom.

Being in this situation, it is easy to conceive what racks of mind she must sustain on the account that had been just given by Mrs. M——;—to be told that Celandine had an amour, and to hear it averr'd by the very woman who had been her rival, was a mere trifle in comparison with what follow'd;—that he was found in the close arbour with Jenny was the thing that stung her to the quick, when she remember'd that Celandine had met herself and sister in the walks, and how instead of squireing them as usual, he had only made a slight compliment and abruptly left them; and that Jenny had excused herself from going out on account of some letters she said she had to write, it appear'd plainly to her, that he went not from the walks but with a design of going to Jenny;—that she stay'd not at home but in expectation of his coming, and the appointment was previously agreed upon between them.

Most women have naturally so good an opinion of themselves, as not to believe easily that the man who has once lov'd them can transfer his affections to another, without some very extraordinary arts put in practice for that purpose by the new object.—Lady Speck thought herself as handsome as Jenny, and therefore concluded that the amorous inclination which Celandine had all at once testified for that young lady, could be owing to nothing but some advances made to him on her part.

How unjust and how cruel a passion is that of jealousy!—It destroys all the nobler principles of the soul,—it eraces thence all the ideas of virtue, religion, and morality; it makes us not only condemn the innocent, and acquit the guilty, but also inspires us with the most savage and inhuman sentiments.—Lady Speck now hated her fair friend more than ever she had loved her;—her beauty,—her wit,—all those accomplishments which had excited her esteem, render'd her now the object of her aversion;—she was almost tempted to wish Mrs. M—— had perpetrated her outrageous design, if not to the destruction of her life, yet, to the defacing of those charms which had triumph'd over her in the heart of Celandine;

and was little less angry with him for having prevented the fatal blow aimed against her rival, than she was for his falshood to herself.

Of all the various agitations which by turns convulse and rend the human heart, there are none which instigate to more pernicious purposes, or bring on, if continued, more disastrous consequences; but the flame, however violent it may flash for the present, can have no long existence in a mind not wholly divested of all good nature and generosity;—cooler and more reasonable sentiments, on a little reflection, soon abated the force of those turbulent emotions which had taken possession of this lady's bosom; but as yet were not powerful enough to suppress them entirely; what effects follow'd, either of the one or the other, will hereafter appear,—but the conflict between them was for this time interrupted, by some company coming in, whom Lady Speck was oblig'd to go down to receive, as they were more her guests than her sister's, and altogether strangers to Jenny.

Chapter II

Contains a farther confirmation of the position advanc'd in the preceding chapter, and also some other particulars exciting the curiosity of the reader.

Lady Speck assumed a countenance as serene as possible to entertain, with her usual politeness, the persons who came to visit her; but in spite of all her endeavours to appear entirely easy, she could not keep herself from darting such ill-natur'd glances on Jenny, whenever she look'd towards her, as must have been taken notice of by that young lady, if she had not been too much engross'd by her own thoughts to be capable of penetrating into those of another.

The company stay'd so late, that the instant they were gone the ladies retir'd to their respective chambers; Jenny, who had her mind no less employed than Lady Speck, with the adventures of the day, was equally pleased to be alone and indulge meditation on what had pass'd.

The history of Mrs. M—— had dwelt very much upon her mind; but what made the most deep impression, was that part of it wherein she related the first motive which occasion'd her fall at once from happiness and from virtue, and consequently drew on her all those dreadful misfortunes with which at present she was encompass'd.

I believe the reader will easily remember, as the thing is of a pretty particular nature, how that unhappy woman in order to revive those ardors of affection in her husband, which she imagin'd were beginning to decay, had recourse to the dangerous stratagem of giving him a rival; and also how by coquetting with Celandine, and treating him with a shew of liking, the counterfeited flame kindled by degrees into a real one, and ended at length in her utter ruin and confusion.

The notions Jenny had of honour and generosity were too refin'd and delicate, not to make her look with the utmost contempt on all kinds of artifice, on what pretences soever they were put in practice:—this conduct of Mrs. M——'s, though considering what ensued, the least guilty part of her character, seem'd to her so highly criminal, as well as weak and mean, that she could not help thinking it worthy of all the punishments it met with.

"'How is it possible," cried she within herself, "that a woman who truly loves virtue can be capable of putting on an appearance so much the reverse of it? What if at that time she had no intentions of gratifying the amorous inclinations of the man she sported with, to encourage them in him was a manifest violation, not only of modesty but likewise of religion, honour, and those solemn obligations she had enter'd into."

"Besides," continued she, "this wretched creature seems not to want sense enough to know the heinousness of the fault she was guilty of, even in this first step to perdition;—yet she run boldly into it, and absolv'd herself on account of the good end she propos'd by it,—to regain the affections of her husband:—Oh! how ridiculous was such an attempt for doing so; as if any man of common reason would love his wife the better for suspecting she was about to commit the worst and most shameful action a woman can be guilty of!"

"I have seen some young ladies," went she still on, "that have made use of these little tricks to inspire jealousy in their lovers; either to make trial of their constancy, or shew their own power by giving pain; this is certainly silly as well as cruel; but what is no more than vanity and folly in them, is downright wickedness in a married woman."

Thus did she pass some time in censuring the conduct of Mrs. M——; but as she was of that happy turn of mind, to convert every thing which she either saw or heard of to her own advantage, and to make fresh improvements in herself by the misbehaviours of others, her reflections carried her yet farther, and remembrance presented her with an incident which happen'd long before she had the power of judging, but which she had heard much discourse of in her extreme youth,—it was this:

A person of great distinction happen'd to be married to a lady very young and beautiful; she was a celebrated wit without being wise, and had the most romantick turn of mind;—fancying herself a Statyra,[5] she expected her husband should approach her with the obsequiousness of an Oroondates;[6]—he was little versed in histories of this nature; and though he loved her very well, treated her as mere woman;—the epithets of angel and goddess were strangers to his mouth; and those he usually saluted her with were plain Madam, or my dear;—this disgusted her even in the first days of their marriage,—she look'd on such a behaviour as an indignity to her charms;—her heart reproach'd the indelicacy of his manners, and half despised him for his want of taste; nor did her tongue restrain itself from testifying how much she was disatisfy'd at every thing he said or did.

The fashion in which he found himself used by her gave him some disquiet at first, but it lasted not long;—though a man of sense, he was naturally indolent to an excess;—he loved his ease too well to part with it on any consideration whatever;—he never thought any thing worth attempting the pursuit of, which was likely to be attended with difficulty;—and as he had never taken the pains to examine what it was that his wife expected from him, so he would have been equally negligent in gratifying her humour, if he had been better acquainted with it.

Their way of living together grew every day still worse and worse; as her haughty sullenness increased, his carelessness of it increased in proportion;—all the love they once had for each other turn'd into a mutual indifference, or rather a mutual aversion;—she sought the food for her vanity among those who were of a disposition to indulge it; and she found not a few to whom the glory of pleasing a lady of her beauty, birth, and accomplishments did not seem well worth all the flatteries they could address her with; the husband, in the mean time, made himself not wretched on account of the gallantries she received, but fled for consolation to the arms of a more obliging and endearing fair.

They continued to live together, however, in the same house; but slept not in the same bed, nor eat at the same table, except for decency sake, when company was there; before whom they always behaved to each other with the greatest good manners and politeness imaginable.

But this was a constraint which neither of them could long support,—they parted by consent;—after which her amours became the general topic of conversation; till shunned by all her kindred, despised by her acquaintance, and slighted by those for whose sake she had sacrificed her reputation, she became sensible of her follies, and sought a reconciliation with her husband; but all her endeavours for that purpose being in vain, she hated a place where she no longer had either friends or admirers, and went a voluntary exile into foreign parts, where grief and remorse soon put an end to her life.

This incident threw Jenny into the most serious contemplations on the human system;—the many observations she had made, convinc'd her that vanity was in a more or less degree inherent to the whole species; and that men as well as women were not exempt from it: and immediately recollecting some passages she had seen which demonstrated this truth, "Good God," cried she, "how can any one be so fond of this idol frame, this poor machine, liable to be wither'd by every inclement blast that issues from the firmament! Let the proud of heart read Gulliver's Voyages to the Houghims,[7] and some other pieces of the same excellent author, and they will see and be ashamed to admire a body which requires such means to be sustain'd."—"No," continu'd she, "it is the mind which ought to be the chief object of our attention; it is there alone we are either beautiful or deform'd; and the pains we take to ornament and embellish that nobler part of us will not be thrown away."

She was so taken up with these philosophic reflections, that she went not to bed till the beams of Aurora[8] darting through the window curtains, reminded her how much she had lost of the time commonly alotted for repose.

It was somewhat more late than ordinary when she rose the next morning;—on her coming down stairs she found the ladies already in the room where they always breakfasted; and guessing, by some circumstances, that she had made them wait, was beginning to apologize for tardiness.

"Indeed, my dear," cried Miss Wingman interrupting her, "we were afraid you were not well, and were just going to send to your chamber:— But pray," continued she very gaily, "let me examine your countenance, and see if that will tell me whether you are quite got over the fright that terrible woman put you into yesterday."

Jenny was about to make some answer; but Lady Speck, who could not forgive her for the part she bore in that adventure, took up the word before the other had time to open her mouth, "The fright was of little consequence," said she with an air which had something of derision in it, "as she was deliver'd from the danger before she could have any apprehensions of it;—but, there were other particulars that happen'd afterwards, which perhaps were of a yet more disagreeable nature, and might make a deeper impression."

These words, and the tone in which they were spoke, gave Jenny an infinity of surprise, but without pausing to form any conjecture on the matter, "You will pardon me, Madam," cried she innocently, "if I am not able to comprehend your ladyship's meaning;—I know of no accident that happen'd afterwards; or indeed, in which I had the least concern."

"How weak is it," reply'd Lady Speck, "in people to endeavour to conceal a passion, which in spite of all they can do will break out in every look and gesture! I pity you from my soul, and had I sooner known the situation of your heart, would have contriv'd some way or other to have prevented Mrs. M—— from being quite so open in her narrative;—it must certainly be a very great shock to you to hear some passages she related;—but, alas, I was intirely ignorant that Celandine loved you, or that you loved Celandine; and little suspected that it was for his sake you so resolutely rejected the offers of Sir Robert Manley."

"I should be sorry, Madam," reply'd Jenny very disdainfully, "that your ladyship, or any one else, should have so contemptible an opinion of my judgement.—I know but little of the gentlemen, yet know enough to make a just distinction between them; and were my hand and heart at my disposal should not hesitate one moment to which of them I should give the preference."

"How cunning now you think you are," said Lady Speck with an affected laugh,—"you speak the truth but avoid mentioning the name: I will however do it for you, and answer in somewhat like the poet's words":

> 'Tis Celandine your heart would leap to meet,
> While Manley lay expiring at your feet.[9]

Scarce had Jenny the power to restrain her passion within the bounds of decency, on finding Lady Speck persisted in so injurious an accusation;—scorn and anger overwhelm'd her soul,—tears gush'd from her eyes,—and rising hastily from her seat, "I will not imagine, Madam," said she, "that you are really in earnest in supposing such a thing; but the jest is of such a nature as I do not think it becomes me to hear the continuance of."

In speaking these words she was about to quit the room; but Miss Wingman, who had been a good deal astonish'd at what her sister had said, ran and pulled her back;—but all her persuasions would have been ineffectual to have detain'd her, if Lady Speck, having vented her ill humour; and now repenting she had gone so far, had not added her intreaties.

"My dear creature," cried she, "I had not the least design to affront you; I only meant to rally you a little on your staying at home, when so fine a day called every body to the walks."—"I should have deserved it, Madam," answer'd she, "if I had deny'd myself the pleasure of attending your ladyship on any other motive than what I really did;—but I assure you I wrote no less than five letters, as your own man can witness, whom, my own being out of the way, I took the liberty to send with them to the post-office."

"I believe it," said Lady Speck, "I believe it, and heartily ask your pardon."—She was going to add something more by way of reparation for the vexation she had given to that young lady, when she was prevented by her woman, who having been sent to a milliner's for some things she wanted, came running into the room with a countenance as confus'd and wild as if she had met some spectre or apparition in her way:

"Oh Madam!" cried she to her lady, "I have the strangest thing to tell you,—the oddest accident;—to be sure I was never so much surprised in all my life." "Prithee at what?" demanded Lady Speck.—"Lord, Madam," return'd she, "I could not have thought such a thing of two such civil well behaved gentlemen."—"What gentlemen?" said Lady Speck, "Explain the mystery at once, and do not keep us in suspence by your unseasonable exclamations."

"Lord, Madam," replied she, "your ladyship will wonder when you know as well as I;—for my part I was so confounded that I scarce know which way I got home.—Just as I was stepping into the milliner's,—bless me, I shall never forget it; but I will tell your ladyship as fast as I can:—Just as I was going into the shop, as I was saying, I heard a great noise in the street, and the sound of several men's voices crying out,—'Bring them along,—bring them along,'—I turn'd about, as any one would do,—out of mere curiosity,—and,—would your ladyship believe it possible?—who should I see but Mr. Lovegrove and Mr. Celandine in the hands of I know not how many rough fellows, and followed by a huge croud of all sorts of people.—I fancy they had been fighting, for both their swords were drawn and carried by one of the men that had hold of Mr. Lovegrove; I cannot directly say how that matter was; but there was a strange confused noise among the mob;—one cried it was a sad thing such broils should happen;—and another that it would be a great prejudice to the town:—and all I could hear distinctly was, that they were going to carry the gentlemen before a justice of peace."

All the ladies were very much concern'd at hearing this intelligence; but Lady Speck seem'd the most affected with it; nor did the others at all wonder at her being so, as Mr. Lovegrove was her declared admirer, and was allow'd by all that knew him to deserve more of her favour than he had as yet experienced.

They were all extremely impatient to know both the occasion and the consequence of this affair; and Lady Speck's woman either having not enquir'd, or not been able to learn to what magistrate the gentlemen were carried, footmen were immediatly dispatch'd to every quarter of the town, in hopes of bringing home that information, which the reader shall presently be made acquainted with.

CHAPTER III

Compleats the character of a modern fine gentleman, or a pretty fellow for the ladies.

I believe there are none into whose hands these volumes shall happen to fall, at least if they consider the story of Mrs. M—— with any attention, but will easily perceive there was enough in it to give a very great alarm to a man so much enamour'd as Mr. Lovegrove.

He had observed, that for some time before, as well as since their coming down to Bath, Celandine had been a constant dangler after Lady Speck.—Love and jealousy are quick-sighted passions;—he thought also, that though she ridiculed and laugh'd at his assiduities, she was not so much displeased with them as she ought to have been.

This had frequently given him some uneasy apprehensions; but as there were several other gentlemen of worth and honour who made their addresses to Lady Speck, as well as himself; and she had never given him any assurance of distinguishing him above his competitors, he thought it would be too presuming in him to call her ladyship's conduct in question; especially in regard to a man who did not publickly profess himself her lover, and whose person, character, and behaviour she always affected to despise.

But now to be told, that he had impudently boasted his coming down to Bath was on the invitation of a woman of quality, from whom he gave some hints of having received very extraordinary favours; and to find that the person to whom he said this had any reason to guess the woman of quality he mention'd was no other than Lady Speck, was such a shocking corroboration of his former suspicions as fired him with the extremest rage.

Whether Lady Speck had in reality granted any favours to Celandine, or whether it was his own idle vanity alone, which had made him talk in the manner he had done, this generous lover thought it would become him to chastise the insolence of such a braggadocia;[10] but in what manner he should do so very much perplex'd him: to send him a challenge on this account he feared would make too great a noise, and consequently displease the lady whose honour he meant to defend.—After much debating within himself, an expedient came into his mind, which he immediately put in execution.

He found, by what he had heard Jenny say to Mrs. M——, that Celandine had taken the liberty to treat that young lady in a manner very unworthy of her character;—this seem'd to him a good pretence for covering the face of his design; and therefore resolv'd to make her quarrel appear as the chief motive of his resentment, touching only obliquely on that he had conceiv'd against him in regard of Lady Speck.

Having well consider'd on all the consequences that might probably attend the step he was about to take, and fully determin'd with himself to pursue it, he wrote to Celandine that same evening in the following terms:

To R. Celandine, Esq;

Sir,
You have affronted a young lady of distinguish'd merit, at present under the protection of the woman I adore; and, it is said, have given room for suspicion of your having also entertain'd thoughts of herself altogether unbecoming of you;—I think it therefore a duty incumbent on me to demand that satisfaction which every gentleman has a right to expect, when injured in the persons of those he professes to esteem.—I shall be glad to see you to-morrow morning about six, in the first field at the end of the walks, where I flatter myself you will not long suffer yourself to be waited for, by

Yours,
E. Lovegrove.

P.S. I shall come alone, for I see no need that any friends, either of yours or mine, should be involv'd in this dispute.

This billet he sent by one of his servants; who, after staying a considerable time, return'd with an answer containing these lines:

To E. Lovegrove, Esq;

Sir,

I am sorry you should desire any thing of me which suits not my humour to comply with;—Lady Speck and Miss Jessamy are both of them very fine women; but upon my soul I think neither of them, or any other woman, worth drawing my sword for;—so must desire you will excuse my refusing to meet you on this score; on any other you may command

Yours,

R. Celandine.

It would be difficult to decide, whether anger or contempt was the most predominant passion in the mind of Mr. Lovegrove on reading the above:—he resolved, however, not to suffer the insolence of that bad man to go unpunish'd, but went very early the next morning to his lodgings, in order either to force from him the satisfaction he required: or still persisting to refuse it, to give him such treatment as men are ordinarily accustom'd to receive after behaving in the manner he had done.

As he was going towards the house he perceived, while at some distance, a post-chaise waiting at the door; and before he could well reach it, saw Celandine just ready to step in;—on this he sprung forward with all the speed he could, and catching Celandine by the arm,—"Stay, Sir," cried he, "you must not think to leave this town without making some atonement for your behaviour in it."

"Sir," replied the other, with some hesitation in his voice,—"I give an account of my actions to no man,—nor has any man a right to inspect into them."—"Every man of honour has a right to inspect into the actions of a villain," rejoin'd Mr. Lovegrove fiercely, "and if you are guilty of such as you have neither the justice to acknowledge, nor the courage to defend, you know the recompence you are to expect."

"I dare fight," said Celandine, and immediately drew his sword, as did Mr. Lovegrove his at the same time; but both were prevented by a great possee[11] of people, who in an instant were gather'd about them, drawn thither by the outcries of Celandine's servants, the postilion,[12] and the people of the house who were come to the door to take leave of their lodger; and it was the expectation of this seasonable interruption, which doubtless inspired the antagonist of Mr. Lovegrove with so much boldness on a sudden.

They had scarce time to make one push before they were disarm'd by the populace; and a constable, who lived hard by, coming to interpose his authority to put an end to the fray, took possession of both their swords, and told them they must give him leave to conduct them to a magistrate;—they readily submitted, and were follow'd by a continually increasing crowd, as Lady Speck's woman had described.

They soon arrived at the house of a gentleman in commission of the peace, who happen'd to be a person of great worth and honour.—Celandine exhibited a most pitious complaint against his adversary;—first, for sending him a challenge to fight on account of things which he said he knew nothing of; and afterwards for assaulting him in the streets, putting a stop to his journey, and occasioning a riot and disturbance in the town.—Mr. Lovegrove was entirely silent till the other had left off speaking, and then related the whole which had pass'd between them naturally as it was.—The magistrate could scarce forbear smiling, but desired to see both the letters; on which Celandine produced the challenge; but Mr. Lovegrove, being unwilling to expose the names of the ladies, which the other had indiscreetly mention'd in his answer, said he had it not about him, and believ'd he had lost it.

After having heard both parties, the worshipful gentleman began to expatiate, in terms befitting his character, on the bad custom of duelling;—he said, that though the too frequent practice of it had render'd it not dishonourable, yet it was directly contrary to the rules both of religion and morality, and to the laws of society as well as those of the land;—after which he recommended to them, and even exacted their mutual promise, to regard each other from that time forward, not as enemies, if they could not do so as friends.

"I will not take his word, Sir," cried Celandine hastily,—"I am convinced he has malice against me in his heart; I go in danger of my life by him, and desire I may be admitted to make oath of it, and that he may be bound over."—This could not be refused, and the book was immediately presented to him.[13]

"Are you, Sir, of the same way of thinking too," said the justice to Mr. Lovegrove.—"No, upon my honour, Sir," reply'd he; "I am not under the least apprehensions on the score of this gentleman; and dare answer for him, that if there were as little danger in his tongue as there is to be fear'd from his sword, he would be the most unhurtful creature breathing."

It was with difficulty the justice restrain'd himself from laughing; but preserving as much an air of gravity as he could on the occasion—"Well then, Sir," said he, "I am compell'd, by the duties of my office, to discharge your adversary, and oblige you to give security for your future behaviour towards him."

On this Celandine thank'd him, and took his leave;—several of the croud, who had burst into the hall, follow'd him with a thousand scurril jests and fleers at his cowardice; but he was too much a man of peace to take any notice of what they said; and making what haste he could to the chaise, which still waited for him, set out for London, probably wishing he had not left it to come down to Bath.

Mr. Lovegrove sent for Lord Huntley and Sir Robert Manley, who immediately came, and all the little formalities of this affair being over, and settled to the satisfaction of the gentleman before whom they were, he threw off the magistrate and assum'd a character more natural to him,—that of a man perfectly well bred and complaisant,—was very pleasant with them on the conduct of Celandine,—compell'd them to stay breakfast with him, and entertain'd them as elegantly as such a repast would admit.

Chapter IV

Relates some passages subsequent to the preceding adventure.

After the gentlemen had quitted the justice's house, each repair'd to his respective lodging, in order to dress for the remainder of the day; but meeting again at the coffee-house, it was agreed to adjourn from thence to make a morning visit to Lady Speck and her fair companions, without mentioning a word of what had happen'd; Mr. Lovegrove being desirous that the whole affair should be kept a secret from them, unless chance should by any way make a discovery of it to them.

Those ladies were all this while in a good deal of uneasiness;—the servants who had been sent out for intelligence were all return'd without being able to bring any thing material for the satisfaction of their curiosity;—Miss Wingman and Jenny had both of them a very great regard for Mr. Lovegrove, the one as having known him a considerable time, and the other as having perceived in him many indications of his being a man truly worthy of esteem.

But Lady Speck had her own reasons for being much more perplex'd than either of them could be;—she had an high esteem for Mr. Lovegrove on account of the amiable qualifications he was possess'd of, and the long and respectful court he had made to her;—the caprice of her destiny had made her find something in the person of Celandine which had attracted but too much of the more tender inclinations of her heart; and to think that any danger threatened either of those gentlemen was an extreme trouble to her.

But what touch'd her yet the more deeply, was the concern she had for her own reputation;—she doubted not but that the quarrel between them was on her score; nor indeed could she well assign any other probable motive for it; especially when she reflected that Mr. Lovegrove, on hearing Mrs. M—— say that Celandine had come to Bath on the invitation of a woman of quality, had given her not only some looks but also several hints, that he entertain'd the most jealous apprehensions that herself was the woman of quality whose favours that fop had so impudently boasted of;—she had good reason therefore to be fearful, that an affair of this nature might occasion her name to be brought in question, and perhaps too, not in the most honourable fashion.

Suspence is a kind of magnifying glass, which represents whatever ill we dread in its most formidable shape;—this poor lady figur'd to herself a thousand distracting images; and though she spoke but little, gave such visible demonstrations of her inward disorders, as could not but be taken notice of, both by Jenny and Miss Wingman.

As neither of these young ladies as yet had ever harbour'd the least suspicion of her having a particular regard for any man, much less of the sentiments that Celandine had inspired her with, they imagined they had now made a discovery; but it was in favour of Mr. Lovegrove, and both of them cried out almost at the same time.—"How happy would Mr. Lovegrove think himself, if he saw how your ladyship is disquieted on his account."

Though Lady Speck affected to be a little peevish at their seeming to suppose her capable of having a tenderness for any man; yet she felt as much satisfaction as the present situation of her mind would admit her to enjoy, in finding they mark'd out Mr. Lovegrove as the object, and that Celandine was quite out of the question with them on that account.

"Indeed, sister," said Miss Wingman, "it has been always my opinion, and I believe all your friends are of the same, that the person of Mr. Lovegrove, his accomplishments, his fortune, and long services, render him not unworthy of your acceptance; and I think you need neither be angry nor ashamed that this accident has discover'd your sensibility of his passion."

"Lord, my dear, how very silly you are," said Lady Speck;—no one man has any charms for me above another;—I am only vex'd that men should fall out,—fight,—and kill one another;—and all this too for nothing, perhaps, or what is next to nothing—some idle punctilio[14] of imaginary honour."

Just as she had ended these words the door was suddenly thrown open by a footman, and Lord Huntley, Sir Robert Manley, and Mr. Lovegrove, came altogether into the room.—"What, ladies," cried the latter of these gentlemen, with an air more than ordinarily gay,—"not yet dress'd?—We came to attend you to the walks, and you are still in your deshabillee."

"We must have been strangely insensible," replied Lady Speck, "to have thought of dress when we were told that two of our acquaintance were going to imbrue their hands in each other's blood."

"Our hands are all clean, I think, Madam," said Mr. Lovegrove;—"But can you add," rejoin'd she hastily, "that your heart is also so?—Can you say you did not rise this morning with an intention to destroy, or be destroyed yourself?"

Here Mr. Lovegrove appearing a little confused, as debating within himself whether it was most proper for him to confess or to deny the fact, Lord Huntley immediately took up the word;—"No, faith, Madam," said his lordship with a smile, "I dare answer so far for my friend, that he arose not this morning with the least animosity to any thing worthy of his sword."

"No ambiguities, good my lord," resumed she;—"I expect a plain answer to my question;—therefore tell me at once, Mr. Lovegrove, how happened your quarrel with Celandine, and which of you was the aggressor?—You find," continued she, perceiving he was still silent, "that we are no strangers to the main point; and consequently have a right to expect you should gratify our curiosity with the particulars."

"It never has been my practice yet, Madam," reply'd Mr. Lovegrove, after a little pause, "to disobey your ladyship in any thing, nor must I now do it in this;—you command me to tell you the motive of my quarrel with Celandine, and I must answer it was on the score of justice and of virtue.—You also ask who was the aggressor; to which I must also answer, that it was Celandine, who by affronting a person lov'd and esteem'd by you, justly merited chastisement, not only from me but from all who have the honour of being acquainted with your ladyship."

"So then," said Jenny, "I find that all this bustle is to be placed on my account;—but I would not have you imagine, Mr. Lovegrove," continued she laughing, "that you are entitled to any acknowledgments from me, since I am indebted for what you have done entirely to the friendship I am honoured with by Lady Speck."

Mr. Lovegrove was about to make some reply, but was prevented by Sir Robert Manley, who, approaching her with the most respectful air,—"Madam," said he, "if others had been as early acquainted with the presumption of Celandine, the glory of being your champion would certainly not have fallen to the lot of Mr. Lovegrove."

"I am glad then," return'd Jenny, "that it happen'd as it did; because otherwise I should have been laid under an obligation which it was not in my power to requite."—"It is of no importance, my dear," interrupted Lady Speck, "either who is the obliger or the obliged;—I only want to be fully informed in the particulars of this foolish transaction."

On this Mr. Lovegrove repeated all that pass'd between himself and Celandine, till their being carried before a magistrate; and would have gone through the whole, but Lord Huntley and Sir Robert Manley assisted him in the rest, and gave so pleasant a detail of Celandine's behaviour on that occasion as was highly diverting to the ladies.

But though Lady Speck laugh'd as well as her sister and Jenny, and affected to appear equally unconcern'd at what she heard; yet there still remain'd something on her spirits which she could not forbear testifying in these or the like terms:

The little narrative being concluded,—"I am very glad," said she, "that no worse consequences attended this adventure;—yet I cannot help being a little concern'd, that any thing should happen to occasion my name, or that of Miss Jessamy, to be mentioned before a magistrate, and such a mob of people as generally croud in to be witnesses of the decision he gives in cases of this nature."

"No, Madam," reply'd Mr. Lovegrove hastily,—"I do assure your ladyship that neither of you have any cause to be in pain on that score;—your names were held too sacred to be quoted as the subjects of a quarrel; and it was for this reason I refused to produce Celandine's answer to the billet I sent him,—he having imprudently, I might say impudently too, inserted them in that scrawl."

"How," cried Lady Speck with the utmost impatience in her voice and eyes,—"let us see on what pretence the creature presumed to take that liberty?"

Though it is more than probable that Mr. Lovegrove was far from being displeased at having this opportunity of convincing Lady Speck in what manner she had been spoken of by Celandine, yet he suffer'd her to repeat her demand several times over before he comply'd with it; and at last seem'd to do so with an extreme reluctance."

"I intended, Madam," said he, "that no eyes but my own should have been witnesses of the unparallel'd audacity it contains;—but as your ladyship commands I should deliver it to you, I neither can not dare be disobedient."

With these words he took the letter he had received from Celandine out of his pocket and presented it to her,—adding, at the same time,— "This, Madam, however will serve to prove, that besides the first motive of my resentment to him he subjoin'd another, not less deserving the punishment I design'd."

Her ladyship snatch'd it out of his hand with emotions which it was not in her power to conceal; but having slightly look'd it over to herself grew a good deal more compos'd; and forcing her countenance into a half smile,—"I doubt not," said she,—"but what Mr. Lovegrove had said of this billet has raised a curiosity in you all for the contents;—I will therefore read it aloud for the advantage of the company."

"Well, ladies,"—cried Lord Huntley as soon as she had done,— "though you have not the good fortune to have your merits peculiarly distinguish'd by this fine gentleman, you ought not to fall under too great humiliation, for you find he includes your whole sex; and plainly avows he looks upon no woman worthy venturing the tremendous discomposure of his well-tied sword knot."[15]

Here follow'd much merriment among them, which had perhaps continued longer, as they were all persons of wit, and had so ample a field for ridicule; but it was now almost noon, and the ladies were not yet dress'd, for which reason the gentlemen thought proper to withdraw, and leave them to consult their glasses on those charms that Celandine had affected to despise.

Jenny and Miss Wingman thought little of this adventure afterwards; but it made a very deep impression on the mind of Lady Speck;— the delicacy Mr. Lovegrove had shewn in laying the stress of his resentment on the affront Celandine had offer'd to her friend, and not on the jealousy which she plainly saw he had conceived of herself, open'd her eyes to those merits in him to which her partial inclination for the other had made her so long blind; and she now beheld both the men such as they truly were, and not such as her unjudging fancy had lately painted them.

Ashamed of her past folly she had no consolation but in the care she had always taken to conceal it from the world:—as for Mr. Lovegrove, whose good opinion she was now most concern'd to preserve, she resolved to behave towards him for the future in such a manner as should intirely dissipate whatever suspicions he might have entertain'd to her prejudice.

It was undoubtedly the good genius, or better angel of this lady, which had brought about, however fortuitous they might seem, such a happy concurrence of events as could not fail of awakening in her a just sense of what she owed to her character, and that esteem she was naturally so ambitious of maintaining.

What advantages she received from this change of humour, and the emanations she was at present enlightened with, will hereafter be demonstrated;—in the mean time there are things of a yet more interesting nature which demand the attention of the reader.

Chapter V

Contains, among other things, an account of a very extraordinary, and no less severe trial of female fortitude and moderation.

According to all the observations which reason and a long experience has enabled me to make, happiness is a thing which ought to be totally erased out of the vocabulary of sublunary enjoyments;—the human heart is liable to so many passions, and the events of fortune so uncertain and precarious, that life is little more than a continued series of anxieties and suspence:—what we pursue as the ultimate of our desires, the summum bonum[16] of all our wishes, fleets before us, dances in the wind, seems at sometimes ready to meet our grasp, at others soaring quite out of reach; or, when attain'd, deceives our expectations, baffles our high-raised hopes, and shews the fancy'd heaven a mere vapour.

Nor is this to be wondered at, or indeed much to be pitied in those who place their happiness in the gratification of their passions, which all of them in general tend to the acquisition of what is far from being a real good;—but there are some, though I fear an inconsiderable number, who, compos'd of more equal elements, wisely avoid the restless aims, the giddy vain pursuits with which they see so many of their fellow creatures so intoxicated and perplex'd;—would fain sit down contented with their lot, whatever it happens to be, and observing this maxim of the poet,

Not toss and turn about their feverish will,
But know their ease must come by lying still.[17]

Yet not even these can find an asylum from cares;—though the soul, like a hermit in his cell, fits quiet in the bosom, unruffled by any tempest of its own, it suffers from the rude blasts of others faults;—envy and detraction are sure to taint it with their envenom'd breath;—treachery, deceit and all kinds of injustice alarm it with the most dreadful apprehensions of impending danger, and shew the necessity of keeping a continual guard against their pernicious enterprises;—but above all, the ingratitude of friends is the most terrible to sustain;—that anguish which proceeds from the detected falshood of a person on whom we depend is almost insupportable; nor can reason or philosophy be always sufficient to defend us from it,—as I remember to have somewhere read,

Fate ne'er strikes deep but when unkindness joins.[18]

This is certainly a very melancholy circumstance; and the situation of the injured person's mind cannot but be very uneasy;—after having placed an entire confidence in any one whom we believe to be our friend,—after having intrusted him with the dearest secrets of our lives, and rely'd upon him for all the services and good offices in his power,—then, I say, to find him base, ungenerous and deceitful, is as poignant an affliction as any to which language can give a name.

I know not whether to be eternally deprived of a real and experienced friend by the stroke of death, be not a less shock than it is to lose one, whom we have always believed as such, by his own infidelity.—Under the former of these misfortunes we have the liberty to indulge many consolitory reflections;—first, that the great law of nature must be obey'd, and that there was an indispensible necessity for us to be one day separated;—secondly, in the hope that the person we lament is a gainer by this change, and much more happy than mortal life could make him;—and thirdly, though it may seem perhaps a wild idea, in supposing a possibility that he may be still a witness of our actions, be pleased at our remembrance of him; and, at the hour of our dissolution, even be appointed our conducter to the celestial mansions:—but under the latter, that of being betrayed by a false friend, we can have no such agreeable images before our eyes;—on the contrary,—grief and despair for ill-requited tenderness and sincerity, accompanied with remorse and shame for having made so unworthy a choice, must be the only subjects of our distracted meditations.

Thus impossible is it, for minds the most serene by nature, to remain always wholly free from inquietudes of one shape or other;—Jenny, the heroine of this history, had a temper not easily discomposed, and well deserved that character which our English Sappho gave of a lady for whom she had a particular veneration.

Chearful as birds that welcome in the spring,
No ill suspecting, nor no danger dreading;
In conscious innocence secure and bless'd,
She liv'd belov'd of all, and loving all.[19]

And yet she met with something, which, if it had not all the effect it would have produced in most others of her sex, was at least sufficient to turn that so lately harmonious frame of mind into a kind of chaos and inextricable confusion.

Those arrows of vexation which the base contrivances of Bellpine had levell'd against her peace, had hitherto proved unsuccessful;—they had either miss'd their aim, or slightly glance'd upon her without doing any real mischief; but she now received a random shot, and from a hand which least design'd to hurt her, that pierced her tender bosom to the quick, and left a wound behind which requir'd a long length of time to heal.

Since the adventure of Celandine the ladies had lived for some days in an uninterrupted scene of gaity;—every day,—almost every hour, brought with it some new pleasure or amusement;—to heighten Jenny's satisfaction she had receiv'd a letter from Jemmy, acquainting her that his business was now near being concluded, and that he should very shortly be with her at Bath;—he wrote to her on this account in terms so positive, that she doubted not but his next would inform her of the day in which he was to set out from London.

In that expectation she sent him an answer full of tenderness, expressing the sincere pleasure she took in the hopes he gave her of seeing him so soon, and desiring he would not let slip the first opportunity that presented itself of fulfilling his promise; though, in effect, she thought this injunction very needless; for she had the perfect confidence in him as to assure herself he would not lose a single moment that might bring him nearer to her.

But behold the swift vicissitude of human affairs; how in one instant are the face of things changed to the reverse of what they were? The ladies had been at a ball, which detain'd them till very late;—on their coming home, Jenny remembering it was the day that the post came in, she ask'd if no letter had been brought for her; and being told there was, and that it lay upon her toylet, she wish'd the ladies a good night and ran hastily to her chamber in order to peruse the letter, which she doubted not but came from her dear Jemmy, with the certainty of his immediate approach.

She was not, indeed, deceived in the former part of her conjecture;—she saw it was Jemmy's hand, and directed as usual.

To Miss Jessamy at Bath.

But what was her amazement,—her consternation,—when breaking the seal and unfolding the paper with all impatience of the most warm affection, she found the contents as follows:

Dear Angel,
When I acquainted you with that curst engagement which an unavoidable necessity has laid me under, I little thought you would have resented it in the manner you now seem to do; especially when I assured you, with the utmost sincerity, that I would break from it as soon as I could find a pretence to do it with decency:—you might, methinks, have known me better than to suspect I would omit any thing in my power to hasten the happy minute of flying to your arms with a heart unencumber'd with any cares but those of pleasing you.

If you return the passion I have for you with half that gratitude you have so inchantingly avow'd, you will repent,—you must by this time repent the pains you cannot but be sensible your cruel billet has inflicted on me.

I flatter myself with being able to see you in a few days at our usual place of meeting; when, if you are just as you are fair, you will be more kind to him who is,

With an unextinguishable flame,
My dear charmer,
Your most devoted,
And faithful servant,
J. Jessamy.

P.S. If I have any friends among the intellectual world,[20] I shall petition them to haunt your nightly dreams with the shadow of me, till propitious fortune throws the substance at your feet.

What now was the condition of Jenny?—she re-examined the seal and the handwriting;—she knew both too well to flatter herself with a possibility of their being counterfeited; nor was it in her power to conceive that the engagement mention'd in the letter could be any other than that between herself and Jemmy.—Where are the words can furnish a description? Where is the heart, not under the same circumstances, that can be truly sensible of what she felt?—Grief and indignation in these first moments were absorbed in wild astonishment, convulsions seiz'd her breast,—her brain grew giddy,—her eyes dazzled, while attempting to look over again some passages in this fatal letter, and her whole frame being agitated with emotions too violent for nature to sustain, she fell back in the chair where she was sitting, and every function ceas'd its operation.

Her maid, who was waiting in her chamber, perceiving this, flew to her assistance, threw some lavender-water[21] on her face, and at the same time scream'd out for help;—Lady Speck and Miss Wingman, being that instant coming up stairs to their apartment, heard the cries, and ran into the room;—they found their fair friend without any signs of breath and motionless;—they took hold of her hands and felt them bedew'd all over, as was her lovely face, with a cold dead damp, like that of the last agonies of departing life.

Surprised and frightened beyond measure, they cut the laceings of her stays,—raised her head,—bent her gently forwards,—apply'd hartshorn[22] to her nostrils and temples, and every other remedy they could think of, till at length, either through their endeavours or the force of nature labouring for itself, she recover'd by degrees, open'd her eyes, and uttered some words, which though inarticulate rejoiced their hearts.

Reason and recollection, however, were not as yet return'd, and Lady Speck finding her disorder still continued very violent, thought proper, late as it then was, to send for a physician, and in the mean time both she and her sister, as well as their women servants, who were call'd in, assisted in putting her into bed, where she was no sooner laid than she grew better; not only her voice but her senses also were enough restor'd to thank the ladies for the trouble they had taken; and to tell them, in order to conceal the real cause, that she believed her disorder was occasion'd by her having danced too much that night.

The physician being come, she notwithstanding suffer'd him to feel her pulse, and promised to follow his prescription, which was only a composing draught for that night; though he departed not without giving some items that his advice would be necessary next day.

The ladies, after having seen her take the dose prepared for her, retir'd and left her to the care of her own maid and Lady Speck's woman, who both sat by her bed-side the whole remainder of the night.

Chapter VI

Treats of many things as unexpected by the persons concern'd in them, as they can be by the reader himself.

Lady Speck and her sister had no sooner quitted Jenny's chamber than she fell into a profound sleep; whether owing to the goodness of her constitution, the doctor's prescription, or the fatigue she had undergone, is uncertain, but she awoke next morning greatly refresh'd, and much more so in spirits than could have been expected.

She now call'd to mind all the particulars that had occasion'd her late disorder; and remembering she had not put up the letter,[23] order'd it should be look'd for and brought to her;—the maid search'd carefully about the room, but it being no where to be found, she concluded that some body must have taken it away; and by that means a secret would be divulg'd which she had much rather should have been eternally conceal'd.

But as this suggestion was only a sudden start of female pride, of which she had as small a share as any of her sex, her good understanding easily got the better of it;—"I think," said she to herself, "the unfaithful man call'd his engagement with me a curst engagement, and promised to break off;—if so, the discovery must be made some time or other;—it is therefore of little importance when, or by what means his perfidiousness is reveal'd."

She was not mistaken indeed,—the letter had dropt from her hand as she fainted,—Miss Wingman, during the confusion, seeing a paper lie on the floor, took it up, and finding Jemmy's name subscrib'd was curious to know the contents, and for that purpose put it into her pocket without any one observing what she did.

She kept not from her sister the knowledge of the petty larceny she had committed, and as soon as they were alone together read it carefully over, examin'd every sentence, and made their own reflections upon the whole, which, prejudiced as they were with a belief of Jemmy's inconstancy, were yet less unfavourable to him in this point than those of his offended mistress.

They were, however, extremely incens'd against Jemmy; and, sincerely pitying the case of their friend, resolved to say and do every thing they could to soften her affliction:—it being near morning when they went to rest, the day was very far advanced before they arose; but they no sooner had quitted their beds than they repair'd directly to Jenny's chamber, and found her much less disconsolate than they had imagined.

As that young lady doubted not but it was either Lady Speck or her sister who had taken away her letter, or at least some person who would not fail of communicating it to them, she had determined, before they came, in what manner she would behave on the occasion.

The sisters, on their part, were not altogether so well prepar'd;—they expected not that she was as yet in a condition to endure much discourse, especially on so tender and critical a point;—they thought it would be time enough to entertain her on that head when the first shock of her misfortune should be over; and had not therefore well consider'd how to break their knowledge of it to her.

This caution in them was certainly very prudent, as well as very kind; but Jenny had too much spirit and resolution not to render it unnecessary;—on their entrance she started up in her bed, and said to them with a smile,—"I guess'd, ladies, that your good nature would bring you hither, so was just going to rise that you might be spared the trouble."

"I am very glad," reply'd Lady Speck, "to find that a disorder which seem'd to threaten the worst consequences is likely to go off so well;—but, my dear Miss Jessamy, I would not have you think of leaving your bed till your health is a little farther re-establish'd;—I will order," added she, "breakfast to be brought in here,—and after that, would fain persuade you to take some repose."

The maid then going out of the room to fetch the utensils for breakfast,—"Instead of this goodness, Madam," said Jenny, "your ladyship ought rather to chide me for my folly;—the inconstancy and ingratitude of mankind are not things so new and strange as to justify that surprise and confusion I was last night involv'd in."

They look'd on each other at these words, but made no answer,—on which Jenny went on,—"I am very sensible, ladies," pursued she, "that neither of you are unacquainted with the cause of my disorder;—the letter

I received last night has inform'd you of all,—nor am I sorry it has done what my tongue, perhaps, might have faulter'd in performing."

"Since I have your pardon, my dear," reply'd Miss Wingman, "I shall make no scruple to confess the theft which my curiosity made me guilty of; and I am the more ready to excuse myself for what I have done, as I am apt to think that the knowledge my sister and I have of this affair may enable us to give you some little consolation under it."

"Yes, my dear Miss Jessamy," rejoin'd Lady Speck, "you must believe that, though greatly interested in all that concerns you, our minds were less disconcerted than yours must naturally be on reading that epistle; and consequently were in a better capacity of judging, and seeing into the heart of him who wrote it."

"And what can you see there, Madam," cried Jenny hastily, "but the most vile ingratitude and perfidiousness?"—"I am going about," said that lady, "not to palliate his crime; but I think it is your duty to thank Heaven, that by this incident of his directing to you what was doubtless intended for another, you are convinced how unworthy he is of your affection."

"Besides," cried Miss Wingman, perceiving Jenny sigh'd and made no answer to what Lady Speck had said,—"methinks it should please you to find, that if Mr. Jessamy has slighted you for the sake of Miss Chit, he slights her also for some other; and she has no less reason to condemn him than yourself."

"Do you not think then that the letter was meant for her?" demanded Jenny hastily.—"No indeed," resumed Lady Speck, "nor will you, when you consider more cooly on the matter, believe that any man, much less one so polite as Mr. Jessamy, would write in such a stile and manner to a woman he intended for a wife.—This woman," pursued she, "is rather some petty mistress whom chance may have thrown in his way."

On this Miss Wingman, after having urged something in defence of what her sister had said, return'd the letter to Jenny, desiring she would examine it again, and then tell them how far she thought their opinion of it was unreasonable or improbable.

Jenny obeyed this injunction with a great deal of readiness; and after having paus'd for some moments on what she had read,—"I confess, ladies," said she, "that the freedom Mr. Jessamy takes with this woman is little becoming of an honourable passion;—but the more base his inclinations are, the more reason have I to resent he should attempt a gratification of them at the expence of that respect due from him to the engagement he has with me."

"Men will say any thing to gain their point this way," said Lady Speck laughing; "and if hereafter you shall find no greater cause of complaint against him than what this letter gives you, I should almost pity his inadvertency in exposing his folly to the only woman from whom it most behoved him to have conceal'd it."

Just as she had ended these words tea and chocolate were brought in,—after which, as the maids were present, no farther discourse pass'd upon this subject;—when breakfast was over, the ladies retired in order to dress; but not without conjuring Jenny to lie still and endeavour to take a little more repose;—she promised to comply, but had nothing less in her head, being glad to be alone, and at liberty to make her own reflections on an event which had occasion'd so great a change both in her sentiments and humour.

As she had imagined, in the first hurry of her spirits on the receipt of this letter, that it was in reality wrote to Miss Chit, and a demonstrative proof of the truth of all that had been told her on that account by Lady Speck and Miss Wingman, it was no inconsiderable alleviation of her trouble, to be now pretty well convinced, that instead of making his honourable addresses to a woman of condition, he was only amusing himself with an affair of gallantry,—a thing not much to be wonder'd at in a gentleman of his years and gay disposition; and her good sense would doubtless have enabled her to forgive it, but for the promise he seem'd to have made to this new object of his flame of breaking through all engagements, that he might devote himself entirely to her.

This, in a man whom she had always look'd upon and regarded as her second self, appeared so treacherous and ungrateful, that resentment got the better of all the tenderness she once had for him, and made her resolve to take him at his word, and be the first to release him from those engagements he had treated in so unworthy a manner.

Thus did the greatness of her spirit refuse to yield to the impulse of grief;—she got out of bed, in spite of all the intreaties of her maid to the contrary,—put on her cloaths,—lock'd safely up the proof of her lover's infidelity in a little casket where she kept her jewels, and would even have gone down into the dining room as usual, but found her limbs too weak to obey the dictates of her will;—she threw herself into an easy chair, and remain'd there for some time, in a situation of mind which only those of my fair readers, who have experienc'd somewhat like the same, can be capable of conceiving.

She was in a deep resvery when the ladies return'd to her chamber;—

she spoke chearfully to them, yet they plainly saw through all the vivacity she assumed, that a heavy melancholy had seated itself upon her heart;—they would not therefore leave her;—they order'd dinner to be served up in that room; and when it was over, call'd for a pack of cards and obliged her to make one at ombre.[24]

They had play'd but a very short time before a servant acquainted the two ladies, that a man was below who said his name was Landy;—that he was just come from London, and had brought letters of the utmost importance, which he was charg'd to deliver the moment of his arrival.

"Bless me,"—"my mother's steward," cried Lady Speck.—"Grant Heaven," rejoin'd Miss Wingman, "that no hurt has happen'd to her ladyship";—with these words they threw the cards out of their hands and ran immediately down stairs.

Jenny, who at another time would have been anxious for any thing that concern'd her friends, was not too much ingross'd with her own affairs to give much regard to the exclamations these ladies had made, and return'd to those reflections they had endeavour'd to divert her from.

It was not long, however, before they both came back, and with countenances which denoted the most extreme surprise.—"Well, Miss Jessamy," said the younger, "I have done my best to console you, now you may do the same kind office to me:—all men are alike perfidious;—there is no faith,—no honour in the whole sex."

"Aye my dear," cried Lady Speck, "such a monstrous piece of villainy is come to light as when you hear will make you forget every thing besides."—"All that you can guess is nothing to it," resumed Miss Wingman;—"but I will keep you no longer in suspence;—you must know I have just received two letters, the one from my guardian, Sir Thomas Welby, and the other from my Mamma;—she would not trust the intelligence they contain'd by the post for fear of a miscarriage, but sent her own steward on purpose to me;—you shall hear them both;—I will begin with that from Sir Thomas."

She then took the letters she mentioned out of her pocket, and read as follows:

To Miss Wingman at Bath.

Dear Miss,

I thank Heaven for putting it in my power to discover to you, I hope time enough to prevent your ruin, as wicked a design as ever enter'd the heart of the most profligate of our sex to attempt against the innocence of yours.

I am ashamed to think that a nobleman of Lord Huntley's birth and personal endowments can be capable of descending to such a low piece of villainy;—yet so it is,—I can assure you, my dear Miss, that nothing is more certain than that he is already married;—his lady I believe is but lately come from Ireland, and is at present lodged at the house of a particular friend of mine;—I both saw and spoke to her ladyship under the pretence of having some business with my lord; she told me he was not in town, which indeed I very well knew, having been informed he had followed you down to Bath.—There are, besides this, many other circumstances to evince the truth; but as they are too numerous, and too long to be inserted in the compass of a letter, I shall defer giving you the detail of them till I have the pleasure of seeing you.—My advice to you is, that you put it not in the power of this unworthy lord to deceive you any farther, but return immediately to London;—Lady Wingman is of the same opinion; but as this letter will be accompanied with one from herself, I doubt not but it will have all the effect it ought to have on your behaviour.—I am

With the best wishes,
My dear charge,
Your very affectionate friend,
And most humble servant,
T. Welby.

Jenny had no time to express any part of her sentiments on this occasion;—Miss Wingman had no sooner ended her guardian's epistle, than she proceeded to that from her mother,—the contents whereof were these:

To Miss Wingman at Bath.

My dear child,
I cannot sufficiently express the trouble I am under on account of Lord Huntley's baseness,—the intelligence of which I first received from our good friend Sir Thomas Welby, and am since but too much confirm'd in the truth of it by some enquiries myself has been at the pains to make;—I must confess it was with difficulty I listened to any reports to his prejudice;—I could not tell how to believe such foul deceit could be couch'd under a form so seemingly adorn'd with every virtue, as well as every accomplishment befitting his birth;—but, my dear Kitty, we are never so easily beguiled as by the appearance of honour and sincerity; I tremble to

think to what dangers you are exposed, while suffering yourself to be entertain'd with the insinuating addresses of a man who can mean nothing but to involve you in eternal wretchedness;—I conjure you therefore,—I command you by all the authority I have over you, never to see him more;—to fly his presence as a serpent that watches to blast your peace and reputation with his envenomn'd breath;—I have sent Landy on purpose to bring you this, and to attend you to London; and hope you will not detain him any longer than is necessary for your getting ready to set out.—Farewell,—that Heaven may have you always under its protection, is the unceasing prayers of,

My dear child,
Your most affectionate mother,
K. Wingman.

P.S. I am not now in a condition to write to your sister; but desire you will give my blessing to her; and let her know that if she stays behind you at Bath, as I suppose she will, she may expect to hear from me in a short time.—In the present confusion of my thoughts, I had almost forgot my compliments to Miss Jessamy, which pray make acceptable to her.

Jenny could scarce find words to express her astonishment at what she heard;—she could not tell how to think Lord Huntley guilty in the manner he was represented; and yet could less believe that Sir Thomas Welby and Lady Wingman, who she knew had always favour'd his pretensions, would write as they had done without having undeniable proofs of the justice of their accusation.

The three ladies had a long conversation together, the event of which will be seen in the succeeding chapter.

Chapter VII

Contains a brief recital of the resolutions taken on the foregoing advice.

Among the many who made their addresses to Miss Wingman, there was none who had been so likely to succeed as Lord Huntley;—she respected him so well, that had the information against him come from any other hands than those it did, she would not have given the least credit to it, but she loved him not enough to reject the admonitions of her friends, or to make her hesitate one moment if she should believe him guilty, or refuse to condemn a person whom they had found worthy of it.

Gay as she was by nature, she testify'd not the least reluctance to obey the commands of her mother in quitting Bath and all its pleasures, and resolved to do so without seeing Lord Huntley before she went, or being at the pains of reproaching him with the crime he was accused of.

But as she seem'd a little desirous that he should some way or other be made acquainted with her knowledge of his perfidiousness, and thought it as great an infringement of her mother's orders to write as to speak to him any more, Lady Speck was so obliging as to tell her she would take that task upon herself at his next visit.

Nor was it by this alone she proved the affection she had for her sister;—"As you were intrusted to my care by my mother," said she, "on our coming down to Bath, I am very loth to part with you till I have seen you safe again in her arms;—therefore," continued she, "if Miss Jessamy consents, I should be glad to return all together to London in the same manner as we left it."

Nothing could have been more agreeable to Jenny than this proposal;—she was not now in a condition to relish the pleasures of Bath, and longed very much to return to a place where persons are at liberty either to see all the world or to live perfectly retired, as suits best with their humour or circumstances.

"I am charm'd with your ladyship's design," cried she, "I could not have been easy to have seen Miss Wingman torn from us in this manner; especially on an occasion which could not afford her any pleasing ideas for the companions of her journey."

Miss Wingman made many acknowledgements to them both for this kind offer, but at first refused to accept it;—"I think myself happy," added she, "in the testimony you give me of your good nature and friendship towards me; but I cannot suffer you to think of leaving this place just in the height of the season, and returning to London, which is now a perfect wilderness, merely because I am obliged to go thither, by a duty which I cannot dispense with."

It is not to be supposed reasonable that this young lady was much in earnest in what she said on this score;—the others, however, were too sincere to take her at her word;—and it was at last agreed that they should all set out together, as soon as every thing could be got ready for their departure.

No company happening to come in, they pass'd the whole evening in Jenny's chamber, where the conversation turning chiefly on the discovery of Lord Huntley's marriage, it suddenly came into Lady Speck's head, that it would be better for her to express her sentiments on that occasion by a letter, than by holding any discourse with a man whom she could scarce think upon with any tolerable degree of patience.

Miss Wingman approving of her intention, her ladyship took Jenny's standish,[25] and immediately wrote to him in the following terms:

To Lord Huntley.

My Lord,

It is with an infinity of astonishment, and little less concern, that I find your lordship's proposal of an alliance with our family, instead of an honour, is the greatest affront that could possibly be offer'd to it;—I thought my sister's birth, fortune, and character had set her above being attempted to be made the dupe either of a vicious inclination or an unmeaning gallantry; for to what else than to gratify one or the other of these propensities, can tend the addresses of a person who has already disposed of himself to another?

This, my lord, is sufficient to convince you that we are perfectly well acquainted with your marriage;—after which I cannot suppose you will even think of continuing your visits; the only reparation you can make for a proceeding so unworthy of you, being to shun henceforward the presence of my much injured sister, and also of all those who have any interest in her happiness or reputation; among the number of whom you cannot doubt is her who is sorry to subscribe herself,

My lord,
Your lordship's
Ill-treated servant,
M. Speck.

This, after having shewn it to Miss Wingman and Jenny for their approbation, she sent by a servant to be left for Lord Huntley; but that nobleman coming not home till very late could do nothing in the affair that night; early the next morning Lady Speck received a billet from him containing these lines:

To Lady Speck.

Madam,

I received yours with more astonishment than you could be capable of feeling at the motive which induced your ladyship to write to me in the manner you did;—so base, and withal so ridiculous a calumny, would have merited only my contempt, had it not reach'd the ears of persons for whom I have the greatest reverence:—Nothing is more easy than for me to clear my innocence in this matter; but as I cannot bear to appear even for one moment guilty in the eyes of my dear adorable Miss Wingman, I beg your ladyship will give me the opportunity of justifying myself by letting me know the name of my accuser;—that villain, who while he stabs me in the back reaches my heart:—in confidence of your ladyship's generosity in this point I will wait on you as soon as I am dress'd, promising at the same time to intrude no more till this cruel aspersion is removed, and I shall be found to be what I truly am,—a man of honour, and,

With the most profound respect,
Madam,
Your ladyship's
Most humble
And most obedient servant,
Huntley.

The two sisters, who had imagined he would have been too much shock'd at the detection of his crime to have gone about to deny it, or to excuse it,—cried out, that he had an unparalell'd assurance;—that to behave in this manner was an aggravation of his guilt; and proved his soul as mean and abject as his principles were corrupt and base.

But Jenny, who was always ready to think the best, and besides had the eyes of her reason less obscured by passion, began immediately to entertain more favourable sentiments;—she found something in this letter, which, in spite of all the appearances against him, made her believe there was a possibility of his being wrong'd;—she could not forbear communicating her opinion to the ladies; and urg'd in the defence of it these arguments:

"Lord Huntley is a man of sense," said she, "and if he was so wicked as to be capable of acting in the manner that has been represented, he could not be so stupidly weak as to desire a farther explanation of it;—certainly he would rather be intirely silent on that head:—if guilty, what would his pretensions to innocence avail?—His making any noise in relation to a fact which, if true, may be so plainly proved, would only serve to make his criminal designs more conspicuous, and expose his villainy to those who otherwise might hear nothing of it."

"All this is very true, my dear," reply'd Lady Speck, "but yet there are some men who have had the impudence and folly, not only to court but even actually marry a second wife while the former has been living, and perhaps too at less distance than 'tis likely Lady Huntley was when he first made his addresses to my sister."

"It will not enter into my head," resumed Jenny, "that Lord Huntley is one of these,—"nor can I think it quite just that a man should be absolutely condemn'd without a fair trial, or even knowing by whom he is accused."

Lady Speck paus'd a little on these words, and then said,—that as she was certain Sir Thomas Welby would not so positively assert a thing, the truth of which he was not well assured of, she was half inclined to grant Lord Huntley's request, though it were only the more to confound him.

Scarce had she done speaking in this manner when her woman came into the room, and told her that Lord Huntley's servant who had brought the letter, and had waited all this time for an answer, begg'd to know if her ladyship had any commands to send by him;—to which, after a short consideration, she reply'd,—"Yes,—he may tell his lord that I shall be at home."

Miss Wingman had not open'd her mouth during this whole debate; but now shew'd, by her countenance, that she was not displeased at the result; and 'tis highly probable felt more impatience than she thought proper to express for what should pass in this important interview.

Chapter VIII

Serves only to render the cause more intricate, and involve the parties concern'd in it in fresh perplexities.

Lady Speck had given orders that when Lord Huntley came he should be admitted, but no farther than the parlour.

It would have been pleasant enough for any one to have observed the meeting of these two;—he approach'd her with a profound reverence, but with a reserve which had something in it very near akin to resentment;—she return'd his salutation with an air all distant and austere; and they stood looking upon one another for the space of near half a minute without speaking.

Lady Speck was the first that broke silence;—"I did not expect, my lord," said she, "that your lordship would have given yourself the trouble of making any visits here, after what I wrote to you last night."

"It is not indeed, Madam, a thing very common with me," answer'd he gravely, "to go to any place where I have been once forbid;—but I am pierc'd in too tender a part to stand upon punctilios;—both my love and honour are wounded,—gash'd,—mangled in a most cruel and infamous degree; and it is only from your ladyship's justice and humanity that I can hope a cure."

"Can you deny, my lord, that you are married," cried she.—"By Heaven!—Not married,—nor contracted,"—return'd he eagerly:—"nor, till I saw your charming sister, defy the whole world to prove I ever made the least proposal of that nature to any woman breathing."

These words, and the manner in which they were deliver'd, began a little to stagger that belief of his infidelity which she till now had thought herself confirm'd in:—"If any part of what your lordship avers be true," said she, "Sir Thomas Welby must certainly have been imposed on by some very extraordinary methods."

"Sir Thomas Welby, Madam," retorted Lord Huntley in great amazement; "is it then possible that he should be my accuser?"—"There required a no less substantial evidence," said she, "to authorize a supposition of your lordship's being guilty of a crime like this:—But you may see what he says," added she, presenting him with Sir Thomas's letter.

He read it hastily to himself, and as soon as he had done so,—"I perceive indeed, Madam," said he, "that some uncommon arts have been put in practice against me,—for what reason I am not able to conceive;—Sir Thomas's veracity is well known to me, and I think he has been inclined to favour my pretensions;—I doubt not therefore but he will readily afford me his assistance in diving to the bottom of this mysterious villainy;—I am sure I shall lose no time, nor spare no pains to bring the dark incendiary to light;—but," pursued he, "I will trouble your ladyship no farther, nor even ask to see the object of my soul's desire till my innocence is fully clear'd, and I have proved myself less unworthy of adoring her."

He concluded these words with a low bow, and went directly out of the room, without waiting to hear what answer she might have made to them.

It was, perhaps, much for her ease that he did so; for she was now in a consternation at his behaviour little inferior to what she felt on the first information of his crime;—his words,—his looks,—his resolution, made a deep impression on her;—she had seen grief and resentment in his countenance, but nothing that betoken'd a consciousness of guilt;—she knew not what to think,—or how to form a right judgement of him, but ran immediately to Jenny and Miss Wingman to impart to them all that had pass'd, and hear their sentiments upon it.

The latter of these young ladies was afraid of giving her opinion, probably lest it should be thought too favourable; but Jenny presently cried, that she could almost lay her life upon his innocence;—"I dare believe," said she, "that I have hit upon the real ground-work of this story;—the woman who would pass for his wife is certainly no other than some cast-off mistress of his, who either in revenge for his deserting her, or to give herself an air, assumes the name of Lady Huntley."

"No, no, Miss Jessamy," interrupted Lady Speck, "it is impossible that Sir Thomas would assert, in such positive terms, a thing of this nature on so slender a foundation,—I know him better,—and there must be something more in it than we can at present see into."

While the ladies were in this dilemma Lord Huntley, who the moment he had left Lady Speck went in search of his two friends, Sir Robert Manley and Mr. Lovegrove, was now complaining to them of the aspersion cast upon him, and declaring his resolution of going to London with all possible expedition, in order to detect the primary author of that calumny cast upon him.

These gentlemen, who had known his lordship for a considerable time, and had never heard any thing like his having consummated a marriage, were very much surprised that so odd a story should be raised, and highly applauded his intention of justifying himself as soon as he was able.

Both of them offer'd to be partakers of his journey;—he told them he was greatly indebted to their friendship on this score; but that he hoped he should soon return to Bath with the proofs of his innocence, and that it would be altogether needless for them to undergo the fatigues of accompanying him.

Sir Robert Manley, however, insisted on going with him;—"As for Lovegrove," said he, "I think he stands better with Lady Speck for some days past than he had ever done before, and it would be pity to take him from her at a time when she seems to be in such favourable dispositions towards him;—but as for me, I have no mistress, at least none that will receive my vows, and consequently can have no pleasure equal to that of proving my sincerity to my friend;—therefore, my dear lord," added he, "if you do not suffer me to go with you in your coach, you shall not hinder me from following you on horseback."

Lord Huntley was at last prevailed upon to take Sir Robert with him on this expedition; but though he hoped to return triumphant from it in four or five days at farthest, he would by no means hear of Mr. Lovegrove's leaving Bath, for never so small a space of time, while Lady Speck continued there.

They all dined together, after which Sir Robert and Mr. Lovegrove left Lord Huntley, the one to give directions to his man for every thing to be got ready for his departure the next morning by break of day, and the other to pay his devoirs to his mistress.

Jenny, who would not be persuaded to keep her chamber any longer, though not quite recover'd enough to go abroad, was now come down into the dining room, and Miss Wingman being resolv'd not to appear again in any public place while she remain'd at Bath, for fear of meeting Lord Huntley; Lady Speck also, in complaisance to them both, would not go out of the house;—so that Mr. Lovegrove, on his coming there, found them all at home.

The first compliments were no sooner over than the conversation began on Lord Huntley's affair;—Mr. Lovegrove left nothing unsaid that he thought might contribute to make them entertain a more favourable opinion of his friend;—he remonstrated to them the improbability of his being guilty in the manner he was represented; and Lady Speck and Miss Wingman, in their turns, remonstrated the improbability that such a story could be raised without some sort of foundation; but Jenny, as she had always done, sided with Mr. Lovegrove, and took the part of the accused.

They were engaged in this dispute when Sir Robert Manley came in,—that gentleman, though expecting to be back in a short time, was too polite to think of going without taking his leave of the ladies; hearing what subject they were upon, he seconded Mr. Lovegrove's arguments, and so warmly defended the cause of his absent friend, that Lady Speck was obliged to cry out,—"Well—well, let us have no more discourse upon this head;—it is time alone that can decide the point between us;—for my part," added she, "I sincerely wish his lordship may be found as innocent as you would persuade us to believe he is."

"This is extremely generous in your ladyship," reply'd Sir Robert; "but Madam," continued he, addressing himself to Miss Wingman, "how happy should I make my friend if I were permitted to carry to him the assurance that you also join'd with your sister in the same kind wish?"

"Lord Huntley may be certain," answer'd she blushing, "that I should be very sorry a crime like what is laid to his charge should be proved on any in the world, much more on a person whom I cannot deny but I once thought highly deserving of my esteem."

There pass'd nothing more of any moment while they were together, which was not very long, for the gentlemen were impatient to return to Lord Huntley, who they knew was alone and stood in need of all the consolation they could give him;—they staid the whole evening with him, and rejoin'd him very early in the morning, at which time he set out with Sir Robert on his journey to London.

Chapter IX

Has in it some things of no small importance, tho' at present they may appear too insignificant to be inserted.

Lord Huntley being gone, and Miss Wingman freed from all those dangers her mother apprehended for her, there seem'd no necessity for that young lady's leaving Bath; yet, as she had received such positive commands to do so, and Landy waited to conduct her, she thought she could not well excuse herself from going:—Jenny, who was now quite weary of the place, having lost all her relish for its pleasures, said all she could to fortify her in this resolution; and between them both Lady Speck was prevail'd upon to think it right.

Accordingly both the sisters wrote to Lady Wingman, giving her an exact account of all that had pass'd in relation to Lord Huntley, and assuring her that they should throw themselves at her feet, as soon as the necessary preparations could be made for their journey.

But before I proceed any farther on the particulars of these ladies adventures, during the short time they had now to stay at Bath, I think it highly proper that the reader should be made fully acquainted with the several dispositions their minds were in at present.

As for Lady Speck, the late behaviour of Celandine had render'd him so dispicable in her eyes, that she wonder'd at herself for having been able ever to endure the conversation of such a fop, and much more to have been won to a liking of his person, the graces of which she now plainly saw were chiefly owing to his milliner and taylor:—Mr. Lovegrove, on the contrary, had shewn so much of the man of honour and of the respectful lover in what he had done, that she hesitated not a moment if she should give him the preference of all others who made their addresses to her; and if she could not as yet entirely overcome her aversion to entering a second time into the bands of marriage, she however resolved not to change her condition except in favour of him.

Miss Wingman was in a situation very different from that of her sister;—this young lady was of a humour extremely gay and volatile;—she had never been at the pains of examining into the emotions of her own heart; but she now found out a secret there which had hitherto been conceal'd as much from herself as from the world;—those alarms with which she had been agitated at first on the accusation against Lord Huntley, and the pleasure she had since felt in the assurances given her by Sir Robert Manley and Mr. Lovegrove, that it would be easy for him to prove his innocence, equally convinced her that he was not altogether so indifferent to her as she had imagined; and this it was which perhaps, more than obedience to her mother's commands, made her so eager to return to London, where she thought she might soon be inform'd of the whole truth of this affair.

But poor Jenny labour'd under sensations of a yet more unquiet nature,—she had the confirmation of her lover's infidelity under his own hand; and whether he was guilty to the degree she had at first believed, of courting another woman upon honourable terms, yet he could not but appear extremely criminal in the attempt of purchasing the favour of one he intended only for a mistress, with the contempt of those solemn engagements he was bound in to herself.

In what other sense, indeed, was it possible for her to understand the first paragraph in that letter, which by his mistake in the superscription had fallen into her hands,—"There is no room for doubt," cried she, "the meaning is obvious and explicit,—his heart renounces the obligation his father laid him under, and which his own perjured tongue a thousand times has sworn he wished no greater blessing than to fulfill."

"The ungrateful man," continued she, "shall find no difficulty in getting rid of me,—I shall spare him the pains of seeking a pretence to break an engagement now grown so irksome to him,—nor shall I envy the woman to whom his faithless heart is next devoted;—I shall always reflect on a distich I remember to have read in the works of old Michael Drayton."

He that can falsify his vows to one,
Will be sincerely just and true to none.[26]

Thus in some moments did she feel a kind of satisfaction in this early discovery of the inconstancy of his temper;—others again presenting her with the idea of what she once believed him, all that was just, generous, virtuous, and sincere, threw her into the most melancholly musings;—every innocent endearment that had passed between them from their tenderest infancy till this great period, came fresh into her memory, and made her deeply regret the finding him so much unworthy either of her love or friendship.

It is certain, that besides the vivacity and flow of spirits which are generally the companions of youth and affluence of fortune, and keep affliction from seizing too forcibly the vitals, she stood in need of all the good understanding she was endued with to enable her to sustain the shock of Jemmy's infidelity with that chearfulness she wish'd to do:—in spite of all her endeavours, she would sometimes fall into resveries which demanded other helps than those she received from within herself, to rouse her from entirely.

Though the natural sprightliness of Lady Speck and her sister was very much abated, in the one by the secret remorse she felt for the encouragement she had given to Celandine, and in the other by her suspence on account of Lord Huntley, yet neither of them were so taken up with their own cogitations as to neglect any thing in their power to dissipate the langour they observed in their fair friend.

But as it was Jemmy who had been the sole cause of her disquiet, so it was to him alone she was now indebted for her relief,—the night before their departure she received a letter from him containing these lines:

To Miss Jessamy at Bath.

My dear, dear Jenny,

I am so happy as just to snatch an opportunity of acquainting you that the wedding is over,—I wish to heaven that the revels for it were so too, that I might be at liberty to get away; for, besides the impatience I am in to see you, I am quite sick of the incessant noisy mirth of those who come to testify their joy on this occasion;—I do not doubt but they take me for the most dull, stupid fellow in the universe;—and indeed how should it be otherwise?—In the midst of dancing,—drinking,—laughing,—romping, I am absent;—my heart is with you at Bath, and representing to me the more true felicities I might enjoy in your dear conversation:—they tell me, this hurry is to continue no longer than six days; but I think that an age, and nothing but my gratitude to my old friend, for the care he has taken of my affairs, should keep me a prisoner here for half that time:—be assured that as soon as I can get free, I shall do little more than pass through London in my way towards you;—so that if I am deprived of participating with you in the pleasures of the place you are in, I shall at least have that of conducting you home,—till when, I hope, I need say nothing to convince you, that I am

Inviolably, and for ever,
My dear Jenny's,
Most affectionate
And devoted
J. JESSAMY.
Ham-Hall

P.S. When we meet, you may expect a particular detail of what passes here, and some description of the bride, who has indeed a fine outside, but I am afraid wants a little of my dear Jenny's understanding;—Harry, however, finds no defect in her as yet, and I heartily wish, for both their sakes, he never may;—every man's lot is not so happy as mine.—Once more, my dear Jenny, adieu for a short time.

This letter was a kind of clue to guide Jenny through the labyrinth of perplexity she had been involved in;—she knew very well that one of the gentlemen, appointed by the last will and testament of Jemmy's father for his executor and trustee, had a seat call'd Ham-Hall in Bedfordshire;—she had also heard that his son was about being married to a young lady of that county with a considerable fortune;—she therefore easily conceived that the engagement mention'd by Jemmy in that former epistle, and which she imagined he had meant with herself, was in reality no other than being obliged to go down into the country on account of this wedding.

She immediately imparted to her two friends the letter she had received, and also gave them at the same time an explanation of the mystery which had given her so much pain;—both of them sincerely congratulated her on the occasion, especially Miss Wingman, who took her in her arms crying out,—"Did not I tell you, my dear, that Mr. Jessamy was not so guilty as you imagined?"—"Aye," replied Jenny,—"but for all that he is not quite innocent, nor will he find me very easy to give him absolution."

"If criminal in no greater matters than a transient amour," rejoin'd Lady Speck, "I think you might forgive him, without putting him to the penance even of a blush by your reproaches.—In good truth we women have nothing to do with the men's affairs in this point before marriage;—and as I now begin to believe, in spite of all I have heard to the contrary, that he addresses no other woman than yourself upon honourable terms, these are but venial transgressions, which you ought to overlook till you have made him your own."

They were discoursing in this pleasant manner when Mr. Lovegrove enter'd;—he came to pass the evening with them, knowing their things being all pack'd up for their journey, they would not go abroad any more while they staid at Bath.

Talking of the hour in which they intended to set out, he said that he was extremely glad to know it, because he would give orders for a post-chaise to be ready exactly at the same time, that he might not have the mortification of being left behind them even for a moment.

Though he directed these words to the ladies in general, yet Lady Speck knew very well they were meant only to herself; and looking on him with the most obliging air,—"No Mr. Lovegrove," said she, "since you will needs be so complaisant as to accompany us, I see no occasion for your travelling in the way you mention;—as your own coach is not here, and there is a vacant place in mine, I am very certain we shall all be pleased to have it so agreeably fill'd."

He was so transported with this offer, that he could not restrain himself from catching hold of her hand and kissing it with the most passionate gestures;—"This is a condescention, Madam," said he, "which I never durst have presumed to hope, much less to have requested; but it is the peculiar property of Heaven to prevent[27] the petitions of its vassals by blessing the most unexpected, as well as undeserved."

Miss Wingman and Jenny, finding they were likely to enter into a conversation which required no sharers, withdrew to a window as if to look at something that pass'd in the street;—how far Mr. Lovegrove improved this opportunity is not material to particularize;—the reader will easily suppose, that neither that, nor Lady Speck's good humour were thrown away upon him.

Chapter X

Is a digression of no consequence to the history, and may therefore either be read or omitted at discretion.

The sun had made but a very short progress in his diurnal course, when Lady Speck, Miss Wingman, and the amiable Jenny, accompanied by Mr. Lovegrove, set out on their journey for London, escorted by Landy and all their men-servants on horseback.

Our fair travellers soon found the advantage they had gain'd by the invitation given to Mr. Lovegrove;—the innate satisfaction that gentleman felt on Lady Speck's obliging behaviour towards him, diffused itself through all his air and features, and added a double vivacity to his conversation;—he was all life,—all gaiety,—all spirits;—he told a thousand diverting stories, and sung as many pretty songs; so that if they had been more inclined to seriousness than they really were, it would have been impossible for them to have indulged any melancholy reflections in his company.

The day was near pass'd over in this agreeable manner, when a sudden stop was put to all their pleasantry;—one of the hindmost wheels of the coach flew off its axis, and but for the coachman's uncommon presence of mind, in restraining the horses that same instant, some mischief might probably have ensued;—all the servants immediately alighted endeavouring to repair the damage, but in vain;—part of the ironwork was broke, and two spokes of the wheel had started[28] with the shock:—this accident happened about five miles from the town where they had design'd to lie that night; but as there was a small village pretty near, it was judged proper to walk thither, as the only expedient in this exigence; which they did with a great deal of alacrity and chearfulness, while the dismember'd machine, though with some difficulty, was dragged after them.

The accommodation they found here was indifferent enough; but what deficiencies are there in nature or in fortune which good humour cannot supply?—The ladies laugh'd heartily at their little pilgrimage, and Mr. Lovegrove made them all scamper about the room by attempting to wipe the dust off their shoes with his handkerchief.

In fine;—their supper,—their lodging, all that to persons of less wit and more affectation would have been matters of the utmost mortification, to them serv'd only as subjects of diversion, and occasions of fresh pleasantry.

They arose next morning in the same chearful temper with which they had lain down; nor did it abate on being told that the workmen who had been sent for to mend the coach could not pretend to make it fit to take the road for several hours:—as the place they were in afforded no other convenience to prosecute their journey, they resolved to make a virtue of necessity, and content themselves with what was without a remedy.—Mr. Lovegrove, however, took upon himself the office of caterer, and was so fortunate as to provide an entertainment somewhat less inelegant than they had been obliged to content themselves with the night before.

But while dinner was getting ready an accident happen'd which contributed to make the time of their abode there seem shorter, by presenting them with a new theme of conversation.

The woman who kept the house, after having gently open'd the door of the room where they were, came in making a curtsy at very step she took, and approach'd the ladies with an,—"I beg pardon,—I hope no offence,—but I have a poor guest below that would have me come up;—I am very tender hearted,—though God knows what she is, or who she is,—for my part I never saw her before last night in my whole life,—so I have nothing to answer for on that account;—and if she be bad it is the worst for herself,—that is all I have to say."

"If you have nothing more to say, mistress," cried Mr. Lovegrove laughing, "I think you are very much to blame to lose your time in telling us so."—"I hope your lordship's worship and all their ladyships will excuse me;—I am but a plain woman;—but God knows my heart I mean no harm;—but as I was saying, a poor young woman, finding I had quality in my house, has been baiting me this two hours I am sure to shew you a snuffbox she had got to sell;—how she came by it I can't tell; but this I must say, that she does not look like a thief; though there are such sad doings in the world that one does not know who to trust."

"Let us see it, however," said Lady Speck.—"Aye, aye," rejoin'd the others, "let us see it by all means";—on this the woman produced the box, tho' not without repeating several times over her former apologies.

The box was a most curious English pebble, set in gold, with a hinge and lining of the same metal;—they handed it from one to the other, and concluded that as it was a toy too genteel for the possession of a person in very abject circumstances, it must either be stolen, or the real owner be reduced by some uncommon distress to the necessity of parting with it.

The bare supposition that this latter might possibly be the case, inspiring them with a good deal of curiosity to know something farther of the matter, they told the woman they would buy the box, but should be glad to see the owner and bargain for it with herself,—on which she went out of the room, but return'd immediately, bringing with her the person in question.

"This," said she, "is the young woman,—she says she come very honestly by the box,—as I told your honours before, I know nothing of the matter,—she is quite a stranger to me, but I shall leave her with you, and if your honour and ladyships worships will be pleased to examine her you may-hap will be better judges than I am;—for my part I have a great deal of business to do and cannot be spared any longer from my bar and my kitchen;—indeed there is nobody but myself to take care of any thing in this house, though I have a husband and a daughter at woman's estate, as I may say, for she is past fourteen, yet all lies upon me, so I hope your honours will excuse me."

It may be easily imagined that all the company were very glad to get rid of her impertinent babble, so readily dismiss'd her; Mr. Lovegrove telling her at the same time, with an ironical complaisance, that he was extremely troubled she had wasted so many of her important minutes on so trivial an occasion.

After this prating woman was gone, the young person she had left behind, and who had enter'd no farther than just within the door, on being desir'd to come forward advanced with a slow and timid air, yet which had nothing in it of the appearance of a conscious guilt;—notwithstanding the disguise of an old fashion'd long ridinghood,[29] which cover'd her whole body, and even hid some part of her lovely face, there was still enough to be seen to prepossess any beholder in her favour.

Her extreme youth, for she seem'd not to have exceeded fifteen or sixteen years at farthest, the delicacy of her complexion, and of those features which she suffer'd to be exposed to view, excited a kind of respectful compassion in the hearts of all those she was at present with.

Mr. Lovegrove, who had undertaken to be the speaker, began with asking her, if she was the owner of the box before them; to which she answering in the affirmative,—"I am very sorry then," said he, "and I am certain that all here are so, that any exigence should oblige you to dispose of it."

"The vicissitudes of fortune, Sir," reply'd she with a becoming assurance, "are too frequently experienced in the affairs of life to raise much wonder, or to know much pity, except from the hearts of a generous few."

"That is true," resumed Mr. Lovegrove; "but you are too young to have been subjected to them by any of those ways the fickle goddess ordinarily takes to shew her power over the world;—the distress you labour under must therefore proceed from some uncommon source, which if you thought proper to communicate, I dare answer you are now among persons who would not only wish, but also make it their endeavour to lessen the weight of your affliction."

She was about to make some reply but was prevented by Lady Speck, who immediately subjoining to what Mr. Lovegrove had said,—"There is nothing wanting," cried she, "but the knowledge of your affairs to make me shew my readiness to serve you,"—The other two ladies spoke much to the same purpose, especially Jenny, who had taken a more than ordinary fancy to this fair one.

After having thank'd them in the politest terms for their goodness to one so altogether a stranger to them;—"The accidents of my life," said she, "are little worthy the attention of this company; but since I am commanded to repeat them I shall make no scruple to obey, on condition I may be permitted to conceal the names of all the persons concern'd in them."

They then assured her that they should content themselves with such things as she thought proper to impart, and, making her sit down, desired she would not delay one moment the satisfaction she had promised, which request she comply'd with, as will be seen in the succeeding chapter.

Chapter XI

Is a continuation of the same digression, which however insignificant it may appear at present, the reader will hereafter perhaps be glad to turn back to the pages it contains.

The young stranger having been made acquainted, before her coming up stairs, of the rank and condition of the persons to whom she was about to be introduced, would not suffer herself to be any farther intreated by them, but began to satisfy the curiosity she had excited in these or the like words:

"I am the daughter of a gentleman," said she, "who by living in his youth above the income of his estate, has been reduced to live below the dignity of his birth, in order that his children may not, at his decease, have too much occasion to regret the situation in which they shall be left.

"It is impossible for any parent to behave with greater tenderness and indulgence, or to be more sincerely anxious for the welfare of his posterity;—sensible of his former mistakes, he has often condescended to tell us, that he looks upon us as persons he has wrong'd, by having wasted what should have render'd comfortable the life he gave:—his affairs, however, are not on so ill a footing but that he supports his family in a genteel tho' not a grand manner; and if he lives a few years longer, it is hoped will be able to leave the estate to my brother, now a student at Cambridge, born to inherit, free from all incumbrance, except myself and a sister some years elder than either of us.

"As for a provision for myself and sister, I have heard him say that his scheme is, as soon as my brother arrives at a proper age, to match him with some woman of fortune, which fortune should be equally divided between us two, and a settlement made for her out of the estate.

"He never flatter'd himself with the expectations of any offers of marriage to our advantage; nor though he gave us all the accomplishments befitting our station in life, yet did he never encourage either of us to imagine that without money we had any thing in us capable of attracting a heart worthy our acceptance.

"But to my great misfortune he found himself mistaken in this point;—a gentleman of a very large estate, happening to see me at a friend's house where I sometimes visited, took an extraordinary fancy to me; and after some necessary enquiries concerning my birth, character and circumstances, came to wait upon my father and ask'd his permission to make his addresses to me; adding at the same time, that he desir'd nothing but myself, and whatever fortune was intended for me might be given to my sister.

"This last was a prevailing argument with my father, who, dear as I believe I then was to him, would perhaps have rather suffer'd me to lose so advantageous a match, than have confess'd his incapacity of giving me a portion.

"But how fatal did this act of generosity in my lover prove to me;—My father, charmed with the proposal, hesitated not to comply with it, provided my consent might be obtain'd, which in his heart he resolved from that moment to compel me to grant, in case he should find me refractory to it.

"It will doubtless seem a little strange to you," continued she, "that I should mention as a misfortune what you might expect a girl in my precarious situation would have rejoiced at, and been elated with as the greatest good that could have befallen her;—the world I know condemns my folly,—I condemn myself,—yet was it as impossible for me to act otherwise, as it is to repent of what I have done.

"You will perhaps imagine that he is some deformed and loathsome creature, but I assure you he is not, for I must do him the justice to acknowledge, that, making an allowance for his age, which by his own account is pretty near fifty, few men can boast of having a more agreeable person;—that he has also a good understanding,—a great deal of ready wit, and is very gracious in conversation;—but all this was insufficient to engage my affection, and I have a certain delicacy in my nature, if I may so call it, which will not permit me, on any consideration whatever, to give my hand where my heart will not go along with it.

"The astonishment I felt on being first inform'd of the new conquest I had made, was succeeded by an adequate proportion of horror at being commanded by my father to receive that gentleman as the person ordain'd by Heaven and him to be my husband, and to look on such an alliance as the greatest blessing that could be bestow'd upon me.

"I blush'd,—I trembled, and had not power to make the least reply, till being urged to speak, I recollected, as well as I was able, my scatter'd senses, and cried, though with a broken and faultering voice, that I was too young to think of marriage; to which my father sternly answer'd,—'Be guided then by those who know how to think for you';—and with these words left me to consider on what he had said.

"The same day my lover dined with us, as I afterwards found, by the appointment of my father, who, as soon as the cloth was taken away, retired to his closet, pretending he had some letters to write, and left me to entertain this guest, or rather to be entertain'd by him with the declaration of his passion.

"He made it, indeed, in the most respectful terms;—he told me, that having lost his wife in bringing a son into the world, he had resolved never to transfer the affection for her to any other woman;—that he devoted near two and twenty years to her memory;—that during the whole time of his widowhood he had never seen that face till mine which had the power to alienate his thoughts from the grave where she lay buried;—but that he no sooner beheld me, than he felt new life and new desires rekindling in him;—remember'd that he was a man, born to enjoy the social delights of pure and virtuous love, and at the same time found it was with me alone he could partake them.

"As this sort of conversation, and indeed every thing relating to love, was entirely new to me, I made but very aukward replies, and was so little able to express my real sentiments to him on that head, that I afterwards found he took what I said as the effects of simplicity and bashfulness, rather than any aversion either to him or his proposals.

"My father, who poor man rejoiced in this opportunity of making my fortune, seem'd highly pleased with the account my lover gave him of my behaviour;—he told me I was a very good girl, and that he doubted not but that I should deserve the happiness Heaven was about to confer upon me:—'But,' said he, 'though the modesty with which I hear you received this first declaration was very becoming in a maid of your years; yet, as we have agreed the wedding shall be consummated in a few days, I would have you grow less reserved on every visit he makes you,—accustom yourself to treat him by degrees with more freedom, to the end that when you are made one, you may not be too much strangers to each other.'

"This so frighted me, that I could not forbear crying out with some vehemence,—'Oh, Sir! I conjure you not to talk in this manner,—I never can think of being married to him.'

"The look my father gave me at these words will always be imprinted on my memory.—'Never think of being married to him!' said he, 'Then never think I am your father;—think rather of being an utter alien,—an outcast from my name and family—think of begging,—starving,—of infamy, contempt and wretchedness.'

"These cruel expressions coming from the mouth of a parent, who till now had always used me with the extremest tenderness, cut me to the very soul;—I threw myself at his feet,—I wept,—I beseech'd him to moderate his passion, and protested, as I might do with the greatest sincerity, that the thoughts of offending him was more terrible to me than those of death itself.

"He appear'd somewhat mollify'd with these submissions;—'Child,' said he, raising me from the posture I was in,—'you cannot be so ignorant as not to know what I do in this affair is wholly for your happiness; though, indeed, whenever Heaven is pleased to call me hence, it would be an infinite satisfaction to me in my dying moments that I left one of my daughters independent.—I could wish,' added he, looking towards my sister who sat at work in the room, 'that she had an offer equally advantageous.'

"'If I had, Sir,' reply'd she pertly, 'I should scarce be so mad or silly as to run the risque of disobliging, you and at the same time of ruining myself by refusing it.'"

The beautiful stranger was in this part of her little history when she found herself oblig'd to break off by seeing dinner brought upon the table;—

she would have withdrawn till the company should be more at leisure; but they insisted, in the most strenuous terms, that she would be their guest; to which, after making some few apologies, she consented.

Chapter XII

Concludes the distressful narrative.

As the waiters were present, nothing was said during the whole time of dinner, concerning the subject which that necessary appendix to life had interrupted; but the cloth was no sooner taken away, than the three ladies, as well as Mr. Lovegrove, testify'd the interest they took in their fair guest's affairs, by their impatience for knowing the event.

She reply'd to the many complaisant things they said to her with such an air and grace as convinced them, more than any thing she had related, that she had indeed been educated in the most genteel manner, and also been accustom'd to converse with persons of the best fashion and greatest politeness.

But though the discourse that pass'd between them, on the score of mere civility, might very well deserve a place in this work, I shall omit the repetition, as it might be apt to make the reader's attention wander from the main point; and only say, that she prosecuted her history in the following terms:

"My father," said she, "now condescended to talk to me in the mildest, and withal in the most pathetic stile;—he endeavoured to allure my young heart by enumerating and displaying the pleasures that attend on wealth and grandeur;—he remonstrated to me, that the circumstances of our family would not permit his children, especially his daughters, to be directed only by inclination in the article of marriage; and that as I could find no possible objection to my lover but being somewhat too old, gratitude for the happiness he was ready to put me in possession of, might very well attone for that defect.

"'You say you cannot love this gentleman,' continued he; 'but pray what is this passion that is call'd love but a vain delusion, an ignis fatuus[30] of the mind that leads all that follow it astray;—suppose, rejecting the certain good, fortune now puts into your power, and you should hereafter fix your fancy either on some one who has not the means of supporting you, or on one who returns not your affections, how truly miserable would be your state!'

"I could find no arguments to oppose against those he urged, and could only answer with my tears,—till being bid to speak, and the command several times repeated, I at last sobb'd out,—that I would make use of my utmost endeavours to obey him.

"I know not whether his menaces at first, and his persuasions afterwards, might not have made me at that time promise to do every thing he would have me; but some company coming in, luckily preserved me from adding to the guilt of disobedience that of deceit.

"These visiters staid with us till very late, so I was reliev'd from any farther persecutions for that night; but the next morning at breakfast they were renew'd, and as I had no heart to consent, nor courage absolutely to refuse, I could only beg him to allow me a little time to bring my mind to a conformity with his will.

"It is certain that my aversion to this match seem'd unreasonable even to myself, and I did all I could to conquer it; but my efforts to that purpose being fruitless, I set myself to consider, whether to live under the everlasting displeasure of a father whom I revered and loved, perhaps turn'd out of doors by him and exposed to poverty and contempt, or to pass my whole life in opulence with the man I hated, would be the least of evils.

"Oh, ladies!—How impossible is it to represent what it was I felt while thus employ'd;—to which soever of these ways I turn'd my thoughts I was all horror and confusion;—the present idea seemed still the worst;—I was distracted,—irresolute, and fluctuated between both; and all I knew of myself was, that I was wholly incapable of supporting either.

"To heighten my affliction, though I had many acquaintance, I had no one friend on whom I could depend for assistance or advice;—my sister, who by the rules of nature should have pitied my distress, rather added to it by all the ways she could invent.

"Indeed she never loved me, and I have reason to believe I owe great part of my father's severity to her insinuations;—I will tell you an incident which confirms me in that belief,—it was this:

"The very Sunday before the misfortune I am now reciting befel me, a young gentleman happened to sit in a pew just opposite to mine,—he fix'd his eyes upon me with so much earnestness, during the whole time of divine service, that I could not help observing him with some confusion;—after we came out of church, turning my head back on some occasion, I perceived he followed me, though at a distance; but when I came near our door, the footman who attended me stepping before to knock, he advanced hastily and came time enough to make me a profound reverence just as I was entering the house;—I was a little confounded, as I had never seen him before;—I return'd his civility, however, and went in;—my sister, who had not been at church that day, was looking out of a window and beheld this passage;—she rallied me a little upon it, and ask'd me who that pretty fellow was that came to the door with me;—I told her the simple truth, and it pass'd off till we were going to bed, when one of the maids told me, in her presence, a fine young gentleman had watched the footman as he was going out on some errand, and ask'd him abundance of questions concerning me;—I thought it a little strange, but said nothing, nor did my sister seem to take much notice of it.

"I thought little of this adventure, but found she afterwards made a handle of it, not only to possess my father with an opinion that I rejected the lover he recommended to me for the sake of one who was my own choice, but also to reproach me as having encouraged a clandestine courtship.

"I mention this only to shew how destitute I was of any consolation whatsoever; but in the midst of perturbations, which almost deprived me of my senses, an expedient started at once into my head, which flatter'd me with some small prospect of relief.

"My lover appeared to be a man who wanted neither good sense nor generosity; and I fancied that if he knew the true state of my heart, the one would shew him the extreme madness of marrying a woman who had so utter a dislike to him, and the other make him ashamed of rendering miserable the person he pretended to love.

"On this foundation I built my hopes, and resolved on his next visit to make him thoroughly acquainted with the deplorable condition to which I was reduced by his unfortunate passion; and to beseech him to withdraw his pretensions as of his own accord, and without hinting to my father that any thing in my behaviour had been the cause.

"But alas!—I had no sooner contriv'd this project, than I found the impracticability of putting it into execution;—my father had a closet which opened from his bed-chamber, was between that and the dining-room, and divided from the latter but by a thin partition.

"Good God," continued this afflicted fair one, "how every thing conspired against me,—my father had always kept the key of this closet himself, but now had given it to my sister, and I soon found for no other purpose than that she should hear from thence what pass'd between me and my lover, and give him an account.

"Though I only suspected this at first, but was certain of it when being call'd down from the chamber where I lay to receive my lover who waited for me in the dining-room, I saw, as I cross'd the stair-case, the shadow of my sister passing hastily into the very closet I have mention'd.

"The old gentleman was in great good humour that day, and perhaps my tears and prayers might have work'd on him the effect I wish'd, had I not been so unhappily disappointed of making the experiment.

"Having taken notice, I suppose, that I wore no watch, though indeed I had one, but it being out of order was sent some time before to be mended he brought with him a fine repeater[31] set round with diamonds, and begg'd me to accept it;—as I knew who was witness of our conversation I durst not refuse his present, and much less talk to him in the manner I had intended.

"I knew not then what course to take, but at last bethought me of employing my pen to give him that information which my tongue was deprived of all opportunity of doing;—accordingly I wrote to him in this manner:

"Sir,

It is only in your power to save me from the worst of miseries,—that of a forced marriage;—my father is inexorable to my tears, and resolute to compel me to be yours; but not all his authority, your merits, nor my just sensibility of them can ever bring my heart to consent to the union you propose:—in fine, I cannot love you as a husband, but shall always regard you as the best of friends, if you forego the claim parental power has given you, and refuse that hand, the acceptance of which would infallibly make you no less wretched than myself;—consider therefore, Sir, what it is you are about, and drive not an unhappy maid to desperation; for be assured I will seek relief in death rather than be

Yours.

"This I folded up, but neither sealed nor directed it, as I designed to slip it into his own hands as he should be going away from his next visit;—but here again my scheme was frustrated, my father coming home before he went away and waiting on him down stairs.

"The ensuing day, however, I thought myself more fortunate;—he came, and business calling him away somewhat before his usual hour, I follow'd to the dining-room door and gave him the paper, saying at the same time,—'I beseech you, Sir, to consider seriously on the contents of this,—and make no mention of it to my father.'

"He look'd very much surprised, and seemed as if about to open what I gave him; but I clapp'd my hand hastily upon his,—crying,—'For Heaven's sake take care what you do, this is no proper place';—and with these words turn'd quick into the room to prevent any questions he might have made.

"My heart flutter'd a little at the step I had taken;—suspence is a very uneasy situation; but as I thought it impossible that any man would venture to marry a woman who had wrote to him in the manner I had done, I grew more composed, and slept much better that night than for several preceding ones.

"But, oh! How short lived was my ease, and how terrible a surcharge of woe did the next day present me with;—my father, who went out soon after breakfast, return'd not till the cloth was laid for dinner, and then only to tell me that he had been with my lover all the morning;—that every thing was concluded between them; and that the marriage should be solemnized at our house the evening of the succeeding day.

"Judge, ladies, of my condition;—the convict at the bar feels not more horror at the sentence of approaching fate, than I did at the event which I had vainly flatter'd myself was far removed from me;—the amazement I was in kept me for some moments in a kind of stupid silence;—my father was so taken up in directing my sister what preparations she should make for this affair that he regarded not my confusion, till grief and despair unloosed my tongue, and I cried out,—'Oh, Sir, did you not say I should have time?'

"'Time,' reply'd he, 'can any time be more lucky for you than this, when you are going to have the same settlement as if you brought ten thousand pounds? Your lover is so pleased with the pretty trick you play'd him last night, that I believe I might have got more for you if I had insisted upon it;—but this was his own offer, and it is very well;—we are going together to my lawyer's to order the writings.' [32]

"My sister then ask'd him if he would not dine, to which he answer'd in the negative, and after giving her some farther instructions, left us to return to his intended son-in-law, who he said waited for him at the chocolate-house.

"Dinner was presently brought in,—I sat down, but could not eat a bit;—my sister, who since the death of my mother had been house-keeper and affected to be very notable, talked of nothing but the hurry she should be in—and what should be the first,—and what should be the second course of the wedding supper; for though there were but two or three friends to be invited, yet my father had order'd that every thing for this dreadful ceremony should be set forth with as much elegance as possible.

"On my making no reply to all she said, she told me I was a sullen fool, and did not deserve my good fortune;—I had no spirit to enter into any altercations with her, so flung from the table and retir'd to my chamber to vent those cruel agitations with which I was now more than ever overwhelm'd.

"The first reflections that occur'd to me were on this hated lover's being pleased with the paper I had given him, and telling my father that I had play'd him a pretty trick.—'What,' cried I to myself, 'is it not enough that he neglects my complaints,—must he also insult me for them, and turn my grief into derision?'

"But I had no time to waste on this subject,—my doom was fix'd, and I must either fly or tamely submit to it;—I resolved on the former whatever should be the consequence, and now thought of nothing but the means of accomplishing it.

"It was not long before I determin'd on what course to take; I have an aunt married to a merchant at Cork,[33]—I believe she will grant me her protection,—I am going, however, to make the experiment, and if she refuses, must content myself to earn my bread either by going to service or working at my needle."

Chapter XIII

May properly enough come under the denomination of an appendix to the three last preceding chapters, as containing some things which ought to have been inserted in them.

The fair fugitive now thought she had related all that was expected from her; but Lady Speck, perceiving she had done speaking, prevented what any of the rest of the company would have said on that occasion, by crying out hastily,—"Madam, you have not given us an account of the manner of your escaping the misfortune you so much dreaded;—we see you here, but know not by what means you are so,—without which your history will be imperfect."

"As I may perhaps have been too circumstantial in some parts of my narrative," reply'd she, "I was cautious not to weary out your patience by any farther particulars of an event so little deserving your regard;—but as you are so good to afford me your attention, I shall readily make you a detail of whatever pass'd from the moment of my resolving to fly my father's house to that of my arrival at a place where I have the honour to be so generously entertain'd; and I am the more glad to do it, as there is indeed one thing which, in common justice to the gentleman who made his addresses to me, I ought not to have omitted."

"As to my departure," pursued she, "nothing was more easy to be accomplish'd;—no one suspected I had any thoughts of it, so no care was taken to prevent my flight, either by confining my person or setting any body to observe my motions;—but I was willing to take such of my things as I could conveniently carry with me; this requir'd some contrivance;—there was no possibility of sending a trunk or portmanteau out of the house, therefore found I was obliged to leave every thing behind me which I could not be the porter of myself.

"My sister was mighty busy all that afternoon in her domestic affairs;—I employ'd that time in looking over my wearing apparel and made the best assortment of them I could, selecting those which I thought I could least support the want of;—my fine laces I cramm'd into a handkerchief, in order to put into my pockets; and the more bulky part of my linnen, with some upper garments, I tied in two pillowcases, and then essay'd whether I could carry them on each side under my hoop-petticoat,[34] and found I could do it very well;—certainly these vast French hoops were invented chiefly for the convenience of those who carry about them what they want should be conceal'd."

Not only Mr. Lovegrove, but the ladies themselves laugh'd heartily at this reflection on their mode;—but they would not interrupt her, and she went on:

"Finding I was able to walk under the burthens I had prepared, at least as far as out of the sight of our house, I put them all together into a large trunk, pack'd up as they were, ready for a march next morning; for I thought it not adviseable to go that night, as lying at any house in town might endanger a discovery, and I knew that no carriage of any kind would set out before day-break.

"After this I sat down and consider'd what more was to be done before I went away,—my father till now had always been most indulgent to me,—humour'd me in every thing; and even this last act of power, cruel as it was, I know was kindly meant;—I could not therefore think of leaving him, perhaps for ever, without letting him see I had not quite forgot the reverence I owed him.

"I then took pen and paper and wrote a letter to him;—I cannot remember exactly the expressions I made use of, but know they were as pathetic as could be dictated by a heart overflowing, as mine was, with filial love and grief.

"I told him that I had exerted the whole force of my endeavours to obey him;—that my reason and the insurmountable aversion I had to the match he proposed, had occasion'd conflicts in my breast which life could scarce sustain; that I fled not from the presence of the best of fathers, but to avoid being guilty of a deed, which would have been yet more grievous to him;—begg'd him to forgive me, and to rest assured that to what exigencies forever I might be reduced in this forlorn and helpless condition, nothing should tempt me to bring disgrace upon my family or dishonour to myself.

"Having finish'd this melancholy epistle, I threw it into the drawer of a little escrutore, designing to take it with me in the morning and send it to my father by the penny-post;[35]—but, good God! How great was my confusion, when happening to look over some writings I have there, I know not for what reason, for I had nothing which I fear'd should be exposed after I was gone, one of the first things I laid my hands on was the very paper I had wrote to my lover, and thought I had given to him.

"I did not presently conceive how this could be;—I knew I had wrote no copy, and that it was the same which I had been certain of having deliver'd to him; but at last I remember'd, that not being able to give it to him on the day I intended, I had put it into this drawer to prevent its being seen by an accident;—and this recollection convinced me, that instead of a letter of complaint he had received from me a foolish love song, though set to very good music, which a lady of my acquaintance had desired me to write out for her, and I thought, as I could not find it, I had dropt it from my pocket,—It began thus:

'Dearest Damon would you shew
What a faithful man can do,
  Love me ever,
  Leave me never.'"

She was proceeding, but Mr. Lovegrove was so highly diverted with this incident, that he could not forbear interrupting her,—"By Heaven,

Madam," said he, "it would have been cruel in you to have made us lose so agreeable a part of your history."

The ladies express'd themselves in much the same manner;—"I cannot help laughing," cried Lady Speck, "to think of the old gentleman's transports on receiving so fond a remonstrance from his young mistress";—"Nor I," subjoin'd Miss Wingman, "at the idea how much he must be mortified when he found himself deceived."—"For my part," said Jenny, in a more serious air, "I pity the poor man, and am heartily sorry for the lady, who but for this mistake might not perhaps have been driven to the necessity of quitting her father's house."

"It is utterly impossible, Madam," reply'd the other, resuming the thread of her discourse, "to know what would have happen'd, had this not been the case;—I was, however, so much shock'd at the thoughts of what I had done, that I resolved to let him continue in his error no longer than I had it in my power to convince him of it;—to this end I inclosed the letter I had design'd for him in another piece of paper, in which I wrote,—I think to this effect:

Sir,

The silly paper, which by mistake I put into your hands, must certainly have given you a very odd opinion both of my understanding and sincerity.

This will, however, undeceive you as to the latter, by shewing you I meant not to disguise the true situation of my heart, which had you sooner known, perhaps I might not have been the wretch I am;—but it is now too late, and all the hopes I flatter'd myself with from your generosity and compassion are vanish'd into air.

Yes, Sir, the agreement made between my father and yourself drives me from all I once thought happiness; but beg you to believe that I shall always retain a grateful sense of the advantages offer'd me by your love, how miserable forever it has made me, and shall never cease to wish you may long enjoy all those blessings in life which cruel destiny denies any part of to

The forlorn, &c.

"To this," continued she, "I added a postscript, to let him know that I left behind me the watch which he had been so good to present me with, and doubted not but my father would return it to him as soon as my flight should be discover'd.

"Having dispatch'd all that I thought necessary for my going, my mind for some moments was as easy and composed as if the preparations I had been making were only for a journey of pleasure;—but alas, the sad occasion soon recoiled upon me, and fill'd me with most gloomy apprehensions.

"My father came home in the evening in so jocose a humour as hinder'd him from observing that melancholy which I could not else have been able to hide from him;—he had, indeed, been drinking more freely than he was accustom'd; and I found also by what he said, that my lover, by toasting my health too plentifully, had render'd himself incapable of waiting on me that night.

"Nothing material happen'd afterwards to the time of my elopement, which every thing seem'd to favour;—my sister went very early in the morning to Covent Garden[36] to buy fruit for the dessert, taking one of the men with her to bring home what purchases she made;—the other was busy in cleaning the plate;—all the maids were in the kitchen, and my father was yet in bed;—so the coast being entirely clear, I tied my paniers[37] to my sides,—stuffed my pockets with as much as they would contain, and went directly out of the house without being seen by any body; though I believe whoever had met me would not have guess'd in what manner I was equipp'd;—I made all the haste I could out of the street however,—stept into the first hackney coach I found, and drove to a place where I remembered to have seen second-hand cloaths hung up for sale,—there I bought this riding-hood, which I thought would be some kind of a disguise.

"Bristol[38] being just opposite to that part of Ireland where my aunt lives, I had no other route to take; but in the hurry of my thoughts, had never once consider'd that as I had secured no place in the stage-coach it was a thousand against one if there would be any room for me in it at this season of the year.

"I did not forget, however, in my way to the inn, to put the letters I had wrote to my father and lover into the penny-post, but found when I came there the coach was not only full but had set out above an hour before;—this put me into great perplexity; but I was now embark'd on an expedition, and must go through it some how or other;—the Windsor[39] stage was just going out, and had a place which I gladly fill'd, in order to be so far on my journey.

"On my arrival there, I was at as great a loss as before; but being told that if I hired a chaise to Maidenhead I might possibly find a place in some one or other of the coaches that put in there,—I took this advice, but would not lie in that town lest I should be seen by some persons of my acquaintance that lived there, so drove on to this village, which I thought would answer my purpose as well, as I should catch the coaches as they pass'd by this morning;—I got up very early that I might be ready for the first, for it was indifferent to me in which I went, provided they took the road I wanted to go; but my hopes deceived me, every one that came this way was full.

"But this was not the only, nor the worst disappointment I met with at this place;—having laid out what loose money I had about me, I thought to have recourse to my purse, in which, besides sufficient to defray the expences of my journey, there was a diamond ring which had been my mother's, and a medal which I set a high value upon;—not finding it presently I was very much alarm'd,—I pull'd every thing out of my pockets that were in them, but the examination only serv'd to convince me that what I sought was lost;—I know not how this accident happen'd, nor is it of any importance.

"It is easy to conceive how terrible a misfortune this was to a person in my present circumstances;—I should have been driven to the last despair, if a thought had not occurr'd to me, that the little box I took the liberty of sending by the woman of the house might be acceptable to some one or other of this company."

Here ended all she had to say, but the conclusion was accompanied with some tears, which notwithstanding robb'd the eyes from which they fell, of no part of their lustre.

Chapter XIV

Contains much matter for edification, but very little for entertainment.

The distresses of a beautiful person have a double influence over the heart,—those misfortunes which the dignity of our nature obliges us to commiserate, excite a more kindly warmth, a more interested concern, in proportion to the loveliness of the object we see labouring under them.

There was something in the air and whole behaviour of this young stranger; which, join'd to the calamity of her present condition, had a kind of magnetic force capable of attracting both respect and compassion in minds less generous and gentle than those of the company she now was with.

They thank'd her for the pleasure she had given them in the recital of her adventures, and at the same time testify'd the most affectionate concern for the event.

Each having express'd some part of their sentiments on this occasion, Lady Speck drew her sister and Jenny aside, and, after a short whisper between themselves, all return'd again to their seats, and the former addressing herself to their unfortunate guest, spoke in this manner:

"We cannot think, Madam," said she, "of depriving you of a thing which an unforeseen necessity has oblig'd you to expose to sale; but if you please to receive a small contribution in lieu of a purchase, we shall take your acceptance as a favour done to ourselves."

With these words her ladyship put six guineas[40] into her hand, which she took, bow'd and blush'd, though not half so much as Jenny did, who was extremely scandaliz'd at the meanness of the present, though she did not think proper to discover her opinion of it at that time.

On this Mr. Lovegrove, who doubtless had his own reflections,—cried hastily out,—"Then, ladies, since you will not buy the box I will,—I have a mind to make a present of it to a lady."—"I protest I will not have it," said Lady Speck;—"Nor I," rejoin'd Miss Wingman;—"Nor I," cried Jenny."—"You need not be under this agitation, ladies," reply'd he smiling, "for I assure you, it neither was nor is my intention to make an offering of it to any of you."

They all looked a little grave at hearing him speak in this manner, but said nothing, while he counted ten guineas out of his purse and presented to the fair fugitive with one hand, and with the other in the same moment took up the snuff-box, which had all this time lain on a sideboard near which he sat;—"This, Madam," said he, "is an equivalent I believe."

He then put the box into his pocket with a very serious air, but immediately taking it out again laid in into the lap of the owner;—"You are the only person, Madam," said he, "to whom I ought to make this present,—be pleased to accept it as a token of my sincere respect for a lady who at your years can have behaved with so much fortitude and resolution."

All the ladies were highly pleased at the gallant turn he had given to this affair; but the obliged person was so much overwhelm'd with the sense she had of such an unexpected act of generosity, that she was able to express her gratitude only in broken and disjointed phrases,—which notwithstanding Mr. Lovegrove would not suffer her to go on with; but ask'd her in what manner she now intended to prosecute her journey.

She reply'd, that as there was no wheel carriage to be procured in that village, she had thoughts of taking a man and horse to conduct her as far as Reading,[41] where she was informed she might be sure of being better accommodated.

Though Mr. Lovegrove had no other view in this question than merely to turn the discourse, it proved a very fortunate one for the young traveller;—on hearing the answer she made,—"You need not," said Lady Speck, "be at the pains or expence of hiring a man and horse, as we have enough of both standing idle;—I doubt not but the woman of the house will readily provide a pillion[42], and you may ride behind one of my servants."

This offer being too convenient, as well as obliging, not to be joyfully accepted, the lady immediately called for one of her servants and gave him orders to do as she had said; adding withal, that when they came to Reading he should use his endeavours to assist the young lady he carried in getting a post-chaise for her to pursue her journey.

A very little time served for the execution of this command; and after the most becoming retributions on the one side, and sincere good wishes on the other, the fair stranger took her leave of a company among whom she had been so providentially thrown in a time of such distress.

Jenny, who had her head and heart a good deal taken up with what had passed, followed her down stairs, and making her step into a little room where they could not be overheard, surprised her with these words:

"I cannot express," said she, with the greatest sweetness in her voice and looks, "how deeply I have been touched with your misfortunes, nor how much ashamed I am of the slender contribution made for their relief;—Lady Speck is very good, and I never was more amazed than to hear her mention so pitiful a sum as two guineas a piece; but as it was agreed to by her sister I could not well oppose it without giving offence;—I shall however never be able to remember this affair without blushing if you do not allow me to make up some part of the deficiency."

She accompanied the latter part of this speech with a present of five guineas, which the other shewed a very great unwillingness to accept,—saying she was already overloaded with favours, and what she had received was more than sufficient for all the purposes she wanted; but Jenny told her that she knew not what accidents might happen to a person at such a distance from her friends, and in fine forced her to take it,—then, after giving her a most cordial embrace, left her and return'd to the company, without taking any notice of the occasion of her leaving them.

She found them animadverting on this adventure, which doubtless had something pretty extraordinary in it;—Lady Speck was just saying how lucky a thing it was for the young stranger that she happen'd to come into the same inn where they were.—"It was so, indeed, Madam," reply'd Jenny, "and I think no less fortunate for us also, as the sight of her distress has given us an opportunity of doing what every one ought to rejoice in having the power to do."

"Nothing can be more just, Madam, than this reflection of yours," said Mr. Lovegrove; "but I am sorry to have observ'd, that there are too many who have greatly the power without being blest with the will to do the least good office: others again, who though of a more beneficent disposition confine their bounties within the narrow compass of their own acquaintance.—Distress is not distress with them, unless the person who labours under it be known to them, forgetting that all mankind are but one great family, descended originally from the same parents; that every individual is a branch from the same stock, and consequently have a kindred right to the protection of each other.

"I was an ear witness not long ago," continued he, "of a very severe, as well as genteel reprimand given to a peer of the first rank by a person in great distress, who had petitioned his lordship for relief, and to whom he sent for an answer,—that he knew nothing of him, and that he never gave any thing to strangers;—on this the unfortunate person reply'd to him that deliver'd the message,—then tell your lord that he will never relieve an angel."

This worthy gentleman would perhaps have farther expatiated on the beauties of a mind extensively benevolent, if he had not been interrupted by Landy, who came up to acquaint them the necessary repairs of the coach were now entirely finish'd;—on hearing this, as there were yet some hours of day-light, they all agreed to go to Maidenhead that night, not only because they were sure of meeting with better accommodation than they had found here, but also for the sake of being so much the farther on their journey.

Every thing being got ready with all imaginable expedition, they departed from that village, where Lady Speck left orders that the servant who had been sent to conduct the young stranger should refresh himself there that night, and follow them early the next morning to Maidenhead.

Chapter XV

Cannot fail of giving a very agreeable sensation to every honest and good-natur'd reader.

Miss Wingman, who besides the natural affection she had for a mother who tenderly loved her, had always been bred in the strictest principles of duty and obedience to her, could not keep herself from being a little uneasy at the delay that had happen'd in their journey, fearing that indulgent parent might be under some apprehensions of her being detained by a worse accident than the real one, a day longer than she expected.

To relieve her as soon as possible, however, from the anxieties she might be under on this score, she made Landy, instead of stopping with them at Maidenhead, proceed directly, and with all the speed he could, towards London;—the honest steward, knowing his lady's temper, was glad to be changed of his commission, assured the young lady that as far as the day was advanced he doubted not but he should be able to reach Windsor that night, and from thence, setting out early the next morning, carry Lady Wingman the joyful news of their approach several hours before the coach could possibly arrive.

This filial observance, in a young lady of Miss Wingman's gay and volatile disposition, appear'd extremely amiable in the eyes both of Jenny and Mr. Lovegrove; but I will not trouble the reader with any repetition of the many compliments they made to her upon this occasion, things of much greater moment requiring to be discuss'd.

Nothing worthy of obtaining a place in this history happening at present, I shall only say they all came to Maidenhead perfectly well pleased with the change of their quarters, and that Mr. Lovegrove, to whose direction every thing was left, took care they should be made full amends that evening for the bad entertainment of the preceding one.

The servant who had been sent to attend the fair fugitive return'd, according to the orders he had received, very early in the morning, and brought an account that he had been so fortunate as to procure a handsome post-chaise for her, which was to carry her quite to Bristol.[43]

Mr. Lovegrove, Jenny, and Miss Wingman were all up and dress'd,—all the equipage was ready; but Lady Speck, who loved to travel at her ease, not rising before her usual hour, they did not set out so soon as some of the company, her sister in particular, were impatient to do.

Notwithstanding this, the high metal[44] of the horses and skill of the conductor brought them to London pretty early in the afternoon;—Lady Speck, who thought herself under an indispensible duty of waiting on her mother before she went home, prevail'd on Jenny and Mr. Lovegrove to accompany them, so the coachman was order'd to drive directly thither.

It cannot be doubted but that the good old lady received her two daughters with all the demonstrations of affection imaginable, and those they brought with them with the greatest complaisance; but after the first salutations were over,—"I am sorry," said she, turning to Lady Speck, that what I wrote to Kitty has made you and Miss Jessamy quit the pleasures of Bath so much sooner than I believe either of you intended."

"I am sorry, Madam," reply'd she, "for the occasion of your ladyship's writing in that manner."—"So am not I, Madam," cried a voice well known to all that were present, and immediately Lord Huntley, follow'd by Sir Thomas Welby, rush'd from an inner room, where they had withdrawn on the ladies coming up.— The late cloud," continued Lord Huntley, "cast upon my honour, I hope will only serve to render it more bright in the eyes of those to whom I most desire it should be conspicuous."

He then paid his compliments to each of the ladies one after another, who were all of them so astonish'd at the sight of him, that they had not the power of uttering one word;—this scene, in effect, was so pleasant, that Sir Thomas Welby laugh'd till his sides shook, and Lady Wingman herself, in spite of her gravity, could not forbear smiling.

As Lord Huntley advanced to embrace Mr. Lovegrove,—"I congratulate you, my dear lord," said that gentleman,—"I congratulate you, since there needs no other proof than seeing your lordship here to assure me that your innocence is fully clear'd."

"Ay, ay," cried Sir Thomas Welby,—"all this bustle has happen'd through my foolish mistake; and I am glad, that besides my fair charge and her mother, here are so many witnesses of my acknowledging it."

"Sir Thomas," reply'd Lord Huntley, "you have so well attoned for representing me more unworthy than I really am, or can be, by the promise you have given me of using your interest to make me more happy than I can ever deserve to be, that I have reason to bless an error so propitious to my hopes."

"The event, I perceive, has prov'd fortunate enough," said Lady Speck;

"but methinks I should be glad to know how it came about to be so, and by what means Sir Thomas was so strangely deceiv'd."

"Strangely indeed, Madam," answer'd he;—"I am ashamed to think of it;—but have a little patience, and you shall be fully acquainted with all the particulars of this very foolish affair;—it is a penance I have enjoin'd myself for my weakness in so rashly giving credit to appearances."

The company now seated themselves, which before they had not done, and Sir Thomas, on seeing the three young ladies and Mr. Lovegrove prepar'd to give their attention to what he had to deliver, began the recital he had promised in these or the like words:

"Happening to call," said he, "at the house of an honest tradesman with whom I have been long acquainted, I was a little surprised, on passing through his shop, to hear a person who came in just after me enquire if Lord Huntley or his lady were at home.

"I staid not to hear what answer was given to the man, but went directly to my friend, who I saw sitting in his counting-house;—the first question I asked him was,—what lodgers he had in his house;—to which he reply'd,—that at present he had the honour of having Lord and Lady Huntley, of the kingdom of Ireland; but should not long be so happy, for they had taken a great house in the new buildings,[45] and only waited till their furniture, which was on the road from West Chester,[46] should arrive.

"The consternation I was in made me put a great many interrogatories to him, some of which I believe were impertinent enough, but he had the good manners, however, to answer succinctly to every thing I ask'd, according to the best of his knowledge:—he told me that Lord Huntley had been in England some time before his lady,—that he had staid but two nights with her in these lodgings before he went out of town, and would not return till his house should be quite completed, and fit for his reception, leaving the care of every thing to her ladyship and the steward.

"He also added, that hearing they intended to furnish one apartment entirely new, he had recommended an upholsterer and cabinet-maker to them for that purpose, and hoped he should have an opportunity of obliging several others of his friends and neighbours by helping them to the custom of this noble Lord.

"As he is of a very communicative disposition he run on, of his own accord, with several other particulars; to which, indeed, I did not give much attention, thinking myself thoroughly convinced in the main point,—that of Lord Huntley's being a married man.

"But notwithstanding all he said served to corroborate that belief in me, I was willing to be still more confirm'd, which I thought I might be by seeing and speaking to the lady herself.

"Accordingly I told my friend, that I was well acquainted with Lord Huntley, though I had not till now heard of his marriage; but that since it was so, and the thing seem'd to be no secret, I should be glad to pay my compliments to her ladyship on that occasion.

"To this he reply'd, that she was the best humour'd woman in the world, and he was sure would take it very kindly:—'Yonder is the steward,' cried he, 'I will let him know your intention';—in speaking these words, and without waiting to hear what I would say, he beckon'd to a person who was that moment coming into the house;—presently the worst countenanced man I ever saw,—but who, on my signifying to him my desire of waiting on Lady Huntley, answer'd with a great deal of civility, that he would see if her ladyship was at leisure to receive the honour of my visit.

"I forgot to send up my name, which blunder occasion'd him to come down again on purpose to ask it;—I made no scruple to inform him who I was, with this addition of being one of Lord Huntley's friends;—he went up again, but staid much longer above the second time than he had done the first;—at last, however, he return'd with leave for my admission.

"I follow'd my conductor, who introduced me to the presence of a very lovely woman indeed, though she had somewhat of a down-cast look in her eyes, which, as well as a good deal of hesitation in her voice in receiving me, I at that time imputed to her modesty, on finding herself accosted by a stranger, but have since found more proper causes to ascribe it to,—those of guilt and fear.

"When the first compliments were past, I took the liberty of asking her to what part of the country my lord was retired;—she seem'd in more confusion than before at this question, which then gave me some surprise; but on reflecting afterwards upon it, I easily found it had proceeded from her want of being prepared with an answer; I was, however, so inconsiderate as to furnish her with one, by mentioning Bath;—on which she presently cried out,—'Yes, Sir, my lord is gone to Bath with some persons of quality, his relations.'

"Having satisfied my curiosity with the sight of this fine lady, I took a pretty hasty leave of her, and went directly to Lady Wingman, to whom I was impatient to communicate the discovery which I thought had been so providentially thrown in my way.

"Her ladyship, as may easily be supposed, was both amazed and troubled; but the result of our conversation was to write immediately to Miss Wingman, and apprise her of the danger we imagined she was in from the addresses of a married man;—my lady would needs send Landy with these dispatches, in order to enforce the contents, and to conduct her daughter up to London.

"I need not tell you the satisfaction Miss Wingman's letter gave us;—her ladyship was now perfectly easy, and I gave myself no farther pains to enquire after Lord and Lady Huntley;—happening, however, to meet my friend one day by accident, he told me that his lordship was expected in town every hour, and that all was ready for their going into their house,—so that he should soon lose his lodgers.

"Things were in this position when I was told one morning, soon after I was out of bed, that Lord Huntley and a gentleman he had brought with him were below and desired to speak with me;—I think I was not more astonish'd on hearing he was married, than I was at his making me a visit;—I ran down notwithstanding to receive him; but more hastened by the perplexity I was in than by any respect I had for him at that time.

"Indeed, my lord," continued Sir Thomas, addressing himself to Lord Huntley, "I can never too much admire your lordship's moderation in behaving towards me as you did, after knowing what I had wrote concerning you to Miss Wingman."—"Oh, Sir Thomas," reply'd that nobleman, "I reserved all my fire for those who I supposed had traduced me to you, and created me an enemy out of my best friend."

Sir Thomas was about to make some return to what Lord Huntley had said; but the ladies cried out,—that they were impatient for the catastrophe of this adventure, and desired he would give a truce to compliments and pursue the thread of his discourse;—on which he told them, they should be obey'd, and went on thus:

"What I have farther to relate," said he, "will be contained in a very short compass;—my lord and I soon came to an eclaircisement,—his lordship repeated to me the heads of my letter to Miss Wingman, and I gave him a faithful account of the reasons on which my accusation was founded;—he requested me to use my endeavours to shew him the villain that had usurp'd his name; I readily complied, and attended his lordship and his friend, who I afterwards found was Sir Robert Manley, to the house where the supposed Lord Huntley and his lady lodg'd.

"My honest friend was luckily at home, but on my desiring to speak with Lord or Lady Huntley, he told me they had left him two days before and were gone to their new house;—on which I ask'd him if he knew Lord

Huntley when he saw him:—'Yes certainly,' reply'd he, somewhat surprised at the question;—'Am I the person,' cried Lord Huntley, stepping forward, that lodged with you and bore the name of Lord Huntley?'—'No, Sir,' answer'd he, 'nor has he any thing of your resemblance.'—'Then,' said I, 'you have been imposed upon,—'tis well if not cheated too; for I assure you this is the real Lord Huntley, and him you have had with you must be an impostor.'

"Never was horror and amazement more strongly painted than in the face of the poor tradesman:—'Then I am undone,' cried he, 'I do not mean for what I shall lose myself, though it is no trifle, but I have drawn in several of my friends to give them credit.'—He then proceeded to inform us that they had taken up plate,—jewels,—houshold furniture, and wearing apparel to a considerable amount, and all through his recommendation;—we pitied his distress,—comforted him the best we could, and told him that as the affair was so recent, it was to be hoped their things might be recover'd.

"Lord Huntley's honour was now fully clear'd, but he could not be content without condign punishment being inflicted on the villain who had assum'd his name and character for purposes so infamous and base;—the defrauded tradesmen were all sent for on this occasion, and as it could not be imagined that the pretended Lord Huntley would either stay long in this town, or venture to appear to any stranger while in it, the best expedient that offer'd was to get a search-warrant to force open the doors of his new habitation; by which means he would not only be apprehended, but also such part of the goods he had taken up, which were not yet embezzled, might be restored to the proper owners.

"A warrant was easily obtain'd on the oath of the several tradesmen, who all went with Lord Huntley, Sir Robert Manley, and myself, to see it put in execution by the officers of justice; but, to our great disappointment, the impostor was flown with the whole gang belonging to him, both male and female:—upon enquiry among the neighbours we found they had been there but one night, which time it may be supposed they had spent in packing up and carrying off what goods had been brought in; the house indeed, is conveniently situated for such a purpose, there being a back door through the stables into another street."

Here Sir Thomas Welby ended his little narrative, what was said upon it will be part of the subject of the succeeding chapter.

Chapter XVI

Treats of more things than one.

After thanking Sir Thomas Welby for the trouble he had given himself in satisfying their curiosity, and congratulating Lord Huntley on the ease he had found in removing the aspersion cast upon him, this amiable company began to enquire what methods had been taken to find out where the impostor and his associates had concealed themselves, in order that they might be brought to justice.

Lord Huntley reply'd, that nothing had been left undone for that purpose;—that not only all the suspected places in London had been search'd, but also letters sent to all those ports in the kingdom which open'd either towards France, Holland or Ireland, with a description of their persons; and affidavits of the frauds they had been guilty of; but that all this had been of no effect, so that those wretches, if they took any of these routes, must have escaped before the intelligence arrived.

"I cannot but confess," said Mr. Lovegrove, "that the impostor shew'd a good deal of address in the management of this affair; for as he had assumed the character of a nobleman whose person he must needs believe was well known, he took care not to be seen by any one but the master of the house where the scene of his villainy was to be transacted, and even by him but just enough to give him room to say he had such a one for his lodger."

"It certainly requires abundance both of courage and policy to form a compleat villain," said Lady Wingman; "and I have often wonder'd that men endued with such great talents should not rather employ them for ends more laudable, as well as more safe for themselves."

"All good qualities, Madam," reply'd Mr. Lovegrove, "lose their very nature when accompanied with a vicious disposition;—some men are born with such an unhappy propensity,—such an innate love of wickedness, that they will do nothing at all unless they can do mischief;—it is in that alone they are capable of exerting the talents they are possessed of;—nothing is more frequent than for a lawyer, who might make a very good figure in a just cause, to chuse to engage himself only in those which require chicanery and artifice; nor for a soldier drummed out of his regiment for cowardice, to become a most bold and hardened villain in robbing on the highway."

"Yet there is a way to correct this propensity you talk of," cried Lady Speck, "otherwise vice would rather be a misfortune than a fault, and consequently deserve less blame than pity."

"Doubtless, Madam," answer'd Mr. Lovegrove; "but it must be done in the most early years of life, and requires more pains than either tutor or pupil are sometimes inclined to take."

This gentleman would perhaps have gone on with some discourse concerning the mistakes of education, and the little care that is too generally taken in giving a right bent to the minds of youth, which might have been of very great service to many of my readers, if it had not been prevented by the sudden entrance of Sir Robert Manley, on which the conversation immediately turn'd on other subjects.

The trusty Landy, according to his promise, having reach'd London pretty early that morning, Lady Wingman took it into her head to surprise her daughters with the sight of Lord Huntley in a place where they could so little expect to find him; and willing also that their common friends should be witnesses of this meeting, made an invitation at the same time to Sir Thomas Welby and Sir Robert Manley; but the latter of these gentlemen not being at home when the message was deliver'd heard not of it till some hours afterwards, which was the cause that he came not with the others.

Welcomes,—congratulations, and all the compliments befitting the present occasion were now renew'd; after which,—"What I have lost," said Sir Robert Manley, "by not being here before, will I hope be made up to the company by the intelligence I bring.—You know, my lord," continued he turning to Lord Huntley, "that we met Celandine in the park yesterday."

"Yes," reply'd that nobleman laughing, "he was all alert and gay, talking to some ladies, when we met him; but I shall never forget how his countenance changed on perceiving us, and how silly and sheepish he look'd as we pass'd by him."

"The secret of his doing so," resumed Sir Robert, "is easy to guess;—the sight of us two doubtless made him imagine that the terrible Mr. Lovegrove was also in town; for I have just now heard that he has pack'd up all his fardles[47] of fopperies, and is gone this very morning to make a second tour, and display them to the best advantage he can among his brethren, the petit-maitres."[48]

"What! Gone to Paris!" cried Mr. Lovegrove:—"Aye verily," reply'd the other, "his diamond tassel now ceases to sparkle in St. James's[49] sun, and his musk and amber to perfume the Mall;[50]—your dreadful idea has driven hence the hero of the mode."

> To the great grief of many a charming toast,
> Who sighs and mourns her dear Pulvilio lost.[51]

"Fye upon you, Sir Robert," said Miss Wingman, giving him a slap over the shoulder with her fan,—"I cannot have so mean an opinion of my sex as to believe that there is even one woman in the world that will regret the absence of such a coxcomb."

"Yes, sister," rejoin'd Lady Speck, "just as one would regret the loss of a squirrel or a monkey who has diverted one with its tricks; for I dare answer no woman ever consider'd him in any other light."

"Perhaps not, Madam," said Lord Huntley; "but as the animals you mention are sometimes very mischievous, so there may be danger in encouraging the follies of Celandine, which every one is not aware of;—there is a certain young lady in this town, by some cried up for one of the greatest beauties in it, who has received a wound in her reputation which will not easily be healed, on account of her acquaintance with him."

"I know who your lordship means," cried Jenny, who was always ready to take part with the absent;—"but dare believe that whoever censures her of having the least tendre[52] for that unworthy trifler does her a great deal of injustice;—it is true he has had the impudence and vanity to follow her to all public places, and even to take some liberties in company, which her excess of good nature kept her from resenting so much as perhaps she ought to have done; yet, in spite of these appearances, I think I may be pretty positive that she heartily hates and despises him."

Mr. Lovegrove, who in all probability had more concern in this discourse than any one of the company except Lady Speck, join'd not in it, but affected to be wholly unattentive during the time it lasted, and seem'd taken up with admiring a fine gold headed cane Sir Thomas Welby had in his hand.

The good baronet, who had all this while been silent, as knowing nothing either of Celandine or the lady mention'd by Lord Huntley could not now, on hearing what Jenny said, forbear testifying his admiration of her generosity in expressions no less polite than they were sincere.

"It is no new thing, Sir Thomas," said Mr. Lovegrove, "to hear Miss Jessamy plead the cause of the accused:—strong as was the indictment laid against Lord Huntley in your letter, I can assure you, it lost half its force by the arguments which this fair advocate urg'd in opposition to it;—scarce could the supposed criminal himself have defended his innocence with more zeal, or in terms more pathetic and efficacious."

It cannot be doubted but that Lord Huntley made the most grateful acknowledgements to that young lady, on being told the part she had taken in his justification.—"But how, Madam," said he to her, "did my charming judge receive the pleas you were so good to offer in my behalf?"

"Oh, my lord," answer'd she with a smile, "this is not a fair question;—a barrister you know never pretends to dive into the sentiments of the court."—He then was about to address something to Miss Wingman, who seem'd in a good deal of confusion at this discourse; but her blushes were instantly reliev'd by the butler coming in to tell Lady Wingman that supper was on the table; on which they all adjourn'd into the next room, and sat down to partake of a very elegant collation which that lady had prepared for their entertainment.

What pass'd during the time of eating would be superfluous to repeat; so I shall only say, that soon after the cloth was taken away, Lady Speck, knowing her mother went early to bed, made a motion to retire, and by, doing so engaged the company to break up to the no small satisfaction of Jenny, who was impatient to get home for reasons which will presently appear.

Chapter XVII

Affords fresh matter to employ the speculation of every curious reader.

By Jemmy's letter from Ham-Hall, Jenny found that the time which he proposed to continue there was elapsed, and therefore doubting not but that he was now in town, sent her servant the minute she came home to acquaint him with her arrival; but she was a good deal surprised when the return of the messenger informed her that after staying but two nights in London he had set out the very day before for Bath.

The gall of this disappointment had an equal portion of sweetness mingled with it;—if she was vex'd at not being able to see him so soon as she had expected, she was no less pleased on the haste he had made to go to

Bath, as she knew he could have no reason to imagine she as yet had left that place.

This being a new proof of the sincerity of his affection towards herself, very much abated her impatience to reproach him with the less honourable addresses he had made elsewhere; and she sometimes even doubted within herself whether she ought ever to give him any shock upon that score.

When the suspicion of an enormous injury is once removed, all lesser ones decrease in magnitude, and seem less deserving our resentment than they really are;—Jenny believing her lover innocent, as to the main point, began now to think little of any thing else he might be guilty of.

The good humour she was in at present with him render'd her mind quite composed; but the time was not yet arrived when she was to remain in any settled state of tranquility;—a letter was brought to her by a person who refused to say either from whom or from whence he came;—it contained these lines:

To Miss Jessamy.

Madam,

The high character I have heard of your good nature and complaisance, makes me not doubt but you are endow'd with an equal share of justice and generosity, especially when those noble virtues are to be exerted in favour of a person of your own sex; and in that confidence take the liberty of intreating you will set me right in an affair on which the whole happiness of my life depends, and which none but yourself can clear up from its present ambiguity.

I have for a considerable time received the most passionate addresses of a gentleman who I very well know the world once look'd upon as destin'd to be yours;—he has gain'd my friends' consent, and, by his merits and assiduities, so great an ascendant over me, that nothing hitherto has hinder'd me from accepting his had but the fears that in doing so I should be accessary to his being guilty of an irreparable injury to you.

After this it may perhaps be needless to tell you that I mean Mr. Jessamy; but as my circumstances require a plain and categorical answer from you on this head, it behoves me to express myself in terms which will admit no room to doubt their meaning;—it is indeed, Madam, no other than he whom I love, and by whom I am equally beloved, and who, while he confesses a former engagement with you, protests at the same time, and with the same seeming sincerity at least, that it is now entirely broken off, and that he is at full liberty to dispose of his person where he has given his heart.

But I have been told, by people more experienced than myself, that men will say and swear any thing to gain their point; I dare therefore depend on nothing but an assurance from yourself of the reality of his professions;—tell me, I beseech you, how far the intended union between you is dissolv'd, and whether I may be his without a crime;—pity a rival who would rather die than invade your property, if once convinced he is so;—ease a suspence which has something in it more distracting,—more cruel, than all that could be inflicted by the last despair on her, who is,

With the greatest respect,
Madam,
Your most obedient,
Though unknown servant.

P.S. I beg an immediate answer, because I have promised to give mine to Mr. Jessamy on his return from Bath, and should be glad to know before he comes in what manner I ought to square my conduct towards him.

On the first reading this letter, new alarms, new doubts, new jealousies, instantly fill'd the head and heart of Jenny; but on a second perusal there seem'd to her something too romantic in the expression, as well as purport of it, for her to believe it founded upon real fact; and she began to fancy it was either intended by her enemies as an insult, or by her friends as a jest;—resolving therefore, that from which quarter soever it came, neither of them should have any room to laugh at her behaviour on the occasion, she took a small piece of paper and wrote in it the following words:

> If I were really possess'd of all the good qualities ascrib'd to me in the letter before me, I know none of them that would oblige me to send any answer to an anonymous epistle;—when the lady who wrote it thinks proper to reveal herself she may depend on the satisfaction she desires; in the mean time she is at liberty to form what conjectures she pleases, and to be directed by them which appear to her to have the greatest probability of being right.

This, without either seal or direction, and only folded in a careless manner, she gave to the messenger who had brought the letter, and bid him carry it to those that sent him.

She set herself down again in order to re-examine the contents of this extraordinary epistle; but the more she did so the less able was she to conceive either the real intention of it, or from what hand it came.

After forming, and as often rejecting a thousand different conjectures, it at last came into her head, that the woman to whom Jemmy had wrote that letter, which she received at Bath by mistake, had contrived this stratagem to create a dissention between them.

"I have heard," said she to herself, "that women of the vile profession I suppose her of, value themselves upon these kind of artifices, and take a pride in the mischief they sometimes occasion;—but certainly," continued she, "those on whom such little tricks have any effect must have a very small share of understanding:—Jemmy, however," added she after a pause, "will see by this the scandal and danger of entering into any sort of intimacy with such abandon'd creatures."

But though it must be acknowledged that there was the appearance of a good deal of reason to confirm her in this last opinion, yet I believe the sagacious reader, by what has been the business of several chapters in the first volume of this work, will easily guess that the letter in question was only an addition to the former attempts made by the invidious Bellpine to dissolve that cement of affection which had so long united the hearts of our two lovers.

It was indeed no other than the base man, who knowing she was in town, by having accidentally met her footman in the morning, had taken this method of corroborating the many others which he before had put in practice.

He waited at a coffee-house in the neighbourhood to see what return Jenny would make by his emissary, which finding not so satisfactory as he wish'd, he went directly to visit her, hoping that by her countenance and behaviour, immediately after the receipt of this letter, he should be able to discover, more than by her answer to it, what effect it had wrought upon her.

It has been already observed that Jemmy had inspired her with the best opinion of this treacherous friend, so she no sooner heard he was below than she ordered he should be introduced, and received him with that sweetness and affability with which she always treated those whom she thought deserving of it.

What company was at Bath,—who made the most brilliant appearance there,—who won, and who lost at play, with other such like matters, employed the first moments of their conversation; but Bellpine, desirous of turning it on something more applicable to his purpose, gave over speaking on these subjects as soon as he could do so without abruptness.

"Mr. Jessamy must certainly be very unhappy, Madam," said he, "on finding you had quitted Bath before his arrival there."—"He deserves little pity on that score," reply'd Jenny;—"you men can always find ways to divert yourselves;—few of you regret the absence of an old friend, when you have so many opportunities of engaging new ones."

Though she spoke these words with a very gay air, yet there was a certain keenness in her looks at the same time which persuaded this watchful observer that his plot had not entirely failed of the success he aimed at.

"I do not pretend, Madam," resum'd he, "to dive into the sentiments of Mr. Jessamy; but I am very sure that if you were free and at liberty to be adored, there are men in the world, who would think no joy equal to that of gazing on you, and of repeating every day,—every hour,—nay, every minute, the influence of your charms."

"It is possible indeed," answer'd she, "that there may be some who would endeavour to make me believe so, and that might even be vain enough to imagine I was pleased with what they said;—it is therefore very fortunate for me that I was disposed on by my parents before I arrived at an age to be tiez'd with such impertinencies."

"It is strange how you have escaped them; however, Madam," said he, "your marriage with Mr. Jessamy being so long delay'd might reasonably tempt those who wish it so to flatter themselves with a belief that it never will be accomplish'd, and that there was somewhat of a disinclination either on the one side or the other."

These words made her not doubt but that the report she had heard so much of concerning Jemmy's inconstancy had also reach'd his ears, and she would certainly have been instigated, if not by female curiosity, by love or jealousy, to enter into some discourse with him on that head, if the intimacy between them had not restrain'd her, as she thought he would not betray to her the secret of his friend, in case he were intrusted with it.

What he said however bringing fresh to her memory the vexation she had lately undergone on this account, her countenance went through several changes in the space of half a minute,—"Whoever should think in the manner you mention," reply'd she, "would discover a great want of judgement;—a conjecture of this nature could be justified only by the behaviour of one or the other of us, and I believe it has been such on both sides as to give no room for suspicion that either of us regreted the agreement made between our parents."

A lady to whom Jenny had sent a card that morning, to give notice of her being in town, that same instant coming in prevented Bellpine from making any answer, and he took his leave soon after, having discovered by this visit that his artifices had given her some uneasiness, but less resentment than was necessary for the success of his design.

CHAPTER XVIII

Is dull enough to please those who take an ill-natur'd delight in finding something to condemn; yet is not without occurrences which will keep awake the attention of such who read with a desire of being agreeably amused.

The lady who came to visit Jenny was extremely good humour'd, but a little too talkative;—she never exceeded the bounds of truth in any thing she said, but gave herself not the trouble of considering how far the truths she utter'd were proper to reveal.

I have observ'd that people of this temper frequently do as much mischief, without designing it, as those of the most malicious intentions are capable of; and though sincerity be among the number of the most valuable virtues, yet there are many circumstances wherein to speak all one knows may produce as bad consequences as to speak more than one knows.

I never happen into the company of either man or woman of this stamp but I have fresh in my memory some lines I formerly read in Browne's works.

Those babbling ecchos of whate'er they hear,
Fame's menial servants, who her tidings bear,
Sow such dissention, kindle such debate,
As turns all sweet to sour, all love to hate.[53]

But to return to my subject;—Bellpine had no sooner left the two ladies together than Jenny's friend began to express some wonder at seeing her in town so much before the time she was expected:—"What," cried she, "is there any disagreement between you and Mr. Jessamy?"

"No, not any," reply'd Jenny, a little startled at the question; "but wherefore do you ask?"—"Nay," resumed the other, "it was only a foolish imagination of my own;—not but I had some reason for it too:—you must know that I thought you had been told something of him that had made you angry,—and so when you heard he was coming down to Bath you immediately flounced up to London."

"All a mistake upon my word," said Jenny; "the ladies I was with had some business in town, and my unwillingness to be left behind was the sole cause of my returning to London so soon.—But pray what put such a thing into your head?"

"I did not think to tell you," answer'd this fair gossip; "but since you press me,—though I am afraid it will vex you,—yet I think too you ought to know it;—and if you will promise me not to fret I will let you into the whole secret."

Jenny then said that she should listen without pain to any thing she had to relate; and gave her many more assurances of her philosophy in this point than she had occasion to do, as the other was no less impatient to disburthen herself of the secret than she was to be made a sharer in it.

"Well,—men will be men," said the lady;—"there is no such a thing as changing nature;—but sure I made the discovery I am going to tell you by the oddest accident that ever was;—I suppose you know Mrs. Comode, the habit-maker."[54]—"No", replied Jenny, "but I have heard of her."

"I buy all my things of her," resumed the other, "she has vast business, and I think the genteelest fancy of any woman of her profession about town; every thing she makes up sets with such an air; you must know I had bespoke a fly petticoat with fringes[55] of her;—it not being sent home according to the time she promised, I called in one morning as I passed that way to see if it was done;—she made a thousand apologies, and said I should have it that day; but I scolded heartily, and insisted upon seeing how near it was finished, on which she ran up to fetch it, leaving me alone in the shop."

"The moment she was gone," continu'd this tale-monger, "I found my garter was slipt,—I durst not venture to tie it up in that place for fear somebody should come in, but was running into a little room behind the shop;—but, Lord, I shall never forget how I was surprised,—I had no sooner push'd open the door than—who do you think I saw there?"

"I cannot guess indeed, my dear, but expect you will inform me," reply'd Jenny,—"Why no other," said she "than the very individual Mr. Jessamy;—do not be uneasy now,—sitting as close to a fine lady as two kernels in a nut-shell, hand in hand, and one of his arms across her shoulder; they were so earnest in discourse, that they either did not hear the door open, or thought it was Mrs. Comode herself; but both seem'd in great confusion, and started from their seats when I came in:—whether Mr. Jessamy saw enough of me to distinguish who I was I know not; for I only cried,—'I ask pardon,' and went out of the room with as much haste as I had enter'd.

"Mrs. Comode came down presently after, and brought the petticoat; but I was in such a consternation at what I had seen, that I could scarce look upon it:—I told her of what had happen'd, but did not say I knew either of the parties;—she appear'd very much shock'd, but made an aukward excuse,—said they were two of her customers that had been walking that morning and came in to beg a pot of tea; on which I took no farther notice, but have had no good opinion of her ever since."

"Some woman of the town, I suppose," said Jenny; "Pray what sort of creature was it he had with him?"—"Nay," answer'd the other, "you cannot think it possible for me to give any particular description of her by the momentary glimpse I had of her; but I cannot say that altogether she look'd like such a person."

Jenny had boasted of so much fortitude that she was a little vex'd she had betray'd any want of it by the question she had ask'd; but she afterwards attoned for it by affecting the most perfect indifference during the rest of the conversation they had together on this subject, which lasted almost the whole time the lady staid.

Nothing is more painful than when the mind is discomposed to be under a necessity of concealing it;—Jenny had been impatient to be alone long before she was so; and found a good deal of ease when she attain'd an opportunity of reflecting at leisure on what she had heard.

The story told her by this lady had not so much affected her as the hint given her by Bellpine, concerning a supposition that the match between her and Jemmy was on the point of being broke off,—this tallying so exactly with the intelligence sent to Lady Speck at Bath, convinced her that such a thing was really talk'd of in town, and could not but very much alarm both her love and pride.

Yet when she remember'd her lover's tender letter from Ham-Hall, and the many others she had received from him while she was at Bath, besides the haste she found he had made in hurrying down to that place in expectation of meeting her there, she could not tell how to think it possible that, if guilty as represented, he could be capable of such deceit.

"There is no answering for the hearts of men," said she, "love is an involuntary passion,—chance or fatality directs the choice, and sometimes a single moment undoes the work of years;—I should not be surprised that Jemmy happen'd to see a face which had more charms for him than mine;—but wherefore then should he carry on the deception with me?—How would it avail his new flame to pretend to prosecute a former one?—No," continued she after pausing a little;—"for him to act in this manner would be as inconsistent with reason and common-sense as with honour and justice; and it would also be the utmost weakness in me to believe it."

Thus did she make herself tolerably easy as to the main part of what was laid to his charge; but as to his having enter'd into an affair of gallantry, she had too plain a proof of that under his own hand writing to admit the least room for doubt, and needed not the confirmation she had just received of it from her friend.

Upon the whole, however, few young ladies in her circumstances would have suffer'd less inquietude; and this must be said of her, that it was much more difficult to raise any tempest in her mind, than it was to calm that tempest after it had been raised.

Neither grief nor anger had the power to affect her long, or to drive her to any excesses while they lasted,—a humour extremely volatile,—a great deal of good nature, and an equal share of understanding, were happily united in her composition, and made her always ready to believe the best, and to forgive the worst.

The small remains of resentment and discontent, on the various occasions that had been given her for both, were entirely dissipated, when, on the evening of the succeeding day, she received a letter from Jemmy,—the contents whereof were as follow:

To Miss Jessamy.

My more than ever dear Jenny,

I have certainly been of late one of the most unlucky fellows in the universe,—first to be detained by a series of cross accidents from following you in a few days, as I proposed;—then, when I had dispatch'd those vexatious affairs, and just upon the wing to fly to Bath, to be dragg'd to another quarter of the kingdom, by one whose intreaties you know I could not well deny;—and lastly, when got free from every care but my impatience to be with you, I arrived here full fraught with the expectations of meeting all my soul holds dear, to find you had left the place scarce twenty-four hours before I came;—judge how sincerely I am mortified:—I suppose the caprice of those you were with carried you so suddenly from hence; but I hope the day is now very near at hand when those who take you will be obliged to take me also; for indeed, my dear Jenny, I am quite weary of this life: whenever I am from you for any length of time I feel methinks as if separated from myself;—the more I see of other women, the more I regret the absence of my dear Jenny:—as I came hither pretty early last night, I went to the Long-room,[56]—there were a great many fine ladies there; but all their beauties are without a charm for me;—I can be gay but not happy in their company;—the power of giving true felicity to Jemmy is reserved only for his dear, dear Jenny.

I give you warning therefore, not to think of delaying any longer a blessing I have been made to hope ever since my first putting on breeches reminded me that if I lived I should be one day a man; but be assured I should have little joy in being so, if it were not for the expectation of being yours by a more tender title than that with which I now subscribe myself,

Unalterably and inviolably,
My dear dear Jenny's
Most passionately devoted,
Most faithful lover,
And ever humble
And obedient servant,
J. Jessamy.

P.S. I would have set out tomorrow morning on my return for London, but my servant got an ugly fall from his horse in coming hither, and is very much bruised, so am willing to give him one day to recover himself; but hope the next to be so far on my journey towards you, as that there will be but a few hours distance between your receiving this and the author of it,—till when I am, my dear dear Jenny,

Yours as above.

Jenny was now in such a great good humour with her lover, that she grew half resolved to consent to his desires for the consummation of their marriage, if it were only to put a final end to those idle reports which had been spread concerning his having an intention to break it off.

But before we bring them together again, it is highly necessary that the reader should be made fully acquainted with the manner in which

Jemmy had passed his time during this little separation, and also to clear up those parts of his conduct which have hitherto appeared mysterious.

Chapter XIX

Returns to what has doubtless been long ago expected, and opens a new scene of various and entertaining occurrences.

I am very much afraid that poor Jemmy has lain for a great while under the displeasure of my fair readers, and that few among them will be quite so ready as Jenny has been to take his bare word for a sufficient proof of his honour, and the sincerity of his passion.

It is high time therefore to let his actions speak for themselves; and if they cannot shew him so wholly blameless as could be wish'd, from the frailties of youth and nature, they will at least defend his character from the more gross imputations of perfidiousness, ingratitude, and deceit.

As I have no view to self-interest in this work,—no time-server, no patron to please, it may be depended on that I shall present my hero such as he truly is, and not like some political historians of a modern date, attempt to mislead the judgment by any false glosses or misrepresentations of facts.

The writers I have been speaking of, will not allow the person on whom fortune has not vouchsafed to smile any one virtue or good quality;—he must be all black, without a single speck of white, even to excite the compassion of the world;—what false steps he may have been guilty of are ascribed to his own innate propensity to evil, not to any inadvertency, nor to the wicked insinuations of those on whom he may unhappily have depended, and who perhaps have found their interest in pushing him on things purposely to betray and ruin him.

Whereas, on the other hand, the man whom a concurrence of fortuitous events, or perhaps some indirect measures of his own or partisans contrivance, have raised to prosperity, shall be mounted on the pinnacle of fame,—his virtues, if he has any, be resounded even to the remotest borders of the earth, and all his vices, though numerous as the hairs upon his head, and glaring with red impiety, be so screen'd and shadow'd over with the incense of panegyric, as not to be discern'd but by a few eagle-eyed observers;—but I shall say no more,—these authors perhaps earn their sustenance by the labour of the pen;—these are not times for truth to go clad in velvet, and there is no serving God and Mammon.[57]

I cannot, however, without great injustice, close this reflection till I have taken notice, that there is one who bravely and almost alone, has courage to enter the lists of battle against an host of adversaries, and attempts to rescue injured innocence from the claws of cruel and all-devouring scandal;—may his honest endeavours meet the success they merit, and in spite of prejudice and partiality open the eyes of too long hood-wink'd reason.

And now—for our Jemmy Jessamy;—nothing is more certain than that he had determined to follow his dear Jenny to Bath, according to his promise, as soon as the affairs which brought his steward to town should be dispatch'd; nor was he less uneasy than one of his letters inserted in a former chapter had intimated to her, on finding himself likely to be detained in London so much longer than he had expected at the time of her departure.

Business of any kind, especially of that sort in which he was now engaged, was no way agreeable to his humour;—to be obliged to sit for hours together reading over leases, bonds and ejectments,[58] instead of poetry and books of diversion;—to converse every day with men of the law instead of the men of pleasure, was extremely distasteful to him; but in the midst of all this he met with something which though he did not think of any very great moment, served however to add to the perplexity of his mind, and involve him in an embarrassment he had never dreamt of.

He was at breakfast one morning when his servant inform'd him, that a gentleman who call'd himself Morgan desir'd to speak with him;—this was a person for whom Jemmy had a very great esteem, not only on account of many good qualities he was possess'd of, but likewise as he knew he had been always highly respected by his father.

He gave orders that he should be immediately introduced, and when he was so, began to testify, with as much sincerity as politeness, how much he thought himself indebted to him for the favour of this visit; but he was soon interrupted by the other, who with an honest plainness replied in these terms:

"Mr. Jessamy," said he, "this is not a visit of mere ceremony;—I come not hither at this time either to make or receive any compliments, but to do you a more essential service, and myself a more real pleasure:—to be free with you," continued he, "I am very much troubled at some things I have heard in relation to you, and would gladly offer you such advice as my long experience of the world may enable me to give you."

Few young people like to have their conduct call'd in question;—Jemmy presently imagined that the old gentleman had been inform'd of some little slights,—some trifling irregularities which company and the gaiety of his own temper might have led him into, and expected to be entertain'd with a grave lesson on that occasion:—he told him, however, he should willingly listen to any instructions he should give him.

"I believe," resumed Mr. Morgan, "that you are convinced I wish you well; but if you are not I hope what I have to say will make you so:—mistake me not," pursued he, seeing the other look very serious,—"I am not going to reprimand you,—I know not as yet whether you deserve it;—I have not seen Miss Jessamy since she was an infant;—I have heard, indeed, a very good character both of her person and accomplishments; but you are the best judge of her merits as well as of your own heart;—I am confident that when your parents agreed upon a marriage between you, they meant not it should render either of you miserable, so have nothing to say as to that;—but whatever be the motive of your breaking with her, I would not have you, methinks, transfer your addresses to any one where there is not a greater probability of being more happy."

Jemmy was so confounded,—so astonish'd at hearing him speak in this manner, that he had not the power, for some moments, of uttering one syllable, and when he had, it was only to cry,—"Breaking with her, Sir,—what,—breaking with Miss Jessamy?"

"You have doubtless your own reasons for so doing," reply'd the good old gentleman; "but let that pass,—I would only have you be wary how you make a second choice;—it is not in my nature to traduce the character of any one;—Miss Chit may be a very deserving young woman for any thing I have to accuse her of; but you know very well that her family is doubtful,—her fortune precarious,—and if she should have any, it will be little for her husband's honour to receive,—besides, this is not the worst, for though she may be virtuous in fact, yet she keeps company with some persons of both sexes, which does not become a woman who has any regard for reputation; in fine, my dear Mr. Jessamy, she is in no respect a fit wife for you."

"A wife for me!" said Jemmy not yet recover'd from this amazement;—"For Heaven's sake, Sir, explain the meaning of all this;—you talk of things which have so little analogy with my intentions, that they never once enter'd into my head or heart;—to break my engagements with Miss Jessamy, or to make my addresses to Miss Chit, are both of them equally inconsistent with my inclination as with my reason; and it is not possible for me to conceive how such chimeras could come into the thoughts of any one."

"As to the first," answer'd Mr. Morgan, "I have heard it mention'd in several companies where I have been, as an event past all dispute; and as to what concerns Miss Chit, I was not only told it by a person who frequently visits her, but also had it confirm'd yesterday at the coffee-house by her own father, who being asked if there was any truth in the report of an intended marriage between his daughter and Mr. Jessamy, reply'd with his usual stiffness and formality, that he believed a treaty of that nature was upon the carpet."

Jemmy, on hearing this, was fully persuaded that so idle a rumour could proceed from nothing but the vanity of that young lady, which so incensed him against her, that he could not forbear, in the first emotions of passion, speaking of her in terms which nothing but the occasion could excuse.

As he was discussing the matter with Mr. Morgan, and convincing that gentleman of the entire fallacy of all he had reproach'd him with, a card was brought from Miss Chit, in which was wrote these words:

> Miss Chit gives her compliments to Mr. Jessamy, and desires his company to a concert to be performed by private hands this evening at her house.

"Now, Sir," said he to Mr. Morgan, "you shall see the little influence the charms of this vain girl has over me,—I will send her a letter instead of a card, and such a one as shall put an effectual stop to all the foolish imaginations she may have conceiv'd on my account."

He then took pen and paper, and without giving himself much time to consider what he was about, wrote to her in these terms:

To Miss Chit.

Madam,

Business denies me the pleasure of accepting your invitation; but I lay hold of this opportunity of taking my leave of you, as I cannot do it in person.

Love and honour summon me to Bath, where my dear Miss Jessamy is gone before; —as it is impossible but you must have heard of my engagements with that lady, you will not wonder that I am in the utmost impatience to follow her.

Whenever you venture on marriage, I wish you all the happiness which I hope very shortly to enjoy in that state, with the admirable lady to whom I am going.—I am,

With thanks for all favours,
Madam,
Your most obedient
humble servant,
J. Jessamy.

This letter, after having shew'd it to Mr. Morgan and received his approbation, Jemmy sent directly away, and gave orders that it should be left for the lady without waiting for any answer.

On talking farther of this affair, they both concluded that the report must have taken rise originally from the vanity of the daughter and the stupidity of the father, who misconstruing the civilities Jemmy treated them with as the effects of an amorous inclination, had boasted of the imaginary conquest to some of their acquaintance,—those again had whisper'd it to others, till it went round, and became, as is common in such cases, the universal secret.

Thus had the artifices of Bellpine made Miss Chit and her father, who were in reality no more than the dupes of his design, appear as the principal contrivers of it;—there is nothing, indeed, in which the judgment is so liable to be deceived, as in endeavouring to discover the first author of a calumny,—those generally take care to stand behind the curtain,—content themselves with the invention, and leave the work of malice to be performed by others,—as one of our poets says:

'Tis difficult, when rumour once is spread,
To trace its windings to their fountainhead.[59]

The injustice which Jemmy and his friend were guilty of in this point, may however have some claim to absolution, as their belief was founded on the most strong probability of truth that could be.

These gentlemen parted not till the clock striking three reminded them of dinner;—Mr. Morgan, being engaged at home, would fain have taken Jemmy with him; but he was not at present in a humour for much company,—therefore desired to be excused from complying with the invitation.

Chapter XX

Is very short, but pithy.

A volatile temper is not always a sufficient security from discontent;—Jemmy loved his dear Jenny even more than he knew he did himself; and to be assured from a mouth whose veracity he was too well convinced of to suspect, that it was said he had quitted her for the sake of Miss Chit, he look'd upon as such an indignity to her merits, as gave him more pain than any censure the supposed change might bring upon himself.

He wrote to her that same night; but as he hoped the idle report which gave him so much vexation could not as yet, at least, have extended itself so far as Bath, he thought it improper to make any mention of it till he should see her in person, and have the better opportunity of proving the falsehood of it;—he complained therefore only of the business that kept him so long from her, and his heart now more than ever overflowing with love and tenderness, his expressions were conformable.

This was the letter which Jenny received immediately after the intelligence given her by Lady Speck and Miss Wingman of his supposed infidelity;—the effects of it have been already shewn, and need not be repeated.

Bellpine, who had been at Miss Chit's concert, was a good deal surprised at not finding Jemmy there, as he knew he had been invited, but much more when that young lady, taking him aside, shew'd him the answer that had been sent to her card, and reproach'd him in terms pretty severe for having endeavour'd to persuade her she was mistress of an heart which she now found was so firmly attach'd to another.

Happy was it for this deceitful man that the time and place would not allow of much discourse, as he had not consider'd that such an event might possibly happen, nor was he prepared with any subterfuge for his proceeding;—the confusion he was in was very great; but it did not make him repent of what he had done, or cease from future projects for the same base end; as will hereafter appear.

It is natural, when the mind is overcharged with thoughts of any kind, to disburthen itself to those who we believe take an interest in our affairs;—Jemmy had not a greater confidence in any one man of his acquaintance than in Bellpine,—it may be supposed, therefore, that he fail'd not to communicate to him the perplexity he was at present under, and the story which had occasion'd it.

That faithless friend affected the utmost astonishment at the recital, and cried out with a shew of the most affectionate zeal;—"Good God!—I hope Miss Jessamy has heard nothing of this."

"I think it scarce possible," reply'd Jemmy, "that such a report can have reach'd her ears at least as yet, in the place where she is; and as I hope to be with her in a few days shall take care to arm her against what she might be told hereafter by relating it myself."

This greatly disconcerted Bellpine;—he had flatter'd himself that Jemmy's affairs would have detain'd him so long in London, that the stratagems laid to inspire her with a belief of his inconstancy would have taken too strong a hold of her heart to be totally removed:—fain he would have dissuaded him from going to Bath, but could find no reasons for that purpose plausible enough to prevent the real motive from being suspected;—chance, however, at present befriended his designs, and did that for him which all his own invention, fertile as it was, could not furnish him with the means of accomplishing.

As Jemmy, in an indolent and uncontemplative mood, was one day loitering in Covent-Garden Piazza,[60] a fine gilt chariot, with two footmen behind it, stopp'd at one of the arches, and just as he was passing, an ancient gentleman and a very young lady alighted out of it, and went into the great auction-house, lately Mr. Cock's, but now occupy'd in the same manner by Mr. Langford.[61]

He started, and was strangely surprised at sight of this lady;—not on account of her beauty, though she was handsome beyond description, but because he thought himself perfectly well acquainted with her face; but where, or at what time, he had been so, he could not presently recollect.

He stood for the space of several minutes endeavouring to recover a more distinct idea of that lovely person; but finding it impossible, he stepp'd to one of the footmen, who was leaning his back against a pillar, and ask'd him to whom that chariot belong'd; and being answer'd—"To Sir Thomas Hardy."—"Then," resumed Jemmy, "I suppose the young lady with him is his daughter."—"No, Sir," replied the fellow with a smile, which he was not able to restrain,—"I assure you she is his wife."

Jemmy on this began to think he had been mistaken;—resolving however to be convinced, he went into the auction room, doubting not but a second and more full view would set him right.

There was a great deal of company, but he presently singled her out, and was now more assured than ever that they were no strangers to each other; when, on fixing his eyes upon her, he perceiv'd her countenance change at sight of him, that she grew pale and red by turns, and betrayed all the marks of the utmost confusion.

Yet all this was not sufficient to enable him to bring back to remembrance what curiosity made him so desirous of retrieving, till the lady, taking the opportunity of her husband's being engaged in looking over some pictures, advanced hastily towards him, and said in a low voice— "What has Mr. Jessamy forgot his Celia of the Woods?"

"Heavens!" cried he, "What a stupid dolt was I?"—"Hush," reply'd she, "take no notice of me here";—she had kept her eyes upon her husband all the time she was speaking to Jemmy, and observing that he now look'd that way rejoin'd him in an instant.

The old baronet kept very close to his fair wife all the rest of the time, yet had she the address to steal a moment just to bid Jemmy meet her at ten the next morning at the end of the Mall next Buckingham house.[62]

He could only give her a bow of assent; and remain'd in a consternation which only can be guess'd at by the knowledge who Celia was, and the intercourse he formerly had with her.

Chapter XXI

Discovers Celia of the Woods on her first acquaintance with Jemmy, and also some other particulars of equal importance.

Though Jemmy, when he was at Oxford, debar'd himself from few of those gay amusements which he saw taken by his fellow collegians, yet he apply'd himself to his studies more closely than most gentlemen commoners[63] think they are under any obligation to do; and, because he would not be interrupted, would frequently steal from the university and pass whole hours together in the fields, either reading or contemplating.

A pretty warm dispute happening to rise one day between two students concerning the true reading of Persius,[64] he was ambitious of becoming more master of the subject than either of them seem'd to be;—accordingly he put the book into his pocket and repair'd to his usual place of retirement.

The evening was fair and pleasant, and he was so much absorb'd in meditation, that he wander'd on to a greater distance from the town than he had been accustom'd, till at last, finding himself a little weary, he sat down at the foot of a large spreading oak.

Here he prosecuted his examination of that crabbed author, but had not long done so before he was interrupted, and his eyes taken off by the sudden appearance of a sight more pleasing.

The tree, which served him at once for a support and screen, was just at the entrance of a little wood;—a rustling among the leaves made him look that way, where he immediately saw a young country maid;—she was neat, tho' plainly dress'd, and had eyes which might vye with any that sparkled in the box or drawing room.

At this view he was not master of himself;—like Carlos at the sight of Angelina in the play,[65] he threw away his book,—started from the posture he was in, and advanced towards the sweet temptation;—she saw him too and fled, but not so fast as not to be easily overtaken.

The first encounter between these two young persons reminds me of a passage I have read in one of our best poets:

As Mahomet was musing in his cell,
Some dull insipid paradice to trace,
A brisk Arabian girl came tripping by,
Passing she shot at him a side-long glance,
And look'd behind as if to be pursu'd;
He took the hint, embraced the flying fair,
And having found his Heaven, he fix'd it there.[66]

It is not to be imagined that Jemmy accosted a maid of her degree with any set speeches or formal salutations;—those charms which in a woman of condition would have inspired him with a respectful awe, served only to fill his heart with the most unwarrantable desires;—he told her she was very pretty, and at the same time attempted to convince her that he thought her so by catching her forcibly in his arms, and giving her two or three hearty kisses.

She struggled,—blush'd,—cried—"Aye, Sir," and desired him to forbear; but our young commoner was not to be so easily rebuffed;—the little repulses she gave him served only the more to inflame his amorous inclination; and he had perhaps completed his conquest, without any farther ceremony, if she had not fallen on her knees, and with tears besaught him to desist.

Jemmy had too much honour and good nature not to be touch'd with a behaviour so moving, and which he had so little reason to expect from the weak efforts she at first had made to repel his caresses.

"Nay,—my dear creature," said he, "I scorn to do any thing by force; but if all the love in the world can make you mine I shall be happy;—tell me therefore," continued he, "who you are, and where you live, that I may see you another time."

"Oh lud, Sir," cried she, "that is impossible";—"What do you think my friends would say, if they should see such a gentleman as you come to visit me?"—"I did not mean so," reply'd he, "but I suppose your father lives here about, and it may be is of some business that might give a pretence for my calling at his house."

"My father keeps a farm," said she, "about six miles off; but I am at present with my uncle, who is a gardener, and lives on the other side the wood."—"That's unlucky," rejoin'd he, "for I have no sort of occasion for any thing in his way.—You must then consent to meet me, my little angel," added he, tenderly pressing her hand.

On this she blush'd,—hung down her head, but made no answer; till he repeating his request, and enforcing it by all the rhetoric he was master of, whether real or feign'd I will not pretend to say, she at last promised to meet him the next evening at the place where they now were.

He received this grant with the greatest shew of transport, but made her swear to the fulfilling it; after which he ask'd her by what name he should think of his dear pretty charmer. "They call me Celia, Sir," said she.—"Then," cried he, "you shall be my Celia of the Woods, and I will be your Jessamy of the plains."

The sun beginning now to withdraw his beams, they were obliged to part; but before they did Celia gave evident indications that her Jessamy had made no slight impression on her young and unexperienced heart.

Jemmy return'd from his evening's excursion with thoughts very full of this new amour, which he flatter'd himself would afford him a most agreeable amusement, without costing much pains in the acquisition.

Besides, the liking he had for this country girl seem'd to him to be no breach of his fidelity to Jenny, or any way interfere with the honourable affections he had for that young lady;—she being then but in her sixteenth year, himself not quite nineteen, and was not intended by their parents that they should marry till he had attain'd the age of one and twenty;—so that it was a long time to the completion of his felicity with her.—I know not whether my fair readers will look upon this as a sufficient excuse for him; but dare answer that those of the other sex will think what he did was no more than a venial transgression.

As for poor Celia, she was in agitations which she had never known nor had the least notion of before;—she was charm'd with the person of Jemmy;—she was quite ravish'd with the kind things he had said to her; and though the liberties he had taken with her at that first interview would have been shocking to her modesty, had they been offer'd by any of those whom she was accustom'd to converse with, yet did that very rudeness in him appear too agreeable to alarm her with any dreadful apprehensions of his repeating it.

More full of joy than fear she long'd for the appointed hour of meeting him again, and hasted to the rendezvous, where she had not waited many minutes before the charmer of her soul appear'd;—he flew to her with open arms, and the transport she felt made her half return the strenuous embrace he gave her.

They sat down together upon a little hillock beneath the shade of some trees which arch'd above their heads and form'd a kind of canopy;—here Jemmy finding her softened to his wish, would fain have finish'd the affair he had made so considerable a progress in; but, on perceiving his intent, she burst a second time into tears,—begg'd he would not ruin her,—confess'd she loved him, but said she could not bear the thoughts of being naught.[67]

He could scarce keep himself from laughing; but as he had promised not to make use of force, fail'd not to urge all the arguments that such a thing would admit of to perswade her that what he requested of her was not naught in itself, but perfectly conformable to the laws of nature.

She was too ignorant, and perhaps also too little inclined to attempt any thing in order to confute what he said on this occasion; but though she refused with less resolution than she had done, yet she would not absolutely consent to his desires:—on which Jemmy, not doubting but the fruit thus ripened would soon fall of itself, told her,—that he was not of a humour to accept of any favours granted with reluctance, and that he would content himself with such as he should find her willing to bestow.

He kept his word, and press'd her no farther at that time;—this the poor innocent creature look'd upon as so great a condescention in him, and thought herself so much obliged by it that she readily allow'd his kisses, his embraces, and in fine every freedom except that only one which he had assured her he would not take without her leave.

Notwithstanding what they call'd the crown of a lover's felicity was wanting, this couple pass'd the time they were together in a manner pleasing enough to both; nor parted without a mutual promise of re-enjoying the same happiness again on the ensuing day.

Jemmy, however, who was of too sanguine and amorous a disposition not to feel a good deal of impatience for the consummation of his wishes, in order to hasten it contrived a stratagem, which, from the ascendant he had gain'd over Celia's heart, gave him no room to doubt would fail of success in making her lovely person no less entirely his,—it was this:

He approach'd her at their next meeting with the most solemn and dejected air;—she had brought him a fine posy selected from the choicest flowers in her uncle's garden, tied together with a piece of green riband;—she was going to present it to him, when perceiving the change in his countenance she started, and asked him if he was not well.

"No Celia," answer'd he, affecting to speak in a very faint voice,—"I am sick,—sick at heart,"—"Indeed I am very sorry," said she, "smell this posy,—I hope it will refresh you, my dear Sir."—"No, Celia," return'd he, "it is not in the power of art or nature to relieve me, you must lose your lover;—I must die, my Celia."—"Now all that's good forbid it," cried she, and wept bitterly.

"I must die," said he again, "or what is worse than death,—never see my Celia more."—Surprised and overwhelm'd with the mingled passions of love and grief at hearing him speak in this manner, she threw her taper[68] arms about his neck, laid her cheek close to his, and begg'd him to tell her what he meant, and the cause of his complaint.

"You, dear cruel maid," answer'd he with a well counterfeited agony,—"it is you which is the cause of my complaint;—and it is you alone can be my cure:—in fine, it is impossible for me to breathe the same air with you and not see you,—yet every time I see you gives fresh tortures to my bleeding heart, by letting me know still more of the Heaven I am deny'd possessing;—I have therefore taken a resolution to banish myself for ever from you, and from this country.—You must then," continued he,—embracing her with the utmost eagerness, "either lose all your Jessamy or give me all my Celia."

The consternation she was in is not to be express'd; but every look,—every motion, betray'd to him the inward trouble of her mind;—she could not speak for several minutes; but at last cried out, with a voice interrupted by sighs,—"Oh Mr. Jessamy, will you,—can you be so barbarous to leave me,—leave me for ever!"

"Call not that barbarous which your unkindness drives me to," rejoin'd he;—"if I loved you with a common passion, I could perhaps be easy under the severe restriction you have laid upon me,—but you are too beautiful, and I too much enamoured.—Oh then throw off at once this cruel coyness,—this unmerited reserve,—generously say you will be all mine, and make both me and yourself completely bless'd."

He utter'd these last words in accents which pierced her to the soul;—she was all confusion,—irresolute for a while,—sometimes looking on him, and sometimes on the ground; but love at length,—prevailing love, got the better of that bashfulness, which 'tis likely had, more than any other principle, till now restrain'd her from yielding to his suit;—she threw herself into his arms, and hiding her head within his bosom,—"I cannot part with you," cried she, "I can deny you nothing,—you have my heart, and must command whatever Celia has to give."

There is strong probability, if it does not amount even to a certainty, that Jemmy would not have given her time for a second thought, which might have revok'd the promise she had made; but his plot, hitherto so successful, was now entirely frustrated by the sudden sound of men's voices at a distance, and which seem'd to approach more near.

"Oh lud," cried she extremely frighted, "I hear my uncle;—if he should come this way and find me with a gentleman, he will tell my father, and I shall be half kill'd;—Dear Mr. Jessamy, make all the haste you can out of the wood;—I will go and face him, and pretend I was going to carry these flowers to a great lady who lives hard by."

Jemmy could not forbear cursing both the uncle and the interruption; but thought proper to comply with Celia's advice, after having exacted an oath from her to meet him again the next day and fulfil her engagement, which she readily gave, and then tripp'd away as fast as her legs could carry her.

Thus did they part, not to see each other again for a much longer time than either of them imagined,—the cause of which will presently be shewn.

Chapter XXII

In which, among other things, it will be found highly proper that some passages formerly inserted should be re-capitulated, in order to form the better understanding of those which are now upon the tapis.

Jemmy return'd to the college in no very good humour, as may be supposed, though the mortification of the disappointment he had received was very much alleviated by the assurance he had of Celia's affection for him; but on his entering into his chambers he met with something which made the adventures of the day, and indeed all that had pass'd between him and the country maid, vanish like a dream from his remembrance.

A letter was presented to him which had been left for him by the post, summoning him immediately to London to receive the last commands and blessing of a dying father;—filial piety and duteous affection now took up all his mind, and he thought of nothing but to be speedy in his obedience to the authoritative mandate.

Accordingly he rose the next morning, by break of day,—rode post, and arrived in London before evening, as has been already related in the beginning of the first volume of this work.

On his going back to the university, after the melancholy solemnity of his father's funeral was over, Celia came again a little into his head; and though he design'd shortly to quit Oxford entirely, yet he thought that for the time he staid he could not have a more agreeable amusement than the prosecution of that amour to divert his affliction for the loss he had sustain'd.

To this end he went to the wood,—ranged through every part of that scene of their loves, but found no Celia there;—he knew her uncle's name, but not directly where he lived; or if he had, would not have thought it proper to go to his house to make any enquiry concerning her;—happening, however, to see a fellow cutting down wood, he ventur'd to ask him if one Mr. Adams, a gardener, did not live somewhere thereabouts,—"Ay, Sir," reply'd the man, "if you turn by that thicket on your right hand you may see his house."—"Nay," said Jemmy carelesly, "I have no business with him,—I have only heard he was a very honest man."—"Ay, Sir," rejoin'd the other, "that he is to be sure, as ever broke bread;—I have known him above these thirty years, and never heard an ill thing of him in my life."

Jemmy finding this fellow seem'd to be of a communicative disposition, demanded of him what family Mr. Adams had.—"Ah, Sir," said the man,—"he has only two boys,—one he brings up to his own business and the other is a gentleman's servant;—his wife,—rest her soul, has been dead two years come Michaelmas[69] next, and he would have been quite helpless if he had not got a brother's daughter of his to look after his things;—but she is gone now;—I know not what the poor man will do,—he must even hire a maid, and there are so few of them good."—"What is his niece dead too," cried Jemmy pretty hastily. "No Sir," answer'd he,—"but she is gone away;—her father, belike, sent for her home,—I know not on what account,—not I; but she has left poor Adams, and he is in a piteous plight."

Jemmy being desirous of receiving as much intelligence as he could of his little mistress, affected to be in some concern for the honest gardener, her uncle, pretending he had heard much in his commendation from those that knew him; and said it was a great pity that the maid should be sent for away, as she was so useful to him, and so notable a manager.

"Ay very handy, indeed Sir," answer'd Mr. Adams's friend,—"she kept every thing in the house so clean and so tight it would have done your heart good to have seen it;—but as to her father's sending for her away,—I don't know,—mayhap he had a mind to have her under his own eye,—he has the character of a parlous-shrewd[70] man, and sees things a great while before they come."

"Was there any danger then to be apprehended in her staying?" demanded Jemmy.—"I can say nothing as to that, Sir,—she is as likely,—as comely a lass as any in the county round,—but I believe very honest;—though she has a kind of a leer with her eyes, and is always simpering and smirking; and you know Sir, that gives encouragement;—there were a power of young fellows that had a hankering after her,—I have heard my wife say a thousand times I believe,—and she is seldom mistaken, that she wish'd Celia might come to good."

"Besides, Sir," continued he, shaking his head, "we are so near the University here, and the young students are most of them wild blades, and spend their time more in running after the girls than on their books."

It must be observed that Jemmy was now in his travelling dress; for had he appeared as a gentleman-commoner, no body can suppose that the countryman would have been so free in his discourse with him, which being once enter'd into he would probably have gone on with till he had related all he knew of the news of the whole parish.

But Jemmy having satisfied his curiosity as fully as he could have desired, and much more than he had any reason to expect, grew quite weary of this kind of conversation, and soon after took leave of his informer, and walk'd back to the college.

He had now lost his Celia of the Woods,—he knew indeed where to find her; but as his stay in Oxford was to be very short, and he had many friends to see before he went away, he had no time to devote to the pursuit of a mistress so far removed;—besides, he knew not what inconveniencies might attend his seeking her at her father's house; and was too indolent in his nature to risque any difficulties for the sake of gratifying a passion such as the beauty of that girl had inspired him with.

After he had quitted the University entirely, and was settled in London, besides the society of his dear Jenny, whom, in spite of the little excursions of his youth, he loved with the most pure and respectful passion, new scenes of life,—new amusements,—new pleasures, crowded upon his senses, and presently obliterated the memory of those he left behind.

Celia, no more was wish'd for, no more thought on by him, how was it possible that after so long a space of time as two whole years, and having seen such a variety of beautiful faces, he should be able to recollect his plain country maid under the character of a fine town lady, blazing with gold and jewels, attended by a splendid equipage, and dignify'd with a title.

This adventure, notwithstanding, served greatly to dissipate all the chagrine which the story invented in relation to his infidelity to Jenny had involved him in;—he could not keep himself from being highly pleased at meeting with a person who had once so many charms for him, nor with finding, by her behaviour towards him, that so prodigious a change of fortune had not made the least change in her sentiments on his account:—in a word, all the long dormant inclinations which he had formerly felt for Celia, now revived in his bosom at sight of Lady Hardy; and he hesitated not a moment whether he should comply with the appointment she had made him.

How uncertain,—how wandering are the passions of mankind,—how yielding to every temptation that presents itself;—seldom are they masters of their own hearts or actions; especially at Jemmy's years; and well may they deceive others in what they are deceived themselves.

When they protest to love no other object than the present, they may, perhaps resolve to be as just as they pretend;—but alas!—This is not in their power, even though it may in their will;—they can no more command their wishes than they can their thoughts, which, as Shakespear tells us,—"Once lost, are gone beyond the clouds."[71]—We often see that to reverse this boasted constancy is the work of but a single minute,—and then in vain their past professions recoil upon their minds;—in vain the idea of the forsaken fair haunts them in nightly visions.

For mighty love, which honour does despise,
For reason shews them a new charmer's eyes.[72]

Chapter XXIII

Contains only such accidents as are too common to excite much wonder.

I would not be understood, by the observations made on the generality of mankind in the close of the preceding chapter, that the vice of inconstancy ought to be imputed to the hero of this history; what in most others is the effect of a love of variety, was produced in him by the too great vivacity and sprightliness of his temper: he had sometimes very strong inclinations, but never a real affection for any but his dear Jenny; and tho' these may have led him into errors which render him not wholly blameless, yet the permanence of his devoirs to that sole object of his honourable passion, shews his character to have in it infinitely more of light than shade.

Let no one therefore pass too severe a censure on his conduct in regard to this fair tempter, either as Celia of the Woods or Lady Hardy;—whatever was the first motive of his addresses to her, curiosity to know how this transformation came about might now, and doubtless had, some share in exciting him to renew his acquaintance with her.

I shall not, however, as I have more than once assured my readers, make any attempts either to palliate or disguise the truth:—Jemmy was punctual to the hour that had been prefix'd by his mistress, yet found her in the Park before him;—she had placed herself on a bench behind the Mall, as being most free from company:—when he first discerned her, she seem'd talking to a young woman who stood waiting near her, but left her ladyship alone before he could come up to them.

"How little possible was it for me to expect this blessing,"—said he approaching her.—"Hold—hold,"—cried she interrupting him,—"we have no time at present for fine speeches, and you will be surprised to find yourself summon'd here only to be told you must be gone."—"I should be indeed surprised,"—rejoin'd he;—"but how have I deserved to be so unhappy?"

"No, no," reply'd she smiling, "you are not unhappy, though I could easily tell you how you deserve to be so;—but this is no place either for a quarrel or a reconciliation:—you must know I could not come out alone for fear of giving suspicion to my old husband, so brought my woman with me; but as soon as I saw you, sent her home under the pretence of fetching my snuffbox, which I left behind me for that purpose;—she will be here again in two minutes, for we live but in the next street, and have a door into the Park;—therefore take this," continued she, "and be careful to do as this directs."

"Let me first examine how I approve of the contents," said he with his accustom'd gaiety,—"You may," answer'd she; "but then you will lose the only moment that I have to tell you, I am as much yours as ever, and that I have not known one joy in life since last we parted."—"Angelic creature!" cried he with a voice and eyes all transport, "oh that I had the opportunity of throwing myself at your feet to thank, as it deserves, this goodness!—Where,—when shall we meet again?"

"The paper I gave you will inform you," reply'd she; "but do not disappoint Lady Hardy in the same manner as you did Celia of the Woods."—"Oh I can clear myself of that" cries he, "it was a sad necessity that drove me from you, and I had no means of conveying a letter to you; but I have sought you since."—"And I have sought you too," rejoin'd she; "but we must talk of this hereafter;—I see my woman coming,—leave me for Heaven's sake, and if you stay in the walks pass carelessly by, and seem not to regard me."—Jemmy had only time to tell her, that he would read the dear mandate, and obey whatever it enjoined.

After speaking these words he retired with as much haste as he could to the other end of the walk, where he examined what had been given him by the lady, and found it contain'd only these few expressive lines:

Go at six this evening precisely to Mrs. Comode, the habit-maker, in * * * street,—she is already apprized of your coming, but knows not your person;—so you have only to say,—you are come for the riband,—on which she will immediately conduct you to

Yours, &c.

It has been observ'd through the course of this history, that Jemmy, in spite of his gay temper, had sometimes the power of thinking very seriously;—the billet he had in his hand, together with the looks and gestures of the lady, fill'd him with reflections which it cannot be supposed she either intended or wish'd to inspire.

To find that the most timid bashfulness,—the most innocent simplicity of mind and manners thus improved, in the compass of so small a space of time, into all the assured airs of a woman who had pass'd her whole life in artifice and intrigue, seem'd to him a thing so strange, so out of nature, that he would never have believed it possible, had he not seen it verified in the character of his Celia, at present Lady Hardy.

This transformation did not render her more amiable in his eyes;—he was, however, punctual to the assignation, though it is pretty certain his curiosity of knowing those accidents which had occasion'd so extraordinary a revolution, both in her circumstances and behaviour, had as great a share in carrying him thither as any other motive.

On his coming to Mrs. Comode's he found the obliging gentlewoman ready to receive him; and, on his giving the appointed signal, led him with a smiling countenance into a back parlour behind the shop, where Lady Hardy already waited his approach.

He was doubtless about to salute her with some fine speech, but she no sooner saw him enter than, starting from her seat, she threw herself at once into his arms, before they were even open to receive her;—"My dear, dear Mr. Jessamy," cried she, with an undescribeable softness in her voice and eyes,— "a few days past how little did I hope this happiness?"

Such love,—such tenderness, in one so young and beautiful, must have warm'd the heart of a dull Stoick,[73] much more that of one endow'd by nature with the most amorous inclinations,—Jemmy must have been as insensible as he was really the reverse, had he not felt the force of such united charms;—he return'd all her transports,—her caresses, with interest;—they said the most passionate and endearing things to each other; but the energy of the expressions, as they were so often interrupted with kisses and embraces, would be lost in the repetition;—for as Mr. Dryden justly says,

Imperfect sentences, and broken sounds,
And nonsense is the eloquence of love.[74]

After the first demonstrations of their mutual joy on this meeting was over,—"I will not," said she, "be so ungenerous to accuse you of a crime of which I know you clear;—I discover'd the melancholy occasion which call'd you in such haste to London;—but tell me, my dear Jessamy," continued she, "did not your heart feel some anguish on finding yourself obliged to leave your Celia just as you had prevail'd upon her to swear she would be yours?"

He could not without being guilty of, as much ill manners as ingratitude, avoid pretending he had suffer'd greatly on that account; but whatever was wanting of sincerity in this assertion he attoned for in the relation he made her of the pains he had taken in searching for her on his return to Oxford.

She laugh'd heartily at the detail he gave her of the conversation he had with the countryman concerning her uncle Adams and the affairs of his family;—"And, now," said she, "I will make you the confidant of every thing that has happen'd to me since I had the pleasure of seeing you."

Jemmy then telling her it was a favour for which he had the utmost impatience, she immediately gave him the satisfaction he desired.

Chapter XXIV

The history of Celia in the Woods prosecuted in that of Lady Hardy, related by herself to Jemmy.

"I will not," said she, "poison the sweets of our present moments with any description of the bitter pangs I suffer'd in not finding you as I expected in the wood;—I had too much dependance on your love and honour to entertain one thought that this disappointment was an act of your own choice; and therefore fear'd that you was either suddenly taken sick, or that some other ill accident had befallen you.

"Under these apprehensions I pass'd the most cruel night that ever was;—nor did the day bring me much more tranquility; though I sometimes flatter'd myself that business,—company, or some such like enemy to love, had kept you from me the evening before, and that you would not fail on this to come and make attonement for the disquiet you had given me.

"Accordingly, in this hope I went about the usual hour to the dear scene of our past meetings;—I threw myself on the little hillock where we had sat—I kiss'd—I embraced the tree you had lean'd against;—I invoked love and all its powers to bring my Jessamy once more to my arms;—and ran to the entrance of the wood, and sent my longing eyes towards town, vainly still expecting your approach;—I envied the little birds that hopped among the boughs above my head, and wish'd to be one of them, that I might fly to the place which I then thought contain'd you, and see in what manner you were employ'd.

"I had like to have forgot," continued she, "I promised that I would not trouble you either with my grief or my despair, yet I am unwarily running into a detail of both;—pardon me,—my dear Jessamy,—and prepare to hear what contrivances my passion for you inspired me with.

"It was almost dark when I left the wood; my uncle was come out of the grounds and at home before me; he chid me for being abroad so late; but I made an excuse which, though not worth your hearing, pass'd well enough upon him:—I rose very early the next morning, and wrote a little letter to you; but when I had done knew not which way to convey it to you, nor indeed how to direct it properly, as I had never heard you say to which of the colleges you belonged.

"Resolved, however, at any rate, and whatever I did, to be satisfied concerning your health, and what was become of you, I went to Oxford under the pretence of buying something I stood in need of;—I was afraid and ashamed to go to the University to ask for you; but believing that you must be known in town, enquired at several great shops, but without any success, till a perriwig-maker[75] directed me to go to a coffee-house, which he said you used every day.

"Here I was informed that you had been sent for to London on account of your father's indispositions, and was gone the day before; but that not having quitted the University, it was expected you would not long be absent,—this intelligence a little comforted me, and I return'd with a satisfaction in my mind, which I believe might spread a more than ordinary glee upon my countenance.

"But however it was, my looks, it seems, were that day ordain'd to do for me what I never had vanity enough to expect from them.

"On my coming home, I found a chariot with two footmen waiting at our door, and within a very old grave gentleman busy in discourse with my uncle;—the latter had some time before got a slip from a fine exotic plant out of a nobleman's garden, which he had rear'd to such perfection that it was now loaded with flowers; and it was concerning the purchase of this, and some other curiosities my uncle's nursery afforded, that had brought this guest to our house.

"I fancy, my dear Jessamy, that you already imagine that the person I am speaking of was no other than Sir Thomas Hardy, whose wife I now am, and who you saw yesterday with me at the auction;—it was he, indeed, whose heart, without designing it, I captivated at first sight."

Jemmy on this could not forbear making some compliments on the force of her charms;—to which she only reply'd, that of how great service soever they had been to her interest, she took no pleasure in looking lovely in any eyes but those of her dear Jessamy,—and then went on with her discourse.

"The old baronet," resumed she, "had his eyes fix'd upon me from the moment I came into the room, and soon took an opportunity of asking my uncle if I was his daughter.—'No, please your honour,' reply'd he, 'she is only my niece;—farmer Adams, one of your honour's tenants, is her father.'"

"'Oh then,' cried Sir Thomas, 'I suppose he has sent her hither to be out of the way of some handsome young man or another whom she may have taken a liking to.'—'No, please your honour,' said my uncle, 'I hope the girl has no such thoughts in her head as yet;—my brother only lets her be here out of kindness to me, to look after my house.'

"'A very pretty house-keeper, indeed,' rejoin'd Sir Thomas; 'and I do not doubt but manages as well as can be expected.'—'For her years, Sir,' said my uncle.—'I dare swear she does,' cried my new lover; 'and if it were not for robbing you, I should be glad to have such a one to look after my affairs.'

"I could not forbear blushing excessively at these words; though I was far from imagining he had any design in them:—he said no more, however, at that time; but having ordered my uncle to bring home the plants he had bought of him, went into his chariot, though not without giving me a very amorous look as he passed by.

"For my part, I should have thought no more of this stuff afterwards, but was very much surprised when I saw him come again the next day;—my uncle happened to be abroad, and I was sitting alone at work in a little room just by the door, which was wide open, and he came directly in.

"'Where is your uncle, my pretty maid,' said he, 'I would buy some things of him':—I reply'd,—that I believed he was not far off, and I would call the boy to go in search of him.—'It is no matter,' return'd he, taking hold of my hand to prevent my doing as I had said;—'and to tell you the truth, I am glad of this opportunity of saying something to you that may be for your advantage.'

"I wonder'd what he meant, but sat down again on his bidding me;—he then told me I was a very pretty maid, and would be more pretty still if I was dress'd as I ought to be.—''Tis a pity,' said he, looking on me from heat to foot, 'that such limbs as these should be employ'd in any hard or servile work.—I know very well that neither your father nor your uncle are able to do much for you; therefore if you will be one of my family, you shall eat and drink of the best,—have fine cloaths, and have no business but to see that the servants do theirs.'

"To all this I answer'd, that I was very much obliged to his honour for the offer he made me, but that I was not accustom'd to the ways of gentlemen, and in no respect qualified for the place he mentioned.

"'Yes,—my dear girl,' cried he, 'you are sufficiently qualified for every thing I shall require of you';—in speaking these words he threw his wither'd hands about my neck, and kiss'd me with a vehemence which one would not think his years capable of.

"I protest to you," continued she, "that I was so foolish as not to apprehend the base design he had upon me till this last action convinced me of it.—I struggled and got loose from an embrace which was then so detestable to me;—I told him that I was not for his purpose, and that I never would be the wicked creature he would have me.

"'You are a little fool, and do not consider the value of the offer you reject,' said he, throwing a handful of guineas into my lap.—'See here,—your pocket shall be always fill'd with these to dispose of as you shall think fit;—you shall have what you please,—do what you please,—command me and my whole estate;—I desire only a little love in recompence.'

"'I despise all you can give or promise,' answer'd I; 'therefore take back your gold or I shall throw it out of doors for your servants to pick up;—poor as I am, I will not sell my honesty.'

"It was not in this manner, my Jessamy," pursued she, looking fondly on him, "that I withstood the attempts you made upon my virtue;—How wide is the difference between love and interest?—My old baronet, however, took my behaviour as the effect of the most pure and perfect virtue;—he was both amazed and charmed with it, and approaching me with looks as respectful as they had lately been presuming;—'Well, my lovely maid,' said he, 'I will not henceforward go about to seduce your innocence,—I love you, but will endeavour to conquer my desires.'

"I answer'd in a tone pretty rude I believe,—that it was the only thing he could oblige me in; on which he stood in a considerative posture for some moments,—at last coming out of it,—'Celia,' said he, looking earnestly on my face,—'it is my desire to do every thing to oblige you; and since that will do it shall come here no more.'—With these words he turn'd from me, and it was with much ado I prevail'd on him to take up his money; but I protested a single piece should not remain behind."

Her ladyship was going on, but Mrs. Comode, who was all complaisance, came in with tea, which occasion'd a small interruption, after which she resumed her discourse, as will be seen in the next chapter.

Chapter XXV

Contains the sequel of Lady Hardy's story, with other matters of some consequence.

"After my old baronet had left me," said she, "and I had leisure to reflect on what had pass'd, though I was far from repenting of having refused the offer he had made of living with him; yet, to confess the truth, I thought there was no necessity for my giving myself the grand airs I had done, and that I might have taken the gold he would have forced upon me, without any breach either of my modesty or virtue; but this it was which, as he has since told me, gave him so high an opinion of my spirit and delicacy, as made him think me worthy of the dignity he was determined to raise me to.

"The third day after that in which he had been with me, a man and horse arrived from my father, with orders to being me home directly.—I cannot tell whether myself or [my] uncle were most surprised at this message, but am certain that both of us were very much so.—'Sure,' said he, 'brother does not intend to take her from me without letting me know that I might provide for myself.'

"'I can say nothing as to that,' reply'd the fellow; 'but I believe she will not come back in haste; for he bid me tell her she must bring all the things away that she has here.'—This convincing him that my father had indeed took it into his head to keep me at home, he complained bitterly of his unkindness, and asked the man a thousand questions concerning my being sent for so suddenly away, in none of which the other was able to give him any satisfaction.

"I was all this while in tears, which my uncle, poor man, imputed to my good-nature and sorrow for leaving him thus destitute; but alas they proceeded from a cause very different from what he imagined,—that of being obliged to remove so much farther from the only place where I could ever hope to see my dear Jessamy again.

"But there was no remedy,—the orders I had received must be submitted to;—I therefore went up to my room,—pack'd up my little wardrobe, which I gave to the man to put before him,—took leave of my uncle,—got upon the pillion, and with an aking heart trotted towards home as fast as the horse thus loaded could carry us.

"On my arrival I found my father waiting at the door to receive me,—he lifted me off the horse himself,—kiss'd me,—said I was a good girl for making such haste to come when he sent for me;—in fine, I never remember to have seen him in such a humour in my whole life:—my mother was the same,—she catch'd me in her arms as soon as she saw me, and cried,—'My dear Celia, thou wert born to be a blessing to us all.'—I was strangely surprised at all this complaisance and joy; but as my parents made many circumlocutions in their discourse before they informed me of the motive, I will tell it you in a more brief manner.

"Sir Thomas Hardy, it seems, had been with my father,—told him he had seen me at my uncle's,—that he liked me, and if he would give his consent would marry me as soon as things could be got ready for that purpose.—You may be sure my father did not make many words to this bargain; and it was agreed between them that I should be immediately sent for home, in order to be cloathed according to the station I was going to enjoy.

"The astonishment I was in at hearing all this is impossible to be express'd; I shall therefore only say, that it was such as almost turn'd my brain, and for a good while allowed me not the power of knowing whether I was most pleased or troubled at an event so prodigious.

"Early the next morning a servant belonging to my lover brought me a portmanteau, in which I found several rolls of various colour'd silks,—a great deal of lace and dresden work, with some pieces of holland[76] of an extraordinary fineness;—in the portmanteau was also a small ivory casket, containing a gold repeating watch and equipage,—a set of diamond buckles for my stays,—a large pearl necklace with a solitaire,[77] and several other trinkets of a considerable value."

"You may believe," continued she, "that my eyes were dazzled with the sight of such things as I had never seen in my whole life before; but I had scarce time to examine them thoroughly before Sir Thomas came himself to visit me;—he told me he was glad to see me at home, and ask'd me how I liked the presents he had made;—I was very much confounded, but had courage enough to reply,—that I liked them very well, expecially as they were accompanied with honourable intentions:—this answer pleased him so much that he could not forbear taking me in his arms, though my father and mother were in the room, saying at the same time,—'my dear girl, I can have nothing for thee but the most honourable intentions; and what I have given thee now are mere trifles in comparison of what I will hereafter make thee mistress of.'

"He staid with us near two hours, and before he went away gave my mother fifty guineas, to pay for making my cloaths, and to provide for me such other things as she should find necessary, earnestly recommending to her to get all ready for our marriage with as much speed as possible.

"He might have spared himself the trouble of this injunction, for never were two people more eagerly anxious for any thing than my poor father and mother to see me disposed of in a manner so infinitely beyond all they could have hoped:—the persons employ'd in equipping me were so much press'd and so well paid, that in a very few days nothing was wanting for my nuptials, which were celebrated by the parson of the parish at my father's house, after which, I was carried to that which is now my home, and as pleasant a seat as any in the whole county.

"During the first week of our marriage my head was so taken up with the coach and six,—number of my servants,—the magnificence of every thing about me,—the title of my ladyship, and the compliments made on that occasion, that I thought of nothing but my new grandeur;—but all these things became less dazling to me as they grew more customary, and all my relish for them vanish'd with their novelty.

"The idea of my dear Jessamy now return'd to my remembrance,—I sigh'd,—I languish'd, and thought I could have exchang'd all my present opulence for one soft hour of love with that first and only charmer of my soul.

"My husband's fondness for me increased every day;—but alas! The endearments of a man of his years are rather disgustful than agreeable; and I have often wish'd, that as it is impossible I should ever have any love for him, that he had less for me, in spite of the advantages I receive by it.

"In this fashion, my dear Jessamy," added she, "I past two whole years,—quite hopeless of ever tasting more substantial joys, till business calling Sir Thomas to London, chance has blest me with the sight of him who never has been absent from my mind."

Jemmy, perceiving she had done, thank'd her for the gratification of his curiosity, and the share he had in her remembrance; and then reminded her that at their last meeting in the wood she had made a promise to him which he had now a right to claim the performance of.

"If I had not intended to pay my debt," reply'd she with a smile, "I should certainly have avoided the presence of my creditor."—"When then," cried he, "where shall we meet? For I suppose this is no proper place for the continuance of our interviews."

"You are mistaken," said she, "Mrs. Comode and I know each other perfectly well;—Sir Thomas carried me to Tunbridge[78] last year,—she kept a shop there at that time,—I bought all my things of her, and we soon grew very intimate;—on my coming to town I renewed my acquaintance with her; and I am very sure of her readiness to oblige me in every thing I desire.

"It falls out a little unlucky, indeed," pursued she, "that we could not go up stairs to day;—but it seems some other company had appointed to drink tea there before Mrs. Comode knew any thing of our coming."

He then begg'd she would prefix a time for their happy meeting;—on which she told him that she was to go the next morning to see Windsor-Castle,[79] and that Sir Thomas proposed staying there two or three days; but that as soon as they return'd he might be sure she would fly to her dear Jessamy with a transport at least equal to his own.

"But how shall I be appriz'd," cried he, "how know when to expect the blissful moment?"—"I have a contrivance for that," answer'd she; "I will send a little note to Mrs. Comode, which you may either call for here, or she shall leave for you on your giving her your directions."

"I will not put her to that trouble," said he, "nor fail to wait on her every morning till the dear mandate shall arrive."—"Then I will take care," rejoin'd she, "to send the evening before in order to prevent you from being previously engaged elsewhere."

Jemmy was beginning to express himself in a very tender manner on this occasion, when the door immediately flew open and a lady rush'd into the room;—perceiving company there she staid not a quarter of a minute, yet long enough to put them both into a good deal of confusion, especially Jemmy, who by this momentary glance discover'd she was one whom he had often seen with Jenny.

This was indeed that same officious friend who had told Jenny the manner in which she had surprised him; but had he known with what moderation that young lady received the intelligence, it would have added, if possible, to the love and admiration he had for her.

But whatever vexation this accident might give him on his own account, he took care to conceal it under the appearance of his great concern for the reputation of his dear Lady Hardy, who, after the first hurry of her spirits was over, seem'd perfectly easy, and endeavoured to make him so,—saying, that as she had been but three weeks in the town, and knew very few people in it, she did not apprehend any danger from this intrusion.

He gave but little attention to what she said on this subject,—second thoughts made him repent his promise of calling every day at Mrs. Comode's, as there was more than a possibility of being met there again by the lady who had just left them, or of being seen by some other of Jenny's acquaintance.

As soon as Mrs. Comode had got rid of her customer, she came in and made an apology for what had happen'd, by relating the accident of the garter, as the lady had told it to her, assuring them withal, that the next time they did her the honour of a visit she would take care they should not be interrupted.

Lady Hardy then told her they had been settling a correspondence together, and was going to say in what manner it was to be conducted; but Jemmy prevented her by crying out,—"Hold, Madam, business or company may detain me from receiving your ladyship's commands so soon as they arrive,—I should be glad therefore that Mrs. Comode would be at the pains to send them directly to me."

The obliging shopkeeper reply'd, that she should always take a pleasure in serving Lady Hardy or any of her friends;—on which he told her his name, and that of the street wherein he lived.

After this nothing material pass'd, and Lady Hardy not judging it proper to stay abroad too long, the lovers separated with a mutual expectation of seeing each other again at the same place in a few days.

Chapter XXVI

Will, in some measure, contribute to reconcile Jemmy to those who may have been offended with him.

How much soever Jemmy might be envy'd by the young amorous sparks of the town for the adventure he was now engag'd in, yet certain it is he felt less satisfaction in it than might have been expected either from his own years and warmth of constitution, or from the beauty and love of his mistress.

Celia of the Woods, it is true, had at first sight inspired him with very strong desires; but then it was a transient flame,—a sudden flash of inclination, which ceased on being absent from the object; the idea of her charms had been long since forgot; and if it return'd, on finding her again in the person of Lady Hardy, it was but a faint resemblance of what he felt before, and could be called little more than the ghost of his first passion.

The reason of this is pretty evident,—there is a charm in innocence more attracting to a nice and delicate heart than any other perfection whatsoever;—the harmless simplicity of the rural maid was not only now all lost in the fine lady, but exchanged for a certain boldness of looks and behaviour, and a spirit for intrigue, no way engaging to the penetrating Jemmy.

Besides, it must be remember'd, that when he first saw Celia he was two years younger, and consequently had less solidity, and perhaps a less sensibility of the merits of Jenny than he has since acquired, by being a more constant witness of them; to this may also be added, that an amour with Lady Hardy was not a thing of his own seeking, but rather in a manner forced upon him;—a circumstance which in most men would have destroyed great part of the relish for it.

From all that has been said, it may very justly be concluded that Jemmy considered the affair he was entering into only as a mere matter of amusement for his senses, without allowing it any share in the affections of his mind; and it is a point which might bear some dispute,—whether had the business which so long detain'd him in London been completed, he would have staid one day longer in respect to Lady Hardy, or have rather chose to have gone directly down to Bath.

An accident altogether unexpected, however, prevented him from being put to the trial, and left him not at liberty to do either the one or the other, by snatching him away at once from the pursuit both of his honourable and dishonourable flame.

The business he had so much complain'd of was adjusted while Lady Hardy was at Windsor, and he now had it in his power either to wait her return to London or to go down to Bath;—he was perhaps debating within himself which of these two he should do when he received a billet from Mrs. Comode, with a small piece of paper inclosed in it;—that from Mrs. Comode contain'd these lines:

To James Jessamy, Esq;

Honour'd Sir,

I just now received the inclosed from the lady you know of;—it was brought by her footman, unseal'd as you see and address'd to me, to prevent all suspicion:—her ladyship has a world of wit; but you will easily comprehend the meaning, and not fail to favour with your company, at the appointed hour, those who so much desire it,—I am

With the profoundest respect,
Honour'd Sir,
Your most devoted,
And most faithful servant
B. Comode.

P.S. You may depend, Sir, that every thing shall be order'd so as you may be here in all the privacy you can wish.

In the other piece of paper he found these words:

To Mrs. Comode.

Dear Mrs. Comode,
I came last night from Windsor, and am in prodigious want of a new robe de chambre,[80] for I am quite weary and sick of those I have by me;—therefore pray get me some patterns of silks, such as you think I shall like;—I will be with you to-morrow at five o'clock precisely to make my choice—I am

Dear Comode,
Yours,
Hardy.

P.S. Be sure you do not fail to get the silks ready against I come.

Whatever uncertainty his mind was in before this turn'd the balance, and he sent his compliments by the bearer to Mrs. Comode, with an assurance that he would wait on her as she desir'd; but he had scarce dispatch'd this message when a footman belonging to one Mr. Ellwood came to let him know his master intreated his company immediately at his house, on business of the utmost importance.

This Mr. Ellwood was one of those gentlemen who had been appointed by Jemmy's father for the trustees and guardians of his minority;—he was a man of great fortune,—great abilities, and yet greater integrity;—our young hero had a thousand obligations to him, particularly in relation to that perplexing affair he had lately been involved in, and which he could not so easily have accomplish'd without his kind assistance.

The eldest son of this worthy person had been a fellow collegian with Jemmy,—they had lived together in the most perfect harmony while at the University; nor had the friendship between them slackened since their quitting it:—they had not now seen each other for a considerable time, the old gentleman, who lived for the most part at his seat in Bedfordshire, having sent for his son in order to make his addresses to a young lady of that county, as heiress to a large estate.

The attachment Jemmy had to this family made him presently comply with the summons that had been sent him;—Mr. Ellwood hearing he was come, met him at the top of the stairs, and with a countenance which express'd the inward satisfaction of his mind,—"Dear Mr. Jessamy," cried he, "I have news to tell you, which I am certain you will participate in the joy of;—my boy has gain'd his point,—the lady has consented, and we must go and see them tack'd together."

Jemmy had heard much talk of this courtship, and that it went on very successfully, but did not think it had been so near a conclusion;—he express'd, however, the interest he took in so felicitious an event in terms the most obliging and sincere.

"I doubt not," said Mr. Ellwood, "but the goodness of your heart makes you pleased with every thing that gives pleasure to your friends; but this is not all we require of you,—Harry must needs have you a witness of his marriage;—he presses me to engage you to accompany me to Ham-Hall;—and here is a letter for you which he sent inclosed in mine;—I have not been so curious or so ill-manner'd as to open it; but I suppose it is on the account I mention:—pray see whether I am mistaken."

Jemmy having taken the letter out of his hand, instantly broke the seal, and read aloud as follows:

To James Jessamy, Esq;

Dear Friend,

I have now done with hopes,—fears, and suspence;—the angel I have so long sollicited has at last consented to be mine; and I am shortly to enjoy a happiness which can have no alloy but the want of your presence.

I would fain flatter myself, that the earnest desire I have to see you on this blest occasion will be sufficient to bring you to Ham-Hall; but lest I should be too vain in this point, have intreated my father, whose influence is questionless more powerful, to omit nothing which may engage you to accompany him; and in this expectation remain,

With the greatest sincerity,
Dear Jessamy,
Your most affectionate friend,
And very humble servant,
H. Ellwood.

This invitation very much disconcerted Jemmy;—the regard he had for those that made it render'd him very unwilling to deny, and the double obligation he had laid himself under, first of meeting Lady Hardy at Mrs. Comode's, and secondly of going down to Bath, made him not well know how to comply.

Mr. Ellwood, on perceiving he paus'd and seem'd in some dilemma, told him he would have no denial, and remonstrated to him that he could have no engagement in town with any persons who were more truly his friends than those who now desir'd his company in Bedfordshire.

Jemmy was a little ashamed at the reluctance he had shewn to this journey, and could find no better excuse for it than that which was indeed the chief motive,—his having promised Jenny to follow her to Bath, and the expectation he knew she was in every day of seeing him arrive.

"If that be all," cried the old gentleman, "the difficulty is easily removed,—you have only to write to her, and relate the occasion that keeps you from her somewhat longer than you intended, and I will answer for her she has good-nature enough to pardon you."

Jemmy, being still desirous of finding some excuse to avoid this invitation, repeated the discourse he had with Mr. Morgan, and the report which was spread about town in relation to his supposed infidelity to Jenny, urging the necessity of his being with her before she should hear any thing of it.

Mr. Ellwood laugh'd at the apprehensions he discover'd on this account,—reply'd, that it was not likely that such an idle story should be told her, especially while she remain'd at so great a distance from the place where it was invented;—"but in case," continued he, "any malicious person should convey the scandal to her, as the thing is utterly without foundation, it may be easily disproved when you come together, and she would allow it a weakness in herself to have given credit to it."

This, with some other arguments, assisted by Jemmy's own unwillingness to disoblige him, soon decided the matter; and as Mr. Ellwood said he purposed to set out very early the next morning, Jenny's lover took his leave to make what preparations were necessary for his departure, as well as to give an account to both his mistresses of what had happened.

Chapter XXVII

Contains, among other particulars, a more full explanation of Jemmy's innocence in some things which had very much the appearance of being criminal.

Jemmy had no sooner taken leave of Mr. Ellwood, than he wrote to Lady Hardy,—telling her that an unavoidable necessity had torn him from his wishes;—that he was compell'd to go into the country the next morning, and consequently must be deprived of the pleasure of meeting her, as he had hoped, according to appointment; but added, that he should return in a very short time, and then enjoy the happiness he languished for;— This he inclosed in another to Mrs. Comode, with an intreaty that she would convey it as directed with all expedition and secrecy.

That necessary friend discharged the trust reposed in her with so much diligence, that on his coming home pretty early from Vaux-Hall,[81] where he had been that evening with some company, he found a letter from Mrs. Comode, with another inclosed in it from Lady Hardy, in answer to his billet;—the contents of both were as follow:

To James Jessamy, Esq;

Honour'd Sir,

I know not what you will find in the inclosed, tho' it was wrote at my house, and I saw it wetted with tears falling from a pair of the most beautiful eyes in the world.—I doubt not, however, but you will soon dry them up:—it would, indeed, be a great pity that two such charming persons should have any cause of complaint against each other.—You will pardon this freedom, as it springs from my zeal for your mutual happiness, to which you may assure yourself I shall always be proud to contribute, being,

With the most profound respect,
Honoured, Sir,
Your very faithful
And obsequious servant,
B. Comode.

By this prelude he easily guess'd what was the purport of the other, so was not surprised at the reproaches it contained.

To James Jessamy, Esq;

Sir,

I have just now received yours by the hands of Mrs. Comode; and Sir Thomas being abroad I have the opportunity of disburthening myself of some part of that mingled astonishment and grief your cruel epistle has involved me in.—Oh, Mr. Jessamy, how can you treat with such indifference a woman who loves you to distraction!—Nothing but yourself could ever have made me believe you were capable of behaving towards me in this manner.—Is this the effect of all your soft professions?—Is this the recompence of the fondness I have shewn to you?—You find me ready to risque every thing for you,—virtue,—duty, reputation;—nay, the dangers of eternal ruin are too weak to deter me from flying to your arms; should any other engagement then,—any business,—any pleasure, have the power to snatch you from me?—The excuses you make might have pass'd well enough with me when I was the ignorant unjudging Celia of the Woods; but time, reading, and observation has now informed me better, and I know what a woman has a right to expect from the man who has a real passion for her;—but I see you are insensible,—ungrateful,—yet still I love you; and, in spite of my resentment, cannot help wishing you a prosperous journey and a safe return.—You promise me that it shall be speedy; but I know not how to give credit to your words; the sooner you come back, however, the more you will be intitled to the forgiveness of

Your too much devoted
Celia.

P.S. Sir Thomas talks of staying in London all next winter;—this would be joyful news to me indeed, if I could flatter myself with a belief you wish'd it so; but dare not hope too much after the cruel disappointment you have given me.

Till the receipt of this Jemmy thought he had done with Lady Hardy till his return from Bedfordshire; but he now found himself under a necessity either of writing to her again, or of giving her cause to complain of his want of politeness as well as love.

With the pleasures of an amorous intrigue there will be always some mixture of fatigue;—Jemmy liked to enjoy the one, but was not of a humour to endure much of the other, especially at present; and the tender reproaches and accusation in this letter seem'd to him so many impertinencies which he would gladly have been able to dispense with himself from answering.

He was also obliged to write to Jenny that same night, in order to give her an account of the motive that carried him to Ham-Hall, at the very instant that he was about to gratify his inclinations in following her to Bath; but this was a task which he was far from feeling any reluctance in the performance of;—so widely different are the effects of an honourable and a dishonourable passion.

This puts me in mind of a very just as well as beautiful hieroglyphic, which I once saw among the paintings of Titian, the capital figures in the piece were two Cupids, the one coming down from Jupiter in a milk-white robe, his sparkling eyes wide open, and garlands in his hands of fresh and unmix'd sweets, ready to crown the brows of every faithful votary:—the other in a garment of a dusky yellow, spatter'd all over with black, seem'd ascending from the earth,—condens'd vapours encircled his head,—a bandage cover'd his eyes, and in his impure hands were wreaths of half-shed faded roses, thinly blended with thorns and prickly briars.[82]

The ancients were extremely fond of expressing their designs by emblems, and this custom, which is as old as the Syriac and Chaldean,[83] is still retain'd throughout the greatest part of Europe in the devices on their shields; so that by looking on the escutcheon of any family, it is easy to know for what great action it was at first distinguish'd;—and this, methinks, should remind those who wear them to act in such a manner as may render themselves worthy of the honours acquir'd for them by their progenitors;—otherwise they are no more, according to the words of a late author, than

Dignify'd dregs of Britain's fall'n race,
Honour's dishonour, and fame's last disgrace.[84]

But this is not a work in which remonstrances are to be expected, nor perhaps would be greatly relish'd;—I shall therefore leave the world such as it is, and without being much of a prophet, one may say is like to be, and return to the subject of my history.

Jemmy wrote a long letter to his dear Jenny, in which he acquainted her with all the particulars relating to the journey he was about to take, in compliance with Mr. Ellwood's invitations; and express'd the utmost discontent at an accident which hinder'd him from going to Bath so soon as he had design'd, and hoped to have done.

Having finish'd this, he set himself about answering the complaint of Lady Hardy, which he did in terms that have no occasion to be repeated, this letter having been already inserted in the fifth chapter of this volume, to which if the reader takes the trouble to turn back he will easily perceive to be the same that by one of the caprices of fortune fell into the hands of Jenny, and threw her into the condition there described.

Jemmy in this point acted like some careless apothecaries, who, by fixing wrong labels on the potions they prepare, frequently destroy one patient by what would have given relief to another;—so he having seal'd both the letters before he wrote the superscription of either, directed that he design'd for Jenny to Lady Hardy; and by consequence that for Lady Hardy to Jenny.

Quite ignorant of the mischief his inadvertency would occasion, he sent a servant with these dispatches,—the one to be left at Mrs. Comode's, and the other at the Post-house.

About five the next morning the impatient Mr. Ellwood call'd on him in his travelling coach;—what unwillingness soever he had testify'd for this expedition, he had taken care that every thing necessary for it should be prepar'd against the coming of his friend, so being entirely ready, they set out together immediately, attended by the servants belonging to both of them.

The coachman having orders to make all the speed he could, the horses being full of spirit, the road good, and no bad accident retarding the progress of their journey, they arrived at Ham-Hall that same evening, where it is not to be doubted but they were received by the intended bridegroom with all the demonstrations imaginable of joy,—of duty to the one, and affection to the other.

The wedding was not solemniz'd till two days after, on account of some writing which had waited for the old gentleman to sign, he having agreed to settle a pretty large part of his estate upon his son at this marriage.

I will not trouble my reader with any description of these nuptials, though they were celebrated with as much magnificence as the rank of the persons and the place they were in would admit of, without incurring the censure of vanity and ostentation;—Jemmy stay'd there eight days, and was then obliged to tear himself away from his kind hosts, who would not have suffer'd him to part so soon but on the score of his impatience to be with Jenny, and the reasons he had given Mr. Ellwood for it.

Chapter XXVIII

Treats of such things as the author is pretty well convinced, from a long series of observations on the human mind, will afford more pleasure than offence, even among some of those who most affect a contrary sensation.

How strangely ignorant are we of our own hearts?—How weak a dependance is there to be placed upon our best resolves?—So true is this maxim of Mr. Dryden's:

Men are but children of a larger growth,
Our appetites as apt to change as theirs,
And full as craving too, and full as vain:[85]

Who that has heard with what reluctance Jemmy went down to Bedfordshire,—the insensibility he express'd for all the gaieties and pleasures of the nuptial feast, and the impatience he had to take his leave of friends who so much desired and valued his company;—who, I say, that has been informed of all this but would have thought that, according to the promise he had made to Jenny in his letter to her from Ham-Hall, he would have done little more in London than just pass through it in his way to Bath?

Yet see the swift vicissitude, and how suddenly the rolling tide of inclination is capable of overturning those designs which even we ourselves have believed were founded on the most solid basis, and impossible to be shaken.

But I will not detain the attention of my reader with any superfluous remarks of my own, the fact I am going to relate will be sufficient of itself to prove the uncertain state of human resolution, and may serve to abate the pride of those who depend too much on their own strength of mind.

Jemmy, who during his stay in the country had his whole soul absorb'd, as it were, in the thoughts of his dear and deserving Jenny, had no sooner reach'd London than his stability began to slacken; and though he did not cease to love her with the same tenderness as ever, yet that burning impatience he had so lately felt to be with her became less fierce on something coming in his way which till he saw had almost slipt his memory.

He came to town in a post-chaise; but how his inclinations stood in regard to Lady Hardy, or whether he would have endeavoured to see her before he went to Bath, is altogether uncertain; something however happen'd which turn'd the balance on her side, and reminded him both of her and the promise he had made in that letter, which he doubted not but she had received.

He alighted at a coffee-house which he was accustom'd to frequent very much; a stop of coaches happening to be in the street, he saw Sir Thomas and Lady Hardy in one of them, just opposite to the door he was going to enter;—she saw him too, and gave him a very significant look, which was all the salutation the place and company she was in would allow of.

A young amorous heart, I think, may with some analogy be compared to tinder, as it is ready to take fire from every spark that falls;—how cool soever Jemmy might have been some moments before, this sight sufficed to revive the glowing embers of desire, and made him think it would not become him to neglect totally so kind and fair a creature.

He supp'd that night with some company he met at the coffee-house; but resolved to send to her by the way of Mrs. Comode the next morning;—the impatience of the lady, nevertheless, prevented his intentions, and on his coming home he was presented with a letter which his people said had been left for him by a porter above an hour before.

He opened it with some eagerness, not doubting from what hand it came, and found as he had imagined, the cover from Mrs. Comode, with these lines:

To James Jessamy, Esq;

Honour'd Sir,

I send you what I dare say will be a welcome present,—your answer to it with the utmost expedition is requested, to be left at my house as usual;—

I beg you, Sir, to believe that I shall always be ready to oblige you and the beautiful party to the utmost of my poor power, being

With the greatest respect,
Sir,
Your most obedient,
And most humble servant
To command,
B. COMODE.

The contents of the inclosed were as follow:

TO JAMES JESSAMY, ESQ;

SIR,
I see you are in town, but am far from assuring myself you have any thoughts of me;—the violence of your passion for your charming Jenny, and the hurry you are in to follow her to Bath, may probably have made you forget that there is such a person in the world as myself;—I send this therefore to desire one more interview, even though it should be to take an everlasting leave;—my happy rival would not certainly regret your giving that satisfaction to a woman who loves you more than perhaps she is capable of doing:—honour and gratitude demand this from you,—to them I appeal, and shall commit my cause.

Since you went out of town, I have another misfortune added to that of having discovered your engagement with Jenny;—Mrs. Comode has lett her lodgings to a person intimately acquainted with my husband, so it is utterly impracticable for me to see you there; and I am reduced, by this piece of ill luck, to desire you will find out some more proper place for our meeting;—whether it be at your own house, or at that of any friend in whom you can confide, is a matter of indifference to me,—only remember that I will not venture to a tavern, bagnio,[86] or any such public place.

As I am convinced your heart, if not wholly lost, is at least divided, I should have little joy in the continuance of an intercourse so dangerous to myself, and so negligently pursued by you;—you need not, therefore, be under any apprehensions of my persecuting you with a passion you seem'd to have ceased desiring any farther proofs of;—happy should I be, indeed, to find myself mistaken in what I have so much cause to fear:—see me once more, however, and fix the yet uncertain fate of her who is,

With too much sincerity,
The unkind Jessamy's
Still affectionate
And devoted,
Celia.

P.S. If you no longer have any love for me, let pity and good nature for that you have inspired me with prevail on you not to keep me in suspence;—I languish, I am distracted, till I receive your answer with an appointment where and when I shall have the opportunity of telling you all my soul is full of.

This passionate epistle gave Jemmy much more pain than pleasure,—not that he was either surprised or troubled at the knowledge he found she had of his engagement with Jenny;—he was sensible a thousand accidents might reveal it to her, nor did he think she had any business to interfere with the honourable addresses he made elsewhere; and, had she ever question'd him upon that subject, would not have evaded or deny'd the truth.

But it vex'd him a good deal, to find that the providing a place for their meeting was required of him;—whatever amorous intrigues he had hitherto been engaged in had been accompany'd with no difficulties,—they had fallen in his way without any pains of his own,—he had never been put to the trouble of forming any contrivances for the carrying them on; and the injunction now laid upon him was a thing no less new than disagreeable to him.

Never had he been so much puzzled in his whole life;—he judged it highly inconvenient, for many reasons, to make an appointment with her at his own house; and as she had excepted against all those he should readily have proposed, he might well be at a very great loss to whom he should apply on such an occasion.

What course he took in this perplexing dilemma, and what consequences attended this adventure, as well as the catastrophe of many others mentioned in this work, the reader, if he has patience to wait, will find fully set forth and explained in the succeeding volume.

End of the Second Volume.

The

HISTORY

of

Jemmy and Jenny Jessamy

Volume III

Contents to the Third Volume

The

HISTORY

of

Jemmy and Jenny Jessamy

CHAPTER I

Shews the character of Jemmy in a light which will be thought worthy approbation by some readers, and equally ridiculed by others.

How much soever Jemmy was taken up on going to bed, with the thoughts of when and where he should meet his mistress, according to her desire, he did not forget next morning an appointment he had made to breakfast with a gentleman, in order to look over some curiosities that had been brought from Rome at the last jubilee.[1]

In his way thither, as he was passing by the door of a great Mercer,[2] he was surprised with the sight of Lady Hardy starting out upon him, and before he had time to speak, or indeed to think whether he ought to do so in that place or not, "Well, Mr. Jessamy," cried she in a low voice, "what answer may I expect to the letter I sent last night?"—"Such a one, Madam," reply'd he, "as I hope will give you no future cause to reproach me."

"I should be glad," said she, and was going on; but something, which will hereafter be discover'd, prevented her, and she ran back into the shop in the greatest hurry and confusion: Jemmy imagined that the sight of some person who knew her had given her this alarm; but as it was improper to follow her, and he did not chuse to saunter about the street in hope of speaking again to her, he went directly to the place where he was expected.

He staid no longer at this visit than mere civility required;—the task enjoin'd him by Lady Hardy ran very much in his head, and he could not be easy till he had found some means or other of performing it.

He was returning home so deeply buried in cogitation, that though he went through the park, which at that time was very full of company, he saw nor took notice of any body in it, till Bellpine meeting him in this unusual musing accosted him with a slap on the shoulder, accompanied by these lines borrow'd from Farquair's *Recruiting Officer*:

Spleen, thou worst of fiends below,
Fly, I conjure thee. by this magic blow.[3]

"What in the name of wonder," pursued he, "has wrought this transformation?—What fair cruel she has the power to engross you to herself, and make you absent amidst a throng of beauties."

The sight of him, together with the salutation he had given him, put Jemmy in mind of something he had never thought on before:—"Faith, Bellpine," answer'd he laughing, "your guess is partly right;—I was thinking of a lady, though no cruel one, and just wishing for such a friend as you."

"Then here I am apropos," cried the other;—"What act of friendship am I to be employ'd in?"—"Come home with me, and I will tell you," reply'd Jemmy.—"With all my heart," said Bellpine, "I will only speak to a couple of gentlemen I see yonder, and be after you in a moment."

Jemmy was now astonish'd at his own stupidity; so anxious as he had been to find a proper place for the consummation of his amour with Lady Hardy, yet he had never once thought of having recourse to Bellpine for that purpose, who was a single man, had handsome lodgings, and look'd upon by him as sufficiently his friend to oblige him in a much greater matter than the use of his apartment for a few hours.

He walked slowly on, and the other overtook him before he reach'd his own door;—as soon as they were come into the house and shut up together, Jemmy told him, that having a small affair of gallantry with a woman of condition, who would not venture to any house of public resort, the favour he requested of him was to lend him his lodgings to entertain her in.

To this the other reply'd, that he was glad of the opportunity of contributing to his pleasures;—"but," said he, "we must be very cautious,—my landlady, you must know, is a formal piece of stuff, and piques herself mightily on the reputation and honesty of her house;—I will therefore sneak privately out before you come, that she may not know I am abroad, and when my man has shew'd you and your fair companion upstairs, he shall tell the old cant that you are relations of mine come to visit me."

Bellpine looked extremely thoughtful all the time he was speaking, which Jemmy interpreting as the effect of his great zeal and care that every thing should be conducted to his satisfaction, heartily embraced and thank'd him for.

The other grew every moment more serious; but asked him on what day and at what hour he intended to bring his mistress;—"That must depend upon herself," said Jemmy, "and what opportunity chance and our good fortune may befriend us with;—but I shall take care to give you timely notice."

"I suppose," resumed Bellpine, "as this affair is to be a mighty secret, I must not be trusted with the name of this fine lady."—"No, friend," reply'd Jemmy, "you must excuse me there;—she is a person of fashion, and a married woman."—"Aye," return'd Bellpine, in a voice scarce articulate, through his inward agitations, "and you might have added too,—a lewd,—a base, and a most ungrateful woman."

"What do you mean, Sir?" demanded Jemmy somewhat startled at his looks and manner of speaking.—"Before I answer you," cried Bellpine, "tell me, I conjure you, by all our friendship,—tell me truly, whether you have yet enjoy'd her?"—"No, upon my honour," reply'd the other still more surprised;—"but wherefore do you ask?—she is perhaps your mistress."

"Would to Heaven," said Bellpine, "that she were mine,—or yours,—or any man's mistress, so she were not my uncle's wife, and dignify'd with the name of Lady Hardy."

Never was any one in a greater consternation than Jemmy was on hearing this;—he had been told, indeed, somewhat concerning his having an uncle who had married a girl of mean extraction, but knew nothing of his name nor of the particulars of the story.—"What," cried he hastily, "is Sir Thomas Hardy your uncle?"

"Yes," reply'd the other sullenly, "he is my mother's brother, and I was always look'd upon as his undoubted heir, but by his marriage with this curst Jezabel I am like to be defraud'd of an estate of upwards of two thousand pounds a year."

Jemmy having by this time a little recovered himself from his surprise, was very much affected with these last words;—"You shall not be a loser by any act of mine," said he; "if Lady Hardy were more handsome than she is, and I loved her more than I ever did, be assured I would henceforth for ever shun her presence, and forego the gratification of my desires, rather than be guilty of attempting any thing which might happen to prove an injury to my friend."

"This is generous, indeed," cried Bellpine embracing him, "and what I could have expected from no man but yourself:—you will pardon, dear Sir," continued he, "the warmth of some expressions I may have let fall;—but I cannot keep my temper in due bounds whenever I think on my uncle's dotage, and the misfortunes I may possibly be reduced to by it."

After many repeated assurances on the one side, and retributions on the other, Jemmy bethought himself of asking him how it came into his head to guess that Lady Hardy, of all womankind, was the mistress he had spoke of, and intended to have brought to his lodgings.

"It can be call'd, indeed, no more than a conjecture," reply'd Bellpine, "yet was it such a conjecture as amounted almost to a certainty; you know," pursued he, "that you spoke to her this morning at the door of a shop in Chandos-street;[4]—I was sitting in a parlour window just opposite to it, and had the opportunity of beholding with what hurry of looks and motion her impudent ladyship flew out to meet you; and how presently after conscious guilt and fear at sight of me, on turning her head that way, made her leave you, and retire with as much precipitation as she had come out."

"This," went he still on, "was enough to give a strange suspicion of your intimacy, and I thought to have asked you by what means you came to be so well acquainted with one of our family; but you prevented me by making a request which confirmed me in what I had so much reason to believe before; and also that you were entirely ignorant of the near relationship between me and that vile woman."

"You do me justice," said Jemmy; "nothing could be farther from my thoughts than that she was your aunt;—I knew her before she had any expectations of being so, and when she was much more innocent than I fear she is at present."

He then, on the desire of the other, related the manner of his first acquaintance with Celia of the Woods, and the many accidents which had interven'd and hinder'd the completion of what at that time he so ardently had desired, and she seem'd not very averse to grant.

On his having finish'd this recital;—"When I consider," said Bellpine, "what you are, and what she was at the time of her acquaintance with you in the wood, I could almost pity her for not being able, even after marriage, to banish an idea so agreeable, and which had made the first impression on her heart; but, my dear friend, it is not for your sake alone that she has transgressed the rules of virtue, and even of decency;—others have proved the too great warmth of her constitution; some unquestionable instances of this have came to my knowledge;—be assured I speak not this out of malice, nor in regard of my uncle's honour would mention it at all, if I did not think it might serve to fortify you in the resolution you have taken of never seeing her any more."

A sort of a contemptuous smile spread itself all over Jemmy's face at this supposition;—he assured Bellpine that there was no occasion for any proofs of that lady's levity to enable him to keep the promise he had made; and that as he never was possess'd of anything more than a transient inclination for her, he could throw it off without feeling the least pain.—"Whatever anecdotes therefore," said he, "you favour me with will only serve to gratify my curiosity."

Bellpine was, however, preparing to recollect the passages he had to relate; but their discourse had already taken up so much time, that before he could begin, a servant came into the room and told his master that dinner was upon table.

"Well then," said Jemmy to his guest, "you must do penance with me,—a batchelor's table is always thinly served; but I indulg'd somewhat too plentifully last night, so mortify to day with a boil'd chicken and small beer."[5]

In speaking these words, he took Bellpine by the hand and led him into another room, where it is not to be doubted but that they found more covers already placed than he had made mention of.

Chapter II

Contains, besides other matters, some farther particulars relating to Lady Hardy, which she did not think proper to make any mention of to Jemmy in the detail she had given him of her adventures.

Dinner was no sooner over,—all the apurtenances of it removed, and the servants withdrawn, than Bellpine began the little narrative he had promised, in these or the like terms:

"It was always my custom," said he, "even from my childhood, to go to Oxfordshire and pay my respects to my uncle three or four times every year; nor did I refrain continuing to give him this mark of my duty and affection after his marriage; though as you may suppose, it was an event which gave me great uneasiness.

"The first time I saw my new aunt I found her busily employed in learning French, music, and dancing; she seem'd, and I believe really was, no less desirous of becoming mistress of those accomplishments than her fond husband was that she should be so, passing all those hours he suffer'd her from his presence either in reading some books which he had presented to her, or in the study of the lessons given her by her masters;—her behaviour was also full of humility and courtesy:—in a word, as much as I was prejudiced against her, which I confess I greatly was, I could see nothing in her to condemn during this visit, which lasted near three weeks, as unwilling that my uncle should think I took any umbrage at the change of his condition.

"I went not down again till six months after, having been detain'd in London by a long fit of sickness, which it was thought would have been my last;—but,—good God, how strange a transformation had happen'd in the family in that time!—On my arrival—most of the old servants were removed, and new ones in their places;—all my aunt's preceptors were dismiss'd; and her ladyship, instead of the tractable obliging creature I had left her, was now grown haughty, sullen and reserved, scarce spoke but in her husband's presence, and then with only an assumed softness:—in fine, every thing was the very reverse of what it had been, except my uncle himself, and he too, I thought, appeared less chearful and satisfied than usual.

"But what the most amaz'd me was, to find that in the change of domesticks was included an old gentlewoman, who had lived with my uncle for seven or eight and twenty years in quality of a house-keeper, and being a distant relation of my father's, and reduced by misfortunes to go to service, had been recommended by my mother to take care of his affairs; which trust she so well discharged, and gave my uncle such content, that he used frequently to say, that as long as they both lived Jamison, for so she is call'd, and he should never part.

"I took the liberty of asking my uncle what was become of her, but he only reply'd, that she was a foolish woman,—that he had discharged her,—and that he had done with her:—I rejoin'd, that I hoped she had been guilty of nothing to incur his displeasure.—'I tell you,' cried he, peevishly, 'she is a foolish impertinent woman,—say no more about her';—I obey'd, but could not keep myself from putting some questions concerning her removal to those of the servants who had lived there in her time, but could get no other answer from any of them than a shake of the head, or a shrug of the shoulder.

"All this increased my wonder; but on hearing she was at present boarded at a little farm-house about three or four miles off, I got one of my uncle's horses and went thither one morning, under pretence of riding for the air.

"Notwithstanding the good creature received me with the greatest joy imaginable, I found the utmost difficulty in prevailing on her to acquaint me with the reason of her having left a place where she had been so useful as well as so much respected; and all I could get from her for a good while was, that Sir Thomas had now no occasion for a house-keeper, having so good a lady, and such like evasive answers; which convincing me there was some mystery in the affair, made me the most sollicitous for an explanation.

"I press'd, however, in such strong terms that she at last consented to satisfy me:—'Your aunt is a base woman,' said she, 'and deserves to be exposed; but as ill as Sir Thomas has used me I should be sorry that he should be made the jest of the county, therefore would not mention what I am going to relate to any person in the world besides yourself, nor even to you if I did not know you would be obliged, for your own sake, to keep it secret.'

"After this, she asked me if I did not remember that the last time I was down there was a young French Hugonot[6] who made part of the family, and had been agreed with by Sir Thomas to teach her ladyship the language for two guineas a month and his board.

"I told her I knew very well there had been such a man, and she proceeded to inform me that this fellow presently grew a prodigious favourite with Lady Hardy,—that she was always praising him, and was so extravagantly silly as even to ask the maids if they did not think Monsieur La Noye was a very handsome man.—'This,' said Mrs. Jamison, 'occasion'd whispers in the family, which were little to her ladyship's advantage; but for my part I really look'd upon her behaviour as the effect of simplicity, and not of guilt, as some of them imagined, till happening to go into the best chamber to see if every thing was in order, as I had made it be clean'd the day before, who did I see there but my lady and this La Noye, upon the bed together;—they had forgot, it seems, to fasten the door, and the posture I surprised them in admitted no doubt of their guilt; I was so thunder-struck that I had not the power to go either forward or backward, but stood motionless as a stock;—the fellow started up and rush'd by me out of the room,—my lady, you may be sure, was in confusion enough,—she ran to me, threw herself at my feet, burst into tears, and cry'd, "Dear Jamison don't betray me."—"Oh, Madam," said I, "I never thought to have seen what I have seen."—"I was half asleep," rejoin'd she, "when he came into the room, and I scarce knew what I did;—therefore, dear Mrs. Jamison do not ruin me,—do not tell Sir Thomas;—indeed I will never be guilty of the like again.'

"I could not forbear interrupting the good woman in this part of her story," said Bellpine, "by venting my indignation in a volley of curses on that scandal to our family; but she conjured me to moderate my passion, and resolve to shew no future marks of it, or protested she would reveal no farther; I gave my promise to do as she desired, and she went on.

"'The deceitful creature,' resumed she, 'hung about me all the time she was speaking with such a shew of innocence and grief, that at last, I am ashamed to say it, her tears,—her seeming penitence,—her humiliation melted me into pity, and I promised never to mention what I had discovered, on condition she would never repeat her offence; and also that she should make some pretence to Sir Thomas for getting the vile seducer of her honour removed out of the family.'

"'This she bound herself by the most solemn imprecation to perform;—but alas!—One day—another, and another, still came on, and pass'd away without any proof, or even probability of the sincerity of her conversion;—she took care, indeed, not to be surprised in the manner she had been; but I easily saw by Sir Thomas's behaviour, and some words he let fall in casual conversation, that there was no thought of parting with this French fellow till her ladyship was made perfect in the language.

"'I express'd my sentiments very plainly to her on this head, on which she told me that monsieur had not taken any freedoms with her since the time I catch'd them together, and that he had sworn never to attempt the like again; and added, that though she would be glad to get rid of him, and could not endure the sight of him, yet she could find no excuse to make to Sir Thomas for leaving off learning French till she was become mistress of it, which she was far from being as yet.

"'This not satisfying me, I renewed my remonstrances to her as often as I had an opportunity; but I soon found that instead of working the effect I aimed at, she rather seem'd more hardened by them;—every time I spoke she answer'd in a more lofty strain; and at last told me that she would not be teaz'd;—that it was sufficient she did not repeat her fault, and as for the rest she knew what was proper to be done, and would not be kept in leading-strings by any servant of her husband's.

"'I now plainly saw, that she was no less wicked though more wary than she had been;—I was troubled at the shame she would bring upon my master, and was debating within myself whether or not I should relate to him the discovery I had made, and all that had pass'd upon it between us, when an unforeseen accident saved me the pains of thinking any farther on the matter.

"'Her ladyship, who, as you may suppose, was never much respected by the servants on account of her birth, became every day less so through the strong suspicion they had of her incontinency; but the insolence of her gallant was intolerable to all of them, especially to Humphrey, who being the oldest servant in the house, except myself, would not submit to the impertinent commands of that French renegado; this causing many quarrels, he resolved to leave Sir Thomas's service; but, before he went, had an opportunity of revenging himself on those who were the occasion of his doing so.

"'I was one morning with Sir Thomas in his closet, settling my accounts, as I always did every month, when this Humphrey came running in and told him that my lady was in the summer-house at the farther end of the garden, and desired he would come to her that minute, for there was a great curiosity to be seen there.—"What little fancy has she got in her head now, I wonder?" said Sir Thomas, "But I'll go."—"Your honour must come immediately," cried the fellow, "or the sight will be gone,"—"Well, well," reply'd he, "she must be humour'd";—in speaking this he threw down the papers, and hurried away as fast as the burthen of his years would let him.

"'I staid some little time in the closet expecting Sir Thomas would soon return; but finding he did not, left it and went down:—I had just got to the bottom of the stairs when he came in follow'd by my lady,—both of them with countenances strangely discomposed.—"Sirrah," said he, very angrily to Humphrey, who happen'd to be in the passage,—"how dare you tell me that your lady wanted to speak with me in the summer-house?"—"Sir," reply'd the fellow, with the greatest assurance,—"I saw my lady and the young Frenchman run thither very fast, so I thought there might be something very extraordinary to be seen,—so made bold to tell your honour of it."—"You are an impudent rascal," cried Sir Thomas, and went up stairs, still followed by my lady.

"'I wonder'd what all this meant, but was soon after inform'd of the whole matter:—the fellow, it seems, being convinced in his own mind that my lady and this Frenchman were too great, had watch'd all their motions, and finding that they retir'd almost every morning into this summer-house, when they knew Sir Thomas was reading, or otherwise employed in his closet, he had taken this method of giving the injured husband an opportunity of detecting them.

"'I did not approve of Humphrey's proceeding in this point, and told him that let the matter be how it would, he must not hope to keep his place after what he had done; he reply'd that he did not care how soon he was discharged,—that he had got money enough to set up an ale-house, and would not stay in any service where he must be insulted by people no better born than himself, and not half so honest.'

"Here," said Bellpine, "I could not forbear interrupting Mrs. Jamison a second time, by asking how the shameful pair behaved on the approach of my uncle.—'All that can be known of that part of the story,' reply'd she, 'I was told by the gardener, who happened to be at work very near the place;—he said that Sir Thomas, on finding the door made fast, knock'd and called to be let in, but no answer being made he beckoned the gardener to him, and bid him clamber up to the window and get in that way; but on his attempting to do so the door was opened by those within, and Sir Thomas having gain'd entrance, the man withdrew and went again to his work;—he told me that the Frenchman came out in a few minutes looking very pale and discomposed, and that neither Sir Thomas nor his lady appeared in a much better condition, though they staid some time after, as he supposed, to talk the business over.

"'What pass'd between them on this score,' pursued Mrs. Jamison, 'is impossible to be known;—all that I can tell you is, that Monsieur La Noye was dismiss'd entirely from the family within two hours after;—that my lady either was or pretended to be very sick, and Sir Thomas appeared in a worse humour than ever I had seen him:—Humphrey was discharged that same day, and the next the poor gardener and two other servants, for what reason I know not, shared the same fate:—indeed, I little thought it would also have been mine; but all the distinction I had to boast of from the rest was, to be the last turn'd off.'"

Bellpine was going on, when Jemmy was called suddenly away to a gentlewoman, who his servant told him was very earnest to speak with him;—who this person was, and what her business, the reader shall not wait long to be inform'd.

Chapter III

If it cannot be said to deserve any encomium, it must at least be allowed to stand in no need of an apology.

This person who Jemmy had been told was so importunate to see him was no other than Mrs. Comode;—Lady Hardy, after having been obliged to leave him so abruptly in the morning, went directly to this woman, and commission'd her to find him either at his own house or where-ever else he could be heard of, in order to excuse her behaviour by relating the accident which had occasion'd it; and also to know of him if he had yet thought of a convenient place for their meeting.

This necessary woman deliver'd her message with the utmost punctuality; and added, that she was extremely sorry for not having at present an apartment to accommodate them with;—"But, your honour may depend," said she, "that nothing in my power shall be wanting to oblige both you and the good lady."

Jemmy received all this with great coolness, and only told her that Lady Hardy should have a full declaration of his sentiments in a letter that same evening,—"Which," said he, "I will direct under a cover to you, as usual, and perhaps will be the last trouble I shall give you."

She seem'd pretty much astonish'd on hearing him speak in this manner, and was going to make some reply; but he told her he had a friend within whom he could not leave alone any longer, so begg'd her pardon, and rung the bell for a servant to open the door.

He paused for some moments before he return'd to Bellpine, considering whether he should inform him of the visit he had just received; but as he was so nearly interested in the honour of Sir Thomas Hardy, he thought it best not to say any thing to him of an affair which was of no consequence in itself, and would only serve to add to the chagrin he was already in.

The other no sooner saw him re-enter the room, and that he was prepared to give attention to what he had to say, than he resumed his discourse in words to this effect:

"There is now little remaining to inform you of," said he, "Mrs. Jamison only told me, that for three or four days after La Noye was dismiss'd, her infamous ladyship kept her chamber; whether by the order of Sir Thomas, or that she was really indisposed, she could not be certain; but during that time her artifices so far prevail'd upon him, that he not only discharged all those servants who he thought had any suspicion of her crime, but also forbad them from ever coming within his doors again on any pretence whatsoever.

"I then ask'd her if she thought my uncle was really convinced of the infidelity of his wife;—'As much as I am myself,' reply'd she, 'though he will not seem to be so, because the excessive fondness he has for her will not suffer him to part from her.'

"'I rather think,' said I, 'that he stands in awe of the just ridicule of the world, for having married, at his years, a girl whose conduct obliged him to get rid of in so short a time.'

"'It may be owing partly to the one, and partly to the other of these motives,' answer'd she; 'but however that may be, I can assure you that he will suffer no body to come near him that he imagines has the least suspicion of her virtue.'

"'This is sufficiently evident in the case of La Noye,' added she; 'but I can give you another instance since the banishment of her Frenchman, she has been catch'd in pretty close conference with a young gentleman, who has been for some time a guest at a neighbouring seat; though Sir Thomas has been told that a fine diamond ring, which her ladyship pretended to have lost, has been seen on the finger of that spark, he only affected to laugh at the intelligence, and has since broke off all acquaintance with the person from whom he received it.'

"This is the sum of that account given me by Mrs. Jamison," said Bellpine to Jemmy, "and I must be in fact as stupid as my uncle affects to be, if I doubted the truth of it:—Judge then, my dear friend," continued he, "of the unhappiness of my situation;—I am every moment in danger of being deprived of my inheritance by the incontinency of this vile woman, and if I make any attempt to detect her infamy am equally in danger of losing it by my uncle's displeasure."

Jemmy could not help agreeing with him, that there was, indeed, somewhat extremely precarious in his case; but told him he ought to console himself with this reflection, that as Lady Hardy had never yet been pregnant, she might in all probability not be so while Sir Thomas Hardy lived.

After this the conversation between them turn'd on various subjects, till Bellpine having an engagement that evening took his leave; but before they parted Jemmy told him that his business in London being now entirely finish'd, he intended to set out the next morning for Bath, where he knew Jenny by this time expected him.

Bellpine was not altogether so much chagrin'd at this intelligence as he would have been some days before; for though he would have been glad to have kept him from Jenny, yet he was pleased at his removing himself out of the way of Lady Hardy:—men who are themselves deceitful, are always slow in giving credit to the sincerity of others;—he had not enough depended on the promise Jemmy had made of breaking off all intercourse with his aunt, till he found him resolved to go from the place she was in, and to which it was not likely he should return till she had left it, as he had heard Sir Thomas say he intended to stay but a few days longer.

But not even this demonstration of his friend's honour towards him had the power of touching his ungrateful heart with any remorse for what he had done, or of obliging him to desist from the prosecution of his wicked attempt to break the union between him and Jenny; as the reader must have observed by the letter he sent to her under the character of a supposed rival, and the invidious hints he threw out in the visit he made her on her arrival in town.

As for Jemmy, he was not much surprised at the account given him of Lady Hardy's conduct;—by the little he had seen of her behaviour since his renewing an acquaintance with her in the character she now bore, he was perfectly convinced that she had a great genius as well as inclination for intrigues, and had also often imagined that an amour, such as she was about to enter into with him, was not a thing in which she was altogether unpracticed.

He was not therefore sorry that his friendship for Bellpine obliged him to discontinue an amorous correspondence with her; and as it was an affair at present not of his own seeking, and he had given into not through the force of passion but merely for the sake of amusement, cannot be supposed to give him any pangs in quitting.

He thought it a great pity, however, that a woman endowed by nature with beauty, wit, and every thing requisite to adorn the station to which she was raised, should know so little how to improve or to deserve the good fortune that had befallen her; and, in this serious humour, remembering the promise he had given to her emissary of making a full declaration of his sentiments by way of letter, sat down immediately and wrote to her in the following manner:

To Lady Hardy.

Madam,

I know not how you will relish this epistle, but am very certain you ought to look upon it as the greatest proof both of love and friendship that can be given by man;—be not therefore startled when I tell you that I must see you no more;—it is for your sake, and yours alone, that I have taken this resolution, and tear myself away from all the joys which beauty, such as yours, has the power of bestowing.

I have well consider'd the consequences which must infallibly attend your entering into an amorous engagement with me, and find that all the love I could offer in return would be too poor a recompence for those innumerable difficulties and dangers to which you would be perpetually exposed by it.

Exert then the whole force of your reason to curb the incroachments of lawless passion in your own heart, and to disdain the shew of it in another;—set a true value on yourself, and believe that no man living can deserve that merely for the gratification of his desires you should sacrifice your honour,—virtue,—reputation,—peace of mind, and, in fine, all that is valuable in your sex.

This advice may appear very odd in a man of my years; but the less you expected it from me the more impression it ought to make on you; you are not only a wife, but also bound by a double obligation to be just;—remember the station for which you were design'd by nature, and be not insensible of that to which you are raised by fortune;—look round on the magnificence of every thing about you;—think to whom you owe it, and let gratitude supply the place of love for a husband who so dearly prizes you.

I allow that old age has something in it extremely disagreeable to youth;—yet, methinks, the many advantages you enjoy might compensate for that one deficiency; and also remind you, that as Sir Thomas, by the course of nature, cannot long be with you, it is only by observing a proper conduct while he lives that you can, after his decease, have any right to expect the honourable addresses of a person capable of making you more happy.

Before I take my leave I have one thing more to add, tho' it be a secret which my sex would hardly forgive me for revealing;—we men are apt to think a woman is never singly kind;—that the favours she grants to one, she is equally liberal of to others; and, in this opinion, are seldom very thankful for the blessings we enjoy;—if you take this truth upon the assurance I give you of it, pride will enable you to forbear making the experiment:—Farewel, believe that, tho' I cease henceforth all correspondence with you, I am,

With the best wishes,
Madam,
Your ladyship's
Most humble and
Obliged servant,
J. Jessamy.

POSTSCRIPT

Madam,
To attempt sending to me again, either by letter or message, will be giving yourself an unprofitable trouble; for, besides the resolution I have made of avoiding a communication which I can neither answer to myself nor the regard I have for you, I shall infallibly leave this town to-morrow morning.

This he sealed up and put under a cover directed to Mrs. Comode, in which he wrote these lines:

Madam,
Pray deliver the inclosed with your accustomed care, and you will oblige

Your humble servant,
J. Jessamy.

It must be owned that the advice contained in the above was very good; but whether Jemmy would have acted in this manner if his passion for the lady had been more strong or his friendship for Bellpine less sincere, is a moot-point, and must be left to the decision of the judicious reader.

Chapter IV

Contains a brief recital of Jemmy's journey and return, with some other particulars, which if not very interesting will be found necessary, however, to be inserted.

The morning dew was yet upon the grass, when Jemmy, attended by one servant, set out for Bath in a post-chaise;[7]—it happened a little unluckily for him that this was the very day that Lady Speck's coach had broke down, and the company been obliged to put up at the first village till it was repaired; but for which accident he might have spared himself part of his journey, and met those upon the road whom he went to seek at a greater distance.

Finding, on his arrival at Bath, that Jenny had left the place, he was no less disappointed and vexed than he had expressed himself to be in the letter he sent to her from thence;—he took a lodging in the same house the ladies had quitted, and put many questions to the mistresses of it concerning the motive of their departing so suddenly; but all she could answer was, that she believed it was on Miss Wingman's account, as the old lady's steward had been sent down, after which they had presently prepared for going.

In order to divert his thoughts, he no sooner had put off his travelling dress than he went to the Long-room;—but as it often happens that seeking pleasure we encounter pain, so it was with Jemmy,—here he met with something which instead of dissipating the gloominess of his mind, served only to render it more heavy.

There was a great deal of company, many of whom Jemmy had a slight acquaintance with, but none with whom he had any intimacy excepting one gentleman, who on the moment of his entering the room ran to embrace him,—"Dear Jack," cried Jemmy to him, "you wonder, I believe, to see me here at this tail of the season."—"No faith," reply'd the other, "I should have wonder'd if I had seen you here before:—I have always observed that married people, and people that are going to break off, are always careful to avoid each other;—they are like buckets in a well,—one up and the other down."

"What do you mean?" demanded Jemmy a little gravely.—"How dull of understanding you affect to be," said the other; "Miss Jessamy left Bath one day,—you come to it the next;—do you think the world don't see into this?—It was not, however, quite so politic, methinks; you should have staid a day longer at least; for sure you must meet, if not clash, upon the road."

"If I had been so fortunate," reply'd Jemmy, "you would not have found me at Bath; for I assure you it was only my impatience to see that lady that brought me hither."—"Then there is nothing in the story of your breaking with her," cried the gentleman, "and going to be married to

Miss Chit?"—"Just as much," return'd he, "as that you are going to be made King of the Romans."

The other was about to make some answer; but all farther discourse between them on this head was prevented for the present, by several gentlemen, who seeing Jemmy at a distance, came that instant towards him to pay their compliments to him on his arrival.

As Jemmy had never been the least sensible that any report was raised of his infidelity to Jenny, till he was told it by Mr. Morgan, he was the more surprised to hear it at Bath, and from the mouth of a person who had left London before he thought such a thing had ever been talked of there.

This making him extremely curious to know who had been his informers, he took an opportunity, when most of the company were engaged at play, to propose to him passing the remainder of the evening together at a tavern, to which the other readily agreed, and they immediately adjourn'd.

They had no sooner seated themselves than Jemmy renewed the conversation which had been interrupted in the Long-room, and desired his friend, in the most earnest terms, to let him know by whom, and in what manner, he had been told so wild and so improbable a story as that of his breaking off with Miss Jessamy, and making his addresses to Miss Chit.

"Faith, my dear Jessamy," reply'd the other, "I am afraid I shall be able to give you but little satisfaction in this point:—I think that the first time I ever heard any thing of it was at White's chocolate-house[8], the day before I left London;—but there being a good deal of company, I cannot for my soul recollect what gentleman began the discourse, though I know I was a good deal surprised at it, remembering that I had heard you express some uneasiness that your affairs in town would not permit you to accompany me to Bath, where, you then said, the best part of yourself, meaning Miss Jessamy, was already gone."

"I must confess," continued he, "that my journey, and one affair or other of my own, put this intelligence quite out of my head; till on my coming hither I found it the discourse of almost all the tea-tables where I have been;—some condemning,—others excusing your change; but every one agreeing in the certainty of the fact."

Here Jemmy could not keep himself from expressing some astonishment, that a thing so utterly without the least foundation in truth should be able to obtain such credit, and more especially that it should already have reach'd to such a distance as Bath.

"For my part," resumed the gentleman, "I see nothing strange in all this;—a story once raised, whether true or false, immediately spreads itself like wildfire, and runs through the ears and tongues of as many as have any acquaintance with the persons concern'd in it.—Do you not know what the poet tells us?

On Eagles wings immortal scandals fly."[9]

"Besides," said he, "Bath is the same thing as London;—people are so perpetually going backwards and forwards, that what is talked on in one place can never be long a secret in the other.—You may also find another reason for the propagation of this rumour;—you cannot suppose that either yourself or Miss Jessamy are so little known, or so indifferent to the world, as that it should not be interested in whatever concerns you."

This compliment was lost upon Jemmy in the humour he was at present;—they were going on, however, with some farther discourse on the same subject, when something else coming that instant into the gentleman's mind, he ask'd him suddenly if he had heard any thing of the hurly-burly that had happen'd in the house where Miss Jessamy and the other ladies lodged;—to which Jemmy answer'd in the negative, and desired to know of what nature.

The other then repeated to him what he had heard from the mouth of common fame;—that a woman, who it was said had been kept by Celandine, and ran mad on his quitting her, had attempted to stab Miss Jessamy;—that Mr. Lovegrove had sent him a challenge on that young lady's account, which he refused to accept; but that some brulée[10] happening between them afterwards, they were both carried before a magistrate, where Mr. Lovegrove, being proved the aggressor, was obliged to give bail; and the other, to avoid being pointed at for a coward, went directly out of town.

"Well, but the occasion, my dear friend," cried Jemmy hastily, "how was Celandine answerable for the fury of his forsaken mistress? Or if he could be so, how came Lovegrove, who all the world knows courts Lady Speck, to be so warm in his resentment on the account of any other woman?"

"Indeed," reply'd the other, "the whole affair seems to me, and to all whom I have heard speak of it, as much a mystery as it can be to yourself:—I can only tell you what happen'd;—but as to the why and the wherefore, it must be left to time, and the parties themselves to unfold."

Jemmy's impatience to know every thing relating to an event in which he thought himself so deeply interested, made him persecute his friend with a thousand questions, which were altogether unavailing, as the other had it not in his power to inform him in any more than he had already done.

Hoping, however, to get better intelligence at home, he took leave of his friend more early than otherwise he would have done, yet came to his lodging too late for what he had proposed;—the gentlewoman of the house was gone to bed, and he was compell'd to defer taking any measures for the satisfaction of his curiosity till the next day.

In the morning the mistress of the house, on his requesting it, drank chocolate with him in his own apartment; but at first was very cautious in her replies to the interrogatories he put to her, till finding he was already informed of the quarrel between Mr. Lovegrove and Celandine, and also on whose account it happen'd, she made no scruple of relating to him all she knew of the transaction of the garden, and the danger Miss Jessamy had been in from the jealous rage of Mrs. M——.

Let any one, who is truly a lover, judge how much Jemmy must be shock'd on hearing the double danger to which his mistress had been exposed; and as he doubted not but his presence would have secur'd her from meeting either with the one or the other of these insults, he severely condemn'd himself for having suffer'd any thing to keep him from her.

He met with several of his acquaintance here, who would fain have detain'd him among them during the remainder of the season; but all the persuasions in the world would not now have prevailed upon him to stay a moment longer than he could conveniently depart.

By way of attonement for the vexation, and perhaps the slights Jenny might have sustain'd through the report of his infidelity, he resolved to shew that he came to Bath only for her sake, and that neither the place nor company had any charms for him now she was gone.

Accordingly he set out for London, after giving one day's rest to his servant, who, as he had wrote to Jenny, was very much hurt by a fall he had received in the journey thither.

Chapter V

Displays love in colours very different from those in which that passion generally appears, and seems calculated chiefly for the entertainment of the young and fair; but will scarcely be displeasing to such as are not so, with this proviso, that they have no share of envy in their composition.

Not the sybils of antiquity, nor those enthusiasts who mounted the hallowed tripod,[11] more mistook for the inspiration of their fictitious deity the frenzy of their own heated imaginations, or were more deceiv'd themselves, or capable of deceiving others, than those lovers are who dignify with the sacred name of a pure and virtuous affection that passion which is excited merely by beauty and the difference of sex.

I have heard of some ladies of that romantic turn of mind as not to be convinced of their lovers sincerity without the most fatal proofs, and have took in good earnest what the humourous poet meant only in ridicule:

He that will hang or beat out's brains,
The devil's in him if he feigns.[12]

But though it is to be hoped that far the greater number are of a more reasonable way of thinking, yet I am afraid that even among some of these the hero of this history will be look'd upon as no more than a half lover at the best;—he could be perfectly easy and gay out of Jenny's company;—nay,—and what is less to be forgiven, amuse the hours of absence from her in an amorous conversation with other women, when with her he has hitherto discovered none of those impatiencies,—those alternate hopes and fears,—those extravagancies which men so frequently put in practice, and which their mistresses are apt to take as the most certain indications of a true and ardent passion.

Yet, in spite of all these deficiencies,—omissions,—commissions, and other sins against the god of love, I doubt not to bring him, by degrees, into the good graces of the most imperious, vain and tyrannic of my fair readers.

It will appear that he loved the object of his honourable flame much more than he knew he did himself;—he had never been sensible of the least jealousy on her account, nor indeed, had taken much pains to prevent that passion from laying hold on her; yet no sooner had he reason to believe she was made acquainted with the story of his falshood, than he felt all the pangs which he supposed had seized her heart on receiving a shock so unexpected.

What was wanting in the violence of that passion he had for her was abundantly made up with tenderness;—he trembled not for himself but her;—conscious of his innocence, he had no cause to dread the reproaches she might meet him with; but was ready to sink under the apprehensions of what she endured, till he was fully clear'd of this unjust accusation.

It was now that he first began to feel that burning impatience to be with her which all lovers pretend to have, though few perhaps, very few, in reality experience;—it was not that he so much languish'd to feast his eyes upon her beauties, or his ears with her wit and engaging conversation, tho' both had charms for him preferable to those of any other woman in the world; but it was to ease her of all suspence in regard to his integrity; and convince her, by the most unquestionable testimony, that he was incapable of love for any but herself.

Let the discreet, and judging part of womankind speak their opinion of a lover such as this, and I believe Jemmy himself might safely appeal to the verdict they would give.

The freedom with which from their infancy they had been accustom'd to converse together abolish'd all manner of ceremony between them; but had more been required, Jemmy's eagerness to see her would not have permitted him to make use of any at this time:—he order'd the postilion to drive directly to the house where she was lodged, and without going home, or having any thoughts of changing his travelling dress, flew up stairs, nor even waited till a servant should apprise her of his arrival.

This, however, being the day in which his letter had made her expect his coming, she had taken care to be at home and alone, judging it improper there should be any witnesses of a conversation which she knew not but might be of too much importance to be divulged.

On seeing him enter the room, she rose hastily from her seat and received the embrace he gave her with the same sweetness and obliging air with which she had always treated him—"My dear,—dear Jenny," cried he, throwing himself a second time upon her bosom,—"how many disappointments have I suffer'd before I could attain the blessing I now enjoy?"

"I should have shared with you in those disappointments," answered she smiling, "if I had not been assured that whatever pleasures you missed the enjoyment of at Bath were very well attoned for by others that you met with in London."

"Cruel sarcasm," rejoin'd he, looking earnestly on her face,—"could I have expected it from a mouth so much used to softness?—If to have been detained from the presence of all my soul holds dear;—if to have been involved in affairs to which my nature is the most averse;—if to have been aspersed,—scandalized,—doubly wounded in my love and honour by a villainous report;—if these are pleasures, I have indeed met with enough to gratify the spleen of my worst enemies, but should methinks excite my Jenny's pity."

"One cannot rightly pity," reply'd she more seriously, "what one is not perfectly acquainted with;—you may perhaps have had some embarassments which you did not think proper to communicate to me, and I was loth to depend too much on what I heard from others."

"The less you have depended," said he, "the more generous you are, and the more fortunate I am;—I need not ask what it is you mean;—I know you have been told that I am inconstant, perfidious;—that, insensible to your merits and the happiness ordained for me by the best of fathers, I have basely transferred my vows and affections to another."

"This story," continued he, perceiving she was silent, "false and absurd as in itself it is, has not only gained strange credit here, but I find has also been carried down to Bath, and cannot have escaped your ears.—I hope you know your Jemmy better than to imagine there was even a possibility of there being the least truth in it; yet the uneasiness you may have felt through your regard for me, in finding it believed by others, has given me a mortification beyond what I am able to express."

"Much pains has indeed been taken," reply'd Jenny, "to perswade both myself and friends, that you no longer thought me worthy of your affection, and were weary of the engagement made for us by our parents; but I assure you that I never gave the least credit to any insinuations of this kind, tho' made in the most specious manner imaginable."

She was going on,—but Jemmy could not forbear interrupting her, by catching her in his arms, and testifying by that action, as well as by the most rapturous expressions, the grateful sense he had of the justice she had done him.

After having indulged him for some moments, "It was not," said she, "that I was thus tenacious of your constancy through any vanity of my own merits, but through a perfect confidence in the sincerity of your heart;—I was far from thinking it impossible that you should cease to love me, but then I also thought it impossible that you would not at the same time cease all professions of it;—I always believed you incapable of deceit, and therefore could not give credit to your change of sentiments in respect to me, while you continued to assure me they were the same as ever."

"Charming,—angelic creature!" cried he, seizing her a second time, and pressing her with the extremest tenderness to his breast. "How beyond all description villainous, as well as stupid, must be the man who could wrong such excelling sweetness,—such unparallel'd goodness!"

Jenny then told him, that whoever had propagated this report must certainly be greatly interested in having it believed, since such uncommon methods had been taken for that purpose,—"as you will presently be convinced," continued she, "by that I have to shew you."

In speaking these words she ran hastily to a little cabinet, and having taken thence the letter which had been sent to Lady Speck at Bath, and that other which she had received herself since her coming to town from a pretended rival, put them both into his hands, and desired him to peruse them.

Jemmy read them over with an equal mixture of rage and astonishment;—he now plainly saw, that to break the union between him and Jenny must have been a thing contrived by some person who was an enemy to both, and could not proceed merely from the vanity of Miss Chit, in imagining him her lover;—much less could he think it possible that any woman was capable of raising such a report, for the sake of revenge, against a man for not loving her, who had never pretended to do so.

He repeated to Jenny, without the least reserve, the motive of his being at first introduced to that young lady's acquaintance, and of the visits he continued to make to her house, till he was informed by Mr. Morgan what the world said of it;—protested, as he might do with the greatest veracity, that he never had the least thought of making an amorous address to her on any score whatever.

They were still upon this topick, and endeavouring, by various conjectures, to fathom the bottom of an affair which seem'd so mysterious to both of them, when a servant came into the room to lay the cloth, Jenny having ordered supper should be served up that night in her own chamber.

This changed the subject of their entertainment for the present; but the business of the table was no sooner over than more and greater matters came upon the carpet.

Chapter VI

Will be found yet more affecting than the former, unless the reader is as dull as perhaps he may think the author.

When our lovers had regained the opportunity of communicating freely to each other all that their minds were charged with, Jemmy, who had thought a good deal of what had been told him concerning the insults Jenny had received from Celandine and his outrageous mistress, began to testify a desire of being fully informed in the particulars of an adventure he had heard but an imperfect account of at Bath.

Jenny hesitated not to comply with his request; but tho' she expatiated, with all the wit and satire she was mistress of, on Celandine's behaviour in regard to the challenge sent him by Mr. Lovegrove, yet she took care to avoid setting his impertinence towards herself in so bad a light as she might have done, and it indeed deserved.

Never had this young lady given a greater demonstration of her prudence, than in thus shadowing over, as much as truth would permit, the insolence of Celandine;—she consider'd that it was not unlikely that Jemmy might some time or other meet him, and think himself obliged to call him to a severe account for an affront offer'd to the woman whom it was so publickly known he was about to marry.

She soon found how necessary had been the precaution she had taken;—Jemmy flew into the extremest rage at the presumption of Celandine, even on hearing it in the manner she recited it; and she was obliged, before she could bring him to any degree of moderation, to remind him that all actions of so egregious a coxcomb proceeded more from folly than design, and merited rather contempt than indignation from a man of sense.

"You see, my dear Jenny," said he, "how many inconveniencies have attended the protraction of our marriage so much beyond the time in which it was expected to have been consumated;—for heaven's sake, therefore, let us put an end to the suspence that every one is in, and convince the world that we indeed are born only for each other."

"Could you then resolve," cryed she, with an air which had something very meaning[ful] in it, "to renounce all the joys of an unhoused condition, as Otway calls a single life,[13] and give up your liberty before fully satiated with the sweets you men find in it?—How would it sound at Mrs. Comode's that Mr. Jessamy was become a husband?"

"Mrs. Comode!" repeated he; she made no answer presently, but went again to her cabinet to fetch the letter he had intended for Lady Hardy, and put it open into his hands.

"How would marriage, my dear Jemmy," resumed she, "agree with the promise you made in this,—of coming to the arms of the kind she to whom you wrote it, with a heart intirely unincumbered with any cares but those of pleasing her?"

The consternation he was in at this sight is utterly impossible to be described; but recovering himself from it as well as he could,—"Before I make any attempt," said he, "either to excuse or justify my conduct in this point, tell me, I conjure you, by what means this letter came into your possession."

"You need but turn the paper," answered she, "and the superscription[14] will inform you":—he did so, and finding it—"To Miss Jessamy at Bath,"—instantly discovered the mistake he had committed, and cried out in the greatest confusion,—"Good God!—How justly is my folly punished!"—then turning to Jenny,—"Yet when known," continued he, "by how odd an accident I was betray'd into this error, you will, I am sure, forgive me."

"I will know nothing farther of this matter," reply'd Jenny, "nor shall I ever think of it hereafter;—all I desire is, that when we marry you will either have no amours, or be more cautious in concealing them;—and in return, I promise never to examine into your conduct,—to send no spies to watch your motions,—to listen to no tales that might be brought me, nor by any methods whatever endeavour to discover more than you would have me."

"Generous creature," rejoin'd he kissing her hand, "yet permit me to assure you, by all my hopes of happiness, that the fault I am now detected in was never eagerly pursued by me;—that it was only an intention;—did not proceed to fact;—and that an angel's form can hereafter never tempt me to swerve, even in thought, from the fidelity I owe my dear forgiving Jenny."

"Make no vows on this last head, I beseech you," said she; "I have heard people much older, and more experienced than ourselves, say that the surest way to do a thing is to resolve against it."

"Besides, my dear Jemmy," added she with the most engaging sprightliness,—"I shall not be so unreasonable to expect more constancy from you than human nature and your constitution will allow; and if you are as good as you can, may very well content myself with your endeavours to be better."

What so much gains upon the soul as to meet endearments where we expected only reproaches, according to the words of a late honourable author?

Kindness has resistless charms,
All things else but faintly warms;
It gilds the lover's servile chain,
And makes the slave grow pleased and vain.[15]

To find Jenny thus turning into pleasantry what would have made other women swell into a storm of rage and jealousy, transported Jemmy almost beyond himself; he thought she was somewhat superior to mortality and half divine, and ascrib'd to her what Mr. Addison makes Juba say to Cato's daughter:

The virtuous Marcia tow'rs above her sex,
True, she is fair, O how divinely fair!
But then the lovely maid improves her charms,
With wisdom, modesty, good-nature,
And sanctity of manners.[16]—

In the exuberance of his present admiration, he gave her such praises as not being able to endure the hearing, she put her hand before his mouth to silence,—"Hold Jemmy," said she, "you cannot entertain me with any thing less agreeable, than encomiums which, thank Heaven, I am not so silly as to imagine I deserve:—If you would oblige me let us change the conversation."

"Oh Jenny,—Jenny,—Jenny," cried he, sending forth a tender sigh between every repetition of her name,—"How is it possible for me to think or speak of any thing but your transcendent goodness and my own unworthiness?"

In pronouncing these last words he fix'd his eyes upon the letter which had given him so much confusion, and he had thrown upon the table after having seen what it was.—Jenny perceiving on what his looks were bent, snatch'd it hastily away, and running to a candle set it immediately on fire.—"This testimonial of your fault," said she, "shall no more rise up against you, and as it consumes, may all remembrance of it for ever be extinguish'd."

The heart of Jemmy was so much overwhelmed with love and gratitude at this action, and the words that accompanied it, that he could not refrain the most extravagant demonstrations of what he felt;—he threw himself at her feet, and embraced her knees with transports not to be described, nor even by himself express'd.

It was with a great deal of difficulty that she made him rise from the posture he was in, and much more that she prevailed on him to talk no more on this affair; to which, on whatever topic she began, he would still return.

The time pass'd so swiftly, as well as sweetly, in this tender intercourse, that the lovers never so much as thought on hours, nor once look'd upon their watches, till the sonorous guardian of the night, with his usual solemnity, thunder'd in their ears,—"Past two o'clock."

It was now that Jemmy first reflected how much he had transgress'd on his dear mistress's repose, and therefore prepared to take an unwilling leave; but she would not suffer him to go till her servant, none of his own being there, had got a chair for him, which being brought, they embraced, kiss'd, and parted, the behaviour of each to the other having imprinted a mutual satisfaction in their minds, greater than ever either of them had before experienced.

Chapter VII

Is very concise, and presents the reader only with some few passages, by way of a preparative for events, shortly to ensue, of an infinitely far greater consequence.

The good-natured reader must certainly be pleased to find, that all the base artifices of Bellpine were so entirely frustrated;—that all his endeavours to dissolve the union between the lovers had only served to cement it the more firmly;—they were now in a fair way of being as happy as could be wish'd; and that the ungenerous contriver of the plots against them had the mortification to see all his labour had been thrown away.

He could not, indeed, any longer flatter himself with the least hopes of success;—the last conversation he had with Jemmy before he went to Bath, and that he had with Jenny on her arrival from that place, convinced him that neither the one nor the other were to be wrought upon by any projects he could frame.

Besides the disappointment of those vain hopes he had entertain'd of becoming one day the master of Jenny's person and fortune, it vexed him to the heart to have lost himself in the good graces of Miss Chit; not that he had any regard for her, on her own account; but because, as has been already observed, he was solliciting for an employment at court, where he knew that young lady had a very great interest.

He had never attempted to visit her since the concert, when, as the reader may remember, she had given him a rebuff which might well make him fearful of approaching her again, without some more plausible pretence than it was in his power to make, to cover the occasion he had given her of offence.

It also fell out, very unluckily for him, that just at this time the post he was endeavouring to procure happened in the disposal of a certain great person, who, it was said, was too nearly allied to Miss Chit to have refused any thing she ask'd;—well therefore might he be chagrin'd at having, by a foolish scheme, incurr'd the displeasure of one so able, and where he had reason to believe, would otherwise have been so ready to serve him.

Miss Chit had, indeed, a great deal of good-nature, and an inclination to afford all the assistance in her power, to any one who she thought either wanted or deserved it;—She had been acquainted with Bellpine for a considerable time, had look'd upon him as a very facetious tea table visiter, and he had not deceived himself in believing she would have exerted her whole interest in his favour.

But all the good-will she once had for him was now justly coverted into an adequate resentment;—she was gay and flighty, but wanted not understanding;—she plainly saw he had imposed upon her on Mr. Jessamy's account, by the answer that gentleman had sent to her card of invitation; and as she was not able to conceive with what design he had made her the dupe, it gave her the more disquiet, and dwelt the longer on her mind.

She likewise found he had told the same story he had done to herself to several of her friends, who were continually teazing her with one question or another concerning this imaginary lover; nor could all her protestations that she knew nothing of the matter, pass with any of them for more than maiden bashfulness.

All this while, however, she knew not how much she suffer'd in the opinion of some people, till a pretty extraordinary chance discover'd it to her.

On account of some apprehensions of an inward decay, she had been advised to drink milk warm from the cow with conserve of roses; and in compliance with this recipe, went every morning into the park, and sat upon a bench while her maid prepared the dose she was to take.

It happen'd that at one of these times two elderly gentlemen came and placed themselves on the same seat;—they took no other notice of her than the compliment of—"By your leave, Madam";—nor did she much regard the near neighbourhood of them, as their age and gravity defended her from the fears of being treated by them with any of those impertinencies she might have had reason enough to expect from the more young and gay.

They talked only of the weather,—the calamity of the times,—and such like common topics of conversation, till he, who appeared to be somewhat the oldest of the two, started up on a sudden and went hastily towards a footman who he saw passing along on the other side of the Mall.

On his return,—"If I am not mistaken," said his friend, "the person you have been speaking to belongs to Mr. Jessamy."—"Yes" reply'd he, "I did not know his master was in town, but it seems he came last night."—"Are you acquainted with him, pray."—"No otherwise," said he, "than by seeing him at a coffee-house where I sometimes go; but I am told he is a very accomplish'd gentleman."—"As any in town," rejoin'd the old gentleman pretty eagerly;—"and I can tell you, has as few of the vices of it."

Before we proceed any farther, it is highly proper to inform the reader, that the person who spoke with so much friendly warmth was no other than that very Mr. Morgan, mention'd in the nineteenth chapter of the second volume of this history, for the remarkable conference he had with Jemmy on account of his supposed infidelity to Jenny.

This hearty well-wisher of Jemmy was about to add something farther in his praise, but was hinder'd from doing so at that time by the others saying, that he had heard some talk of the match between him and Miss Jessamy was broke off, and that he made his addresses at present to a young lady call'd Miss Chit.

"Nothing in it, upon my word, Sir," reply'd Mr. Morgan a little peevishly;—"all an idle story, raised by the vain girl herself:—I heard it too, and I believe was the first that told him of it; but I never saw a man so much surprised and vexed.—She wanted to draw him in, I suppose;—she has a good voice, it seems, and plays on the harpsichord;—he made her some few visits on that score, and she was so silly as either to believe him really in love with her, or to endeavour to make others believe so if she could;—that is all, upon my honour, Sir."

It is easy to conceive what Miss Chit must feel on being witness of this discourse:—on hearing Mr. Jessamy named, she had sat longer than else she would have done, out of mere curiosity of knowing what would be said of him, but little expected to hear such a character of herself;—she as yet, however, restrain'd the passion she was in, and Mr. Morgan went on.

"Thank Heaven I have no daughters," resumed he; "formerly a young maid was ready to blush to death at being told a man was in love with her; but now, forsooth, the girls are as proud of a new lover as they are of a new suit of cloaths, and want as much to shew it;—but, a-lack-a-day, Miss Chit quite miss'd her mark in my friend Jessamy;—he loves music, 'tis true; but is not to be sung or play'd out of his senses."

She could now hold out no longer;—"Do you know this Miss Chit, Sir," demanded she, "whom you speak of in this contemptuous manner?"—"No truly, Madam," answer'd he; "but if I did, should make no scruple to tell her my mind on this occasion."—"If you had the least acquaintance with her," return'd she, "you would find she stood in no need of any lessons you could give.—I can assure you she despises the thoughts of drawing in any man;—she is above it;—and as for boasting of her lovers, has too many who are really such for her to be vain on any imaginary single one."

With these words she quitted the bench, and casting a disdainful look on Mr. Morgan took hold of her maid's arm and tripp'd down the walk with the utmost precipitation.

What the gentlemen said of her after she was gone, or whether Mr. Morgan had any guess that she was the person he had been speaking of is not material, I shall only say that the affronted lady went home in the greatest agitations;—that she wept,—raved,—curst Bellpine as the primary cause of all this, and at last took a resolution to do what will presently be shewn.

Chapter VIII

Contains a most extraordinary, as well as unexpected turn in the lovers affairs, not fit to be read by those who have very tender hearts or watery eyes.

The joy one feels on being forgiven an offence which one repents, and is heartily ashamed of, can be surpass'd by nothing but that most sublime satisfaction which must fill the mind of the person who forgives;—both our lovers were equally pleased with themselves and with each other, and there wanted but one thing to complete the felicity of either.

As for Jenny, it cannot be supposed that she wished a supremer happiness than what she now enjoy'd in a full assurance of the affection and sincerity of her dear Jemmy; but we will not pretend to say that his desires were altogether so much circumscrib'd,—he thought it was now high time to fulfil the agreement made between their parents, and the more so, as it would be the only sure way of totally silencing the present invidious report, and of preventing all others of the like nature from being propagated hereafter.

This last, he thought, would be a prevailing motive with her, and therefore resolved to omit neither that nor any other argument which all the love and wit he was master of could furnish him with, to gain her consent to a speedy celebration of their nuptials.

The pleasing contemplations on Jenny's behaviour towards him the evening before,—her thousand amiable qualities, and the idea of that happiness he hoped shortly to be in full possession of, kept him in bed somewhat longer than was his custom; but he was no sooner up and dress'd, than he hasted to the apartment of that dear mistress who had been the sole object both of his dreams and waking thoughts.

He found Miss Wingman with her, but was not sorry he did so; for as he knew that lady was acquainted with the story of his imaginary falshood, by the letter which had been sent to Lady Speck, he made no scruple of saying to Jenny great part of what he would have done, had she not been present; nor was Jenny at all displeased that this young lady should be witness how little foundation there was for the reports which had been spread.

"Indeed, my dear," said Miss Wingman, on hearing him press the completion of their marriage,—"I think you ought not to refuse compliance with Mr. Jessamy's desires, if it were only to make him some amends for the vexation he must have endured in the late scandal thrown upon him."

"First be generous yourself, before you direct others to be so," reply'd Jenny laughing; "Mr. Jessamy cannot have suffer'd more, or with less reason, than Lord Huntley has done; and when I see you inclined to make a reparation, I may perhaps be prevailed upon to follow your example."

"I do not know how soon I may be obliged to it," resumed that lady, "for Sir Thomas Welby and my mamma are so ashamed, and concern'd at the injury they have done my lord by their unjust suspicions, that, by way of attonement, they are for making a present of me to him, almost whether I will or not."

"Excellent, i'faith," cried Jemmy, "you are caught, my dear Jenny, and have made a promise without knowing you did so;—I shall, however, be obliged to watch and pray for Lord Huntley's happiness, as I find my own so much depends upon it."

They went on in the same strain of pleasantry all the time Miss Wingman staid; but after she was gone Jemmy began to renew his suit with more seriousness, and had the pleasure to find it was not altogether rejected, though not immediately comply'd with.

"It is not owing to the want of affection for you," said she with the most enchanting softness, "but rather to an excess of it, that I would yet a little longer protract what you at present seem so earnestly to desire;—men are often deceived in their own hearts;—I speak not to reproach you for any amours you may have been engaged in, or that I am jealous of any you may hereafter be engaged in;—no,—my dear Jemmy, I should not think that even marriage gave me a right to censure, or to pry into your actions; it is for your own sake alone that I would have you forbear making a vow of constancy till you are very certain of being quite out of love with variety; but rather continue in a condition which allows you full liberty to pursue whatever pleasures you think fit, without having any occasion to condemn yourself."

"I should be ready to condemn myself to everlasting horrors," cried he, "could I be capable of lavishing one tender thought on any but she who so well deserves all, and much more than I can pay.—I confess I have been guilty of some follies; but in all my amusements with your sex, my heart had never the least share;—no,—that was always,—is,—and ever must be intirely,—unchangeably,—inviolably devoted to my only dear, dear Jenny."

They were in the midst of this tender conversation, when the persons with whom Jenny boarded, hearing Jemmy was above, sent to intreat he would honour them with his company at dinner that day; which invitation, for the sake of not being separated from Jenny, he willingly accepted.

These people were well-bred; and perfectly chearful, but the lovers liking no company so well as that of each other, staid no longer with them than decency demanded, and Jemmy had again an opportunity of repeating his sollicitations, which he did in the most pressing and emphatic terms.

How far he would have been able to prevail is uncertain;—Jenny's servant came into the room, and told her that a young lady, who called herself Miss Chit, was in a chair at the door, and desired leave to wait on her.

On hearing the name of Miss Chit, Jemmy and Jenny look'd upon each other with the utmost astonishment.—"Are you acquainted with her?" cried he—"Not in the least," answer'd she, "nor can imagine what should bring her here;—but go," said she to the man, "and shew her up."

They had no time to form any conjectures, the lady immediately came in, and Jenny rose to receive her with her accustom'd politeness, but mixt with a certain reserve, which she neither could nor endeavour'd to throw off.

"You are doubtless surprised, Madam," said Miss Chit, "at receiving a visit from one so much a stranger to you, but you will pardon the liberty I have taken when you know the necessity that obliged me to it."—"I cannot suppose, Madam," reply'd Jenny, "that you would have given yourself this trouble without being induced by some extraordinary motive."—

"An extraordinary one, indeed, Madam," resumed the other; "and I am very glad to meet you here, Mr. Jessamy," continued she, addressing herself to Jemmy,—"as what I have to say to this lady concerns you also."—"You are certainly in the right, Madam," added he very gravely; "for whatever relates to this lady must infallibly concern me too."

"I never believed the contrary, Sir," said Miss Chit, "nor doubted of the sincerity of your attachment to one so deserving of it;—and it was, in some measure, to do justice to you, that brought me hither, as well as to vindicate myself from the most cruel aspersion that ever was laid on any one of my sex."

No reply being made to these words, she went on,—"It is scarce possible," said she, "that either of you can have escaped the hearing a report, which absurd as it is, has been strangely propagated about town, concerning the intended marriage between you being broke off; but you perhaps may be ignorant that your pretended friend Bellpine was the sole author of this invention."

"Bellpine," cried they both out at the same time,—"Sure, Madam, you mistake."—"Yes,—Bellpine," rejoined she, "for what base ends I know not, would fain have had me so weak as to believe Mr. Jessamy was not only false to his first vows, but also false on my account:—I pretend not to be free from the follies my sex are charged with, yet was never vain enough to believe a man in love with me till he had told me so himself; and therefore gave no credit to all he said and swore upon that subject:—his artifices, however, wrought so far upon my father, and all those of my friends with whom he had any acquaintance, that wherever I went I was entertain'd with no other discourse than my imaginary conquest;—I was very much amazed at all this; but other thoughts kept it from dwelling much upon my mind, till this morning I was grosly affronted by being told that I myself had spread about this foolish story, as having flatter'd myself that the few visits Mr. Jessamy had favoured me with were made on the account of his having a passion for me."

"It is no matter, Madam," cried Jemmy, "by whom or in what manner this ridiculous story has been propagated;—but tell me, was it from Bellpine that you were first informed of this pretended villainy?"

"Yes, Sir," answered she, "it was by him—and him alone, that your character has been traduced, Miss Jessamy without doubt disquieted, and myself attempted to be deceived; as you will presently be convinced if you have patience to listen to the monstrous detail I can give you of his behaviour."

She then went on, and gave a succinct account of all the particulars she knew of Bellpine's conduct in this affair, which, as the reader is already perfectly acquainted with, need not be here repeated.

Jenny opened not her lips, but listened with the greatest attention to all she said;—but Jemmy could not keep himself from interrupting her almost at every sentence by some vehement exclamation, and when he spoke not, discovered by his gestures all the marks of an over-boiling rage.

"Well, Madam," cried he, perceiving she had done,—"I see that Bellpine has been the Boutefeu;[17]—for what reason he has been so, it belongs to me to penetrate":—he said no more, but snatching up his hat, which lay on a table near him, flew down stairs without taking any other leave.

Jenny, having observed the agitations he had been in, was extremely frighted at this last action;—she ran and opened the door, which he had flung after him as he went, and called as loud as she could to him to come back; but he either heard not, or would not at that time obey her summons.

She then stamp'd with both her feet, and rung the bell for the footman with such violence as snapp'd the wire by which it hung;—"Run," cry'd she, "overtake Mr. Jessamy, who is just gone out of the house;—tell him I must needs speak with him, and desire he will return this instant."

It is not to be doubted but that the fellow did his best; but notwithstanding all the speed he made, the person he pursued was gone quite out of sight:—this increasing the ferment on Jenny's spirits,—"I wish, Madam," said she to Miss Chit, "you had reserved the story you have been telling till you had found me alone;—it is dangerous to let one gentleman know too much of the injuries he has sustained from another."

"I should be sorry, Madam," reply'd that young lady, "that what I meant well should prove the contrary; but I flatter myself the event will give me no cause for repentance;—Mr. Jessamy, I hope, will only examine Bellpine on this affair;—he is not worthy of his sword;—nor, as base men are generally cowards, will scarcely be provoked to meet it."

Jenny making no answer, and continuing to walk about the room in a disordered motion, the other easily perceived her company was not desired, so took her leave without much ceremony on either side.

Impossible is it to describe the apprehensions, the alarms, which shook the tender heart of Jenny for what might be the consequences of the discovery Miss Chit had made;—she figured to herself all that was terrible on the occasion, and could scarce bear up under the ideas of her own formation.

But if she suffer'd so much through the fears of what might, or might not happen, what must the cruel certainty inflict, when in about three hours after she saw Jemmy enter the room with a countenance pale and confused, and his cloaths sprinkled in many places with blood!—"Oh Heavens!" cry'd she, "What have you been doing?"—"An act of justice," reply'd he, "which I can repent of for no other reason than as it compels me to be once more separated from you.—I know not but I have kill'd the villain Bellpine, and prudence requires that I should be out of the way for a short time."—"But whither will you go?" demanded she in a voice scarce articulate,—"Where can you be safe?"—"I have already taken care of that," answered he, "all is prepared for my departure, and I but stay to snatch one dear embrace."

"Go then,—Oh go!" cry'd she, "And hazard not your safety on a moment's delay."—Tho' she spoke this with all the courage she could assume, yet she could not so well conceal the trembling of her whole frame, while he held her in his arms, but that he found, and was pierced with them to the soul;—"I cannot go," said he, "and leave you thus."—"You must,—you must," rejoin'd she,—"your presence, while this danger threatens you, is much more terrible to me than your absence can be."

He then told her, that a boat waited to carry him that night to Greenwich,—that he should take a post-chaise from thence to Dover, and hoped to be in Calais before that time the next day:—on hearing this, she in a manner forced him from her arms, and never was there a more tender, tho' hasty parting, than between those two so equally loving and beloved.

Chapter IX

Is inserted for no other purpose than merely to gratify the curiosity of the reader.

The event which once more separated our lovers is of so interesting a nature, that I believe there are but very few who will not be desirous of knowing those particulars concerning it which Jemmy had no opportunity of relating to his fair mistress, in the short time his safety allow'd him to stay with her.

But first,—as some people may be apt to think that Miss Chit, in making the discovery she had done, had a view to the consequences which ensued; and that in mere spite to Jemmy for not loving her, and to Bellpine for having imposed upon her, she had taken this method of revenging herself on both;—in justice to her character I must therefore beg leave to observe, that if this had been the case, she would rather have chose to have wrote the whole matter to Jemmy, with whom she was acquainted, than have gone in person to a lady to whom she had never spoke in her whole life, and from whom she could not be certain of meeting a very candid reception.

On hearing herself accused in the manner she had been by Mr. Morgan, and not doubting but that Jenny, as the party most concerned, had been equally severe upon her on that occasion, she came, in the heat of her passion, to clear herself to that lady from the imputation of a vanity of which she was indeed not guilty; and to convince her, by relating the whole proceeding of Bellpine in this affair, that she neither was, nor ever imagined herself her rival in Jemmy's affections.

It is true, that on seeing him there she might have forbore making any mention of Bellpine, or the business on which she came;—but then, what other excuse could she have made to Jenny for this visit, at least she was not at that time prepared with any, so that it must be allow'd the mischief she did sprung more from inadvertency than design?

As for Jemmy, no body, I believe, will either wonder at or condemn his just indignation, on finding himself thus treacherously dealt with, by a person he had loved and so much confided in;—the laws both of honour and of nature obliged him to demand some satisfaction for the injury that had been done him; and he must have been little of a lover, and indeed little of a man, not to have resented it in the manner he did.

Fired with a rage impossible to be express'd, he had not patience to wait the dull formality of a challenge; but the moment he left Jenny's apartment flew in search of that infamous traducer of his reputation.

As he knew most of the houses frequented by Bellpine, he went from one to another enquiring for him, but without success; and was just going home in order to send him a summons to meet him the next morning, when in his way thither he saw, by the light of the lamps, for it was then dark, the person he had vainly sought for, coming out of a tavern with another gentleman arm in arm.—"Bellpine," cried he, "Jemmy," rejoin'd the other, "What, left Bath so soon?"—"Yes," resumed Jemmy,—"and must needs speak with you this instant."—"I was going to supper with this gentleman," said Bellpine, "but will put off my engagement if your business be of any importance."—"It is," reply'd Jemmy, "and cannot be delay'd."

Bellpine perceiving by his manner of speaking that he had somewhat more than ordinary in his mind, and perhaps imagining it might be some new incident relating to Lady Hardy, excused himself to his friend for quitting him, and they went into the tavern and up into the same room where he, Bellpine, and the other gentleman had been drinking.

The bottles and glasses were not yet removed, but as soon as they were so, and fresh wine brought in,—"Now, my dear friend, your pleasure," said Bellpine.—"To tell you that you are a villain!" reply'd Jemmy,—"a most consummate villain."—"A villain, Sir," retorted Bellpine.—"Yes,—I again repeat the name," cried Jemmy,—"A villain,—a base incendiary, or you would not, by the most monstrous of all falshoods, have defamed the character of one you call'd your friend,—and endeavour'd to break the bands of union between two hearts inseparably link'd by love and honour."

Conscious guilt now stared this base man in the face, and assisted the reproaches of his injured friend;—he affected, however, an intire ignorance of what he was accused of, and would fain have seem'd to take as only a jest what the other said to him.

But our hero was in too great a heat to endure this trifling; he told him that he had learned the truth of every thing from Miss Chit;—that she was now with Jenny, and insisted that he should either go with him to those two ladies,—renounce all he said, and ask pardon on his knees, or with his sword defend the injustice he had done.

To this he sullenly reply'd, that he knew of no obligation he was under to do either the one or the other.—"Then you are a coward,—a scoundrel, and poltroon," cry'd Jemmy, "and deserve to be used as such";—with these words he took one of the glasses, which the drawer had fill'd before he left the room, and threw full in his face;—the other could not now be any longer passive,—both their swords were out in an instant,—they made several thrusts, and Bellpine had the advantage of having the first hit by wounding his antagonist in the arm; but this slight hurt was soon return'd with double interest,—Jemmy making a furious push ran him quite through the body;—he fell immediately, crying out,—"Oh, I am kill'd."

Jemmy ran to him, but he spoke no more, nor shewed the least signs of life; on which he thought it behoved him to make the best of his way out of the house, which he did directly; though not without ordering a drawer, as he pass'd by the bar, to go up to the gentleman above.

After he had got out of that street he stood still awhile, to consider what course he should take in case Bellpine was really dead; and on reflecting how much circumstances were against him, found it most adviseable to leave England, till he should hear whether the wound he had given him was mortal or not.

Having resolved on this, he called upon a surgeon of his acquaintance and directed him to go immediately to the tavern where he had left Bellpine, contenting himself with having his own arm, which had only a flesh would, dressed and bound up by the apprentice.

He then went home and made his servants get every thing ready for his departure;—they loved their master too well not to be very expeditious in executing his command; and, indeed, as it was not likely but that what had happened would presently be known, there was no time to be lost;—the danger he was in, however, would not prevent him from biding adieu to his dear Jenny, as has been already said.

As for Bellpine, he was not dead, nor speechless, as he had fain'd to be, but finding himself deeply pierced had fallen out of policy to prevent his enemy from giving a second blow;—so apt are men of mean minds to judge of others by themselves.

A surgeon had been sent for by the people of the tavern before Jemmy's friend arrived;—both these gentlemen coming almost at the same time examined, the wound together; but neither of them could pretend as yet to give his opinion how far it might be dangerous.

The condition he was in not permiting him to be put either into a coach or chair, they were obliged to lay him on a mattress, and cover'd close over with blankets, make him be carried by two fellows on a bier to his lodgings;—both the surgeons immediately follow'd, saw him into bed, and gave exact directions in what manner he should be order'd till they should attend him again the next morning, which they did very early, as believing his case extremely dangerous.

To their care, and the secret remorse of his own conscience for having so justly incurr'd the misfortune now fallen upon him, we shall leave him for a time, and return to subjects more capable of affecting the heart of every generous reader.

Chapter X

Treats of divers things, some of little, some of greater consequence; but none that will afford much matter of entertainment to those who read for no other end than merely to divert themselves.

Every passion of the human mind gains double energy by our own endeavours to conceal it;—like fire, which being smother'd for a time bursts out at last with greater violence;—Jenny, who had behav'd with so much seeming resolution while Jemmy was with her, could not see him turn his back to leave her; she knew not for how long, and on so dreadful an occasion, without falling into the extremest agonies;—all her moderation, almost all her reason, forsook her at this juncture.—"He is gone!" cried she, "He is gone!—Perhaps for ever, and I am left to waste my youth in unavailing grief:—but what of that,—selfish that I am,—in comparison of him; how small a share of pity is my due?—His single loss is all I have to mourn, while he, dear unhappy wanderer, is driven at once from his native country,—from love,—from friendship,—fortune, without any other companion than the dire reflection of having embrued his hands in the blood of a fellow creature.—Bellpine was wicked," continued she, "but justice might have overtaken him without the guilt of him he had wrong'd.—Oh what is honour!—'This impatience of indignities,' as the poet calls it:

> This raging fit of virtue in the soul,
> This painful burthen, which great minds must bear,
> Obtain'd with danger, and possess'd with fear."[18]

This was the manner in which the generous and truly amiable Jenny lamented the accident that had happen'd;—she wept not for the absence of her lover, but for the occasion that enforced it;—such was the delicacy of her soul, that his real infidelity would not have inflicted on her the thousandth part of those agonies she now endured on his having so fatally resented the aspersion; and so dear was he to her, that she would have wish'd to see him even unfaithful rather than unhappy.

It might perhaps be too affecting, tho' all that could be said would be far short of the truth of what she suffer'd during this whole cruel night;—the morning, however, brought her some consolation;—she heard that Bellpine was not dead, and to find that he had not been killed upon the spot, as Jemmy had imagined, affording her some hopes that his wounds might not be mortal, gave her as much satisfaction as a person in her circumstances was capable of feeling.

The whole adventure being presently blaz'd abroad, all her friends, and more of her acquaintance than, at that time, she wish'd to see, came to visit her, and made their compliments of condolance;—among the number of the former were Lady Speck, Miss Wingman, Mr. Lovegrove, and Sir

Robert Manley. After having express'd their concern for the accident, as it might give Mr. Jessamy much trouble, especially if his antagonist should die, they told her that Lord Huntley was to give them a concert that evening upon the river, and would fain have persuaded her to have accompanied them, in order, as they said and really meant, to divert those melancholy thoughts which could not but rise in her mind on what had happen'd.

It is not to be imagined that she gave the least ear to so unseasonable an invitation; but they continuing to press her with a great deal of earnestness to accept it;—"Oh," said she, bursting into tears, which hitherto she had restrain'd in their presence,—"can you think me capable of making one in a party of pleasure, while the liberty, perhaps the life of him ordain'd to be my husband is in danger?—No,—till I know him safe, music would be discord to my ears, and every thing that gives joy to others add to my affliction."

On hearing this, Sir Robert Manley could not forbear breaking into a kind of rhapsody,—"Happy Mr. Jessamy," cried he, "by his very misfortunes rendered yet more blest in the proofs of such exalted tenderness."

Mr. Lovegrove said little less in praise of her constancy and generosity; and the ladies afterwards gave over urging her any farther on the subject they had done, but employ'd the whole time they staid with her in discourses more suitable to her present humour.

But what was most of all obliging to her, was a promise the two gentlemen made of taking care to inform themselves, from day to day, of the true condition of Bellpine's wounds, and letting her have an exact account, to the end she might transmit it to Mr. Jessamy, and enable him the better to judge what course he had to take.

Several others of her acquaintance, who hearing what had happen'd, came to visit her on that occasion, and those among them who were most apprehensive on Jemmy's account, forbore to speak their sentiments in her presence; but, on the contrary, all joined to comfort her with hopes which they were far from entertaining themselves;—so that she pass'd this night with somewhat more tranquility than she had done the preceding one.

Between her broken slumbers, however, a thousand melancholy reflections return'd upon her mind;—her thoughts pursued the dear unhappy fugitive in his wanderings, they painted him to her troubled imaginations in the most forlorn and pitious moving figure, thus traveling by night, and exposed to dangers almost equal to those from which he fled;—nor when her eyes, doubly fatigued with tears and watching, were closed again in sleep, did the sad ideas intirely quit her head.

The next day brought with it something which threw her into fresh agitations,—she was no sooner up than her maid presented her with a letter, which had been left for her by a footman sometime before she had quitted her bed, she having lain that morning longer than was her usual custom.

She was a little surprised as not knowing the hand on the superscription; but, on her opening it, found it from Miss Chit, and contain'd the following lines:

To Miss Jessamy.

Madam,

I am extremely sorry to send you any intelligence that may add to the disquiet I am sensible you are already under; but there are some cases in which it is absolutely necessary that even the most painful truths should be reveal'd;—you will find this relating to Mr. Jessamy, is so; and therefore do not condemn, as an over officiousness in me, what I now take the liberty to communicate.

One of the surgeons who attends Bellpine has declared, that, according to the best of his judgment, his patient cannot live; on which a search-warrant is issued out against Mr. Jessamy, it being already known that he has absconded from his house.

This, Madam, my father heard last night at a coffee-house; and moreover, that the people of the tavern, as well as a gentleman who it seems was with Bellpine when he was met by Mr. Jessamy, have offer'd to depose that he took him aside, prevail'd with him to leave his company, and go with him into a private room, where he soon after left him for dead.

I cannot pretend to any understanding in such matters; but they say, that in the eye of the law these circumstances will make the affair appear very black on the side of Mr. Jessamy, and that the fact will not be consider'd as a rencounter, or a fair duel, but as a downright premeditated murder.

As I cannot suppose that to whatever place Mr. Jessamy is retired you are ignorant of it, I thought it highly proper to give you this intimation, to the end you may apprise him of the greatness of his danger, and warn him to keep extremely close;—indeed I should never have forgiven myself, if by neglecting to do so any worse accident, than what has already happen'd, should ensue;—but I will trouble you no farther, than to assure you that I am,

With all due respect,
Madam,

Your most obedient,
Humble servant,
S. Chit.

P.S. My poor father is troubled beyond measure at this event, and swears that, old as he is, if he had sooner been convinced of the baseness of Bellpine, which till now he never was, he would have taken upon himself to punish it.

Jenny had but just finish'd the reading this epistle, when she was convinced of the truth of the intelligence it contain'd,—the officers of justice came in,—produced their warrant, and one of them very civilly intreated her leave to do what, by virtue of their commission, they were impowered to have done without it.

She seem'd a little surprised notwithstanding, and said, with an air of some resentment, that it seemed very odd to her that they should come to search her lodgings for a gentleman;—to which another of them, more surly than he who had spoke first, replied,—that they had orders to search not only her lodgings, but all that house, and every other which Mr. Jessamy had been known to frequent.

She said no more, but suffer'd them to pass wherever they would, and they discharged their duty with so much diligence, as to leave no place unlook'd into, that was big enough to have concealed a much less person than him they sought for.

Tho' Jenny had nothing to apprehend on this score, yet the sight of these men, and the errand they came upon, was an extreme shock to her; but she presently received another yet greater, when the person with whom she boarded told her, without considering the consequence of what he said, that he was credibly informed that notice had been sent to all the ports to prevent Mr. Jessamy from making his escape out of the kingdom.

These words struck her with such a horror, that she was very near falling into fits; and it was not in the power of all that both he and his wife could say afterwards to pacify her grief, or to make her be persuaded that Mr. Jessamy must needs be in Calais before any orders to stop him could arrive at Dover.

They remonstrated to her, that if he travelled all night, as it was not to be doubted but he did, he would certainly reach the port by the next day at noon; and as there was always some one or other of the packets ready, might embark the same hour he came;—"So that, my dear Miss," cried he merrily, "you may depend upon it your lover long before now has been regaling himself with good burgundy, and some quelque-chose or other, a-la-mode de France."[19]

She could not help allowing the reasonableness of his arguments;—but imagination, that creative faculty, which has the power to raise us to the utmost pinnacle of happiness, or sink us into the lowest depths of despair, form'd so many accidents which might retard her dear Jemmy's journey, and render him too late to avoid the pursuit made after him, that she could not think she ought to flatter herself with the hopes of his being safe till she was positively assured he was so.

Chapter XI

Contains some occurrences deserving the attention of the reader.

In a continual rack of thought, to which all the persuasions of her friends could not give the least intermission, did the fair heroine of this history pass her nights and days, till Jemmy, being safely arrived at Calais, sent her the following epistle:

To Miss Jessamy.

My for ever dear, dear Jenny.

The concern I saw you under on my departure has hung more heavy on my spirits than even the occasion that inforced it; but I assure you that none of your commands have been lost upon me, I have taken all the precautions that human prudence could suggest not to render your kind wishes unavailing, and preserve a life which I am so happy as to know you set some value upon.

The date of this will inform you that I have now reach'd an asylum, from whence it is not in the power of my enemies to snatch me;—but perhaps, after all, I might have spared your tender heart the cruel alarm I have given it, and myself the trouble of coming hither:—since I left London I have sometimes been tempted to hope that Bellpine is not dead, and that it was no more than a swoon in which I left him;—if so, with what transport shall I soon return to thank my dear Jenny for all her unequal goodness?

It is you,—and you alone,—my everlasting charmer,—that can make either my life or liberty a blessing; and when this cursed affair is once over, I shall then doubly taste the sweets of both;—for oh,—my soul,—I now feel that the apprehensions of being deprived of you, are infinitely more terrible to me than those of becoming an exile,—an outlaw—a vagabond.

But I will not turn the eyes of my imagination that way;—my reason, my resolution faulter at it,—and as Otway says,

> Madness lies there, and Hell is in the thought.[20]

I will rather endeavour to believe the best, and that the first intelligence I receive from England will intirely banish these sad ideas from my mind;—but whatever I suffer, or shall hereafter suffer, I beg my dear Jenny will exert all her fortitude to repel the invasions of an over-much grief and pity;—let your answer to this assure me, that you bear with moderation this sudden turn in our late blest condition, which is the only consolation can at present be received by him who is,

With a love unutterable,
Soul of my soul,
Your most faithfully,
And most passionately
Devoted lover and servant,
J. JESSAMY.

P.S. In the distraction of my thoughts I had like to have sent this away without informing you where an answer might find me,—pardon therefore the wildness of my brain, and direct for me at Monsieur Grandsine's, the Silver Lion in Calais.

The joy which filled the affectionate heart of Jenny, on finding her dear Jemmy had so happily avoided all the pursuit might be made after him, was so great, that for a time it intirely dissipated all her other anxiety.

But the ease she enjoy'd was momentary,—all the information the enquiries that her friends could procure was, that tho' Bellpine was not dead, he was far from being out of danger, and the consideration on what consequences his death must produce, in case his wound should prove mortal, rendered her incapable of enjoying any lasting or perfect satisfaction.

It cannot be supposed that she contented herself with once perusing a letter she had so much languished for;—she read it over and over, and the oftener she did so, the more a flood of tenderness poured in upon her soul; but the reader will be better able to judge, by her own words, of the disposition she was in, than by any description I am able to give of it.

After having well weighed what apprehensions they were which seem'd to give him the most pain, she thought herself obliged, both by love and gratitude, to make use of her utmost endeavours to remove them, as will be seen in the answer she gave to his letter, which was wrote in the following terms:

To James Jessamy, Esq;

My very dear Jemmy,

I congratulate you on your fortunate arrival at Calais;—you cannot more rejoice on finding yourself in a place of safety, than I have done in the knowledge that you are so;—I have also the pleasure to acquaint you, that Bellpine still lives,—I wish I could lengthen the intelligence by adding, that there are hopes of his recovery, but that is a satisfaction as yet denied us.

But wherefore, my dear Jemmy, do you wound my heart with apprehensions for which you have not the least ground;—do you know so little of your Jenny as to believe that any change of circumstances can change her sentiments in regard to you?—No,—if the vain supposition of losing me disturbs your peace, henceforth be perfectly at rest; for be assured, that wherever you are I will be.

Take not this as a flight of sudden passion, which I may hereafter be tempted to repent of and retract, but as the firm and determinate resolution of my soul, founded on the principles of honour, of duty, and of justice, as well as inclination.

Love for each other, my dear Jemmy, was the first lesson taught us in our most early years, and I have too long been accustomed to the practice, to be capable of swerving from it;—should therefore the fate of Bellpine, which Heaven forbid, be such as our worst fears suggest, you have no more to do, on the news of it, than to go directly into Paris, and provide a proper place for my reception;—and there, if you continue to desire it, the English Ambassador's Chaplain may fulfil the engagement made for us between our parents.

Farewell,—I flatter myself that you will find some satisfaction in the assurance I now give you of being,

With all the tenderness,
You can wish or expect,
My dear Jemmy,

Sincerely faithfully,
And ever yours,
J. JESSAMY.

P.S. I must do our common friends the justice to let you know they are greatly affected at your misfortune, all of them, at least that I see;—indeed if they were not, they would find little welcome from me.—Once more adieu,—I expect to hear from you again by the first post.

Jenny, not doubting but what she had wrote would afford great relief to the anxieties of her lover; found in that thought sufficient to calm those she had felt within herself;—such is the effect of a real tenderness, as to make us take pleasure in every thing that we imagine will give pleasure to the person beloved.

And now let those readers, who in the beginning of this history were apt to look on Jemmy and Jenny as two insensibles, acknowledge their mistake, and be convinced that flames which burn with rapidity at first are soonest wasted, and that a gentle, and almost imperceptible glow of a pure affection, when once raised up by any extraordinary incident, sends forth a stronger and more lasting heat.

I remember to have formerly read a little pamphlet, entitled, "Reflections on the different effects of love,"[21] which contains many pretty observations on the subject I am speaking of; but I know of none more just than this of Mr. Dryden:

Love various minds does variously inspire,
He stirs in gentle nature's gentle fire,
Like that of incense on the altars laid;
But raging flames tempestuous souls invade;
A fire which every wind of passion blows,
With pride it mounts, and with revenge it glows.[22]

It may easily be perceived, by those who consider the motives on which the events of this history depend, that our lovers were not thus stirred up by accidents relating merely to themselves, but by such as concerned each other;—Jemmy had not fought with Bellpine but for the discontent and affronts which he thought his dear Jenny had suffer'd thro' his base artifices;—nor would Jenny have discovered any part of the warmth she now did, had she not been invigorated by the perplexity and danger of her Jemmy.

Nothing certainly can be more truly worthy of admiration than the love,—the constancy,—the generosity, of this amiable lady, who at her years could so readily renounce her native country,—kindred, and all the amusements to which her youth had been accustomed, and resolve to live in a perpetual banishment, if by the death of Bellpine, the man ordain'd to be her husband in his more prosperous circumstances, should now be reduced to the condition of an exile.

Nor was Jemmy, gay and unthinking as he has sometimes appeared, at all inferior to his charming mistress, in giving her the most unquestionable and exalted proofs of the sincerity and disinterestedness of his passion, as the next chapter will declare.

Chapter XII

Recites a passage which will certainly be extremely agreeable to all the ladies; it is much to be feared, however, that there are but very few of them who can, with any reason, flatter themselves with experiencing the like.

Jenny, who had the mortification of hearing every day that Bellpine grew rather worse than better, began to call to mind every trifling accident that had happen'd to give her any disgust in England, to the end that she might have the less love for it, and be more reconciled to the thoughts of leaving it for ever;—she found it, indeed, a thing of no great difficulty to conquer all the reluctance she might at first have on that score;—the society of the man she loved, and by whom she was so much beloved, was an over-balance for all she was about to quit for his sake, and her whole mind was now taken up with the manner in which she should order her affairs so as to be prepared to go whenever the circumstances of things should call her.

Her resolution being settled, her thoughts by degrees became so too, and she now enjoy'd more serenity than she had known since the accident that drove Jemmy from her; but the post not bringing her a letter as she expected, some part of her former discontents began to revive in her;—she was, however, too well assured of his punctuality not to impute this disappointment to some other cause than his neglect.

She soon found that she had done him no more than justice in this point;—Mr. Morgan came the next morning to visit her;—as she had not seen him since she was a girl, his coming at this juncture a little surprised her, and he kept her in suspence for some time, by making her a thousand compliments, after the fashion of old men, on the improvements he found in her stature and beauty, before he related to her the business which had brought him thither.

At last, tho' not till after many circumlocutions, by way of prelude,—"I have a present for you, my pretty lady," said he;—"I received a letter last night from my good friend Mr. Jessamy, and something inclosed for you, which he commission'd me to deliver into your own hands;—here it is," continued he, giving her a packet, "take it, I believe it will not be displeasing to you."

"I have no apprehensions of receiving any thing that can be so, either from him or you, Sir," reply'd she, "you will therefore, pardon my impatience to see what it contains."—"Aye,—aye," cryed he, "read it by all means,—I would have you read it while I am here."

He then retired to a window and took up a book while she opened the packet, in which was a large parchment, heavy with the weight of seals, and a letter from Jemmy containing these lines:

To Miss Jessamy.

With what words,—O thou more than woman,—thou angel of thy sex,—shall I express that rush of joyous astonishment,—that extacy which on the reading your dear letter overwhelm'd my heart!—Can you then resolve to leave your native country, with all the charms you once found in it?—Can you do this for my unworthy sake,—consent to share my fate, and live in exile with your Jemmy?—Yes,—I know you can,—you have said it, and will not promise without meaning to perform.

Thus transcendently blest in your affection, the goods of fortune would be below my care if you had no interest in them;—nor would even life itself be of any estimation with me were it not dear to you;—but as they both are yours, eternally devoted to you, they ought not to be neglected by me.

On my relating my affair with Bellpine in all its unhappy circumstances, to a lawyer who happen'd to come over with me, he told me I ought to take proper methods for securing my estate in case the wound I had given should prove mortal;—I approved of his advice, and as there is no English attorney at Calais, he has been so good as to draw up an instrument for that purpose himself,—which is the same I now send to you.

You will find by it, my dear Jenny, that I am no longer possess'd of any lands or hereditaments;[23]—you are the mistress of all that once was mine;—to whom, indeed, should I commit my estate but to her who has my soul in keeping?

I have wrote to Mr. Morgan and Mr. Ellwood to assist you in whatever cares may attend this accession, and also to my steward and housekeeper to receive their orders henceforward from you, who have now the only right to command and to direct their services.

What remittances I may have occasion for I shall become your petitioner to grant, and doubt not but your charity will extend itself as far as you think my wants may reasonably require;—I am sure that I can feel none the thousandth part so great as that of your dear society, which, without my daring to ask, you have already promised to relieve.

I should be glad methinks, however, to know the certainty of my doom;—that is,—whether I may have hope of returning to England, or must content myself with being a denizen of France; tho' in whatever place my lot is cast, fate will find it very difficult to render me unhappy, while permitted to subscribe myself,

With the most pure and perfect passion,
My dearest Jenny's,
Fervently and unalterably
Devoted Servant,
J. Jessamy.

P.S. I need not tell my dear Jenny with how much impatience I shall long for the arrival of the next mail, and every mail till we are so happy as to meet again.

Having read the letter, she unfolded the writing which accompany'd it, and found it was a deed of conveyance to herself of Jemmy's whole estate, both real and personal;—as she knew not well the nature of these things, nor for what end this had been done, it threw her into so deep a revery that she forgot Mr. Morgan was in the room.

But that gentleman, perceiving she had done reading, returned to the seat he had lately quitted, and, taking her by the hand, ask'd her with a smile what she thought of the gift her lover had made her.—"Indeed, Sir," answered she, "I know not what to think; and should be at a very great loss how to behave on the occasion, if I did not depend on being directed by one or other of the two worthy persons mentioned in Mr. Jessamy's letter."

He then explained to her all she wanted to know, and concluded with some compliments on the confidence Mr. Jessamy reposed in her;—"If ever I see him again," said he pleasantly, "I shall tell him that he relies much on his own merit to imagine he can secure the affection of so fine a lady after endowing her with a fortune which may entitle her to the addresses of the first nobleman in the kingdom."

"He need not be very vain," returned she, "to be intirely free from all apprehensions on that score.—But, Sir," continued she, "there is another danger which perhaps he has not thought of;—I have a kinsman, who, tho' a very distant one, is yet my heir in case I die unmarried, and would certainly, after my demise, seize on every thing which could be proved had been in my possession at that time."

"Demise," cry'd Mr. Morgan, "how can such a thought come into your head?—A virgin in her bloom talk of dying!"—"Things more unlikely, Sir, have come to pass," said she, "and I am for leaving nothing to chance, especially on such an account as this;—as the first proof, therefore, of that assistance Mr. Jessamy makes me hope for from you, I must intreat you will provide me an able lawyer that I may make my will, and be bequeathing back to Mr. Jessamy his own estate, with my whole fortune annexed to it, unite both according as our parents always intended they should be."

Mr. Morgan looked on her with the highest admiration all the time she was speaking; but making no immediate answer she went on, insisting that he would do as she desired, to which he at last consented, and promised to bring an attorney with him in the afternoon; they had some farther conversation together, in which Jenny display'd herself so well, without aiming to do so, that he departed quite amazed and charmed to find such generosity, such justice, and such prudence in a person of her years.

When she was left alone, and had leisure to reflect on what Jemmy had done, it did not seem at all strange to her that he should have reposed so much confidence in her, because she thought there was not a possibility for any woman in the world to be wicked enough to abuse such a trust; but she wonder'd at the haste he made to execute a deed of this nature, which she could see no necessity for on the score of what had passed between him and Bellpine, at least as yet.

After a little pause,—"It must certainly be," cry'd she, "that the dear, the generous man, has caused this instrument to be drawn up merely for my sake, that if any unforeseen accident should snatch him suddenly from the world, I should then remain in an undisturbed possession of all he left behind;—no other motive can have induced him to act in this manner; and it was only the secret sympathy of my soul with his that has put it into my head to make a will in his favour."

It pleased her to think she had found a way to be even with him in his tender care, and longed for the return of Mr. Morgan, that she might put in execution what she had devised.

That gentleman came in the afternoon, and according to the promise she had exacted from him, brought with him an able lawyer of his particular acquaintance, whom, as soon as the first civilities were over, she immediately set to work upon the business for which she had desired his presence.

The writing being intirely finished in all its forms, and witnessed by Mr. Morgan and the people of the house, whom Jenny had ordered to be called up for that purpose, she deposited it in Mr. Morgan's hands, desiring him to keep it till she should die, unless some accident should oblige her to demand it back;—this he assured her he would do, still affecting to smile, tho' admiring within himself a precaution so uncommon in a young lady.

But whatever either he or his friend the lawyer might think of her on this occasion, they were afterwards convinced, by the vivacity and sprightliness of her conversation and behaviour, during the whole time they continued with her, that it was not by any melancholy vapours she had been instigated to the step she had taken, and which appeared so extraordinary to them, as indeed it well might do to persons who never had an opportunity of being acquainted with the greatness of her mind.

Chapter XIII

Affords less matter either of instruction or entertainment than many of the former; though perhaps more of both than can be found in some other late histories of the same nature with this.

How preferable are the enjoyments of the mind to those of the body! Persons of a truly delicate way of thinking find a much greater pleasure in their own contemplations, on a delightful subject, than those of less refined ideas are capable of tasting in the utmost gratification of the senses.

Our amiable Jenny felt a more perfect satisfaction in the proof she had received of her lover's affection, and in that she had just shewn of her own for him, than she had ever known when with him, and no cross accident had interven'd to oblige either of them to exert, and display their mutual tenderness.

She was in a most delightful situation of mind on this occasion, when Mr. Morgan made her another morning visit, on a business which he doubted not but would greatly add to her contentment,—it was this:

The sincere good-will he had towards Jemmy had made him indefatigable in his endeavours to find out the true state of Bellpine's condition;—he had gone and sent several times to the house where he lodged, without being able to get any satisfactory account, sometimes being told one thing, and sometimes another;—they even refused to let him know who were the surgeons that attended him;—this however he got intelligence of from the people of the tavern where the accident had happened;—the first to whom he applied seemed a little uneasy at the questions he put to him,—made very short and evasive answers, the plainest of which was,—"That if the gentleman lived, it would be a miracle."

Mr. Morgan, not contenting himself with this, went directly to the other, who was the same that had been sent by Jemmy, and whom he found of a much more communicative disposition, tho' less able to give him information he desired;—he said, that on examining the wound, he had thought it a very bad one, but when he went the next morning to visit Mr. Bellpine, he was told by somebody about him that there was no need of his attendance, and that he was not permitted to stay in the room even while the first dressings were taken off, tho' he had earnestly requested it.—Mr. Morgan than asked him, if he apprehended the wound to be mortal, by what he had seen of it at first.—"I then thought it so," reply'd the surgeon, "for had it been as I imagined he must have died in twelve hours;—but as he has lived till now, I think I may safely pronounce him out of danger, except a fever takes him."

He then went on, and gave so many reasons, from the structure of the human body, to prove that if Bellpine's wound had been mortal, he must have died long before the time which had elapsed since his receiving it, that the hearty old gentleman was quite convinced, and run immediately to make Jenny partaker of the joyful news.

She was, indeed, extremely pleased; but said, she could not conceive what motive should induce Bellpine or his friends to give out that he was still in danger if he was not really so.—"Spite," cry'd Mr. Morgan, "nothing but spite,—as my friend Lee somewhere has it:

> Spite, by the Gods, proud spite, and burning envy."[24]

"I see into his design," continued he, "as well as if I were of his cabinet council;—the venemous revengeful rascal thinks, as long as he can make people believe his life is despaired of, Mr. Jessamy will be obliged to keep out of the way; but he may be out in his politics,—the surgeon assures me that he will depose upon oath that the wound is not mortal; and if so, Mr. Jessamy may come over as soon as he pleases,—bail will be taken for him."

"Ah, Sir, let him not trust to that," cried Jenny hastily, "and I beseech you do not advise him to it when you write."—"I advise him, Madam," answered he, "not I, indeed,—I shall only tell him what I think,—he may do as he pleases."

"You may be certain, Sir," resumed she, "that I should greatly rejoice in Mr. Jessamy's return, if he could come without any hazard either of his life or liberty;—but you must pardon me if I am not altogether so sanguine in this matter as you seem to be:—I am apt to hope and believe with you, that Bellpine is not in so dangerous a way as is pretended;—but then, methinks, we ought not to build too much upon the asseveration of this surgeon, whose judgement we cannot be sure is infallible."

Mr. Morgan was about to say something in answer to this but was prevented, Jenny's servant open'd the door instantly, and told her that Lady Speck was just coming up stairs, on which he took his leave for that time.

After the usual salutations at a first meeting were over, and they had seated themselves,—"If the heart is to be judged by the countenance," said Lady Speck, looking earnestly on her fair friend, "I may hope, my dear, that yours is somewhat less depress'd than it has been of late."

On her speaking in this manner, Jenny made no scruple to repeat to her all she had been told by Mr. Morgan in regard to Bellpine's condition, and also the reasons which both of them had assigned for his causing it to be reported so much worse than in effect it was.

"Bellpine must certainly be one of the most mischievous fellows in the universe," said Lady Speck, "and since you have not got a more perfect intelligence of his situation, I may venture to let you know that nothing can be more terrible than the account given of it by his servant, both to Sir Robert and Mr. Lovegrove, who I assure you did not fail to make the enquiries they promised when they were here last;—and it has been only because they were unwilling either to deceive you, or to be the bearers of an unwelcome truth, that they have deny'd themselves the pleasure of waiting on you for some days."

Jenny express'd herself in the most grateful terms for the generous concern those gentlemen had seem'd to take in her affairs; and then began to turn the conversation on some other topick; but there was something in the behaviour of Bellpine which appeared so peculiar as well as base, in the opinion of Lady Speck, that she could talk of little else all the time she staid, which indeed was not very long, her ladyship being in her deshabille, and in haste to go home to dress for dinner.

She was no sooner gone, than Jenny's servant acquainted her that a lady, who call'd herself Sophia, had been to wait on her.—"Sophia," cried she hastily,—"why then did you not shew her up?"—"You had company, Madam," answer'd he, "and she said she rather chose to wait on you when you were quite alone, and that she would come again in the afternoon to see if you were so."

If the reader has forgot this young lady he may have recourse to the second chapter of the first volume, where he will find her character at large; and now need only to be told that Jenny, who had not heard of her being in town, was extremely glad that she should have a person near her in whom she placed more confidence than in most others of her acquaintance.

The pleasure of this friend's return did not however make her forget that it was post day, and that she had an obligation to discharge which could not be dispensed with by any other; and therefore, to prevent any interruption which delay might occasion, sat down immediately and wrote the following lines:

To James Jessamy, Esq;

My dear Jemmy,

I received the trust you reposed in me of which I shall be a very faithful steward; but I have just heard something which makes me hope you might have spared yourself that trouble;—your worthy friend Mr. Morgan will write to you the particulars, and perhaps subjoin some advice, which tho' I am certain he means well, cannot consent you should comply with;—so much as I prize your presence I should tremble to behold you here while there remains even the most distant menace either to your life or liberty.

A little time, of course, must put an end to our suspense,—till then therefore, I conjure you, content yourself with the assurance I have given you, and now again repeat, that if you cannot come to me, I will go to you, and endeavour, by every thing in my power, to soften the asperity of all other losses.

I fear, indeed, you pass your days in a manner uncomfortable enough,—without friends,—without acquaintance,—without any companion but your own melancholy thoughts,—nothing to please, or even to amuse your mind:—I am ignorant of the place you are in,—I only know it is on the sea-coast;—there, methinks, I see you often wandering, casting a wishing eye towards what you left behind, and almost cursing fortune for the deprivation.—Tell me, my Jemmy, does my fancy paint your situation such as it is?—I shall rejoice to find myself deceived, and to hear that Calais is not wanting in matters of agreeable entertainment;—believe you can give no account so welcome to me as that of your being perfectly easy;—endeavour, at least, to make yourself so, I beseech you, till the circumstances of things permit you to be happy, and to make happy all your friends, particularly her who is,

With an unfeign'd affection,
Dear Jemmy,
Yours eternally,
J. Jessamy.

P.S. I cannot close this without once more conjuring you, not for your own sake but mine, not to think of returning till we shall be well assured that Bellpine has left his chamber.

She soon found how much she had been in the right to lay hold of the first opportunity to prepare the above, otherwise she might have been prevented from doing it at all that day; for Sophia, who had a great deal to say to her, came very early in the afternoon.

Chapter XIV

Contains a very strange and detestable instance of perfidiousness and ingratitude, in a person of the most honourable vocation.

These two young ladies, who from their childhood had preserved an entire friendship for each other, could not meet after an absence of many months without the utmost demonstrations of affection on both sides;—after which Jenny gently reproached the other as having been very remiss of late in writing to her, and that whenever she did so her letters had been short, reserved, and such as ordinarily pass between persons who converse together merely through complaisance.

"Your charge would be very just," said Sophia, "had it been in my power to have acted otherwise than I did;—but, indeed, my dear Miss Jessamy, I had nothing to write except such things as were utterly improper for me to communicate by the post;—I am now, however," continued she with a deep sigh, "come to tell you all, as well as to take my everlasting leave."

These words, and the manner in which they were delivered, threw Jenny into so great an astonishment, that she had not the power of asking an explanation of them, which the other perceiving, saved her the trouble of speaking and went on:

"Yes," continued she, "I shall very shortly be removed from all that ever yet have known me,—shall quit England as soon as the vessel that is to carry me is ready to put to sea, which I hope will be in a very few days;—nor, when you have heard my unhappy story, will you think it strange that I should be impatient to go from a place where I have received such cruel injustice as perhaps no woman but myself ever met with."

"Heavens! Of what nature?" cried Jenny with some eagerness. "Of a most monstrous,—and, I believe, unprecedented one," replied she; "but I will keep you no longer in suspence,—you shall at once be let into the secret of those wrongs I have sustain'd, and of the folly which exposed me to them."

Finding Jenny made no answer, but was prepared to give attention to what she was about to say, she wiped off some tears, which, in spite of her endeavours to restrain them, fell from her eyes; and then began the recital she had promised in the following terms:

The History of Sophia

"You may remember, my dear Miss Jessamy," said she, "in what a rage my brother flew out of the house after the ridiculous adventure you were witness of the last time you favoured me with a visit;—he then went no farther than to a gentleman's seat about four miles distant; but from thence proceeded to London, where he continued full three months:—on his return he appeared very pensive and discontented, which I at first imputed to the disappointment he had received from the lady you saw; but I soon found it arose from a quite different cause;—he had, it seems, mortgaged the best part of his estate to discharge some debts he had contracted at play, the only vice I know him guilty of; but to which he has always been too much addicted;—he had the generosity, however, to pay my fortune which was but five and twenty hundred pounds, into the bank; he now gave me the bills, and told me that he must go and live in the southern parts of France till he had retrieved his circumstances, and that he had spoke to a gentleman about letting his house; but added, that I should be welcome to stay in it, and have the use of every thing till a tenant could be found, if I chose to do so.—This offer, having my own reasons for it, I gladly accepted of;—he had before prepared every thing for his departure, and in four days left me to myself.

"You will doubtless wonder that I should chuse to remain in a great lone house without any companion, and be at the expence of keeping two maids and a man servant, which the income of my little fortune could ill afford, rather than come to town, where I might have been boarded in a genteel family and lived much cheaper, and more agreeably in the opinion of every body but myself.—I will tell you my reason for all this,—it was love,—love, that fatal frenzy of our sex,—that sure destruction of all that is dear to womankind;—I ought to blush even at the remembrance I ever was directed by it, much more to confess the shameful folly."

"Hold, my dear Sophia," cry'd Jenny interrupting her,—"take care what you say;—Mr. Dryden was certainly as good a judge of human nature as you can pretend to be, and he tells us that:

Loves an heroic passion, which can find
No room in any base degen'rate mind;
It kindles all the soul with honour's fire
To make the lover worthy his desire."[25]

"And I am of opinion that a virtuous love, such as I doubt not but yours was, ought never to be repented or ashamed of."

"I allow the truth of what you say," answer'd Sophia; "but then it must be a love conducted by prudence, and for a worthy object;—mine, alas, had neither the one nor the other of these excuses to plead in its defence,—as you will presently be convinced."

Here she stopp'd to give passage to some sighs which had been labouring in her bosom;—after which, growing a little more composed, she went on in the prosecution of her narrative.

"While my brother was at London," resumed she, "I unfortunately, as it has proved, happen'd into the acquaintance of a young officer in the army, called Willmore,[26]—the first time I saw him was at a gentleman's house about a mile distant from ours, where I sometimes visited:—tho' there were several other ladies in company he seemed to take a particular notice of me, and I could not avoid doing so of him;—he has, indeed, every thing in his person that can attract the eye and captivate the heart;—he is handsome,—well-made,—genteel,—has abundance of wit and vivacity, and tho' he talks a great deal never speaks but to the purpose."

"When I took my leave, he would needs see me home, tho' I had a servant with me, and but three little fields to cross;—I refused this offer, but must own I could not help being very well pleased that he persisted in it.—In fine, he came home with me, and though as we walk'd he entertain'd me only with common subjects of conversation, yet he treated them in such a manner as appear'd to me very agreeable.

"Among other things, happening to tell me that he had lodgings at Windsor, and was almost always there when not obliged to be with the regiment, I said it was a thing seldom heard of, that a gay young gentleman like him should prefer a little country town to the pleasures of London;—to which he reply'd, that hunting and reading were his favourite pleasures;—'The one,' said he, 'I frequently take with very good company; and the other I am here more at liberty to indulge myself in than I could possibly be in London':—He then ask'd me if I took any delight in the latter of these amusements, and on my answering that I did,—'Because, Madam,' rejoin'd he, 'I have all the public papers and new pamphlets constantly sent down to me as they come out, and if you will give me leave will wait on you with such of them as I shall find worthy your perusal.'

"Though I plainly saw this was no more than a pretence to visit me, yet I thought it so handsome a one, and afforded me so good an excuse for granting him the permission he desir'd, that I hesitated not to tell him, that I should readily accept, and be thankful for the favour he mention'd.

"This was the method he took to introduce himself;—he was almost every day bringing me some new book or other; and, in return for this civility, I lent him such as he chose to read out of my brother's collection, which is esteem'd a very good one;—at first our conversation turned chiefly on the subjects with which we had mutually obliged each other; but after a few visits he threw off that constraint he had hitherto been under, and profess'd himself my lover.

"As I have already confess'd the liking I had of his person, you will not expect to hear that I received the declaration of his passion with any disdain,—on the contrary, I am afraid I listen'd to it with too visible an approbation;—but however that might be,—for indeed I do not well remember how I behaved at that time,—all that I know is, that I forbad not his addresses.

"I will not give you the trouble of hearing, nor myself the confusion of repeating, how very easily I was won to give credit to every thing he said in relation to his pretended passion, for such you will find it was, and not only pretended for the sake of gallantry and amusement, but for the carrying on a design the most low, base, and dishonourable that ever enter'd the heart of man, much less of a gentleman, to conceive or put in practice.

"It was in the height of his courtship that my brother came home;—the hurry of his affairs,—the discontent he was in, and the short time he staid, hinder'd me from saying any thing to him concerning my new lover; but you now may perceive the motive which induced me so readily to embrace the offer he made me of staying in his house after he was gone;—I knew Willmore was fond of the country, and I dreaded lest I should see him less frequently in town;—fool that I was, not to consider that a man who truly loved would follow me any where.

"As we grew more familiar in conversation, I found he was much better acquainted with the circumstances of our family than I could have thought he was;—among other things, he one day mention'd my brother's late miscarriage, and ask'd me, with some concern, whether it had been of any prejudice to my fortune;—I told him that it had not, and related to him how tender he had been of me in that point,—at which he seem'd extremely pleased, and said no more upon that subject.

"Soon after this he went to London, where he staid upwards of a week,—a much longer time than ever he had done since my acquaintance with him;—the same day which brought him again to Windsor brought him also to visit me; but though his expressions were, I think, more endearing and more passionate than ever they had been, I perceived there was a certain air of melancholy about him, which very much affected me;—I could not forbear taking notice of it to him, and ask'd him, with more tenderness than perhaps became me, if any ill accident had happen'd to him since he left me;—he told me not any;—but added, that he had been a little vex'd, and could not help thinking himself a very unlucky fellow.

"On my farther desiring him to let me know the occasion of his chagrin, he told me—that he could not content himself with the condition of a subaltern;—that he had never enter'd into the army but with the hope of rising in it;—nor had accepted of a lieutenancy, which was the commission he then bore, but with the expectation of being soon a captain.—'Now,' said he, 'just at this juncture an old officer has got leave to sell out,—and I might have his commission for about a thousand guineas[27] and my own in exchange, which I have a gentleman ready to purchase.—This it is, my dear Sophia,' added he, 'that has so much disconcerted me; for though I have offer'd a very large premium, and my bond to pay the money quarterly, I can no way raise it.'

"'Bless me,' cried I, 'have you no friends,—no relations who on such an occasion would not advance that sum?'—'Yes, several,' answer'd he, 'who would do it for a word speaking; but they are all of them either out of the kingdom, or at their country seats I know not how far off, and the thing must be done immediately or not at all; and Heaven knows whether I shall ever meet with such an opportunity again.'

"Indeed, my dear Miss Jessamy," continued she, "I thought it a great pity that any man, much more the person I loved and intended to make my husband, should lose so considerable an advantage through the want of what was in my power to supply him with;—I did not consider much on the matter, but stepp'd to my cabinet and took out bank bills to the amount of a thousand pounds, which I put directly into his hands,—'There, Mr. Willmore,' said I, 'is the sum you stand in need of, and I hope it will not come too late to lay out in the purchase you mention.'

"Tho' I believe he saw enough into my weakness to expect I would do as I did, yet he seem'd equally surprised as transported with it,—'Well, my dear Sophia,' cry'd he, kissing my hand,—'this is generous indeed, and truly like yourself,—but I hope,' continued he, 'you will soon consent to reap some part of the benefit of the favour you have conferr'd; and, as promotions in the army must come by degrees, who knows but you may one day see your lover,—I flatter myself long before then your husband, at the head of a regiment instead of a company!'

"I reply'd, that I wish'd him success for his own sake, and as to what related to myself we would talk of that hereafter;—he then told me that he would go to London very early the next morning, and at his return bring with him a bond in exchange for the bills I had obliged him with,—'which,' added he with a gay air, 'if you should not think sufficient, I am ready to give you my person as a collateral security.'"

She was in this part of her story when the tea equipage, that important article of a lady's drawing-room, was brought in, on which she was obliged to break off till it should be removed.

CHAPTER XV

Is only a continuance of the same story.

The ladies having finished their little regale, and the gentleman-usher of the ceremony[28] withdrawn with his tea-kettle and lamp, Jenny began to testify some impatience for the knowledge of an event which as yet she could have no other room to guess at than by the exclamations of Sophia.

"If I had not been infatuated, to a degree beyond whatever woman was," resumed that lady, "I must have seen that whatever Willmore pretended, his head was much more taken up with the thoughts of his commission than of his passion for me; for after the first retributions were over, he talk'd of little else during the whole time he staid.

"He took his leave, however, in a manner tender enough, and I remained perfectly satisfied with his behaviour, as well as with myself for what I had done:—so high an idea had I both of his love and honour, that when, instead of seeing him again in five or six days, as he had made me expect, I heard nothing of him in three whole weeks, I was far from entertaining the least suspicion of him, nor felt any other alarms than what proceeded from my fears that some ill accident might have befallen him.

"But at last he removed all my apprehensions on that score by sending me a letter, or rather billet,[29] containing these lines:

TO MISS SOPHIA * * * * * *.

MADAM,

I have at last accomplished my affairs, which took me up more time and expence than I imagin'd;—all is now over, however, and there remains but one thing more to make me compleatly happy:—I shall be at Windsor in a few days, and will then give myself the pleasure of waiting on you, till when, believe me,

With great respect,
Madam,
Your most humble, and
Obedient servant,
G. WILLMORE.

"You look astonish'd, my dear Miss Jessamy," pursued she, perceiving Jenny did so, "and well, indeed, you may;—Did ever man write such a letter to a woman he courted,—who he knew loved him, and from whom he had received so great an obligation?—Yet,—would you think it possible!—Not even this open'd my blinded eyes;—I doubted not but by the one thing remaining to make him completely bless'd, he meant the consummation of our marriage; and the kindness of that expression sufficed with me to attone for all the cold indifference of the rest.

"Eight days more, from the time of my receiving this epistle, were elapsed without my seeing or hearing any thing farther of him;—but when, at the expiration of that time, he came, whatever doubts might have been beginning to rise in my mind, they all vanish'd as soon as he appear'd, and were succeeded by a double portion of satisfaction.

"I know not whether it was owing to his being so long absent from me, or whether the success of his affairs had diffused a more than ordinary sprightliness through all his air, but methought he look'd more charming, more engaging than ever;—the passion he pretended to have for me seemed also to be increased even to a romantic height; and after telling me that his own lawyer being out of town, and not chusing to employ any other, he had not brought the bond he promised;—'But what occasion,' cry'd he, eagerly kissing my hand, 'is there for the formality of a bond, when you have my heart,—my soul in your possession?—When myself and all I am, or ever shall be master of, is entirely at your command,—never happy till you accept the offer.'

"In fine, he continued to press me so closely on the article of marriage all that whole evening, that before we parted I made him a kind of half promise;—and to confess the truth, for I will hide nothing from you, I was at that time so much softened by the artifices he put in practice, that if I did not say positively,—I would be his,—it was owing rather to my bashfulness than want of inclination to comply.

"Indeed when I came to reason with myself, I thought it would be a piece of silly nicety to keep him any longer in suspence;—that his family,—his person,—his accomplishments, and the post he had now obtain'd, might intitle him to a woman of a larger fortune than I was mistress of;—and that, putting love entirely out of the question, no body would condemn the choice I made of him.

"In a word, my dear, having thus fix'd my resolution, the next visit assured him of my consent, and I told him that I was ready to give him my hand as soon as every thing necessary for that ceremony could be prepared.

"I have often heard him, in casual conversation, express a great dislike of public weddings; and he now represented, that for our to be so must infallibly be attended with many inconveniencies;—'For besides,' said he, 'the ridiculous bustle of drums,—trumpets,—epithilamiums,[30] that always disturb the slumbers of people on the first going to bed together with a licence, there are so many young officers of my acquaintance, who would come the next morning to congratulate my happiness, as I know would be shocking to the modesty of my dear Sophia.'

"Finding I approved of what he said,—'For the reasons I have mentioned,' resumed he, 'Windsor would be the most improper place in the world,—we both are so well known there, that the moment we are tack'd the bells would immediately proclaim what we had been about;—the thing can be done no where with so much privacy as in London;—and to tell you the truth, though perhaps you will laugh at my superstition,' continued he, 'my father and mother were married at Ely chapel,[31]—their whole lives was a series of love and joy,—and I should like, methinks, that my happiness should be fix'd at the same altar theirs was.'

"I could not, indeed, forbear rallying him a little on this whim, but replied, that I had not the least objection to the place he mentioned; but, on the contrary, should chuse that the ceremony should be performed there, rather than in any parish church whatever.

"He then told me, that having flatter'd himself with finding me no less just to his passion than I now had been, he had already made some preparations which he hoped would not be displeasing to me:—I ask'd him of what nature,—to which he reply'd, that he had an aunt, an excellent good old lady, whom he had made the confidant of his courtship to me;—that by the character he had given her of me she approved highly of the match, and that we should be welcome to an apartment in her house, 'till we could take one for ourselves, and get it fitted up for our reception.'

"To this he added, that she was a widow of a handsome jointure;[32]—

that her eldest son had a large estate in Somersetshire, and her youngest was a captain in the Navy;—that she had two daughters, who were both unmarried and lived with her;—that they kept the best of company;—'So that, my dear,' continued he, 'you will find you do not marry into a family you will have any cause to be ashamed of.'

"He said a great deal more in praise of these relations, all which I took for gospel, and was so much charmed with the character of my aunt,—that was to be,—and two young cousins, that I almost longed to be with them; and it was presently concluded between us that I should go with him to London the next day;—that he should introduce me to these ladies;—that he should leave me with them for that night, and return in the morning with a ring and licence, in order to put the last hand to the business of his courtship.

"Every thing being thus settled, as I then thought, much for my convenience and satisfaction, I slept that night without the least forebodings of the mischief that was just ready to fall upon me;—about eleven the next morning a chariot, by Willmore's order, came to the door;—I told my maids I was going on some business to London, but should come back in a few days, as I knew I was obliged to do, on account of delivering up the keys of the house, and all that was in it, to the person whom my brother had intrusted with the care of his affairs, so took nothing with me but some linnen and a wrapping gown;[33]—I took up Willmore at the corner of a back lane, where he waited by appointment for me, and we drove directly to London.

"We alighted at the door of a handsome house in one of the streets near Hatton-Garden,[34] and were immediately shew'd up into the dining-room, where we found a grave old gentlewoman, whose appearance answered very well to the description Willmore had given of her;—he presented me to her with these words:—'This, Madam,' said he, 'is the lady I spoke of, and who has at last consented to make me happy.'—She received me with a great shew of respect and kindness, but accompany'd with a certain stiffness, which I thought had something of affectation in it; but this I imputed merely to the time in which she had been educated, according to the silly notion, that people of the last age were less free in their conversation than those of ours.

"The room we were in was very genteely furnished; but what most attracted my eyes, were the pictures of five or six young ladies, very different in their features and complexions, but all of them extremely handsome;—I could not forbear expressing my admiration of these pieces to the old lady, who told me that two of them were drawn for her daughters, and the other for her nieces and cousins; and added, that she hoped one day to have the honour of seeing mine there;—I reply'd, that I should make but an ill figure among so many beauties, on which she made me many compliments not worth repeating.

"Chocolate and biscuits were the first things presented to us, and were soon after succeeded by a bottle of madeira;—the old lady said, that she was disconcerted beyond measure; that not being certain of my coming she was not provided in the manner she would have been for my reception; and particularly that she had given her daughters leave to go on a party of pleasure with some persons of quality; but added, that they would be at home in a day or two, and hoped her family would then be more agreeable to me:—I was of her opinion, indeed, as to this last article; but could not avoid telling her, that nothing could be wanting where she was:—this drew on so many compliments in return, that I should have been very much embarrass'd to reply, if Willmore, the only thing I have to thank him for, had not given a turn to the conversation.

"Soon after lighting the candles supper was served in, which consisted of several small dishes, all in a foreign taste; when the cloth was taken away, and bottles and glasses set upon the table, the old lady began the king's health in a bumper,—then another to the prince of Wales, and a third to the duke of Cumberland[35];—these having gone round, Willmore ran to the sideboard, fetch'd a large water-glass, which filling to the brim,—'Here is the noble duke again,' cried he, 'we cannot toast his health too often;—here is to his royal highness, and prosperity to the army—may they increase and multiply till every housekeeper in London and Westminster has at least half a dozen of them quarter'd at once upon him.'[36]

"I cannot say that I was pleased with any thing which shew'd a tendency to the manifest destruction of the constitution and liberties of my country; but I thought myself about to be the wife of a soldier, and that it would not become me to make any objection:—I only repeat these circumstances to you, to let you see what company I was among.

"The night growing pretty far advanced, Willmore began to talk of going home, and desired a coach might be called; but his kind relation told him, she could not bear he should think of such a thing,—said, that as the girls were abroad he might lie in their bed without the least trouble to any one in the family,—reminded him that it was a long and very ugly way from Hatton-Garden to his lodgings at Whitehall,[37] and bid him consider how many desperate fellows lay in wait for the purses, and even lives of gentlemen who expose themselves, as he would do, to their villainous attacks;—he seeming to laugh at all this, and insisting that a coach should be called, she renewed her remonstrances, and begg'd of me to second them; which I readily did, having heard such frightful stories of street-robberies, that I was in more real terror for him than she affected to be.

"I no sooner spoke than he pull'd off his sword, and said my commands were not to be disputed, he would stay;—'But, Madam,' continued he, turning to the old lady, 'I am afraid we have kept you up beyond your hour.'—'I am never weary of good company,' answer'd she; 'but for this sweet young lady's sake, who may want repose after her journey, I think it may be proper for us to retire';—in speaking these words she rung her bell for a servant to shew Willmore to his chamber;—she would needs attend me herself into that allotted for me, and see me into bed; but whether she did this out of complaisance, or a far different motive, you will presently be judge."

Here the melancholy Sophia stopp'd to take breath; and as it is very possible the reader will be glad to do so too, I shall defer giving the catastrophe of this adventure till the next chapter.

There is a maxim which I have always thought worthy of being observed by every writer, that an old author has delivered down to posterity in these lines:

Too much of one thing the vex'd mind will cloy,
It asks a relaxation e'en from joy.[38]

Chapter XVI

Contains the sequel of Sophia's story.

"Tho' the old lady," resumed Sophia, pursuing the thread of her discourse, "shew'd a most tender care in tucking the cloaths about me, and drawing close the curtains of the bed, I found it impossible, after she was gone, to compose myself to rest;—it was not the thoughts of what I was about to do, nor the step I had taken towards it, that kept me waking, for I accused myself not of the least imprudence in that affair, nor once imagined that the condition I was going to enter into would not render me perfectly happy; but it was a strange mixture of ideas, which I then thought nothing to the purpose, and could not account for, but have since ascribed, and ever must ascribe, to the goodness of my guardian angel, which prevented me from falling into a state which must have deprived me of the power of resisting the worst mischief that could have happen'd to me.

"Finding I could not sleep, the moon shining extremely bright, I got out of bed and throwing on my wrapping gown I went to the window which looked into a pretty large garden, the air was sweet and serene, and the beams of my favourite planet glittering among the trees and plants afforded a very delightful prospect, and fill'd me with solemn contemplations on the beauties of nature, and the bounties for which we are indebted to the Great Author of our being.

"How long I should have remained in this pleasing resvery I know not, if I had not been disturbed by fancying I heard something behind me in the chamber;—on turning my head hastily about, in order to convince myself, I saw the figure of a man in a nightgown and cap, but could not distinguish the face, he being in the dark part of the room;—I shriek'd out, 'Hush,—hush,'said he advancing;—I then found it was Willmore; and tho' less frighted than before, was equally astonished,—'Willmore,' cried I, 'what brings you here?'

"'I should rather ask,' said he, 'what brings you out of bed at this unseasonable hour?—Come,—come, my dear',—pursued, he going to lay hold on me,—'let me replace these tender limbs where they will be exposed to less inconveniencies.'—'Stand off,'—rejoin'd I,—'and tell me what you mean by this intrusion?'

"'Can a man intrude on what is his own?' cried he,—'Are you not already mine by love,—and will not to-morrow make you so by law?—Away then with this idle coyness;—there should now be no reserve between us;—be as wise as you are fair, and generously grant to night what to-morrow will give me power to seize;—leave nothing for the parson but to confirm the gift your inclination has previously bestowed;—this is the marriage of the souls, that of the hands is mere matter of form;—this alone can assure me of your affection, and by consequence engage the continuance of mine.'

"You will perhaps wonder, my dear Miss Jessamy," pursued she, "that I had patience to listen to so impudent a declaration, and did not rather attempt to put a stop to it by expressing the just abhorrence and disdain I had of his behaviour; but, indeed, I was so much shock'd and confounded, that I believe, had he run on in the same strain even longer than he did, I should not have had the power to make the least reply.

"Misconstruing, I suppose, my silence as a half approbation of what he had been urging, he took me in his arms, kiss'd, and press'd me to his bosom with the utmost vehemence, though I cannot say with any indecency.—I struggled,—burst into a flood of tears, but as yet was able to bring out no more than,—'Oh Mr. Willmore, I never could have believed you would talk to me in this manner.'

"'I talk to you as a man of reason as well as a lover,' answer'd he, 'and I would have you behave like a woman who has some share of both;—I do not despair, however,' added he with an affected laugh, 'but to find my arguments will have more efficacy with you when we are in bed.'

"While he was speaking these words he made an offer of forcing me from the place where I was standing, and this action it was which first rous'd me from the stupid lethargy which amazement at his proceeding had thrown me into,—'Base man,' cried I, 'unworthy of my least regard;—be assured I will rather plunge myself headlong from this window than be exposed one moment longer to such audacious insults;—therefore be gone,—leave me this instant, or I will raise the whole family with my shrieks.'

"'Mighty well, Madam,' said he with an air of derision,—''tis mighty well;—I see the respect you have for me;—and now will let you into the secret of my acting in the manner I have done;—you must know, that being perfectly acquainted with the sham tenderness with which your sex frequently impose upon us men, I made a resolution never to give up my liberty to any woman who would not convince me of her love by permitting me to enjoy her before marriage.'

"'Monster,—villain,'—cried I, and was going on, but he prevented me.—'No hard names, I beseech you, Madam,' said he, 'we men have as much vanity as you women can have,—and have as good a right too as yourselves to it;—we are as well pleased as you with being loved, and as malicious as you when we find we are not so;—you take pride in triumphing over us, when you fancy you have us in your power, and whenever we have you in ours we should be asses not to make use of it;—you happen to be in mine, and tho' you do not love me, nor I care two pence for you, I shall not take all this pains for nothing, nor come here to lie alone to night.'

"In concluding this fine speech,—he flew upon me like a lion, and sure it was providence alone which in that dreadful moment inspired me with an unusual strength and courage;—I broke from the hold he had taken on me, and ran screaming into the next room; but that would have availed me little, if in pursuing me his feet had not tangled in the carpet, and he fell at full length upon the floor,—this gave me opportunity to pull down the bars of one of the windows, open the shutter, and throw up the sash;—the villain's sword, which he had pull'd off on our persuading him to stay all night, lay just at my hand, I drew it, resolved to run it into his heart, if by no other means I could escape the violence he threatened;—he soon recover'd himself from the accident and was with me;—I stood on my defence with his own weapon pointed against his breast, calling out at the same time,—a rape,—thieves, murder,—fire, and every thing that I thought might alarm the neighbourhood;—he would fain have come near enough to me to have wrested the sword out of my hand, but I kept it still waving, and I could perceive he was pretty fearful of encountering the point:—the noise I made, however, brought the woman of the house up stairs,—she came running into the room with a candle in her hand, and affected to be greatly surprised to see Willmore there, and myself in the posture I was.

"Had I been in any other situation than such as I then was, I must have laugh'd excessively at the sight of this old beldam, just risen from her bed, her head so cased with napkins that it almost rivalled the size of her enormous belly, which, stripp'd of the penthouse of her hoop-petticoat shew'd itself in its full magnitude,—the flannel bandages about her gouty legs, exposed by the shortness of a little red petticoat, which scarce reach'd below her knees, and her bow'd out back cover'd only with a thin toylet,[39] which I suppose she had snatch'd up in the hurry of hearing me call out, render'd her certainly the most grotesque figure that ever eyes beheld.

"Though it was doubtless this wretch's fears of being exposed, and not any compassion for me that brought her to my relief, yet it must be owned her coming was very seasonable at this juncture, as my spirits as well as strength must inevitably have fail'd in a short time, and left me entirely destitute of all defence.

"'By what vile arts soever I have been decoy'd into your house,' said I, as soon as I saw her enter,—'I expect to be protected in it, and if I am not so, nothing but your murdering me shall prevent my applying to a magistrate for justice.'

"In spite of the confusion I was in myself, I could perceive she was most terribly alarm'd at my words, and the posture in which she found me.—'You shall not be murder'd,—you shall not be hurt,' cried she, in a hoarse trembling voice,—'no harm shall come to you in my house:—but pray what has happen'd to put you into this disorder?'—'Ask that villain there, who calls himself your nephew,' return'd I, 'and thank him for the ill opinion I have of every thing that is here.'

"On this she took Willmore by the arm, and drew him to a corner of the room, where they talked together for the space of several minutes, but in such low and grumbling accents that I could hear nothing of what was said, till he, raising his voice a little, cried,—'It is not that I care a straw for the girl, but I hate to be baulk'd.'—She then spoke something to him very softly, on which he flung from her, and went out of the room, casting a most malicious look at me as he pass'd by.

"As soon as he was gone,—'Dear Madam,' said she, approaching me, 'I am afflicted to the last degree that any thing should happen to disconcert you in my house,—sure the captain was drunk; but all is over now, he is gone up to his own chamber, and I am sure, after what I have said to him, will not come down again to night;—therefore I beseech you give me leave to help you into bed,—you will certainly get cold in the night air.'

"I would have thanked her, for indeed I thought it best to behave civilly till I had got out of that cursed house, but I had not the power of speaking; the late terror I had been in being now a little subsided, a flood of other mingled passions overwhelm'd my heart, I threw myself into a chair and was ready to faint;—seeing my condition she ran and fetch'd a bottle of cordial water, which I took a little of and found myself refresh'd;—all she could say, however would not persuade me to go into bed;—I told her that the greatest obligation she could confer upon me, was to leave me to myself for the remainder of the night;—on which she retired, after giving me, on my desiring it, the keys of the dining-room and bed-chamber doors.

"When I had secured myself as much as locks could make me, I began to give a loose to emotions, which, had they not found a vent in tears, must certainly have burst my heart, and left me dead upon the spot; but I will not prolong my already too tedious narrative with any description of what I suffer'd, I shall only say, that I continued in a condition little inferior to madness till break of day, without once reflecting that I was almost naked, or of the dangers to which my health was exposed.

"At last, however, I recover'd my senses enough to get on my cloaths, and to think of going from a place which had been the scene of so much horror to me:—hearing the maids were up, I ventured to unfasten my door and went down into the parlour, where I desired a wench that was sweeping the entry to call a coach for me, which she promised, but I found instead of doing so she went up directly to her mistress and told her my request, for the old beldam immediately came down, and asked me, in her fawning tone, if I would not please to stay breakfast; which I refusing,—'I hope Madam,' said she, 'you will take nothing amiss from me, I am sorry to the very soul that you should meet with any thing in my house to disoblige you;—I do assure you I have rattled the captain soundly about it,—he confesses he was in liquor, and will beg your pardon.'

"'I want no submissions from him,' answer'd I, 'nor will I ever see him more;—but you may tell him, that I expect he will send me a bond for the money he borrow'd of me.'—'I am quite a stranger,' cried she, 'to all affairs between you; but I will go up directly and let him know what you say';—with these words she left me, I suppose with the intent she mentioned.

"The moment she was gone, a hackney coach came to the door,—two young women gaily dress'd, bolted out of it;—I presently knew them, by the pictures I had seen above, for those she called her daughters; though, indeed, their faces had nothing of that innocence which the painter had bestowed upon them;—they stared at me as they passed by the parlour door, but said nothing, and ran singing up stairs;—in fine,—they had all the marks of their profession about them; and the very sight of them would have convinced me, if I had doubted of it before, into what sort of a house the villain Willmore had seduced me.

"The coach that brought them not being yet gone from the door, I thought best to take this opportunity of going away, without waiting to hear what answer Willmore would give to my message by his pretended aunt,—I was just stepping in when she came down, and told me that the captain was asleep at present, but that as soon as he awoke she would not fail to deliver to him what I had said.—I replied, that it was no matter, I should find other means to send to him,—and then bid the coachman drive to Piccadilly.

"The fatigue I had sustain'd the night before, and the hurry of spirits I was still in, render'd me very unfit to be seen by any of my acquaintance, I therefore resolved to go directly home, and as I knew not but the stage might be already set out, or if not so was equally uncertain of getting a place in it, I hired a chariot at Bullamor's:—I found myself very much indisposed during all this little journey, and on my arrival grew so extremely ill that I was obliged to be let blood;[40] but this was far from giving me any relief, I fell the next morning into a fever, in which I continued eleven days, without hope of recovery.

"If the extremest bitterness of heart,—if shame and remorse for having ever loved a man so unworthy of it,—if rage and disdain at the insults I had received, were capable of killing I could not have surviv'd;—yet so it was,—my distemper left me at the expiration of the time I mentioned, and I regain'd my health, though, indeed, by very slow degrees, for it was near a month before I was able to quit my chamber.

"In all this time I received no bond, nor even letter from Willmore; therefore, as soon as I was fit to see company, I sent for a lawyer who was a friend of my brother's, and when he was at home had often visited at our house;—I told him my unhappy story, as far as relates to the money I had lent, and desired he would commence a prosecution against Willmore on that account;—but when he found that I had neither bond, promissory note, nor other obligation under his own hand-writing, nor even any one witness of the loan, he assured me at once, that if the gentleman had not honour enough to pay the debt I must infallibly lose it, for law could give me no relief:—perceiving I was extremely shock'd at what he said, he told me that if I would make a demand of the money in writing he would carry it to him, and hear what answer he would make to it;—though it was death to me to set pen to paper to such a villain, my unwillingness that he should run away with almost half of my fortune made me comply with this proposal, and I wrote to him, as near as I can remember, in these terms:

To Capt. George Willmore.

Sir,

I have employ'd this gentleman to take such security as he shall think sufficient from you, for a thousand pounds lent you by me on the fourth day of last month; or, on your refusing to give it, to pursue such methods as the law provides to compel you to do justice to

The ill-treated,
Sophia, * * *

"The lawyer approved of what I wrote,—said he would argue with Willmore upon it, and as soon as he had done so wait on me again with the result of their conversation.

"As he had told me, and I myself had always believed, that the recovery of my money depended wholly on the honour of the person to whom I had lent it, you may suppose I could not flatter myself with the least hopes of success, so was not disappointed, when, at the end of ten days, my lawyer return'd and gave an account that the monster Willmore had utterly denied the whole affair, and treated both me and my demand with the greatest contempt.

"'I am very much surprised, Madam,' said this gentleman to me, 'that you should venture so large a sum of money in the hands of any one without an acknowledgment of the receipt in some shape or other, much more in those of a person such as Captain Willmore;—for to deal plainly with you, I have enquired into his character, and find he is one of those sparks who are distinguish'd by the name of bucks,[41]—a species of the creation who are scarce worthy of the name of men, yet would fain be thought heroes;—fellows that run about the streets with great clubs in their hands, and swords by their sides as long as themselves, frighting women and children, and affecting to be ridiculously terrible.'

"I was a little picqued at this description of a man who had once appeared but too agreeable to me;—I said nothing, however, but that since it was so, I must be content to lose my money;—I was willing, notwithstanding, to make some farther enquiry what could be done; and accordingly, as soon as he was gone, came to London, where I had the advice of three several council; but they all agreeing in what the first had told me, I was convinced that all attempts to do myself justice would be in vain, and only serve to expose me to the ridicule of the world.

"England now grew hateful to me, and I took a resolution to leave it, and throw myself into a new scene of life;—a young lady of my acquaintance being lately gone to a convent at Brussels, I wrote to her, desiring she would make an agreement for me with the superiors, which she having done very much to my satisfaction, I discharged the servants in the country, gave up the house to my brother's friend, and have now nothing to do but to depart.

"In the midst of all these embarrassments," continued she, "I did not forget my dear Miss Jessamy;—I was twice to wait on you, but was informed you were at Bath, and not expecting your return till the end of the season, I despaired of the satisfaction I have now enjoyed, both in seeing you, and in disburthening myself of that load of afflictions with which I have been oppress'd since last I had the pleasure of your company."

Chapter XVII

In which the reader is not to expect any extraordinary matters.

Sophia could not put a period to her recital without letting fall some tears;—Jenny, who was all good-nature, though she did not approve of her conduct in some parts of it, said many obliging things for her consolation;—and after expressing her detestation of the almost unexampled baseness and ingratitude of Willmore, told her, among other things, that tho' she was extremely sorry to be deprived of her conversation, she could not but highly applaud the resolution she had taken of retiring into a monastery, as change of place, and a way of living so entirely new to her, might by degrees wear out the remembrance of whatever had been disagreeable to her in the past.

"Besides," said that amiable lady with a smile, "you will perhaps hear of many adventures parallel to your own among the holy sisterhood; for I have been told, and am apt to think with some truth, that the convents are greatly indebted, for being crowded as they are, to the inconstancy and ingratitude of the other sex."

The other agreeing with her in this point, they were beginning to enter into a discourse concerning the swift transition which sometimes happens from the flesh to the spirit, from an enthusiasm in love to an enthusiasm in devotion, when Sophia on a sudden recollecting herself, cried out,—"But my dear Miss Jessamy, I have been so engross'd by my own affairs that I forgot, till now, to enquire into yours;—I flatter myself, however, that you have no reason to complain of woes you so well know how to pity in another."

"Indeed," replied Jenny, "I have had my share of anxieties too, though of a nature far different from yours";—and then repeated to her the whole story of that confusion which both herself and Jemmy had been involv'd in, through the report raised by Bellpine; as also the unhappy consequences which had attended the discovery of his baseness.

They continued talking together upon this subject till Sophia thought it a proper time to retire; but Jenny would not suffer her to go till she had given her promise to see her again before she left the kingdom.

Her unhappy adventure had made a very great impression on the mind of our young heroine;—she sincerely loved her, and pitied her misfortune; but could not help thinking it both strange and blameable in her to entertain so violent a passion for a man whose character she knew so little of.—"People make their own unhappiness, and then lament it," cried she somewhat peevishly; "sure I never could have been so indiscreet"; but this thought no sooner came into her head than it was check'd by another;—"Yet how vain am I to flatter myself with such an imagination, or presume so far on my own strength of reason; as the poet truly says,

When things go ill, each fool presumes to advise,
And if more happy, thinks himself more wise."[42]

"How can I be certain," pursued she, "that in the same circumstances I should not have acted in the same manner that poor Sophia has done?—I have been defended from the misfortune that has befallen her;—first, by my father's care in training me up to love where interest and convenience would accompany my passion,—and afterwards by the well proved fidelity of the man ordain'd for me:—had I been left to my own choice, who knows what might have happen'd?—I remember to have read a passage somewhere which may remind the fortunate part of the world, that they ought not to think they are so through their own merits, but the prevalence of their stars:

With prosperous gales life's vessel smoothly glides,
And on the smiling waves triumphant rides;
But when rough storms from adverse quarters roar,
How difficult to gain the wish'd for shore?"[43]

Thus did the knowledge of her friend's mistake, instead of making her set any value upon herself for not having been guilty of the like error, serve only to fill her with the warmest gratitude to Heaven that had not exposed her to the like danger.

Happy would it be, both for themselves and others, if all those ladies who know themselves free from the weakness incident to some others of their sex were of Jenny's way of thinking; but I shall say no more upon this head,—the reader must have sufficiently observ'd, through all her actions, the sweetness and candour of her disposition;—therefore, according to the words of the inspired writer,

Let her own works praise her in the gates.[44]

She was every day expecting her unfortunate friend to make her a second visit to take leave, when she received one from another person, on the same ceremony, which tho' she thought she had no manner of concern in at that time, proved afterwards matter of much satisfaction to her.

Sir Robert Manley had a sudden call to Paris, on account of the death of an uncle, who disliking the times had retired thither some time ago, carrying with him all his effects, which were very considerable;—it was this gentleman, tho' his business required haste, that could not think of leaving the kingdom without first waiting on Jenny, to know if she had any commands in his power to execute at the place he was going to.

She thank'd him in the most obliging terms, but told him she had no affairs in Paris, nor did not know of any acquaintance she had at present in all France, except Mr. Jessamy, who was no farther than Calais.

"I shall pass through Calais, Madam," answer'd he, "perhaps stay a night or two there;—I shall doubtless see Mr. Jessamy,—at least it will be in my power so to do, if you permit me to acquaint him that I have the honour to be known to you, and to carry to him the joyful news of your being in good health."

Tho' she had the highest esteem for this gentleman, on account of his many amiable qualities, as well as for his birth, fortune and accomplishments, yet always keeping in mind the declaration he had once made of a passion for her, she maintained a greater reserve towards him than to any other of her acquaintance,—and now only reply'd coldly, that if chance should bring them together, Mr. Jessamy would certainly think himself honour'd in the company of a gentleman of his character.

As he was to take post for Dover the next morning, and had many friends to see before his departure, the visit he made here was very short; but he had not been gone an hour before Jenny found she had need of his service at Calais, and began a little to repent she had received the offer he had made her with so much indifference;—a letter was brought her from Jemmy containing these lines:

To Miss Jessamy.

Dearest and only dear,

Nothing but your commands could have kept me here, after what Mr. Morgan has wrote to me;—instead of this you would not have seen me at your feet.—Oh Jenny!—Tender generous soul:—but I will not wound your delicacy either with thanks or praises;—indeed all the tribute I could pay of both would be too mean for the occasion.

You desire to know in what manner I pass my time while banish'd from you, and I will give you an exact account:—your ideas of my sea-coast promenades are just; but for the rest I am not quite so unhappy as your fancy represents.—They say Calais is the sink of France;—but if it is—what must be the garden?—the streets, indeed, are for the most part narrow and ill paved; but there is a square, call'd La Place, spacious, airy, and very commodious for walking; and the ramparts afford as delectable a prospect as imagination can well figure out:—then the air is so serene and pure,—the water good,—the wine excellent, and the inhabitants, even to the lowest degree of the people, extremely polite, an instance of which I experienced a few nights past, and must acquaint you with it.

Having seen all that is worthy of observation in the town, curiosity led me to pass the gates, which I had no sooner done than I found myself at the entrance of three great roads;—that before me, as I have since been informed, is the high way to Paris;—that on the right hand to St. Omers;—and on the left to Bologne;—the good order in which they are kept, and two triangles of beautiful fields which separate the one from the other, took my eye extremely;—the evening was very pleasant,—every thing about me indulged contemplation, and I wandered on to a considerable distance, when a soldier came running almost breathless after me, and being obliged to stop and turn about by his repeated calling to me, he accosted me with a very low bow, and told me, that perceiving I was a stranger, he thought it his duty to acquaint me that the gates were always shut at eight o'clock and the keys carried to the governor; that it was very near that hour, and if I did not immediately return I should find it very difficult, if not impossible, to re-enter the town;—on this I mended my pace according to his advice; but tho' I went as fast as I could, came but just time enough to go over the first draw-bridge, which they were preparing to take up;—I now saw the danger I had escaped,—thanked the honest soldier for his intelligence, and offer'd him a piece of money, on which he drew back and surprised me with this answer:—"No Sir," said he, "the honour of serving you is a sufficient recompence,—we soldiers never take money but from the king our master."—Judge, my dear Jenny, of the courtesy of the French nation in general by the sample I have given you of it in this soldier.

I will not, however, so far deceive either myself or you, as not both to think and say, that if I were to continue here for any length of time, I should not be very much at a loss for company, the town consisting chiefly of trading people, who are entirely taken up with their several avocations, so that excepting the officers of the army, and some few friars, there is little conversation suitable to the taste of an Englishman.

I was yesterday at St. Omers, to take a view of that famous seminary of jesuits,[45] which has given to the world so many prime-ministers, bishops, cardinals and popes; but as I staid but a few hours there I saw scarce any thing of the place, except the college, which is indeed a very fine one; and I only tell you this to shew you that I neglect no opportunity of amusing myself.

I also intend to make a visit to Bologne to-morrow, as I am told there are several English gentlemen there at present, for some of whom I have a particular regard.—I may perhaps stay two or three days; but if I should transgress the time of the mail coming in, shall leave orders for letters with my direction to be sent after me;—I would not be deprived one moment of the pleasure of hearing from you for all the enjoyments the world can give;—for know, my dear Jenny, it is not the park,—the plays,—the operas,—the assemblies, nor the company at White's,[46] but it is your dear society alone I languish for, and which I trust to heaven I shall soon be bless'd with;—till when call every soft idea of love and tenderness to your imagination, and let them tell you how much I am,

Beyond what words can speak,
My dear, dear Jenny,
Your most passionate admirer,
And eternally devoted
Lover and servant,
J. JESSAMY.

P.S. I remember you have a little picture which was drawn for you some years ago, and came as near the life as any thing of art can do;—it would be a very great pleasure to me if you could contrive a way to send it to me without much trouble to yourself;—for though, as you may be certain, your image is indelibly fix'd upon my heart, I should be glad, methinks, to feast my eyes as well as mind with your dear resemblance.

Jenny was now heartily sorry this letter had not arriv'd before Sir Robert Manley took his leave, as she might have engag'd him to be the bearer of the picture Jemmy requested of her.

She resolved, however, rather than not comply with the desire of a person so dear to her, to take the liberty of sending to that gentleman, and intreating the favour of speaking with him, if possible, before he set out on his journey.

Sir Robert was not at home when her servant went, nor received the message that had been left for him till it was too late to wait on her that night; but would not go out of town without obeying her summons, and came pretty early the next morning.

Jenny could not repeat, without blushing, the motive which had induced her to send for him; but after having said all, and indeed much more than was necessary, to apologize for what she had done;—"Madam," answer'd he, "I know not how to thank, as it deserves, the confidence you repose in me; but you must own, that in doing me this favour you put my honour to the severest trial:—How are you sure that a trust such as your picture may not tempt me to be base?"

"I will venture that," said she gaily, "and should be glad to be quite as sure you will pardon the trouble I give you on this occasion."—On this Sir Robert said many gallant things; but concluded with a promise of delivering his charge safe into the hands of the happy person for whom it was intended,—and then took leave, as time pressed him to depart, and his chaise and servants had all this while waited for him at the door.

Chapter XVIII

Contains none of those beautiful digressions, those remarks, or reflections which a certain would-be critic pretends are so much distinguish'd in the writings of his two favorite authors; yet, it is to be hoped, will afford sufficient to please all those who are willing to be pleased.

The smallest trifle, if requested by a friend, is a business of importance to the truly tender and sincere;—Jenny was as much pleased with having found an opportunity of sending her picture to Jemmy, as some ladies would be with being presented themselves with one set round with diamonds.

She contented not herself, however, with having obliged him in this particular, she knew he would also expect an immediate answer to his letter; and accordingly, that same evening, wrote to him in the following terms:

To James Jessamy, Esq;

My dear Jemmy,

I rejoice to hear that Calais is less irksome to you than by the description has been given me of sea-port towns I fear'd it was;—you could not oblige me more than in telling me that you endeavour to make it as agreeable as possible, and that you support this banishment with some tolerable degree of patience.

Would to Heaven it were any way consistent with the affection I have for you to invite you home; but all the accounts our friends as yet have been able to get, in relation to Bellpine's condition, are so very dubious and imperfect, that till we are more assured I dare not even indulge a wish of seeing you here:—Perplexing circumstance! That compels me to be thus anxious for the welfare of a villain who has attempted to destroy my peace, and that of him whose happiness I prize above my own.

As you desire to have my picture; I have intreated the favour of Sir Robert Manley to deliver it to you as he passes through Calais in his way to Paris;—he has the character of a person of great sense and honour, and I believe deserves it;—he talks of staying a day or two in the place where you are, and if so, I am apt to think his conversation, while thus destitute of company, will be at least equally agreeable to that little token that introduces him to your acquaintance.

I have seen so few people since you went away, that I have nothing to relate worthy your attention, except what you know already, that I am,

With the most tender affection,
Dear Jemmy,
Your's entirely,
And for ever,
J. Jessamy.

P.S. I will not ask your picture in return, because I know not whether the place you are in affords any artists of that kind; and besides,—flatter myself that fate will order it so that you will not be obliged to continue there long enough to have it drawn.

Had Jenny deferr'd this letter till the next day, it is certain she would have wrote in a quite different manner;—pretty early in the morning Mr. Morgan came and brought her the joyful news that Bellpine had been seen walking about his chamber and looking through the window.

Mr. Lovegrove also made her a visit the same day, and confirm'd what the old gentleman had said; as did several others of her friends, who had been industrious in sifting out the truth of an affair which they knew was of so much consequence to her peace.

Two or three days put the veracity of this intelligence beyond all dispute,—the surgeon who had all this time attended Bellpine, no longer denied but that his patient was out of danger from his wound, and the people of the house confess'd to those who enquired into the matter, that he had quitted his bed, and it was expected would soon go abroad for the air.

Jenny, who was fully informed of every thing that pass'd on this occasion, was beginning to entertain the most pleasing ideas of seeing her dear Jemmy within a very short space of time, and waited for a letter from him with less patience than ever she had done before, as the answer she should send him to it would be accompanied with an assurance that all the apprehensions his friends had for him were removed, and he might now return with safety.

She figured to herself the extacy with which her lover would receive this information,—the haste he would make to obey the welcome summons, and the mutual joy of their happy meeting;—thus was she amused, as Shakespear elegantly expresses it,

> Lull'd in the day, dreams of a mind in love.[47]

But when the wish'd-for letter arrived, she found the delightful prospect she had form'd was, for the present, quite obscured, as the reader will see in these lines:

To Miss Jessamy.

My Soul's Treasure,

You have not only given me the resemblance of your angelic self, but at the same time given me a friend, for whom, next to that I ought to bless and thank you;—you will doubtless wonder how I am become so well acquainted with the virtues of Sir Robert Manley in the short time we have been together;—I will tell you then,—he has made me the confidante of the passion he had for you,—your behaviour on his declaring it, and the noble conquest he gain'd over himself when you so generously avowed your fidelity to me, and dependance on mine to you.

But oh, my Jenny,—how could I curse that dog Bellpine!—How could I repeat, a thousand and a thousand times the blow I have given him, when I look back upon that scene of wretchedness into which I might have been inevitably plung'd by his base arts?—Your ears continually fill'd with reports of my perfidiousness and ingratitude,—a rival of such dangerous merit, encouraged by them to make his addresses to you; what must have become of me, if the most unparallel'd constancy on your side, and the strictest adherence to justice and honour on his, had not secured my hopes?—But, thanks to both, the storm is overblown,—the danger is past, and I should give up all myself to joy, and forgive the wretch whose vile attempts to ruin me have the more confirm'd my happiness.

And now, my dearest,—I am to inform you that to-morrow I remove myself farther from you,—my new friend tells me, that I might have seen Paris,—all the royal palaces, and every thing deserving observation, in the time I have been here; and is surprised that I did not take this opportunity of going to a place which affords so much to excite the curiosity of a stranger;—in fine, he has seduced me to accompany him;—I would not have you think, however, that I yielded to his persuasions but in the assurance he gave me that he had often heard you lament the solitude of my condition, and wish me in a more agreeable situation.

Though I dare take his word, yet I should be glad of receiving a farther confirmation from yourself;—a line from your dear hand will be a joyful welcome to me on my arrival at that great city to which I am going:—I know you too well to doubt of your kind compliance with this request, as it is the only thing which can enable me to relish any amusements that may present themselves to me.

Our worthy friend, who is willing to contribute all he can to my satisfaction, writes this night to Mr. Waters, a banker in Paris, to desire that if any letters directed for me are left at his house, they shall be taken care of.—Farewel,—believe that wherever I am, my heart is always with you, and that I never can be other than,

With inviolable love and truth,
My dear Jenny,
Your most passionately,
And most tenderly
Devoted lover,
And servant,
J. JESSAMY.

P.S. Sir Robert lays a strict injunction upon me to engage your pardon for the tales he has told me, and to make his compliments and best wishes acceptable to you.

How would some ladies have swell'd at this disappointment?—I believe I know those who would have thrown the letter from them with the utmost disdain,—perhaps torn it, and cried out—"How dare the fellow use me thus?—He ought to have asked me leave before he went away;—he does not deserve that I should ever see him more,"—and a thousand such like reproaches;—but the reader has seen too much of Jenny to expect this sort of behaviour in her;—at first, indeed, it gave a little check to her late flow of spirits, to find her lover was every day going farther from her, at a time when she had hoped he would be approaching towards her; but she soon recover'd herself, and, on well weighing the motives that induced him to leave Calais, found she had more reason to approve than to condemn him for it.

Though in his letters to her he had dissembled his chagrin, for fear she should be too much affected with it, yet she was sensible that for a man of his gay temper to be so long pent up in such a place as Calais, could not but be very irksome to him; and as he yet was ignorant of the hopes his friends had of his returning soon to England, neither wonder'd at, nor was angry that he so readily embraced Sir Robert Manley's proposal of passing the time of his absence in a manner so much more capable of improving his mind, as well as of gratifying his senses.

This was the way in which she argued with herself in defence of her lover's proceedings; and upon the whole, was not sorry to be deprived of his company for a while longer, as he was gone to view the magnificence of a place so famous throughout Europe, and so much the mode for all young persons of condition to be acquainted with.

Chapter XIX

Which, the author thinks it highly proper to acquaint the public, is much of a piece with the foregoing; so that every one may be at liberty either to read or not, according to the satisfaction the other has afforded.

Jenny had lived almost as retired as a woman in the first month of her widowhood, ever since Jemmy had been obliged to fly the kingdom on the wound he had given Bellpine; but now finding he was out of all danger, either of life or liberty, on that score, by the recovery of his antagonist, and also that he was gone to regale himself in a place so abounding with all sorts of pleasures, she began to resume her former chearfulness and vivacity, appeared in public places as she had been accustom'd, and return'd all the visits that were made to her.

Her intimacy with Lady Speck and Miss Wingman was very much

increased since she had been at Bath with them, by the participation they had in her secrets, and she in theirs:—as these ladies were continually entertain'd by their lovers with all manner of diversions, she was never left out of any of them, except by her own choice.

Though no one was fonder of all innocent pleasures, and was less reserv'd and unconstrain'd in conversation, yet she did not suffer the gaities of life to interfere with her more serious reflections;—the duties of love and friendship, next those of Heaven, were always her peculiar care, and she never neglected the discharge of them on any pretence whatever.

It cannot therefore be supposed that she omitted the gratification of her dear Jemmy's request;—she calculated, as well as she was able from the accounts [that] had been given her of the route to Paris, on what day he would be there, and sent a letter to meet him on his arrival;—the contents of what she wrote to him were these:

To James Jessamy, Esq;

My dear Jemmy,

I hope this will find you in good health and spirits, after the fatigue of your long journey;—I am so well pleased with your having taken it, that I should extremely condemn myself for not having advised you to it sooner, if what I confess was owing to my want of thought, had not proved for the best, by occasioning you to go in such good company.

I am told that Bellpine is judg'd to be out of danger;—but that is now a matter of no moment,—whatever may be wrote to you on that head, remember, that as I may never see Paris myself I shall expect from you a very exact account of all the curiosities the place affords;—therefore, if you would oblige me, you must not think of coming home till you are well assured that you can have left nothing behind you unobserv'd.

Good night,—repose, at present, must be more beneficial to you than any thing I could say, which would all amount to no more than a repetition of my being,

With the most unfeigned affection,
My dear Jemmy,
As much yours at this distance
As when nearer,
J. Jessamy.

P.S. Pray let Sir Robert know I think of him with the most just respect.

Tho' this letter was somewhat shorter than those she usually wrote to him, yet the few lines it contain'd discovered, without her designing to do so, such a well establish'd fund of tenderness in her soul, as cannot but be discernable to every understanding reader.

She was entirely eased of all her apprehensions for him on the score of the wound he had given Bellpine, and doubtless wish'd as ardently to see him again as the most violent of her sex could have done; but there was a certain delicacy in her passion, which render'd every thing that gave him pleasure an adequate satisfaction to herself, nor could she ever have been truly happy without knowing he was so.

Besides, she consider'd that for him to leave such a place as Paris immediately, and without being able, at his return, to give any description of the royal palaces,—colleges,—convents, and other things she had heard much talk of, must infallibly expose him to the raillery of all his acquaintance,—she knew that they would say it was for her sake he did so;—that they would call him a romantic lover;—tell him that he was so much the devotee of Cupid, that he could not support the least absence from his mistress; with such like stuff;—and would have chose he should even love her less, rather than that he should give any proofs of love which might call in question his good sense.

How easy,—how contented must be the man who has a mistress of this way of thinking! And how happy is it also for herself, as it is the almost certain means of securing the lasting esteem, as well as affection, of the man she loves?

Jemmy, at least, was a proof of the truth of this observation;—the gay and sprightly manner in which he answed'd his dear Jenny's epistle, shew'd he was highly pleased with the injunction she laid upon him in it;—these were his words:

To Miss Jessamy.

Dearest Jenny,

I received yours two hours after my arrival,—I need not tell you with what pleasure;—but because I have no words to thank the kindness of it as I ought, nor any thing more material to fill up my letter, shall give you a brief recital of our journey, in which we met with something drole enough to make you laugh, if I do not spoil it in the description.

We had not been long in the first inn we baited at, when the drawer told us there was an English gentleman in the house, who hearing we were his countrymen begg'd leave to join us;—this we readily granted, flattering ourselves that the evening would pass more agreeably by the addition of a third person in company;—a young spark was presently usher'd in, dress'd fitter for the drawing-room than the road;—after the first compliments were over, he cried out in a very theatric tone,

Thro' Purgatory first we pass,
And then arrive at Heaven's high Mass.[48]

We stared at him, but he immediately explained himself, and told us in plain prose, that after the purgatory of an odious sea-sickness, and the villainous jolt of a post-chaise, he had at last attain'd the heaven of being admitted into the company of persons whom he knew, by their equipage, must be men of good sense and taste.

We found him very communicative;—he had not been half an hour before he gave us the history of his life; but so larded with scraps of poetry and tags of plays, that it was not altogether intelligible; we pick'd out enough, however, to know that he had been intended for the law; but that not liking the business, nor indeed any business, he had left his master before he had served out half his clerkship; and unexpectedly coming into the possession of an estate, by the death of a relation, he applied himself to the study of the Belles Lettres, meaning poetry,—in which he imagin'd himself a great proficient:—he told us that he had read every thing worth reading in English, and was now come to France to perfect himself in that language, for the better understanding of Racine, Crebillion,[49] and some other authors whom he had heard much talk'd on.

I have known some men, who either having no genius of their own, or are too indolent to exert it, have thus set up both for wits and critics upon the shoulders of others; but I never found one so strongly possess'd with this poetical frenzy as the fellow I am telling of.

Sir Robert, in a sarcastical humour, wrote his character extempore in these lines, which I find no fault with, but that they are not half severe enough:

Sure he was born when nature was in chime,
Whate'er you say, he answers still in rhyme;
Knows all the bards,—from Shakespear's lofty flow,
Down to the jingle of time-serving Row,[50]
And Fielding's Rosamond[51] in puppet show;
Has all fam'd Laureat Colley's Odes[52] by heart,
Can point out what is dull, and what is smart;
Erects himself a wit, on their foundation,

And proves his arguments from found quotation;
Memory supplies judgement and fancy's want,
You miss not these, while that's predominant.

In fine, my dear Jenny, there never was a more egregious coxcomb; but the poor creature was diverting, and complaisant to such an excess, that it was not in our power to affront him:—we had him with us quite up to Paris, and perhaps should not have got rid of him here very easily, if it had not come into Sir Robert's head to recommend him to a coffee-house, where he told him he would find a great many petit-maitres, much of his own turn of mind.

This is the only adventure that happen'd to us on the road, except an instance of puritanical hypocrisy, which may serve to strengthen that contempt I know you already have for those pretended zealots:—happening to stop at a cabaret[53] on the road for some refreshment, another post-chaise came to the door at the same time, out of which alighted one of the most noted and most impudent courtezans that ever stroll'd St. Jame's-Park;—she was handed out by a person in laced cloaths, bag wig,[54] feather in his hat, and a long sword by his side; but the conventicle[55] leer distinguish'd him thro' this disguise, and I presently knew him for a wealthy citizen of London,—a strong Presbyterian,—and who passes for a saint among his congregation;—as I had some little acquaintance with him, having once bought some things of him, I stepp'd towards him,—call'd him by his name, and told him I was surprised to see him in France;—never was poor mortal so confused,—so shock'd;—at first, I believe, he would have denied he was the person; but not having courage, he begg'd I would not expose him, by telling any body where, or in what company I had seen him;—I promised I would not, and left him; but still so disconcerted, that I dare say it would be some time before he could recover himself to be good company with his mistress.

I leave you to laugh; for whatever tender things I have to say to you must be deferr'd till another opportunity, my paper affording room for no more, than that I am,

Eternally, truly, and passionately,
My soul's best joy,
Your most devoted
Friend, lover,
And servant,
J. Jessamy.

The satisfaction Jenny felt in reading this letter, as indeed in all others she received from the same hand, need not be told to those who have faithful and affectionate hearts; and to those of rougher natures would be but impertinent; I shall therefore say no more on this head, but pass on to matters of a very different kind.

Chapter XX

Makes a short pause in the history, in order to present the reader with the detail of a matrimonial contest on a pretty particular occasion.

A very celebrated French author[56] tells us, in his treatise on the human mind, that what we commonly call humour is no more than nature in odd circumstances:—"Humour," says he, "is made up of three qualities,—an ambition of appearing peculiar, a strong attachment to some one trifle, and an obstinate perseverance in whatever it inclines to;—all these three," he still goes on, "are in nature; but then it is in nature perverted, unregulated by reason, and consequently in odd circumstances."

How far he is right in this definition I dare not take upon me to determine; but it is certain, that one daily sees a great many people whose characters and manners cannot otherwise be very easily accounted for.

When any two of these humourists meet together in company, and some subject happens to be started in which they differ in opinion, how farcical would be the dispute between them, if not liable to be attended with worse mischiefs than mutual altercations;—both of them vehemently tenacious of what he imagines is right, and equally impatient of contradiction, they foam,—they fret,—they rail,—affect to despise each other, and frequently from such beginnings the most lasting animosities arise; though perhaps the thing in question is a mere bagatelle; or, if not so, of no more consequence to either of them than what is doing in the farthest parts of Ethiopia, or the Desarts of Arabia.

But how much soever we may laugh at such idle quarrels between persons who are strangers, or only casually acquainted with each other, it must afford a very melancholy reflection when we see the same effects on those who are most near, either by blood or alliance.

Of all tyes, that of marriage requires the strictest unanimity; yet how many do we find, who, merely for the gratification of some ridiculous caprice of their own, endeavour to render miserable the person whom, by all laws, both human and divine, they are bound to make it their study to oblige, and turn that state, which should be all love and harmony, into one of discord and confusion.

The people with whom Jenny lived were of this unhappy class;—they had little to discompose them, except the perverseness of their own humours; but this indulged was sufficient to involve them in greater inquietudes than fortune could otherwise have inflicted on them:—without the least understanding in political affairs, they took it into their heads to attach themselves to different parties, not thro' principle or interest, but merely because they had a mind to do so:—this opposition of humour, for it could not be call'd sentiment, occasioned perpetual jars between them, in which they were sometimes so loud and disturbing, that Jenny had more than once threaten'd to quit their house; and it was, perhaps, the fear of losing so beneficial a boarder that kept them within any tolerable bounds.

It is very strange, and would be incredible, if daily experience did not evince the truth, that people of a genteel education,—naturally complaisant, and of a social disposition in other things, should suffer themselves to be so much influenced by some one favourite humour as to throw off all love,—all good manners,—all decency, and act like the most rude unpolish'd creatures in the universe.

Yet thus it sometimes proves,—neither the husband nor the wife I am speaking of were ignorant how to behave themselves agreeably to the world and to each other; but unfortunately happening to be of a different way of thinking in one particular point, their passions got the better of all other considerations, and both of them seem'd divested of reason, and equally even of common civility, as will be seen in the instance I am going to relate.

The wife was now lying-in of a first child, which happen'd to prove a daughter; Jenny, who had promised to be one of the sponsors at the font,[57] frequently stept into the room to enquire after the health of the new-made mother and her infant;—as she was going on this good-natur'd and charitable errand, she heard the husband's voice within exceeding loud, and found they were at very high words; but this did not hinder her entering, not doubting but her presence would allay the storm, as it had done many times before.

But this couple were at this time raised to a pitch too high to be easily quell'd;—"A man," cried he, "had better be buried alive than be married to a fool,—an idiot":—"And a woman," retorted she with equal bitterness, "had better be in her grave than married to a man who, without the least share of reason, fancies he has more than any body else."

"Fye," said Jenny, "is this a time for quarrelling,—when one should expect to see only mutual endearments? Pray what has occasion'd this dissention? Some trifle, I will lay my life,"—"No, Madam," answer'd he, "it is no trifle, I assure you, but the most serious thing that can be:—Would you believe it, Miss Jessamy," continued he pointing to his wife,—"that unnatural mother there would make me hate the infant she has brought into the world."

"Regard not what he says, Miss Jessamy," cried she, "let him not lay the blame of his own venemous heart on me;—for he may be assured, that if he has his will, I would see the little creature, dear as it now is to me, sprawling,—dying at my feet, rather than act a mother's part."—"And if your peevish obstinacy prevails," rejoin'd he, "it never shall know me for a father,—shall never share my blessing or my substance."

"Bless me," said Jenny, "what horrid menaces are these to the poor helpless innocent?—But still I am in the dark as to the meaning."—Both the husband and the wife had their mouths open at the same time to make answer to this demand; but the weak condition of the woman having taken away some part of her usual volubility, he had the advantage of speaking first.—"The dispute between us, Madam," said he, "is concerning the name by which the child shall be baptised,—I am desirous it should be Charlot, and she, in downright opposition to me, will needs have it call'd Wilhelmina."

"Oh Heavens!" cried Jenny with a sort of a scornful smile, "is all this contention about a name?"—"A name, Madam," resumed he eagerly,—"a name is not so trifling a thing as you seem to think it:—I am an Englishman, Madam,—I love my country, and will have no foreign names in my family."[58]

"It is a small mark of your loving your country," bawl'd she out as loud as she was able, "when your child is to have a horrid,—papish,—jacobite[59] name;—but she shall never be made a christian on such terms;—I had a thousand times rather see her an atheist, an infidel, or any thing, than an odious jacobite."

"Both of you are certainly mad," said Jenny, "and put constructions upon things which no people in the world, except yourselves, would ever think of;—as if the name of a person were the symbol of a party:—but even if it were so, how can Charlot be accounted papish?—Or Wilhelmina, outlandish?—The one, as I take it, being the feminine of Charles and the other of William, which are both English, and also good Protestant names."[60]

"Your derivation, Madam, is extremely right as to the one," replied the husband; "but not as to the other;—Charlot is indeed the feminine of Charles; but, in our language, the feminine of William would be Willamina or Willamana, not Wilhelmina;—that hel in the middle shews it is not of English extraction."

Jenny laugh'd heartily at this definition, though she could not but allow it to be just;—on which the wife said somewhat sullenly,—that she did not care to what country the name most properly belong'd, if it were even the Hotentots, provided it did not savour of jacobitism;—and then beginning to inveigh afresh against her husband's principles, provok'd him to be no less severe on those she profess'd.

While they were railling, a thought came into Jenny's head which luckily put an end to this ridiculous controversy, and was, perhaps, the only way that could have done it:—"I have been considering on this matter," said she, "not that I pretend to decide which of you is in the right; for as the thing appears to me you are both equally in the wrong; but as I am to be god-mother to the child, and it is the very first time I have ever taken that charge upon me, I think I might have expected the compliment of giving the name."

At these words the husband and wife looked on each other with a good deal of confusion, which lasted for some minutes;—after which,—"Indeed, Madam," said he, turning to Jenny, "our unpoliteness well deserves this reprimand;—but it is not yet too late, I hope, to make attonement;—the honour you do us claims at least the retaliation you mention,—be pleased, therefore, to bestow upon the child what name you shall think proper,—I shall readily acquiesce to whatsoever you make choice of, even though it should be Wilhelmina."

"Nor will I oppose Miss Jessamy," rejoined the wife very gravely; "but flatter myself she will not call my poor baby the cursed name of Charlot";—she said no more, but could not utter these few words without letting fall some tears of spite, which Jenny, as good-natured as she was, did not regard with much compassion.

"Since then you consent to leave this important matter to my decision," answer'd she with a smile, you may depend that I shall present my little god-daughter at the font neither by the name of Charlot or Wilhelmina; but in compliment to a person who is much nearer to me than any Charles or William in the world, I shall call it Jemima."

"I understand your reason for that, Madam, perfectly well," said the wife, "I know Mr. Jessamy's name is James; and I assure you that I have so high a respect for that gentleman on his own account, as well as yours, that I shall be proud to have my child call'd after him."

"I hold up both my hands in token of approbation," cried the husband; and was so well pleased with the choice Jenny had made, that he would doubtless have added something more, if he had not been prevented by the fears of rouzing certain imaginations in his wife's head, which he was glad to find had not yet enter'd there, on account of the name Jenny had mention'd.[61]

Thus was this mighty controversy, at last, happily adjusted through the interposition of Jenny, to the entire satisfaction of one of the parties concern'd, and without giving the other the least cause to think herself aggriev'd.

The next day having before been agreed upon for the performance of the ceremony, the infant was made a christian by that name which the fair and discreet mediator had proposed.

Nothing happening afterwards of consequence enough to trouble the reader with the repetition of, I shall now return to the thread of my history, which it is more than possible some may condemn me for having interrupted.

Chapter XXI

Is very proper to be read in an easy chair, either soon after dinner, or at night just going to rest.

Those people who are justly look'd upon as the most fortunate, cannot pass through life without having their anxieties on some score or other,—frequent rubs in the way to our desires,—disappointments and vexations of various kinds attend the whole race of man; they are inherent to our very species, and none can be said to be always totally exempt from them:—it is a certain and exstablish'd maxim, that as no one was ever so completely wretched as not to have some intervals of joy, so no one was ever so happy as not to have some portion of bitter mingled with the sweets of life;—Sir Robert Howard thus accounts for the fluctuating state of human affairs:

One gains by what another is bereft,
The frugal destinies have only left
A common bank of happiness below,
Maintain'd like nature, by an ebb and flow.[62]

The celebrated Mr. Dryden also expresses himself on the same subject in this manner:

Good after evil, after pain delight,
Alternate, like the scenes of day and night.[63]

And another author of a more modern date, though no less worthy estimation than either of the former, tells us, and his words are true:

Eternal changes on our beings wait,
Life's certain dow'r, the chequer-work of fate.[64]

But though misfortunes are common to every one, yet they fall lighter or heavier according to the disposition of the person they lay hold on;—dull and sluggish minds are apt to sink beneath the weight of the most trifling ill; whereas the more active and spirituous, not only bear up with fortitude amidst the greatest, but also feel a pleasure in their deliverance from them, which they had never known had they been ignorant of affliction.

To find ourselves triumphant over difficulties,—to have escaped some threatened calamity,—to be raised from a state of mourning into one of joy and gladness, enhances our sensibility of happiness, and gives us a double relish in the possession, as old Broome in one of his commedies observes:

Past woes the present blessing more endear.[65]

But I might have spared myself the trouble of quoting authors, to prove the truth which is in the experience of almost every one, in a more or less proportion;—the heroine of this history, however, must doubtless be sensible of it in a much higher degree than many others, as she was posses'd of a greater share of vivacity and sprightliness.

The apprehensions,—the terrors, which this amiable young lady had lately labour'd under for the safety of Jemmy, being now entirely dissipated, by hearing from all hands that Bellpine was perfectly recover'd; the satisfaction,—the transport, that succeeded those anxieties was such, as without having suffer'd the other she never would have experienced.

Besides, without this accident she might possibly never have been acquainted with the true tenderness of her own heart for him, nor with the sincerity of his affection for her; and it was the full conviction of both these which could alone enable her to taste the douceurs[66] of love and friendship in that elevated manner she now did.

To this, therefore, though it seem'd the worst of mischiefs when it happen'd, did she owe the happiness she now enjoy'd; and to this also was Jemmy indebted for that soft communication of hearts which the volatileness of both their tempers had before deny'd them the blessing of partaking.

Her heart, however, was not so much taken up with love and gladness, as not to afford some room for commiseration to the misfortunes she saw others suffer;—Sophia being now ready to depart, came to take her last farewel, and the dejection which appeared in the voice and countenance of that unhappy lady, touch'd her very deeply.

"Then you are resolved to leave us, my dear Sophia": said she embracing her;—"It was my fix'd determination when last I saw you," answer'd the other sighing, "but if it had not been so I have met with enough to convince me I had no other part to take."—"Can any new insults have been offer'd to you?" demanded Jenny hastily.—"None," replied she, "that can exceed the baseness of those I had before received from that most consummate of all villains Willmore, and this last only serves to prove he is incorrigible."

"Happening to have some business the other day to cross the park," continued she, "I met Willmore in the narrow passage leading from thence to Spring-Garden,—he had two persons with him, who I suppose, by their habits, were officers in the army;—they were all three arm in arm, and took up so much of the way that it was impossible for me to pass by them without brushing;—Willmore was next to me, and I could not, though I confess it was indiscreet, omit this opportunity of asking him, how he had the assurance to deny the debt he owed me?—'Child, don't expose yourself;—I wonder your friends let you go loose in this manner,'—cried he; and without staying to hear what farther I would say, went on:—just as they had pass'd by me, I heard one of those that were with him say,—'Who is she?'—'A poor distracted creature that follows me about,' reply'd the monster, on which they all set up a horse-laugh.

"I was frighted almost to death lest they should turn back, and also of being used by the populace, as I perceived several people, hearing what they had said, stood still to stare at me;—I pluck'd my hood over my face, and ran as fast as I was able to take shelter in a shop at the corner of the place, where I had certainly fainted away if the master of it, seeing the condition I was in, had not brought me a glass of water.

"Judge now, my dear Miss Jessamy," added she, "if to remain in a place where I must expect to be made the public ridicule, would not be a folly in me even greater than that which has subjected me to it?"

"I have already testified," replied Jenny, "how much I approved your resolution of retiring, at least for a time; but I would wish to see you do so without pain,—I would not have you stay, but would have you carry no sad ideas with you, and when you quit the scene of your misfortunes, quit the remembrance of them also."

Tears were the only answer which the disconsolate Sophia was able to make for some time to this kind advice;—but recovering herself as soon as possible,—"Ah, my dear Miss Jessamy," said she, "a heart so perfectly at ease as yours, is little able to comprehend the horrors mine must feel, thus doubly oppress'd with shame and unavailing rage."

The good-natured Jenny then remonstrated to her, that as she had been guilty of no crime, she had no cause to take any shame to herself;—"you have been cruelly imposed upon, indeed," said she; "but if you have believed too much, it was the sincerity of your own heart that would not suffer you to suspect another's could be base;—and as for the loss of so considerable a part of your fortune by the injustice of Willmore, that misfortune will seem less to you when compared with what worse evils you might have sustain'd, if marriage had bestowed the whole of what you are mistress of, as well as your person, on a man of such abandon'd principles."

The fair afflicted acknowledged the justice of these arguments, particularly the last; and confess'd that to a virtuous woman the lowest and most abject station in life was infinitely preferable to being the wife of a man who had neither honour nor humanity.

In discourses of this nature did these two ladies pass most of the time they were together;—on parting, Jenny oblig'd the other to accept of a small diamond ring in token of her friendship,—conjured her to write often to her, and assured her that there were very few things which could afford her more real satisfaction than to hear that her tranquility was perfectly restored.

The last embrace was accompanied with tears on both sides, and Jenny, after being left alone, could not restrain her eyes from letting fall a second shower;—"Poor Sophia," cried she, "what cruel star presided at thy nativity, and subjected thee to such dreadful and undeserv'd misfortunes!"

But afterwards, on beginning to reflect more deeply on the source of that lady's unhappiness.—"Yet how unjust and silly is it in us," said she, "to lay the blame of our misdeeds on destiny?—'Tis our own actions make our fate;—else to what end is reason given us?—Wherefore are we endued with the power of thinking,—of judging,—of comparing, but to defend our hearts from any dangerous impressions?

"Fate,—fortune," continued she, "the irrestible decrees of over-ruling powers, to which people impute whatever calamities they suffer, are only mention'd to excuse the inadvertencies they have been guilty of;—so strictly true is the inimitable Cowley's observation on this head:

'Tis our own wisdom moulds our state,
Our faults or virtues make our fate."[67]

Thus justly did the considerative Jenny reason within herself on the condition of Sophia; though she had always preserved a very tender friendship for that lady, and sincerely commiserated her present misfortunes, yet she could not absolve from blame the conduct which had reduced her to them;—for a young woman, who wanted not understanding, to have resign'd her heart,—trusted her fortune, and afterwards her person, in the hands of a man whom she had known but a short space of time, and whose character and principles she was utterly unacquainted with, seem'd to her an indiscretion no less inexcusable than it was strange.

"I do not like that sort of love," said she, "which comes at once upon us, and is inspired merely by exterior perfections:—beauty may attract the eye; but, in my opinion, is not sufficient to engage the heart:—the face is not always the index of the mind;—those qualifications, which alone merit our affections, are not presently to be discover'd; and I am amazed how any woman can resolve to give up her liberty to a man, without being able to alledge something farther in justification of her choice than his having an agreeable person."

These were the dictates of her severer reason; but they were soon overpower'd by the more prevailing softness of her nature, and swallow'd up amidst a flood of pity.—"Yet—why do I think this way," cried she again, "the circumstances of my fortune have render'd me no competent judge of the passion I pretend to condemn?—Much certainly may be said in defence of poor Sophia,—her heart was tender, unprepossess'd, and ready to receive the first impression;—she had convers'd little with the world, was entirely ignorant of the artifices which the villainous part of mankind are capable of putting in practice to deceive our sex, and had no friend to advise or warn her against the danger;—I should therefore, perhaps, be no less inexcusable in censuring this unhappy creature, than she is in having yielded to that fatal impulse, by which so many, and some too of the best understanding, have been seduced."

She was in the depth of these meditations, when a servant from Lady Wingman came to acquaint her, that her company was immediately desir'd at her house; and also that her ladyship insisted, that, putting off all other engagements, she would resolve to pass the whole evening with her.

Jenny dismiss'd the fellow with her compliments, and an assurance that she would accept the invitation her ladyship favour'd her with as soon as she could get herself ready, she being then in an entire deshabille, not having intended to go abroad that day.

Accordingly she call'd her maid that same moment to her assistance, and as she never wasted much time in dressing, was soon equipp'd for the performance of her promise; but remembering it was post-day, would not, on any consideration, omit answering her dear Jemmy's letter, therefore sat down and wrote to him in the following terms:

To James Jessamy, Esq;

My dear Jemmy,

I always receive every thing that comes from you with an inexpressible satisfaction; but your last afforded me a more than double potion, as the strain in which you write assures me that the air of Paris has already begun to dissipate some part of those melancholy ideas you carry'd with you, which I shall love it for as long as I live.

I flatter myself that by the time this reaches your hand you will have visited some of those fine places which are so much talk'd of here, and expect you will give me a short sketch of every thing you see, in order to prepare my attention for a more particular description of it hereafter;—in the mean time I shall bottle up all the occurrences that shall happen to fall in my way, to entertain you with on your return.

I have nothing worth your notice at present to acquaint you with, except that I am happy in the frequent visits of your two very sincere friends,—Mr. Ellwood and Mr. Morgan;—I need not tell you, when either of them are with me, on what the conversation chiefly turns;—they easily perceive they can talk on no subject so pleasing to me as yourself; and I am perfectly well convinced, by the warmth with which they speak of you, that it is not altogether owing to their complaisance to me, but in a great measure to gratify their own inclinations, that your name and virtues are so often mentioned.

Lady Wingman has just now sent for me in very great haste,—I know not as yet on what occasion, but would not disoblige her ladyship by being too tardy in complying with her request,—so must bid you adieu for this time: be assured I am, and ever shall be,

With the sincerest, tenderest affection,
My dear Jemmy,
As much as you can wish or expect,
Yours,
J. JESSAMY.

P.S. The accounts I have concerning Bellpine are very favourable;—but let not this intelligence hasten your return one moment sooner than you are quite weary of the place you are in.

She had but just seal'd this up and order'd her servant to carry it to the post, when a second messenger from Lady Wingman arrived, and presented her with a little billet from Lord Huntley, folded in the shape of a true lover's knot, and contained these lines:

TO MISS JESSAMY.

MADAM,

Come,—charmer come,—but leave your cares behind,
To your friends happiness be all resign'd:
Haste to congratulate rewarded love;
A bliss you'll one day give,—and Jemmy prove,
In the same manner as does

Madam,
Your most obedient servant,
The transported
HUNTLEY.

Jenny easily found by this rhapsody, that his lordship's marriage with Miss Wingman was agreed upon, if not already celebrated, and as she had a very great respect both for the one and the other of them, bid her chairmen make all the haste they could to carry her to the scene of joy.

Chapter XXII

Contains, among sundry interesting and entertaining particulars, a certain proposal, agreement, and resolution,—sudden,—unexpected,—highly important to one of the parties concerned, and no less pleasing to the others.

Jenny, being shew'd up into lady Wingman's great drawing-room, found Lady Speck,—Miss Wingman,—Lord Huntley,—Mr. Lovegrove, and Sir Thomas Welby, with her ladyship; the highest gaiety appear'd in all their countenances, except in those of Miss Wingman and Mr. Lovegrove, who both look'd extremely serious, tho' for very different reasons.

This had, indeed, been a pretty extraordinary day,—Lady Wingman having consented to give her daughter to Lord Huntley, and Sir Thomas Welby highly approving of that union between them, the marriage articles were that morning signed; and it was either that the intended bride thought it became her to look grave on this occasion, or that the thoughts of being so near entering into a new scene of life made her really so, which caused an unusual sedateness in her behaviour.

As to Mr. Lovegrove,—the encouragement he had lately received from Lady Speck, and the knowledge that she had discarded all her lovers except himself, had given him courage that day to press her in more strong terms than ever he had done before, for the completion of his wishes; at which she had seem'd very much offended, and told him that the man who had not love and patience enough to wait til she discover'd an inclination to change her condition, should find that she never would do so in his favour.

This cruel rebuff, from a mistress he had courted for so long a time, did not however hinder him from waiting on her to Lady Wingman's, having before received an invitation from her ladyship to come there; but it cast, notwithstanding, such a dejection on his spirits, as was not in his power to conceal, though he attempted it as much as possible.

But Jenny had not presently an opportunity to observe this change in him, or to make her compliments to any of the company;—she had scarce returned the first salutations of Lady Wingman, before Lord Huntley catching fast hold of both her hands,—"Dear Miss Jessamy," cried he, "you were so good to take part in my distresses at Bath, and I flatter myself will no less do so in the assurance I now have of being shortly the happiest man in the world."

"Shortly, my lord," reply'd she, "you surprise me;—I imagin'd by the billet I just now received that the ceremony was over, and that your lordship was already a bridegroom."

On this Sir Thomas Welby took up the word,—"No, Madam," said he, "I have not yet given up my fair charge; but have promised to put her entirely into his lordship's possession on Tuesday next,—according to the institution,—till death do them part;—and it was to engage you to be witness of this form, that your company was desired."

"That is not all, Sir Thomas," cried Lady Speck, "we have something more than being present at the wedding to require of Miss Jessamy."—"Yes," rejoined Miss Wingman,—"something that I fancy will be much more agreeable to herself."

"There is hardly a possibility," answer'd Jenny, "for either of you to require any thing of me that will not be agreeable;—but I am very much at a loss to guess what can be more so than to behold an union which affords so fair a prospect of lasting happiness, to persons for whom I have the greatest honour and esteem."

Lord Huntley was just opening his mouth in order to make some return to this compliment, but was prevented by Lady Speck, who briskly cried out,—"You must know, Miss Jessamy, that we have all taken it into our heads to go to Paris,—and are resolved to have you with us."

"To Paris, Madam!" demanded Jenny strangely amazed;—"Pray what does your ladyship mean?"—"We all mean alike," said Miss Wingman smiling,—"and are determined to take no denial;—you must needs go with us and fetch home Mr. Jessamy."

All the presence of mind Jenny was usually mistress of, could not now enable her to recover herself enough from the astonishment she was in to desire an explanation of all this; nor even to ask whether what they had said to her was meant in earnest or in jest.—The ladies laugh'd heartily; but Lord Huntley, pitying her confusion, took upon himself to unfold the mystery.

He told her that his dear Miss Wingman, having an utter aversion to those formal visits of congratulation, always made to persons of condition on their marriage, and believing she should be no less troubled with them in the country than in town, had testified a desire of going to France;—that Lady Speck, approving of the motion, had promised to accompany them;—and, in fine, that it was agreed among them to set out for Dover, in order to embark for Calais, immediately after the ceremony was perform'd.

Lady Wingman confirmed what Lord Huntley had said, and added, that as her daughters so earnestly desir'd Miss Jessamy would accompany them, she joined her entreaties they might not be refused this satisfaction.

That flutter which had seiz'd on Jenny's heart at the first mention of this tour to Paris was not quite gone off, yet she answer'd, with her accustom'd sprightliness,—that since the ladies did her the honour to invite her, she should not be so much an enemy to herself as to refuse making one in so agreeable a party.

Then turning to Mr. Lovegrove, who had not spoke all this while,—"I suppose, Sir," said she, "you are to be one of the company."—"Yes, Madam," reply'd he, casting at the same time a kind of reproachful look on Lady Speck!—"Lord Huntley and Miss Wingman have been so good to insist on my doing so, and I should obey their commands with an infinity of pleasure, if I could flatter myself that my presence was no less acceptable to every one that goes."

"I understand you, Sir," cried Lady Speck, "and so I believe do all here;—this is because I did not ask you to go:—indeed I thought—the knowledge I went was sufficient to engage you, by whomsoever the invitation was given."—"You thought right, Madam," return'd he;—"yet I should have been glad to have attended you by your own permission."

"Well,—well," said she, "since you are so particular, and oblige me to be so too, I will give you your humour for once, and tell you, that without you I should lose half the satisfaction I propose to myself in this excursion."

"This is an assurance, Madam," answer'd he in a transported accent, "as much beyond my expectations as my power of ever deserving it, and demands all the acknowledgments of my future life."—"I expect no more," return'd she with a smile, "than that you will not presume too far upon it."

Had they been alone, he doubtless would have thrown himself at her feet, and said a thousand fine things to her on the occasion; but the presence of so many witnesses obliged him to defer his raptures till a more convenient opportunity allowed him to indulge them.

To prevent him, however, from saying any thing more than she wish'd him to do at that time, she went on,—"I fancy," cry'd she, "that to see the behaviour of Mr. Jessamy on so unexpected a meeting with his mistress will afford a good deal of pleasantry to us all."

"I had the honour, Madam," said Lord Huntley, "to have just the same thought with your ladyship; it must needs be an admirable scene, if we can prevail with Miss Jessamy not to apprize her lover of her coming."—Jenny, who was willing to give her friends this satisfaction, and besides was herself extremely delighted with the conceit, laughed heartily, and protested she would observe as much secrecy in this point as his lordship could desire.

After this they fell into some discourse concerning their intended journey,—in what manner they should set out,—what route they were to take,—by what number of servants it would be necessary they should be attended,—and such like particulars; which having settled, so as to be most for the ease and convenience of the ladies, Lord Huntley, who knew Paris perfectly well, farther added,—that it would be highly proper a large Hotel should be hired for their reception on their arrival;—and that as Sir Robert Manley was luckily there, he would write to him and beg that favour of him.

This proposal seemed too commodious to be rejected, only Lady Speck said, that she fear'd it would destroy their design of surprising Mr. Jessamy; for as Jenny had told of the intimacy that was now grown between him and Sir Robert, it could scarce be doubted, but that the latter would inform his new friend what company he might soon expect to see.

"Not if I request him to the contrary, Madam," reply'd Lord Huntley, "which I shall do in the strongest terms I am able, as you shall all be witness of," continued he, "if Lady Wingman will favour me with her standish, and forgive the liberty I take of writing in her presence."

He had no sooner spoke than Miss Wingman ran herself into the next room, and fetched all the necessary utensils wanting for him to do as he had said, and he then sat down to a side-table, and wrote in the following manner:

To Sir Robert Manley.

Dear Sir Robert,

What so much testifies the excess of any passion as the being unable to express it!—It is utterly impossible for me to describe the present transport of my soul; but you will easily conceive it, when I tell you that my so-long-adored Miss Wingman has at last consented to be mine.

Next Tuesday is fixed upon to make me the happiest of mankind, and it is also agreed upon, that, for the sake of avoiding those troublesome formalities usual on such occasions, we shall that same day set out on our way for France, where, it is no compliment to assure you, my felicity will receive no inconsiderable addition by your being a witness of it.

We shall come to Paris accompanied by Lady Speck, Mr. Lovegrove, and a third person, whose name I am not at liberty to mention; but if you chance to guess at, must insist upon it your not acquainting Mr. Jessamy with any part of your conjectures on that head; and, upon second thoughts, it will be still better, if, to prevent all suspicion in him, you keep him in an entire ignorance that any of us are expected.

You will, perhaps, laugh at this injunction, but I make it at the request of the ladies, whose desires I know you always take a pleasure in complying with:—I write this in their presence;—they all send their compliments, and, as well as Mr. Lovegrove, join with me in intreating a favour of a more serious nature;—which is,—that you will be so good as to employ some person, who knows the town, to hire a handsome hotel, with all other proper accommodations for us, against our arrival, that the fair travellers may meet with no more embarrassments at the end of the journey, than they would do in stepping into their own country seat.

I shall not pretend to direct your choice in the situation of a place,—I am convinced you will fix on such a one as you shall find most agreeable;—neither will I attempt any apology for the trouble I give you,—I am too well acquainted with your heart to think I stand in need of any, and hope you are enough so with mine to assure yourself that I am,

With the greatest friendship
and esteem,
Dear Sir Robert,
Your most obedient,
And most humble servant,
Huntley.

P.S. I beg leave to recommend as much expedition in this affair as possible; for tho' we propose travelling at our ease, we shall certainly, barring accidents, be with you in twelve days at farthest, from the date hereof.

After having read this to the company, and received their approbation of it, he sealed it up, in order to have it carried to the post; but Jenny, finding they should not reach Paris in less than twelve days, desired that errand might be deferred for a few minutes:—she considered, that before the expiration of the time his lordship mentioned, Jemmy would certainly, not only write to her, but also expect an answer from her; and thinking herself under an obligation to prevent him from entertaining any uneasy apprehensions on that disappointment, begged leave to take up the pen Lord Huntley had laid down, and write a few lines to him.

"Ah, Madam," cry'd Lord Huntley, "how are we sure you will not undo all I have been doing, and apprize Mr. Jessamy of our plot upon him."—"No, upon my honour," replied she laughing;—"but if you will not take my word, Miss Wingman and Lady Speck, if her ladyship will give herself that trouble, shall read what I write to him."

She said no more, but sat down to the table,—whence she returned in a very small space of time, and, according to her promise, submitted to Miss Wingman's perusal, what she had been writing:—this little epistle was as follows:

To James Jessamy, Esq;

Dear Jemmy,

You will wonder at receiving two letters from me by one post, but I cannot suffer that any pains you take on my account should be thrown away:—I have engaged myself to see my charming friend, Miss Wingman, give her hand to Lord Huntley, and also to accompany the happy pair in an excursion they propose to make immediately after their marriage:—according to the manner in which they have regulated the route we are to take, it will be ten or twelve days before we stay at any one place scarce longer than merely for necessary refreshment; so that it will be absolutely impossible for me to give you any exact directions where to send to me during that time.

I beg, therefore, that you will not think of writing till you hear from me again, which, you may be certain, will be as soon as I shall find myself in a situation to hope an answer from you; till when content yourself with the assurance, that, wherever I am, I shall always be,

With the greatest tenderness,
My dear Jemmy,
Your most affectionate,
And most faithful
J. Jessamy.

Miss Wingman, on reading this, declared to her sister and the whole company, that Jenny had betray'd no part of their design; but, on the contrary, had wrote in such a manner as would rather prevent, than raise any suspicion in Mr. Jessamy of the truth;—and, in fine, that she had done no more than what love,—friendship,—politeness,—and even good-nature, demanded from a person in her circumstances.

The remainder of the evening was chiefly taken up with conversation on their intended journey, which afforded an ample field for wit and pleasantry;—they separated not till it was very late, and even Lady Wingman and Sir Thomas Welby seemed to have forgot their age and gravity, to participate, in some measure, in the good-humour and sprightliness of those who were fired with more gay and sanguine expectations.

Chapter XXIII

Contains, among other particulars of less moment, an incident, which, to every reader of a distinguishing capacity, must certainly appear as extraordinary as it did to our fair heroine herself, or indeed any other in the whole history.

An excess of satisfaction is sometimes as great an enemy to repose as an excess of grief; so little is human nature able to sustain the violence of any passion:—tho' Jenny went not into bed till almost the time in which she usually arose, yet could she not submit that those pleasing ideas she was now possessed of should be lost in sleep and an inactivity of thought.

Never, indeed, had she experienced a contentment more sincere,—a joy more perfect than that she now felt;—scarce could Lord Huntley himself long with greater impatience for the day which was to put him in possession of his wishes, than she did for the arrival of it as it was the day in which she was to set out on so agreeable a journey, the end of which promised her such an infinity of pleasure in surprising her dear Jemmy with her unexpected presence.

It is certain that so agreeable a tour, taken in the company of persons of such high rank and fortune, and who, she was convinced, had a perfect friendship for her;—the going to a place so famous for its variety of amusements, had something in it extremely ravishing to a young heart, had love been entirely out of the question;—yet, it is no less certain, that this last was the prevailing motive;—the verb by which all desires of her soul was governed, and the rest no more than mere adjectives:—that was the grand structure her expectation formed, the others no more than exterior embellishments.

Tasso, the Italian poet, seems to have, in my opinion, a very just notion of this passion, when he makes Armida, in his celebrated piece of Godfridus, say,

> Love, the great aim of all created beings!
> The source and center of our hopes and fears!
> From that they flow,—in that they terminate.[68]

I know not whether, in my translation of this passage, I have done the original all the justice it deserves; but how much soever I may have wronged that great author in the expression, am pretty certain that I cannot be mistaken in his meaning.

I believe, however, that very few of my readers, especially those of the softer sex, will stand in need of any comment on the present disposition of Jenny's heart,—their own will sufficiently inform them what her's must feel in the pleasing idea of rushing unexpectedly,—undreamt of,—unthought of, upon a lover so deservingly beloved,—who she knew languished to behold her, and whom she languished to behold.

But notwithstanding all the pretty images she pictured in her mind, on account of this meeting, she suffered not herself to be so much engrossed by them as to neglect the settling her affairs in a proper manner before she went away:—she sent for Mr. Morgan and Mr. Ellwood, told them she was going out of town for some time, but without acquainting either of them to what place, and desired that they would give, during her absence, such directions to Jemmy's steward and housekeeper as should be found necessary.

She had also some business to dispatch before her departure, in relation to remittances and accounts, with those gentlemen, who were her own trustees, and this with some articles, concerning what habits and ornaments she should carry with her, was, as any one may suppose, sufficient employment for the short space of time between her agreeing to go on this journey and her taking it.

There were very few of her acquaintance of whom she took any leave, and none to whom she imparted the route she was about to pursue,—telling them only that she had engaged herself to take a little ramble into the country with Lady Speck and Miss Wingman; though the sole motive she had for preserving such secrecy in this point, was to avoid the railleries she must have expected to be treated with, in case they had known she was going to the place which Jemmy had made choice of for his refuge.

She was returned to her apartment, after having paid the above mentioned compliment to those, who, by their age or condition, most exacted it from her;—every necessary preparation for her journey was already made, and it was the eve of that important day in which she was to set out, and she had nothing now to do but indulge contemplations on the happy consequence.

The humour she was in, at present, was so serene and sweet, that one would have thought there was scarce a possibility for any thing to have discomposed her;—yet did the compass of a very few minutes serve to dissipate all the sunny chearfulness of her mind, and convert the late calm into a sudden tempest of disdain and indignation.

Her footman came hastily into the room, and told her, that a gentleman in a chair begg'd leave to speak with her, if at home and alone,—"Who is he," cry'd she; "He did not send up his name," reply'd the fellow; "but by the glimpse I had of him between the curtains I think it is Mr.——."

Before he could pronounce the name, Bellpine rush'd in;—he had justly doubted of admittance, and resolute to see her, had got out of his chair and follow'd the servant directly up stairs.—Jenny was astonished, and started at the sight of him; but he prevented her from speaking by a profound reverence, accompany'd by these words: "I fear'd, Madam," said he, "the disadvantageous opinion you have been inspir'd with of my principles and behaviour, might have excited you to deny me the privilege of saying something to you of much more consequence than the life which has been so cruelly attack'd, and so miraculously preserved, and which not to have utter'd I should have died a double death."

"If you have been attack'd," reply'd she, looking on him with the extremest scorn, "you justly merited it;—and if preserv'd, must be as vain as you are base, to imagine it any mark of Heaven's favour to yourself:—but to what pretence," demanded she, "to what new artifice, to disturb my quiet, am I indebted for this unexpected, this unwelcome visit?"

"Ah, Madam,"cry'd he, casting his eyes round the room to see if the servant was withdrawn, and finding he was so, "great as my offences are," went he on, "they rise not to that enormous height as a wish to perservere in them:—I rather come," continued he, putting one knee to the ground, "like a repentant sinner, to throw myself at the throne of mercy, and, in this humble posture, confess my crimes, and implore forgiveness."

"There is no need of confession where the facts are fully proved," said she with the same contempt as before; "you have already received the punishment of them from a hand best able to inflict it, and have nothing to fear from my resentment."

"Yet, Madam," resumed he, "I have much to hope from your forgiveness;—it is that indeed on which my soul's eternal peace depends;—it is not that I dread a second blow from Mr. Jessamy, should he be inclin'd to repeat it, even were I certain his better fortune would again give him the advantage over me, and his revengeful sword bathe itself in my heart's best blood;—nor is the remembrance of my wounds, nor all the painful circumstances of my tedious cure, that is capable of giving me the least alarm;—but it is the sad remorse that I have been guilty of any thing to forfeit that portion of esteem I once was favour'd with by you, which, like a vulture, preys upon my vitals, and fills me with ideas too terrible for nature to sustain;—oh, therefore, have compassion,—vouchsafe to say you hate me not;—that you pardon all I have done, and while I live, I will live only in the study how to deserve such goodness."

His words,—the seeming contrition in which he utter'd them,—his pathetic gestures,—his pale and dejected countenance,—altogether gave him such a pity-moving air as made Jenny lose much of the fierceness she had assum'd:—"Mr. Jessamy," said she, "is a person whose friendship you have so grossly abused; whom chiefly you have wrong'd; and if he can be brought to forgive the mischief you intended for us both, I shall easily remit that part of it which concerns myself;—therefore pray rise,—I am neither accustomed to receive, nor desire any such submissions."

"No, Madam," reply'd this artful dissembler, "I must not quit this humble posture till I have disclosed the whole of my transgression;—it is not enough that you pardon the faults I have been guilty of, without you vouchsafe also the same grace to the motive which induced me to commit them."

"Motive," cried she hastily, "what motive but the most fiendlike disposition could tempt any man to behave as you have done?"—"Yes, Madam," rejoined he, "there is one, which if I were as certain you would absolve as I am that the whole world besides would applaud me for, I should be the most bless'd among my sex:—it was love, Madam,—love of the most angelic being that Heaven ever form'd that has render'd me the criminal I seem."

Finding she made no answer, as indeed it was impossible she should in the present confusion of her thoughts on so amazing a declaration,—"Yes,—charming Miss Jessamy," went he still on, "if I have been base,—ungrateful,—false to the rules of honour and of friendship, it was your lovely self that made me so."—At these words she cried out,—"Me, villain,—me!"—she as yet was able to bring forth no more, and he had the opportunity of replying.

"Blame not," said he, "the effects of your beauty, but rather pity a passion which made me deaf to every other consideration:—the more I have forgot the principles to which my youth were bred;—the more I have erred, the more I have proved the unbounded violence of my love; and even those very transgressions have some claim to a grateful recompence from you."

"Monstrous unheard of impudence," returned she, a little recovered from her surprize, "had you the vanity and folly to imagine, that if your wicked arts had succeeded to separate me from Mr. Jessamy, I should ever have descended to cast my eyes on you?"

"I am a gentleman, Madam," answer'd he, rising from the posture he had all this time been in, "of as good a family as Mr. Jessamy, and heir to an estate not inferior to his:—I knew, indeed, you were designed for him in your childhood, but was ignorant that your partial fancy preferred him to all other men; and therefore hoped"—"I will hear no more," interrupted she, "nor suffer in my sight a wretch, whose unexampled baseness renders him even below my anger."

In speaking this she rang her bell, and the footman immediately coming up—"Shew this gentleman down," said she, "and take care he enters here no more."—On this, Bellpine's late paleness turned to a fiery red:—"You might have saved yourself this charge, Madam," cry'd he, "I shall not trouble you with a second visit";—and then flung out of the room without the least mark either of that love, or that humility, which he had, but a few moments before, taken so much pains to counterfeit.

It may, perhaps, seem strange to some people, that a man of so much subtilty as Bellpine, should venture to take a step which could reasonably promise nothing less than the mortification he received; but a very small share of observation is sufficient to inform us, that those who are most cunning in deceiving others, are frequently deceived themselves by their own vanity;—as was the case with him.

The civilities which, on Jemmy's recommendation, he had been treated with by this lady, had made him imagine, on his first acquaintance with her, that she considered him with an extraordinary regard, and that it would not be very difficult to improve that regard into a softer passion, if a favourable opportunity should once offer for his attempting it.

The precariousness of his circumstances, as has already been observed,—the largeness of her fortune,—and, it is probable, some share of inclination to her person, made him presently envy the friend who introduced him; and to endeavour, by all possible methods, how ungenerous and wicked soever, to exclude him from a happiness he wished to be in possession of himself.—The reader has seen how all the plots for this purpose were defeated, and how at last he began to despair of ever being able to succeed.

On his recovering, however, his former views began to retake possession of his mind;—he thought things could not be worse with him than they were, and that it would be worth his while to try at least if by one bold push he could not retrieve all.

The report he had caused to be spread concerning the imminent danger he was in from his wound, he found had made Jemmy keep abroad, which was the sole end he proposed by it;—being also told that Jenny appear'd with the same gaiety as ever, he had flatter'd himself with the hopes that absence and this accident had somewhat wean'd her affection from its former object, and that she had vanity enough to make her pleased with what he had done, when he should tell her it was occasioned only by the violence of a passion she had inspired him with.

But the contempt with which our heroine treated this declaration, notwithstanding his disappointment and vexation he conceived at it, forced him to confess that there are women who set no value on such effects of their beauty as they find not accompanied with honour and virtue.

Chapter XXIV

Gives a very succinct account of the happy accomplishment of an affair, as yet quite unthought-of by the reader; and also of another which has been long ago expected, with other particulars of less consequence.

Jenny was so much disconcerted at Bellpine's visit, and the manner in which she had been entertain'd by him, that it was a considerable time before she was able to bring back her temper to its accustomed serenity; and when the emotions of anger and disdain were a little subsided, they yet left a certain heaviness upon her spirits, which made her fall into reflexions of the most serious nature.

"How greatly," said she, "does the name of love suffer by the unworthiness of its pretended votaries? How is that passion, which in reality refines the mind, and fills it only with sublime ideas, made the veil to cover the most foul and most detestable designs, and also an excuse for the worst of villainies when perpetrated?"

"That woman must certainly be very weak," continued she, "who believes herself truly belov'd by a man who has recourse to dishonourable means for the accomplishment of his wishes:—if this wretch has in earnest been instigated to act as he has done by any inclination for me, they must be of such a sort as I should blush to inspire; and I am amazed that my sex should plume themselves, as I have seen some do, in addresses which either have no meaning at all, or such as are not consistent with their virtue or reputation to encourage."

Her maid now coming in to ask some questions concerning the packing up of her things, she started from the resvery she had been in, and went into her dressing-room to give the necessary directions, where busying herself in assisting in the execution of her own orders, the pleasing thoughts of her journey drove those of Bellpine pretty much out of her head, tho' not so entirely but that the remembrance of his complicated impudence and hypocrisy would sometimes intervene.

It would be superfluous to trouble the reader with a detail of those avocations in which she pass'd the remainder of that evening, as nothing happen'd of consequence enough to afford either much delight or improvement.

Ten the next morning being the hour appointed to celebrate the nuptials of Lord Huntley and Miss Wingman, she arose pretty early,—dress'd herself in a rich riding habit, and went to Lady Wingman's in a chair, leaving her maid, who was to attend her in this expedition, to follow with the luggage in a hackney coach.

She found all the company already there, except the reverend divine, who also came in a few minutes after;—Sir Thomas Welby presented the bride, and the ceremony was instantly perform'd; but the wedded pair had scarce time to receive the benediction of Lady Wingman, and the congratulations of those friends who were present, before Mr. Lovegrove took Lady Speck by the hand and led her towards Sir Thomas, saying,—"Sir, I must intreat the favour of you to become a father a second time this morning, and bestow a blessing on me which my whole life shall thank you for."

"How is this!" cried the old baronet very much astonish'd, as was every one in the room:—"Is it possible!" added the new-married Lady Huntley; "Sister, are you in earnest,—really going to be married to Mr. Lovegrove?"

"Even so, indeed, my dear sister," reply'd Lady Speck laughing, "I have suffer'd him too long as a lover not to make a husband of him at last."—Then turning to Lady Wingman,—"I beg pardon, Madam," continued she, "for not consulting your ladyship in this affair; but you gave me away once, and now I thought myself at liberty to make my own choice."

"Indeed, daughter," said that lady, "it is a choice which I should long ago have made for you myself, if, as you justly say, I had not lost my right of directing your inclinations, by your having been married before;—however, I must do you the justice to acknowledge, you exercise not the power you now have over your actions but in favour of a gentleman, who you were very certain would not only receive my approbation, but that of every one who has any acquaintance with his merit."

It is not to be doubted but that Mr. Lovegrove, who is one of the most polite men on earth, return'd this compliment from the mother of his mistress in terms full of submission and respect.

Lord Huntley, his fair bride, and Jenny, were all this while got together, expressing to each other the most glad surprise at this event;—"It affords me," said the former, "a double portion of satisfaction, to see my friends happiness go hand in hand with mine";—which Mr. Lovegrove overhearing, just as he had done speaking to Lady Wingman,—"My dear lord," cried he, "though yesterday I thought myself as far remov'd from the completion of my wishes as I now am near, I protest to your lordship that I found room in my heart to rejoice in your good fortune while despairing of my own."

"Aye,—aye,—we are all very well pleased," said Sir Thomas Welby; "but do not let us make the reverend gentleman wait any longer.—Come, my fair daughter elect," pursued he, taking Lady Speck by the hand, "put yourself under my jurisdiction for a minute or two, that I may consign my short-liv'd authority to one whose every command, I dare answer, you will find a pleasure in obeying."

Here the remembrance of some disagreeable passages in her former marriage made Lady Speck shudder a little at the thoughts of venturing on a second;—but she had great experience of Mr. Lovegrove's temper;—she had promised to be his, both in private and now before all this company,—so threw off all apprehensions, and advanced with her usual sprightliness towards the clergyman, who had his book ready open'd in order to begin the ceremony.

Jenny, who till this morning had never happen'd to be present at these sacred rites, was fill'd with the most solemn meditations during the performance, especially on the repetition for this second couple;—she found something so binding in the contract,—so awful in the injunction laid on the married persons by the ordinance, that she was amaz'd to think there could be any one hardy enough to infringe it.

She thought, nevertheless; that the obligation would make a greater impression, and have more weight with those who enter'd into it, if celebrated in a place consecrated to divine worship, than in one which was usually the scene of feasting,—dancing,—and all kinds of pleasantry, if no worse:—"Marriage," said she within herself, "is the great action of our lives,—the hinge on which our happiness or misery, while we have breath, depends;—the more respect we pay to the institution, the more we shall be careful to observe its rules; and I can see no justifiable reason for avoiding to solemnize it in the temple of him who first ordain'd, and who alone has power to render it a blessing."[69]

These reflections frequently recurr'd to her mind, but she had no opportunity at present to proceed in them;—Mr. Lovegrove, now put in possession of the happiness he so long had sought, was already receiving the felicitations of his friends; and she, who sincerely rejoiced in his good fortune, would not be slow in testifying the sense she had of it.

Lady Wingman, who was a great lover of old customs, had prepar'd a rich cake, which Sir Thomas Welby immediately broke over the heads of the bridegrooms and their brides;[70]—the servants were all call'd in to partake of this oblation to Ceres,[71]—after which they went down to see if the equipage was ready for setting out.

The leave this happy company took of Lady Wingman and Sir Thomas Welby was very short, as it was not past one o'clock, and they purposed to reach Sittingbourn[72] that evening;—they went all together in a landau, chusing to sit close rather than be separated;—their women attendants, which were also five in number, were cramm'd into Lady Speck's old travelling coach, with such things as they knew their ladies would require for present use upon the road, and the more heavy baggage placed behind and before it.

Notwithstanding the privacy with which these weddings had been conducted, a crowd of Mendicants having got a scent of what was doing, had gather'd about the house, and hung upon the doors and even wheels of the landau; but Lord Huntley and Mr. Lovegrove throwing out handfuls of money for them to scramble for, the machine was soon freed from this incumbrance and drove away, escorted by nine servants on horseback, valets included.

Chapter XXV

Contains a great deal of business in a very narrow compass.

Life affords but few amusements which are more agreeable than travelling, when in a party of select friends who have all of them their hearts at ease, and think of nothing but to divert themselves:—the company, which now set out from Lady Wingman's, were in a situation as near to perfect happiness as can be tasted on this side eternity;—Jenny was the only person in a state of expectation, yet was she no less alert and gay than those who had already obtain'd the ultimate of their desires.

When they had got free from the tumultuous din,—the smoak,—the stench, and rugged stones of London,—"I begin already," said this amiable lady with a smile, "to taste the pleasures of this journey; but you little suspect how much I have been tempted not to take it; and when I make you the confidants of an adventure that happen'd to me last night, you will confess I am a woman of great resolution in keeping the promise I gave of accompanying you."

On this they all cried to her not to keep them in suspence;—"I will not," resumed she,—"and hope you will not think me too vain a boaster, when I tell you at once that I have made a new conquest,—have gain'd a heart all flaming and adoration,—a lover who for my sake has done such things as I believe no man besides himself ever did or would do"

"Nobody doubts the power of your charms, my dear," said Lady Speck; "but pray who is this lover?—For he must be one of whom you are either very fond, or think not worth concealing."—"I dare answer by her looks," subjoin'd Lord Huntley, "that he is the latter;—but pray, Madam, let us have his name."

"I will not put your lordship, nor any of the company, to the trouble of guessing," reply'd Jenny; "for should you all go to work upon that task, it would certainly last till we came to Paris, and even then be as far from being accomplish'd as now:—know then, that the hero of my true romance,—the man who dies for me, is call'd—Bellpine."

"Bellpine!—Bellpine!—Impossible," repeated they all several times over;—"He could not sure have the impudence," cried Lady Huntley; "but, dear creature let us have the whole story,—it must, however, be very entertaining."

Jenny then related to them Bellpine's visit, his discourse, and the manner of his behaviour towards her; and this she did with so much wit and spirit as could not be extremely pleasing to the company;—they laugh'd heartily at some passages in the recital; and their mirth would have been yet more complete, had it not been somewhat check'd by their astonishment at his unparallel'd impudence and deceit.

"For my part," said Lord Huntley, "tho' I cannot but own that there was somewhat very extraordinary in the declaration he made to Miss Jessamy, yet it is certain that love was the only excuse he could alledge for what he had done; and I am apt also to think it might be the real motive too, when I remember what Mr. Dryden says upon this subject:

That love, all sense of right and wrong confounds,
Strong love and proud ambition have no bounds."[73]

Mr. Lovegrove reply'd, that he had the honour to agree with his lordship's sentiments in this point;—"But," cried Lady Speck, "would any man besides himself, after the most plain detection of his villainy, have had the folly and the arrogance to appear before a woman whom he was conscious had so much reason both to detest and scorn him?"

"Perhaps, Madam," answer'd he, "Mr. Bellpine had been just reading Shakespear's *Richard the Third*, and flatter'd himself with being able to say like that prince, after courting Lady Ann,

Was ever woman in this humour woo'd?
Was ever woman in this humour won?"[74]

"But," continued he, "tho' I can very easily believe that love might be one inducement, yet I can scarce think it was the only one;—I have been told that Mr. Bellpine's circumstances are not in the most prosperous condition;—he might hope to mend them by Miss Jessamy's fortune;—and it therefore appears to me extremely probable, that the lady's money had, at least, as great an influence over him as her eyes."

From this they fell into a conversation concerning the practice of fortune-hunting, and the stratagems to which men of desperate circumstances and enterprising heads have sometimes recourse, in order to gain their point;—this was a copious subject, and afforded a great variety of diverting stories, no way to the advantage either of the deceiver or deceived;—these, with some animadversions of the company upon them, lasted till they arriv'd at Sittingbourn,[75] where a servant having been sent before, as indeed the same care was afterwards taken at every stage, they found an elegant entertainment ready prepar'd against their coming.

The next day they dined at Canterbury, reach'd Dover the same evening, and the ensuing morning embark'd for Calais, to which port a prosperous gale safely conducted them in a few hours.

But there is no necessity to oblige my readers to accompany them through the whole course of their journey to Paris, as no material incident happen'd in it:—on the very dawning of that day which was to conclude their progress, Lord Huntley sent a servant to Paris in order to apprize Sir Robert Manley of their approach; and, as he doubted not but he had provided a place for the reception, to take directions from him where they should alight, and then to return with his answer to a little town within two leagues of the city, where they intended to bait and would stay for him;—this was easily perform'd, as the fellow had an excellent horse under him, and set out several hours before the company.

Sir Robert was at dinner with Jemmy and some other gentlemen, when a waiter of the house inform'd him that there was a man on horseback at the door who intreated to speak with him, and said he came from Lord Huntley, on which he arose up immediately and went down.

Jemmy started at the name of Lord Huntley, but not being able to assure himself that his ears had not deceiv'd him, ran to the window which commanded the court-yard, where he indeed saw Sir Robert talking with a man who he knew by his livery belong'd to that nobleman, and seem'd as if but just come off a journey;—this put a sudden thought into his head, which, pleasing as it was, he durst not too much encourage, for fear of a disappointment.

"What," cried he to Sir Robert on his returning into the room, "is Lord Huntley in Paris?"—"No," reply'd the other, "but very near it,—he will be here by night."—"I hear he is married," return'd Jemmy strangely agitated; "I suppose he brings his lady with him."—"I shall soon see that," said Sir Robert with a smile;—"for I must go to meet him, and shall be glad if you will accompany me."

"I am always ready to attend you any where, Sir Robert," answer'd he; "but there is but little of a compliment in my doing so at this time; because I cannot help flattering myself with meeting some company to whom I am better known than either to Lord Huntley or his lady."—Sir Robert could not keep himself from laughing at these words, but made no reply, and only said he must send out to hire a chariot immediately; on which a gentleman, who was present, told him he had one at the door that should be perfectly at his service, and as he seemed in haste, and the horses were ready put to, desired he would make use of it.

Sir Robert, for the reasons urged by the gentleman, readily accepted his offer, and after taking leave of the company, and giving some private orders to a servant, went with Jemmy into the chariot, which, though it carried them with all imaginable celerity, seemed yet too slow to the impatience of one of them.

On their arrival they were presently ushered into the room, where our travellers had but just got in before them:—Jemmy flew to Jenny, as if no other person had been present, and throwing himself upon her bosom, cried in the utmost extacy,—"My dear, dear Jenny, this is an unhoped-for blessing."—"My dear Jemmy," return'd she, "I did not expect to see you till I came to Paris;—but I am fairly caught in my own snare, I thought to have surprised you, and am surprised myself."

On this he fell a second time upon her neck, and who knows how long, forgetful of every thing but love and joy, he might have continued in that tender situation, if Sir Robert Manley, having by this time paid his compliments to Lord Huntley, Mr. Lovegrove, and their ladies, had not advanced to do the same to Jenny, saying,—"Dear Jessamy, you must not think as yet of engrossing this lady wholly to yourself." These words reminding Jemmy of what was due from him to the rest of the company, which debt he discharged with an air of freedom and politeness too natural to him for his late transports to render less so.

They staid no longer here than was necessary to take some refreshment; and on their arrival at Paris were conducted by Sir Robert to the hotel he had hired for them, which they found so handsome and commodious, that they told him he was certainly the best quarter-master in Europe.

After having led them through several apartments, he brought them into a spacious room, where a table (being already set out) was immediately covered, by directions he had before-hand given, with the most exquisite viands of the season.—This was a piece of gallantry which, as well as they knew Sir Robert, they had little expected, or even thought on.

Some hours were past in a continual round of wit and pleasantry, intermixed with more serious demonstrations of love, gratitude, and friendship; but the gentlemen remembering how long a journey the ladies had come, thought it would be neither kind nor complaisant to keep them from their beds too late; though it may easily be supposed, that Jemmy took a very reluctant leave of his dear Jenny, and that she also would have willingly spared some time from her repose to have been entertained by a lover, so much and so deservedly beloved.

Chapter XXVI

Affords less than perhaps may be expected, yet enough to satisfy a reasonable reader.

Jemmy's impatience to entertain his fair mistress, brought him next morning to visit her in her own apartment; but as their conversation consisted only of such things as the reader is already well acquainted with, it would be needless to repeat it here, so I shall only say, that all which can be conceived of soft and tender, passed between them;—he thought that he could never sufficiently acknowledge the proofs she had given him of her affection;—nor she too much return those she had received from him:—Sweet are the charms of mutual love, when inspired by merit, and accompanied by virtue.

Neither of them, however, suffered themselves to be so far absorb'd in mutual endearments as to forget the respect owing to their friends;—Jenny had no sooner heard that the company had left their chambers than she proposed joining them; and Jemmy had conceived so high an idea of Lord Huntley and Mr. Lovegrove, on the character given of them by Sir Robert Manley, that he rejoiced in this opportunity of entering into a more particular acquaintance with them.

On their going into the dining-room they found Sir Robert Manley was also come to pay the salutations of the morning, and enquire how they intended to pass the day; to which the ladies reply'd, that they could not pass it more agreeably than in the situation he had provided for them, especially as their women had not yet had time to regulate their things in a proper manner to appear in public, and that if he and Mr. Jessamy would give them their company, they should think it no confinement to stay at home:—This being readily agreed to,—feasting,—cards, and conversation engrossed the hours till the night was pretty far advanced;—nor were the gentlemen permitted to depart without a promise of returning the next day.

Lord Huntley and Mr. Lovegrove had hitherto been entire strangers to Jemmy, but they now found enough in his conversation to make them think themselves happy in his acquaintance; and he, as well as Sir Robert Manley, was never left out in any party of pleasure formed by them.

In fine, though they continued in different lodgings, they seemed but as one family;—they all went together to visit the churches and convents,—to the opera,—the comedy,—the thuileries,[76]—the gardens of Luxemberg,[77]—made frequent tours to Marli,—Fontainbleau,—and Versailles;[78]—not a day passed over without some new amusement, and time slid on in a perpetual round of pleasure.

Lord Huntley, who had been several times before at Paris, had a pretty large acquaintance among persons of the best fashion;—these hearing of his marriage and arrival, came to visit him, and likewise introduced their wives and daughters to the ladies, so that there was frequently a very large and brilliant assembly of both sexes at the hotel.

Lady Huntley and Lady Speck had their share of admiration among the connoisseurs; but Jenny seemed, in the eyes of most of them, greatly to outshine both her fair companions;—she was toasted and distinguished by the name of—La Belle Angloise:[79]—Jemmy was ravished at the fine things he heard said of her; and the more so, as he found she was not the least elated by the praises she received.

This crowd of company,—this incessant hurry of accumulated diversions, however, deprived our lover of the opportunity of entertaining his dear mistress in private, as often as the pleasure he took in her conversation above all others made him wish to do; and it is probable this restriction fill'd him with more impatience than ever he felt before for the consummation of their marriage.

One day, when he found himself alone with her, he fail'd not to press her in the most strong terms he was able on that article; but she reply'd,—that it was then neither a fit time nor place for such a thing,—and that she wish'd he would not think of it till they should return to England.

"Why not a fit time and place, my dear Jenny," said he, "can there be any time or place unfit to solemnize a covenant made so long ago for us by our parents?—A covenant which I hope the expectations of fulfilling has always been equally agreeable to ourselves;—remember," continued he, kissing her hand, "the transporting promise you made in one of your kind epistles,—that if I could not go to you,—you would come to me, and the ambassador's chaplain should complete my happiness."

"When I made that promise," answer'd she, "I meant nothing more than to observe it religiously;—and should have contented myself to have lived in a continual banishment with you;—but, my dear Jemmy, the case, thank Heaven, is now quite alter'd,—the circumstances of our affairs have changed their face,—the wretch Bellpine is recover'd,—no danger threatens your return, and as we have been here already near two months, it cannot be supposed shall stay much longer;—wherefore then should we hurry thus precipitately into a marriage, while in a foreign land and absent from the greatest part of our friends?"

She had scarce ended these words when Lady Huntley came into the room; but on seeing them together was about to retire immediately, crying, she would not interrupt their conversation;—Jenny call'd to her to stay, and Jemmy recollecting how much she had been his friend, in a discourse of the like nature just after her coming from Bath, told her that her ladyship's presence would be so far from giving any interruption, that it was highly necessary to decide a little dispute between him and Miss Jessamy.

"I guess the subject," answer'd she with a smile; "and if I am to be arbiter, shall not fail to give it on your side the question, as I shall then be sure of obliging both parties."—"You may be mistaken," cry'd Jenny, and was going on; but Jemmy, who would have the advantage of being first heard, remonstrated to the fair judge all the inquietudes of an ever hoping,—ever expecting, and never gratified passion, and all the anxieties attending impatience and suspence;—the manner in which he express'd himself had so much of the humorous in it, mix'd with the pathetic, as made both the ladies laugh heartily:—Jenny, in her turn, repeated the reasons she had for denying her lover's request, in terms no less sprightly;—after which,—"Well" said Lady Huntley, "this is a moot point, and I must even leave it where I found it, and the room, that you may agree upon it between yourselves."

She was going to do as she said, and had turn'd away for that purpose;—"Hold, Lady Huntley," cried Jenny, "you must not depart till I have convinced you of my generosity to this unreasonable man":—"here," continued she to Jemmy, "is my hand, which I faithfully promise to give you before a parson as soon as we arrive at London, and things can be got ready for the ceremony":—Jemmy receiv'd and kiss'd it with the greatest satisfaction.

"This is as it should be," said Lady Huntley; "and to heighten your contentment, Mr. Jessamy, I can tell you that I believe you will very shortly have an opportunity to demand the performance of this promise;—for my part I begin to be weary of Paris;—Mr. Lovegrove, I can perceive, is so too; and if we can persuade Lady Speck to be of the same opinion, I know I can easily bring my lord into it."

She was going on when Lord Huntley came in with a letter in his hand;—"Oh, my dear," cried he, "I have been looking for you through all the rooms;—I have just receiv'd a letter from Sir Thomas Welby."—"I hope mamma is well," cried she hastily,—"and no ill accident has happen'd."—"Not in the least," return'd he, "but far on the contrary;—Sir Thomas only writes to let us know that his son is married, and will very shortly bring his bride to visit us in Paris."

"I am astonish'd," cried Lady Huntley;—"Mr. Welby married!—I do not understand how such a thing can be;—he took leave of mamma and I just after my coming from Bath, and told us he was to set out on his travels next day, and I thought that he was gone:—sure he must either have made a very short tour, or have stopp'd in his progress and have pick'd up a wife by the way."

"I know nothing of the particulars," resum'd his lordship;—"but you shall hear what Sir Thomas says on the occasion":—with these words he look'd over the letter,—and singling out that part of it which he thought would most satisfy her curiosity, read as follows:

> I thought him too young to marry; but found his inclinations so much divided between love and travelling, that the latter would have afforded him neither pleasure nor improvement without the gratification of the former, so consented to both;—he was married last week, and two days ago set out on his rambles, and has taken his bride with him:—as they intend to stay some time at Paris, in their way to Italy and other parts, he will have the honour to present her to the ladies, and I flatter myself she will appear not unworthy of their countenance and friendship.

"Well, this is strange," said she, perceiving he had done; "but does not mention to whom he is married."—"Not a syllable," reply'd he; "but we shall soon know more of the matter;—for I find by the date of this letter, which I did not observe before, that it has been retarded, by some accident or another, in the post; and the young gentleman, by the time mention'd of his leaving London, must infallibly be already arriv'd, or very near."

These words had but just escap'd his lips, when a servant came hastily into the room and said, that a gentleman, who call'd himself Welby, was in the great salon with Lady Speck and Mr. Lovegrove, and they sent him to let his lordship know it.

On this Lord and Lady Huntley went to receive their new guest; but Jemmy and Jenny, having no acquaintance with him, thought themselves excused from paying their compliments to him at this time.

Chapter XXVII

Contains a very remarkable occurrence.

Mr. Welby made his first visit very short; but was not suffer'd to depart without engaging himself to come again the next day and bring his lady with him, whom they were not a little impatient to see, as Sir Thomas had mention'd her so handsomly in his letter.

The daughters of Lady Wingman had a sincere regard for this young gentleman, not only as he was the son of Sir Thomas Welby, but also on the score of his own good qualities; and, willing to testify it by all the marks in their power, gave orders to those who had the management of their houshold affairs, to omit nothing proper for the entertainment of the new wedded pair.

Three was the appointed hour, and had not elapsed as many minutes when their expected guest appear'd;—the bride seem'd very lovely in the eyes of Lord Huntley, Jemmy, and Sir Robert Manley; but there was something in her, which much more than her beauty, attracted those of Mr. Lovegrove and the three ladies,—each of these was perfectly convinced that they had been acquainted with her face, though when or where none of them could recollect;—but when she spoke, in returning the salutations they severally gave her, her voice immediately eased them in the suspence they had been in, and presented her to their remembrance for the fair stranger whom accident and distress had brought into their company, at the village where they had been obliged to lie on their return from Bath.

Great was their astonishment, nor was that of Mrs. Welby less; but as they had too much politeness to betray any part of theirs, or take the least notice they had ever seen her before, so she had too much generosity not to avow her remembrance of them.

"It was with a great deal of pleasure I came," said Mrs. Welby, "to pay my respects to the friends of Mr. Welby; but how infinitely would that pleasure have been enhanced, had it been possible for me to have foreseen I should have met the only persons to whom I have been so highly obliged in the extremest exigence in my life";—then perceiving they made no other reply, as indeed they were not yet enough recover'd from their surprize to do it:—"You may not, perhaps," resumed she, "be able presently to distinguish in the wife of Mr. Welby the once forlorn, the distress'd fugitive;—but this will be to me a perpetual memento of your goodness."

In speaking these last words she took out of her pocket the snuff-box she had exposed to sale at the inn, and which Mr. Lovegrove had bought and return'd to her with so much gallantry;—on sight of it,—"It will be a lasting honour to me, Madam," said that gentleman, "that you still retain a trifle not otherwise worthy your acceptance than by being before in your possession."

The two sisters now first acknowledged their remembrance of her, with many compliments on the change of her condition; and Jenny, who had been impatient to do so, congratulated her good fortune with the extremest warmth:—those of the company who were not in the secret, were surprised at these salutations; but Mr. Welby most of all, which his fair wife perceiving,—"You have introduced me," said she, "to persons whom I little hoped to have met at Paris, but would have gone much farther to have seen;—I shall at leisure make you acquainted with the obligations I have to them."

Dinner being that instant serv'd up broke off all farther speech upon this head; but the ladies were all the time in the utmost impatience to know the bottom of an affair which at present seem'd so mysterious to them, and as soon as the cloth was remov'd, left the gentlemen to their burgundy and drew Mrs. Welby into another room, not doubting but she would readily satisfy their curiosity, which she accordingly did in the following manner:

The Sequel of the Fair Stranger's Adventures.

"What you desire of me," said she, "is so little worthy your attention, that I shall be as brief as possible in the repetition;—you already know the catastrophe of my fate in seeing me the wife of the most generous man on earth;—as for the accidents that made me so, they will only serve to shew that when we think ourselves farthest remov'd from happiness we are often nearest to it.

"You may remember, ladies, that I told you my design was to cross the sea from Bristol to Cork;—I got safe, without the least molestation, to the end of my journey; but was fortunately prevented from embarking on my voyage by this means:

"I had scarce time to enquire if any vessel was bound for my intended port, when the aunt to whom I was going landed from thence;—she came into the same inn where I was,—we were mutually astonish'd at the sight of each other; but I soon related to her the whole of my unlucky story, and the dissappointment it was to me to see her come to England in the very moment I was flying for refuge to her in Ireland, at which she seem'd equally surprised and troubled.

"At first she highly blam'd me for resisting so foolishly my good fortune, as she term'd it; but, perceiving I burst into tears at her reproaches, became more gentle:—she told me, however, that it would be quite improper for me to go to her house while she was out of it, as my uncle had never seen me, and I was an entire stranger to every one in the family;—'But,' said she, 'you shall go back to London with me,—I shall see your father soon after I come there,—will talk to him concerning you, and doubt not but I shall be able to mitigate matters between you, so as you may go home again without being forced to marry against your inclinations.'

"This did not very well please me, as I knew my father's positive temper, and fear'd the success of her negotiation in this point; however, as I had no other course to take, I was oblig'd to submit to her directions, and the next day we set out together in the stage coach for London.

"On our arrival we were lodg'd at the house of an eminent banker in the city, who had before been apprisd of my aunt's coming by letters for that purpose:—she told him nothing more of me than that I was her niece, nor did he think it his business to ask any questions, but treated me with a great deal of civility and respect; and, as I was a perfect stranger in that part of the town, I thought myself as secure there as if I had been in Ireland.

"The next day my aunt went to visit my father; but he happen'd to be gone out of town for a few days, and she found only my sister, who, on her making some enquiry for me, told her—that I was an impudent slut,—that after having promised to marry a gentleman of great worth and fortune, and every thing being prepared for the ceremony, I had run away in a most scandalous manner on the very day it was to have been perform'd;—that nobody knew what was become of me;—that I had almost broke my father's heart, and was a disgrace to all that belong'd to me.

"As I knew the bitterness of my sister's nature, and the small portion of good-will she always had for me, I was not at all surpriz'd when my aunt return'd with this intelligence;—I was only sorry my father was not at home, that I might have known in what manner he resented my behaviour; for as I had never failed in the dutious love of a child to a parent, the thoughts of having been compell'd to incur his displeasure gave me the most severe affliction and remorse.

"While I was in this suspence an accident befel me, which, tho' I thought little of at that time, proved afterwards to be of the greatest importance of my whole life.

"My aunt was gone one day to her lawyer, on the business which had brought her to England,—I was sitting reading at a window, when a servant at the banker's shew'd a gentleman into the room, and desir'd him to sit down, saying he expected his master home in a few minutes;—I rose from my seat at the entrance of this stranger, but was pretty much surpriz'd when I presently recollected he was the person who had follow'd me from church one Sunday to my father's door:—you may remember, ladies," continued she, "that I mention'd this incident to you on account of my sister's reproaching me with it afterwards."

"I remember it perfectly well," said Lady Speck; "and I dare answer that no part of your story was lost on any of us:—but pray proceed; for I already begin to trace the oddness of this event."—Mrs. Welby smil'd and went on:

"I would have left the room," resum'd she, "but an unaccountable something rivetted my feet;—the gentleman at first seem'd in more confusion than myself, but he soon recover'd from it; and seeing I had a book in my hand approach'd me, and with an air the most gay, yet respectful,—'May I presume, Madam,' said he, 'to ask what author is so happy as to engage your contemplations?'—I reply'd, it was only a novel, entitled, *Love and Duty reconciled*;[80]—this, he has since told me, he look'd upon as a prosperous omen to his hopes;—but he had no opportunity then to say anything farther,—the banker came that instant in,—begg'd his pardon for having made him wait, and told him, that as they should now be too late for the office, if he would accept of a bad dinner with him they would go together in the afternoon;—the gentleman very readily agreed;—while they were talking my aunt came in, and the cloth being already spread we all sat down to table.

"My aunt was so much disconcerted that she could scarce eat, which the banker taking notice of, she burst into the most vehement exclamations against her lawyer;—the young gentleman, who by this time had found how nearly she was related to me, ask'd her many questions concerning the behaviour of the person she complain'd of, and she then gave him a long detail of particulars, which, as they are no way material to my story, I shall not trouble you with a repetition of; and shall only tell you, that she concluded with saying, that Mr. Dally was one of the most base as well as most unmannerly men in the world.—'Mr. Dally,' cry'd he, 'I know him well, my father has been long his client, and I believe is the best friend he has:—if you will permit me to wait on you to him, I dare almost promise to engage him to do you justice.'—She was quite transported at this offer and joyfully accepted it, on which he assur'd her he would come the next morning and attend her to Mr. Dally's chambers; there pass'd no more, soon after dinner he went out with the banker on the business they had been talking of, which I afterwards found was to the Million Bank,[81] where he had some money left him on the death of a relation.

"On the banker's return my aunt could not forbear asking the name of the gentleman who had been so obliging to her, to which he reply'd, that he was the only son of Sir Thomas Welby, and then ran into great encomiums both on the father and the son, tho' no more than what I have since experienced they justly merit:—I was, however, very much confounded, for I must now acquaint you, ladies, that Sir Thomas Welby is the person, the history of whose liking of me I have already told you, since it was he I took so much pains to fly."

Here they all cry'd out in the utmost amazement, almost at the same time,—"What, Madam, Sir Thomas Welby, my guardian," said Lady Huntley; "was it to him you should have been married?"

"The same, indeed," reply'd she; "nor is it strange you should be ignorant such a thing was in agitation; for even had it been effected it was to have been kept a secret from his own family till I had been carried home and set at the head of it; but I shall now proceed to the more agreeable part of my narrative;—Mr. Welby came according to his promise, and usher'd my aunt to the lawyer's;—she return'd about noon in very high spirits;—told me that Mr. Welby's presence, and what he said, had wrought a wonderful effect;—that the lawyer was now as civil as before he had been rude; and that her business would be dispatch'd in a very short time:—'But, my dear niece,' said she, 'I have something better than all this to inform you of;—this fine young gentleman is violently in love with you;—he has made me the confidant of his passion, and engag'd my interest.—What now,' pursued she, seeing me look a little grave, 'surely you will not withstand your fortune a second time?'—I reply'd, that I could see little advantage in that gentleman's affections, since it was impossible his father would ever give a sanction to it.—'Pish,—what then,' resum'd she; 'when once you are married to him the father will easily be brought to forgive what cannot be recall'd.'—I urged the vanity of hoping a father would ever forgive a son for marrying the woman he had a mind to himself; but she made slight of all I said, and then told me, that as it was not proper the banker should as yet be let into the secret, she had promised to give Mr. Welby a meeting that afternoon, and to bring me with her:—'Neither your pride nor modesty,' continued she, 'has any cause to be alarm'd, for I shall pretend it is all my doing, and that you knew nothing of seeing him.'

"I was very averse to this meeting; but she was positive, and I was fearful of disobliging her, as I had no other friend but herself whom I could rely upon for making my peace with my father:—in fine, we went, Drapers-garden[82] was the place of rendezvous; Mr. Welby was there before us,—he affected, as had been contrived between my aunt and him, to have come there by chance, which a little saved my blushes:—after walking a turn or two, talking on ordinary matters, he proposed going to Ranelagh[83]—my aunt reply'd, that she had never seen the place, and could not do it in better company;—it did not become me to oppose what she had agreed to,—a coach waited which carried us directly thither;—it was very early in the evening and the company were not yet come, so we had the gardens to ourselves:—my aunt was so much in his interest, or rather mine, that she gave him all the opportunities the place would admit of to declare his passion to me, which he did in the most pathetic terms, while she pretended to amuse herself with looking on the story of Pamela,[84] painted on the walls:—I was far from giving any encouragement to what he said, yet, by an irresistible impulse, was prevented from treating it with the severity I wish'd to have done.

"But why should I detain your attention by particulars?—This meeting was productive of a second,—that of a third,—and so on, for a succession of several days; till at last, finding in myself an inclination to be too much pleased with his addresses, and dreading the consequence, I resolv'd to put an end to them.

"I took the first opportunity of being alone with him to tell him that I had consider'd of the honour he did me, and found it impossible for me to accept the hand he offer'd, so intreated him to withdraw his affection, if in reality he had so much for me as he pretended, and talk to me no more upon that subject;—the manner in which I spoke convincing him I was in earnest, he seem'd much amaz'd,—made such replies as might be expected from a lover, accused destiny, and the influence of ill stars,—complain'd of his want of power to please me, and laid the blame of my refusal on my aversion to his person;—this struck me, and in the sincerity of my soul,— 'No, Sir,' said I, 'wrong not your own merits, or my just sense of them, so far as to harbour such a thought:—I blush not to confess, that of all mankind you have the presence in my heart;—but what avails it when there is a bar between us, which all the love in the world, on both sides, would never be able to surmount!'—'Ah, Madam,' cried he hastily, 'what bar?'— I then told him that I was determin'd never to marry without the consent of parents:—'If that be all,' rejoin'd he briskly, 'I do not despair but to be able to make such proposals to your father as he will not disdain to listen to.'—'However that may be,' answer'd I, 'you, Sir, have a father too,—it is his consent I chiefly mean, and without his permission of the continuance of your addresses, be assured I will not receive them.'

"He now seem'd much disconcerted,—sigh'd, and was silent for several minutes.—'Well, Madam,' said he, 'you shall be obey'd;—my thoughts were lately bent on travelling,—every thing was ready for my design; but on the sight of you love laid a sudden embargo on my feet, and I then made a thousand excuses to my father for deferring my voyage; but I will now confess to him the whole truth, and implore his sanction to my vows;— he is generous,—I am his only son,—he loves me, and I may perhaps succeed;—I will, at least, make trial of my fate, and to-morrow you will see me either the most happy or the most miserable of men.'

"He parted from me with great emotions, nor was I less disquieted; but I acquainted not my aunt with this conversation, knowing she would severely chide me, and think, as indeed I did myself, that the step I had taken would entirely overthrow what she had taken so much pains to promote:—I neither saw nor heard any thing of my lover all the next day, and this confirm'd me in what before I scarce doubted;—I pass'd the night in anxieties enough; but the next morning found my condition revers'd, in a manner which I could never have imagin'd;—soon after breakfast my father's footman came in a great hurry to acquaint me that my father commanded me to return home immediately;—I was in a strange surprize;—I knew not before he was in town,—could not guess by what means he was directed where to find me, and was in the utmost dilemma whether I ought to rejoice or tremble at being sent for;—I would fain have staid for my aunt, who was just gone out, to have taken her with me; but the fellow told me that his orders were to bring me that instant, so I said no more but obey'd the summons.

"On my arrival my father met me in the parlour,—I threw myself at his feet and begg'd forgivness;—'Rise, my child,' said he, embracing me,—'I do forgive you;—the hand of Heaven has been in what you have done, and directed all your steps;—your fears of a forced marriage are now over,—Sir Thomas has resign'd his claim to one fitter for your years;—they are both here, and wait your presence to ratify the contract I have already made for you.'

"Judge, ladies, what I felt;—I was no longer at a loss for the happy event; the sudden surcharge of unexpected joy rushing in at once upon me was more than I could well support;—I was almost fainting when my father led me into the next room, where sat Sir Thomas Welby and his son; the latter, as I have since heard, was in much the same condition as myself; but the former pitying my confusion, took me by the hand with these words, deliver'd in the most sprightly tone,—'Come, daughter,' said he, 'for such you now are,—your father has given you to me, and the least I can do, to attone for the troubles I have occasion'd you, is to give my son to you, and hope you will not refuse to accept the present';—as he spoke this he join'd my hand with his son's,—and added,—'Take each other, and be as happy as love and the mutual consent of parents can make you':—Neither of us could speak for some time; but when we had recover'd ourselves enough to do so, the acknowledgments we made were very well receiv'd by both the old gentlemen.

"As there wanted but little preparations for a marriage so much desired on all sides, the ceremony was perform'd in three days after; and I have now nothing more to acquaint you with, but that Mr. Welby still persisting in his desire of seeing foreign parts, I have gladly consented to accompany him in his travels."

Chapter XXVIII

Concludes this history, and all the author thinks fit, at present, to intrude upon the public.

After Mrs. Welby had finish'd the account of her adventures, and receiv'd the praises due to her conduct thro' the whole of them, they all return'd into the dining-room; where, finding Mr. Welby had entertain'd the gentlemen in much the same manner as his wife had done the ladies, the conversation on this subject became general; and when they discoursed more at large on the odd circumstances of what they had heard related, and consider'd the generosity of Sir Thomas Welby,—the dissinterested passion of his son, and the extraordinary discretion of the young lady, they were at loss to say which of the three characters had the greatest claim to admiration.

These new comers now found themselves so happy in the society of those they were among, that, till the expiration of full three weeks, they seem'd not to remember they had any farther course to steer; nor did their friends think it too great an act of complaisance either to revisit with them all the places they had been at before, or to stay in Paris so much longer than they had intended, or would have done, but for so agreeable an addition to their company.

At length, however, they were oblig'd to separate,—Mr. Welby and his fair wife began their progress towards the Alps, in order to pass into Italy; and the other gentlemen and ladies, now equally impatient to be at home as they had been to go abroad, set out in a few days after on their return to England, where they happily arriv'd without meeting any accidents to retard their journey.

This agreeable company now ceased to be of one family,—Lord Huntley and Mr. Lovegrove took their ladies home, and Sir Robert Manley and our lovers returned to their respective habitations, to receive the visits of those friends and acquaintance from whom they had so long been absent;—Jemmy, however, was seldom from his dear Jenny, and had now a full opportunity to remind her of the promise she had made him; and that amiable lady, thinking they had sufficiently prov'd the love and sincerity of each other, no longer sought excuses to delay what he desir'd.

But before we bring them to the altar, it may not be improper to acquaint the reader with something concerning Bellpine, as he was the person who had taken so much pains to hinder their felicity from being ever compleated, and has, on that score, made too considerable a figure in this history to be wholly dropp'd.

The expences of his way of living having by much exceeded the slender income of his patrimony, he found himself obliged to mortgage, for near half the value, in order to discharge several debts, which had began to be very troublesome to him, and had exposed him to repeated insults.

But this was a trifling misfortune, when compared with that which soon ensued:—Lady Hardy had declar'd herself pregnant, which so enrag'd him, that not remembring the advice given him by the old housekeeper, he plainly accused his aunt of incontinency, and for proofs of his allegation against her, related all the good woman had reveal'd to him, and also all he knew concerning the passion she pretended to have felt for Jemmy.

But he was presently convinced of the error he had been guilty of in this rash behaviour;—Sir Thomas, either not believing, or not seeming to do so, treated all he said as a base forgery, and flew into the extremest rage,—forbad him coming any more into his presence, or even to think of him as an uncle, and at the same time bound himself by the most solemn imprecation, that whether the child his lady went with should live or die, to take such measures as should infallibly prevent the villain, who had so infamously traduced her, from ever inheriting any part of his estate.

Thus undone in all his future expectations, and reduced to an incapacity of living in a fashion equal to his birth, and much more to that of his ambition, it is not to be doubted but that he suffer'd all that despair and enervate[85] rage could inflict upon him.

In this condition, the only method his invention could supply him with to avoid poverty, and its sure attendant, the contempt of the world, was to sell an estate, which he found by much too inconsiderable for his support, and get into the army;—he accordingly did so, paid off the mortgage upon it, and with the remainder of the money he receiv'd for the purchase bought a captain of foot's commission in a marching regiment, which, to add to his mortification, was presently after order'd to one of the plantations in the West-Indies, and he was obliged to leave England, with all its dear delights, and embark for the Creolian coast some weeks before our lovers and their friends return'd from France,—a punishment which his own pride and luxury had brought upon him, and was justly due to the complicated vices of so bad a heart.

Jemmy was little affected at this piece of intelligence; but Jenny, who thought him capable of every thing that was base and wicked, and had not been altogether free from apprehensions of some mischief which his revenge and malice might possibly be productive of, could not forbear rejoicing, in spite of all the good-nature she was endow'd with, that a man of such dangerous propensities was so far remov'd.

Among other occurrences of less importance to her peace than this of Bellpine, she was also inform'd that Mrs. Marlove, whom if the reader has forgot, he may find mention'd [in] the beginning of this work, was now separated from her husband, having first made him, by her over delicacy and capricious temper, heartily weary of a state he had enter'd into with transport and the prospect of a lasting happiness.—She heard also that the marriage of Rodophil's mistress with the captain having been discover'd, her father oblig'd them to live together; but that they agreed so ill that the contentions between them made much diversion for their neighbours;—and that Miss Chit had quarrel'd with her great friend Lady Fisk, on the score of a young nobleman who had made his addresses to both, and equally despised both, tho' neither could suffer herself to believe so—and that the animosity of these fair rivals was arriv'd to such a height, that they made no scruple of betraying to the world all the failings each had been guilty of, and of which they had been mutually the confidants.

But our amiable Jenny had now done enquiring into the follies and mistakes of her sex, as she had seen enough of both to know how to avoid them; and all the preparations for giving herself to Jemmy being now ready, their marriage was solemnized, by her own desire, in the Abbey church of Westminster, in the presence of Lord Huntley, Mr. Lovegrove and their ladies, Sir Robert Manley, and some other friends, among whom Mr. Ellwood and Mr. Morgan were not left out.

It would be needless to repeat the satisfaction which this happy catastrophe[86] gave to every one who took any interest in the welfare of our accomplish'd lovers, or the sincere congratulations the new united pair receiv'd upon it;—I shall therefore leave them, after the hurry of feasting and visiting was over, to enjoy, in calm retirement, the more pure and lasting sweets of a well govern'd and perfect tenderness.

FINIS

Notes to the Novels

Volume I

1. *still will grow* "The Lyceum," from a volume of verse by Samuel Whyte (1733–1811), *The Shamrock: or Hibernian Cresses* (1722).

2. *breaking up* that is, when school vacations arrived

3. *according to the forms of law* In English law a female orphan could choose her legal guardian at fourteen. As Blackstone puts it: A female "at fourteen is at years of legal discretion, and may choose a guardian." See William Blackstone, *Commentaries on the Laws of England*, I, 451 (*A Facsimile of the First Edition of 1765–1769*, in 4 Volumes, Chicago: The University of Chicago Press, 1979).

4. *pluretic fever* pleurisy: inflammation of the pleura, the membraneous sacs containing the lungs, a disease characterized by pain in the chest or side, with fever, loss of appetite, etc.; usually caused by a chill, or occurring as a complication of other diseases (scarlatina, rheumatic fever, phthisis, etc.).

5. *landau and six* a four-wheeled, closed carriage with facing seats and a roof, here drawn by six horses

6. *last cast* in the figurative sense, the last effort or try

7. *hoydenish* from *hoyden*, a high-spirited or impudent girl or woman

8. *endued* endowed

9. *licenses* marriage licenses. To end the custom whereby a simple exchange of vows before a clergyman constituted a legal marriage (often called "Fleet Marriages" because the Fleet Prison in London was the best known place where such marriages were performed), Lord Hardwicke's Marriage Act of 1753 specified that only marriages conducted in the Church of England by "banns" or by means of a license and before witnesses were legal. Under the traditional system of banns, the following announcement was read on three consecutive Sundays in the parish church or churches of the bride and groom: "I publish the Banns of marriage between [groom's name] of [his parish] and [bride's name] of [her parish]. If any of you know cause or just impediment why these two persons should not be joined together in Holy Matrimony, ye are asked to declare it." To avoid this waiting period, a license could be purchased from a bishop, but this was expensive, ten shillings.

10. *eclaircisement* *eclaircissement:* explanation, clarification [French]

11. *tilt-work* duelling, sword fighting

12. *kind compliance* misquoted slightly, from John Dryden (1631–1700), *Amphitryon; or, The Two Socia's. A Comedy* (1690), Act IV.

13. *Vaux-Hall* a popular London pleasure ground on the south bank of the Thames that featured walks, arcades, and supper alcoves, as well as fireworks and other spectacular displays.

14. *beau monde* the fashionable world, high society

15. *keeping* that is, she has become a man's mistress, supported by him for sexual favors.

16. *Mrs. Becky* "Mrs." was a title given to both married and unmarried women; "Miss" was properly restricted to young girls.

17. *French capuchin* a hooded cloak, in this case an elaborately embroidered one, modeled on the habit of the religious order called Capuchins.

18. *fifty guineas* a guinea was (originally) a gold coin worth one pound and one shilling. Although modern equivalence in purchasing power is very difficult to establish, fifty guineas was in the mid-eighteenth century a very large sum of money, nearly six thousand pounds in modern purchasing power or about ten thousand dollars, more than the annual wages, for example, of a skilled workman at the time.

19. *play* gambling

20. *blow'd upon* made stale, old-fashioned, hackneyed

21. *in fine* in the end

22. *five pieces* that is, the five guineas Mrs. Frill has charged each of her customers who have signed up for the raffle of the expensive French capuchin

23. *short sack* a loose gown or dress

24. *sensible* well aware of something

25. *Cowley* Abraham Cowley (1618–1667), English poet. These lines are from *The Mistress* (1647), "Inconstancy," lines 19–28. The Roman poet Ovid (Publius Ovidius Naso, 43 B.C.–A.D. 17) was known for, among other poetic works, his *Amores*, a series of poems about love.

26. *others counter part* Haywood seems to be misquoting these lines from Samuel Butler (one of her favorite poets), *Hudibras*, Part III (1678): For nothing else has pow'r to settle / Th' interests of Love perpetual. / An Act and Deed that makes one Heart / Become another's Counter-part" (Canto I, ll. 923–26).

27. *deed of settlement on her by way of dower* Dower is the portion of an estate, traditionally one-third, that a widow is entitled to for her lifetime upon the death of her husband, but Jenny's father is following the new practice of a marriage settlement that allocated a sum (not always as much as the widow's one-third) in lieu of dower.

28. *escrutore* a writing desk

29. *Ranelagh* London pleasure gardens founded in 1742 in Chelsea that were, like Vauxhall Gardens, the scene for fashionable masquerades, concerts, fireworks, and other diversions.

30. *music on the river tonight* Jemmy and his friends have arranged to hire a barge or boat and some musicians to entertain their lady friends with a floating concert.

31. *chair* portable, enclosed or "sedan" chair mounted on horizontally placed parallel poles and carried by two men and serving as a kind of urban taxi cab in the eighteenth century.

32. *equipage* carriage and horses, liveried servants, etc.

33. *mall* a road through Hyde Park, bordered by trees and grass, that was a fashionable promenade for fashionable people in eighteenth-century London

34. *rout* a party or ball

35. *doux yeux* literally, soft eyes, looks [French], flirting or languishing glances

36. *fleering* sneering, scoffing

37. *Colly* Colley Cibber (1671–1757), actor, playwright, manager, and autobiographer was widely ridiculed for his choice of words in praising the performance given by Anne Oldfield (1688–1730) in his comedy, *The Provok'd Husband* (1728). "'Tis not enough," he wrote in the play's preface, "to say she here *outdid* her usual *Outdoing*." In his later autobiography, he explained his solecism this way: "A most vile Jingle, I grant it! You may well ask me, How could I possibly commit such Wantonness to Paper? I have no Excuse for it, but that, like a Lover in the Fulness of his Content, by endeavouring to be floridly grateful, I talked Nonsense" (*Apology for the Life of Colley Cibber*, ed. B.R.S. Fone, Ann Arbor: Univ. of Michigan Press, 1968, p. 34).

38. *Covent-Garden* Originally a convent garden owned by the Benedictines of Westminster, the site was laid out in the 1630s as a "piazza," or residential square (the first of its kind in London), to the design of Inigo Jones. A fruit and vegetable market was established there in 1670. It was a fashionable residential neighborhood in the seventeenth century but by the 1750s, thanks to the neighboring playhouses, taverns, and gambling dens, it became a rather unsavory and even dangerous area, much frequented by prostitutes.

39. *Bartholomew-Fair* a fair held each August in the northwestern part of London in Smithfield Market, the London Central Meat Market

40. *watch-house* sometimes called a round-house, a place in a particular parish where those accused of crimes could be kept overnight until charges were heard the next day

41. *alfresco* out of doors

42. *pacquet* the news or gossip that the ladies have brought

43. *buckle* to fasten hair in curls

44. *raparties* repartees: swift and witty retorts

45. *laceings of her stays* a laced underbodice or corset, stiffened by strips of whale-bone (sometimes of metal or wood) worn very tightly by women to give shape and support to the figure

46. *malapert* bold, outspoken, insolent

47. *brulée* quarrel [French]

48. *degagée* free and easy, relaxed and self-confident [French]

49. *vainly sought abroad* I am unable to find the source of this quotation.

50. *dissembled joys* John Dryden, *The Indian Emperour, Or, The Conquest of Mexico by the Spaniards* (1667), I, ii.

51. *window* that is, a window seat

52. *blind goddess* Jemmy must mean Fortune, proverbially represented as blind

53. *doit* a small Dutch coin worth about one quarter of a cent

54. *picquet* a card game for two people with a pack of thirty-two cards in which all the cards below the seven are omitted and in which points are scored on groups or combinations of cards

55. *solitaire* usually a diamond or gemstone set in a ring, although Jemmy's remark a few pages later as he gives it back to Liberia and fastens it seductively around her neck indicates that Haywood means us to see it as a stone set in a necklace. A solitaire was also a loose necktie or broad ribbon worn by men in the eighteenth century.

56. *point . . . quatorze* terms from picquet: point is the number of cards of the most numerous suit in one's hand after discarding; quatorze is a set of four similar cards (aces, kings, queens, knaves, or tens) held by one player, which count as fourteen.

57. *hackney* a chair for hire

58. *phlegm* possessing an unemotional, clam disposition; derived from the theory of the four humors of ancient physiology whereby temperament is determined by the preponderance of one of the four elements: phlegm, blood, choler, and black bile.

59. *dearly bought* misquoted slightly, from Dryden's *Aureng-Zebe* (1676), Act IV: "Prudence, thou vainly in our Youth art sought, / And with Age purchas'd art too dearly bought."

60. *Mr. Hoyle* Sir Edmund Hoyle (d. 1769) compiled a reference book of rules for card games, *A Short Treatise on the Game of Whist* (1742), to which in subsequent editions were added rules for other card games such as quadrille and picquet, as well as rules for chess and backgammon. Later editions, such as the fourteenth from 1765, which I consulted, provide a table of "Calculations directing, with moral Certainty, how to play well any Hand or Game, by showing the Chances of your Partner's having 1, 2, or 3 certain cards."

61. *deshabillee* casual or lounging dress, from French, *déshabillé*, undressed

62. *These ladies . . . those perfections which each possess'd in so lavish an abundance* The Gunning sisters were famous Irish beauties of the day; their mother was the daughter of the Sixth Viscount Mayo. Called "the Beauties," they appeared in London in 1751, and according to Horace Walpole they caused a sensation in London that year: "There are mobs at their doors to see them get into their chairs; and people go early to get places at the theatres when it is known they will be there." They were soon pronounced, Walpole had written earlier that year to Horace Mann, "the handsomest women alive." See Walpole to Horace Mann, March 23, 1752, and June 18, 1751, *Yale Edition of Horace Walpole's Correspondence*, XX, 311–12, 260 (New Haven: Yale University Press, 1960). Maria, Countess Coventry (1733–1760) married

George William, Sixth Earl of Coventry; her sister, Elizabeth (1734–1790) married James, Duke of Hamilton surreptitiously one midnight, February 14, 1752.

63. *Not the silver Doves . . . consent to move* Edmund Waller (1606–1687), "On the Friendship betwixt Two Ladies" (lines 17–24)

64. *route* usually "rout," a gathering of fashionable people, usually featuring card games

65. *quadrille* a card game played by four persons with forty cards, the eights, nines, and tens of the ordinary pack being discarded. Quadrille began to take the place of ombre as the fashionable card game about 1726, and was in turn superseded by whist.

66. *jointure* property set aside to be used for the support of a wife after her husband's death

67. *levees* levee, a reception held by a person of high rank in the morning, upon arising from bed. From the French noun, levée, a raising or lifting.

68. *Those free from guile . . . That others will be false* Haywood appears to be misquoting herself here, and these lines echo a character's observations in her play, *Frederick, Duke of Brunswick-Lunenburgh. A Tragedy* (1729): "Those free from Guile themselves, with Pain believe / The Fraud of others." Act II, scene i.

69. *The wretch . . . her voice, he dies* misquoted, from George Granville, Baron Lansdowne (1667–1735), "Mira Singing" (1736): "Who from her wit, or from her beauty flies, / If with her voice she overtakes him, dies."

70. *Orpheus* musician and poet from Greek myth whose songs could charm wild beasts. When his wife, Eurydice, was killed by a serpent's bite Orpheus went to the underworld after her and by the magic of his music persuaded Hades to let her go. But Hades warned Orpheus to not look back at her as he went back to earth, and when he did Eurydice slipped back to the nether world.

71. *White's* Founded by Francis White in 1693 in St. James Street, White's was a fashionable chocolate and coffee house, one of many in London, that was popular as a place for fashionable gentlemen to gamble.

72. *Oroondates and Statyra* a heroic character in Madeline de Scudery's romance *Artamène ou le Grand Cyrus* (1649–1653); *Statyra*: Alexander the Great's wife in *The Rival Queens; or The Death of Alexander the Great* (1677) by Nathaniel Lee (1653?–1692).

73. *chocolate house* that is, a shop where chocolate and coffee were served, popular gathering places in eighteenth-century London, such as White's (see above, note 71).

74. *Handel's last oratorio* George Frideric Handel (1685–1759), German-born English composer, turned in the late 1730s from writing operas in the Italian baroque style to sacred oratorios, based on scriptural stories. The most famous of these is *Messiah* (1741). Haywood may be referring to his last oratorio, *Jeptha*, performed at Covent Garden in 1752.

75. *devoirs* courteous attention, compliments (from French, *devoir*, to owe, a duty)

76. *closet* a small private room for reading, writing letters, or other solitary activities

77. *morelles* edible mushrooms, sometimes called sponge mushrooms

78. *s'death* an archaic and midly blasphemous oath, a short form of "God's Death"

79. *pitty-patties* little pies or pasties, usually filled with meat such as veal but here part of dessert and filled with something sweet

80. *Clamours . . . haunts forsake* John Dryden, *Aureng-Zebe: A Tragedy* (1676), Act II.

81. *enthusiast* a deeply or intensely religious person, with a negative connotation of fanaticism in the mid-eighteenth century

82. *give her the bonjour* to wish her good morning [French]

83. *Small jealousies . . . put out the fire* slightly misquoted, from John Dryden, *Aureng-Zebe: A Tragedy* (1676), Act IV: "Small jealousies, 'tis true, inflame desire; / Too great, not fan, but quite blow out the fire."

84. *false should find us so* I am unable to find the source of this quotation.

85. *ban-boxes* band-box: a rounded box originally designed to hold collars but then and now used for any small articles of clothing

86. *gentlemen collectors of the road* Eighteenth-century roads were dangerous and lawless, and thieves (highwaymen) were a real problem.

87. *Maidenhead* a town about twenty-five miles west of London, the first leg on the trip to Bath

88. *Jehu* a fast or furious driver, in this case a coachman. A traditional allusion to 2 Kings 9.20: "the driving is like the driving of Jehu the son of Nimshi, for he driveth furiously."

89. *the mischievious little deity* Cupid; Ceres and Bacchus are the gods respectively of agriculture or fertility and of wine

90. *post-chaise* a traveling carriage, either hired from one post or stage to another, or drawn by horses so hired, usually having a closed body, and seating for from two to four persons, the driver or postilion riding on one of the horses.

91. *cantato . . . recitativo* the first would seem to refer to an aria that is sung, the latter is a style of musical declamation, intermediate between singing and ordinary speech, commonly employed in the dialogue and narrative parts of operas and oratorios.

92. *retributions* here and elsewhere in the novel used in the now rare sense of a payment in return

93. *Gold! . . . valiant* misquoted slightly and abridged from Shakespeare's *Timon of Athens* (1623), Act IV, scene iii:

> What is here?
> Gold? yellow, glittering, precious gold? No, gods,
> I am no idle votarist: roots, you clear heavens!
> Thus much of this will make black white, foul fair,
> Wrong, right, base noble, old young, coward valiant.
> Ha, you gods! why this? what this, you gods?
> Why, this
> Will lug your priests and servants from your sides,
> Pluck stout men's pillows from below their heads:
> This yellow slave
> Will knit and break religions, bless the accursed,
> Make the hoar leprosy adored, place thieves
> And give them title, knee and approbation
> With senators on the bench: this is it
> That makes the wappen'd widow wed again;
> She, whom the spital-house and ulcerous sores
> Would cast the gorge at, this embalms and spices
> To the April day again. Come, damned earth,
> Thou common whore of mankind, that put'st odds
> Among the route of nations, I will make thee
> Do thy right nature.

94. *Hence 'tis . . . money too* Samuel Butler (1612–1680), slightly altered, from *Hudibras, The Third and Last Part* (1677), Canto I, ll. 1–4.

95. *Unhurt . . . into nature go* misquoted slightly and expanded from Abraham Cowley, "The Dissembler" (1647).

96. *fierty* *fièrté*, pride [French]

97. *Man is but man . . . work upwards first* slightly misquoted from John Dryden, *Cleomenes: The Spartan Hero. A Tragedy* (1692), Act III, Scene i.

98. *long room* one of the two (lower) assembly rooms at Bath on the Grand (now North) Parade, where fashionable guests gathered for socializing. Haywood must be referring to one of the ball rooms remodeled around 1749, one of which was said to be by a visitor in 1766 about 90 feet long and 35 feet wide.

99. *Clodio in the play* most likely a reference to a character in Cibber's 1702 play, *Love makes a Man: Or, The Fop's Fortune. A Comedy.*

100. *clasp'd the dame* I am unable to find the source of this quotation.

101. *beau monde* high society, fashionable people

102. *once fear to lose* Haywood may here be misquoting some lines from Lewis Theobald's "The Happy Captive, An English Opera" (1741): "What most we value, most we fear to lose" (I, vi).

103. *endued* endowed

104. *night-mob* an indoor cap worn by women in the eighteenth century

105. *Bedlam* from Bethlehem (Hospital of St. Mary of Bethlehem), the hospital for the insane in London

106. *racks* the instrument of torture, the rack, which stretched the body

107. *A singing, dancing . . . ne'er enjoyed* Nicholas Rowe's *The Fair Penitent* (1703), misquoted and adapted from Act II, scene ii:

> Away, no Woman cou'd descend so low:
> A skipping, dancing, worthless Tribe you are,
> Fit only for your selves, you Herd together;
> And when the circling Glass warms your vain Hearts,
> You talk of Beauties that you never saw,
> And fancy Raptures that you never knew.

108. *Were you, ye fair . . . can never love you less* *The Fair Penitent*, Act I, scene ii.

109. *du coeur* of the heart [French]

Volume II

1. *upon the tapis* on (upon) the tapis [from French sur le tapis], on the carpet, under discussion or consideration

2. *arts of the toylet* the toilette or dressing table, where a lady applied her makeup and arranged herself to be seen in pubic

3. *Marriage, thou curse . . . marriage enemies* Dryden's *The Conquest of Granada*, Part II (1672), Act III.

4. *bagatelle* a trifle, an unimportant or playful thing

5. *Statyra* see note 72 to Volume I

6. *Oroondates* see note 72 to Volume I

7. *Gulliver's Voyages to the Houghims* Jonathan Swift's satirical narrative, *Gulliver's Travels* (1726); the fourth book is a "Voyage to the Country of the Houyhnhnms" (rational beings in the shape of horses who keep as cattle irrational creatures called Yahoos, who are debased human beings).

8. *Aurora* Roman goddess of the dawn

9. *expiring at your feet* I have been unable to trace the source of this quotation.

10. *braggadocia* braggart, usually "braggadocio"

11. *possee* normally posse—an amateur or volunteer band bent on apprehending or punishing criminals

12. *postilion* a rider of one of the horses drawing a coach, who helps to guide them

13. *book was immediately presented to him* the Bible, to swear the oath on

14. *punctilio* a fine point of etiquette

15. *well-tied sword knot* a ribbon or tassel tied to the hilt of a sword (originally the thong

with which the hilt was fastened to the wrist, but later used chiefly as a mere ornament and in the eighteenth century sometimes fantastically elaborated).

16. *summum bonum* the greatest or supreme good [Latin]

17. *Not toss and turn . . . by lying still* misquoted from Dryden's *The Indian Emperor, Or, The Conquest of Mexico by the Spaniards* (1673), Act IV:

> We toss and turn about our Feaverish will,
> When all our ease must come by lying still:
> For all the happiness Mankind can gain
> Is not in pleasure, but in rest from pain.

18. *Fate ne'er . . . joins* Dryden's *Secret Love, Or The Maiden-Queen* (1668), Act IV, scene ii. "That her fair hand with Destiny combines!— / Fate ne're strikes deep, but when unkindness joynes!"

19. *English Sappho . . . Chearful as birds . . . and loving all* The poet and novelist Charlotte Lennox (1727–1804) was sometimes referred to as the English Sappho, just as in an earlier period Aphra Behn received that compliment. In the *Gentleman's Magazine* for November 1750, an anonymous poem appears "To Mrs. Charlotte Lennox, On reading her Poems," and offers this praise:

> Admiring Greece, which boasts the Sapphic muse,
> To thee the second wreath would not refuse:
> But Britain, emulous of ancient fame,
> May equal honours for her Sappho claim.

But I am unable to find the lines Haywood quotes in Lennox's poems or in Behn's.

20. *intellectual world* the world of spirits, of disembodied creatures

21. *lavender-water* a perfume compounded with alcohol and ambergris from the distilled flowers of lavender

22. *hartshorn* smelling salts

23. *put up the letter* put it away out of plain sight

24. *ombre* a popular eighteenth-century card game played by three persons, with forty cards, the eights, nines, and tens of the ordinary pack being thrown out

25. *standish* an inkwell

26. *old Michael Drayton . . . true to none* Michael Drayton (1563–1631). I am unable to find these lines in his work. Haywood may be thinking of Drayton's most famous sonnet, that begins, "Since there's no help, come let us kiss and part," and speaks of the canceling of vows in lines 5–8: "Shake hands for ever, cancel all our vows, / And when we meet at any time again, / Be it not seen in either of our brows / That we one jot of former love retain."

27. *prevent* to anticipate

28. *started* come loose

29. *ridinghood* a large hood originally worn for riding, but in later use becoming an article of outdoor apparel for women and children

30. *ignis fatuus* something that misleads or deludes [Latin: foolish fire]

31. *repeater* a watch or a clock with a mechanism that strikes the hour

32. *writings* the marriage settlement, a legal document

33. *Cork* a city in southern Ireland

34. *hoop-petticoat* a petticoat or skirt stiffened and expanded by hoops of whalebone or cane or other materials

35. *penny-post* an organization for sending letters or packages at an ordinary charge of a penny each, established around 1680 for London and its environs within a radius of ten miles

36. *Covent Garden* see note 38 in Volume I

37. *paniers* panniers, an overskirt puffed out at the hips, but originally bags or baskets carried on each side by a beast of burden. Transferred to mean underskirt padding on each side, the word is here being brought back closer to its origin.

38. *Bristol* see note 43 below

39. *Windsor* a town on the south bank of the River Thames to the west of London. The modern town is dominated by Windsor Castle, a royal residence.

40. *six guineas* although Jenny is described as surprised by "the meanness of the present," in fact in terms of purchasing power in the mid-eighteenth century, six pounds and six shillings was a considerable sum, worth perhaps as much as a hundred times that today, or in modern purchasing power over a thousand dollars.

41. *Reading* city in Berkshire, thirty-eight miles west of London

42. *pillion* a pad or cushion for an extra rider behind the saddle

43. *Bristol* a port city 120 miles west of London at the confluence of the Rivers Avon and Frome

44. *high metal* that is, high mettle, spirited and energetic

45. *new buildings* The reference is probably not to a specific set of buildings but, rather, to the new residential development that was taking place throughout the middle decades of the eighteenth century to the west and northwest of the City of London, in areas such as Bloomsbury and Marylebone.

46. *West Chester* Chester is a port city, on the River Dee, in western England, in Cheshire

47. *fardles* bundles, burdens

48. *petit-maitre* an effeminate man, a fop or dandy [French: "little master"]

49. *St. James's* an area of London surrounding the London royal palace built for Henry VIII in the sixteenth century. With the destruction of Whitehall Palace in 1698, St. James's became the main London residence of the sovereign until the royal family moved to the grander and larger Buckingham Palace after St. James's burned down in the early nineteenth century.

50. *Mall* see note 33, Volume I

51. *To the great grief . . . her dear Pulvilio lost* I have not been able to find the source of this quotation, although "pulvilio" means powder (for the hair) and the term is a name for a fop.

52. *tendre* tender feelings [French]

53. *Those babbling ecchos . . . all sweet to sour, all love to hate* I am unable to trace the source of this quotation. Haywood may be thinking of Isaac Hawkins Browne (1705–1760) or William Browne (1590–1665).

54. *habit-maker* dress maker

55. *fly petticoat with fringes* A petticoat was in the eighteenth century an underskirt, but I am unable to discover just what a fly petticoat would have been. It might have been a petticoat with the hooks covered with a fly, as modern trousers and skirts are.

56. *Long-room: at Bath* see note 98 in Volume I

57. *God and Mammon* part of Jesus's teaching as narrated in Matthew 6:24: "No man can serve two masters: for either he will hate the one and love the other; or else he will hold to the one, and despise the other. Ye cannot serve God and mammon." See also Luke 16:13. Mammon is actually the Aramaic word for "riches," although most English translations of the Bible turned it into a personification rather than translating it.

58. *ejectments* the act or process of ejecting a person from his holding, that is to say, removing a tenant

59. *'Tis difficult . . . to their fountainhead* I have been unable to trace the source of this quotation.

60. *Covent-Garden Piazza* see note 38 in Volume I

61. *Mr. Cock's . . . Langford* Christopher Cock was the first major auctioneer in London. By 1735, he had established an auctioneering business in the piazzas in London's Covent Garden, selling the property of deceased and bankrupt individuals, including personal effects and real estate. Cock was one of the first auctioneers not only to advertise extensively, but also to court the nobility as patrons. Abraham Langford was an auctioneer and print and bookseller

in Covent Garden 1748–1777, whose firm took over from Cock and operated as Cock and Langford in 1748–1749.

62. *Buckingham house* the present day Buckingham Palace, then the mansion of the Duke of Buckingham

63. *gentleman commoner* one of a privileged class of undergraduates formerly recognized in the Universities of Oxford and Cambridge. They were distinguished from ordinary students by special academic dress, a separate dining table, by various immunities with respect to lectures, etc., and by the payment of higher fees.

64. *Persius* Roman satirist (34–62 A.D.).

65. *Carlos . . .* [and] *Angelina in the play* characters in a comedy by Colley Cibber (1671–1757), *Love makes a Man: Or, The Fop's Fortune* (1702).

66. *As Mahonet . . . he fix'd it there* from John Dryden's *Don Sebastian, King of Portugal: A Tragedy* (1690), Act IV, scene i.

67. *naught* wickedness, evil, moral wrong, mischief

68. *taper* an adjective, meaning tapering, diminishing gradually in breadth or thickness toward one extremity, becoming more slender

69. *Michaelmas* September 29, the feast of the archangel St. Michael

70. *parlous-shrewd* very or unusually shrewd

71. *Once lost . . . beyond the clouds* I am unable to find these lines in Shakespeare. Haywood, quoting from memory, may be thinking here of some lines in John Dryden's and Nathaniel Lee's *Oedipus; A Tragedy* (1678), II, i: 'Tis lost, / Like what we think can never shun remembrance; / Yet of a sudden's gone beyond the Clouds.

72. *For mighty love . . . a new charmer's eyes* adapted or misremembered from lines in John Dryden's *Aureng-Zebe* (1675): "For mighty Love, who Prudence does despise, / For Reason, show'd me Indamora's Eyes." (Act II)

73. *dull Stoick* philosophical school dating back to the teachings of Zeno of Citium (third century B.C.) which stressed the necessity of indifference to adversity and the cultivation of a self-sufficient virtue as the basis of happiness rather than any material or worldly possession. Here the emphasis is on the popular misconception of what was thought to be the Stoic philosopher's claim to be impervious to emotion or physical feeling.

74. *Imperfect sentences . . . the eloquence of love* I am unable to find these lines in Dryden's works, although it is possible that Haywood is misremembering some lines in *The Indian Emperour, or, The Conquest of Mexico by the Spaniards*, which convey something of the same sentiment: "Your Gallants sure have little Eloquence, / Failing to move the Soul, they Court the Sence, / With Pomps, and Trains, and in a crowd they Woo, / When true Felicity is but in two; / But can such Toys your Womens passion move? / This is but noise and tumult, 'tis not Love" (II, iii).

75. *perriwig-maker* usually spelled "periwig," a wig, an artificial imitation of a head of hair (or part of one), worn by both men and women

76. *dresden work . . . holland* Dresden was famous for its intricate and luxurious lace; holland is lace originally made in the province of Holland in the Netherlands.

77. *solitaire* see note 55, Volume I

78. *Tunbridge* city about thirty-five miles southeast of London in the county of Kent, usually called Tunbridge Wells (or Royal Tunbridge Wells), and a fashionable spa with medicinal springs

79. *Windsor-Castle* English royal residence outside of London near Maidenhead in the county of Berkshire

80. *robe de chambre* a dressing gown

81. *Vaux-Hall* London pleasure gardens. See note 13, Volume I.

82. *among the paintings of Titian . . . thinly blended with thorns and prickly briars* I have looked at reproductions of all of Titian's paintings and consulted several art historians and can only conclude that Haywood is thinking of another painting. There is no painting by Titian that features two Cupids, although *The Worship of Venus* has many Cupids or putti in it. Haywood is

clearly thinking of another painting, perhaps by Veronese, one of Titian's contemporaries, but I have not been able to find it.

83. *Syriac and Chaldean* languages spoken in biblical times in Babylonia and in Syria

84. *and fame's last disgrace* I have not been able to find the source of this quotation.

85. *Men are but children . . . full as vain* Dryden's *All for Love Or, The World Well Lost* (1678), Act IV.

86. *bagnio* literally, a bathing house [Italian, bagno], but in common eighteenth-century usage a brothel or place to have a sexual assignation

Volume III

1. *Rome at the last jubilee* Since the fifteenth century, the Roman Catholic Church has every twenty-five years celebrated a "Jubilee," a year in which pilgrims are encouraged to visit Rome to earn "plenary indulgences" (remission of punishment in the afterlife for sins, if there is sincere repentance) by visiting the four great basilicas, St. Peter's, St. John's Lateran, St. Mary Major, and St. Paul-without-the-Walls. Haywood must be referring to the Jubilee of 1750.

2. *Mercer* shop that deals in textile fabrics, especially silks, velvets, and other costly materials

3. *Spleen . . . blow* from George Farquhar's play *The Recruiting Officer* (1706), Act I, Scene i.

4. *Chandos-street* street near Regent's Park in a newly fashionable western part of London

5. *small beer* beer of a weak or inferior quality

6. *Hugonot* Huguenots: French Protestants, many of whom had emigrated to England and other Protestant countries in the seventeenth century to escape religious persecution, especially after the revocation in 1685 by Louis XIV of the 1598 Edict of Nantes (which had granted them a measure of religious liberty).

7. *post-chaise* see note 90, Volume I

8. *White's chocolate house* see note 71 Volume I

9. *On eagles wings . . .* from *The Gentle Shepherd* (1725), a play by the Scottish poet Allan Ramsay (1686–1758)

10. *brulée* see note 47, Volume I

11. *sybils . . . mounted the hallowed tripod* Sybils were in Greek and Roman mythology and religion women given the power of prophesy by the god Apollo; the hallowed tripod was a three-legged chair at the shrine of Apollo at Delphi, on which the priestess seated herself to deliver oracles.

12. *He that will . . . he feigns* slightly misquoted from Samuel Butler, *Hudibras* (Part II, 1663), Canto I: "For he that hangs, or beats out's brains, / The Devils in him if he feigns."

13. *Otway calls a single life* The only reference in Otway's plays that I can find is the following from *Friendship in Fashion* (1678): "Thus Madam you freely enjoy all the pleasures of a single life, / and ease your self of that wretched formal Austerity which commonly attends / a married one. / Mrs. Goody: Who would not hate to be one of those simpring Saints / that enter into Marriage as they would go into a Nunnery, where they / keep very strict to their Devotion for a while, but at last turn as errant / Sinners as e're they were" (III, i). Haywood may be thinking of Shakespeare's Othello, who does use the phrase in I, ii as he speaks to Iago: "But that I love the gentle Desdemona, / I would not my unhoused free condition / Put into circumscription and confine / For the sea's worth."

14. *superscription* envelopes did not yet exist at the time, and letters were folded and the address or superscription written on the blank outside

15. *And makes the slave grow pleased and vain* Haywood is quoting freely from a volume

published in 1682 by "Ephelia," *Female Poems*, and from a poem entitled "Song: Give me leave to rail at you":

Kindness has resistless charms,
All besides but weakly move;
Fiercest anger it disarms,
And clips the wings of flying love.
Beauty does the heart invade,
Kindness onely can the heart persuade:
It guilds the lovers servile chain,
And makes the slave grow pleas'd again.

16. *Cato's daughter . . . sanctity of manners* the lines (slightly misquoted) are from Joseph Addison's *Cato* (1713), Act I, Scene iv:

True, she is fair, (Oh, how divinely fair!)
But still the lovely Maid improves her Charms
With inward Greatness, unaffected Wisdom,
And Sanctity of Manners.

17. *Boutefeu* firebrand, firebug [French], from the obsolete French word, "bouter," meaning to put or set

18. *This raging fit . . . possess'd with fear* slightly misquoted from John Dryden's *The Indian Emperour; or The Conquest of Mexico by the Spaniards* (1667), Act II, Scene ii: "A raging fit of Vertue in the Soul; / A painful burden which great minds must bear, / Obtain'd with danger, and possest with fear."

19. *quelque-chose . . . a-la-mode de France* something or other in the French style

20. *Madness . . . Hell is in the thought* no such line seems to appear in Otway's plays, although these from *Venice Preserv'd* (1682), Act I, Scene i, may be the ones Haywood was thinking of:

Oh I will love thee, even in Madness love thee:
Tho my distracted Senses should forsake me,
I'd find some intervals, when my poor heart
Should swage it self and be let loose to thine.
Though the bare Earth be all our Resting-place.

21. *"Reflections on the different effects of love"* a work by Haywood herself, *Reflections on the various effects of Love, . . . intermix'd with the latest amours . . . of persons of . . . rank . . . of a certain island adjacent to the kingdom of Utopia, . . . by the author of the Mercenary Lover, etc.* (London, 1726).

22. *Love various minds . . . and with revenge it glows* slightly misquoted, from John Dryden, *Tyrannick Love, Or The Royal Martyr. A Tragedy* (1670), Act II, Scene i:

Love various minds does variously inspire:
He stirs in gentle Natures gentle fire;
Like that of Incense on the Altars laid:
But raging flames tempestuous Souls invade.
A fire which every windy passion blows;
With pride it mounts, and with revenge it glows.

23. *hereditaments* a legal term signifying whatever may be inherited

24. *Spite, by the Gods, proud spite, and burning envy* quoted from Nathaniel Lee, *The Rival Queens, Or The Death of Alexander the Great* (1677), Act IV, Scene i.

25. *Loves an heroic passion . . . lover worthy his desire* quoted, accurately, from John Dryden's *The Conquest of Granada*, Part II (1672), Act I, Scene i.

26. *Willmore* the name of the rake hero of Aphra Behn's play "The Rover" (1677, 1681).

27. *a thousand guineas* an enormous amount of money; in current purchasing power about one hundred and ten thousand pounds or about one hundred and ninety thousand dollars

28. *gentleman-usher of the ceremony* servant who served the tea

29. *billet* love letter, French for "letter"

30. *epithilamiums* marriage songs or poems

31. *Ely chapel* the most famous chapel in England with this name is the Lady Chapel at Ely Cathedral in Cambridgeshire, the largest chapel in the British Isles, completed in 1349. But Willmore's parents can hardly have been married privately there. Haywood's reference may be to St. Ethelreda, which was a private chapel, part of Ely Palace, the London town house of the Bishop of Ely, on Ely Place in the center of London.

32. *jointure* money set aside by a husband for his wife in the event of their separation by death or divorce

33. *wrapping gown* night gown or bath robe

34. *Hatton-Garden* street in East Central London, near Clerkenwell, not a fashionable address at the time

35. *duke of Cumberland* William Augustus, Duke of Cumberland and Frederick, Prince of Wales were King George II's two eldest sons, the latter a fierce enemy of his father

36. *quarter'd at once upon him* householders could be compelled to house soldiers, there being few permanent barracks in eighteenth-century England, when the army was largely disbanded during times of peace. Willmore's enthusiasm for such quartering in peacetime (and Sophia's worry about the political and constitutional dangers of such views) is a sign for mid-eighteenth-century readers of his unsoundness.

37. *Whitehall* street near St. James's Palace, a much more fashionable neighborhood than Hatton Garden

38. *Too much of one thing . . . relaxation e'en from joy* I have not been able to find the source of this quotation.

39. *toylet* a towel or cloth thrown over the shoulders during hair-dressing, also a shawl

40. *let blood* Blood-letting was used in the eighteenth century as a traditional medical treatment for a range of conditions, including fevers, inflammations, diseases, and hemorrhages.

41. *bucks* according to the *Oxford English Dictionary*, in the eighteenth century the word indicated masculine high spirits or even rowdiness of conduct rather than elegance of dress or physical attractiveness, as it came to signify in the nineteenth century.

42. *When things go ill . . . thinks himself more wise* Charles Sedley, *Antony and Cleopatra: A Tragedy* (1677), Act I, Scene ii.

43. *With prosperous gales . . . to gain the wish'd for shore* I have not been able to find the source of this quotation.

44. *Let her own works praise her in the gates* Favor is deceitful, and beauty is vain: but a woman that feareth the Lord, she shall be praised. Give her of the fruit of her hands; and let her own works praise her in the gates. (Proverbs 31: 30–31).

45. *St. Omers, . . . famous seminary of jesuits* founded for the training of English Jesuits in 1592, twenty-four miles from Calais, in the province of Artois

46. *White's* see note 71, Volume I

47. *Lull'd . . . a mind in love* This line does not occur in Shakespeare's works, as far as I can tell.

48. *Thro' Purgatory . . . Heaven's high Mass* This may be a reference to a line in "The Blunderer: Or, the Counter-Plots. A Comedy" (1739) by Henry Baker (1698–1744) and James Miller (1706–44): "If your soul is in Purgatory and wants Masses, why you shall have 'em upon my Word" (Act I, scene v).

49. *Racine, Crebillion* Jean Racine (1639–1699), French neoclassical dramatist; Prosper Jolyot de Crébillon (1674–1762), French dramatist

50. *Row* Nicholas Rowe (1674–1718), English dramatist, named poet laureate in 1715. In the early eighteenth century he enjoyed political patronage for his strong Whig views.

51. *Fielding's Rosamond* In his puppet theater in Panton Street, near the Haymarket, Henry Fielding staged among other plays *Fair Rosamond* (1748), a satiric treatment of contemporary life.

52. *Colley's Odes* Colly Cibber, actor, playwright, and poet laureate from 1731 for George II, produced annual odes (much ridiculed by literary critics) as birthday tributes to the sovereign.

53. *cabaret* restaurant, although in this case Jemmy must mean an inn.

54. *bag wig* wig fashionable in the eighteenth century; the back-hair was enclosed in an ornamental bag

55. *conventicle* Although the word can mean any assembly or meeting, in the eighteenth century in England it was most often applied to dissenting (that is, non–Church of England) meeting houses, often with a pejorative implication. Or as the *OED* puts it, "a religious meeting or assembly of a private, clandestine, or illegal kind; a meeting for the exercise of religion otherwise than as sanctioned by the law." Jemmy's phrase "conventicle leer" conveys contempt for what he implies is the sanctimonious hypocrisy of the merchant class religious dissenter.

56. *French author* I have not been able to find the source of this quotation.

57. *sponsors at the font* that is, as one of the godparents at the baptism of the child

58. *no foreign names in my family* Since the English royal family and the current occupant of the throne (George II) were Germans and continued to rule there as Electors of Hanover, this is a charged political joke.

59. *jacobite* adherent of the deposed Stuart family, living in exile in France since James II (Jacobite from Jacobus, Latin for James) had been forced to abdicate in 1688

60. *English, and also good protestant names* Charlot is the feminine of Charles, and the Stuarts were English, although Charles II was a crypto-Catholic. Wilhelmina is the feminine of Wilhelm or William, and King William III was certainly a Dutch Protestant but only half English, on his mother's side.

61. *the name Jenny had mention'd* Jemima is the feminine of James (Jemmy's proper name, of course) but also the name of the last Stuart king, James II, and of his successors, his son and grandson, the Old Pretender and the New Pretender, as they were called. So Jenny has in fact chosen a Jacobite name.

62. *One gains . . . by an ebb and flow* Sir Robert Howard, *The Indian-Queen, A Tragedy* (1665), Act II, Scene i.

63. *Good after evil . . . like the scenes of day and night* misquoted slightly from John Dryden, *Tales from Chaucer. Palamon and Arcite; or The Knight's Tale* (1700)

64. *Eternal changes . . . the chequer-work of fate* I have not been able to trace the source of this quotation.

65. *Past woes . . . the present blessing more endear* I have not been able to trace the source of this quotation.

66. *douceurs* softness, tenderness [French]

67. *'Tis our own wisdom . . . make our fate* adapted from Abraham Cowley (1618–1667), "Destinie": "'Tis their own Wisdom molds their State, / Their Faults and Virtues make their Fate."

68. *Tasso . . . Armida . . . in that they terminate* Torquato Tasso (1544–1595), Italian author of *Gerusalemme Liberata* (1575), an epic poem describing the First Crusade led by Godfrey of Boulogne, which captured Jerusalem in 1099. The poem was first translated into English by Edward Fairfax (c. 1575–1635) in 1600 as *Jerusalem Delivered.* Armida is the niece of Hidraort, the Prince of Damascus, who at the instigation of Satan sends her to the Christian camp to attempt to seduce their chiefs. However, I am unable to find in Fairfax's translation or for that matter in the Italian original any lines that match these.

69. *the temple of him who first ordain'd, and who alone has power to render it a blessing* Lord Hardwicke's Marriage Act of 1754 for the Better Preventing of Clandestine Marriages required

among other things that marriages could only be carried out in licensed buildings—which were churches and chapels of the Church of England. So Jenny's reservations about getting married anywhere but in church are in line with the new regulations shortly to be enacted.

70. *rich cake, which Sir Thomas Welby immediately broke over the heads of the bridegrooms and their brides* an old custom signifying a hope for fertility, related to the current practice of throwing rice or confetti at the newly married couple, in which small cakes were broken over the heads of the couple or in some cases a small cake broken over the head of the bride.

71. *Ceres* Roman goddess of the harvest and fertility

72. *Sittingbourn* see below, note 75 for their route to Paris

73. *That love . . . proud ambition have no bounds* slightly misquoted, from John Dryden, *Palamon and Arcite; or, The Knight's Tale* (1700), "But love the sense of right and wrong confounds; / Strong love and proud ambition have no bounds."

74. *Was ever woman . . . in this humour won?* Shakespeare, *Richard III*, Act I, Scene ii. In Shakespeare's play at this point, Richard has caused the death of the Lady Anne's husband and he woos her successfully as she mourns over his coffin.

75. *Sittingbourn* The party is traveling southeast to Sittingbourn, further southeast to Canterbury and then to Dover, from which they embark for France, to Calais, from where it is a southern journey to Paris, about 190 miles or 306 kilometers.

76. *thuileries* on the east side of the present Place de la Concorde, the royal palace of the Tuileries, and the Jardin des Tuileries, laid out in 1664 as the French king's pleasure gardens

77. *gardens of Luxemberg* On the left bank of Paris, the Jardin du Luxembourg was laid out in 1613 as the garden for the Palais du Luxembourg, built in 1620–1621.

78. *Marli,—Fontainbleau,—and Versailles* Marly-le-Roi, west of Paris, where Louis XIV built a palace and gardens as a retreat from his court at Versailles; Fontainebleau, a royal palace thirty-five miles southeast of Paris, begun after 1528 for Francis I; Versailles, twelve miles southwest of Paris, enormous and sumptuous palace and gardens built by Louis XIV, who from 1672 onward expanded tremendously the hunting lodge built there in 1624 by Louis XIII.

79. *La Belle Angloise* the Beautiful Englishwoman

80. *Love and Duty reconciled* novella published in 1692 by William Congreve, *Incognita or Love and Duty Reconciled.*

81. *Million Bank* Although founded as a bank in 1695, this firm quickly specialized in purchasing and trading in government life annuities. In the South Sea Bubble financial crash of 1720, it was one of the major holders of government securities that lost most of their value.

82. *Drapers-garden* street in the City of London, near the present Bank of England

83. *Ranelagh* see note 29 in Volume I

84. *Pamela* Samuel Richardson's *Pamela* (1740), the famous novel about a servant girl who marries her master. The illustrations of the novel were actually at another pleasure garden, Vauxhall, where two scenes from the novel were among a series of canvases decorating the supper boxes there painted by Francis Hayman and adapted from his illustrations for the 1742 edition of the novel that Richardson had commissioned. See the introduction by Tom Keymer and Peter Sabor to *The Pamela Controversy: Criticisms and Adaptations of Samuel Richardson's Pamela 1740–1750*, vol. 2, "Prose Criticisms, Verbal Representations (London: Pickering & Chatto, 2001), xxxix.

85. *enervate* enervated, depleted, deprived of strength

86. *catastrophe* used in a neutral sense to mean simply a conclusion

Selected Bibliography

Primary Texts:

Backscheider, Paula, ed. *Selected Fiction and Drama of Eliza Haywood.* New York: Oxford University Press, 1999.

Backscheider, Paula, and John J. Richetti, eds. *Popular Fiction by Women, 1660–1730: An Anthology.* New York: Oxford University Press, 1996. Includes two Haywood novellas, "Fantomina" and "The British Recluse."

Haywood, Eliza. *Anti-Pamela*, vol. III of Thomas Keymer and Peter Sabor (ed.). *The Pamela Controversy: Criticisms and Adaptations of Samuel Richardson's Pamela, 1740–1750.* London: Pickering and Chatto, 2001.

———. *The History of Miss Betsy Thoughtless*, ed. Christine Blouch. Peterborough, Ontario: Broadview Press, 1998.

———. *The History of Miss Betsy Thoughtless*, ed. Beth Fowkes Tobin. Oxford: Oxford University Press, 1997.

———. *The Injur'd Husband; or, The Mistaken Resentment* and *Lasselia; or, The Self-Abandon'd*, ed. Jerry C. Beasley. Lexington: University Press of Kentucky, 1999.

———. *Life's Progress Through the Passions: Or, The Adventures of Natura.* London, 1748.

———. *Love in Excess, or, The Fatal Enquiry*, ed. David Oakleaf. Peterborough, Ontario: Broadview Press, 1994.

———. *Selected Works of Eliza Haywood.* 4 vols. London: Pickering and Chatto, 2000. Vol. I, *Miscellaneous Writings, 1725–43*; vol. II, *Epistles for the Ladies*; vol. III, *The Wife, the Husband, and the Young Lady*; vol. IV, *The Dramatic Historiographer* and *The Parrot.*

———. *The Works of Mrs. Eliza Haywood: Consisting of Novels, Letters, Poems, and Plays*, 4 vols. London: Browne and Champman, 1724.

Rudolph, Valerie C., ed. *The Plays of Eliza Haywood.* New York: Garland Publishing Co., 1983.

Spacks, Patricia, ed. *Selections from The Female Spectator.* New York: Oxford University Press, 1999.

Secondary Works:

Backscheider, Paula. "The Shadow of an Author: Eliza Haywood," *Eighteenth-Century Fiction* 11 (1998): 79–102.

Ballaster, Ros. *Seductive Forms: Women's Amatory Fiction from 1684 to 1740*. Oxford: The Clarendon Press, 1992.

Beasley, Jerry C. "Eliza Haywood," *Dictionary of Literary Biography* 39, 251–58.

Blouch, Christine. "Eliza Haywood and the Romance of Obscurity," *Studies in English Literature 1500–1900* 31 (1991): 535–51.

Bowers, Toni O'Shaughnessy. "Sex, Lies, and Invisibility: Amatory Fiction from the Restoration to Mid-Century," *The Columbia History of the British Novel*, ed. John Richetti. New York: Columbia University Press, 1994.

Elwood, J. R. "Henry Fielding and Eliza Haywood: A Twenty-Year War," *Albion* 5 (1973): 184–92.

Erickson, James P. "*Evelina* and *Betsy Thoughtless*," *Texas Studies in Literature and Language* 6 (1964): 96–103.

Hollis, Karen. "Eliza Haywood and the Gender of Print," *Eighteenth Century: Theory and Interpretation* 38 (1997): 43–62.

Ingrassia, Catherine. *Authorship, Commerce, and Gender in Early Eighteenth-Century England: A Culture of Paper Credit*. Cambridge: Cambridge University Press, 1998.

King, Kathryn R. "Spying upon the Conjurer: Haywood, Curiosity, and 'the novel' in the 1720s," *Studies in the Novel* 30 (1998): 447–64.

Nestor, Deborah J. "Virtue Rarely Rewarded: Ideological Subversion and Narrative Form in Haywood's Later Fiction," *Studies in English Literature 1500–1900* 34 (1994): 579–98.

Richetti, John J. *The English Novel in History 1700–1780*. London: Routledge, 1999.

———. "Ideas and Voices: The New Novel in Eighteenth-Century England," *Eighteenth-Century Fiction* 12 (2000): 327–44.

———. *Popular Fiction Before Richardson: Narrative Patterns 1700–1739*. Oxford: The Clarendon Press, 1969; rpt., with new introduction by the author, 1992.

———. "Voice and Gender in Eighteenth-Century Fiction," *Studies in the Novel* 19 (1987): 263–72.

Saxton, Kirsten T., and Rebecca P. Bocchicchio, eds. *The Passionate Fictions of Eliza Haywood: Essays on Her Life and Work*. Lexington: University Press of Kentucky, 2000.

Schofield, Mary Anne. *Eliza Haywood*. Boston: Twayne Publishers, 1985.

Schultz, Dieter. "'Novel,' 'Romance,' and Popular Fiction in the First Half of the Eighteenth Century," *Studies in Philology* 70 (1973): 77–91.

Spencer, Jane. *The Rise of the Woman Novelist: From Aphra Behn to Jane Austen*. Oxford: Basil Blackwell, 1986.

Todd, Janet. *The Sign of Angellica: Women, Writing and Fiction, 1660–1800*. New York: Columbia University Press, 1989.

Warner, William B. "Formulating Fiction: Romancing the General Reader in Early Modern Britain," in *Cultural Institutions of the Novel*, eds. Deidre Lynch and William Warner. Durham, N.C.: Duke University Press, 1996.

Whicher, George Frisbie. *The Life and Romances of Mrs. Eliza Haywood*. New York: Columbia University Press, 1915.